MW01067806

An Ornament to His Profession

Charles L. Harness

edited by Priscilla Olson

The NESFA Press
Post Office Box 809
Framingham, MA 01701
1998

FIRST EDITION
Second printing, February 1999

International Standard Book Number:
1-886778-09-4

Copyright Acknowledgments

Author Dedication:

For my brother, Blandford

Contents

An Ornament
to His Profession

An Ornament

Priscilla Olson

"Throw-away ideas" . . .

Both David Hartwell and George Zebrowski use this term in their analyses of Charles Harness' work. They're absolutely right, of course. Harness uses ideas as ornaments and he is *extravagant*—almost wasteful—with them. His stories are veritable jungles of intriguing ideas, rich and tangled. Compared to this opulence, the works of many other writers seem but arid wastelands.

Read just a few of the stories included in this collection and enjoy the visit! While you explore these luxuriant environments, discover some of his repeating motifs: spiders and their related symbolism (reputedly due to early experiences with tarantulas); a penchant for poetry (notably Coleridge and Poe), music, and other expressions of the arts; chess; law (particularly patent); and history.

And this book is just a small selection of his fifty years of writing science fiction. Fifty years—pretty neat!

And that's fifty years of a most unusual writer, indeed. Does Charles Harness write like a romantic version of A. E. van Vogt? A proto-cyberpunk cross between Jack Vance and Roger Zelazny? Part of the old *Analog* crew? His writing is difficult to characterize. His plots are generally baroque and convoluted. The reader is frequently thrown immediately into an active, sometimes confusing, and always complicated situation, and finds out what is happening (or has happened) as the work progresses. There are few totally happy endings, and nightmarish, dreamlike scenes abound. Additionally, while some of Harness' material may seem to be merely escapist super-science idea stories, recurrent serious (and often mystical and/or metaphysical) interrelated themes are apparent:

Transformation, change, transcendence, evolution

Love and redemption

Destruction and rebirth, death and transfiguration, grand beginnings and epic endings

"Art versus science" (and their interdependence)

Overall, Harness writes about the hard stuff. He writes about creative people making a difference in a complicated universe. About humanity and hope.

It's pretty powerful stuff, and it's first rate SF as well—and people just don't seem to know this! Many of my proofreaders, all NESFA members (a very well-read group), were unfamiliar with this material. One told me, "Hey, these are really *really* good!" Another confided that some stories made her cry. "Did you really hate them that much?" I asked, shocked. "No," she said. "They were *wonderful.*"

And they are both wonderful and wonder-*filled.*

I hope you think so too.

Priscilla Olson, Editor

CHARLES HARNESS: NEW REALITIES

DAVID G. HARTWELL

I have been a fan of Charles Harness since I first read *Flight Into Yesterday* in the Ace Double edition, and read Damon Knight's insightful review. I was aware at that time that he sometimes published short fiction, but it wasn't until more than ten years later, in the mid-60s, that I came across *The Rose,* a Berkley paperback reprint of a British hardcover containing the title novella and two other stories, "The New Reality" and "The Chessplayers."

"Wow," I said to myself, and was a convert. I didn't find *The Ring of Ritornel* until years later, but by the mid-70s I was an editor and could buy new Harness fiction to publish. I did *Wolfhead* (1978) at Berkley and *The Catalyst* (1980) and *Firebird* (1981) at Pocket Books. I wanted to do a short story collection at that time, but could not. It's a long boring business story. Harness retired from his day job in the '80s, and has actually published more since that time than before. He is still active and writing, with recent stories published in the magazines, a new one in this book, and perhaps more to come.

Charles Harness entered the field in the late 1940s and is one of the impressive talents in SF who wrote too little in any one decade to bring him to the forefront of the field. Even worse, his masterpieces, *The Rose* and *Flight Into Yesterday,* were published in such a way as to deemphasize their achievements, at least for a time, and marginalize their contributions. The first was published only in *Authentic,* an English SF magazine, that had no circulation in the USA, and was generally unknown for more than ten years. The second was published first in *Startling Stories* in 1949 and then in 1953 by a marginal hardcover publisher, and so received little review attention, and then sold off to the Ace Doubles, where it became a minor treasure to readers under the title *The Paradox Men.* Lots of people were eager to see Harness's next novel, but it didn't appear, nor did any new stories for years, and he began to be forgotten, just as the SF of John D. MacDonald and Alfred Coppel began to be forgotten when they moved on out of SF.

The resuscitation of *The Rose* as a lost classic, with a fine, articulate introduction by Michael Moorcock, made Harness in effect one of the precursors of the

New Wave generation, along with Alfred Bester, Theodore Sturgeon, and Philip K. Dick. Many readers discovered Harness for the first time in the paperback collection, and also read his new novel, *The Ring of Ritornel* (1968)—but *The Paradox Men* was long out of print in the US, though not in the UK, so his reputation was not fully restored. And although he published a few stories, in the mid-60s, he again disappeared for a decade. His next novel, *Wolfhead*, appeared in 1978.

He's been active in six decades of SF now, but never a central figure. Long ago he chose to make his career as a patent attorney for W. R. Grace the center of his professional life, and writing a sideline, just as Wallace Stevens, for instance, had a full career as an insurance executive while writing poetry. Or Cordwainer Smith, who kept his personal and professional life completely separate from his occasional SF, and who did not become recognized as an important writer until after his death. I am not going to try to prove that Harness is as important as Cordwainer Smith, but Harness certainly deserves a higher ranking than he has at present, somewhere below Zenna Henderson and only perhaps slightly above Mack Reynolds.

It seems to me Charles Harness, in stories such as "Time Trap," "Stalemate in Time," "The New Reality," and "Child by Chronos" started his career on the same track as Alfred Bester and Philip K. Dick, as a writer adapting the paradoxes and complexities of A. E. van Vogt to a new kind of story, that plays games with time and the nature of reality. One might with some justice see these stories as a bridge between van Vogt's work and the new Bester and Dick stories of the early fifties. Time dilation, time paradoxes, colorful and dramatic surprises abound, and more sentiment than usual in such stories at the time. And then there is *Flight Into Yesterday* and *The Rose*.

Damon Knight, in his review of *Flight Into Yesterday* reprinted in *In Search of Wonder*, said "Harness told me in 1950 that he had spent two years writing the story, and had put into it every fictional idea that occurred to him during the time. He must have studied his model [van Vogt] with painstaking care." Knight's point is that Harness surpasses van Vogt in SF: "all this, packed even more tightly than the original, symmetrically arranged, the loose ends tucked in, and every outrageous twist of the plot fully justified both in science and in logic." Brian W. Aldiss is also a partisan of it: "This novel may be considered as the climax to the billion year spree . . . I call it Wide Screen Baroque . . . Harness's novel has a zing of its own, like whiskey and champagne, the drink of the Nepalese sultans." Michael Moorcock, though, in an essay about *The Rose*, calls that work Harness's "greatest novel," and says "although most of Harness's work is written in the magazine style of the time and at first glance appears to have only the appeal of colorful escapism, reminiscent of A. E. van Vogt or James Blish of the same period, it contains nuances and 'throw away' ideas that show a serious (never earnest) mind operating at a much deeper and broader level than its contemporaries."

Moorcock goes on to say, "*The Rose* [is] crammed with delightful notions— what some SF readers call 'ideas'—but these are essentially icing on the cake of Harness's fiction. [His] stories are what too little science fiction is—true stories of ideas, coming to grips with the big abstract problems of human existence and attempting to throw fresh, philosophical light on them."

I see these works, like the central works of Jack Vance, and Alfred Bester, and Cordwainer Smith, as Space/Time Grand Opera. He approached this level of intensity in some of his later novels, but never equalled these two again. His best mature novel, *The Catalyst,* is in a different mode altogether, clean and slick.

Harness is a writer who returns to certain themes and ideas: he likes to play with time paradoxes, with chess, with logic, with science (as opposed to technology), with history, with the law (especially patent law—he wrote a series of patent law stories in collaboration with Theodore L. Thomas published in *Astounding* in the '50s). His characters are most often motivated by love, or ideas, or ideals, or all three. He writes SF for grown-ups who like to play with speculative ideas. He is willing, like Bester and Dick, to be a bit clunky or gorgeously absurd sometimes, if it keeps the game alive. I think "The Chessplayers" is a good example, and "George Washington Slept Here."

What Harness is is a science fiction storyteller of impressive talents. "George Washington Slept Here," for instance, reminds me of the stories of James Tiptree, Jr., or Hilbert Schenck, and is quite different from his early stories. As is "The Tetrahedron." One would expect a good writer to grow and change in interesting ways. "The Araqnid Window," on the other hand, reminds me of the hybrid SF stories in 1920s adventure pulps, for instance the work of Francis Stevens. It is full of surprises, coincidences, drama, a lost city, and has a volcano erupt just in time. "Summer Solstice" is his best alternate history SF story, a thread you can see in Harness's work growing from the '60s onward, in such stories as "Probable Cause" and "Quarks at Appomattox."

I mentioned *The Catalyst* earlier. That mode of realistic, character-driven SF about patent law and big corporations and cutting edge technology shows up in the major stories of the '60s, most especially in "An Ornament to His Profession" and "The Alchemist," both fantasy stories (one is about a deal with the devil, the other is a clever psi-powers story about industrial chemistry) that appeared in the 1960s in John W. Campbell's *Analog* (!); but is also evident in "The Million Year Patent" and "Probable Cause" (a story that combines a Supreme Court drama involving time paradoxes, with historical references to the JFK and Lincoln assassinations).

Over fifty years of publishing SF in six different decades and it seems as if Harness started out as Bester and Dick, and ended up as Tiptree or Hilbert Schenck, erring on the side of sentiment—spending some time as Algis Budrys, alternating with Roger Zelazny in the middle, ca '66–'86 (the Zelazny stream in his fiction is much more evident in his novels, but begins in *The Rose* and continues through *Wolfhead* and *Firebird* and perhaps *The Venetian Court* and *Lurid Dreams,* and is mythic, heroic, and romantic, as in the early Zelazny). In any of the various periods of his writing, he is always just a bit over the top into outrageousness, that van Vogtian goshwow firecracker effect that makes one go "oooh" and "aaah." For all the intelligence and cleverness and rationality, finally the appeal is emotional.

So here is Charles Harness back in his place in the living history of contemporary SF. There is a new story here too, but I won't spoil any surprises.

David G. Hartwell
Pleasantville, NY

The Rose *is about my brother Billy—Blandford Bryan Harness. Billy was nine years older than I, and the age gap precluded the comradely rapport of brothers born closer together. No matter. Maybe he knew me only as a noisy kid, often in his way. But I knew him, as the acolyte knows the demi-god. He was a fine artist; he studied art at TCU, then at the Chicago Art Institute. He wrote short stories but never submitted any for publication. Much much later, I used the plots of several of those stories in my own work. He was a fair mechanic; he kept our ancient Hudson tuned and running. He was many things. No palette of adjectives really illustrates him. He was mocking, wry, sardonic, frequently scornful.*

He was killed by two brain tumors. Inoperable, the surgeons said, though God knows they tried. He died at home, in his bed. Mother sat there and held his hand. We all heard his last gasp. He was 26.

I began work on The Rose *almost twenty years later. It had been a rough season for me. In the lab where I worked then, a dear friend, a world-class chemist, had been passed over for promotion, and we knew he would now resign. He had been like an older brother to me, a tremendous help when I was just getting started in the patent department. In fact, looking back, he very nearly filled the vacancy left by Billy. His departure was prolonged and painful. Writing* The Rose *helped me deal with it, like some sort of catharsis. So I finished it and it went out to market.*

Every SF market in the U.S. turned it down. John Campbell: "I know only one tune, 'Pop Goes the Weasel.' " Forrest Ackerman finally sold it in England to Authentic Science Fiction *magazine. After that everybody wanted it, and it's been printed in the U.S. and in six or seven foreign languages.*

The tale (as indeed the story itself says) is plotted around a short story, "The Nightingale and the Rose," by Oscar Wilde. This was in a little fabrikoid-bound volume I found among Billy's books after he died. I was so impressed, I actually memorized the story—2,500 words.

The picture of Billy I love best: He and I are trying to play checkers on the breakfast-room table. Little Brother Pat keeps interfering. Billy in calm silence unlatches the window screen. picks a puzzled Pat up carefully, lowers him out the window, relatches the screen, returns to the game. It was all so smooth, so ceremonial, so right, that I think little Pat took it as a rare honor.

Wherever a mind could go, Billy had been. He could answer Goethe's question in Mignon: *Yes, he knew the land where the lemon trees grow. And the other things. He had sailed to Byzantium. He had heard the mermaids sing. And the very best of all, he had loved, and been loved.*

The perfect Ruy Jacques.

THE ROSE

CHAPTER ONE

Her ballet slippers made a soft slapping sound, moody, mournful, as Anna van Tuyl stepped into the annex of her psychiatrical consulting room and walked toward the tall mirror.

Within seconds she would know whether she was ugly.

As she had done half a thousand times in the past two years, the young woman faced the great glass squarely, brought her arms up gracefully and rose upon her tip-toes. And there resemblance to past hours ceased. She did not proceed to an uneasy study of her face and figure. She could not. For her eyes, as though acting with a wisdom and volition of their own, had closed tightly.

Anna van Tuyl was too much the professional psychiatrist not to recognize that her subconscious mind had shrieked its warning. Eyes still shut, and breathing in great gasps, she dropped from her toes as if to turn and leap away. Then gradually she straightened. She must force herself to go through with it. She might not be able to bring herself here, in this mood of candid receptiveness, twice in one lifetime. It must be now.

She trembled in brief, silent premonition, then quietly raised her eyelids.

Somber eyes looked out at her, a little darker than yesterday: pools plowed around by furrows that today gouged a little deeper—the result of months of squinting up from the position into which her spinal deformity had thrust her neck and shoulders. The pale lips were pressed together just a little tighter in their defense against unpredictable pain. The cheeks seemed bloodless, having been bleached finally and completely by the Unfinished Dream that haunted her sleep, wherein a nightingale fluttered about a white rose.

As if in brooding confirmation, she brought up simultaneously the pearl-translucent fingers of both hands to the upper borders of her forehead, and there pushed back the incongruous masses of newly-gray hair from two tumorous bulges—like incipient horns. As she did this she made a quarter turn, exposing to the mirror the humped grotesquerie of her back.

Then, by degrees, like some netherworld Narcissus, she began to sink under the bizarre enchantment of that misshapen image. She could retain no real awareness that this creature was she. That profile, as if seen through witch-opened eyes, might have been that of some enormous toad, and this flickering metaphor paralyzed her first and only forlorn attempt at identification.

19

In a vague way, she realized that she had discovered what she had set out to discover. She was ugly. She was even very ugly.

The change must have been gradual, too slow to say of any one day: Yesterday I was not ugly. But even eyes that hungered for deception could no longer deny the cumulative evidence.

So slow—and yet so fast. It seemed only yesterday that had found her face down on Matthew Bell's examination table, biting savagely at a little pillow as his gnarled fingertips probed grimly at her upper thoracic vertebrae.

Well, then, she was ugly. But she'd not give in to self-pity. To hell with what she looked like! To hell with mirrors!

On sudden impulse she seized her balancing tripod with both hands, closed her eyes, and swung.

The tinkling of falling mirror glass had hardly ceased when a harsh and gravelly voice hailed her from her office. "Bravo!"

She dropped the practice tripod and whirled, aghast. "Matt!"

"Just thought it was time to come in. But if you want to bawl a little, I'll go back out and wait. No?" Without looking directly at her face or pausing for a reply, he tossed a packet on the table. "There it is. Honey, if I could write a ballet score like your *Nightingale and the Rose,* I wouldn't care if my spine was knotted in a figure eight."

"You're crazy," she muttered stonily, unwilling to admit that she was both pleased and curious. "You don't know what it means to have once been able to pirouette, to balance *en arabesque.* And anyway"—she looked at him from the corner of her eyes—"how could anyone tell whether the score's good? There's no Finale as yet. It isn't finished."

"Neither is the Mona Lisa, 'Kubla Khan,' or a certain symphony by Schubert."

"But this is different. A plotted ballet requires an integrated sequence of events leading up to a climax—to a Finale. I haven't figured out the ending. Did you notice I left a thirty-eight-beat hiatus just before the Nightingale dies? I still need a death song for her. She's entitled to die with a flourish." She couldn't tell him about The Dream—that she always awoke just before that death song began.

"No matter. You'll get it eventually. The story's straight out of Oscar Wilde, isn't it? As I recall, the student needs a red rose as admission to the dance, but his garden contains only white roses. A foolish, if sympathetic, nightingale thrusts her heart against a thorn on a white rose stem, and the resultant ill-advised transfusion produces a red rose . . . and a dead nightingale. Isn't that about all there is to it?"

"Almost. But I still need the nightingale's death song. That's the whole point of the ballet. In a plotted ballet, every chord has to be fitted to the immediate action, blended with it, so that it supplements it, explains it, unifies it, and carries the action toward the climax. That death song will make the difference between a good score and a superior one. Don't smile. I think some of my individual scores are rather good, though of course I've never heard them except on my own piano. But without a proper climax, they'll remain unintegrated. They're all variants of some elusive dominating leitmotiv—some really marvelous theme

I haven't the greatness of soul to grasp. I know it's something profound and poignant, like the *Liebestod* theme in *Tristan*. It probably states a fundamental musical truth, but I don't think I'll ever find it. The nightingale dies with her secret."

She paused, opened her lips as though to continue, and then fell moodily silent again. She wanted to go on talking, to lose herself in volubility. But now the reaction of her struggle with the mirror was setting in, and she was suddenly very tired. Had she ever wanted to cry? Now she thought only of sleep. But a furtive glance at her wristwatch told her it was barely ten o'clock.

The man's craggy eyebrows dropped in an imperceptible frown, faint, yet craftily alert. "Anna, the man who read your *Rose* score wants to talk to you about staging it for the Rose Festival—you know, the annual affair in the Via Rosa."

"I—an unknown—write a Festival ballet?" She added with dry incredulity: "The Ballet Committee is in complete agreement with your friend, of course?"

"He *is* the Committee."

"What did you say his name was?"

"I didn't."

She peered up at him suspiciously. "I can play games, too. If he's so anxious to use my music, why doesn't *he* come to see *me?*"

"He isn't that anxious."

"Oh, a big shot, eh?"

"Not exactly. It's just that he's fundamentally indifferent toward the things that fundamentally interest him. Anyway, he's got a complex about the Via Rosa—loves the district and hates to leave it, even for a few hours."

She rubbed her chin thoughtfully. "Will you believe it, I've never been there. That's the rose-walled district where the ars-gratia-artis professionals live, isn't it? Sort of a plutocratic Rive Gauche?"

The man exhaled in expansive affection. "That's the Via, all right. A six-hundred-pound chunk of Carrara marble in every garret, resting most likely on the grand piano. Poppa chips furiously away with an occasional glance at his model, who is momma, posed *au naturel.*"

Anna watched his eyes grow dreamy as he continued. "Momma is a little restless, having suddenly recalled that the baby's bottle and that can of caviar should have come out of the atomic warmer at some nebulous period in the past. Daughter sits before the piano keyboard, surreptitiously switching from Czerny to a torrid little number she's going to try on the trap-drummer in Dorran's Via orchestra. Beneath the piano are the baby and mongrel pup. Despite their tender age, this thing is already in their blood. Or at least, their stomachs, for they have just finished an *hors d'oeuvre* of marble chips and now amiably share the *pièce de résistance,* a battered but rewarding tube of Van Dyke brown."

Anna listened to this with widening eyes. Finally she gave a short amazed laugh. "Matt Bell, you really love that life, don't you?"

He smiled. "In some ways the creative life is pretty carefree. I'm just a psychiatrist specializing in psychogenetics. I don't know an arpeggio from a dry point etching, but I like to be around people that do." He bent forward earnestly. "These artists—these golden people—they're the coming force in society. And you're one of them, Anna, whether you know it or like it. You and your kind are going to inherit the earth—only you'd better hurry if you don't want Martha Jacques and her National Security scientists to get it first. So the battle lines converge in Renaissance II. Art versus Science. Who dies? Who lives?" He looked thoughtful, lonely. He might have been pursuing an introspective monologue in the solitude of his own chambers.

"This Mrs. Jacques," said Anna. "What's she like? You asked me to see her tomorrow about her husband, you know."

"Darn good-looking woman. The most valuable mind in history, some say. And if she really works out something concrete from her Sciomnia equation, I guess there won't be any doubt about it. And that's what makes her potentially the most dangerous human being alive: National Security is fully aware of her value, and they'll coddle her tiniest whim—at least until she pulls something tangible out of Sciomnia. Her main whim for the past few years has been her errant husband, Mr. Ruy Jacques."

"Do you think she really loves him?"

"Just between me and you, she hates his guts. So naturally she doesn't want any other woman to get him. She has him watched, of course. The Security Bureau co-operates with alacrity, because they don't want foreign agents to approach *her* through *him*. There have been ugly rumors of assassinated models . . . But I'm digressing." He cocked a quizzical eye at her. "Permit me to repeat the invitation of your unknown admirer. Like you, he's another true child of the new Renaissance. The two of you should find much in common—more than you can now guess. I'm very serious about this, Anna. Seek him out immediately—tonight—now. There aren't any mirrors in the Via."

"Please, Matt."

"Honey," he growled, "to a man my age you aren't ugly. And this man's the same. If a woman is pretty, he paints her and forgets her. But if she's some kind of an artist, he talks to her, and he can get rather endless sometimes. If it's any help to your self-assurance, he's about the homeliest creature on the face of the earth. You'll look like de Milo alongside him."

The woman laughed shortly. "I can't get mad at you, can I? Is he married?"

"Sort of." His eyes twinkled. "But don't let that concern you. He's a perfect scoundrel."

"Suppose I decide to look him up. Do I simply run up and down the Via paging all homely friends of Dr. Matthew Bell?"

"Not quite. If I were you I'd start at the entrance—where they have all those queer side-shows and one-man exhibitions. Go on past the vendress of love philters and work down the street until you find a man in a white suit with polka dots."

"How perfectly odd! And then what? How can I introduce myself to a man whose name I don't know? Oh, Matt, this is so silly, so *childish* . . ."

He shook his head in slow denial. "You aren't going to think about names when you see him. And your name won't mean a thing to him, anyway. You'll be lucky if you aren't 'hey you' by midnight. But it isn't going to matter."

"It isn't too clear why you don't offer to escort me." She studied him calculatingly. "And I think you're withholding his name because you know I wouldn't go if you revealed it."

He merely chuckled.

She lashed out: "Damn you, get me a cab."

"I've had one waiting half an hour."

CHAPTER TWO

"Tell ya what the professor's gonna do, ladies and gentlemen. He's gonna defend not just one paradox. Not just two. Not just a dozen. No, ladies and gentlemen, the professor's gonna defend *seventeen,* and all in the space of one short hour, without repeating himself, and including a brand-new one he has just thought up today: 'Music owes its meaning to its ambiguity.' Remember, folks, an axiom is just a paradox the professor's already got hold of. The cost of this dazzling display . . . don't crowd there, mister . . ."

Anna felt a relaxing warmth flowing over her mind, washing at the encrusted strain of the past hour. She smiled and elbowed her way through the throng and on down the street, where a garishly lighted sign, bat-wing doors, and a forlorn cluster of waiting women announced the next attraction:

"FOR MEN ONLY. Daring blindfold exhibitions and variety entertainments continuously."

Inside, a loudspeaker was blaring: "Thus we have seen how to compose the ideal end-game problem in chess. And now, gentlemen, for the small consideration of an additional quarter . . ."

But Anna's attention was now occupied by a harsh cawing from across the street.

"Love philters! Works on male or female! Any age! Never fails!"

She laughed aloud. Good old Matt! He had foreseen what these glaring multifaceted nonsensical stimuli would do for her. Love philters! Just what she needed!

The vendress of love philters was of ancient vintage, perhaps seventy-five years old. Above cheeks of wrinkled leather her eyes glittered speculatively. And how weirdly she was clothed! Her bedraggled dress was a shrieking purple. And under that dress was another of the same hue, though perhaps a little faded. And under *that,* still another.

"That's why they call me Violet," cackled the old woman, catching Anna's stare. "Better come over and let me mix you one."

But Anna shook her head and passed on, eyes shining. Fifteen minutes later, as she neared the central Via area, her receptive reverie was interrupted by the outburst of music ahead.

Good! Watching the street dancers for half an hour would provide a highly pleasant climax to her escapade. Apparently there wasn't going to be any man in a polka-dot suit. Matt was going to be disappointed, but it certainly wasn't her fault she hadn't found him.

There was something oddly familiar about that music.

She quickened her pace, and then, as recognition came, she began to run as fast as her crouching back would permit. This was *her* music—the prelude to Act III of her ballet!

She burst through the mass of spectators lining the dance square. The music stopped. She stared out into the scattered dancers, and what she saw staggered the twisted frame of her slight body. She fought to get air through her vacuously-wide mouth.

In one unearthly instant, a rift had threaded its way through the dancer-packed square, and a pasty white face, altogether spectral, had looked down that open rift into hers. A face over a body that was enveloped in a strange flowing gown of shimmering white. She thought he had also been wearing a white academic mortarboard, but the swarming dancers closed in again before she could be sure.

She fought an unreasoning impulse to run.

Then, as quickly as it had come, logic reasserted itself; the shock was over. Odd costumes were no rarity on the Via. There was no cause for alarm.

She was breathing almost normally when the music died away and someone began a harsh harangue over the public address system. "Ladies and gentlemen, it is our rare good fortune to have with us tonight the genius who composed the music you have been enjoying."

A sudden burst of laughter greeted this, seeming to originate in the direction of the orchestra, and was counter-pointed by an uncomplimentary blare from one of the horns.

"Your mockery is misplaced, my friends. It just so happens that this genius is not I, but another. And since she has thus far had no opportunity to join in the revelry, your inimitable friend, as The Student, will take her hand, as The Nightingale, in the final *pas de deux* from Act III. That should delight her, yes?"

The address system clicked off amid clapping and a buzz of excited voices, punctuated by occasional shouts.

She must escape! She must get away!

Anna pressed back into the crowd. There was no longer any question about finding a man in a polka-dot suit. *That* creature in white certainly wasn't he. Though how could he have recognized her?

She hesitated. Perhaps he had a message from the other one, if there really was one with polka dots.

No, she'd better go. This was turning out to be more of a nightmare than a lark. Still—

She peeked back from behind the safety of a woman's sleeve, and after a moment located the man in white.

His pasty-white face with its searching eyes was much closer. But what had happened to his *white* cap and gown? *Now,* they weren't white at all! What optical fantasy was this? She rubbed her eyes and looked again.

The cap and gown seemed to be made up of green and purple polka dots on a white background! So he was her man!

She could see him now as the couples spread out before him, exchanging words she couldn't hear, but which seemed to carry an irresistible laugh response.

Very well, she'd wait.

Now that everything was cleared up and she was safe again behind her armor of objectivity, she studied him with growing curiosity. Since that first time, she had never again got a good look at him. Someone always seemed to get in the way. It was almost, she thought, as though he was working his way out toward her, taking every advantage of human cover, like a hunter closing in on wary quarry, until it was too late . . .

He stood before her.

There were harsh clanging sounds as his eyes locked with hers. Under that feral scrutiny the woman maintained her mental balance by the narrowest margin.

The Student.

The Nightingale, for love of The Student, makes a Red Rose. An odious liquid was burning in her throat, but she couldn't swallow.

Gradually she forced herself into awareness of a twisted sardonic mouth framed between aquiline nose and jutting chin. The face, plastered as it was by white powder, had revealed no distinguishing features beyond its unusual size. Much of the brow was obscured by the many tassels dangling over the front of his travestied mortar-board cap. Perhaps the most striking thing about the man was not his face, but his body. It was evident that he had some physical deformity, to outward appearances not unlike her own. She knew intuitively that he was not a true hunchback. His chest and shoulders were excessively broad, and he seemed, like her, to carry a mass of superfluous tissue on his upper thoracic vertebrae. She surmised that the scapulae would be completely obscured.

His mouth twisted in subtle mockery. "Bell said you'd come." He bowed and held out his right hand.

"It is very difficult for me to dance," she pleaded in a low hurried voice. "I'd humiliate us both."

"I'm no better at this than you, and probably worse. But I'd never give up dancing merely because someone might think I look awkward. Come, we'll use the simplest steps."

There was something harsh and resonant in his voice that reminded her of Matt Bell. Only . . . Bell's voice had never set her stomach churning.

He held out his other hand.

Behind him the dancers had retreated to the edge of the square, leaving the center empty, and the first beats of her music from the orchestra pavilion floated to her with ecstatic clarity.

Just the two of them, out there . . . before a thousand eyes . . .

Subconsciously she followed the music. There was her cue—the signal for the Nightingale to fly to her fatal assignation with the white rose.

She must reach out both perspiring hands to this stranger, must blend her deformed body into his equally misshapen one. She must, because he was The Student, and she was The Nightingale.

She moved toward him silently and took his hands.

As she danced, the harsh-lit street and faces seemed gradually to vanish. Even The Student faded into the barely perceptible distance, and she gave herself up to The Unfinished Dream.

CHAPTER THREE

She dreamed that she danced alone in the moonlight, that she fluttered in solitary circles in the moonlight, fascinated and appalled by the thing she must do to create a Red Rose. She dreamed that she sang a strange and magic song, a wondrous series of chords, the song she had so long sought. Pain buoyed her on excruciating wings, then flung her heavily to earth. The Red Rose was made, and she was dead.

She groaned and struggled to sit up.

Eyes glinted at her out of pasty whiteness. "That was quite a *pas*—only more *de seul* than *de deux*," said The Student.

She looked about in uneasy wonder.

They were sitting together on a marble bench before a fountain. Behind them was a curved walk bounded by a high wall covered with climbing green, dotted here and there with white.

She put her hand to her forehead. "Where are we?"

"This is White Rose Park."

"How did I get here?"

"You danced in on your own two feet through the archway yonder."

"I don't remember . . ."

"I thought perhaps you were trying to lend a bit of realism to the part. But you're early."

"What do you mean?"

"There are only white roses growing in here, and even *they* won't be in full bloom for another month. In late June they'll be a real spectacle. You mean you didn't know about this little park?"

"No. I've never even been in the Via before. And yet . . ."

"And yet what?"

She hadn't been able to tell anyone—not even Matt Bell—what she was now going to tell this man, an utter stranger, her companion of an hour. He had to be told because, somehow, he too was caught up in the dream ballet.

She began haltingly. "Perhaps I *do* know about this place. Perhaps someone told me about it, and the information got buried in my subconscious mind until I wanted a white rose. There's really something behind my ballet that Dr. Bell didn't tell you. He couldn't, because I'm the only one who knows. The *Rose* music comes from my dreams. Only, a better word is nightmares. Every night the score starts from the beginning. In the dream, I dance. Every night, for months and months, there was a little more music, a little more dancing. I tried to get it out of my head, but I couldn't. I started writing it down, the music and the choreography."

The man's unsmiling eyes were fixed on her face in deep absorption.

Thus encouraged, she continued. "For the past several nights I have dreamed almost the complete ballet, right up to the death of the nightingale. I suppose I identify myself so completely with the nightingale that I subconsciously censor her song as she presses her breast against the thorn on the white rose. That's where I always awakened, or at least, always did before tonight. But I think I heard the music tonight. It's a series of chords . . . thirty-eight chords, I believe. The first nineteen were frightful, but the second nineteen were marvelous. Everything was too real to wake up. The Student, The Nightingale, The White Roses."

But now the man threw back his head and laughed raucously. "You ought to see a psychiatrist!"

Anna bowed her head humbly.

"Oh, don't take it too hard," he said. "My wife's even after *me* to see a psychiatrist."

"Really?" Anna was suddenly alert. "What seems to be wrong with you? I mean, what does she object to?"

"In general, my laziness. In particular, it seems I've forgotten how to read and write." He gave her widening eyes a sidelong look. "I'm a perfect parasite, too. Haven't done any real work in months. What would *you* call it if you couldn't work until you had the final measures of the *Rose,* and you kept waiting, and nothing happened?"

"Hell."

He was glumly silent.

Anna asked, hesitantly, yet with a growing certainty. "This thing you're waiting for . . . might it have anything to do with the ballet? Or to phrase it from your point of view, do you think the completion of my ballet may help answer your problem?"

"Might. Couldn't say."

She continued quietly, "You're going to have to face it eventually, you know. Your psychiatrist is going to ask you. How will you answer?"

"I won't. I'll tell him to go to the devil."

"How can you be so sure he's a *he?*"

"Oh? Well, if he's a *she,* she might be willing to pose *al fresco* an hour or so. The model shortage is quite grave, you know, with all of the little dears trying to be painters."

"But if she doesn't have a good figure?"

"Well, maybe her face has some interesting possibilities. It's a rare woman who's a total physical loss."

Anna's voice was very low. "But what if *all* of her were very ugly? What if your proposed psychiatrist were me, *Mr. Ruy Jacques?*"

His great dark eyes blinked, then his lips pursed and exploded into insane laughter. He stood up suddenly. "Come, my dear, whatever your name is, and let the blind lead the blind."

"Anna van Tuyl," she told him, smiling.

She took his arm. Together they strolled around the arc of the walk toward the entrance arch.

She was filled with a strange contentment.

Over the green-crested wall at her left, day was about to break, and from the Via came the sound of groups of diehard revelers, breaking up and drifting away, like specters at cock-crow. The cheerful clatter of milk bottles got mixed up in it somehow.

They paused at the archway while the man kicked at the seat of the pants of a specter whom dawn had returned to slumber beneath the arch. The sleeper cursed and stumbled to his feet in bleary indignation.

"Excuse us, Willie," said Anna's companion, motioning for her to step through. She did, and the creature of the night at once dropped into his former sprawl.

Anna cleared her throat. "Where now?"

"At this point I must cease to be a gentleman. *I'm* returning to the studio for some sleep, and *you* can't come. For, if your physical energy is inexhaustible, mine is not." He raised a hand as her startled mouth dropped open. "Please, dear Anna, don't insist. Some other night, perhaps."

"Why, you—"

"Tut tut." He turned a little and kicked again at the sleeping man. "I'm not an utter cad, you know. I would never abandon a weak, frail, unprotected woman in the Via."

She was too amazed now even to splutter.

Ruy Jacques reached down and pulled the drunk up against the wall of the arch, where he held him firmly. "Dr. Anna van Tuyl, may I present Willie the Cork."

The Cork grinned at her in unfocused somnolence.

"Most people call him the Cork because that's what seals in the bottle's contents," said Jacques. "*I* call him the Cork because he's always bobbing up. He looks like a bum, but that's just because he's a good actor. He's really a Security man tailing me at my wife's request, and he'd only be too delighted for a little further conversation with you. A cheery good morning to you both!"

A milk truck wheeled around the corner. Jacques leaped for its running board, and he was gone before the psychiatrist could voice the protest boiling up in her.

A gurgling sigh at her feet drew her eyes down momentarily. The Cork was apparently bobbing once more on his own private alcoholic ocean.

Anna snorted in mingled disgust and amusement, then hailed a cab. As she slammed the door, she took one last look at Willie. Not until the cab rounded the corner and cut off his muffled snores did she realize that people usually don't snore with their eyes half-opened and looking at you, especially with eyes no longer blurred with sleep, but hard and glinting.

CHAPTER FOUR

Twelve hours later, in another cab and in a different part of the city, Anna peered absently out at the stream of traffic. Her mind was on the coming conference with Martha Jacques. Only twelve hours ago Mrs. Jacques had been just a bit of necessary case history. Twelve hours ago Anna hadn't really cared whether Mrs. Jacques followed Bell's recommendation and gave her the case. Now it was all different. She wanted the case, and she was going to get it.

Ruy Jacques—how many hours awaited her with this amazing scoundrel, this virtuoso of liberal—nay, loose—arts, who held locked within his remarkable mind the missing pieces of their joint jigsaw puzzle of The Rose?

That jeering, mocking face—what would it look like without makeup? Very ugly, she hoped. Beside his, her own face wasn't too bad.

Only—he was married, and she was en route at this moment to discuss preliminary matters with his wife, who, even if she no longer loved him, at least had prior rights to him. There were considerations of professional ethics even in thinking about him. Not that she could ever fall in love with him or any other patient. Particularly with one who had treated her so cavalierly. Willie the Cork, indeed!

As she waited in the cold silence of the great ante-chamber adjoining the office of Martha Jacques, Anna sensed that she was being watched. She was quite certain that by now she'd been photographed, x-rayed for hidden weapons, and her fingerprints taken from her professional card. In colossal central police files a thousand miles away, a bored clerk would be leafing through her dossier for the benefit of Colonel Grade's visigraph in the office beyond.

In a moment—

"Dr. van Tuyl to see Mrs. Jacques. Please enter door B-3," said the tinny voice of the intercom.

She followed a guard to the door, which he opened for her.

This room was smaller. At the far end a woman, a very lovely woman, whom she took to be Martha Jacques, sat peering in deep abstraction at something on the desk before her. Beside the desk, and slightly to the rear, a moustached man in plain clothes stood, reconnoitering Anna with hawk-like eyes. The description fitted what Anna had heard of Colonel Grade, Chief of the National Security Bureau.

Grade stepped forward and introduced himself curtly, then presented Anna to Mrs. Jacques.

And then the psychiatrist found her eyes fastened to a sheet of paper on Mrs. Jacques' desk. And as she stared, she felt a sharp dagger of ice sinking into her spine, and she grew slowly aware of a background of brooding whispers in her mind, heart-constricting in their suggestions of mental disintegration.

For the thing drawn on the paper, in red ink, was—although warped, incomplete, and misshapen—unmistakably a rose.

"Mrs. Jacques!" cried Grade.

Martha Jacques must have divined simultaneously Anna's great interest in the paper. With an apologetic murmur she turned it face down. "Security regulations, you know. I'm really supposed to keep it locked up in the presence of visitors." Even a murmur could not hide the harsh metallic quality of her voice.

So *that* was why the famous Sciomnia formula was sometimes called the "Jacques Rosette": when traced in an ever-expanding wavering red spiral in polar co-ordinates, it was . . . a Red Rose.

The explanation brought at once a feeling of relief and a sinister deepening of the sense of doom that had overshadowed her for months. So you, too, she thought wonderingly, seek The Rose. Your artist-husband is wretched for want of it, and now you. But do you seek the same rose? Is the rose of the scientist the true rose, and Ruy Jacques' the false? What *is* the rose? Will I ever know?

Grade broke in. "Your brilliant reputation is deceptive, Dr. van Tuyl. From Dr. Bell's description, we had pictured you as an older woman."

"Yes," said Martha Jacques, studying her curiously. "We really had in mind an older woman, one less likely to . . . to—"

"To involve your husband emotionally?"

"Exactly," said Grade. "Mrs. Jacques must have her mind completely free from distractions. However"—he turned to the woman scientist—"it is my studied opinion that we need not anticipate difficulty from Dr. van Tuyl on that account."

Anna felt her throat and cheeks going hot as Mrs. Jacques nodded in damning agreement: "I think you're right, Colonel."

"Of course," said Grade, "*Mr.* Jacques may not accept her."

"That remains to be seen," said Martha Jacques. "He might tolerate a fellow artist." To Anna: "Dr. Bell tells us that you compose music, or something like that?"

"Something like that," nodded Anna. She wasn't worried. It was a question of waiting. This woman's murderous jealousy, though it might some day destroy her, at the moment concerned her not a whit.

Colonel Grade said: "Mrs. Jacques has probably warned you that her husband is somewhat eccentric; he may be somewhat difficult to deal with at times. On this account, the Security Bureau is prepared to triple your fee, if we find you acceptable."

Anna nodded gravely. Ruy Jacques and money, too!

"For most of your consultations you'll have to track him down," said Martha Jacques. "He'll never come to you. But considering what we're prepared to pay, this inconvenience should be immaterial."

Anna thought briefly of that fantastic creature who had singled her out of a thousand faces. "That will be satisfactory. And now, Mrs. Jacques, for my preliminary orientation, suppose you describe some of the more striking behaviorisms that you've noted in your husband."

"Certainly. Dr. Bell, I presume, has already told you that Ruy has lost the ability to read and write. Ordinarily that's indicative of advanced dementia praecox, isn't it? However, I think Mr. Jacques' case presents a more complicated picture, and my own guess is schizophrenia rather than dementia. The dominant and most frequently observed psyche is a megalomanic phase, during which he tends to harangue his listeners on various odd subjects. We've picked up some of these speeches on a hidden recorder and made a Zipf analysis of the word-frequencies."

Anna's brows creased dubiously. "A Zipf count is pretty mechanical."

"But scientific, undeniably scientific. I have made a careful study of the method, and can speak authoritatively. Back in the forties, Zipf of Harvard proved that in a representative sample of English, the interval separating the repetition of the same word was inversely proportional to its frequency. He provided a mathematical formula for something previously known only qualitatively: that a too-soon repetition of the same or similar sound is distracting and grating to the cultured mind. If we must say the same thing in the next paragraph, we avoid repetition with an appropriate synonym. But not the schizophrenic. His disease disrupts his higher centers of association, and certain discriminating neural networks are no longer available for his writing and speech. He has no compunction against immediate and continuous tonal repetition."

"A rose is a rose is a rose . . ." murmured Anna.

"Eh? How did you know what this transcription was about? Oh, you were just quoting Gertrude Stein? Well, I've read about her, and she proves my point. She admitted that she wrote under autohypnosis, which we'd call a light case of schizo. But she could be normal, too. My husband never is. He goes on like this all the time. This was transcribed from one of his monologues. Just listen:

"Behold, Willie, through yonder window the symbol of your mistress' defeat: The Rose! The rose, my dear Willie, grows not in murky air. The smoky metropolis of yester-year drove it to the country. But now, with the unsullied skyline of your atomic age, the red rose returns. How mysterious, Willie, that the rose continues to offer herself to us dull, plodding humans. We see nothing in her but a pretty flower. Her regretful thorns forever declare our inept clumsiness, and her lack of honey chides our gross sensuality. Ah, Willie, let us become as birds! For only the winged can eat the fruit of the rose and spread her pollen . . ."

Mrs. Jacques looked up at Anna. "Did you keep count? He used the word 'rose' no less than five times, when once or twice was sufficient. He certainly had no lack of mellifluous synonyms at his disposal, such as 'red flower', 'thorned plant', and so on. And instead of saying 'the red rose returns' he should have said something like 'it comes back.' "

"And lose the triple alliteration?" said Anna, smiling. "No, Mrs. Jacques, I'd re-examine that diagnosis very critically. Everyone who talks like a poet isn't necessarily insane."

A tiny bell began to jangle on a massive metal door in the right-hand wall.

"A message for me," growled Grade. "Let it wait."

"We don't mind," said Anna, "if you want to have it sent in."

"It isn't *that*. That's my private door, and I'm the only one who knows the combination. But I told them not to interrupt us, unless it dealt with this specific interview."

Anna thought of the eyes of Willie the Cork, hard and glistening. Suddenly she knew that Ruy Jacques had not been joking about the identity of the man. Was the Cork's report just now getting on her dossier? Mrs. Jacques wasn't going to like it. Suppose they turned her down. Would she dare seek out Ruy Jacques under the noses of Grade's trigger men?

"Damn that fool," muttered Grade. "I left strict orders about being disturbed. Excuse me."

He strode angrily toward the door. After a few seconds of dial manipulation, he turned the handle and pulled it inward. A hand thrust something metallic at him. Anna caught whispers. She fought down a feeling of suffocation as Grade opened the cassette and read the message.

The Security officer walked leisurely back toward them. He stroked his moustache coolly, handed the bit of paper to Martha Jacques, then clasped his hands behind his back. For a moment he looked like a glowering bronze statue. "Dr. van Tuyl, you didn't tell us that you were already acquainted with Mr. Jacques. Why?"

"You didn't ask me."

Martha Jacques said harshly: "That answer is hardly satisfactory. How long have you known Mr. Jacques? I want to get to the bottom of this."

"I met him last night for the first time in the Via Rosa. We danced. That's all. The whole thing was purest coincidence."

"You are his lover," accused Martha Jacques.

Anna colored. "You flatter me, Mrs. Jacques."

Grade coughed. "She's right, Mrs. Jacques. I see no sex-based espionage."

"Then maybe it's even subtler," said Martha Jacques. "These platonic females are still worse, because they sail under false colors. She's after Ruy, I tell you."

"I assure you," said Anna, "that your reaction comes as a complete surprise to me. Naturally, I shall withdraw from the case at once."

"But it doesn't end with that," said Grade curtly. "The national safety may depend on Mrs. Jacques' peace of mind during the coming weeks. I *must* ascertain your relation with Mr. Jacques. And I must warn you that if a compromising situation exists, the consequences will be most unpleasant." He picked up the telephone. "Grade. Get me the O.D."

Anna's palms were uncomfortably wet and sticky. She wanted to wipe them on the sides of her dress, but then decided it would be better to conceal all signs of nervousness.

Grade barked into the mouthpiece. "Hello! That you, Packard? Send me—"

Suddenly the room vibrated with the shattering impact of massive metal on metal.

The three whirled toward the sound.

A stooped, loudly dressed figure was walking away from the great and inviolate door of Colonel Grade, drinking in with sardonic amusement the stuporous faces turned to him. It was evident he had just slammed the door behind him with all his strength.

Insistent squeakings from the teleset stirred Grade into a feeble response. "Never mind . . . it's Mr. Jacques . . ."

CHAPTER FIVE

The swart ugliness of that face verged on the sublime. Anna observed for the first time the two horn-like protuberances on his forehead, which the man made no effort to conceal. His black woolen beret was cocked jauntily over one horn;

the other, the visible one, bulged even more than Anna's horns, and to her fascinated eyes he appeared as some Greek satyr; Silenus with an eternal hangover, or Pan wearying of fruitless pursuit of fleeting nymphs. It was the face of a cynical post-gaol Wilde, of a Rimbaud, of a Goya turning his brush in saturnine glee from Spanish grandees to the horror-world of Ensayos.

Like a phantom voice, Matthew Bell's cryptic prediction seemed to float into her ears again: ". . . much in common . . . more than you guess . . ."

There was so little time to think. Ruy Jacques must have recognized her frontal deformities even while that tasselated mortarboard of his Student costume had prevented her from seeing his. He must have identified her as a less advanced case of his own disease. Had he foreseen the turn of events here? Was he here to protect the only person on earth who might help him? That wasn't like him. He just wasn't the sensible type. She got the uneasy impression that he was here solely for his own amusement—simply to make fools of the three of them.

Grade began to sputter. "Now see here, Mr. Jacques. It's impossible to get in through that door. It's my private entrance. I changed the combination myself only this morning." The moustache bristled indignantly. "I must ask the meaning of this."

"Pray do, Colonel, pray do."

"Well, then, what is the meaning of this?"

"None, Colonel. Have you no faith in your own syllogisms? No one can open your private door but you. Q.E.D. No one did. I'm not really here. No smiles? Tsk tsk! Paragraph 6, p. 840 of the Manual of Permissible Military Humor officially recognizes the paradox."

"There's no such publication—" stormed Grade.

But Jacques brushed him aside. He seemed now to notice Anna for the first time, and bowed with exaggerated punctilio. "My profound apologies, madame. You were standing so still, so quiet, that I mistook you for a rose bush." He beamed at each in turn. "Now isn't this delightful? I feel like a literary lion. It's the first time in my life that my admirers ever met for the express purpose of discussing my work."

How could he know that we were discussing his "composition," wondered Anna. *And how did he open the door?*

"If you'd eavesdropped long enough," said Martha Jacques, "you'd have learned we weren't admiring your 'prose poem.' In fact, I think it's pure nonsense."

No, thought Anna, he couldn't have eavesdropped, because we didn't talk about his speech after Grade opened the door. There's something here—in this room— that *tells* him.

"You don't even think it's poetry?" repeated Jacques, wide-eyed. "Martha, coming from one with your scientifically developed poetical sense, this is utterly damning."

"There *are* certain well recognized approaches to the appreciation of poetry," said Martha Jacques doggedly. "You ought to have the autoscanner read you some books on the aesthetic laws of language. It's all there."

The artist blinked in great innocence. "*What's* all there?"

"Scientific rules for analyzing poetry. Take the mood of a poem. You can very easily learn whether it's gay or somber just by comparing the proportion of low-pitched vowels—*u* and *o*, that is—to the high-pitched vowels—*a, e,* and *i*."

"Well, what do you know about that!" He turned a wondering face to Anna. "And she's right! Come to think of it, in Milton's *L'Allegro*, most of the vowels are high-pitched, while in his *Il Penseroso*, they're mostly low-pitched. Folks, I believe we've finally found a yardstick for genuine poetry. No longer must we flounder in poetastical soup. Now let's see." He rubbed his chin in blank-faced thoughtfulness. "Do you know, for years I've considered Swinburne's lines mourning Charles Baudelaire to be the distillate of sadness. But that, of course, was before I had heard of Martha's scientific approach, and had to rely solely on my unsophisticated, untrained, uninformed feelings. How stupid I was! For the thing is crammed with high-pitched vowels, and long *e* dominates: 'thee', 'sea', 'weave', 'eve', 'heat', 'sweet', 'feet' . . ." He struck his brow as if in sudden comprehension. "Why, it's gay! I must set it to a snappy polka!"

"Drivel," sniffed Martha Jacques. "Science—"

"—is simply a parasitical, adjectival, and useless occupation devoted to the quantitative restatement of Art," finished the smiling Jacques. "Science is functionally sterile; it creates nothing; it says nothing new. The scientist can never be more than a humble camp-follower of the artist. There exists no scientific truism that hasn't been anticipated by creative art. The examples are endless. Uccello worked out mathematically the laws of perspective in the fifteenth century; but Kallikrates applied the same laws two thousand years before in designing the columns of the Parthenon. The Curies thought they invented the idea of 'half-life'—of a thing vanishing in proportion to its residue. The Egyptians tuned their lyre-strings to dampen according to the same formula. Napier thought he invented logarithms—entirely overlooking the fact that the Roman brass workers flared their trumpets to follow a logarithmic curve."

"You're deliberately selecting isolated examples," retorted Martha Jacques.

"Then suppose you name a few so-called scientific discoveries," replied the man. "I'll prove they were scooped by an artist, every time."

"I certainly shall. How about Boyle's gas law? I suppose you'll say Praxiteles knew all along that gas pressure runs inversely proportional to its volume at a given temperature?"

"I expected something more sophisticated. That one's too easy. Boyle's gas law, Hooke's law of springs, Galileo's law of pendulums, and a host of similar hogwash simply state that compression, kinetic energy, or whatever name you give it, is inversely proportional to its reduced dimensions, and is proportional to the amount of its displacement in the total system. Or, as the artist says, impact results from, and is proportional to, displacement of an object within its milieu. Could the final couplet of a Shakespearean sonnet enthrall us if our minds hadn't been conditioned, held in check, and compressed in suspense by the preceding fourteen lines? Note how cleverly Donne's famous poem builds up to its crash line, 'It tolls for thee!' By blood, sweat, and genius, the Elizabethans lowered the entropy of their creations in precisely the same manner, and with precisely the same result, as when Boyle compressed his gases. And the method was long old when *they* were young. It was old when the Ming artists were painting the barest suggestions of landscapes on the disproportionate backgrounds of their vases. The Shah Jahan was aware of it when he designed the long eye-restraining reflecting pool before the Taj Mahal. The Greek tragedians knew it. Sophocles' *Oedipus* is still unparalleled in its suspensive pacing toward climax. Solomon's imported Chaldean architects knew the effect to be gained by spacing the Holy of Holies at a distance from the temple pylae, and the Cro-Magnard magicians with malice aforethought painted their marvelous animal scenes only in the most inaccessible crannies of their limestone caves."

Martha Jacques smiled coldly. "Drivel, drivel, drivel. But never mind. One of these days soon I'll produce evidence you'll be *forced* to admit art can't touch."

"If you're talking about Sciomnia, there's *real* nonsense for you," countered Jacques amiably. "Really, Martha, it's a frightful waste of time to reconcile biological theory with the unified field theory of Einstein, which itself merely reconciles the relativity and quantum theories, a futile gesture in the first place. Before Einstein announced *his* unified theory in 1949, the professors handled the problem very neatly. They taught the quantum theory on Mondays, Wednesdays, and Fridays and the relativity theory on Tuesdays, Thursdays, and Saturdays. On the Sabbath they rested in front of their television sets. What's the good of Sciomnia, anyway?"

"It's the final summation of all physical and biological knowledge," retorted Martha Jacques. "And as such, Sciomnia represents the highest possible aim of human endeavor. Man's goal in life is to understand his environment, to analyze it to the last iota—to know what he controls. The first person to understand Sciomnia may well rule not only this planet, but the whole galaxy—not that he'd want to, but he could. That person may not be me—but will certainly be a scientist, and not an irresponsible artist."

"But, Martha," protested Jacques. "Where did you pick up such a weird philosophy? The highest aim of man is *not* to analyze, but to synthesize—to *create*. If you ever solve all of the nineteen sub-equations of Sciomnia, you'll be at a dead end. There'll be nothing left to analyze. As Dr. Bell the psychogeneticist says, overspecialization, be it mental, as in the human scientist, or dental, as in the saber-tooth tiger, is just a synonym for extinction. But if we continue to create, we shall eventually discover how to transcend—"

Grade coughed, and Martha Jacques cut in tersely: "Never mind what Dr. Bell says. Ruy, have you ever seen this woman before?"

"The rose bush? Hmm." He stepped over to Anna and looked squarely down at her face. She flushed and looked away. He circled her in slow, critical appraisal, like a prospective buyer in a slave market of ancient Baghdad. "Hmm," he repeated doubtfully.

Anna breathed faster; her cheeks were the hue of beets. But she couldn't work up any sense of indignity. On the contrary, there was something illogically delicious about being visually pawed and handled by this strange leering creature.

Then she jerked visibly. What hypnotic insanity was this? This man held her life in the palm of his hand. If he acknowledged her, the vindictive creature who passed as his wife would crush her professionally. If he denied her, they'd know he was lying to save her—and the consequences might prove even less pleasant. And what difference would her ruin make to *him?* She had sensed at once his monumental selfishness. And even if that conceit, that gorgeous self-love urged him to preserve her for her hypothetical value in finishing up the Rose score, she didn't see how he was going to manage it.

"Do you recognize her, Mr. Jacques?" demanded Grade.

"I do," came the solemn reply.

Anna stiffened.

Martha Jacques smiled thinly. "Who is she?"

"Miss Ethel Twinkham, my old spelling teacher. How are you, Miss Twinkham? What brings you out of retirement?"

"I'm not Miss Twinkham," said Anna dryly. "My name is Anna van Tuyl. For your information, we met last night in the Via Rosa."

"Oh! Of course!" He laughed happily. "I seem to remember now, quite indistinctly. And I want to apologize, Miss Twinkham. My behavior was execrable, I suppose. Anyway, if you will just leave the bill for damages with Mrs. Jacques, her lawyer will take care of everything. You can even throw in ten per cent, for mental anguish."

Anna felt like clapping her hands in glee. The whole Security office was no match for this fiend.

"You're getting last night mixed up with the night before," snapped Martha Jacques. "You met Miss van Tuyl last night. You were with her several hours. Don't lie about it."

Again Ruy Jacques peered earnestly into Anna's face. He finally shook his head. "Last night? Well, I can't deny it. Guess you'll have to pay up, Martha. Her face *is* familiar, but I just can't remember what I did to make her mad. The bucket of paint and the slumming dowager was *last* week, wasn't it?"

Anna smiled. "You didn't injure me. We simply danced together on the square, that's all. I'm here at Mrs. Jacques' request." From the corner of her eye she watched Martha Jacques and the colonel exchange questioning glances, as if to say, "Perhaps there is really nothing between them."

But the scientist was not completely satisfied. She turned her eyes on her husband. "It's a strange coincidence that you should come just at this time. Exactly why *are* you here, if not to becloud the issue of this woman and your future psychiatrical treatment? Why don't you answer? What is the matter with you?"

For Ruy Jacques stood there, swaying like a stricken satyr, his eyes coals of pain in a face of anguished flames. He contorted backward once, as though attempting to placate furious fangs tearing at the hump on his back.

Anna leaped to catch him as he collapsed.

He lay cupped in her lap moaning voicelessly. Something in his hump, which lay against her left breast, seethed and raged like a genie locked in a bottle.

"Colonel Grade," said the psychiatrist quietly, "you will order an ambulance. I must analyze this pain syndrome at the clinic immediately."

Ruy Jacques was hers.

CHAPTER SIX

"Thanks awfully for coming, Matt," said Anna warmly.

"Glad to, honey." He looked down at the prone figure on the clinic cot. "How's our friend?"

"Still unconscious, and under general analgesic. I called you in because I want to air some ideas about this man that scare me when I think about them alone."

The psychogeneticist adjusted his spectacles with elaborate casualness. "Really? Then you think you've found what's wrong with him? Why he can't read or write?"

"Does it have to be something *wrong?*"

"What else would you call it? A . . . *gift?*"

She studied him narrowly. "I might—and you might—if he got something in return for his loss. That would depend on whether there was a net gain, wouldn't it? And don't pretend you don't know what I'm talking about. Let's get it out in the open. You've known the Jacques—both of them—for years. You had me put on his case because you think he and I might find in the mind and body of the other a mutual solution to our identical aberrations. Well?"

Bell tapped imperturbably at his cigar. "As you say, the question is, whether he got enough in return—enough to compensate for his lost skills."

She gave him a baffled look. "All right, then, I'll do the talking. Ruy Jacques opened Grade's private door, when Grade alone knew the combination. And when he got in the room with us, he knew what we had been talking about. It was just as though it had all been written out for him, somehow. You'd have thought the lock combination had been pasted on the door, and that he'd looked over a transcript of our conversation."

"Only, he can't read," observed Bell.

"You mean, he can't read . . . *writing?*"

"What else is there?"

"Possibly some sort of thought residuum . . . in *things.* Perhaps some message in the metal of Grade's door, and in certain objects in the room." She watched him closely. "I see you aren't surprised. You've known this all along."

"I admit nothing. You, on the other hand, must admit that your theory of thought-reading is superficially fantastic."

"So would writing be—to a Neanderthal cave dweller. But tell me, Matt, where do our thoughts go after we think them? What is the extra-cranial fate of those feeble, intricate electric oscillations we pick up on the encephalograph? We know they can and do penetrate the skull, that they can pass through bone, like radio waves. Do they go on out into the universe forever? Or do dense substances like Grade's door eventually absorb them all? Do they set up their wispy patterns in metals, which then begin to vibrate in sympathy, like piano wires responding to a noise?"

Bell drew heavily on his cigar. "Seriously, I don't know. But I will say this: your theory is not inconsistent with certain psychogenetic predictions."

"Such as?"

"Eventual telemusical communication of all thought. The encephalograph, you know, looks oddly like a musical sound track. Oh, we can't expect to convert overnight to communication of pure thought by pure music. Naturally, crude transitional forms will intervene. But *any* type of direct idea transmission that involves the sending and receiving of rhythm and modulation as such is a cut higher than communication in a verbal medium, and may be a rudimentary step upward toward true musical communion, just as dawn man presaged true words with allusive, onomatopoeic monosyllables."

"There's your answer, then," said Anna. "Why should Ruy Jacques trouble to read, when every bit of metal around him is an open book?" She continued speculatively, "You might look at it this way. Our ancestors forgot how to swing through the trees when they learned how to walk erect. Their history is recapitulated in our very young. Almost immediately after birth, a human infant can hang by his hands, ape-like. And then, after a week or so, he forgets what no human infant ever really needed to know. So now Ruy forgets how to read. A great pity. Perhaps. But if the world were peopled with Ruys, they wouldn't need to know how, for after the first few years of infancy, they'd learn to use their metal-empathic sense. They might even say, 'It's all very nice to be able to read and write and swing about in trees when you're *quite* young, but after all, one matures.' "

She pressed a button on the desk slide viewer that sat on a table by the artist's bed. "This is a radiographic slide of Ruy's cerebral hemispheres as viewed from above, probably old stuff to you. It shows that the 'horns' are not mere localized growths in the prefrontal area, but extend as slender tracts around the respective hemispheric peripheries to the visuo-sensory area of the occipital lobes, where they turn and enter the cerebral interior, there to merge in an enlarged ball-like juncture at a point over the cerebellum where the pineal 'eye' is ordinarily found."

"But the pineal is completely missing in the slide," demurred Bell.

"That's the question," countered Anna. "*Is* the pineal absent—or, are the 'horns' actually the pineal, enormously enlarged and bifurcated? I'm convinced that the latter is the fact. For reasons presently unknown to me, this heretofore small, obscure lobe has grown, bifurcated, and forced its destructive dual limbs not only through the soft cerebral tissue concerned with the ability to read, but also has gone on to skirt half the cerebral circumference to the forehead, where even the hard frontal bone of the skull has softened under its pressure." She looked at Bell closely. "I infer that it's just a question of time before I, too, forget how to read and write."

Bell's eyes drifted evasively to the immobile face of the unconscious artist. "But the number of neurons in a given mammalian brain remains constant after birth," he said. "These cells can throw out numerous dendrites and create increasingly complex neural patterns as the subject grows older, but he can't grow any more of the primary neurons."

"I know. That's the trouble. Ruy can't grow more brain, but he has." She touched her own 'horns' wonderingly. "And I guess I have, too. *What*—?"

Following Bell's glance, she bent over to inspect the artist's face, and started as from a physical blow.

Eyes like anguished talons were clutching hers.

His lips moved, and a harsh whisper swirled about her ears like a desolate wind: ". . . The Nightingale . . . in death . . . greater beauty unbearable . . . but *watch . . . THE ROSE!*"

White-faced, Anna staggered backwards through the door.

CHAPTER SEVEN

Bell's hurried footsteps were just behind her as she burst into her office and collapsed on the consultation couch. Her eyes were shut tight, but over her labored breathing she heard the psychogeneticist sit down and leisurely light another cigar.

Finally she opened her eyes. "Even *you* found out something that time. There's no use asking me what he meant."

"Isn't there? Who will dance the part of The Student on opening night?"

"Ruy. Only, he will really do little beyond provide support to the prima ballerina, The Nightingale, that is, at the beginning and end of the ballet."

"And who plays The Nightingale?"

"Ruy hired a professional—La Tanid."

Bell blew a careless cloud of smoke toward the ceiling. "Are you sure *you* aren't going to take the part?"

"The role is strenuous in the extreme. For me, it would be a physical impossibility."

"Now."

"What do you mean—*now?*"

He looked at her sharply. "You know very well what I mean. You know it so well your whole body is quivering. Your ballet première is four weeks off—but you know and I know that Ruy has already seen it. Interesting." He tapped coolly at his cigar. *"Almost as interesting as your belief he saw you playing the part of The Nightingale."*

Anna clenched her fists. This must be faced rationally. She inhaled deeply, and slowly let her breath out. "How can even *he* see things that haven't happened yet?"

"I don't know for sure. But I can guess, and so could you if you'd calm down a bit. We do know that the pineal is a residuum of the single eye that our very remote sea-going ancestors had in the center of their fishy foreheads. Suppose this fossil eye, now buried deep in the normal brain, were reactivated. What would we be able to see with it? Nothing spatial, nothing dependent on light stimuli. But let us approach the problem inductively. I shut one eye. The other can fix Anna van Tuyl in a depthless visual plane. But with two eyes I can follow you stereoscopically, as you move about in space. Thus, adding an eye adds a dimension. With the pineal as a third eye I should be able to follow you through time. So Ruy's awakened pineal should permit him at least a hazy glimpse of the future."

"What a marvelous—and terrible—gift."

"But not without precedent," said Bell. "I suspect that a more or less reactivated pineal lies behind every case of clairvoyance collected in the annals of parapsychology. And I can think of at least one historical instance in which the pineal has actually tried to penetrate the forehead, though evidently only in monolobate form. All Buddhist statues carry a mark on the forehead symbolic of an 'inner eye.' From what we know now, Buddha's 'inner eye' was something more than symbolic."

"Granted. But a time-sensitive pineal still doesn't explain the pain in Ruy's hump. Nor the hump itself, for that matter."

"What," said Bell, "makes you think the hump is anything more than what it seems—a spinal disease characterized by a growth of laminated tissue?"

"It's not that simple, and you know it. You're familiar with 'phantom limb' cases, such as where the amputee retains an illusion of sensation or pain in the amputated hand or foot?"

He nodded.

She continued: "But you know, of course, that amputation isn't an absolute prerequisite to a 'phantom.' A child born armless may experience phantom limb sensations for years. Suppose such a child were thrust into some improbable armless society, and their psychiatrists tried to cast his sensory pattern into their own mold. How could the child explain to them the miracle of arms, hands, fingers—things of which he had occasional sensory intimations, but had never seen, and could hardly imagine? Ruy's case is analogous. He is four-limbed and presumably springs from normal stock. Hence the phantom sensations in his hump point toward a *potential organ*—a foreshadowing of the future, rather than toward memories of a limb once possessed. To use a brutish example, Ruy is like the tadpole rather than the snake. The snake had his legs briefly, during the evolutionary recapitulation of his embryo. The tadpole has yet to shed his tail and develop legs. But one might assume that each has some faint phantom sensoria of legs."

Bell appeared to consider this. "That still doesn't account for Ruy's pain. I wouldn't think the process of growing a tail would be painful for a tadpole, nor a phantom limb for Ruy—if it's inherent in his physical structure. But be that as it may, from all indications he is still going to be in considerable pain when that narcotic wears off. What are you going to do for him *then?* Section the ganglia leading to his hump?"

"Certainly not. Then he would *never* be able to grow that extra organ. Anyhow, even in normal phantom limb cases, cutting nerve tissue doesn't help. Excision of neuromas from limb stumps brings only temporary relief—and may actually aggravate a case of hyperaesthesia. No, phantom pain sensations are central rather than peripheral. However, as a temporary analgesic, I shall try a two per cent solution of novocaine near the proper thoracic ganglia." She looked at her watch. "We'd better be getting back to him."

CHAPTER EIGHT

Anna withdrew the syringe needle from the man's side and rubbed the last puncture with an alcoholic swab.

"How do you feel, Ruy?" asked Bell.

The woman stooped beside the sterile linens and looked at the face of the prone man. "He doesn't," she said uneasily. "He's out cold again."

"Really?" Bell bent over beside her and reached for the man's pulse. "But it was only two per cent novocaine. Most remarkable."

"I'll order a counter-stimulant," said Anna nervously. "I don't like this."

"Oh, come, girl. Relax. Pulse and respiration normal. In fact, I think you're nearer collapse than he. This is very interesting . . ." His voice trailed off in musing surmise. "Look, Anna, there's nothing to keep both of us here. He's in no danger whatever. I've got to run along. I'm sure you can attend to him."

I know, she thought. You want me to be alone with him.

She acknowledged his suggestion with a reluctant nod of her head, and the door closed behind his chuckle.

For some moments thereafter she studied in deep abstraction the regular rise and fall of the man's chest.

So Ruy Jacques had set another medical precedent. He'd received a local anesthetic that should have done nothing more than desensitize the deformed growth in his back for an hour or two. But here he lay, in apparent coma, just as though under a general cerebral anaesthetic.

Her frown deepened.

X-ray plates had showed his dorsal growth simply as a compacted mass of cartilaginous laminated tissue (the same as hers) penetrated here and there by neural ganglia. In deadening those ganglia she should have accomplished nothing more than local anaesthetization of that tissue mass, in the same manner that one anaesthetizes an arm or leg by deadening the appropriate spinal ganglion. But the actual result was not local, but general. It was as though one had administered a mild local to the radial nerve of the forearm to deaden pain in the hand, but had instead anaesthetized the cerebrum.

And that, of course, was utterly senseless, completely incredible, because anaesthesia works from the higher neural centers down, not vice versa. Deadening a certain area of the parietal lobe could kill sensation in the radial nerve and the hand, but a hypo in the radial nerve wouldn't knock out the parietal lobe of the cerebrum, because the parietal organization was neurally superior. Analogously, anaesthetizing Ruy Jacques' hump shouldn't have deadened his entire cerebrum, because certainly his cerebrum was to be presumed neurally superior to that dorsal malformation.

To be presumed . . .

But with Ruy Jacques, presumptions were—invalid.

So *that* was what Bell had wanted her to discover. Like some sinister reptile of the Mesozoic, Ruy Jacques had *two* neural organizations, one in his skull and one on his back, the latter being superior to, and in some degree controlling, the one in his skull, just as the cerebral cortex in human beings and other higher animals assists and screens the work of the less intricate cerebellum, and just as the cerebellum governs the still more primitive medulla oblongata in the lower vertebrata, such as in frogs and fishes. In anaesthetizing his hump, she had disrupted communications in his highest centers of consciousness, and in anaesthetizing the higher, dorsal center, she had apparently simultaneously deactivated his "normal" brain.

As full realization came, she grew aware of a curious numbness in her thighs, and of faint overtones of mingled terror and awe in the giddy throbbing in her forehead. Slowly, she sank into the bedside chair.

For as this man was, so must she become. The day lay ahead when *her* pineal growths must stretch to the point of disrupting the gray matter in her occipital lobes, and destroy her ability to read. And the time must come, too, when *her* dorsal growth would inflame her whole body with its anguished writhing, as it had done his, and try with probable equal futility to burst its bonds.

And all of this must come—soon; before her ballet première, certainly. The enigmatic skein of the future would be unraveled to her evolving intellect even as it now was to Ruy Jacques'. She could find all the answers she sought . . . Dream's end . . . the Nightingale's death song . . . The Rose. And she would find them whether she wanted to or not.

She groaned uneasily.

At the sound, the man's eyelids seemed to tremble; his breathing slowed momentarily, then became faster.

She considered this in perplexity. He was unconscious, certainly; yet he made definite responses to aural stimuli. Possibly she had anaesthetized neither member of the hypothetical brain-pair, but had merely cut, temporarily, their lines of intercommunication, just as one might temporarily disorganize the brain of a laboratory animal by anaesthetizing the pons Varolii linking the two cranial hemispheres.

Of one thing she was sure: Ruy Jacques, unconscious, and temporarily mentally disintegrate, was not going to conform to the behavior long standardized for other unconscious and disintegrate mammals. Always one step beyond what she ever expected. Beyond man. Beyond genius.

She arose quietly and tiptoed the short distance to the bed.

When her lips were a few inches from the artist's right ear, she said softly: "What is your name?"

The prone figure stirred uneasily. His eyelids fluttered, but did not open. His wine-colored lips parted, then shut, then opened again. His reply was a harsh, barely intelligible whisper: "Zhak."

"What are you doing?"

"Searching . . ."

"For what?"

"A red rose?"

"There are many red roses."

Again his somnolent, metallic whisper: "No, there is but one."

She suddenly realized that her own voice was becoming tense, shrill. She forced it back into a lower pitch. "Think of that rose. Can you see it?"

"Yes . . . yes!"

She cried: *"What is the rose?"*

It seemed that the narrow walls of the room would clamor forever their outraged metallic modesty, if something hadn't frightened away their pain. Ruy Jacques opened his eyes and struggled to rise on one elbow.

On his sweating forehead was a deep frown. But his eyes were apparently focused on nothing in particular, and despite his seemingly purposive motor reaction, she knew that actually her question had but thrown him deeper into his strange spell.

Swaying a little on the dubious support of his right elbow, he muttered: *"You are not the rose . . . not yet . . . not yet . . ."*

She gazed at him in shocked stupor as his eyes closed slowly and he slumped back on the sheet. For a long moment, there was no sound in the room but his deep and rhythmic breathing.

Without turning from her glum perusal of the clinic grounds framed in her window, Anna threw the statement over her shoulder as Bell entered the office. "Your friend Jacques refuses to return for a check-up. I haven't seen him since he walked out a week ago."

"Is that fatal?"

She turned blood-shot eyes on him. "Not to Ruy."

The man's expression twinkled. "He's your patient, isn't he? It's your duty to make a house call."

"I certainly shall. I was going to call him on the visor to make an appointment."

"He doesn't have a visor. Everybody just walks in. There's something doing in his studio nearly every night. If you're bashful, I'll be glad to take you."

"No thanks. I'll go alone—early."

Bell chuckled. "I'll see you tonight."

CHAPTER NINE

Number 98 was a sad, ramshackled, four-story, plaster-front affair, evidently thrown up during the materials shortage of the late forties.

Anna took a deep breath, ignored the unsteadiness of her knees, and climbed the half dozen steps of the front stoop.

There seemed to be no exterior bell. Perhaps it was inside. She pushed the door in and the waning evening light followed her into the hall. From somewhere came a frantic barking, which was immediately silenced.

Anna peered uneasily up the rickety stairs, then whirled as a door opened behind her.

A fuzzy canine muzzle thrust itself out of the crack in the doorway and growled cautiously. And in the same crack, farther up, a dark wrinkled face looked out at her suspiciously. "Whaddaya want?"

Anna retreated half a step. "Does he bite?"

"Who, Mozart? Nah, he couldn't dent a banana," the creature added with anile irrelevance. "Ruy gave him to me because Mozart's dog followed him to the grave."

"Then this is where Mr. Jacques lives?"

"Sure, fourth floor, but you're early." The door opened wider. "Say, haven't I seen you somewhere before?"

Recognition was simultaneous. It was that animated stack of purple dresses, the ancient vendress of love philters.

"Come in, dearie," purred the old one, "and I'll mix you up something special."

"Never mind," said Anna hurriedly. "I've got to see Mr. Jacques." She turned and ran toward the stairway.

A horrid floating cackle whipped and goaded her flight, until she stumbled out on the final landing and set up an insensate skirling on the first door she came to.

From within an irritated voice called: "Aren't you getting a little tired of that? Why don't you come in and rest your knuckles?"

"Oh." She felt faintly foolish. "It's me—Anna van Tuyl."

"Shall I take the door off its hinges, doctor?"

Anna turned the knob and stepped inside.

Ruy Jacques stood with his back to her, palette in hand, facing an easel bathed in the slanting shafts of the setting sun. He was apparently blocking in a caricature of a nude model lying, face averted, on a couch beyond the easel.

Anna felt a sharp pang of disappointment. She'd wanted him to herself a little while. Her glance flicked about the studio.

Framed canvases obscured by dust were stacked willy-nilly about the walls of the big room. Here and there were bits of statuary. Behind a nearby screen, the disarray of a cot peeped out at her. Beyond the screen was a wire-phono. In the opposite wall was a door that evidently opened into the model's dressing alcove. In the opposite corner stood a battered electronic piano which she recognized as the Fourier audiosynthesizer type.

She gave an involuntary gasp as the figure of a man suddenly separated from the piano and bowed to her.

Colonel Grade.

So the lovely model with the invisible face must be—Martha Jacques.

There was no possibility of mistake, for now the model had turned her face a little, and acknowledged Anna's faltering stare with complacent mockery.

Of all evenings, why did Martha Jacques have to pick *this* one?

The artist faced the easel again. His harsh jeer floated back to the psychiatrist: "Behold the perfect female body!"

Perhaps it was the way he said this that saved her. She had a fleeting suspicion that he had recognized her disappointment, had anticipated the depths of her gathering despair, and had deliberately shaken her back into reality.

In a few words he had borne upon her the idea that his enormously complex mind contained neither love nor hate, even for his wife, and that while he found in her a physical perfection suitable for transference to canvas or marble, that nevertheless he writhed in a secret torment over this very perfection, as though in essence the woman's physical beauty simply stated a lack he could not name, and might never know.

With a wary, futile motion he laid aside his brushes and palette. "Yes, Martha is perfect, physically and mentally, and knows it." He laughed brutally. "What she doesn't know, is that frozen beauty admits of no plastic play of meaning. There's nothing behind perfection, because it has no meaning but itself."

There was a clamor on the stairs. "Hah!" cried Jacques. "*More* early-comers. The word must have got around that Martha brought the liquor. School's out, Mart. Better hop into the alcove and get dressed."

Matthew Bell was among the early arrivals. His face lighted up when he saw Anna, then clouded when he picked out Grade and Martha Jacques.

Anna noticed that his mouth was twitching worriedly as he motioned to her. "What's wrong?" she asked.

"Nothing—yet. But I wouldn't have let you come if I'd known *they'd* be here. Has Martha given you any trouble?"

"No. Why should she? I'm here ostensibly to observe Ruy in my professional capacity."

"You don't believe that, and if you get careless, *she* won't either. So watch your step with Ruy while Martha's around. And even when she's not around. Too many eyes here—Security men—Grade's crew. Just don't let Ruy involve you in anything that might attract attention. So much for that. Been here long?"

"I was the first guest—except for *her* and Grade."

"Hmm. I should have escorted you. Even though you're his psychiatrist, this sort of thing sets her to thinking."

"I can't see the harm of coming here alone. It isn't as though Ruy were going to try to make love to me in front of all these people."

"That's exactly what it is as though!" He shook his head and looked about him. "Believe me, I know him better than you. The man is insane . . . unpredictable."

Anna felt a tingle of anticipation . . . or was it of apprehension? "I'll be careful," she said.

"Then come on. If I can get Martha and Ruy into one of their eternal Science-versus-Art arguments, I believe they'll forget about you."

Chapter Ten

"I repeat," said Bell, "we are watching the germination of another Renaissance. The signs are unmistakable, and should be of great interest to practicing sociologists and policemen." He turned from the little group beginning to gather about him and beamed artlessly at the passing face of Colonel Grade.

Grade paused. "And just what are the signs of a renaissance?" he demanded.

"Mainly climatic change and enormously increased leisure, Colonel. Either alone can make a big difference—combined, the result is multiplicative rather than additive."

Anna watched Bell's eyes rove the room and join with those of Martha Jacques, as he continued: "Take temperature. In seven thousand B.C. *homo sapiens*, even in the Mediterranean area, was a shivering nomad; fifteen or twenty centuries later a climatic upheaval had turned Mesopotamia, Egypt, and the Yangtse valley into garden spots, and the first civilizations were born. Another warm period extending over several centuries and ending about twelve hundred A.D. launched the Italian Renaissance and the great Ottoman culture, before the temperature started falling again. Since the middle of the seventeenth century, the mean temperature of New York City has been increasing at the rate of about one-tenth of a degree per year. In another century, palm trees will be commonplace on Fifth Avenue." He broke off and bowed benignantly. "Hello, Mrs. Jacques. I was just mentioning that in past renaissances, mild climates and bounteous crops gave man leisure to think, and to create."

When the woman shrugged her shoulders and made a gesture as though to walk on, Bell continued hurriedly: "Yes, *those* renaissances gave us the Parthenon, *The Last Supper,* the Taj Mahal. *Then,* the *artist* was supreme. But this time it might not happen that way, because we face a simultaneous technologic and climatic optimum. Atomic energy has virtually abolished labor as such, but without the international leavening of common art that united the first Egyptian, Sumerian, Chinese, and Greek cities. Without pausing to consolidate his gains, the scientist rushes on to greater things, to Sciomnia, and to a Sciomnic power source"—he exchanged a sidelong look with the woman scientist—"a machine which, we are informed, may overnight fling man toward the nearer stars. When that day comes, the artist is through . . . unless . . ."

"Unless what?" asked Martha Jacques coldly.

"Unless this Renaissance, sharpened and intensified as it has been by its double maxima of climate and science, is able to force a response comparable to that of the Aurignacian Renaissance of twenty-five thousand B.C., to wit, the flowering of the Cro-Magnon, the first of the modern men. Wouldn't it be ironic if our greatest scientist solved Sciomnia, only to come a cropper at the hands of what may prove to be one of the first primitive specimens of *homo superior*—her husband?"

Anna watched with interest as the psychogeneticist smiled engagingly at Martha Jacques' frowning face, while at the same time he looked beyond her to catch the eye of Ruy Jacques, who was plinking in apparent aimlessness at the keyboard of the Fourier piano.

Martha Jacques said curtly: "I'm afraid, Dr. Bell, that I can't get too excited about your Renaissance. When you come right down to it, local humanity, whether dominated by art or science, is nothing but a temporary surface scum on a primitive backwoods planet."

Bell nodded blandly. "To most scientists Earth is admittedly commonplace. Psychogeneticists, on the other hand, consider this planet and its people one of the wonders of the universe."

"Really?" asked Grade. "And just what have we got here that they don't have on Betelgeuse?"

"Three things," replied Bell. "One—Earth's atmosphere has enough carbon dioxide to grow the forest-spawning grounds of man's primate ancestors, thereby ensuring an unspecialized, quasi-erect, manually-activated species capable of indefinite psychophysical development. It might take the saurian life of a desert planet another billion years to evolve an equal physical and mental structure. Two—that same atmosphere had a surface pressure of 760 mm of mercury and a mean temperature of about 25 degrees Centigrade—excellent conditions for the transmission of sound, speech, and song; and those early men took to it like a duck to water. Compare the difficulty of communication by direct touching of antennae, as the arthropodic pseudo-hominidal citizens of certain airless worlds must do. Three—the solar spectrum within its very short frequency range of 760 to 390 millimicrons offers seven colors of remarkable variety and contrast, which our ancestors quickly made their own. From the beginning, they could see that they moved in multichrome beauty. Consider the ultra-sophisticate dwelling in a dying sun system—and pity him for he can see only red and a little infra-red."

"If that's the only difference," snorted Grade, "I'd say you psychogeneticists were getting worked up over nothing."

Bell smiled past him at the approaching figure of Ruy Jacques. "You may be right, of course, Colonel, but I think you're missing the point. To the psychogeneticist it appears that terrestrial environment is promoting the evolution of a most extraordinary being—a type of *homo* whose energies beyond the barest necessities are devoted to strange, unproductive activities. And to what end? We don't know—yet. But we can guess. Give a psychogeneticist Eohippus and the grassy plains, and he'd predict the modem horse. Give him Archeopteryx and a dense atmosphere, and he could imagine the swan. Give him *h. sapiens* and a two-day work week, or better yet, Ruy Jacques and a no-day work week, and what will he predict?"

"The poorhouse?" asked Jacques, sorrowfully.

Bell laughed. "Not quite. An evolutionary spurt, rather. As *sapiens* turns more and more into his abstract world of the arts, music in particular, the psychogeneticist foresees increased communication in terms of music. This might require certain cerebral realignments in *sapiens,* and perhaps the development of special membranous neural organs—which in turn might lead to completely new mental and physical abilities, and the conquest of new dimensions—just as the human tongue eventually developed from a tasting organ into a means of long-distance vocal communication."

"Not even in Ruy's Science/Art diatribes," said Mrs. Jacques, "have I heard greater nonsense. If this planet is to have any future worthy of the name, you can be sure it will be through the leadership of her scientists."

"I wouldn't be too sure," countered Bell. "The artist's place in society has advanced tremendously in the past half-century. And I mean the minor artist—who is identified simply by his profession and not by any exceptional reputation. In our own time we have seen the financier forced to extend social equality to the scientist. And today the palette and musical sketch pad are gradually toppling the test tube and the cyclotron from their pedestals. In the first Renaissance the merchant and soldier inherited the ruins of church and feudal empire; in this one we peer through the crumbling walls of capitalism and nationalism and see the artist . . . or the scientist . . . ready to emerge as the cream of society. The question is, *which one?*"

"For the sake of law and order," declared Colonel Grade, "it must be the scientist, working in the defense of his country. Think of the military insecurity of an art-dominated society. If—"

Ruy Jacques broke in: "There is only one point on which I must disagree with you." He turned a disarming smile on his wife. "I really don't see how the scientist fits into the picture at all. Do you, Martha? For the artist is *already* supreme.

He dominates the scientist, and if he likes, he is perfectly able to draw upon his more sensitive intuition for those various restatements of artistic principles that the scientists are forever trying to fob off on a decreasingly gullible public under the guise of novel scientific laws. I say that the artist is aware of those 'new' laws long before the scientist, and has the option of presenting them to the public in a pleasing art form or as a dry, abstruse equation. He may, like da Vinci, express his discovery of a beautiful curve in the form of a breath-taking spiral staircase in a *chateau* at Blois, or, like Dürer, he may analyze the curve mathematically and announce its logarithmic formula. In either event he anticipates Descartes, who was the first mathematician to rediscover the logarithmic spiral."

The woman laughed grimly. "All right. *You're* an artist. Just what scientific law have *you* discovered?"

"I have discovered," answered the artist with calm pride, "what will go down in history as 'Jacques' Law of Stellar Radiation.' "

Anna and Bell exchanged glances. The older man's look of relief said plainly: "The battle is joined; they'll forget you."

Martha Jacques peered at the artist suspiciously. Anna could see that the woman was genuinely curious but caught between her desire to crush, to damn any such amateurish "discovery" and her fear that she was being led into a trap. Anna herself, after studying the exaggerated innocence of the man's wide, unblinking eyes, knew immediately that he was subtly enticing the woman out on the rotten limb of her own dry perfection.

In near-hypnosis Anna watched the man draw a sheet of paper from his pocket. She marveled at the superb blend of diffidence and braggadocio with which he unfolded it and handed it to the woman scientist.

"Since I can't write, I had one of the fellows write it down for me, but I think he got it right," he explained. "As you see, it boils down to seven prime equations."

Anna watched a puzzled frown steal over the woman's brow. "But each of these equations expands into hundreds more, especially the seventh, which is the longest of them all." The frown deepened. "Very interesting. Already I see hints of the Russell diagram . . ."

The man started. "What! H. N. Russell, who classified stars into spectral classes? You mean he scooped me?"

"Only if your work is accurate, which I doubt."

The artist stammered: "But—"

"And here," she continued in crisp condemnation, "is nothing more than a restatement of the law of light-pencil wavering, which explains why stars twinkle and planets don't, and which has been known for two hundred years."

Ruy Jacques' face lengthened lugubriously.

The woman smiled grimly and pointed. "These parameters are just a poor approximation of the Bethe law of nuclear fission in stars—old since the thirties." The man stared at the scathing finger. "Old . . . ?"

"I fear so. But still not bad for an amateur. If you kept at this sort of thing all your life, you might eventually develop something novel. But this is a mere hodgepodge, a rehash of material any real scientist learned in his teens."

"But, Martha," pleaded the artist, "surely it isn't *all* old?"

"I can't say with certainty, of course," returned the woman with malice-edged pleasure, "until I examine every sub-equation. I can only say that, fundamentally, scientists long ago anticipated the artist, represented by the great Ruy Jacques. In the aggregate, your amazing Law of Stellar Radiation has been known for two hundred years or more."

Even as the man stood there, as though momentarily stunned by the enormity of his defeat, Anna began to pity his wife.

The artist shrugged his shoulders wistfully. "Science versus Art. So the artist has given his all, and lost. Jacques' Law must sing its swan song, then be forever forgotten." He lifted a resigned face toward the scientist. "Would you, my dear, administer the *coup de grâce* by setting up the proper coordinates in the Fourier audiosynthesizer?"

Anna wanted to lift a warning hand, cry out to the man that he was going too far, that the humiliation he was preparing for his wife was unnecessary, unjust, and would but thicken the wall of hatred that cemented their antipodal souls together.

But it was too late. Martha Jacques was already walking toward the Fourier piano, and within seconds had set up the polar-defined data and had flipped the toggle switch. The psychiatrist found her mind and tongue to be literally paralyzed by the swift movement of this unwitting drama, which was now toppling over the brink of its tragicomic climax.

A deep silence fell over the room.

Anna caught an impression of avid faces, most of whom—Jacques' most intimate friends—would understand the nature of his little playlet and would rub salt into the abraded wound he was delivering his wife.

Then in the space of three seconds, it was over.

The Fourier-piano had synthesized the seven equations, six short, one long, into their tonal equivalents, and it was over.

Dorran, the orchestra leader, broke the uneasy stillness that followed. "I say, Ruy old chap," he blurted, "just what is the difference in 'Jacques' Law of Stellar Radiation' and 'Twinkle, twinkle, little star'?"

Anna, in mingled amusement and sympathy, watched the face of Martha Jacques slowly turn crimson.

The artist replied in amazement. "Why, now that you mention it, there does seem to be a little resemblance."

"It's a dead ringer!" cried a voice.

" 'Twinkle, twinkle' is an old continental folk tune," volunteered another. "I once traced it from Haydn's 'Surprise Symphony' back to the fourteenth century."

"Oh, but that's quite impossible," protested Jacques. "Martha has just stated that science discovered it first, only two hundred years ago."

The woman's voice dripped *aqua regia*. "You planned this deliberately, just to humiliate me in front of these . . . these clowns."

"Martha, I assure you . . . !"

"I'm warning you for the last time, Ruy. If you ever again humiliate me, I'll probably kill you!"

Jacques backed away in mock alarm until he was swallowed up in a swirl of laughter.

The group broke up, leaving the two women alone. Suddenly aware of Martha Jacques' bitter scrutiny, Anna flushed and turned toward her.

Martha Jacques said: "Why can't you make him come to his senses? I'm paying you enough."

Anna gave her a slow wry smile. "Then I'll need your help. And you aren't helping when you deprecate his sense of values—odd though they may seem to you."

"But Art is really so *foolish!* Science—"

Anna laughed shortly. "You see? Do you wonder he avoids you?"

"What would *you* do?"

"*I?*" Anna swallowed dryly.

Martha Jacques was watching her with narrowed eyes. "Yes, you. *If you wanted him?*"

Anna hesitated, breathing uneasily. Then gradually her eyes widened, became dreamy and full, like moons rising over the edge of some unknown, exotic land. Her lips opened with a nerveless fatalism. She didn't care what she said:

"I'd forget that I want, above all things, to be beautiful. I would think only of him. I'd wonder what he's thinking, and I'd forsake my mental integrity and try to think as he thinks. I'd learn to see through his eyes, and to hear through his ears. I'd sing over his successes, and hold my tongue when he failed. When he's moody and depressed, I wouldn't probe or insist that-I-could-help-you-if-you'd-only-let-me. Then—"

Martha Jacques snorted. "In short, you'd be nothing but a selfless shadow, devoid of personality or any mind or individuality of your own. That might be all right for one of your type. But for a scientist, the very thought is ridiculous!"

The psychiatrist lifted her shoulders delicately. "I agree. It *is* ridiculous. What *sane* woman at the peak of her profession would suddenly toss up her career to merge—you'd say 'submerge'—her identity, her very existence, with that of an utterly alien male mentality?"

"What woman, indeed?"

Anna mused to herself, and did not answer. Finally she said: "And yet, that's the price; take it or leave it, they say. What's a girl to do?"

"Stick up for her rights!" declared Martha Jacques spiritedly.

"All hail to unrewarding perseverance!" Ruy Jacques was back, swaying slightly. He pointed his half-filled glass toward the ceiling and shouted: "Friends! A toast! Let us drink to the two charter members of the Knights of the Crimson Grail." He bowed in saturnine mockery to his glowering wife. "To Martha! May she soon solve the Jacques Rosette and blast humanity into the heavens!"

Simultaneously he drank and held up a hand to silence the sudden spate of jeers and laughter. Then, turning toward the now apprehensive psychiatrist, he essayed a second bow of such sweeping grandiosity that his glass was upset. As he straightened, however, he calmly traded glasses with her. "To my old school-teacher, Dr. van Tuyl. A nightingale whose secret ambition is to become as beautiful as a red red rose. May Allah grant her prayers." He blinked at her beatifically in the sudden silence. "What was that comment, doctor?"

"I said you were a drunken idiot," replied Anna. "But let it pass." She was panting, her head whirling. She raised her voice to the growing cluster of faces. "Ladies and gentlemen, I offer you the third seeker of the grail! A truly great artist. Ruy Jacques, a child of the coming epoch, whose sole aim is not aimlessness, as he would like you to think, but a certain marvelous rose. Her curling petals shall be of subtle texture, yet firm withal, and brilliant red. It is this rose that he must find, to save his mind and body, and to put a soul in him."

"She's right!" cried the artist in dark glee. "To Ruy Jacques, then! Join in, everybody. The party's on Martha!"

He downed his glass, then turned a suddenly grave face to his audience. "But it's really such a pity in Anna's case, isn't it? Because her cure is so simple."

The psychiatrist listened; her head was throbbing dizzily.

"As any *competent* psychiatrist could tell her," continued the artist mercilessly, "she has identified herself with the nightingale in her ballet. The nightingale isn't much to look at. On top it's a dirty brown; at bottom, you might say it's a drab gray. But ah! The soul of this plain little bird! Look into my soul, she pleads. Hold me in your strong arms, look into my soul, and think me as lovely as a red rose."

Even before he put his wine glass down on the table, Anna knew what was coming. She didn't need to watch the stiffening cheeks and flaring nostrils of Martha Jacques, nor the sudden flash of fear in Bell's eyes, to know what was going to happen next.

He held out his arms to her, his swart satyr-face nearly impassive save for its eternal suggestion of sardonic mockery.

"You're right," she whispered, half to him, half to some other part of her, listening, watching. "I *do* want you to hold me in your arms and think me beautiful. But you can't, because you don't love me. It won't work. Not here. Here, I'll prove it."

As from miles and centuries away, she heard Grade's horrified gurgle.

But her trance held. She entered the embrace of Ruy Jacques, and held her face up to his as much as her spine would permit, and closed her eyes.

He kissed her quickly on the forehead and released her. "There! Cured!"

She stood back and surveyed him thoughtfully. "I wanted you to see for yourself, that nothing can be beautiful to you—at least not until you learn to regard someone else as highly as you do Ruy Jacques."

Bell had drawn close. His face was wet, gray. He whispered: "Are you two insane? Couldn't you save this sort of thing for a less crowded occasion?"

But Anna was rolling rudderless in a fatalistic calm. "I had to show him something. Here. Now. He might never have tried it if he hadn't had an audience. Can you take me home now?"

"Worst thing possible," replied Bell agitatedly. "That'd just confirm Martha's suspicions." He looked around nervously. "She's gone. Don't know whether that's good or bad. But Grade's watching us. Ruy, if you've got the faintest intimations of decency, you'll wander over to that group of ladies and kiss a few of them. May throw Martha off the scent. Anna, you stay here. Keep talking. Try to toss it off as an amusing incident." He gave a short strained laugh. "Otherwise you're going to wind up as the First Martyr in the Cause of Art."

"I beg your pardon, Dr. van Tuyl."

It was Grade. His voice was brutally cold, and the syllables were clipped from his lips with a spine-tingling finality.

"Yes, Colonel?" said Anna nervously.

"The Security Bureau would like to ask you a few questions."

"Yes?"

Grade turned and stared icily at Bell. "It is preferred that the interrogation be conducted in private. It should not take long. If the lady would kindly step into the model's dressing room, my assistant will take over from there."

"Dr. van Tuyl was just leaving," said Bell huskily. "Did you have a coat, Anna?"

With a smooth unobtrusive motion Grade unsnapped the guard on his hip holster. "If Dr. van Tuyl leaves the dressing room within ten minutes, alone, she may depart from the studio in any manner she pleases."

Anna watched her friend's face become even paler. He wet his lips, then whispered, "I think you'd better go, Anna. Be careful."

CHAPTER ELEVEN

The room was small and nearly bare. Its sole furnishings were an ancient calendar, a clothes tree, a few stacks of dusty books, a table (bare save for a roll of canvas patching tape), and three chairs.

In one of the chairs, across the table, sat Martha Jacques.

She seemed almost to smile at Anna; but the amused curl of her beautiful lips was totally belied by her eyes, which pulsed hate with the paralyzing force of physical blows.

In the other chair sat Willie the Cork, almost unrecognizable in his groomed neatness.

The psychiatrist brought her hand to her throat as though to restore her voice, and at the movement, she saw from the corner of her eye that Willie, in a lightning motion, had simultaneously thrust his hand into his coat pocket, invisible below the table. She slowly understood that he held a gun on her.

The man was the first to speak, and his voice was so crisp and incisive that she doubted her first intuitive recognition. "Obviously, I shall kill you if you attempt any unwise action. So please sit down, Dr. van Tuyl. Let us put our cards on the table."

It was too incredible, too unreal, to arouse any immediate sense of fear. In numb amazement, she pulled out the chair and sat down.

"As you may have suspected for some time," continued the man curtly, "I am a Security agent."

Anna found her voice. "I know only that I am being forcibly detained. What do you want?"

"Information, Doctor. What government do you represent?"

"None."

The man fairly purred. "Don't you realize, Doctor, that as soon as you cease to answer responsively, I shall kill you?"

Anna van Tuyl looked from the man to the woman. She thought of circling hawks, and felt the intimations of terror. What could she have done to attract such wrathful attention? She didn't know. But then, *they* couldn't be sure about *her*, either. This man didn't want to kill her until he found out more. And by that time, surely he'd see that it was all a mistake.

She said: "Either I am a psychiatrist attending a special case, or I am not. I am in no position to prove the positive. Yet, by syllogistic law, you must accept it as a possibility until you prove the negative. Therefore, until you have given me an opportunity to explain or disprove any evidence to the contrary, you can never be certain in your own mind that I am other than what I claim to be."

The man smiled, almost genially. "Well put, Doctor. I hope they've been paying you what you are worth." He bent forward suddenly. "Why are you trying to make Ruy Jacques fall in love with you?"

She stared back with widening eyes. "What did you say?"

"Why are you trying to make Ruy Jacques fall in love with you?"

She could meet his eyes squarely enough, but her voice was now very faint: "I didn't understand you at first. You said . . . that I'm trying to make him fall in love with me." She pondered this for a long wondering moment, as though the idea were utterly new. "And I guess . . . it's true."

The man looked blank, then smiled with sudden appreciation. "You *are* clever. Certainly, you're the first to try *that* line. Though I don't know what you expect to gain with your false candor."

"False? Didn't you mean it yourself? No, I see you didn't. But Mrs. Jacques does. And she hates me for it. But I'm just part of the bigger hate she keeps for *him*. Even her Sciomnia equation is just part of that hate. She isn't working on a biophysical weapon just because she's a patriot, but more to spite *him*, to show him that her science is superior to—"

Martha Jacques' hand lashed viciously across the little table and struck Anna in the mouth.

The man merely murmured: "Please control yourself a bit longer, Mrs. Jacques. Interruptions from outside would be most inconvenient at this point." His humorless eyes returned to Anna. "One evening a week ago, when Mr. Jacques was under your care at the clinic, you left stylus and paper with him."

Anna nodded. "I wanted him to attempt automatic writing."

"What is 'automatic writing'?"

"Simply writing done while the conscious mind is absorbed in a completely extraneous activity, such as music. Mr. Jacques was to focus his attention on certain music composed by me while holding stylus and paper in his lap. If his recent inability to read and write was caused by some psychic block, it was quite possible that his subconscious mind might bypass the block, and he would write—just as one 'doodles' unconsciously when talking over the visor."

He thrust a sheet of paper at her. "Can you identify this?"

What was he driving at? She examined the sheet hesitantly. "It's just a blank sheet from my private monogrammed stationery. Where did you get it?"

"From the pad you left with Mr. Jacques."

"So?"

"We also found another sheet from the same pad under Mr. Jacques' bed. It had some interesting writing on it."

"But Mr. Jacques personally reported nil results."

"He was probably right."

"But you said he wrote something?" she insisted; momentarily her personal danger faded before her professional interest.

"I didn't say *he* wrote anything."

"Wasn't it written with that same stylus?"

"It was. But I don't think he wrote it. It wasn't in his handwriting."

"That's often the case in automatic writing. The script is modified according to the personality of the dissociated subconscious unit. The alteration is sometimes so great as to be unrecognizable as the handwriting of the subject."

He peered at her keenly. "This script was perfectly recognizable, Dr. van Tuyl. I'm afraid you've made a grave blunder. Now, shall I tell you in *whose* handwriting?"

She listened to her own whisper: "Mine?"

"Yes."

"What does it say?"

"You know very well."

"But I don't." Her underclothing was sticking to her body with a damp clammy feeling. "At least you ought to give me a chance to explain it. May I see it?"

He regarded her thoughtfully for a moment, then reached into his pocket sheaf. "Here's an electrostat. The paper, texture, ink, everything, is a perfect copy of your original."

She studied the sheet with a puzzled frown. There were a few lines of scribblings in purple. But it *wasn't* in her handwriting. In fact, it wasn't even handwriting—just a mass of illegible scrawls!

Anna felt a thrill of fear. She stammered: "What are you trying to do?"

"You don't deny you wrote it?"

"Of course I deny it." She could no longer control the quaver in her voice. Her lips were leaden masses, her tongue a stone slab. "It's—unrecognizable . . ."

The Cork floated with sinister patience. "In the upper left-hand corner is your monogram: 'A.v.T.,' the same as on the first sheet. You will admit that, at least?"

For the first time, Anna really examined the presumed trio of initials enclosed in the familiar ellipse. The ellipse was there. But the print within it was—gibberish.

She seized again at the first sheet—the blank one. The feel of the paper, even the smell, stamped it as genuine. It had been hers. But the monogram! "Oh no!" she whispered.

Her panic-stricken eyes flailed about the room. The calendar . . .s ame picture of the same cow . . . *but the rest* . . . ! A stack of books in the corner . . . titled in gold leaf . . . gathering dust for months . . . the label on the roll of patching tape on the same . . . even the watch on her wrist.

Gibberish. She could no longer read. She had forgotten how. Her ironic gods had chosen this critical moment to blind her with their brilliant bounty.

Then take it! And play for time!

She wet trembling lips. "I'm unable to read. My reading glasses are in my bag, outside." She returned the script. "If *you'd* read it, I might recognize the contents."

The man said: "I thought you might try this, just to get my eyes off you. If you don't mind, I'll quote from memory:

" '—what a queer climax for the Dream! Yet, inevitable. Art versus Science decrees that one of us must destroy the Sciomniac weapon; but that could wait until we become more numerous. So, what I do is for him alone, and his future depends on appreciating it. Thus, Science bows to Art, but even Art isn't all. The Student must know the one greater thing when he sees the Nightingale dead, for only then will he recognize . . .' "

He paused.

"Is that all?" asked Anna.

"That's all."

"Nothing about a . . . rose?"

"No. What is 'rose' a code word for?"

Death? mused Anna. Was the rose a cryptolalic synonym for the grave? She closed her eyes and shivered. Were those really *her* thoughts, impressed into the mind and wrist of Ruy Jacques from some grandstand seat at her own ballet three weeks hence? But after all, why was it so impossible? Coleridge claimed 'Kubla Khan' had been dictated to him through automatic writing. And that English mystic, William Blake, freely acknowledged being the frequent amanuensis for an unseen personality. And there were numerous other cases. So, from some unseen time and place, the mind of Anna van Tuyl had been attuned to that of Ruy Jacques, and his mind had momentarily forgotten that both of them could no longer write, and had recorded a strange reverie.

It was then that she noticed the—whispers.

No—not whispers—not exactly. More like rippling vibrations, mingling, rising, falling. Her heart beats quickened when she realized that their eerie pattern was soundless. It was as though something in her mind was suddenly vibrating *en rapport* with a subetheric world. Messages were beating at her for which she had no tongue or ear; they were beyond sound—beyond knowledge, and they swarmed dizzily around her from all directions. From the ring she wore. From the bronze buttons of her jacket. From the vertical steam piping in the corner. From the metal reflector of the ceiling light.

And the strongest and most meaningful of all showered steadily from the invisible weapon The Cork grasped in his coat pocket. Just as surely as though she had seen it done, she knew that the weapon had killed in the past. And not just once. She found herself attempting to unravel those thought residues of death—once—twice—three times . . . beyond which they faded away into steady, undecipherable time-muted violence.

And now that gun began to scream: "Kill! Kill! Kill!"

She passed her palm over her forehead. Her whole face was cold and wet. She swallowed noisily.

CHAPTER TWELVE

Ruy Jacques sat before the metal illuminator near his easel, apparently absorbed in the profound contemplation of his goatish features, and oblivious to the mounting gaiety about him. In reality he was almost completely lost in a soundless, sardonic glee over the triangular death-struggle that was nearing its climax beyond the inner wall of his studio, and which was magnified in his remarkable mind to an incredible degree by the paraboloid mirror of the illuminator.

Bell's low urgent voice began hacking at him again. "Her blood will be on your head. All you need to do is to go in there. Your wife wouldn't permit any shooting with you around."

The artist twitched his misshapen shoulders irritably.

"*Maybe*. But why should I risk my skin for a silly little nightingale?"

"Can it be that your growth beyond *sapiens* has served simply to sharpen your objectivity, to accentuate your inherent egregious want of identity with even the best of your fellow creatures? Is the indifference that has driven Martha nearly insane in a bare decade now too ingrained to respond to the first known female of your own unique breed?" Bell sighed heavily. "You don't have to answer. The very senselessness of her impending murder amuses you. Your nightingale is about to be impaled on her thorn—for nothing—as always. Your sole regret at the moment is that you can't twit her with the assurance that you will study her corpse diligently to find there the rose you seek."

"Such unfeeling heartlessness," said Jacques in regretful agreement, "is only to be expected in one of Martha's blunderings. I mean The Cork, of course. Doesn't he realize that Anna hasn't finished the score of her ballet? Evidently has no musical sense at all. I'll bet he was even turned down for the policemen's charity quarter. You're right, as usual, doc. We must punish such philistinism." He tugged at his chin, then rose from the folding stool.

"What are you going to do?" demanded the other sharply.

The artist weaved toward the phono cabinet. "Play a certain selection from Tchaikovsky's *Sixth*. If Anna's half the girl you think, she and Peter Ilyitch will soon have Mart eating out of their hands."

Bell watched him in anxious, yet half-trusting frustration as the other selected a spool from his library of electronic recordings and inserted it into the playback sprocket. In mounting mystification, he saw Jacques turn up the volume control as far as it would go.

CHAPTER THIRTEEN

Murder, a one-act play directed by Mrs. Jacques, thought Anna. With sound effects by Mr. Jacques, But the facts didn't fit. It was unthinkable that Ruy would do anything to accommodate his wife. If anything, he would try to thwart Martha. But what was his purpose in starting off in the finale of the first movement of the *Sixth?* Was there some message there that he was trying to get across to her? There was. She had it. She was going to live. If—

"In a moment," she told The Cork in a tight voice, "you are going to snap off the safety catch of your pistol, revise slightly your estimated line of fire, and squeeze the trigger. Ordinarily you could accomplish all three acts in almost instantaneous sequence. At the present moment, if I tried to turn the table over on you, you could put a bullet in my head before I could get well started. But in another sixty seconds you will no longer have that advantage, because your motor nervous system will be laboring under the superimposed pattern of the extraordinary Second Movement of the symphony that we now hear from the studio."

The Cork started to smile, then he frowned faintly. "What do you mean?"

"All motor acts are carried out in simple rhythmic patterns. We walk in the two-four time of the march. We waltz, use a pickaxe, and manually grasp or replace objects in three-four rhythm."

"This nonsense is purely a play for time," interjected Martha Jacques. "Kill her."

"It is a fact," continued Anna hurriedly. (Would that Second Movement never begin?) "A decade ago, when there were still a few factories using hand-assembly methods, the workmen speeded their work by breaking down the task into these same elemental rhythms, aided by appropriate music." (There! It was beginning! The immortal genius of that suicidal Russian was reaching across a century to save her!) "It so happens that the music you are hearing *now* is the Second Movement that I mentioned, and it's neither two-four nor three-four but *five*-four, an oriental rhythm that gives difficulty even to skilled occidental musicians and dancers. Subconsciously you are going to try to break it down into the only rhythms to which your motor nervous system is attuned. But you can't. Nor can *any* occidental, even a professional dancer, unless he has had special training"— her voice wobbled slightly—"in Delcrozian eurhythmics."

She crashed into the table.

Even though she had known that this must happen, her success was so complete, so overwhelming, that it momentarily appalled her.

Martha Jacques and The Cork had moved with anxious, rapid jerks, like puppets in a nightmare. But their rhythm was all wrong. With their ingrained four-time motor responses strangely modulated by a five-time pattern, the result was inevitably the arithmetical composite of the two: a neural beat, which could activate muscle tissue only when the two rhythms were in phase.

The Cork had hardly begun his frantic, spasmodic squeeze of the trigger when the careening table knocked him backward to the floor, stunned, beside Martha

Jacques. It required but an instant for Anna to scurry around and extract the pistol from his numbed fist.

Then she pointed the trembling gun in the general direction of the carnage she had wrought and fought an urge to collapse against the wall.

She waited for the room to stop spinning, for the white, glass-eyed face of Martha Jacques to come into focus against the fuzzy background of the cheap paint-daubed rug. And then the eyes of the woman scientist flickered and closed.

With a wary glance at the weapon muzzle, The Cork gingerly pulled a leg from beneath the table edge. "You have the gun," he said softly. "You can't object if I assist Mrs. Jacques?"

"I *do* object," said Anna faintly. "She's merely unconscious . . . feels nothing. I want her to stay that way for a few minutes. If you approach her or make any unnecessary noise, I will probably kill you. So—both of you must stay here until Grade investigates. I know you have a pair of handcuffs. I'll give you ten seconds to lock yourself to that steam pipe in the corner—hands *behind* you, please."

She retrieved the roll of adhesive patching tape from the floor and fixed several strips across the agent's lips, following with a few swift loops around the ankles to prevent him stamping his feet.

A moment later, her face a damp mask, she closed the door leisurely behind her and stood there, breathing deeply and searching the room for Grade.

He was standing by the studio entrance, staring at her fixedly. When she favored him with a glassy smile, he simply shrugged his shoulders and began walking slowly toward her.

In growing panic her eyes darted about the room. Bell and Ruy Jacques were leaning over the phono, apparently deeply absorbed in the racing clangor of the music. She saw Bell nod a covert signal in her direction, but without looking directly at her. She tried not to seem hurried as she strolled over to join them. She knew that Grade was now walking toward them and was but a few steps away when Bell lifted his head and smiled.

"Everything all right?" said the psychogeneticist loudly.

She replied clearly: "Fine. Mrs. Jacques and a Security man just wanted to ask some questions." She drew in closer. Her lips framed a question to Bell: "Can Grade hear?"

Bell's lips formed a soft, nervous guttural: "No. He's moving off toward the dressing room door. If what I suspect happened behind that door is true, you have about ten seconds to get out of here. And then you've got to hide." He turned abruptly to the artist. "Ruy, you've got to take her down into the Via. Right now—*immediately*. Watch your opportunity and lose her when no one is looking. It shouldn't be too hard in that mob."

Jacques shook his head doubtfully. "Martha isn't going to like this. You know how strict she is on etiquette. I think there's a very firm statement in Emily Post that the host should never, never, *never* walk out on his guests before locking up the liquor and silverware. Oh, well, if you insist."

CHAPTER FOURTEEN

"Tell ya what the professor's gonna do, ladies and gentlemen. He's gonna defend not just one paradox. Not just two. But seventeen! In the space of one short hour, and without repeating himself, and including one he just thought up five minutes ago: 'Security is dangerous.' "

Ruy frowned, then whispered to Anna: "That was for us. He means Security men are circulating. Let's move on. Next door. They won't look for a woman there."

Already he was pulling her away toward the chess parlor. They both ducked under the For Men Only sign (which she could no longer read), pushed through the bat-wing doors, and walked unobtrusively down between the wall and a row of players. One man looked up briefly out of the corner of his eye as they passed.

The woman paused uneasily. She had sensed the nervousness of the barker even before Ruy, and now still fainter impressions were beginning to ripple over the straining surface of her mind. They were coming from that chess player: from the coins in his pocket; from the lead weights of his chess pieces; and especially from the weapon concealed somewhere on him. The resonant histories of the chess pieces and coins she ignored. They held the encephalographic residua of too many minds. The invisible gun was clearer. There was something abrupt and violent, alternating with a more subtle, restrained rhythm. She put her hand to her throat as she considered one interpretation: *Kill—but wait.* Obviously, he'd dare not fire with Ruy so close.

"Rather warm here, too," murmured the artist. "Out we go."

As they stepped out into the street again, she looked behind her and saw that the man's chair was empty.

She held the artist's hand and pushed and jabbed after him, deeper into the reveling sea of humanity.

She ought to be thinking of ways to hide, of ways to use her new sensory gift. But another, more imperative train of thought continually clamored at her, until finally she yielded to a gloomy brooding.

Well, it was true. She wanted to be loved, and she wanted Ruy to love her. And he knew it. Every bit of metal on her shrieked her need for his love.

But—was she ready to love him? No! How could she love a man who lived only to paint that mysterious, unpaintable scene of the nightingale's death, and who loved only himself? He was fascinating, but what sensible woman would wreck her career for such unilateral fascination? Perhaps Martha Jacques was right, after all.

"So you got him!"

Anna whirled toward the crazy crackle, nearly jerking her hand from Ruy's grasp.

The vendress of love-philters stood leaning against the front center pole of her tent, grinning toothily at Anna.

While the young woman stared dazedly at her, Jacques spoke up crisply: "Any strange men been around, Violet?"

"Why, Ruy," she replied archly, "I think you're jealous. What kind of men?"

"Not the kind that haul you off to the alcoholic ward on Saturday nights. Not city dicks. Security men—quiet—seem slow, but really fast—see everybody—everything."

"Oh, *them*. Three went down the street two minutes ahead of you."

He rubbed his chin. "That's not so good. They'll start at that end of the Via and work up toward us until they meet the patrol behind us."

"Like grains of wheat between the millstones," cackled the crone. "I *knew* you'd turn to crime, sooner or later, Ruy. You were the only tenant I had who paid the rent regular."

"Mart's lawyer did that."

"Just the same, it looked mighty suspicious. You want to try the alley behind the tent?"

"Where does it lead?"

"Cuts back into the Via, at White Rose Park."

Anna started. "White rose?"

"We were there that first night," said Jacques. "You remember it—big rose-walled cul-de-sac. Fountain. Pretty, but not for us, not now. Has only one entrance. We'll have to try something else."

The psychiatrist said hesitantly: "No, wait."

For some moments she had been struck by the sinister contrast between this second descent into the Via and the irresponsible gaiety of that first night. The street, the booths, the laughter seemed the same, but really weren't. It was like a familiar musical score, subtly altered by some demoniac hand, raised into some harsh and fatalistic minor key. It was like the second movement of Tchaikovsky's *Romeo and Juliet:* all the bright promises of the first movement were here, but repetition had transfigured them into frightful premonitions.

She shivered. That second movement, that echo of destiny, was sweeping through her in ever faster tempo, as though impatient to consummate its assignation with her. Come safety, come death, she must yield to the pattern of repetition.

Her voice had a dreamlike quality: "Take me again to the White Rose Park."

"What! Talk sense! Out here in the open, you may have a chance."

"But I *must* go there. Please, Ruy. I think it's something about a white rose. Don't look at me as though I were crazy. Of course I'm crazy. If you don't want to take me, I'll go alone. But I'm going."

His hard eyes studied her in speculative silence, then he looked away. As the stillness grew, his face mirrored his deepening introspection. "At that, the possibilities are intriguing. Martha's stooges are sure to look in on you. But will they be able to see you? Is the hand that wields the pistol equally skilled with the brush and palette? Unlikely. Art and Science again. Pointillist school versus police school. A good one on Martha—if it works. Anna's dress is green. Complement of green is purple. Violet's dress should do it."

"My dress?" cried the old woman. "What are you up to, Ruy?"

"Nothing, luscious. I just want you to take off one of your dresses. The outer one will do."

"Sir!" Violet began to sputter in barely audible gasps.

Anna had watched all this in vague detachment, accepting it as one of the man's daily insanities. She had no idea what he wanted with a dirty old purple dress, but she thought she knew how she could get it for him, while simultaneously introducing another repetitive theme into this second movement of her hypothetical symphony.

She said: "He's willing to make you a fair trade, Violet."

The spluttering stopped. The old woman eyed them both suspiciously. "Meaning what?"

"He'll drink one of your love potions."

The leathery lips parted in amazement. "*I'm* agreeable, if *he* is, but I know he isn't. Why, that scamp doesn't love any creature in the whole world, except maybe himself."

"And yet he's ready to make a pledge to his beloved," said Anna.

The artist squirmed. "I like you, Anna, but I won't be trapped. Anyway, it's all nonsense. What's a glass of acidified water between friends?"

"The pledge isn't to me, Ruy. It's to a Red Rose."

He peered at her curiously. "Oh? Well, if it will please you . . . All right, Violet, but off with that dress before you pour up."

Why, wondered Anna, do I keep thinking his declaration of love to a red rose is my death sentence? It's moving too fast. Who—what—is The Red Rose? The Nightingale dies in making the white rose red. So *she*—or I—can't be The Red Rose. Anyway, The Nightingale is ugly, and The Rose is beautiful. And why must The Student have a Red Rose? How will it admit him to his mysterious dance?

"Ah, Madame De Medici is back." Jacques took the glass and purple bundle the old woman put on the table. "What are the proper words?" he asked Anna.

"Whatever you want to say."

His eyes, suddenly grave, looked into hers. He said quietly; "If ever The Red Rose presents herself to me, I shall love her forever."

Anna trembled as he upended the glass.

CHAPTER FIFTEEN

A little later they slipped into the Park of the White Roses. The buds were just beginning to open, and thousands of white floreate eyes blinked at them in the harsh artificial light. As before, the enclosure was empty, and silent, save for the chattering splashing of its single fountain.

Anna abandoned a disconnected attempt to analyze the urge that had brought her here a second time. It's all too fatalistic, she thought, too involved. If I've entrapped myself, I can't feel bitter about it. "Just think," she murmured aloud, "in less than ten minutes it will all be over, one way or the other."

"Really? But where's my red rose?"

How could she even *consider* loving this jeering beast? She said coldly: "I think you'd better go. It may be rather messy in here soon." She thought of how her body would look, sprawling, misshapen, uglier than ever. She couldn't let him see her that way.

"Oh, we've plenty of time. No red rose, eh? Hmm. It seems to me, Anna, that you're composing yourself for death prematurely. There really is that little matter of the rose to be taken care of first, you know. As The Student, I must insist on my rights."

What made him be this way? "Ruy, please . . ." Her voice was trembling, and she was suddenly very near to tears.

"There, dear, don't apologize. Even the best of us are thoughtless at times. Though I must admit, I never expected such lack of consideration, such poor manners, in *you*. But then, at heart, you aren't really an artist. You've no appreciation of form." He began to untie the bundled purple dress, and his voice took on the argumentative dogmatism of a platform lecturer. "The perfection of form, of technique, is the highest achievement possible to the artist. When he subordinates form to subject matter, he degenerates eventually into a boot-lick, a scientist, or, worst of all, a Man with a Message. Here, catch!" He tossed the gaudy garment at Anna, who accepted it in rebellious wonder.

Critically, the artist eyed the nauseating contrast of the purple and green dresses, glanced momentarily toward the semi-circle of white-budded wall beyond, and then continued: "There's nothing like a school-within-a-school to squeeze dry the dregs of form. And whatever their faults, the pointillists of the impressionist movement could depict color with magnificent depth of chroma. Their palettes held only the spectral colors, and they never mixed them. Do you know why the Seines of Seurat are so brilliant and luminous? It's because the water is made of dots of pure green, blue, red, and yellow, alternating with white in the proper proportion." He motioned with his hand, and she followed as he walked slowly on around the semi-circular gravel path. "What a pity Martha isn't here to observe our little experiment in tricolor stimulus. Yes, the scientific psychologists finally gave arithmetical vent to what the pointillists knew long before them— that a mass of points of any three spectral colors—or of one color and its complementary color—can be made to give any imaginable hue simply by varying their relative proportion."

Anna thought back to that first night of the street dancers. So *that* was why his green and purple polka-dot academic gown had first seemed white!

At his gesture, she stopped and stood with her humped back barely touching the mass of scented buds. The arched entrance was a scant hundred yards to her right. Out in the Via an ominous silence seemed to be gathering. The Security men were probably roping off the area, certain of their quarry. In a minute or two, perhaps sooner, they would be at the archway, guns drawn.

She inhaled deeply and wet her lips.

The man smiled. "You hope I know what I'm doing, don't you? So do I."

"I think I understand your theory," said Anna, "but I don't think it has much chance of working."

"Tush, child." He studied the vigorous play of the fountain speculatively. "The pigment should never harangue the artist. You're forgetting that there isn't really such a color as white. The pointillists knew how to simulate white with alternating dots of primary colors long before the scientists learned to spin the same colors on a disc. And those old masters could even make white from just two colors: a primary and its complementary color. Your green dress is our primary; Violet's purple dress is its complementary. Funny, mix 'em as pigments into a homogeneous mass, and you get brown. But daub 'em on the canvas side by side, stand back the right distance, and they blend into white. All you have to do is hold Vi's dress at arm's length, at your side, with a strip of rosebuds and green leaves looking out between, and you'll have that white rose you came here in search of."

She demurred: "But the angle of visual interruption won't be small enough to blend the colors into white, even if the police don't come any nearer than the archway. The eye sees two objects as one only when the visual angle between the two is less than sixty seconds of arc."

"That old canard doesn't apply too strictly to colors. The artist relies more on the suggestibility of the mind rather than on the mechanical limitations of the retina. Admittedly, if our lean-jawed friends stared in your direction for more than a fraction of a second, they'd see you not as a whitish blur, but as a woman in green holding out a mass of something purple. But they aren't going to give your section of the park more than a passing glance." He pointed past the fountain toward the opposite horn of the semi-circular path. "I'm going to stand over *there,* and the instant someone sticks his head in through the archway, I'm going to start walking. Now, as every artist knows, normal people in Western cultures absorb pictures from left to right, because they're levo-dextro readers. So our agent's first glance will be toward you, and then his attention will be momentarily distracted by the fountain in the center. And before he can get back to you, I'll start walking, and his eyes will have to come on to me. His attentive transition, of course, must be sweeping and imperative, yet so smooth, so subtle, that he will suspect no control. Something like Alexander's painting, *Lady on a Couch,* where the converging stripes of the lady's robe carry the eye forcibly from the lower left margin to her face at the upper right."

Anna glanced nervously toward the garden entrance, then whispered entreatingly. "Then you'd better go. You've got to be beyond the fountain when they look in."

He sniffed. "All right, I know when I'm not wanted. That's the gratitude I get for making you into a rose."

"I don't care a tinker's damn for a *white* rose. Scat!"

He laughed, then turned and started on around the path.

As Anna followed the graceful stride of his long legs, her face began to writhe in alternate bitterness and admiration. She groaned softly. "You—*fiend!* You gorgeous, egotistical, insufferable unattainable FIEND! You aren't elated because you're saving my life; *I* am just a blotch of pigment in your latest masterpiece. *I hate you!*"

He was past the fountain now, and nearing the position he had earlier indicated.

She could see that he was looking toward the archway. She was afraid to look there.

Now he must stop and wait for his audience.

Only he didn't. His steps actually hastened.

That meant . . .

The woman trembled, closed her eyes, and froze into a paralytic stupor through which the crunch of the man's sandals filtered as from a great distance, muffled, mocking.

And then, from the direction of the archway, came the quiet scraping of more footsteps.

In the next split second she would know life or death.

But even now, even as she was sounding the iciest depths of her terror, her lips were moving with the clear insight of imminent death. "No, I don't hate you. I love you, Ruy. I have loved you from the first."

At that instant a blue-hot ball of pain began crawling slowly up within her body, along her spine, and then outward between her shoulder blades, into her spinal hump. The intensity of that pain forced her slowly to her knees and pulled her head back in an invitation to scream.

But no sound came from her convulsing throat.

It was unendurable, and she was fainting.

The sound of footsteps died away down the Via. At least Ruy's ruse had worked.

And as the mounting anguish spread over her back, she understood that all sound had vanished with those retreating footsteps, forever, because she could no longer hear, nor use her vocal cords. She had forgotten how, but she didn't care.

For her hump had split open, and something had flopped clumsily out of it, and she was drifting gently outward into blackness.

CHAPTER SIXTEEN

The glum face of Ruy Jacques peered out through the studio window into the night-awakening Via.

Before I met you, he brooded, loneliness was a magic, ecstatic blade drawn across my heart strings; it healed the severed strands with every beat, and I had all that I wanted save what I had to have—the Red Rose. My search for that Rose alone matters! I must believe this. I must not swerve, even for the memory of you, Anna, the first of my own kind I have ever met. I must not wonder if they killed you, nor even care. They must have killed you . . . It's been three weeks.

Now I can see the Rose again. Onward into loneliness.

He sensed the nearness of familiar metal behind him. "Hello, Martha," he said, without turning. "Just get here?"

"Yes. How's the party going?" Her voice seemed carefully expressionless.

"Fair. You'll know more when you get the liquor bill."

"Your ballet opens tonight, doesn't it?" Still that studied tonelessness.

"You know damn well it doesn't." His voice held no rancor. "La Tanid took your bribe and left for Mexico. It's just as well. I can't abide a prima ballerina who'd rather eat than dance." He frowned slightly. Every bit of metal on the woman was singing in secret elation. She was thinking of a great triumph—something far beyond her petty victory in wrecking his opening night. His searching mind caught hints of something intricate, but integrated, completed—and deadly. Nineteen equations. The Jacques Rosette. Sciomnia.

"So you've finished your toy," he murmured. "You've got what you wanted, and you think you've destroyed what I wanted."

Her reply was harsh, suspicious. "How did you know, when not even Grade is sure? Yes, my weapon is finished. I can hold in one hand a thing that can obliterate your whole Via in an instant. A city, even a continent would take but a little longer. Science versus Art! Bah! This concrete embodiment of biophysics is the answer to your puerile Renaissance—your precious feather-bed world of music and painting! You and your kind are helpless when I and my kind choose to act. In the final analysis Science means *force*—the ability to control the minds and bodies of men."

The shimmering surface of his mind was now catching the faintest wisps of strange, extraneous impressions, vague and disturbing, and which did not seem to originate from metal within the room. In fact, he could not be sure they originated from metal at all.

He turned to face her. "How can Science control all men when it can't even control individuals—Anna van Tuyl, for example?"

She shrugged her shoulders. "You're only partly right. They failed to find her, but her escape was pure accident. In any event, she no longer represents any danger to me or to the political group that I control. Security has actually dropped her from their shoot-on-sight docket."

He cocked his head slightly and seemed to listen. "*You* haven't, I gather."

"You flatter her. She was never more than a pawn in our little game of Science versus Art. Now that she's off the board, and I've announced checkmate against you, I can't see that she matters."

"So Science announces checkmate? Isn't that a bit premature? Suppose Anna shows up again, with or without the conclusion of her ballet score? Suppose we find another prima? What's to keep us from holding *The Nightingale and the Rose* tonight, as scheduled?"

"Nothing," replied Martha Jacques coolly. "Nothing at all, except that Anna van Tuyl has probably joined your former prima at the South Pole by this time, and anyway, a new ballerina couldn't learn the score in the space of two hours, even if you found one. If this wishful thinking comforts you, why, pile it on!"

Very slowly Jacques put his wine glass on the nearby table. He washed his mind clear with a shake of his satyrish head, and strained every sense into receptivity. Something was being etched against that slurred background of laughter and clinking glassware. Then he sensed—or heard—something that brought tiny beads of sweat to his forehead and made him tremble.

"What's the matter with you?" demanded the woman.

As quickly as it had come, the chill was gone.

Without replying, he strode quickly into the center of the studio.

"Fellow revelers!" he cried. "Let us prepare to double, nay, *re*-double our merriment!" With sardonic satisfaction he watched the troubled silence spread away from him, faster and faster, like ripples around a plague spot.

When the stillness was complete, he lowered his head, stretched out his hand as if in horrible warning, and spoke in the tense spectral whisper of Poe's Roderick Usher:

"Madmen! I tell you that she now stands without the door!"

Heads turned; eyes bulged toward the entrance.

There, the door knob was turning slowly.

The door swung in, and left a cloaked figure framed in the doorway.

The artist started. He had been certain that this must be Anna.

It *must* be Anna, yet it could not be. The once frail, cruelly bent body now stood superbly erect beneath the shelter of the cloak. There was no hint of spinal deformity in this woman, and there were no marring lines of pain about her faintly smiling mouth and eyes, which were fixed on his. In one graceful motion her hands reached up beneath the cloak and set it back on her shoulders. Then, after an almost instantaneous *demi-plié,* she floated twice, like some fragile flower dancing in a summer breeze, and stood before him *sur les pointes,* with her cape billowing and fluttering behind her in mute encore.

Jacques looked down into eyes that were dark fires. But her continued silence was beginning to disturb and irritate him. He responded to it almost by reflex, refusing to admit to himself his sudden enormous happiness: "A woman without a tongue! By the gods! Her sting is drawn!" He shook her by the shoulders, roughly, as though to punish this fault in her that had drawn the familiar acid to his mouth.

Her arms moved up, cross-fashioned, and her hands covered his. She smiled, and a harp-arpeggio seemed to wing across his mind, and the tones rearranged themselves into words, like images on water suddenly smooth:

"Hello again, darling. Thanks for being glad to see me."

Something in him collapsed. His arms dropped and he turned his head away. "It's no good, Anna. Why'd you come back? Everything's falling apart. Even our ballet. Martha bought out our prima."

Again that lilting cascade of tones in his brain: "I know, dear, but it doesn't matter. I'll sub beautifully for La Tanid. I know the part perfectly. And I know the Nightingale's death song, too."

"Hah!" he laughed harshly, annoyed at his exhibition of discouragement and her ready sympathy. He stretched his right leg into a mocking *pointe tendue.* "Marvelous! You have the exact amount of drab clumsiness that we need in a Nightingale. And as for the death song, why of course you and you alone know how that ugly little bird feels when"—his eyes were fixed on her mouth in sudden, startled suspicion, and he finished the rest of the sentence inattentively, with no real awareness of its meaning—"when she dies on the thorn."

As he waited, the melody formed, vanished, and reformed and resolved into the strangest thing he had ever known: "What you are thinking is true. My lips do not move. I cannot talk. I've forgotten how, just as we both forgot how to read and write. But even the plainest nightingale can sing, and make the white rose red."

This was Anna transfigured. Three weeks ago he had turned his back and left a diffident disciple to an uncertain fate. Confronting him now was this dark angel bearing on her face the luminous stamp of death. In some manner that he might never learn, the gods had touched her heart and body, and she had borne them straightway to him.

He stood, musing in alternate wonder and scorn. The old urge to jeer at her suddenly rose in his gorge. His lips contorted, then gradually relaxed, as an indescribable elation began to grow within him.

He could thwart Martha yet!

He leaped to the table and shouted: "Your attention, friends! In case you didn't get all this, we've found a ballerina! The curtain rises tonight on our première performance, as scheduled!"

Over the clapping and cheering, Dorran, the orchestra conductor, shouted: "Did I understand that Dr. van Tuyl has finished the Nightingale's death song? We'll have to omit that tonight, won't we? No chance to rehearse . . ."

Jacques looked down at Anna for a moment. His eyes were very thoughtful when he replied: "She says it won't be omitted. What I mean is, keep that thirty-eight-rest sequence in the death scene. Yes, do that, and we shall see . . . what we shall see . . ."

"Thirty-eight rests as presently scored, then?"

"Yes. All right, boys and girls. Let's be on our way. Anna and I will follow shortly."

Chapter Seventeen

Now it was a mild evening in late June, in the time of the full blooming of the roses, and the Via floated in a heady, irresistible tide of attar. It got into the tongues of the children and lifted their laughter and shouts an octave. It stained the palettes of the artists along the sidewalks, so that, despite the bluish glare of the artificial lights, they could paint only in delicate crimsons, pinks, yellows, and whites. The petalled current swirled through the side-shows and eternally new exhibits and gave them a veneer of perfection; it eddied through the canvas flap of the vendress of love philters and erased twenty years from her face. It brushed a scented message across the responsive mouths of innumerable pairs of lovers, blinding them to the appreciative gaze of those who stopped to watch them.

And the lovely dead petals kept fluttering through the introspective mind of Ruy Jacques, clutching and whispering. He brushed their skittering dance aside and considered the situation with growing apprehension. In her recurrent Dreams, he thought, Anna had always awakened just as The Nightingale began her death song. But now she knew the death song. So she knew the Dream's end. Well, it must not be so bad, or she wouldn't have returned. Nothing was going to happen, not really. He shot the question at her: There was no danger any more, was there? Surely the ballet would be a superb success? She'd be enrolled with the immortals.

Her reply was grave, yet it seemed to amuse her. It gave him a little trouble; there were no words for its exact meaning. It was something like: "Immortality begins with death."

He glanced at her face uneasily. "Are you looking for trouble?"

"Everything will go smoothly."

After all, he thought, she believes she has looked into the future and has seen what will happen.

"The Nightingale will not fail The Student," she added with a queer smile. "You'll get your Red Rose."

"You can be plainer than that," he muttered. "Secrets . . . secrets . . . Why all this you're-too-young-to-know business?"

But she laughed in his mind, and the enchantment of that laughter took his breath away. Finally he said: "I admit I don't know what you're talking about. But if you're about to get involved in anything on my account, forget it. I won't have it."

"Each does the thing that makes him happy. The Student will never be happy until he finds the Rose that will admit him to his Dance. The Nightingale will never be happy until the Student holds her in his arms and thinks her as lovely as a Red Rose. I think we may both get what we want."

He growled: "You haven't the faintest idea what you're talking about."

"Yes, I have, especially right now. For ten years I've urged people not to inhibit their healthy inclinations. At the moment I don't have any inhibitions at all. It's a wonderful feeling. I've never been so happy, I think. For the first and last time in my life, I'm going to kiss you."

Her hand tugged at his sleeve. As he looked down into that enchanted face, he knew that this night was hers, that she was privileged in all things, and that whatever she willed must yield to her.

They had stopped at the temporarily-erected stage-door. She rose *sur les pointes,* took his face in her palms, and like a hummingbird drinking her first nectar, kissed him on the mouth.

A moment later she led him into the dressing-room corridor.

He stifled a confused impulse to wipe the back of his hand across his lips. "Well . . . well, just remember to take it easy. Don't try to be spectacular. The artificial wings won't take it. Canvas stretched on duralite and piano wire calls for adagio. A fast pirouette, and they're ripped off. Besides, you're out of practice. Control your enthusiasm in Act I, or you'll collapse in Act II. Now, run on to your dressing room. Cue in five minutes!"

CHAPTER EIGHTEEN

There is a faint, yet distinct anatomical difference in the foot of the man and that of the woman, which keeps him earthbound, while permitting her, after long and arduous training, to soar *sur les pointes.* Owing to the great and varied beauty of the arabesques open to the ballerina poised on her extended toes, the male danseur at one time existed solely as a shadowy *porteur,* and was needed only to supply unobtrusive support and assistance in the exquisite *enchaînements* of the ballerina. Iron muscles in leg and torso are vital in the danseur, who must help maintain the illusion that his whirling partner is made of fairy gossamer, seeking to wing skyward from his restraining arms.

All this flashed through the incredulous mind of Ruy Jacques as he whirled in a double *fouette* and followed from the corner of his eye the gray figure of Anna van Tuyl, as, wings and arms aflutter, she pirouetted in the second *enchaînement* of Act I, away from him and toward the *maître de ballet*.

It was all well enough to give the illusion of flying, of alighting apparently weightless, in his arms—that was what the audience loved. But that it could ever *really* happen—*that* was simply impossible. Stage wings—things of grey canvas and duralite frames—couldn't subtract a hundred pounds from one hundred and twenty.

And yet . . . it had seemed to him that she had actually flown.

He tried to pierce her mind—to extract the truth from the bits of metal about her. In a gust of fury he dug at the metal outline of those remarkable wings.

In the space of seconds his forehead was drenched in cold sweat, and his hands were trembling. Only the fall of the curtain on the first act saved him as he stumbled through his exit *entrechat*.

What had Matt Bell said? "To communicate in his new language of music, one may expect our man of the future to develop specialized membranous organs, which, of course, like the tongue, will have dual functional uses, possibly leading to the conquest of time as the tongue has conquered space."

Those wings were not wire and metal, but flesh and blood.

He was so absorbed in his ratiocination that he failed to become aware of an acutely unpleasant metal radiation behind him until it was almost upon him. It was an intricate conglomeration of matter, mostly metal, resting perhaps a dozen feet behind his back, showing the lethal presence of his wife.

He turned with nonchalant grace to face the first tangible spawn of the Sciomnia formula.

It was simply a black metal box with a few dials and buttons. The scientist held it lightly in her lap as she sat at the side of the table.

His eyes passed slowly from it to her face, and he knew that in a matter of minutes Anna van Tuyl—and all Via Rosa beyond her—would be soot floating in the night wind.

Martha Jacques' face was sublime with hate. "Sit down," she said quietly.

He felt the blood leaving his cheeks. Yet he grinned with a fair show of geniality as he dropped into the chair. "Certainly. I've got to kill time somehow until the end of Act III."

She pressed a button on the box surface.

His volition vanished. His muscles were locked, immobile. He could not breathe.

Just as he was convinced that she planned to suffocate him, her finger made another swift motion toward the box, and he sucked in a great gulp of air. His eyes could move a little, but his larynx was still paralyzed.

Then the moments began to pass, endlessly, it seemed to him.

The table at which they sat was on the right wing of the stage. The woman sat facing into the stage, while his back was to it. She followed the preparations of the troupe for Act II with moody, silent eyes, he was straining ears and metal-empathic sense.

Only when he heard the curtain sweeping across the street-stage to open the second act did the woman speak.

"She *is* beautiful. And so graceful with those piano-wire wings, just as if they were part of her. I don't wonder she's the first woman who ever really interested you. Not that you really *love* her. You'll never love anyone."

From the depths of his paralysis he studied the etched bitterness of the face across the table. His lips were parched, and his throat a desert.

She thrust a sheet of paper at him, and her lip curled. "Are you still looking for that rose? Search no further, my ignorant friend. There it is—Sciomnia, complete, with its nineteen sub-equations."

The lines of unreadable symbols dug like nineteen relentless harpoons ever deeper into his twisting, racing mind.

The woman's face grimaced in fleeting despair. "Your own wife solves Sciomnia and you condescend to keep her company until you go on again at the end of Act III. I wish I had a sense of humor. All I knew was to paralyze your spinal column. Oh, don't worry. It's purely temporary. I just didn't want you to warn her. And I know what torture it is for you not to be able to talk." She bent over and turned a knurled knob on the side of the black steel box. "There, at least you can whisper. You'll be completely free after the weapon fires."

His lips moved in a rapid slur. "Let us bargain, Martha. Don't kill her. I swear never to see her again."

She laughed, almost gaily.

He pressed on. "But you have all you really want. Total fame, total power, total knowledge, the body perfect. What can her death and the destruction of the Via give you?"

"Everything!"

"Martha, for the sake of all humanity to come, don't do this thing! I know something about Anna van Tuyl that perhaps even Bell doesn't—something she has concealed very adroitly. That girl is the most precious creature on earth!"

"It's precisely because of that opinion—which I do not necessarily share—that I shall include her in my general destruction of the Via." Her mouth slashed at him: "Oh, but it's wonderful to see you squirm. For the first time in your miserable thirty years of life you really want something. You've got to crawl down from that ivory tower of indifference and actually plead with me, whom you've never even taken the trouble to despise. You and your damned art. Let's see it save her now!"

The man closed his eyes and breathed deeply. In one rapid, complex surmise, he visualized an *enchaînement* of postures, a *pas de deux* to be played with his wife as an unwitting partner. Like a skilled chess player, he had analyzed various variations of her probable responses to his gambit, and he had every expectation of a successful climax. And therein lay his hesitation, for success meant his own death.

Yes, he could not eradicate the idea from his mind. Even at this moment he believed himself intrigued more by the novel, if macabre, possibilities inherent in the theme rather than its superficial altruism. While seeming to lead Martha through an artistic approach to the murder of Anna and the Via, he could, in a startling, off-key climax, force her to kill him instead. It amused him enormously to think that afterward, she would try to reduce the little comedy to charts and graph paper in an effort to discover how she had been hypnotized.

It was the first time in his life that he had courted physical injury. The emotional sequence was new, a little heady. He could do it; he need only be careful about his timing.

After hurling her challenge at him, the woman had again turned morose eyes downstage, and was apparently absorbed in a grudging admiration of the second act. But that couldn't last long. The curtain on Act II would be her signal.

And there it was, followed by a muffled roar of applause. He must stall her through most of Act III, and then . . .

He said quickly: "We still have a couple of minutes before the last act begins, where The Nightingale dies on the thorn. There's no hurry. You ought to take time to do this thing properly. Even the best assassinations are not purely a matter of science. I'll wager you never read De Quincey's little essay on murder as a fine art. No? You see, you're a neophyte, and could do with a few tips from an old hand. You must keep in mind your objects: to destroy both the Via and Anna. But mere killing won't be enough. You've got to make *me* suffer too. Suppose you shoot Anna when she comes on at the beginning of Act III. Only fair. The difficulty is that Anna and the others will never know what hit them. You don't give them the opportunity to bow to you as their conqueror."

He regarded her animatedly. "You see, can't you, my dear, that some extraordinarily difficult problems in composition are involved?"

She glared at him, and seemed about to speak.

He continued hastily: "Not that I'm trying to dissuade you. You have the basic concept, and despite your lack of experience, I don't think you'll find the problem of technique insuperable. Your prelude was rather well done: freezing me *in situ,* as it were, to state your theme simply and without adornment, followed immediately by variations of dynamic and suggestive portent. The finale is already implicit; yet it is kept at a disciplined arm's length while the necessary structure is formed to support it and develop its stern message."

She listened intently to him, and her eyes were narrow. The expression on her face said: "Talk all you like. This time, you won't win."

Somewhere beyond the flimsy building-board stage wing he heard Dorran's musicians tuning up for Act III.

His dark features seemed to grow even more earnest, but his voice contained a perceptible burble. "So you've blocked in the introduction and the climax. A beginning and an end. The *real* problem comes now: how much—and what kind—of a middle? Most beginning murderesses would simply give up in frustrated bafflement. A few would shoot the moment Anna floats into the white rose garden. In my opinion, however, considering the wealth of material inherent in your composition, such abbreviation would be inexcusably primitive and garish—if not actually vulgar."

Martha Jacques blinked, as though trying to break through some indescribable spell that was being woven about her. Then she laughed shortly. "Go on. I wouldn't miss this for anything. Just when *should* I destroy the Via?"

The artist sighed. "You see? Your only concern is the *result*. You completely ignore the *manner* of its accomplishment. Really, Mart, I should think you'd show more insight into your first attempt at serious art. Now please don't misunderstand me, dear. I have the warmest regard for your spontaneity and enthusiasm: to be sure, they're quite indispensable when dealing with hackneyed themes, but headlong eagerness is not a substitute for method, or for art. We must search out and exploit subsidiary themes, intertwine them in subtle counterpoint with the major motifs. The most obvious minor theme is the ballet itself. That ballet is the loveliest thing I've ever seen or heard. Nevertheless, *you* can give it a power, a dimension, that even Anna wouldn't suspect possible, simply by blending it contrapuntally into your own work. It's all a matter of firing at the proper instant." He smiled engagingly. "I see that you're beginning to appreciate the potentialities of such unwitting collaboration."

The woman studied him through heavy-lidded eyes. She said slowly: "You *are* a great artist—and a loathsome beast."

He smiled still more amiably. "Kindly restrict your appraisals to your fields of competence. You haven't, as yet, sufficient background to evaluate me as an artist. But let us return to your composition. Thematically, it's rather pleasing. The form, pacing, and orchestration are irreproachable. It is adequate. And its very adequacy condemns it. One detects a certain amount of diffident imitation and over-attention to technique common to artists working in a new medium. The over-cautious sparks of genius aren't setting us aflame. The artist isn't getting enough of his own personality into the work. And the remedy is as simple as the diagnosis: the artist must penetrate his work, wrap it around him, give it the distilled, unique essence of his heart and mind, so that it will blaze up and reveal his soul, even through the veil of unidiomatic technique."

He listened a moment to the music outside. "As Anna wrote her musical score, a hiatus of thirty-eight rests precedes the moment the nightingale drops dying from the thorn. At the start of that silence, you could start to run off your nineteen sub-equations in your little tin box, audio-Fourier style. You might even route the equations into the loudspeaker system, if our gadget is capable of remote control."

For a long time she appraised him calculatingly. "I finally think I understand you. You hoped to unnerve me with your savage, over-accentuated satire, and make me change my mind. So you aren't a beast, and even though I see through you, you're even a greater artist than I at first imagined."

He watched as the woman made a number of adjustments on the control panel of the black box. When she looked up again, her lips were drawn into hard purple ridges.

She said: "But it would be too great a pity to let such art go to waste, especially when supplied by the author of 'Twinkle, twinkle, little star.' And you will indulge an amateur musician's vanity if I play *my* first Fourier composition *fortissimo*."

He answered her smile with a fleeting one of his own. "An artist should never apologize for self-admiration. But watch your cueing. Anna should be clasping the white rose thorn to her breast in thirty seconds, and that will be your signal to fill in the first half of the thirty-eight-rest hiatus. Can you see her?"

The woman did not answer, but he knew that her eyes were following the ballet on the invisible stage and Dorran's baton, beyond, with fevered intensity.

The music glided to a halt.

"Now!" hissed Jacques.

She flicked a switch of the box.

They listened, frozen, as the multi-throated public address system blared into life up and down the two miles of the Via Rosa.

The sound of Sciomnia was chill, metallic, like the cruel crackle of ice heard suddenly in the intimate warmth of an enchanted garden, and it seemed to chatter derisively, well aware of the magic that it shattered.

As it clattered and skirled up its harsh tonal staircase, it seemed to shriek: "Fools! Leave this childish nonsense and follow me! I am Science! I AM ALL!"

And Ruy Jacques, watching the face of the prophetess of the God of Knowledge, was for the first time in his life aware of the possibility of utter defeat.

As he stared in mounting horror, her eyes rolled slightly upward, as though buoyed by some irresistible inner flame, which the pale translucent cheeks let through.

But as suddenly as they had come, the nineteen chords were over, and then, as though to accentuate the finality of that mocking manifesto, a ghastly aural afterimage of silence began building up around his world.

For a near eternity it seemed to him that he and this woman were alone in the world, that, like some wicked witch, she had, through her cacophonic creation, immutably frozen the thousands of invisible watchers beyond the thin walls of the stage wings.

It was a strange, yet simple thing that broke the appalling silence and restored sanity, confidence, and the will to resist to the man: from somewhere far away, a child whimpered.

Breathing as deeply as his near paralysis would permit, the artist murmured: "Now, Martha, in a moment I think you will hear why I suggested your Fourier broadcast. I fear Science has been had once mo—"

He never finished, and her eyes, which were crystallizing into question marks, never fired their barbs.

A towering tidal wave of tone was engulfing the Via, apparently of no human source and from no human instrument.

Even he, who had suspected in some small degree what was coming, now found his paralysis once more complete. Like the woman scientist opposite him, he could only sit in motionless awe, with eyes glazing, jaw dropping, and tongue cleaving to the roof of his mouth.

He knew that the heart strings of Anna van Tuyl were one with this mighty sea of song, and that it took its ecstatic timbre from the reverberating volutes of that god-like mind.

And as the magnificent chords poured out in exquisite consonantal sequence, now with a sudden reedy delicacy, now with the radiant gladness of cymbals, he knew that his plan must succeed.

For, chord for chord, tone for tone, and measure for measure, the Nightingale was repeating in her death song the nineteen chords of Martha Jacques' Sciomnia equations.

Only now those chords were transfigured, as though some Parnassian composer were compassionately correcting and magically transmuting the work of a dull pupil.

The melody spiraled heavenward on wings. It demanded no allegiance; it hurled no pronunciamento. It held a message, but one almost too glorious to be grasped. It was steeped in boundless aspiration, but it was at peace with man and his universe. It sparkled humility, and in its abnegation there was grandeur. Its very incompleteness served to hint at its boundlessness.

And then it, too, was over. The death song was done.

Yes, thought Ruy Jacques, it is the Sciomnia, rewritten, recast, and breathed through the blazing soul of a goddess. And when Martha realizes this, when she sees how I tricked her into broadcasting her trifling, inconsequential effort, she is going to fire her weapon—at *me*.

He watched the woman's face go livid, her mouth work in speechless hate.

"You *knew!*" she screamed. "You did it to humiliate me!"

Jacques began to laugh. It was a nearly silent laughter, rhythmic with mounting ridicule, pitiless in its mockery.

"Stop that!"

But his abdomen was convulsing in rigid helplessness, and tears began to stream down his cheeks.

"I warned you once before!" yelled the woman. Her hand darted toward the black box and turned its long axis toward the man.

Like a period punctuating the rambling, aimless sentence of his life, a ball of blue light burst from a cylindrical hole in the side of the box.

His laughter stopped suddenly. He looked from the box to the woman with growing amazement. He could bend his neck. His paralysis was gone.

She stared back, equally startled. She gasped: "Something went wrong! *You should be dead!*"

The artist didn't linger to argue.

In his mind was the increasingly urgent call of Anna van Tuyl.

CHAPTER NINETEEN

Dorran waved back the awed mass of spectators as Jacques knelt and transferred the faerie body from Bell's arms into his own.

"I'll carry you to your dressing room," he whispered. "I might have known you'd over-exert yourself."

Her eyes opened in the general direction of his face; in his mind came the tinkling of bells: "No . . . don't move me."

He looked up at Bell. "I think she's hurt! Take a look here!" He ran his hands over the seething surface of the wing folded along her side and breast: It was fevered fire.

"I can do nothing," replied the latter in a low voice. "She will tell you that I can do nothing."

"Anna!" cried Jacques. "What's wrong? What happened?"

Her musical reply formed in his mind. "Happened? Sciomnia was quite a thorn. Too much energy for one mind to disperse. Need two . . . three. Three could dematerialize weapon itself. Use wave formula of matter. Tell the others!

"*Others?* What are you talking about?" His thoughts whirled incoherently.

"Others like us. Coming soon. Bakine, dancing in streets of Leningrad. In Mexico City . . . the poetess Orteza. Many . . . this generation. *The Golden People.* Matt Bell guessed. Look!"

An image took fleeting form in his mind. First it was music, and then it was pure thought, and then it was a crisp strange air in his throat and the twang of something marvelous in his mouth. Then it was gone. "What was that?" he gasped.

"The Zhak symposium, seated at wine one April evening in the year 2437. Probability world. May . . . not occur. Did you recognize yourself?"

"Twenty-four thirty-seven?" His mind was fumbling.

"Yes. Couldn't you differentiate your individual mental contour from the whole? I thought you might. The group was still somewhat immature in the twenty-hundreds. By the fourteenth millennium . . ."

His head reeled under the impact of something titanic.

". . . your associated mental mass . . . creating a star of the M spectral class . . . galaxy now two-thirds terrestrialized . . ."

In his arms her wings stirred uneasily; all unconsciously he stroked the hot membranous surface and rubbed the marvelous bony framework with his fingers. "But, Anna," he stammered, "I do not understand how this can be."

Her mind murmured in his. "Listen carefully, Ruy. Your pain . . . when your wings tried to open and couldn't . . . you needed certain psychoglandular stimulus. When you learn how to"—here a phrase he could not translate—"afterwards, they open . . ."

"When I learn—*what?*" he demanded. "What did you say I had to know, to open my wings?"

"One thing. The one thing . . . must have . . . to see The Rose."

"Rose—rose—*rose!*" he cried in near exasperation. "All right, then, my dutiful Nightingale, how long must I wait for you to make this remarkable Red Rose? I ask you, where is it?"

"Please . . . not just yet . . . in your arms just a little longer . . . while we finish ballet. Forget yourself, Ruy. Unless . . . leave prison . . . own heart . . . never find The Rose. Wings never unfold . . . remain a mortal. Science . . . isn't all. Art isn't . . . one thing greater . . . Ruy! I can't prolong . . ."

He looked up wildly at Bell.

The psychogeneticist turned his eyes away heavily. "Don't you understand? She has been dying ever since she absorbed that Sciomniac blast."

A faint murmur reached the artist's mind. "So you couldn't learn . . . poor Ruy . . . poor Nightingale . . ."

As he stared stuporously, her dun-colored wings began to shudder like leaves in an October wind.

From the depths of his shock he watched the fluttering of the wings give way to a sudden convulsive straining of her legs and thighs. It surged upward through her blanching body, through her abdomen and chest, pushing her blood before it and out into her wings, which now appeared more purple than gray.

To the old woman standing at his side, Bell observed quietly: "Even *homo superior* has his death struggle . . ."

The vendress of love philters nodded with anile sadness. "And she knew the answer . . . lost . . . lost . . ."

And still the blood came, making the wing membranes thick and taut.

"Anna!" shrieked Ruy Jacques. "You *can't* die. I won't let you! I love you! *I love you!*"

He had no expectation that she could still sense the images in his mind, nor even that she was still alive.

But suddenly, like stars shining their brief brilliance through a rift in storm clouds, her lips parted in a gay smile. Her eyes opened and seemed to bathe him in an intimate flow of light. It was during this momentary illumination, just before the lips solidified into their final enigmatic mask, that he thought he heard, as from a great distance, the opening measures of Weber's *Invitation to the Dance*.

At this moment the conviction formed in his numbed understanding that her loveliness was now supernal, that greater beauty could not be conceived or endured.

But even as he gazed in stricken wonder, the blood-gorged wings curled slowly up and out, enfolding the ivory breast and shoulders in blinding scarlet, like the petals of some magnificent rose.

My first story. I had just finished law school and had a little spare time to try to write. This effort brought together several interesting themes. I remembered in physics class at George Washington University the remarkable standing wave in a vibrating wire. Add to that a fascinating case we had in criminal law, where the defendant had assaulted a man in Kentucky and thought he had killed him (but hadn't), and had then hauled the supposed corpse into Tennessee, where the man actually died, and then he cut off his head. His defense to a charge of murder was, in Kentucky mere assault, no homicide. In Tennessee, no homicide, he merely mutilated a corpse. Alas, the unimaginative judge and jury couldn't see it, and they hanged him.

And time travel! I discovered what treasure lay here, and I used it again and again. As will be seen.

This story went far in paying for my daughter's entry into the world.

TIME TRAP

The Great Ones themselves never agreed whether the events constituting Troy's cry for help had a beginning. But the warning signal did have an end. The Great Ones saw to that. Those of the Great Ones who claim a beginning for the story date it with the expulsion of the evil Sathanas from the Place of Suns, when he fled, horribly wounded, spiraling evasively inward, through sterechronia without number, until, exhausted, he sank and lay hidden in the crystallizing magma of a tiny new planet at the galactic rim.

General Blade sometimes felt that leading a resistance movement was far exceeding his debt to decent society and that one day soon he would allow his peaceful nature to override his indignant pursuit of justice. Killing a man, even a very bad man, without a trial, went against his grain. He sighed and rapped on the table.

"As a result of Blogshak's misappropriation of funds voted to fight the epidemic," he announced, "the death toll this morning reached over one hundred thousand. Does the Assassination Subcommittee have a recommendation?"

A thin-lipped man rose from the gathering. "The Provinarch ignored our warning," he said rapidly. "This subcommittee, as you all know, some days ago set an arbitrary limit of one hundred thousand deaths. Therefore this subcommittee now recommends that its plan for killing the Provinarch be adopted at once. Tonight is very favorable for our plan, which, incidentally, requires a married couple. We have thoroughly catasynthesized the four bodyguards who will be with him on this shift and have provided irresistible scent and sensory stimuli for the woman. The probability for its success insofar as assassination is concerned is about seventy-eight percent; the probability of escape of our killers is sixty-two per cent. We regard these probabilities as favorable. The Legal Subcommittee will take it from there."

Another man arose. "We have retained Mr. Poole, who is with us tonight." He nodded gravely to a withered little man beside him. "Although Mr. Poole has been a member of the bar but a short time, and although his pre-legal life—some seventy years of it—remains a mystery which he does not explain, our catasynthesis laboratory indicates that his legal knowledge is profound. More important, his persuasive powers, tested with a trial group of twelve professional evaluators, sort of a rehearsal for a possible trial, border on hypnosis. He has also suggested an excellent method of disposing of the corpse to render identification difficult. According to Mr. Poole, if the assassinators are caught, the probability of escaping the devitalizing chamber is fifty-three per cent."

"Mr. Chairman!"

General Blade turned toward the new speaker, who stood quietly several rows away. The man seemed to reflect a gray inconspicuousness, relieved only by a gorgeous rosebud in his lapel. Gray suit, gray eyes, graying temples. On closer examination, one detected an edge of flashing blue in the grayness. The eyes no longer seemed softly unobtrusive, but icy, and the firm mouth and jutting chin seemed polished steel. General Blade had observed this phenomenon dozens of times, but he never tired of it.

"You have the floor, Major Troy," he said.

"I, and perhaps other League officers, would like to know more about Mr. Poole," came the quiet, faintly metallic voice. "He is not a member of the League, and yet Legal and Assassination welcome him in their councils. I think we should be provided some assurance that he has no associations with the Provinarch's administration. One traitor could sell the lives of all of us."

The Legal spokesman arose again. "Major Troy's objections are in some degree merited. We don't know who Mr. Poole is. His mind is absolutely impenetrable to telepathic probes. His fingerprint and eye vein patterns are a little obscure. Our attempts at identification"—he laughed sheepishly—"always key out to yourself, Major. An obvious impossibility. So far as the world is concerned, Mr. Poole is an old man who might have been born yesterday! All we know of him is his willingness to co-operate with us to the best of his ability—which, I can assure you, is tremendous. The catasynthesizer has established his sympathetic attitude beyond doubt. Don't forget, too, that he could be charged as a principal in this assassination and devitalized himself. On the whole, he is our man. If our killers are caught, we must use him."

Troy turned and studied the little lawyer with narrowing eyes; Poole's face seemed oddly familiar. The old man returned the gaze sardonically, with a faint suggestion of a smile.

"Time is growing short, Major," urged the Assassination chairman. "The Poole matter has already received the attention of qualified League investigators. It is not a proper matter for discussion at this time. If you are satisfied with the arrangements, will you and Mrs. Troy please assemble the childless married couples on your list? The men can draw lots from the fish bowl on the side table. The red ball decides." He eyed Troy expectantly.

Still standing, Troy looked down at the woman in the adjacent seat. Her lips were half-parted, her black eyes somber pools as she looked up at her husband.

"Well, Ann?" he telepathed.

Her eyes seemed to look through him and far beyond. "He will make you draw the red ball, Jon," she murmured, trancelike. "Then he will die, and I will die. But Jon Troy will never die. Never die. Never die. Nev—"

"Wake up, Ann!" Troy shook her by the shoulder. To the puzzled faces about them. he explained quickly, "My wife is something of a seeress." He 'pathed again: "Who is *he?*"

Ann Troy brushed the black hair from her brow slowly. "It's all confused. *He* is someone in this room—" She started to get up.

"Sit down, dear," said Troy gently. "If I'm to draw the red ball, I may as well cut this short." He slid past her into the aisle, strode to the side table, and thrust his hand into the hole in the box sitting there.

Every eye was on him.

His hand hit the invisible fish bowl with its dozen-odd plastic balls. Inside the bowl, he touched the little spheres at random while he studied the people in the room. All old friends, except—Poole. That tantalizing face. Poole was now staring like the rest, except that beads of sweat were forming on his forehead.

Troy swirled the balls around the bowl; the muffled clatter was audible throughout the room. He felt his fingers close on one. His hands were perspiring freely. With an effort he forced himself to drop it. He chose another, and looked at Poole. The latter was frowning. Troy could not bring his hand out of the bowl. His right arm seemed partially paralyzed. He dropped the ball and rolled the mass around again. Poole was now smiling. Troy hesitated a moment, then picked a ball from the center of the bowl. It felt slightly moist. He pulled it out, looked at it grimly, and held it up for all to see.

"Just 'path that!" whispered the jail warden reverently to the night custodian.

"You know I can't telepath," said the latter grumpily. "What are they saying?"

"Not a word all night. They seem to be taking a symposium of the best piano concertos since maybe the twentieth century. Was Chopin twentieth or twenty-first? Anyhow, they're up to the twenty-third now, with Darnoval. Troy reproduces the orchestra and his wife does the piano. You'd think she had fifty years to live instead of five minutes."

"Both seem nice people," ruminated the custodian. "If they hadn't killed the Provinarch, maybe they'd have become famous 'pathic musicians. She had a lousy lawyer. She could have got off with ten years sleep if he'd half tried." He pushed some papers across the desk. "I've had the chamber checked. Want to look over the readings?"

The warden scanned them rapidly. "Potential difference, eight million; drain rate, ninety vital units/minute; estimated period of consciousness, thirty seconds; estimated durance to nonrecovery point, four minutes; estimated durance to legal death, five minutes." He initialed the front sheet. "That's fine. When I was younger they called it the 'vitality drain chamber.' Drain rate was only two v.u./min. Took an hour to drain them to unconsciousness. Pretty hard on the condemned people. Well, I'd better go officiate."

When Jon and Ann Troy finished the Darnoval concerto they were silent for a few moments, exchanging simply a flow of wordless, unfathomable perceptions between their cells. Troy was unable to disguise a steady beat of gloom. "We'll have to go along with Poole's plan," he 'pathed, "though I confess I don't know what his idea is. Take your capsule now."

His mind registered the motor impulses of her medulla as she removed the pill from its concealment under her armpit and swallowed it. Troy then perceived her awareness of her cell door opening, of grim men and women about her. Motion down corridors. Then the room. A clanging of doors. A titanic effort to hold their fading contact. One last despairing communion, loving, tender.

Then nothing.

He was still sitting with his face buried in his hands, when the guards came to take him to his own trial that morning.

"This murder," announced the People's advocate to the twelve evaluators, "this crime of taking the life of our beloved Provinarch Blogshak, this heinous deed— is the most horrible thing that has happened in Niork in my lifetime. The creature charged with this crime"—he pointed an accusing finger at the prisoner's box—"Jon Troy has been psyched and has been adjudged integrated at a preliminary hearing. Even his attorney"—here bowing ironically to a beady-eyed little man at counsels' table—"waived the defense of nonintegration."

Poole continued to regard the Peoples' advocate with bitter weariness, as though he had gone through this a thousand times and knew every word that each of them was going to say. The prisoner seemed oblivious to the advocate, the twelve evaluators, the judge, and the crowded courtroom. Troy's mind was blanked out. The dozen or so educated telepaths in the room could detect only a deep beat of sadness.

"I shall prove," continued the inexorable advocate, "that this monster engaged our late Provinarch in conversation in a downtown bar, surreptitiously placed a lethal dose of *skon* in the Provinarch's glass, and that Troy and his wife—who, incidentally, paid the extreme penalty herself early this—"

"Objection!" cried Poole, springing to his feet. "The defendant, not his wife, is now on trial."

"Sustained," declared the judge. "The advocate may not imply to the evaluators that the possible guilt of the present defendant is any way determined by the proven guilt of any past defendant. The evaluators must ignore that implication. Proceed, advocate."

"Thank you, Your Honor." He turned again to the evaluators' box and scanned them with a critical eye. "I shall prove that the prisoner and the late Mrs. Troy, after poisoning Provinarch Blogshak, carried his corpse into their sedan, and that they proceeded then to a deserted area on the outskirts of the city. Unknown to them they were pursued by four of the mayor's bodyguards, who, alas, had. been lured aside at the bar by Mrs. Troy. Psychometric determinations taken by the police laboratory will be offered to prove it was the prisoner's intention to dismember the corpse and burn it to hinder the work of the police in tracing the crime to him. He had got only as far as severing the head when the guards' ship swooped up and hovered overhead. He tried to run back to his own ship, where his wife was waiting, but the guards blanketed the area with a low-voltage stun."

The advocate paused. He was not getting the reaction in the evaluators he deserved, but he knew the fault was not his. He was puzzled; he would have to conclude quickly.

"Gentlemen," he continued gravely, "for this terrible thing, the Province demands the life of Jon Troy. The monster must enter the chamber tonight." He bowed to the judge and returned to counsels' table.

The judge acknowledged the retirement and turned to Poole. "Does the defense wish to make an opening statement?"

"The defense reiterates its plea of 'not guilty' and makes no other statement," grated the old man.

There was a buzz around the advocates' end of the table. An alert defense with a weak case always opened to the evaluators. Who was this Poole? What did he have? Had they missed a point? The prosecution was committed now. They'd have to start with their witnesses.

The advocate arose. "The prosecution offers as witness Mr. Fonstile."

"Mr. Fonstile!" called the clerk.

A burly, resentful-looking man blundered his way from the benches and walked up to the witness box and was sworn in.

Poole was on his feet. "May it please the court!" he croaked.

The judge eyed him in surprise. "Have you an objection, Mr. Poole?"

"No objection, Your Honor," rasped the little man, without expression. "I would only like to say that the testimony of this witness, the bartender in the Shawn Hotel, is probably offered by my opponent to prove facts which the defense readily admits, namely, that the witness observed Mrs. Troy entice the four bodyguards of the deceased to another part of the room, that the present defendant surreptitiously placed a powder in the wine of the deceased, that the deceased drank the wine and collapsed, and was carried out of the room by the defendant, followed by his wife." He bowed to the judge and sat down.

The judge was nonplussed. "Mr. Poole, do you understand that you are responsible for the defense of this prisoner, and that he is charged with a capital offense?"

"That is my understanding, Your Honor."

"Then if prosecution is agreeable, and wishes to elicit no further evidence from the witness, he will be excused."

The advocate looked puzzled, but called the next witness, Dr. Warkon, of the Provincial Police Laboratory. Again Poole was on his feet. This time the whole court eyed him expectantly. Even Troy stared at him in fascination.

"May it please the court," came the now-familiar monotone, "the witness called by the opposition probably expects to testify that the deceased's finger prints were found on the wineglass in question, that traces of deceased's saliva were identified in the liquid content of the glass, and that a certain quantity of *skon* was found in the wine remaining in the glass."

"And one other point, Mr. Poole," added the Peoples' advocate. "Dr. Warkon was going to testify that death from *skon* poisoning normally occurs within thirty seconds, owing to syncope. Does the defense concede that?"

"Yes."

"The witness is then excused," ordered the judge.

The prisoner straightened up. Troy studied his attorney curiously. The mysterious Poole with the tantalizing face, the man so highly recommended by the League, had let Ann go to her death with the merest shadow of a defense. And now he seemed even to state the prosecution's case rather than defend the prisoner.

Nowhere in the courtroom did Troy see a League member. But then, it would be folly for General Blade to attempt his rescue. That would attract unwelcome attention to the League.

He had been abandoned, and was on his own. Many League officers had been killed by Blogshak's men, but rarely in the devitalizing chamber. It was a point of honor to die weapon in hand. His first step would be to seize a blaster from one of the guards, use the judge as a shield, and try to escape through the judge's chambers. He would wait until he was put on the stand. It shouldn't be long, considering how Poole was cutting corners.

The advocate was conferring with his assistants. "What's Poole up to?" one of them asked. "If he is going on this far, why not get him to admit all the facts constituting a prima facie case: malice, intent to kill, and all that?"

The advocate's eyes gleamed. "I think I know what he's up to now," he exulted. "I believe he's forgotten an elementary theorem of criminal law. He's going to admit everything, then demand we produce Blogshak's corpse. He must know it was stolen from the bodyguards when their ship landed at the port. No corpse, no murder, he'll say. But you don't need a corpse to prove murder. We'll hang him with his own rope!" He arose and addressed the judge.

"May it please the court, the prosecution would like to ask if the defense will admit certain other facts which I stand ready to prove."

The judge frowned. "The prisoner pleaded not guilty. Therefore, the court will not permit any admission of the defense to the effect that the prisoner did kill the deceased, unless he wants to change his plea." He looked inquiringly at Poole.

"I understand, Your Honor," said Poole. "May I hear what facts the learned prosecutor wishes me to accede to?"

For a moment the prosecutor studied his enigmatic antagonist like a master swordsman.

"First, the prisoner administered a lethal dose of *skon* to the deceased with malice aforethought, and with intent to kill. Do you concede that?"

"Yes."

"And that the deceased collapsed within a few seconds and was carried from the room by the defendant and his wife?"

"We agree to that."

"And that the prisoner carried the body to the city outskirts and there decapitated it?"

"I have already admitted that."

The twelve evaluators, a selected group of trained experts in the estimation of probabilities, followed this unusual procedure silently.

"Then Your Honor, the prosecution rests." The advocate felt dizzy, out of his depth. He felt he had done all that was necessary to condemn the prisoner. Yet Poole seemed absolutely confident, almost bored.

"Do you have any witnesses, Mr. Poole?" queried the judge.

"I will ask the loan of Dr. Warkon, if the Peoples' advocate will be so kind," replied the little man.

"I'm willing." The advocate was beginning to look harassed. Dr. Warkon was sworn in.

"Dr. Warkon, did not the psychometer show that the prisoner intended to kill Blogshak in the tavern and decapitate him at the edge of the city?"

"Yes, sir."

"Was, in fact, the deceased dead when he was carried from the hotel?"

"He had enough *skon* in him to have killed forty people."

"Please answer the question."

"Well, I don't know. I presume he was dead. As an expert, looking at all the evidence, I should say he was dead. If he didn't die in the room, he was certainly dead a few seconds later."

"Did you feel his pulse at any time, or make any examination to determine the time of death?"

"Well, no."

Now, thought the advocate, comes the *no corpse, no murder*. If he tries that, I've got him.

But Poole was not to be pushed.

"Would you say the deceased was dead when the prisoner's ship reached the city limits?"

"Absolutely!"

"When you, as police investigator, examined the scene of the decapitation, what did you find?"

"The place where the corpse had lain was easily identified. Depressions in the sand marked the back, head, arms, and legs. The knife was lying where the prisoner dropped it. Marks of landing gear of the prisoner's ship were about forty feet away. Lots of blood, of course."

"Where was the blood?"

"About four feet away from the head, straight out."

Poole let the statement sink in, then:

"Dr. Warkon, as a doctor of medicine, do you realize the significance of what you have just said?"

The witness gazed at his inquisitor as though hypnotized. "Four feet . . . jugular spurt—" he muttered to no one. He stared in wonder, first at the withered, masklike face before him, then at the advocate, then at the judge. "Your Honor, the deceased's heart was still beating when the prisoner first applied the knife. The poison didn't kill him!"

An excited buzz resounded through the courtroom.

Poole turned to the judge. "Your honor, I move for a summary judgment of acquittal."

The advocate sprang to his feet, wordless.

"Mr. Poole," remonstrated the judge, "your behavior this morning has been extraordinary, to say the least. On the bare fact that the prisoner killed with a knife instead of with poison, as the evidence at first indicated, you ask summary acquittal. The court will require an explanation."

"Your Honor"—there was a ghost of a smile flitting about the prim, tired mouth—"to be guilty of a crime, a man must intend to commit a crime. There must be a *mens rea*, as the classic expression goes. The act and the intent must coincide. Here they did not. Jon Troy intended to kill the Provinarch in the bar of the Shawn Hotel. He gave him poison, but Blogshak didn't die of it. Certainly up to the time the knife was thrust into Blogshak's throat, Troy may have been guilty of assault and kidnapping, but not murder. If there was any murder, it must have been at the instant he decapitated the deceased. Yet what was his intent on the city outskirts? He wanted to mutilate a corpse. His intent was not to murder, but to mutilate. We have the act, but not the intent—no *mens rea*. Therefore the act was not murder, but simply mutilation of a corpse—a crime punishable by fine or imprisonment, but not death."

Troy's mind was whirling. This incredible, dusty little man had freed him.

"But Troy's a murderer!" shouted the advocate, his face white. "Sophisms can't restore a life!"

"The court does not recognize the advocate!" said the judge harshly. "Cut those remarks from the record," he directed the scanning clerk. "This court is guided by the principles of common law descended from ancient England. The learned counsel for the defense has stated those principles correctly. Homicide is not murder if there is no intent to kill. And mere intent to kill is not murder if the poison doesn't take effect. This is a strange, an unusual case, and it is revolting for me to do what I have to do. I acquit the prisoner."

"Your Honor!" cried the advocate. Receiving recognition, he proceeded. "This . . . this felon should not escape completely. He should not be permitted to make a travesty of the law. His own counsel admits he has broken the statutes on kidnapping, assault, and mutilation. The evaluators can at least return a verdict of guilty on those counts."

"I am just as sorry as you are," replied the judge, "but I don't find those counts in the indictment. You should have included them."

"If you release him, Your Honor, I'll re-arrest him, and frame a new indictment."

"This court will not act on it. It is contrary to the Constitution of this Province for a person to be prosecuted twice on the same charge or on a charge which should have been included in the original indictment. The Peoples' advocate is estopped from taking further action on this case. This is the final ruling of this court." He took a drink of water, wrapped his robes about him, and strode through the rear of the courtroom to his chambers.

Troy and Poole, the saved and the savior, eyed one another with the same speculative look of their first meeting.

Poole opened the door of the 'copter parked outside the Judiciary Building
and motioned for Troy to enter. Troy froze in the act of climbing in.

A man inside the cab, with a face like a claw, was pointing a blaster at his chest.
The man was Blogshak!

Two men recognizable as the Provinarch's bodyguards suddenly materialized
behind Troy.

"Don't give us any trouble, Major," murmured Poole easily. "Better get in."

The moment Troy was pushed into the subterranean suite he sensed Ann was
alive—drugged insensate still, but alive, and near. This knowledge suppressed
momentarily Blogshak's incredible existence and Poole's betrayal. Concealing his
elation, he turned to Poole.

"I should like to see my wife."

Poole motioned silently to one of the guards, who pulled back sliding doors.
Beyond a glass panel, which was actually a transparent wall of a tile room, Ann
lay on a high white metal bed. A nurse was on the far side of the bed, exchanging
glances with Poole. At some unseen signal from him the nurse swabbed Ann's
left arm and thrust a syringe into it.

A shadow crossed Troy's face. "What is the nurse doing?"

"In a moment Mrs. Troy will awaken. Whether she stays awake depends on you."

"On me? What do you mean?"

"Major, what you are about to learn can best be demonstrated rather than
described. Sharg, the rabbit!"

The beetle-browed man opened a large enamel pan on the table. A white rabbit eased its way out, wrinkling its nose gingerly. Sharg lifted a cleaver from the
table. There was a flash of metal, a spurt of blood, and the rabbit's head fell to
the floor. Sharg picked it up by the ears and held it up expectantly. The eyes
were glazed almost shut. The rabbit's body lay limp in the pan. At a word from
Poole, Sharg carefully replaced the severed head, pressing it gently to the bloody
neck stub. Within seconds the nose twitched, the eyes blinked, and the ears perked
up. The animal shook itself vigorously, scratched once or twice at the bloody
ring around its neck, then began nibbling at a head of lettuce in the pan.

Troy's mind was racing. The facts were falling in line. All at once everything
made sense. With knowledge came utmost wariness. The next move was up to
Poole, who was examining with keen eyes the effect of his demonstration on
Troy.

"Major, I don't know how much you have surmised, but at least you cannot
help realizing that life, even highly organized vertebrate life, is resistant to death
in your presence."

Troy folded his arms but volunteered nothing. He was finally getting a glimpse
of the vast and secret power supporting the Provinarch's tyranny, long suspected
by the League but never verified.

"You could not be expected to discover this marvelous property in yourself except by the wildest chance," continued Poole. "As a matter of fact, our staff discovered it only when Blogshak and his hysterical guards reported to us, after your little escapade. But we have been on the lookout for your type for years. Several mutants with this characteristic have been predicted by our probability geneticists for this century, but you are the first known to us—really perhaps the only one in existence. One is all we need.

"As a second and final test of your power, we decided to try the effect of your aura on a person in the devitalizing chamber. For that reason we permitted Mrs. Troy to be condemned, when we could easily have prevented it. As you now know, your power sustained your wife's life against a strong drain of potential. At my instruction she drugged herself in her cell simply to satisfy the doctor who checked her pulse and reflexes afterwards. When the staff—my employers—examined her here, they were convinced that you had the mutation they were looking for, and we put the finishing touches on our plans to save you from the chamber."

Granting I have some strange biotic influence, thought Troy, still something's wrong. He says his bunch became interested in me *after* my attempt on Blogshak. *But Poole was at the assassination meeting!* What is his independent interest?

Poole studied him curiously. "I doubt that you realize what tremendous efforts have been made to insure your presence here. For the past two weeks the staff has hired several thousand persons to undermine the critical faculties of the four possible judges and nine hundred evaluators who might have heard your case. Judge Gallon, for example, was not in an analytical mood this morning because we saw to it that he won the Province Chess Championship with his Inner Gambit—a prize he has sought for thirty years. But if he had fooled us and given your case to the evaluators, we were fairly certain of a favorable decision. You noticed how they were not concentrating on the advocate's opening statement? They couldn't; they were too full of the incredible good fortune they had encountered the previous week. Sommers had been promoted to a full professorship at the Provincial University. Gunnard's obviously faulty thesis on space strains had been accepted by the *Steric Quarterly*—after we bought the magazine. But why go on? Still, if the improbable had occurred, and you had been declared guilty by the evaluators, we would simply have spirited you away from the courtroom. With a few unavoidable exceptions, every spectator in the room was a trained staff agent ready to use his weapons—though in the presence of your aura, I doubt they could have hurt anyone.

"Troy, the staff had to get you here, but we preferred to do it quietly. Now, why are you here? I'll tell you. Your aura, we think, will keep—" Poole hesitated. "Your aura will keep . . . *It* . . . from dying during an approaching crisis in its life stream."

"It? What is this 'it'? And what makes you so sure I'll stay?"

"The staff has not authorized me to tell you more concerning the nature of the entity you are to protect. Suffice to say that It is a living, sentient being. And I think you'll stay, because the hypo just given Mrs. Troy was pure *skon*."

Troy had already surmised as much. The move was perfect. If he stayed near her, Ann, though steeped in the deadliest known poison, would not die. But why had they been so sure he would not stay willingly, without Ann as hostage? He 'pathed the thought to Poole, who curtly refused to answer.

"Now, Major, I'm going to turn this wing of the City Building over to you. For your information, your aura is effective for a certain distance within the building, but just how far I'm not going to tell you. However, you are not permitted to leave your apartment at all. The staff has demoted the Provinarch, and he's now the corporal of your bodyguard. He would be exceedingly embarrassed if you succeeded in leaving. Meals will be brought to you regularly. The cinematic and micro library is well stocked on your favorite subjects. Special concessions may even be made as to things you want in town. But you can never touch your wife again. That pane of glass will always be between you. A psychic receptor tuned to your personality integration is fixed within Mrs. Troy's room. If you break the glass panel, or in any other way attempt to enter the room, the receptor will automatically actuate a bomb mechanism imbedded beneath Mrs. Troy's cerebellum. She would be blown to little bits—each of them alive as long as you were around. It grieves us to be crude, but the situation requires some such safeguard."

"When will my wife recover consciousness?"

"Within an hour or so. But what's your hurry? You'll be here longer than you think."

The little lawyer seemed lost in thought for a moment. Then he signaled Blogshak and the guards, and the four left. Blogshak favored Troy with a venomous scowl as he closed and locked the door.

There was complete and utter silence. Even the rabbit sat quietly on the table, blinking its eyes at Troy.

Left alone, the man surveyed the room, his perceptions palping every square foot rapidly but carefully. He found nothing unusual. He debated whether to explore the wing further or to wait until Ann awakened. He decided on the latter course. The nurse had left. They were together, with just a sheet of glass between. He explored Ann's room mentally, found nothing.

Then he walked to the center table and picked up the rabbit. There was the merest suggestion of a cicatrix encircling the neck.

Wonderful, but frightful, thought Troy. Who, what, am I?

He put the rabbit back in the box, pulled a comfortable armchair against the wall opposite the glass panel, where he had a clear view of Ann's room, and began a methodical attempt to rationalize the events of the day.

He was jolted from his reverie by an urgent 'pathic call from Ann. After a flurry of tender perceptions, each unlocked his mind to the other.

Poole had planted an incredible message in Ann's ESP lobe.

"Jon," she warned, "it's coded to the Dar—... I mean, it's coded to the notes and frequencies of our last concerto, in the death house. You'll have to synchronize. I'll start."

How did Poole know we were familiar with the concerto? thought Troy.

"Think on this carefully, Jon Troy, and guard it well," urged Poole's message. "I cannot risk my identity, but I am your friend. It—the Outcast—has shaped the destinies of vertebrate life on Earth for millions of years, for two purposes. One is a peculiar kind of food. The other is . . . you. You have been brought here to preserve an evil life. But I urge you, develop your latent powers and destroy that life!

"Jon Troy, the evil this entity has wreaked upon the Earth, entirely through his human agents thus far, is incalculable. It will grow even worse. You thought a sub-electronic virus caused the hundred thousand deaths which launched you on your assassination junket. Not so! The monster in the earth directly beneath you simply drained them of vital force, in their homes, on the street, in the theater, anywhere and everywhere. Your puny League has been fighting the Outcast for a generation without the faintest conception of the real enemy. If you have any love for humanity, search Blogshak's mind today. The staff physicians will be in this wing of the building today, too. Probe them. This evening, if I am still alive, I shall explain more, in person, free from Blogshak's crew."

"You have been wondering about the nature of the being whose life you are protecting," said Poole in a low voice, as he looked about the room. "As you learned when you searched the minds of the physicians this morning, he is nothing human. I believe him to have been wounded in a battle with his own kind, and that he has lain in his present pit for millions of years, possibly since pre-Cambrian times. He probably has extraordinary powers even in his weakened state, but to my knowledge he has never used them."

"Why not?" asked Troy.

"He must be afraid of attracting the unwelcome attention of those who look for him. But he has maintained his life somehow. The waste products of his organic metabolism are fed into our sewers daily. He has a group of physicians and physicists—a curious mixture!—who keep in repair his three-dimensional neural cortex and run a huge administrative organization designed for his protection."

"Seems harmless enough, so far," said Troy.

"He's harmless except for one venomous habit. I thought I told you about it in the message I left with Ann. You must have verified it if you probed Blogshak thoroughly."

"But I couldn't understand such near cannibalism in so advanced—"

"Certainly not cannibalism! Do we think of ourselves as cannibals when we eat steaks? Still, that's my main objection to him. His vitality must be maintained by the absorption of other vitalities, preferably as high up the evolutionary scale as possible. Our thousands of deaths monthly can be traced to his frantic hunger for vital fluid. The devitalizing department, which Blogshak used to run, is the largest section of the staff."

"But what about the people who attend him? Does he snap up any of them?"

"He hasn't yet. They all have a pact with him. Help him, and he helps them. Every one of his band dies old, rich, evil, and envied by their ignorant neighbors. He gives them everything they want. Sometimes they forget, like Blogshak, that society can stand just so much of their evil."

"Assuming all you say is true—how does it concern my own problem, getting Ann out of here and notifying the League?"

Poole shook his head dubiously. "You probably have some tentative plans to hypnotize Blogshak and make him turn off the screen. But no one on the staff understands the screen. None of them can turn it off, because none of them turned it on. The chief surgeon believes it to be a direct, focused emanation from a radiator made long ago and known now only to the Outcast. But don't think of escaping just yet. You can strike a tremendous, fatal blow without leaving this room!

"This afternoon," Poole continued with growing nervousness, "there culminates a project initiated by the Outcast millennia ago. Just ninety years ago the staff began the blueprints of a surgical operation on the Outcast on a scale which would dwarf the erection of the Mechanical Integrator. Indeed, you won't be surprised to learn that the Integrator, capable of planar sterechronic analysis, was but a preliminary practice project, a rehearsal for the main event."

"Go on," said Troy absently. His sensitive hearing detected heavy breathing from beyond the door.

"To perform this colossal surgery, the staff must disconnect for a few seconds all of the essential neural trunks. When this is done, but for your aura, the Outcast would forever after remain a mass of senseless protoplasm and electronic equipment. With your aura they can make the most dangerous repairs in perfect safety. When the last neural is down, you simply suppress your aura and the Outcast is dead. Then you could force your way out. From then on, the Earth could go its merry way unhampered. Your League would eventually gain ascendancy and—"

"What about Ann?" asked Troy curtly. "Wouldn't she die along with the Outcast?"

"Didn't both of you take an oath to sacrifice each other before you'd injure the League or abandon an assignment?"

"That's a nice legal point," replied Troy, watching the corridor door behind Poole open a quarter of an inch. "I met Ann three years ago in a madhouse, where I had hidden away after a League assignment. She wasn't mad, but the stupid overseer didn't know it. She had the ability to project herself to other probability worlds. I married her to obtain a warning instrument of extreme delicacy and accuracy. Until that night in the death house, I'd have abided by League rules and abandoned her if necessary. But no longer. Any plan which includes her death is out. Suffering humanity can go climb a tree."

Poole's voice was dry and cracking. "I presumed you'd say that. You leave me no recourse. After I tell you who I am, you will be willing to turn off your aura even at the cost of Ann's life. I am your . . . agh—"

A knife whistled through the open door and sank in Poole's neck. Blogshak and Sharg rushed in. Each man carried an ax.

"You dirty traitor!" screamed Blogshak. His ax crashed through the skull of the little old man even as Troy sprang forward. Sharg caught Troy under the chin with his ax handle. For some minutes afterward Troy was dimly aware of chopping, chopping, chopping.

Troy's aching jaw finally awoke him. He was lying on the sofa, where his keepers had evidently placed him. There was an undefinable raw odor about the room. The carpet had been changed.

Troy's stomach muscles tensed. What had this done to Ann? He was unable to catch her ESP lobe. Probably out wandering through the past, or future.

While he tried to touch her mind, there was a knock on the door, and Blogshak entered with a man dressed in surgeon's white.

"Our operation apparently was a success, despite your little mishap," 'pathed the latter to Troy. "The next thirty years will tell us definitely whether we did this correctly. I'm afraid you'll have to stick around until then. I understand you're great chums with the Provinarch—ex-Provinarch, should I say? I'm sure he'll entertain you. I'm sorry about Poole. Poor fellow! Muffed his opportunities. Might have risen very high on the staff. But everything works out for the best, doesn't it?"

Troy glared at him wordlessly.

"Once we're out of here," 'pathed Troy in music code that afternoon, "we'll get General Blade to drop a plute fission on this building. It all revolves around the bomb under your cerebellum. If we can deactivate either the screen or the bomb, we're out. It's child's play to scatter Blogshak's bunch."

"If I had a razor," replied Ann, "I could cut the thing out. I can feel it under my neck muscles."

"Don't talk nonsense. What can you give me on Poole?"

"He definitely forced you to choose the red ball at the League meeting. Also, he knew he was going to be killed in your room. That made him nervous."

"Did he *know* he was going to be killed, or simply anticipated the possibility?"

"He knew. *He had seen it before!*"

Troy began pacing restlessly up and down before the glass panel, but never looking at Ann, who lay quietly in bed apparently reading a book. The nurse sat in a chair at the foot of Ann's bed, arms folded, implacably staring at her ward.

"Puzzling, very puzzling," mused Troy. "Any idea what he was going to tell me about my aura?"

"No."

"Anything on his identity?"

"I don't know—I had a feeling that I . . . we— No, it's all too vague. I noticed just one thing for certain."

"What was that?" asked Troy. He stopped pacing and appeared to be examining titles on the bookshelves.

"He was wearing your rosebud!"

"But that's crazy! I had it on all day. You must have been mistaken."

"You know I can't make errors on such matters."

"That's so." Troy resumed his pacing. "Yet, I refuse to accept the proposition that both of us were wearing my rosebud at the same instant. Well, never mind.

While we're figuring a way to deactivate your bomb, we'd also better give a little thought to solving my aura.

"The solution is known—we have to assume that our unfortunate friend knew it. Great Galaxy! What our League biologists wouldn't give for a chance at this! We must change our whole concept of living matter. Have you ever heard of the immortal heart created by Alexis Carrel?" he asked abruptly.

"No."

"At some time during the Second Renaissance, early twentieth century, I believe, Dr. Carrel removed a bit of heart tissue from an embryo chick and put it in a nutrient solution. The tissue began to expand and contract rhythmically. Every two days the nutrient solution was renewed and excess growth cut away. Despite the catastrophe that had overwhelmed the chick—as a chick—the individual tissue lived on independently because the requirements of its cells were met. This section of heart tissue beat for nearly three centuries, until it was finally lost in the Second Atomic War."

"Are you suggesting that the king's men can put Humpty Dumpty together again if due care has been taken to nourish each part?"

"It's a possibility. Don't forget the skills developed by the Muscovites in grafting skin, ears, corneas, and so on."

"But that's a long process—it takes weeks."

"Then let's try another line. Consider this: The amoeba lives in a fluid medium. He bumps into his food, which is generally bacteria or bits of decaying protein, flows around it, digests it at leisure, excretes his waste matter, and moves on. Now go on up the evolutionary scale past the coelenterates and flatworms, until we reach the first truly three-dimensional animals—the coelomates. The flatworm had to be flat because he had no blood vessels. His food simply soaked into him. But cousin roundworm, one of the coelomates, grew plump and solid, because his blood vessels fed his specialized interior cells, which would otherwise have no access to food.

"Now consider a specialized cell—say a nice long muscle cell in the rabbit's neck. It can't run around in stagnant water looking for a meal. It has to have its breakfast brought to it, and its excrement carried out by special messenger, or it soon dies."

Troy picked a book from the shelf and leafed through it idly.

Ann wondered mutely whether her nurse had been weaned on a lemon.

"This messenger," continued Troy, "is the blood. It eventually reaches the muscle cell by means of a capillary—a minute blood vessel about the size of a red corpuscle. The blood in the capillary gives the cell everything it needs and absorbs the cell waste matter. The muscle cell needs a continuously fresh supply of oxygen, sugar, amino-acids, fats, vitamins, sodium, calcium, and potassium salts, hormones, water, and maybe other things. It gets these from the hemoglobin and plasma, and it sheds carbon dioxide, ammonium compounds, and so on. Our cell can store up a little food within its own boundaries to tide it over for a number of hours. But oxygen it must have, every instant."

"You're just making the problem worse," interposed Ann. "If you prove that blood must circulate oxygen continuously to preserve life, you'll have yourself out on a limb. If you'll excuse the term, the rabbit's circulation was decisively cut off."

"That's the poser," agreed Troy. "The blood didn't circulate, but the cells didn't die. And think of this a moment: Blood is normally alkaline, with a pH of 7.4. When it absorbs carbon dioxide as a cell excretion, blood becomes acid, and this steps up respiration to void the excess carbon dioxide, via the lungs. But so far as I could see, the rabbit didn't even sigh after he got his head back. There was certainly no heavy breathing."

"I'll have to take your word for it; I was out cold."

"Yes, I know." Troy began pacing the room again. "It isn't feasible to suppose the rabbit's plasma was buffered to an unusual degree. That would mean an added concentration of sodium bicarbonate and an increased solids content. The cellular water would dialyze into the blood and kill the creature by simple dehydration."

"Maybe he had unusual reserves of hemoglobin," suggested Ann. "That would take care of your oxygen problem."

Troy rubbed his chin. "I doubt it. There are about five million red cells in a cubic millimeter of blood. If there are very many more, the cells would oxidize muscle tissue at a tremendous rate, and the blood would grow hot, literally cooking the brain. Our rabbit would die of a raging fever. Hemoglobin dissolves about fifty times as much oxygen as plasma, so it doesn't take much hemoglobin to start an internal conflagration."

"Yet the secret must lie in the hemoglobin. You just admitted that the cells could get along for long periods with only oxygen," persisted Ann.

"It's worth thinking about. We must learn more about the chemistry of the cell. You take it easy for a few days while I go through Poole's library."

"Could I do otherwise?" murmured Ann.

". . . thus the effect of confinement varies from person to person. The claustrophobe deteriorates rapidly, but the agoraphobe mellows, and may find excuses to avoid the escape attempt. The person of high mental and physical attainments can avoid atrophy by directing his every thought to the destruction of the confining force. In this case, the increment in mental prowess is 3.1 times the logarithm of the duration of confinement measured in years. The intelligent and determined prisoner can escape if he lives long enough."
— J. and A. T., *An Introduction to Prison Escape,* 4th Edition, League Publishers, p. 14.

In 1811 Avogadro, in answer to the confusing problems of combining chemical weights, invented the molecule. In 1902 Einstein resolved an endless array of incompatible facts by suggesting a mass-energy relation. Three centuries later, in the tenth year of his imprisonment, Jon Troy was driven in near-despair to a similar stand. In one sure step of dazzling intuition, he hypothesized the viton.

"The secret goes back to our old talks on cell preservation," he explained with ill-concealed excitement to Ann. "The cell can live for hours without proteins and salts, because it has means of storing these nutrients from past meals. But oxygen it must have. The hemoglobin takes up molecular oxygen in the lung capillaries, ozonizes it, and, since hemin is easily reduced, the red cells give up oxygen to the muscle cells that need it, in return for carbon dioxide. After it takes up the carbon dioxide, hemin turns purple and enters the vein system on the way back to the lungs, and we can forget it.

"Now, what is hemin? We can break it down into etiopyrophorin, which, like chlorophyll, contains four pyrrole groups. The secret of chlorophyll has been known for years. Under a photon catalyst of extremely short wave length, such as ultraviolet light, chlorophyll seizes molecule after molecule of carbon dioxide and synthesizes starches and sugars, giving off oxygen. Hemin, with its etiopyrophorin, works quite similarly, except that it doesn't need ultraviolet light. Now—"

"But animal cell metabolism works the other way," objected Ann. "Our cells take up oxygen, and excrete carbon dioxide."

"It depends which cells you are talking about," reminded Troy. "The red corpuscle takes up carbon dioxide just as its plant cousin, chlorophyll, does, and they both excrete oxygen. Oxygen is just as much an excrement of the red cell as carbon dioxide is of the muscle cell."

"That's true," admitted Ann.

"And that's where the viton comes in," continued Troy. "It preserves the status quo of cell chemistry. Suppose that an oxygen atom has just been taken up by an amino-acid molecule within the cell protoplasm. The amino-acid immediately becomes unstable, and starts to split out carbon dioxide. In the red corpuscle, a mass of hemin stands by to seize the carbon dioxide and offer more oxygen. But the exchange never takes place. Just as the amino-acid and the hemin reach toward one another, their electronic attractions are suddenly neutralized by a bolt of pure energy from me: the viton! Again and again the cells try to exchange, with the same result. They can't die from lack of oxygen, because their individual molecules never attain an oxygen deficit. The viton gives a very close approach to immortality!"

"But *we* seem to be getting older. Perhaps your vitons don't reach every cell?"

"Probably not," admitted Troy. "They must stream radially from some central point within me, and of course they would decrease in concentration according to the inverse square law of light. Even so, they would keep enough cells alive to preserve life as a whole. In the case of the rabbit, after the cut cell surfaces were rejoined, there were still enough of them alive to start the business of living again. One might suppose, too, that the viton accelerates the re-establishment of cell boundaries in the damaged areas. That would be particularly important with the nerve cells."

"All right," said Ann. "You've got the viton. What are you going to do with it?"

"That's another puzzler. First, what part of my body does it come from? There must be some sort of a globular discharge area fed by a relatively small but impenetrable duct. If we suppose a muscle controlling the duct—"

"What you need is an old Geiger-Müller," suggested Ann. "Locate your discharge globe first, then the blind spot on it caused by the duct entry. The muscle has to be at that point."

"I wonder—" mused Troy. "We have a burnt-out cinema projection bulb around here somewhere. The vacuum ought to be just about soft enough by now to ionize readily. The severed filament can be the two electron poles." He laughed mirthlessly: "I don't know why I should be in a hurry. I won't be able to turn off the viton stream even if I should discover the duct-muscle."

Weeks later, Troy found his viton sphere, just below the cerebral frontal lobe. The duct led somewhere into the pineal region. Very gingerly he investigated the duct environment. A small but dense muscle mass surrounded the entry of the duct to the bulk of radiation.

On the morning of the first day of the thirty-first year of their imprisonment, a few minutes before the nurse was due with the *skon* hypo, Ann 'pathed to Troy that she thought the screen was down. A joint search of the glass panel affirmed this.

Ann was stunned, like a caged canary that suddenly notices the door is open—she fears to stay, yet is afraid to fly away.

"Get your clothes on, dear," urged Troy. "Quickly now! If we don't contact the League in the next ten minutes, we never shall."

She dressed like an automaton.

Troy picked the lock on the corridor door noiselessly, with a key he had long ago made for this day, and opened the portal a quarter of an inch. The corridor seemed empty for its whole half-mile length. There was a preternatural pall of silence hanging over everything. Ordinarily, someone was always stirring about the corridor at this hour. He peered closely at the guard's cubicle down the hall. His eyes were not what they once were, and old Blogshak had never permitted him to be fitted with contacts.

He sucked in his breath sharply. The door of the cubicle was open, and two bodies were visible on the floor. One of the bodies had been a guard. The green of his uniform was plainly visible. The other corpse had white hair and a face like a wrinkled, arthritic claw. It was Blogshak.

Two mental processes occurred within Troy. To the cold, objective Troy, the thought occurred that the viton flow was ineffective beyond one hundred yards. Troy the human being wondered why the Outcast had not immediately remedied this weak point in the guard system. Heart pounding, he stepped back within the suite. He seized a chair, warned Ann out of the way, and hurled it through the glass panel. Ann stepped gingerly through the jagged gap. He held her for a moment in his arms. Her hair was a pure white, her face furrowed. Her body seemed weak and infirm. But it was Ann. Her eyes were shut and she seemed to be floating through time and space.

"No time for a trance now!" He shook her harshly, pulling her out of the room and down the corridor. He looked for a stair. There was none.

"We'll have to chance an autovator!" he panted, thinking he should have taken some sort of bludgeon with him. If several of the staff should come down with the 'vator, he doubted his ability to hypnotize them all.

He was greatly relieved when he saw an empty 'vator already on the subterranean floor. He leaped in, pulling Ann behind him, and pushed the bottom to close the door. The door closed quietly, and he pushed the button for the first floor.

"We'll try the street floor first," he said, breathing heavily. "Don't look around when we leave the 'vator. Just chatter quietly and act as though we owned the place."

The street floor was empty.

An icy thought began to grow in Troy's mind. He stepped into a neighboring 'vator, carrying Ann with him almost bodily, closed the door, and pressed the last button. Ann was mentally out, but was trying to tell him something. Her thoughts were vague, unfocused.

If they were pursued, wouldn't the pursuer assume they had left the building? He hoped so.

A malicious laughter seemed to follow them up the shaft.

He gulped air frantically to ease the roar in his ears. Ann had sunk into a semi-stupor. He eased her to the floor. The 'vator continued to climb. It was now in the two hundreds. Minutes later it stopped gently at the top floor, the door opened, and Troy managed to pull Ann out into a little plaza.

They were nearly a mile above the city.

The penthouse roof of the City Building was really a miniature country club, with a small golf course, swimming pool, and club house for informal administrative functions. A cold wind now blew across the closely cut green. The swimming pool was empty. Troy shivered as he dragged Ann near the dangerously low guard rail and looked over the city in the early morning sunlight.

As far as he could see, nothing was moving. There were no cars gliding at any of the authorized traffic levels, no 'copters or transocean ships in the skies.

For the first time, Troy's mind sagged, and he felt like the old man he was.

As he stared, gradually understanding, yet half-unbelieving, the rosebud in his lapel began to speak.

Mai-kel condensed the thin waste of cosmic gas into several suns and peered again down into the sterechron. There could be no mistake—there was a standing wave of recurrent time emanating from the tiny planet. The Great One made himself small and approached the little world with cautious curiosity. Sathanas had been badly wounded, but it was hard to believe his integration had deteriorated to the point of permitting oscillation in time. And no intelligent life capable of time travel was scheduled for this galaxy. Who, then? Mai-kel synchronized himself with the oscillation so that the events constituting it seemed to move at their normal pace. His excitement multiplied as he followed the cycle.

It would be safest, of course, to volatilize the whole planet. But then, that courageous mite, that microscopic human being who had created the time trap would be lost. Extirpation was indicated—a clean, fast incision done at just the right point of the cycle.

Mai-kel called his brothers.

Troy suppressed an impulse of revulsion. Instead of tearing the flower from his coat, he pulled it out gently and held it at arm's length, where he could watch the petals join and part again, in perfect mimicry of the human mouth.

"Yes, little man, I am what you call the Outcast. There are no other little men to bring my message to you, so I take this means of—"

"You mean you devitalized every man, woman, and child in the province . . . in the whole world?" croaked Troy.

"Yes. Within the past few months, my appetite has been astonishingly good, and I have succeeded in storing within my neurals enough vital fluid to carry me into the next sterechron. There I can do the same, and continue my journey. There's an excellent little planet waiting for me, just bursting with genial bipedal life. I can almost feel their vital fluid within me, now. And I'm taking you along, of course, in case I meet some . . . old friends. We'll leave now."

"Jon! Jon!" cried Ann, from behind him. She was standing, but weaving dizzily. Troy was at her side in an instant. "Even *he* doesn't know who Poole is!"

"Too late for any negative information now, dear," said Troy dully.

"But it isn't negative. If *he* doesn't know, then he won't stop you from going back." Her voice broke off in a wild cackle.

Troy looked at her in sad wonder.

"Jon," she went on feverishly, "your vitons help preserve the status quo of cells by preventing chemical change, but that is only part of the reason they preserve life. Each viton must also contain a quantum of time flow, which dissolves the vital fluid of the cell and reprecipitates it into the next instant. This is the only hypothesis which explains the preservation of the giant neurals of the Outcast. There was no chemical change going on in them which required stabilization, but something had to keep the vital fluid alive. Now, if you close the duct suddenly, the impact of unreleased vitons will send you back through time in your present body, as an old man. Don't you understand about Poole, now, Jon? You will go back thirty years through time, establish yourself in the confidence of both the League and the staff, attend the assassination conference, make young Troy choose the red ball again, defend him at the trial, and then die in that horrible room again. You have no choice about doing this, *because it has already happened!* Good-by, darling! You are Poole!"

There was an abrupt swish. Ann had leaped over the guard rail into space.

A gurgle of horror died in Troy's throat. Still clutching the now-silent rose in his hand, he jammed the viton muscle with all his will power. There was a sickening shock, then a flutter of passing days and nights. As he fell through time, cold fingers seemed to snatch frantically at him. But he knew he was safe.

As he spiraled inward, Troy-Poole blinked his eyes involuntarily as though reluctant to abandon a languorous escape from reality. He was like a dreamer awakened by having his bedclothes blown off in an icy gale.

He slowly realized that this was not the first time he had suddenly been bludgeoned into reality. Every seventy years the cycle began for him once more. He knew now that seventy years ago he had completed another identical circle in time. And the lifetime before that, and the one prior. There was no beginning and no ending. The only reality was this brief lucid interval between cycles, waiting for the loose ends of time to cement. He had the choice at this instant to vary the life stream, to fall far beyond Troy's era, if he liked, and thus to end this existence as the despairing toy of time. What had he accomplished? Nothing, except retain, at the cost of almost unbearable monotony and pain, a weapon pointed at the heart of the Outcast, a weapon he could never persuade the young Troy to use, on account of Ann. Troy old had no influence over Troy young. Poole could never persuade Troy.

Peering down through the hoary wastes of time, he perceived how he had hoped to set up a cycle in the time stream, a standing wave noticeable to the entities who searched for the Outcast. Surely with their incredible intellects and perceptions this discrepancy in the ordered universe would not go unnoticed. He had hoped that this trap in the time flow would hold the Outcast until relief came. But as his memory returned he realized that he had gradually given up hope. Somehow he had gone on from a sense of duty to the race from which he had sprung. From the depths of his aura-fed nervous system he had always found the will to try again. But now his nervous exhaustion, increasing from cycle to cycle by infinitesimal amounts, seemed overpowering.

A curious thought occurred to him. There must have been, at one time, a Troy without a Poole to guide—or entangle—him. There must have been a beginning—some prototype Troy who selected the red ball by pure accident, and who was informed by a prototype staff of his tremendous power. After that, it was easy to assume that the first Troy "went back" as the prototype Poole to scheme against the life of the Outcast.

But searching down time, Troy-Poole now found only the old combination of Troy and Poole he knew so well. Hundreds, thousands, millions of them, each preceding the other. As far back as he could sense, there was always a Poole hovering over a Troy. Now he would become the next Poole, enmesh the next Troy in the web of time, and go his own way to bloody death. He could not even plan a comfortable suicide. No, to maintain perfect oscillation of the time trap, all Pooles must always die in the same manner as the first Poole. There must be no invariance. He suppressed a twinge of impatience, at the lack of foresight in the prototype Poole.

"Just this once more," he promised himself wearily, "then I'm through. Next time I'll keep on falling."

General Blade sometimes felt that leading a resistance movement was far exceeding his debt to decent society and that one day soon he would allow his peaceful nature to override his indignant pursuit of justice. Killing a man, even a very bad man, without a trial, went against his grain. He sighed and rapped on the table.

"As a result of Blogshak's misappropriation of funds to fight the epidemic," he announced, "the death toll this morning reached over one hundred thousand. Does the Assassination Subcommittee have a recommendation?"

A thin-lipped man rose from the gathering. "The Provinarch ignored our warning," he said rapidly. "This subcommittee, as you all know, some days ago set an arbitrary limit of one hundred thousand deaths. Therefore this subcommittee now recommends that its plan for killing the Provinarch be adopted at once. Tonight is very favorable for our—"

A man entered the room quietly and handed General Blade an envelope. The latter read it quickly, then stood up. "I beg your pardon, but I must break in," he announced. "Information I have just received may change our plans completely. This report from our intelligence service is so incredible that I won't read it to you. Let's verify it over the video."

He switched on the instrument. The beam of a local newscasting agency was focused tridimensionally before the group. It showed a huge pit or excavation which appeared to move as the scanning newscaster moved. The news comments were heard in snatches. "No explosion . . . no sign of any force . . . just complete disappearance. An hour ago the City Building was the largest structure in . . . now nothing but a gaping hole a mile deep . . . the Provinarch and his entire council were believed in conference . . . no trace—"

General Blade turned an uncomprehending face to the committee. "Gentlemen, I move that we adjourn this session pending an investigation."

Jon Troy and Ann left through the secret alleyway. As he buttoned his topcoat against the chill night air, he sensed that they were being followed. "Oh, hello?"

"I beg your pardon, Major Troy, and yours, madam. My name is Poole, Legal Subcommittee. You don't know me—yet, but I feel that I know you both very well. Your textbook on prison escape has inspired and sustained me many times in the past. I was just admiring your boutonniere, Major. It seems so lifelike for an artificial rosebud. I wonder if you could tell me where I might buy one?"

Troy laughed metallically. "It's not artificial. I've worn it for weeks, but it's a real flower, from my own garden. It just won't die."

"Extraordinary," murmured Poole, fingering the red blossom in his own lapel. "Could we run in here for a cocktail? Bartender Fonstile will fix us something special, and we can discuss a certain matter you really ought to know about."

The doorman of the Shawn Hotel bowed to the three as they went inside.

STALEMATE IN SPACE

One

At first there was only the voice, a monotonous murmur in her ears.

"Die now—die now—die now—"

Evelyn Kane awoke, breathing slowly and painfully. The top of the cubicle was bulging inward on her chest, and it seemed likely that a rib or two was broken. How long ago? Years? Minutes? She had no way of knowing. Her slender right hand found the oxygen valve and turned it. For a long while she lay, hurting and breathing helplessly.

"Die now—die now—die now—"

The votron had awakened her with its heart-breaking code message, and it was her duty to carry out its command. Nine years after the great battle globes had crunched together, the mentors had sealed her in this tiny cell, dormant, unwaking, to be livened only when it was certain her countrymen had either definitely won—or lost.

The votron's telepathic dirge chronicled the latter fact. She had expected nothing else.

She had only to find the relay beside her cot, press the key that would set in motion gigantic prime movers in the heart of the great globe, and the conquerors would join the conquered in the wide and nameless grave of space.

But life, now doled out by the second, was too delicious to abandon immediately. Her mind, like that of a drowning person, raced hungrily over the memories of her past.

For twenty years, in company with her great father, she had watched *The Defender* grow from a vast metal skeleton into a planet-sized battle globe. But it had not grown fast enough, for when the Scythian globe, *The Invader,* sprang out of black space to enslave the budding Terran Confederacy, *The Defender* was unfinished, half-equipped, and undermanned.

The Terrans could only fight for time and hope for a miracle.

The Defender, commanded by her father, Gordon, Lord Kane, hurled itself from its orbit around Procyon and met *The Invader* with its giant fission torpedoes.

And then, in an intergalactic proton storm beyond the Lesser Magellanic Cloud, the globes lost their bearings and collided. Hordes of brute-men poured through the crushed outer armor of the stricken *Defender*. The prone woman stirred uneasily. Here the images became unreal and terrible, with the recurrent vision of death. It had taken the Scythians nine years to conquer *The Defender's* outer shell. Then had come that final interview with her father.

"In half an hour our last space port will be captured," he had telepathed curtly. "Only one more messenger ship can leave *The Defender*. Be on it."

"No. I shall die here."

His fine tired eyes had studied her face in enigmatic appraisal. "Then die usefully. The mentors are trying to develop a force that will destroy both globes in the moment of our inevitable defeat. If they are successful, you will have the task of pressing the final button of the battle."

"There's an off-chance you may survive," countered a mentor. "We're also working on a means for your escape—not only because you are Gordon's daughter, but because this great proton storm will prevent radio contact with Terra for years, and we want someone to escape with our secret if and when our experiments prove successful."

"But you must expect to die," her father had warned with gentle finality.

She clenched her fingernails vehemently into her palms and wrenched herself back to the present.

That time had come.

With some effort she worked herself out of the crumpled bed and lay on the floor of her little cubicle, panting and holding her chest with both hands. The metal floor was very cold. Evidently the enemy torpedo fissionables had finally broken through to the center portions of the ship, letting in the icy breath of space. Small matter. Not by freezing would she die.

She reached out her hand, felt for the all-important key, and gasped in dismay. The mahogany box containing the key had burst its metal bonds and was lying on its side. The explosion that had crushed her cubicle had been terrific.

With a gurgle of horror she snapped on her wrist luminar and examined the interior of the box.

It was a shattered ruin.

Once the fact was clear, she composed herself and lay there, breathing hard and thinking. She had no means to construct another key. At best, finding the rare tools and parts would take months, and during the interval the invaders would be cutting loose from the dead hulk that clutched their conquering battle globe in a metallic *rigor mortis*.

She gave herself six weeks to accomplish this stalemate.

Within that time she must know whether the prime movers were still intact, and whether she could safely enter the pile room herself, set the movers in motion, and draw the moderator columns. If it were unsafe, she must secure the unwitting assistance of her Scythian enemies.

Still prone, she found the first-aid kit and taped her chest expertly. The cold was beginning to make itself felt, so she flicked on the chaudiere she wore as an undergarment to her Scythian woman's uniform. Then she crawled on her elbows and stomach to the tiny door, spun the sealing gear, and was soon outside. Ignoring the pain and pulling on the side of the imitation rock that contained her cell, she got slowly to her feet. The air was thin indeed, and frigid. She turned the valve of her portable oxygen bottle almost subconsciously, while exploring the surrounding blackened forest as far as she could see. Mentally she was alert for roving alien minds. She had left her weapons inside the cubicle, except for the three things in the little leather bag dangling from her waist, for she knew that her greatest weapon in the struggle to come would be her apparent harmlessness.

Four hundred yards behind her she detected the mind of a low-born Scythe, of the Tharn sun group. Very quickly she established it as that of a tired, brutish corporal, taking a mop-up squad through the black stumps and forlorn branches of the small forest that for years had supplied oxygen to the defenders of this sector.

The corporal could not see her green Scythian uniform clearly, and evidently took her for a Terran woman. In his mind was the question: Should he shoot immediately, or should he capture her? It had been two months since he had seen a woman. But then, his orders were to shoot. Yes, he would shoot.

Evelyn turned in profile to the beam-gun and stretched luxuriously, hoping that her grimace of pain could not be detected. With satisfaction, she sensed a sudden change of determination in the mind of the Tharn. The gun was lowered, and the man was circling to creep up behind her. He did not bother to notify his men. He wanted her first. He had seen her uniform, but that deterred him not a whit. Afterwards, he would call up the squad. Finally, they would kill her and move on. Women auxiliaries had no business here, anyway.

Hips dipping, Evelyn sauntered into the shattered copse. The man moved faster, though still trying to approach quietly. Most of the radions in the mile-high ceiling had been destroyed, and the light was poor. He was not surprised when he lost track of his quarry. He tip-toed rapidly onward, picking his way through the charred and fallen branches, thinking that she must turn up again soon. He had not gone twenty yards in this manner when a howl of unbearable fury sounded in his mind, and the dull light in his brain went out.

Breathing deeply from her mental effort, the woman stepped from behind a great black tree trunk and hurried to the unconscious man. For I.Q.'s of 100 and less, telepathic cortical paralysis was quite effective. With cool efficiency and no trace of distaste she stripped the odorous uniform from the man, then took his weapon, turned the beam power down very low, and needled a neat slash across his throat. While he bled to death, she slipped deftly into the baggy suit, clasped the beam gun by the handle, and started up the sooty slope. For a time, at least, it would be safer to pass as a Tharn soldier than as any kind of a woman.

Two

The Inquisitor leaned forward, frowning at the girl before him.

"Name?"

"Evelyn Kane."

The eyes of the inquisitor widened. "So you admit to a Terran name. Well, Terran, you are charged with having stolen passage on a supply lorry, and you also seem to be wearing the uniform of an infantry corporal as well as that of a Scythian woman auxiliary. Incidentally, where is the corporal? Did you kill him?"

He was prepared for a last-ditch denial. He would cut it short, have the guards remove her, and execution would follow immediately. In a way, it was unfortunate. The woman was obviously of a high Terran class. No—he couldn't consider that. His slender means couldn't afford another woman in his quarters, and besides, he wouldn't feel safe with this cool murderess.

"Do you not understand the master tongue? Why did you kill the corporal?" He leaned impatiently over his desk.

The woman stared frankly back at him with her clear blue eyes. The guards on either side of her dug their nails into her arms, as was their custom with recalcitrant prisoners, but she took no notice.

She had analyzed the minds of the three men. She could handle the inquisitor alone or the two guards alone, but not all three.

"If you aren't afraid of me, perhaps you'd be so kind as to send the guards out for a few minutes," she said, placing a hand on her hip. "I have interesting information."

So that was it. Buy her freedom by betraying fugitive Terrans. Well, he could take the information and then kill her. He nodded curtly to the guards, and they walked out of the hut, exchanging sly winks with one another.

Evelyn Kane crossed her arms across her chest and felt her broken rib gingerly. The inquisitor stared up at her in sadistic admiration. He would certainly be on hand for the execution. His anticipation was cut short with a horrible realization. Under the paralyzing force of a mind greater than his own, he reached beneath the desk and switched off the recorder.

"Who is the Occupational Commandant for this Sector?" she asked tersely. This must be done swiftly before the guards returned.

"Perat, Viscount of Tharn," replied the man mechanically.

"What is the extent of his jurisdiction?"

"From the center of the Terran globe, outward four hundred miles radius."

"Good. Prepare for me the usual visa that a woman clerk needs for passage to the offices of the Occupational Commandant."

The inquisitor filled in blanks in a stiff sheet of paper and stamped a seal at its bottom.

"You will add in the portion reserved for 'comments,' the following: 'Capable clerk. Others will follow as they are found available.' "

The man's pen scratched away obediently.

Evelyn Kane smiled gently at the impotent, inwardly raging inquisitor. She took the paper, folded it, and placed it in a pocket in her blouse. "Call the guards," she ordered.

He pressed the button on his desk, and the guards re-entered.

"This person is no longer a prisoner," said the inquisitor woodenly. "She is to take the next transport to the Occupational Commandant of Zone One."

When the transport had left, neither inquisitor nor guards had any memory of the woman. However, in the due course of events, the recording was gathered up with many others like it, boxed carefully, and sent to the Office of the Occupational Commandant, Zone One, for auditing.

Evelyn was extremely careful with her mental probe as she descended from the transport. The Occupational Commandant would undoubtedly be high-born and telepathic. He must not have occasion to suspect a similar ability in a mere clerk.

Fighting had passed this way, too, and recently. Many of the buildings were still smoking, and many of the radions high above were either shot out or obscured by slowly drifting dust clouds. The acrid odor of radiation-remover was everywhere.

She caught the sound of spasmodic small-arms fire.

"What is that?" she asked the transport attendant.

"The Commandant is shooting prisoners," he replied laconically.

"Oh."

"Where did you want to go?"

"To the personnel office."

"That way." He pointed to the largest building of the group—two stories high, reasonably intact.

She walked off down the gravel path, which was stained here and there with dark sticky red. She gave her visa to the guard at the door and was admitted to an improvised waiting room, where another guard eyed her stonily. The firing was much nearer. She recognized the obscene coughs of a Faeg pistol and began to feel sick.

A woman in the green uniform of the Scythe auxiliary came in, whispered something to the guard, and then told Evelyn to follow her.

In the anteroom a gray cat looked her over curiously, and Evelyn frowned. She might have to get rid of the cat if she stayed here. Under certain circumstances the animal could prove her deadliest enemy.

The next room field a foppish little man, evidently a supervisor of some sort, who was studying her visa.

"I'm very happy to have you here, S'ria—ah—" he looked at the visa suspiciously—"S'ria Lyn. Do sit down. But as I was just remarking to S'ria Gerek, here"—he nodded to the other woman, who smiled back—"I wish the field officers would make up their august minds as to whether they want you or don't want you. Just why did they transfer you to H.Q.?"

She thought quickly. This pompous little ass would have to be given some answer that would keep him from checking with the inquisitor. It would have to be something personal. She looked at the false black in his eyebrows and side-burns, and the artificial way in which he had combed hair over his bald spot.

She crossed her knees slowly, ignoring the narrowing eyes of S'ria Gerek, and smoothed the back of her braided yellow hair. He was studying her covertly.

"The men in the fighting zones are uncouth, S'rin Gorph," she said simply. "I was told that *you*, that is, I mean—"

"Yes?" He was the soul of graciousness. S'ria Gerek began to dictate loudly into her mechanical transcriber.

Evelyn cleared her throat, averted her eyes, and with some effort, managed a delicate flush. "I meant to say, I thought I would be happier working for—working here. So I asked for a transfer."

S'rin Gorph beamed. "Splendid. But the occupation isn't over, yet, you know. There'll be hard work here for several weeks yet, before we cut loose from the enemy globe. But you do your work well"—winking artfully—"and I'll see that—"

He stopped, and his face took on a hunted look of mingled fear and anxiety. He appeared to listen.

Evelyn tensed her mind to receive and deceive a mental probe. She was certain now that the Zone Commandant was high-born and telepathic. The chances were only fifty-fifty that she could delude him for any length of time if he became interested in her. He must be avoided if at all possible. It should not be too difficult. He undoubtedly had a dozen personal secretaries and/or concubines and would take small interest in the lowly employees that amused Gorph.

Gorph looked at her uncertainly. "Perat, Viscount of the Tharn Suns, sends you his compliments and wishes to see you on the balcony." He pointed to a hallway. "All the way through there, across to the other wing."

As she left, she heard all sound in the room stop. The transcribing and calculating machines trailed off into a watchful silence, and she could feel the eyes of the men and women on her back. She noticed then that the Faeg had ceased firing.

Her heart was beating faster as she walked down the hall. She felt a very strong probe flooding over her brain casually, palping with mild interest the artificial memories she supplied: Escapades with officers in the combat areas. Reprimands. Demotion and transfer. Her deception of Gorph. Her anticipation of meeting a real Viscount and hoping he would let her dance for him.

The questing probe withdrew as idly as it had come, and she breathed a sigh of relief. She could not hope to deceive a suspicious telepath for long. Perat was merely amused at her "lie" to his under-supervisor. He had accepted her at her own face value, as supplied by her false memories.

She opened the door to the balcony and saw a man leaning moodily on the balustrade. He gave no immediate notice of her presence.

The five hundred and sixth heir of Tharn was of uncertain age, as were most of the men of both globes. Only the left side of his face could be seen. It was gaunt and leathery, and a deep thin scar lifted the corner of his mouth into a satanic smile. A faint paunch was gathering at his abdomen, as befitted a warrior turned to boring paper work. His closely cut black hair and the two sparkling red-gemmed rings—apparently identical—on his right hand seemed to denote a certain fastidiousness and unconscious superiority. To Evelyn the jeweled fingers bespoke an unnatural contrast to the past history of the man and were symptomatic of a personality that could find stimulation only in strange and cruel pleasures.

In alarm she suddenly realized that she had inadvertently let her appraisal penetrate her uncovered conscious mind, and that this probe was there awaiting it.

"You are right," he said coldly, still staring into the court below. "Now that the long battle is over, there is little left to divert me."

He pushed the Faeg across the coping toward her. "Take this."

He had not as yet looked at her.

She crossed the balcony, simultaneously grasping the pistol he offered her and looking down into the courtyard. There seemed to be nearly twenty Terrans lying about, in pools of their own blood.

Only one man—a Terran officer of very high rank—was left standing. His arms were folded somberly across his chest, and he studied the killer above him almost casually. But when the woman came out, their eyes met, and he started imperceptibly.

Evelyn Kane felt a horrid chill creeping over her. The man's hair was white, now, and his proud face lined with deep furrows, but there could be no mistake. It was Gordon, Lord Kane.

Her father.

The sweat continued to grow on her forehead, and she felt for a moment that she needed only to wish hard enough, and this would be a dream. A dream of a big, kind, dark-haired man with laugh-wrinkles about his eyes, who sat her on his knee when she was a little girl and read bedtime stories to her from a great book with many pictures.

An icy, amused voice came through: "Our orders are to kill all prisoners. It is entertaining to shoot down helpless men, isn't it? It warms me to know that I am cruel and wanton, and worthy of my trust."

Even in the midst of her horror, a cold, analytical part of her was explaining why the Commandant had called her to the balcony. Because all captured Terrans had to be killed, he hated his superiors, his own men, and especially the prisoners. A task so revolting he could not relegate to his own officers. He must do it himself, but he wanted his underlings to know he loathed them for it. She was merely a symbol of that contempt. His next words did not surprise her.

"It is even more stimulating to require a shuddering female to kill them. You are shuddering, you know?"

She nodded dumbly. Her palm was so wet that a drop of sweat dropped from it to the floor. She was thinking hard. She could kill the Commandant and save her father for a little while. But then the problem of detonating the pile remained, and it would not be solved more quickly by killing the man who controlled the pile area. On the contrary if she could get him interested in her—

"So far as our records indicate," murmured Perat, "the man down there is the last living Terran within *The Defender*. It occurred to me that our newest clerk would like to start off her duties with a bang. The Faeg is adjusted to a needle-beam. If you put a bolt between the man's eyes, you may dance for me tonight, and perhaps there will be other nights—"

The woman seemed lost in thought for a long time. Slowly, she lifted the ugly little weapon. The doomed Terran looked up at her peacefully, without expression. She lowered the Faeg, her arm trembling.

Gordon, Lord Kane, frowned faintly, then closed his eyes. She raised the gun again, drew cross hairs with a nerveless wrist, and squeezed the trigger. There was a loud, hollow cough, but no recoil. The Terran officer, his eyes still closed and arms folded, sank to the ground, face up. Blood was running from a tiny hole in his forehead.

The man leaning on the balustrade turned and looked at Evelyn, at first with amused contempt, then with narrowing, questioning eyes.

"Come here," he ordered.

The Faeg dropped from her hand. With a titanic effort she activated her legs and walked toward him.

He was studying her face very carefully.

She felt that she was going to be sick. Her knees were so weak that she had to lean on the coping.

With a forefinger he lifted up the mass of golden curls that hung over her right forehead and examined the scar hidden there, where the mentors had cut into her frontal lobe. The tiny doll they had created for her writhed uneasily in her waist purse, but Perat seemed to be thinking of something else, and missed the significance of the scar completely.

He dropped his hand. "I'm sorry," he said with a quiet weariness. "I shouldn't have asked you to kill the Terran. It was a sorry joke." Then: "Have you ever seen me before?"

"No," she whispered hoarsely. His mind was in hers, verifying the fact.

"Have you ever met my father, Phaen, the old Count of Tharn?"

"No."

"Do you have a son?"

"No."

His mind was out of hers again, and he had turned moodily back, surveying the courtyard and the dead. "Gorph will be wondering what happened to you. Come to my quarters at the eighth metron tonight."

Apparently he suspected nothing.

Father. Father. I had to do it. But we'll all join you, soon. Soon.

Three

Perat lay on his couch, sipping cold purple *terif* and following the thinly-clad dancer with narrowed eyes. Music, soft and subtle, floated from his communications box, illegally tuned to an officers' club somewhere. Evelyn made the rhythm part of her as she swayed slowly on tiptoe.

For the last thirty "nights"—the hours allotted to rest and sleep—it had been thus. By "day" she probed furtively into the minds of the office staff, memorizing area designations, channels for official messages, and the names and authorizations of occupational field crews. By night she danced for Perat, who never took his eyes from her, nor his probe from her mind. While she danced it was not too difficult to elude the probe. There was an odd autohypnosis in dancing that blotted out memory and knowledge.

"Enough for now," he ordered. "Careful of your rib."

When he had first seen the bandages on her bare chest, that first night, she had been ready with a memory of dancing on a freshly waxed floor, and of falling.

Perat seemed to be debating with himself as she sat down on her own couch to rest. He got up, unlocked his desk, and drew out a tiny reel of metal wire, which Evelyn recognized as being feed for an amateur stereop projector. He placed the reel in a projector that had been installed in the wall, flicked off the table luminar, and both of them waited in the dark, breathing rather loudly.

Suddenly the center of the room was bright with a ball of light some two feet in diameter, and inside the luminous sphere were an old man, a woman, and a little boy of about four years. They were walking through a luxurious garden, and then they stopped, looked up, and waved gaily.

Evelyn studied the trio with growing wonder. The old man and the boy were complete strangers. *But the woman—!*

"That is Phaen, my father," said Perat quietly. "He stayed at home because he hated war. And that is a path in our country estate on Tharn-R-VII. The little boy I fail to recognize, beyond a general resemblance to the Tharn line."

"But—*can you deny that you are the woman?*"

The stereop snapped off, and she sat wordless in the dark.

"There seemed to be some similarity—" she admitted. Her throat was suddenly dry. Yet, why should she be alarmed? She really didn't know the woman.

The table luminar was on now, and Perat was prowling hungrily about the room, his scar twisting his otherwise handsome face into a snarling scowl.

"Similarity! Bah! That loop of hair over her right forehead hid a scar identical to yours. I have had the individual frames analyzed!"

Evelyn's hands knotted unconsciously. She forced her body to relax, but her mind was racing. This introduced another variable to be controlled in her plan for destruction. She *must* make it a known quantity.

"Did your father send it to you?" she asked.

"The day before you arrived here. It had been *en route* for months, of course."

"What did he say about it?"

"He said, 'Your widow and son send greetings. Be of good cheer, and accept our love.' What nonsense! He knows very well I'm not married and that—well, if I have ever fathered any children, I don't know about them."

"Is that all he said?"

"That's all, except that he included this ring." He pulled one of the duplicate jewels from his right middle finger and tossed it to her. "It's identical to the one he had made for me when I entered on my majority. For a long time it was thought

that it was the only stone of its kind on all the planets of the Tharn suns, a min-eralogical freak, but I guess he found another. But why should I want two of them?"
Evelyn crossed the room and returned the ring.

"Existence is so full of mysteries, isn't it?" murmured Perat. "Sometimes it seems unfortunate that we must pass through a sentient phase on our way to death. This foolish, foolish war. Maybe the old count was right."

"You could be court martialed for that."

"Speaking of courts martial, I've got to attend one tonight—an appeal from a death sentence." He arose, smoothed his hair and clothes, and poured another glass of *terif*. "Some fool inquisitor can't show proper disposition of a woman prisoner."

Evelyn's heart skipped a beat. "Indeed?"

"The wretch insists that he could remember if we would just let him alone. I suppose he took a bribe. You'll find one now and then who tries for a little extra profit."

She must absolutely not be seen by the condemned inquisitor. The stimulus would almost certainly make him remember.

"I'll wait for you," she said indifferently, thrusting her arms out in a languor-ous yawn.

"Very well." Perat stepped to the door, then turned and looked back at her. "On the other hand, I may need a clerk. It's way after hours, and the others have gone."

Beneath a gesture of wry protest, she swallowed rapidly.

"Perhaps you'd better come," insisted Perat.

She stood up, unloosened her waist purse, checked its contents swiftly, and then followed him out.

This might be a very close thing. From the purse she took a bottle of perfume and rubbed her ear lobes casually.

"Odd smell," commented Perat, wrinkling his nose.

"Odd scent," corrected Evelyn cryptically. She was thinking about the earnest faces of the mentors as they instructed her carefully in the use of the "perfume." The adrenalin glands, they had explained, provided a useful and powerful stimu-lant to a man in danger. Adrenalin slowed the heart and digestion, increased the systole and blood pressure, and increased perspiration to cool the skin. But there could be too much of a good thing. An overdose of adrenalin, they had pointed out, caused almost immediate edema. The lungs filled rapidly with the serum and the victim . . . drowned. The perfume she possessed overstimulated, in some unknown way, the adrenals of frightened persons. It had no effect on inactive adrenals.

The question remained—who would be the more frightened, she or the con-demned inquisitor?

She was perspiring freely, and the blonde hair on her arms and neck was stand-ing stiffly when Perat opened the door for her and they entered the Zone Provost's chambers.

One glance at the trembling creature in the prisoner's chair reassured her. The ex-inquisitor, shorn of his insignia, shabby and stubble-bearded, sat huddled in his chair and from time to time swept his grave tormentors with glazed eyes. He looked a long while at Evelyn.

She got out her bottle of perfume idly and held it open in her warm hand. The officers and judge-provost were listening to the opening address of the prosecution and took no notice of her.

More and more frequently the condemned man turned his gaze to Evelyn. She poured a little of the scent on her handkerchief. The prisoner coughed and rubbed his chin, trying to think.

The charges were finally read, and the defense attorney began his opening statement. The prisoner, now coughing more frequently, was oblivious to all but the woman. Once she thought she saw a flicker of recognition in his eyes, and she fanned herself hurriedly with her handkerchief.

The trial droned on to a close. It was a mere formality. The prosecutor summed up by proving that a Terran woman had been captured, possibly named Evelyn Kane, turned over to the defendant for registration and disposal, and that the defendant's weekly accounts failed to show a receipt for the release of the woman. Q.E.D., the death sentence must be affirmed.

The light in the prisoner's eyes was growing clearer, despite his bronchial difficulties. He began now to pay attention to what was said and to take notice of the other faces. It was as though he had finally found the weapon he wanted, and patiently awaited an opportunity to use it.

The defense was closing. Counsel for the prisoner declared that the latter might have been the innocent victim of the escapee, Evelyn Kane, possibly a telepathic Terran woman, because only a fool would have permitted a prisoner to escape without attempting to juggle the prison records, unless his mind had been under telepathic control. They ought to be looking for Evelyn Kane now, instead of wasting time with her victim. She might be anywhere. She might even be in this building. He bowed apologetically to Evelyn, she smiled at the faces suddenly looking at her with new interest.

The man in the prisoner's chair was peering at Evelyn through half-closed eyes, his arms crossed on his chest. He had stopped coughing, and the fingers of his right hand were tapping patiently on his sleeve.

If Perat should at this moment probe the prisoner's mind . . .

Evelyn, in turning to smile at Perat, knocked the bottle from the table to the floor, where it broke in a liquid tinkle. She put her hands to her mouth in contrite apology. The judge-provost frowned, and Perat eyed her curiously. The prisoner was seized with such a spasm of coughing that the provost, who had stood to pronounce sentence, paused in annoyance. The wracking ceased.

The provost picked up the Faeg lying before him.

"Have you anything to say before you die?" he asked coldly.

The ex-inquisitor stood and turned a triumphant face to him. "Excellency, you ask, where is the woman prisoner who escaped from me? Well, I can tell you . . ."

He clutched wildly at his throat, coughed horribly and bent in Evelyn Kane's direction.

"She . . ."

His lips, which were rapidly growing purple, moved without saying anything intelligible, and he suddenly crashed over the chair and to the floor.

The prison physician leaped to him, stethoscope out. After a few minutes, he stood up, puzzled and frowning, in the midst of a strained silence. "Odd, very odd," he muttered.

"Did the prisoner faint?" asked the judge-provost incuriously, lowering the Faeg.

"The prisoner's lungs are filled with liquid, apparently the result of hyperactive adrenals," commented the baffled physician. "He's dead, and don't ask me to explain why."

Evelyn smothered a series of hacking coughs in her handkerchief as the court broke up in excited groups. From the corner of her eye she saw that Perat was studying her thoughtfully.

Four

Two weeks later, very late at "night," Perat lay stretched gloomily on his sleeping couch. On the other side of the room Evelyn was curled luxuriously on her own damasked lounge, her head propped high. She was scanning some of the miniature stereop reels that Perat had brought from his far-distant home planet.

"Those green trees and hedges . . . so far away," she mused. "Do you ever think about seeing them again?"

"Of late, I've been thinking about them quite a bit."

What did he mean by that?

"I understood it would be months before the field crews cut us loose from the Terran ship," she said.

"Indeed?"

"Well? Won't it?"

Perat turned his moody face toward her. "No, it won't. The field crews have been moving at breakneck speed, on account of some unfounded rumor or other that the Terran ship is going to explode. On orders from our High Command, we pull out of here by the end of the working day tomorrow. Within twenty metrons from now, our ship parts company with the enemy globe."

The scar on her forehead was throbbing violently. There was no time now to send the false orders to the field crew she had selected. She must think a bit.

"It seems, then, this is our last night together."

"It is."

She rose from her couch and walked the room like a caged beast.

"You can hardly take me, a commoner, back with you . . ."

With growing shock she realized that she was more than half sincere in her request.

"It is not done. It is unlike you to suggest it."

"Well, that's that, I suppose." She stopped and toyed idly with a box of chessmen on his table. "Would you care for a game of Terran chess? I'll try to play very intelligently, so that you won't be too terribly bored."

"If you like. But there are more interesting . . ."

"Do you think," she interrupted quickly, "that you could beat me without sight of the board or pieces?"

"What do you mean by that?"

"I just thought it would be more interesting for you. I'll take the board over to my bed, and you call out your moves and I'll tell you my replies. I'll see the board, but you won't."

"A curious variant."

"But you must promise to keep out of my mind; otherwise you would know my plans."

He smiled. "Set up the pieces. What color do you want?"

"I'll defend. Give me black."

She loosed her waist-purse, took a handkerchief from it, and set the purse on the deep carpet in the shadow of her table. She unfolded the chessboard in front of her on the couch and quickly placed the pieces. "I'm ready," she announced.

Indeed, everything was in readiness now except that she didn't know where the cat was. She regretted bitterly not having killed that innocent mouser weeks ago.

"Pawn to king four," announced Perat, gazing idly at the ceiling.

She made the move and replied, "Pawn to king three."

From the unlaced purse hidden on the floor a tiny head thrust itself out, followed soon by a pair of miniscule shoulders.

"Have you studied this Terran game?" queried Perat curiously, "or don't you know enough to seize the center on your first move?"

"Have I made an error already? Was that the wrong move?"

"It's the first move in a complete defensive system, but few people outside of Terrans understand it. Pawn to queen four."

She had blundered in attempting the French Defense, but it was not too late to convert to something that could be expected of a Scythian woman beginner. "Pawn to queen three."

The gray doll was out of the purse, sidling through the shadows to the door, which stood slightly ajar.

"So you don't know the book moves, after all. You would really have astonished me if you had moved your queen pawn two squares. I'll play pawn to king bishop four. Will you have some *terif?*"

He spun around upright and reached for the decanter, looking full at the door . . . and the tiny figure.

Evelyn was up at once, cutting off his line of vision. "Yes, I think I will have one."

Telepathically she ordered the little creature to dash through the crack in the doorway. She heard the faint rustle behind her as she picked up the glass Perat poured.

"You know," he said thoughtfully, "for a moment I thought I saw your little doll . . ."

She looked at him dubiously. "Really, Perat? It's in my purse."

He stepped lithely to the door and flung it open. Far down the hall there was the faintest suggestion of a scuffle.

"A mouse, I guess." He returned to his bed, but it was plain that he was unsatisfied.

The game wore on for half a metron. Perat's combinations were met with almost sufficient counter-combinations, so that the issue hung in doubt for move after move.

"You've improved considerably since yesterday," he admitted grudgingly.

"Not at all. It's your playing 'blind' that makes us even. No cheating! Keep out of my mind! It isn't fair to know what I'm planning."

Oh, by the merciful god of Galaxus, if he'll stay out of my mind and the cat out of the communications room for another five minutes!

"All right, all right. I'll win anyway," he muttered, as he concluded a combination that netted him the black queen. "You could gracefully resign right now."

Evelyn studied the position carefully. She had made a grave miscalculation—the queen loss had definitely not been a part of the plan. She must contrive a delaying action that would invoke an oral argument.

"Bishop to queen rook eight," she murmured. Her telepathic probe, focused on the bit of nervous tissue that the mentors had cut from her frontal lobe and given to her mannikin as a brain, continued its tight control. In Gorph's office, far down the wing, the little creature was hopping painstakingly from one key to another of the dispatch printing machine.

"*. . . takes priority over all other pending projects . . .*"

"Your game is hopeless," scowled Perat. "I'm a queen and the exchange up on you."

"I always play the game out," replied Evelyn easily. "You never know what might happen. Your move."

"*. . . five horizontal columns of metallic trans-scythium nine hundred xedars long will be found in a Terran storeroom, our area code . . .*"

"All right, then. Queen takes pawn."

"Pawn to queen knight seven," replied Evelyn. It was her sole remaining pawn, and she hoped to use it in an odd way.

Perat checked with his queen at queen bishop four, and Evelyn's king slid to safety at queen knight eight. Perat moved his rook from queen knight five to queen five.

"Do you intend to mate with rook to queen's square next move?" asked Evelyn demurely.

"*. . . under the strictest secrecy. Therefore you are ordered not to communicate . . .*"

"Nothing can prevent it," observed the Viscount of Tharn somberly. He had already lost all interest in the game and was contemplating the ceiling tapestries.

With a lurch she brought her telepathic probe to rest, ready to prepare a false front for his searching mind. She must keep him out a moment longer, or all was lost.

"But it's my move, and I have no move," she objected, focusing her probe again.

"... signed, Perat, Viscount of Tharn, Commandant, Occupation Zone One."

Through that distant fragment of her mind she sensed that something was watching the doll with feral interest.

The cat.

"So? No move? Then you lose," replied Perat.

"But my king isn't in check. You told me yourself that when my king was not in check, and I had no legal move, that I was stalemated, and the game was a draw."

In that other room, her telepathic contact guided the little figure down the table leg. Slowly now, don't excite the cat into pouncing. She had only seconds left, but it should suffice to place the dispatch in Gorph's incoming box. The pompous little supervisor would send it by the first jet messenger without doubt or question, and the field crew would proceed to draw the five columns.

Pain daggered into her right leg!

The cat had seized her homunculus by the thigh; she knew the tiny bone had been crushed. She caught fleet, dizzy impressions of the animal striding off proudly with the little creature between its jaws. The letter lay where it had fallen, under the dispatch machine, almost invisible.

The doll ceased her blind writhing and drew a tiny black cylinder from her belt. The cat's right eye loomed huge above her.

Mentally, Perat studied the chessboard position with growing interest.

"Idiotic Terran game," he growled. "Only a Terran would conceive of the idea of calling a crushing defeat a drawn battle. I'm sorry I taught you the game. It's really quite—*what was that?*"

"Sounded like the cat, didn't it?" responded Evelyn.

Her tiny *alter ego* had dropped from those destructive jaws and was dragging itself slowly back to the dispatch. It found the message and picked it up.

"Do you think something could have hurt it?" asked Evelyn.

The doll struggled toward Gorph's desk, leaving behind a thin red trail.

Then several things happened. Hot swords sizzled in Evelyn's back, and she knew the enraged feline had broken the spinal column of the doll. With throbbing intuition she collapsed her telepathic tentacle.

Too late.

Perat's probe was already in her mind, and she knew that he had caught the full impact of her swift telepathic return. She lay there limply. Her rib, now almost healed, began to ache dully.

The man continued to lie motionless, staring heavy-lidded at the ceiling. Gradually, his mind withdrew itself from hers.

"So you're high-born," he mused aloud. "I should have known, but then you concealed it very adroitly, didn't you?"

She sat up against the wall. Her heart was pounding almost audibly. He was relentless. "No Scythian would play chess the way you did. Only a Terran would play for a draw after total defeat."

"I play chess well, so I am a Terran?" she whispered through a dry throat.

Perat turned his handsome gray eyes from the ceiling and smiled at her. His mouth lifted venomously as he watched her begin to tremble.

"Pour me a *terif,*" he ordered.

She arose, feeling that she must certainly collapse the next instant. She forced her legs to move, step by step, to the table by his couch. There she picked up the *terif* decanter and tipped it to fill his glass. The dry clatter of bottle on glass betrayed her shaking hands.

"One for you, too, my dear Lyn."

She held the decanter several inches above her glass to avoid that horrible clatter, and managed to spill quite a bit on the table.

Perat held his glass up to touch hers. "A toast," he smiled, "to a mysterious and beautiful lady!"

He drank prone, she standing. She knew she would spill her drink if she tried to recross to her couch.

"So you're a Terran? Then why did you kill the Terran officer on the balcony?"

She was so relieved that she sank limply to the floor beside him.

"Why should I tell you? You wouldn't believe anything I told you now, or that you found in my mind." She smiled up at him.

"True, true. Quite a dilemma. Should I shoot you now and possibly bring the rage of a noble Scythian house down about my ears, or should I submit you to mechanical telepathic analysis?"

"I am yours, Viscount," she laughed. "Shoot me. Analyze me. Whatever you wish."

She knew her gaiety was forced, and that it had struck a false note. The iron gate of doubt had clanged shut between them. From now on he would contain her mind in the mental prison of his own. The dispatch beside Gorph's desk could have no further aid from her. Anyway, the cat had undoubtedly carried off the doll.

"What a strange woman you are," he murmured. A brief shadow crossed his face. "With you, for a little while, I have been happy. But in a few metrons, of course, you will depart under close arrest for the psych center, and I'll be on my way back to the Tharn suns."

Within half a metron the office force would begin straggling into the Administration offices and her letter would be found and given to a puzzled Gorph, who would then query Perat as to whether it should not be in the incoming box for urgent matters. But what would Gorph do if his superior refused to communicate with him or anyone else for a full metron? The first messenger jet left very soon, and there was no other for four metrons. Would Gorph send it on the first jet, or would he wait? It was a chance she'd have to take.

She got up from the floor and sat down on the couch beside the Viscount of Tharn. "Perat," she began hesitantly, "I know you must send me away. I'm sorry, because I don't want to leave you so soon, and you do not want me to leave you until the last moment, either. Anything else that I would tell you, you might doubt, so I say nothing more. I would like to dance for you. When I dance, I tell the truth."

"Yes, dance, but take care of your rib," assented the man moodily.

She filled his glass again with a sure hand and replaced it on the table. Then she unloosed the combs in her hair and let it fall in a profusion of curls about her shoulders, where it scintillated in a myriad sparkling semicircles in the soft light of the table luminar.

She shook her shoulders to scatter her hair, and unhurriedly released the clasp of her outer lounging gown. The heavy robe fell about her feet, leaving her clad only in a thin, flowing undergarment, which she smoothed languidly while she kicked off her slippers. Her mouth was now half-parted, her eyelids drooping and slumbrous. Perat was still staring at the ceiling, but she knew his mind was flowing unceasingly over her body.

"I must have music," she whispered. The man made no protest when she pressed the controls on his communications box to receive the slow and haunting dance music from the officers' club in the next zone.

The main avenue of access to Perat was now cut. And Gorph was a bolder man than she thought if he dared knock on the door of his chief while she was inside.

She began to sway and to chant. *The Song of Karos, the Great God of Scythe, Father of Tharn folk, Dweller in Darkness . . .*"

Perat's glass halted, then proceeded slowly to his lips. Of course, no educated nobleman admitted a belief in the ancient religion of the Scythes, but how good it was to hear it sung and danced again! Not since his boyhood, when his mother had dragged him to the temple by main force . . . He placed one palm behind his head and continued to sip and to think, as this strange, lovely woman unraveled with undulant body and husky voice the long, satisfying story of his god.

As she postured sinuously, Evelyn breathed a silent prayer of thanks to the dead mentors who had crammed her to bursting with Scythe folklore.

The luminous metron dial revolved with infinite slowness.

Five

One metron had passed when Perat laid his empty glass on the table, without releasing it.

"Enough of dancing," he murmured with cold languor, cutting his communications box back to its authorized channel. "Come here, my dear. I wish you to kiss me."

Evelyn glided instantly to the silken couch, tossing her hair back over her shoulders and ignoring the fact that her rib was alive with pain. She knelt over the reclining man and kissed him on the mouth, running her fingers lightly down his right arm. He relinquished his glass at her touch, and she refilled it absently.

Only then did she notice that something was wrong.

His left hand was no longer beneath his head, but was concealed in the mass of cushions that overflowed his couch in a mute, glittering cascade.

Perat swirled his glass silently, apparently watching only the tiny flashes of iridescence flowing from his jewelled right hand.

Evelyn thought: What made him suspicious? There's something in his left hand. If I only dared probe . . . But he'd know I was afraid, and I'm not supposed to be afraid. Anyway, in a little while it won't matter. If the field crew has started pulling the columns, they should be through in half a metron. If they haven't started, they never will, and nothing will matter then, anyway.

The man's face was inscrutable when he finally spoke. "You couldn't have gone on much longer, anyway, on account of your rib."

"It was becoming a little painful."

"Twice you nearly fainted."

So he had noticed that.

He continued mercilessly. "Why were you so anxious to keep me shut up for a whole metron?"

"I wanted to amuse you. We have so little time left, now."

"So I thought, until your rib began to trouble you. The reaction of an ordinary woman would have been to stop."

"Am I an ordinary woman?"

"Decidedly not. That's why the situation has become so interesting."

"I don't understand, Perat." She sat down beside him, forcing him to move his legs so that his left hand was jammed under the cushion.

"A little while ago, I decided to contact Gorph's mind." He took a sip. "It seems he had been trying to reach me through the communications box."

"He had?" She pictured Gorph's old-womanish anxiety. He had found the sealed message, then, but hadn't been able to verify it because his chief had been listening to a tale of gods. Had he or had he not sent the message by the early jet? It had to be! Possibly all five of the columns had been drawn by now, but she couldn't assume it. The strain-pile would not erupt for a full Terran hour after the fifth column had been drawn. From now until death, of one sort or another, she must delay, delay, delay.

Her blue eyes were widely innocent and puzzled, but the nerves of her arms were going dead with over-tension. Perhaps if she threw the *terif* in his eyes with her left hand and crushed the numbing supraclavicular nerve with her thumb . . .

Perat turned his head for the first time and looked her full in the face.

"Gorph says he sent the message," he said tonelessly.

She looked at him blankly, then casually removed her hand from his knee and dropped it in her lap. He must absolutely not be alarmed until she knew more. "Apparently I'm supposed to know what you're talking about."

He turned back to the ceiling. "Gorph says someone prepared a priority dispatch with my signature, and he sent it out. I don't suppose you have any idea who did it?"

Time! Time!

"When I was Gorph's assistant, there was a young officer—I can't remember his name—who sometimes forged your signature to urgent actions when Gorph was out. This is true, Perat. My mind is open to you."

He fastened his luminous gray eyes on her. "I presume you're lying, but . . ." His mental probe skimmed rapidly over her cortical association centers. Her skill was strained to the utmost, setting up false memories of each of thousands of synaptic groups just ahead of Perat's probe. On some of the groups she knew she had made blunders, but apparently she preserved the general impression by strengthened verification in subsequent nets. She wove a brief tale of a young officer in charge of metals salvage who had sent an order to a field group to recover some sort of metal, and since Gorph had been out, and H.Q. needed the metal urgently, the officer did not wait for official authorization. His probe then searched her visual lobe thoroughly, but with growing skepticism. She offered him only indistinct memories of the dead officer's identity.

"Who was the man?" asked Perat as a matter of form, sipping his *terif* absently.

"Sub-leader Galen, I think." That would give him pause. He knew she had offered no visual memory of Galen. He would wonder why she was lying.

"Are you sure?"

She wanted to look at the time-dial on the wall, but dared not. From the corner of her eye she saw Perat's left arm tense, then relax warily. His mental probe had fastened grimly to her mind again, though he must know it would be effort wasted. She conjured up an image of Sub-leader Galen in the act of telling her he was handling a very urgent matter and that he'd tell the Viscount later what he'd done. Then the face of the young officer changed to another of the staff, then another, then still another. Then back to Galen.

"No, I'm not sure."

Perat smiled thinly. "You wished to gain time, and I wished to idle it away. I suppose we have both been fairly successful."

The communications box beside the bed jangled.

"Yes?" cried Perat, all alert.

As his mouth was forming the word, his probe was collapsing within her mind, and her own flashed briefly into his mind. The hand under the pillow held a Faeg, aimed at her chest. But the safety catch was still on.

"Excellency?" came Gorph's tinny voice.

"Yes, Gorph? Have you replaced the columns?"

"Replaced" . . . ? That seemed to indicate that the field crew had followed her forged order, then returned the columns by Perat's countercommand, relayed telepathically through Gorph. But once all the great rods were drawn, replacing them did not halt the strain pile. The negative potential would keep on increasing geometrically with time, as planned, to the final goal of joint catastrophe and stalemate.

Some sort of knowledge was drumming silently at her threshold of consciousness. Something she couldn't quite grasp. About the woman in the stereop? Possibly. It would come to her soon.

Ignoring Perat's gloating smile, she looked casually at the metron dial, and her heart leaped with elation, for the dial had ceased revolving. Electrons must be flowing from the center of the ship through the walls, outward toward the surface two thousand miles away, and the massive currents were probably jamming all the wall circuits.

Within minutes, *finis.*

Could she really rest, now? She was beginning to feel very tired, almost sleepy. Her duty had been done, and nothing could ever be important again.

Gorph was answering his master over the speaker: "Yes, Your Excellency, we got them back, that is to say, excepting that one of the five is only half-way out of its cradle."

Life was good, life was beautiful. She almost yawned. Most certainly all of the columns had been pulled out, and then four had been replaced and something had broken down with the fifth. But they had all been out, and that was the only thing that mattered.

"What happened, Gorph?" asked Perat, sipping at his *terif* again. His eyes were fastened on his mistress.

She knew that he had pulled the safety catch on the Faeg.

"When the crew took the rods out, the prime mover broke down on the fifth one, when it was only half-way out. They brought in another mover and got the other four rods back in, and now they're trying to repair the first mover and push the fifth rod back."

(The fifth rod had not been completely drawn. Oh Almighty Heaven!)

"Very well, Gorph. I need not repeat that none of the rods are to be moved out again, unless I appear to you personally. I'll talk to you later."

The box went dead.

Perat, now taking no notice of Evelyn, finished his *terif* leisurely. She sat at his side, breathing woodenly. She had done all that she could do. All five rods had not been withdrawn, and they never would be, now.

"If all Terran women are like you," he began slowly, "I cannot understand how you Terrans lost this battle." He did not expect an answer, and did not wait for one. His hard eyes seemed softened somewhat by a curious admiration. "Only your own gods know what you have endured in your attempt to start the pile."

She looked up wretchedly.

He went on: "Yes, we learned in the nick of time, didn't we? Our physicists told Gorph that the great rods were the core of a pile that could have converted both ships into pure energy, with not a shred of matter left over—something that all the fission piles in the two galaxies couldn't do. It seems that the pile, if activated, would have introduced sufficient energy into the low-packing-fraction atoms, from iron on down to helium, to transform them completely from matter into radiation.

"Unpleasant thought! Now the Scythian plan will be modified slightly. We shall wait until we tear our globe away from yours, *far* away, and then prime movers left behind in your ship here can pull the columns again, all five, this time. Our globe then proceeds into the Terran Confederacy, and the war will be over. But of course, you'll know nothing about that."

He regarded her wearily. "I'm sorry, Lyn—or is it 'Evelyn Kane'? If you had been of Tharn-blood, or even of the Scythian federacy, I would have married you."

She listened to him with only half a mind. Some strange, inaudible thing was trying to reach her. Something she couldn't grasp, but ought to grasp. What had the mentors told her to be ready for? Exhaustion lay like a paralyzing blanket over her inert mind.

"You killed your countryman that day," he intoned, "just to ingratiate yourself with me. He was very generous to you. When he saw that you wouldn't shoot him with his eyes open, he closed them. Who was he?"

"Gordon, Lord Kane. My father."

The *terif* glass shook, and the man's face became perceptibly paler. He breathed stridently for a while before speaking again.

This time he seemed to be calling with earnest finality to the forbidding deity of his own warlike homeland, announcing a newcomer at the dark portals of the god: *"This woman . . . !"*

Evelyn Kane did not shriek when the Faeg-bolt tore through her rib and lungs. Even when she sank to the floor, the pain-lines in her own face were much better controlled than those in Perat's.

Then as she lay quietly on the thick, gilded carpet, with consciousness rapidly fading and returning with the regularity of her heart beats, she realized what had been calling to her. The piezo crystal in her waist pouch, still hidden in the shadows of her table, had been activated, and had brought into focus within the room the dim, transparent outlines of a small space ship.

Perat saw it too, and his eyes widened as they traced it quickly from wall to wall.

"It's real . . ." whispered Evelyn between clenched lips. "Mentors wanted me . . . return in it . . . to Terra . . . secret of pile . . ."

A strange light was growing over Perat's face. "Of course! So that's why your father tried so hard at the last to break through our blockade and get a ship through! If the secret of the strain-pile had ever reached Terra, all the Tharn suns—indeed, the whole Scythe federation—would be novae by now! By Karos, it was a narrow thing!"

There was a soft gurgling in Evelyn's throat.

He flung his pistol away and sat down beside her, lifting her head to his chest. "I'll call the physician," he rasped through contorted lips.

She slid a cold palm over his hot cheek, caressing it lightly. "No . . . we die . . ."

He stiffened. *"We?"*

She continued to stroke his cheek dreamily. "Die with you . . ."

He shook her. "What are you talking about!" he cried. "The pile isn't going to erupt!"

"Crystal focuses . . . ship . . . only when pile . . ."

His face blanched.

She whispered again, so softly that he had to bend his ear to her lips. *"You escape . . . get in ship . . ."*

He stared at her incredulously. "You'd let me get away with the pile secret!"

She relaxed in his arms, smiling sleepily, while the tiny red trickle from the corner of her mouth grew wider. "Stupid of me."

She shivered. ". . . cold . . ."

The Viscount of the Tharn Suns, the greatest star-cluster in the Scythe federation, knotted his jaw muscles feverishly and gnawed at his lower lip. Somehow or other the strain-pile had been energized. Probably the terrific proton storm that had hidden both ships for years had compensated for the unrealized potential of the undrawn fifth rod. It was his duty to the federation to throw this woman to the floor and take refuge between the shadowy, shimmering walls of the escape ship. He must carry the secret of the pile to safety with him. He had only seconds.

He looked down distractedly at the small creature who was destroying the proud ships that two great civilizations had spent a generation in building. She seemed to be in a deep, peaceful sleep. The only sign of life was a faint pulse in her throat.

She was the only woman that he had ever found whose companionship he could have . . . enjoyed hour after hour. He almost thought, "could have loved."

The room was growing quite warm. The tremendous currents coursing through the walls were swiftly growing stronger.

Another thought occurred to him: How had those Terran mentors planned for their escape ship to avoid the holocaust? Any matter within millions of miles would be destroyed. It was evident, then, that wherever the ship was, it was *not* within the danger zone.

Suddenly he understood everything.

With a queer smile, in which ribald surmise and tenderness fought for supremacy, he picked the woman up, carried her into the phantom vessel, placed her on the pilot's lounge, and strapped her in. From his waist-pouch he took a hypodermic syringe, removed the sheath from the needle, and thrust it into her arm. Her face twinged briefly, but she did not waken. He threw a blanket over her and then strode quickly to the controls. They were fairly simple, and he had no difficulty in switching the automatic drive to the general direction of the Tharn sun cluster. He wrote a hasty note on the pilot's navigation pad, and then turned again to the woman. He removed one of his duplicate jeweled rings and slipped it on her finger. His father would recognize it and would believe her.

Then he bent over her and kissed her lightly on the lips.

"Perhaps I love you too, my dearest enemy," he whispered gently. "Educate our son-to-be in the ways of peace."

Again outside the ship, he spun the space lock that sealed her in. The ship's walls were now growing opaque and he could no longer see inside.

His communications box was jangling furiously in a dozen different keys, and anxious, querulous voices were pouring through it into the room. He snapped it off, loosened his collar, filled his glass to overflowing with the last of the *terif,* and cut off the table luminar. His stereop projector next had his attention.

He lay on his couch in the darkness of his death cell, studying with the keenest satisfaction his wife, son, and father, while they waved at him happily from the radiant stereop sphere.

Those Terran mentors had planned well. The escape ship would not be affected by the nearing cataclysm, because it was really in a different time plane—at least five years in the past. The catastrophe would simply release it to its original continuum, whence it would proceed with its precious cargo to the Tharn suns.

Odd effect, that time shift. He wished now he'd read more of the theories of that ancient Terran, Einstein, who claimed that simultaneity was an illusion—that "now" here could be altogether different from "now" in other steric areas. His son, unborn as yet "here," was more than four years old "there"—on the planet Tharn-R-VII, where the lad played in his grandfather's gardens.

And then there was the mystery of the rings. The old count had not had another ring made, of course. The ring the count had sent with the stereop coils must have been the same one that Perat had just placed on the finger of his bride. The ring sent with the stereops was merely his original ring brought back in the relooping of a time-line. In his "now" there was only one ring—the one he was wearing. In Evelyn's "now" there was the same ring, but that was logical, because her "now" would soon be five years earlier than his. Owing to this five-year relooping of time, it had been possible for the ring to exist in duplicate for six weeks. But very soon, in his "now," it would be destroyed for good.

He pressed the repeat button on the stereop and started the coil again. The boy had an engaging grin, rather like his own (he would indulge a final vanity), but without the scar. He hoped there would never be another war to disfigure or kill his son. It was up to the next generation.

As he swirled his *terif,* he smiled and thought of the note he had left on the pilot's pad: *Name him after your father—Gordon.*

"*. . . failed to find any survivors, or for that matter, any trace whatever of either globe, if one excepts the supernova that appeared for a quarter metron some thirty years ago at the far margin of the proton storm. We of the Armistice Commission therefore unanimously urge that further hostilities by either side would necessarily be indecisive . . .*"

—Scythe-Terran Armistice, History and Tentative Provisions (excerpts): Gordon of Tharn, Editor-in-Chief and Primary Scythian Delegate.

THE NEW REALITY

CHAPTER I
Raid for the Censor

Prentiss crawled into the car, drew the extension connector from his concealed throat mike from its clip in his right sleeve, and plugged it into the ignition key socket.

In a moment he said curtly: "Get me the Censor."

The seconds passed as he heard the click of forming circuits. Then: "E speaking."

"Prentiss, honey."

"Call me 'E,' Prentiss. What news?"

"I've met five classes under Professor Luce. He has a private lab. Doesn't confide in his graduate students. Evidently conducting secret experiments in comparative psychology. Rats and such. Nothing overtly censorable."

"I see. What are your plans?"

"I'll have his lab searched tonight. If nothing turns up, I'll recommend a drop."

"I'd prefer that you search the lab yourself."

A. Prentiss Rogers concealed his surprise and annoyance. "Very well."

His ear button clicked a dismissal.

With puzzled irritation he snapped the plug from the dash socket, started the car, and eased it down the drive into the boulevard bordering the university.

Didn't she realize that he was a busy Field Director with a couple of hundred men under him fully capable of making a routine night search? Undoubtedly she knew just that, but nevertheless was requiring that he do it himself. Why?

And why had she assigned Professor Luce to him personally, squandering so many of his precious hours, when half a dozen of his bright young physical philosophers could have handled it? Nevertheless E, from behind the august anonymity of her solitary initial, had been adamant. He'd never been able to argue with such cool beauty, anyway.

A mile away he turned into a garage on a deserted side street and drew up alongside a Cadillac.

Crush sprang out of the big car and silently held the rear door open for him. Prentiss got in. "We have a job tonight."

His aide hesitated a fraction of a second before slamming the door behind him. Prentiss knew that the squat, asthmatic little man was surprised and delighted. As for Crush, he'd never got it through his head that the control of human knowledge was a grim and hateful business, not a kind of cruel lark.

"Very good, sir," wheezed Crush, climbing in behind the wheel. "Shall I reserve a sleeping room at the Bureau for the evening?"

"Can't afford to sleep," grumbled Prentiss. "Desk so high now I can't see over it. Take a nap yourself, if you want to."

"Yes, sir. If I feel the need of it, sir."

The ontologist shot a bitter glance at the back of the man's head. No, Crush wouldn't sleep, but not because worry would keep him awake. A holdover from the days when all a Censor man had was a sleepless curiosity and a pocket Geiger, Crush was serenely untroubled by the dangerous and unfathomable implications of philosophical nucleonics. For Crush, "ontology" was just another definition in the dictionary: "The science of reality."

The little aide could never grasp the idea that unless a sane world-wide pattern of nucleonic investigation were followed, some one in Australia—or next door—might one day throw a switch and alter the shape of that reality. That's what made Crush so valuable; he just didn't know enough to be afraid.

Prentiss had clipped the hairs from his nostrils and so far had breathed complete silence. But now, as that cavernous face was turned toward where he lay stomach-to-earth in the sheltering darkness, his lungs convulsed in an audible gasp.

The mild, polite, somewhat abstracted academic features of Professor Luce were transformed. The face beyond the lab window was now flushed with blood, the thin lips were drawn back in soundless demoniac amusement, the sunken black eyes were dancing with red pinpoints of flame.

By brute will the ontologist forced his attention back to the rat.

Four times in the past few minutes he had watched the animal run down an inclined chute until it reached a fork, choose one fork, receive what must be a nerve-shattering electric shock, and then be replaced in the chute-beginning for the next run. No matter which alternative fork was chosen, the animal always had been shocked into convulsions.

On this fifth run the rat, despite needling blasts of compressed air from the chute walls, was slowing down. Just before it reached the fork it stopped completely.

The air jets struck at it again, and little cones of up-ended gray fur danced on its rump and flanks.

It gradually ceased to tremble; its respiration dropped to normal. It seemed to Prentiss that its eyes were shut.

The air jets lashed out again. It gave no notice, but just lay there, quiescent, in a near coma.

As he peered into the window, Prentiss saw the tall man walk languidly over to the little animal and run a long hooklike forefinger over its back. No reaction.

The professor then said something, evidently in a soft slurred voice, for Prentiss had difficulty in reading his lips.

"—when both alternatives are wrong for you, but you *must* do something, you hesitate, don't you, little one? You slow down and you are lost. You are no longer a rat. Do you know what the universe would be like if a *photon* should slow down? You don't? Have you ever taken a bite out of a balloon, little friend? Just the tiniest possible bite?"

Prentiss cursed. The professor had turned and was walking toward the cages with the animal, and although he was apparently still talking, his lips were no longer visible.

After re-latching the cage door the professor walked toward the lab entrance, glanced carefully around the room, and then, as he was reaching for the light switch, looked toward Prentiss' window.

For a moment the investigator was convinced that by some nameless power the professor was looking into the darkness, straight into his eyes.

He exhaled slowly. It was preposterous.

The room was plunged in darkness.

The investigator blinked and closed his eyes. He wouldn't really have to worry until he heard the lab door opening on the opposite side of the little building.

The door didn't open. Prentiss squinted into the darkness of the room.

Where the professor's head had been were now two mysterious tiny red flames, like candles.

Something must be reflecting from the professor's corneas. But the room was dark; there was no light to be reflected. The flame-eyes continued their illusion of studying him.

The hair was crawling on the man's neck when the twin lights finally vanished and he heard the sound of the lab door opening.

As the slow heavy tread died away down the flagstones to the street, Prentiss gulped in a huge lungful of the chill night air and rubbed his sweating face against his sleeve.

What had got into him? He was acting like the greenest cub. He was glad that Crush had to man the televisor relay in the Cadillac and couldn't see him.

He got to his hands and knees and crept silently toward the darkened window. It was a simple sliding sash, and a few seconds sufficed to drill through the glass and insert a hook around the sash lock. The rats began a nervous squeaking as he lowered himself into the darkness of the basement room.

His ear-receptor sounded. "The prof is coming back!" wheezed Crush's tinny voice.

Prentiss said something under his breath, but did not pause in drawing his infra-red scanner from his pocket.

He touched his fingers to his throat-mike. "Signal when he reaches the bend in the walk," he hissed. "And be sure you get this on the visor tape."

The apparatus got his first attention.

The investigator had memorized its position perfectly. Approaching as closely in the darkness as he dared, he "panned" the scanner over some very interesting apparatus that he had noticed on the table.

Then he turned to the books on the desk, regretting that he wouldn't have time to record more than a few pages.

"He's at the bend," warned Crush.

"Okay," mumbled Prentiss, running sensitive fingers over the book bindings. He selected one, opened it at random, and ran the scanner over the invisible pages. "Is this coming through?" he demanded.

"Chief, *he's at the door!*"

Prentiss had to push back the volume without scanning any more of it. He had just relocked the sash when the lab door swung open.

CHAPTER II
Clues from History

A couple of hours later the ontologist bid a cynical good-morning to his receptionist and secretaries and stepped into his private office. He dropped with tired thoughtfulness into his swivel chair and pulled out the infrared negatives that Crush had prepared in the Cadillac darkroom. The page from the old German diary was particularly intriguing. He laboriously translated it once more:

> As I got deeper into the manuscript, my mouth grew dry, and my heart began to pound. This, I knew, was a contribution the like of which my family has not seen since Copernicus, Roger Bacon, or perhaps even Aristotle. It seemed incredible that this silent little man, who had never been outside of Königsberg, should hold the key to the universe—the *Critique of Pure Reason*, he calls it. And I doubt that even he realizes the ultimate portent of his teaching, for he says we cannot know the real shape or nature of anything, that is, the Thing-in-Itself, the Ding-an-Sich, or *noumenon*. He holds that this is the ultimate unknowable, reserved to the gods. He doesn't suspect that, century by century, mankind is nearing this final realization of the final things. Even this brilliant man would probably say that the Earth was round in 600 B.C., even as it is today. But *I* know it was flat, then—as truly flat as it is truly round today. What has changed? Not the Thing-in-Itself we call the Earth. No, it is the mind of man that has changed. But in his preposterous blindness, he mistakes what is really his own mental quickening for a broadened application of science and more precise methods of investigation—

Prentiss smiled.

Luce was undoubtedly a collector of philosophic incunabula. Odd hobby, but that's all it could be—a hobby. Obviously the Earth had never been flat, and in fact hadn't changed shape substantially in the last couple of billion years. Certainly any notions as to the flatness of the Earth held by primitives of a few thousand years ago or even by contemporaries of Kant were due to their ignorance rather than to accurate observation, and a man of Luce's erudition could only be amused by them.

Again Prentiss found himself smiling with the tolerance of a man standing on the shoulders of twenty centuries of science. The primitives, of course, did the best they could. They just didn't know. They worked with childish premises and infantile instruments.

His brows creased. To assume they had used childish premises was begging the question. On the other hand, was it really worth a second thought? All he could hope to discover would be a few instances of how inferior apparatus coupled perhaps with unsophisticated deductions had oversimplified the world of the ancients. Still, anything that interested the strange Dr. Luce automatically interested him, Prentiss, until the case was closed.

He dictated into the scriptor:

"Memorandum to Geodetic Section. Rush a paragraph history of ideas concerning shape of Earth. Prentiss."

Duty done, he promptly forgot it and turned to the heavy accumulation of reports on his desk.

A quarter of an hour later the scriptor rang and began typing an incoming message.

To the Director. Re your request for brief history of Earth's shape. Chaldeans and Babylonians (per clay tablets from library of Assurbanipal), Egyptians (per Ahmes papyrus, ca. 2700 B.C.). Cretans (per inscriptions in royal library at Knossos, ca. 1300 B.C.), Chinese (per Chou Kung ms., ca. 1100 B.C.), Phoenicians (per fragments at Tyre, ca. 900 B.C.), Hebrews (per unknown Biblical historian, ca. 850 B.C.), and early Greeks (per map of widely-traveled geographer Hecataeus, 517 B.C.) assumed Earth to be flat disc. But from the 5th century B.C. forward Earth's sphericity universally recognized . . . .

There were a few more lines, winding up with the work done on corrections for flattening at the poles, but Prentiss had already lost interest. The report threw no light on Luce's hobby and was devoid of ontological implications.

He tossed the script into the waste basket and returned to the reports before him.

A few minutes later he twisted uneasily in his chair, eyed the scriptor in annoyance, then forced himself back to his work.

No use.

Deriding himself for an idiot, he growled at the machine:

"Memorandum to Geodetic. Re your memo history Earth's shape. How do you account for change to belief in sphericity after Hecataeus? Rush. Prentiss."

The seconds ticked by.

He drummed on his desk impatiently, then got up and began pacing the floor.

When the scriptor rang, he bounded back and leaned over his desk, watching the words being typed out.

Late Greeks based spherical shape on observation that mast of approaching ship appeared first, then prow. Not known why similar observation not made by earlier seafaring peoples. . . .

Prentiss rubbed his cheek in perplexity. What was he fishing for?

He thrust the half-born conjecture that the Earth really had once been flat into his mental recesses.

Well, then how about the heavens? Surely there was no record of their having changed during man's brief lifetime.

He'd try one more shot and quit.

"Memo to Astronomy Division. Rush paragraph on early vs. modern sun size and distance."

A few minutes later he was reading the reply:

> Skipping Plato, whose data are believed baseless (he measured sun's distance at only twice that of moon), we come to earliest recognized "authority." Ptolemy (Almagest, ca. 140 A.D., measured sun radius as 5.5 that of Earth (as against 109 actual); measured sun distance at 1210 (23,000 actual). Fairly accurate measurements date only from 17th and 18th centuries. . . .

He'd read all that somewhere. The difference was easily explained by their primitive instruments. It was insane to keep this up.

But it was too late.

"Memo to Astronomy. Were erroneous Ptolemaic measurements due to lack of precision instruments?"

Soon he had his reply:

> To Director: Source of Ptolemy's errors in solar measurement not clearly understood. Used astrolabe precise to 10 seconds and clepsydra water clock incorporating Hero's improvements. With same instruments, and using modern value of pi, Ptolemy measured moon radius (0.29 earth radius vs. 0.273 actual) and distance (59 Earth radii vs. 60 1/3 actual). Hence instruments reasonably precise. And note that Copernicus, using quasi-modern instruments and technique, "confirmed" Ptolemaic figure of sun's distance at 1200 Earth radii. No explanation known for glaring error.

Unless, suggested something within Prentiss' mind, the sun were closer and much different before the 17th century, when Newton was telling the world where and how big the sun *ought* to be. But *that* solution was too absurd for further consideration. He would sooner assume his complete insanity.

Puzzled, the ontologist gnawed his lower lip and stared at the message in the scriptor.

In his abstraction he found himself peering at the symbol "pi" in the scriptor message. *There*, at least, was something that had always been the same, and would endure for all time. He reached over to knock out his pipe in the big circular ash tray by the scriptor and paused in the middle of the second tap. From his desk he fished a tape measure and stretched it across the tray, Ten inches. And then around the circumference. Thirty-one and a half inches. Good enough, considering. It was a result any curious schoolboy could get.

He turned to the scriptor again.

"Memo to Math Section. Rush paragraph history on value of pi. Prentiss."

He didn't have to wait long.

To Director. Re history "pi." Babylonians used value of 3.00. Aristotle made fairly accurate physical and theoretical evaluations. Archimedes first to arrive at modern value, using theory of limits. . . .

There was more, but it was lost on Prentiss. It was inconceivable, of course, that pi had grown during the two millennia that separated the Babylonians from Archimedes. And yet, it was exasperating. Why hadn't they done any better than 3.00? Any child with a piece of string could have demonstrated their error. Countless generations of wise, careful Chaldean astronomers, measuring time and star positions with such incredible accuracy, all coming to grief with a piece of string and pi. It didn't make sense. And certainly pi hadn't grown, any more than the Babylonian 360-day year had grown into the modern 365-day year. It had always been the same, he told himself. The primitives hadn't measured accurately, that was all. That *had* to be the explanation.

He hoped.

He sat down at his desk again, stared a moment at his memo pad, and wrote:

Check history of gravity—acceleration. Believe Aristotle unable detect acceleration. Galileo used same instruments, including same crude water clock, and found it. Why? . . . Any reported transits of Vulcan since 1914, when Einstein explained eccentricity of Mercury orbit by relativity instead of by hypothetical sunward planet? . . . How could Oliver Lodge detect an ether-drift and Michelson not? Conceivable that Lorentz contraction not a physical fact before Michelson experiment? . . . How many chemical elements were predicted before discovered?

He tapped absently an the pad a few times, then rang for a research assistant. He'd barely have time to explain what be wanted before he had to meet his class under Luce.

And he still wasn't sure where the rats fitted in.

CHAPTER III
Imperiled World

Curtly Professor Luce brought his address to a close.

"Well, gentlemen," he said, "I guess we'll have to continue this at our next lecture. We seem to have ran over a little; class dismissed. Oh, Mr. Prentiss!"

The investigator looked up in genuine surprise. "Yes, sir?" The thin gun in his shoulder holster suddenly felt satisfyingly fat.

He realized that the crucial moment was near, that he would know before he left the campus whether this strange man was a harmless physicist, devoted to his life-work and his queer hobby, or whether he was an incarnate danger to mankind. The professor was acting out of turn, and it was an unexpected break.

"Mr. Prentiss," continued Luce from the lecture platform, "may I see you in my office a moment before you leave?"

Prentiss said, "Certainly." As the group broke up he followed the gaunt scientist through the door that led to Luce's little office behind the lecture room. At the doorway he hesitated almost imperceptibly; Luce saw it and bowed sardonically. "After you, sir!"

Then the tall man indicated a chair near his desk. "Sit down, Mr. Prentiss." For a long moment the seated men studied each other.

Finally the professor spoke. "About fifteen years ago a brilliant young man named Rogers wrote a doctoral dissertation at the University of Vienna on what he called . . . 'Involuntary Conformation of Incoming Sensoria to Apperception Mass.' "

Prentiss began fishing for his pipe. "Indeed?"

"One copy of the dissertation was sent to the Scholarship Society that was financing his studies. All others were seized by the International Bureau of the Censor, and accordingly a demand was made on the Scholarship Society for its copy. But it couldn't be found."

Prentiss was concentrating on lighting his pipe. He wondered if the faint trembling of the match flame was visible.

The professor turned to his desk, opened the top drawer, and pulled out a slim brochure bound in black leather.

The investigator coughed out a cloud of smoke.

The professor did not seem to notice, but opened the front cover and began reading: " '—a dissertation in partial fulfillment of the requirements for the degree of Doctor of Philosophy at the University of Vienna. A. P. Rogers, Vienna, 1957.' " The man closed the book and studied it thoughtfully. "Adam Prentiss Rogers—the owner of a brain whose like is seen not once in a century. He exposed the gods—then vanished."

Prentiss suppressed a shiver as he met those sunken, implacable eye-caverns. The cat-and-mouse was over. In a way, he was relieved.

"Why did you vanish then, Mr. Prentiss-Rogers?" demanded Luce. "And why do you now reappear?"

The investigator blew a cloud of smoke toward the low ceiling. "To prevent people like you from introducing sensoria that *can't* be conformed to our present apperception mass. To keep reality as is. That answers both questions, I think."

The other man smiled. It was not a good thing to see. "Have you succeeded?"

"I don't know. So far, I suppose."

The gaunt man shrugged his shoulders. "You ignore tomorrow, then. I think you have failed, but I can't be sure, of course, until I actually perform the experiment that will create novel sensoria." He leaned forward. "I'll come to the point, Mr. Prentiss-Rogers. Next to yourself—and possibly excepting the Censor—I know more about the mathematical approach to reality than anyone else in the world. I may even know things about it that you don't. On other phases of it I'm weak—because I developed your results on the basis of mere logic rather than insight. And logic, we know, is applicable only within inde-terminate limits. But in developing a practical device—an actual machine—for the wholesale alteration of incoming sensoria, I'm enormously ahead of you. You saw my apparatus last night, Mr. Prentiss-Rogers? Oh, come, don't be coy."

Prentiss drew deeply on his pipe. "I saw it."

"Did you understand it?"

"No. It wasn't all there. At least, the apparatus on the table was incomplete. There's more to it than a Nicol prism and a goniometer."

"Ah, you are clever! Yes, I was wise in not permitting you to remain very long—no longer than necessary to whet your curiosity. Look, then! I offer you a part-nership. Check my data and apparatus; in return you may be present when I run the experiment. We will attain enlightenment together. We will know all things. We will be gods!"

"And what about two billion other human beings?" said Prentiss, pressing softly at his shoulder holster.

The professor smiled faintly. "Their lunacy—assuming they continue to exist at all—may become slightly more pronounced, of course. But why worry about them?" The wolf-lip curled further. "Don't expect me to believe this aura of al-truism, Mr. Prentiss-Rogers. I think you're afraid to face what lies behind our so-called 'reality.' "

"At least I'm a coward in a good cause." He stood up. "Have you any more to say?"

He knew that he was just going through the motions. Luce must have real-ized he had laid himself open to arrest half a dozen times in as many minutes: The bare possession of the missing copy of the dissertation, the frank admis-sion of plans to experiment with reality, and his attempted bribery of a high Censor official. And yet, the man's very bearing denied the possibility of being cut off in mid-career.

Luce's cheeks fluffed out in a brief sigh. "I'm sorry you can't be intelligent about this, Mr. Prentiss-Rogers. Yet, the time will come, you know, when you must make up your mind to go—*through,* shall we say? In fact, we may have to depend to a considerable degree on one another's companionship—*out there.* Even gods have to pass the time of day occasionally, and I have a suspicion that you and I are going to be quite chummy. So let us not part in enmity."

Prentiss' hand slid beneath his coat lapel and drew out the snub-nosed auto-matic. He had a grim foreboding that it was futile, and that the professor was laughing silently at him, but he had no choice.

"You are under arrest," he said unemotionally. "Come with me."

The other shrugged his shoulders, then something like a laugh, soundless in its mockery, surged up in his throat. "Certainly, Mr. Prentiss-Rogers."

He arose.

The room was plunged into instant blackness.

Prentiss fired three times, lighting up the gaunt chuckling form at each flash.

"Save your fire, Mr. Prentiss-Rogers. Lead doesn't get far in an intense dia-magnetic screen. Study the magnetic damper on a lab balance the next time you're in the Censor Building!"

Somewhere a door slammed.

Several hours later Prentiss was eyeing his aide with ill-concealed distaste. Crush knew that he had been summoned by E to confer on the implications of Luce's escape, and that Crush was secretly sympathizing with him. Prentiss couldn't endure sympathy. He'd prefer that the asthmatic little man tell him how stupid he'd been.

"What do you want?" he growled.

"Sir," gasped Crush apologetically, "I have a report on that gadget you scanned in Luce's lab."

Prentiss was instantly mollified, but suppressed any show of interest. "What about it?"

"In essence, sir," wheezed Crush, "it's just a Nicol prism mounted on a goni-ometer. According to a routine check it was ground by an obscure optician who was nine years on the job, and he spent nearly all of that time on just one face of the prism. What do you make of that, sir?"

"Nothing, yet. What took him so long?"

"Grinding an absolutely flat edge, sir, so he says."

"Odd. That would mean a boundary composed exclusively of molecules of the same crystal layer, something that hasn't been attempted since the Palomar reflector."

"Yes, sir. And then there's the goniometer mount with just one number on the dial—forty-five degrees."

"Obviously," said Prentiss, "the Nicol is to be used only at a forty-five-degree angle to the incoming light. Hence it's probably extremely important—why, I don't know—that the angle be *precisely* forty-five degrees. That would require a perfectly flat surface, too, of course. I suppose you're going to tell me that the goniometric gearing is set up very accurately."

Suddenly Prentiss realized that Crush was looking at him in mingled suspi-cion and admiration.

"Well?" demanded the ontologist irritably. "Just what is the adjusting mecha-nism? Surely not geometrical? Too crude. Optical, perhaps?"

Crush gasped into his handkerchief. "Yes, sir. The prism is rotated very slowly into a tiny beam of light. Part of the beam is reflected and part refracted. At exactly forty-five degrees it seems, by Jordan's law, that exactly half is reflected and half refracted. The two beams are picked up in a photocell relay that stops the rotating mechanism as soon as the luminosities of the beams are exactly equal."

Prentiss tugged nervously at his ear. It was puzzling. Just what was Luce going to do with such an exquisitely-ground Nicol? At this moment he would have given ten years of his life for an inkling to the supplementary apparatus that went along with the Nicol. It would be something optical, certainly, tied in somehow with neurotic rats. What was it Luce had said the other night in the lab? Something about slowing down a photon. And then what was supposed to happen to the universe? Something like taking a tiny bite out of a balloon, Luce had said.

And how did it all interlock with certain impossible, though syllogistically necessary conclusions that flowed from his recent research into the history of human knowledge?

He wasn't sure. But he *was* sure that Luce was on the verge of using this mysterious apparatus to change the perceptible universe, on a scale so vast that humanity was going to get lost in the shuffle. He'd have to convince E of that.

If he couldn't, he'd seek out Luce himself and kill him with his bare hands, and decide on reasons for it afterward.

He was guiding himself for the time being by pure insight, but he'd better be organized when he confronted E.

Crush was speaking. "Shall we go, sir? Your secretary says the jet is waiting."

The painting showed a man in a red hat and black robes seated behind a high judge's bench. Five other men in red hats were seated behind a lower bench to his right, and four others to his left. At the base of the bench knelt a figure in solitary abjection.

"We condemn you, Galileo Galilei, to the formal prison of this Holy Office for a period determinable at Our pleasure; and by way of salutary penance, We order you, during the next three years, to recite once a week the seven Penitential Psalms."

Prentiss turned from the inscription to the less readable face of E. That oval olive-hued face was smooth, unlined, even around the eyes, and the black hair was parted off-center and drawn over the woman's head into a bun at the nape of her neck. She wore no make-up, and apparently needed none. She was clad in a black, loose-fitting business suit, which accentuated her perfectly molded body.

"Do you know," said Prentiss coolly, "I think you like being Censor. It's in your blood."

"You're perfectly right. I *do* like being Censor. According to Speer, I effectively sublimate a guilt complex as strange as it is baseless."

"Very interesting. Sort of expiation of an ancestral guilt complex, eh?"

"What do you mean?"

"Woman started man on his acquisition of knowledge and self-destruction, and ever since has tried futilely to halt the avalanche. In you the feeling of responsibility and guilt runs exceptionally strong, and I'll wager that some nights you wake up in a cold sweat, thinking you've just plucked a certain forbidden fruit."

E stared icily up at the investigator's twitching mouth. "The only pertinent question," she said crisply, "is whether Luce is engaged in ontologic experiments, and if so, are they of a dangerous nature."

Prentiss sighed. "He's in it up to his neck. But just *what*, and how dangerous, I can only guess."

"Then guess."

"Luce thinks he's developed apparatus for the practical, predictable alteration of sensoria. He hopes to do something with his device that will blow physical laws straight to smithereens. The resulting reality would probably be unrecognizable even to a professional ontologist, let alone the mass of humanity."

"You seem convinced he can do this."

"The probabilities are high."

"Good enough. We can deal only in probabilities. The safest thing, of course, would be to locate Luce and kill him on sight. On the other hand, the faintest breath of scandal would result in Congressional hamstringing of the Bureau, so we must proceed cautiously."

"If Luce is really able to do what he claims," said Prentiss grimly, "and we let him do it, there won't be any Bureau at all—nor any Congress, either."

"I know. Rest assured that if I decide that Luce is dangerous and should die, I shall let neither the lives nor careers of anyone in the Bureau stand in the way, including myself."

Prentiss nodded, wondering if she really meant it.

The woman continued, "We are faced for the first time with a probable violation of our directive forbidding ontologic experiments. We are inclined to prevent this threatened violation by taking a man's life. I think we should settle once and for all whether such harsh measures are indicated, and it is for this that I have invited you to attend a staff conference. We intend to reopen the entire question of ontologic experiments and their implications."

Prentiss groaned inwardly. In matters so important the staff decided by vote. He had a brief vision of attempting to convince E's hard-headed scientists that mankind was changing "reality" from century to century—that not too long ago the earth had been "flat." Yes, by now he was beginning to believe it himself!

"Come this way, please?" said E.

CHAPTER IV
A Changing World

Sitting at E's right was an elderly man, Speer, the famous psychologist. On her left was Goring, staff advisor on nucleonics; next him was Burchard, brilliant chemist and Director of the Western Field, then Prentiss, and then Dobbs, the renowned metallurgist and Director of the Central Field.

Prentiss didn't like Dobbs, who had voted against his promotion to the directorship of Eastern.

E announced: "We may as well start this inquiry with an examination of fundamentals. Mr. Prentiss, just what is reality?"

The ontologist winced. He had needed two hundred pages to outline the theory of reality in his doctoral thesis, and even so, had always suspected his examiners had passed it only because it was incomprehensible—hence a work of genius.

"Well," he began wryly, "I must confess that I don't know what *real* reality is. What most of us call reality is simply an integrated synthesis of incoming sensoria. As such it is nothing more than a working hypothesis in the mind of each of us, forever in a process of revision. In the past that process has been slow and safe. But we have now to consider the consequences of an instantaneous and total revision—a revision so far-reaching that it may thrust humanity face-to-face with the true reality, the world of Things-in-Themselves—Kant's *noumena*. This, I think, would be as disastrous as dumping a group of children in the middle of a forest. They'd have to relearn the simplest things—what to eat, how to protect themselves from elemental forces, and even a new language to deal with their new problems. There'd be few survivors.

"That is what we want to avoid, and we can do it if we prevent any sudden sweeping alteration of sensoria in our present reality."

He looked dubiously at the faces about him. It was a poor start. Speer's wrinkled features were drawn up in a serene smile, and the psychologist seemed to be contemplating the air over Prentiss' head. Goring was regarding him with grave, expressionless eyes. E nodded slightly as Prentiss' gaze travelled past her to a puzzled Burchard, thence to Dobbs, who was frankly contemptuous.

Speer and Goring were going to be most susceptible. Speer because of his lack of a firm scientific background, Goring because nucleonics was in such a state of flux that nucleic experts were expressing the gravest doubts as to the validity of the laws worshipped by Burchard and Dobbs. Burchards was only a faint possibility. And Dobbs?

Dobbs said: "I don't know what the dickens you're talking about." The implication was plain that he wanted to add: "And I don't think you do, either."

And Prentiss wasn't so sure that he did know. Ontology was an elusive thing at best.

"I object to the term 'real reality,' " continued Dobbs. "A thing is real or it isn't. No fancy philosophical system can change *that*. And if it's real, it gives off predictable, reproducible sensory stimuli not subject to alteration except in the minds of lunatics."

Prentiss breathed more easily. His course was clear. He'd concentrate on Dobbs, with a little side-play on Burchard. Speer and Goring would never suspect his arguments were really directed at them. He pulled a gold coin from his vest pocket and slid it across the table to Dobbs, being careful not to let it clatter. "You're a metallurgist. Please tell us what this is."

Dobbs picked up the coin and examined it suspiciously. "It's quite obviously a five-dollar gold piece, minted at Fort Worth in Nineteen Sixty-Two. I can even give you the analysis, if you want it."

"I doubt that you could," said Prentiss coolly. "For you see, you are holding a counterfeit coin minted only last week in my own laboratories especially for this conference. As a matter of fact, if you'll forgive my saying so, I had you in mind when I ordered the coin struck. It contains no gold whatever—drop it on the table."

The coin fell from the fingers of the astounded metallurgist and clattered on the oaken table top.

"Hear the false ring?" demanded Prentiss.

Pink-faced, Dobbs cleared his throat and peered at the coin more closely. "How was I to know that? It's no disgrace, is it? Many clever counterfeits can be detected only in the laboratory. I knew the color was a little on the red side, but that could have been due to the lighting of the room. And of course, I hadn't given it an auditory test before I spoke. The ring is definitely dull. It's obviously a copper-lead alloy, with possibly a little amount of silver to help the ring. All right, I jumped to conclusions. So what? What does that prove?"

"It proves that you have arrived at two separate, distinct, and mutually exclusive realities, starting with the same sensory premises. It proves how easily reality is revised. And that isn't all, as I shall soon—"

"All right," said Dobbs testily. "But on second thought I admitted it was a phony, didn't I?"

"Which demonstrates a further weakness in our routine acquisition and evaluation of pre-digested information. When an unimpeachable authority tells us something as a fact, we immediately, and without conscious thought, *modify* incoming stimuli to conform with that *fact*. The coin suddenly acquires the red taint of copper, and rings false to the ear."

"I would have caught the queer ring anyhow," said Dobbs stubbornly, "with no help from 'an unimpeachable authority.' The ring would have sounded the same, no matter what you said."

From the corner of his eye Prentiss noticed that Speer was grinning broadly. Had the old psychologist divined his trick? He'd take a chance.

"Dr. Speer," he said, "I think you have something interesting to tell our doubting friend."

Speer cackled dryly. "You've been a perfect guinea pig, Dobbsie. The coin was genuine."

The metallurgist's jaw dropped as he looked blankly from one face to another. Then his jowls slowly grew red. He flung the coin to the table. "Maybe I am a guinea pig. I'm a realist, too. I think this is a piece of metal. You might fool me as to its color or assay, but in essence and substance, it's a piece of metal." He glared at Prentiss and Speer in turn. "Does anyone deny that?"

"Certainly not," said Prentiss. "Our mental pigeonholes are identical in that respect; they accept the same sensory definition of 'piece of metal,' or 'coin.' Whatever this object is, it emits stimuli that our minds are capable of registering and abstracting as a 'coin.' But note: we make a coin out of it. However, if I could shuffle my cortical pigeonholes, I might find it to be a chair, or a steamer trunk, possibly with Dr. Dobbs inside, or, if the shuffling were extreme, there might be no semantic pattern into which the incoming stimuli could be routed. There wouldn't be anything there at all!"

"Sure," sneered Dobbs. "You could walk right through it."

"Why not?" asked Prentiss gravely. "I think we may do it all the time. Matter is about the emptiest stuff imaginable. If you compressed that coin to eliminate the space between its component atoms and electrons, you couldn't see it in a microscope."

Dobbs stared at the enigmatic gold-piece as though it might suddenly thrust out a pseudopod and swallow him up. Then he said flatly: "No. I don't believe it. It exists as a coin, and only as a coin—whether I know it or not."

"Well," ventured Prentiss, "how about you, Dr. Goring? Is the coin real to you?"

The nucleist smiled and shrugged his shoulders. "If I don't think too much about it, it's real enough. And yet . . ."

Dobb's face clouded. "And yet what? Here it is. Can you doubt the evidence of your own eyes?"

"That's just the difficulty." Goring leaned forward. "My eyes tell me, here's a coin. Theory tells me, here's a mass of hypothetical disturbances in a hypothetical sub-ether in a hypothetical ether. The indeterminacy principle tells me that I can never know both the mass and position of these hypothetical disturbances. And as a physicist I know that the bare fact of observing something is sufficient to change that something from its pre-observed state. Nevertheless, I compromise by letting my senses and practical experience stick a tag on this particular bit of the unknowable. X, after its impact on my mind (whatever *that* is!) equals coin. A single equation with two variables has no solution. The best I can say is, it's a coin, but probably not really—"

"Hah!" declared Burchard. "I can demonstrate the fallacy of *that* position very quickly. If our minds make this a coin, then our minds make this little object an ash-tray, that a window, the thing that holds us up, a chair. You might say we make the air we breathe, and perhaps even the stars and planets. Why, following Prentiss' idea to its logical end, the universe itself is the work of man—a conclusion I'm sure he doesn't intend."

"Oh, but I do," said Prentiss.

Prentiss took a deep breath. The issue could be dodged no longer. He had to take a stand. "And to make sure you understand me, whether you agree with me or not, I'll state categorically that I believe the apparent universe to be the work of man."

Even E looked startled, but said nothing.

The ontologist continued rapidly, "All of you doubt my sanity. A week ago I would have, too. But since then I've done a great deal of research in the history of science. And I repeat, *the universe is the work of man*. I believe that man began his existence in some incredibly simple world—the original and true *noumenon* of our present universe. And that over the centuries man expanded his little world into its present vastness and incomprehensible intricacy solely by dint of imagination.

"Consequently, I believe that what most of you call the 'real' world has been changing ever since our ancestors began to think."

Dobbs smiled superciliously. "Oh, come now, Prentiss. That's just a rhetorical description of scientific progress over the past centuries. In the same sense I might say that modern tranportation and communications have shrunk the earth. But you'll certainly admit that the physical state of things has been substantially constant ever since the galaxies formed and the earth began to cool, and that the simple cosmologies of early man were simply the result of lack of means for obtaining accurate infomation?"

"I *won't* admit it," rejoined Prentiss bluntly. "I maintain that their information was substantially accurate. I maintain that at one time in our history the earth was flat—as flat as it is now round—and no one living before the time of Hecataeus, though he might have been equipped with the finest modern instruments, could have proved otherwise. His mind was *conditioned* to a two-dimensional world. Any of us present, if we were transplanted to the world of Hecataeus, could, of course, establish terrestrial sphericity in short order. Our minds have been conditioned to a three-dimensional world. The day may come a few millennia hence when a four-dimensional Terra will be commonplace even to schoolchildren; they will have been intuitively conditioned in relativistic concepts."

He added slyly: "And the less intelligent of them may attempt to blame our naive three-dimensional planet on our grossly inaccurate instruments, because it will be as plain as day to them that their planet has four dimensions!"

CHAPTER V
Sentence Is Passed

Dobbs snorted at this amazing idea.

The other scientists stared at Prentiss with an awe which was mixed with incredulity.

Goring said cautiously: "I follow up to a certain point. I can see that a primitive society might start out with a limited number of facts. They would offer theories to harmonize and integrate those facts, and then those first theories would require that new, additional facts exist, and in their search for those secondary facts, extraneous data would turn up inconsistent with the first theories. Secondary theories would then be required, from which hitherto unguessed facts should follow, the confirmation of which would discover more inconsistencies. So the pattern of fact to theory to fact to theory, and so on, finally brings us into our present state of knowledge. Does that follow from your argument?"

Prentiss nodded.

"But won't you admit that the facts were there all the time, and merely awaited discovery?"

"The simple, unelaborated *noumenon* was there all the time, yes. But the new fact—man's new interpretation of the *noumenon,* was generally pure invention—a mental creation, if you like. This will be clearer if you consider how rarely a new fact arises before a theory exists for its explanation. In the ordinary scientific investigation, theory comes first, followed in short order by the 'discovery' of various facts deducible from it."

Goring still looked skeptical. "But that wouldn't mean the fact wasn't there all the time."

"Wouldn't it? Look at the evidence. Has it never struck you as odd in how many instances very obvious facts were 'overlooked' until a theory was propounded that required their existence? Take your nuclear building blocks. Protons and electrons were detected physically only after Rutherford had showed they had to exist. And then when Rutherford found that protons and electrons were not enough to build all the atoms of the periodic table, he postulated the neutron, which of course was duly 'discovered' in the Wilson cloud chamber."

Goring pursed his lips. "But the Wilson cloud chamber would have shown all that prior to the theory, if anyone had only thought to use it. The mere fact that Wilson didn't invent his cloud chamber until nineteen twelve and Geiger didn't invent his counter until nineteen thirteen, would not keep sub-atomic particles from existing before that time."

"You don't get the point," said Prentiss. "The primitive, ungeneralized *noumenon* that we today observe as subatomic particles existed prior to nineteen twelve, true, *but not sub-atomic particles.*"

"Well, I don't know. . . ." Goring scratched his chin. "How about fundamental forces? Surely electricity existed before Galvani? Even the Greeks knew how to build up electrostatic charges on amber."

"Greek electricity was nothing more than electrostatic charges. Nothing more could be created until Galvani introduced the concept of the electric current."

"Do you mean the electric current didn't exist at all before Galvani?" demanded Burchard. "Not even when lightning struck a conductor?"

"Not even then. We don't know much about pre-Galvanic lightning. While it probably packed a wallop, its destructive potential couldn't have been due to its delivery of an electric current. The Chinese flew kites for centuries before Franklin theorized that lightning was the same as galvanic electricity, but there's no recorded shock from a kite string until our learned statesman drew forth one in seventeen sixty-five. *Now,* only an idiot flies a kite in a storm. It's all according to pattern: theory first, then we alter 'reality' to fit."

Burchard, persisted. "Then I suppose you'd say the ninety-two elements are figments of our imagination."

"Correct," agreed Prentiss. "I believe that in the beginning there were only four *noumenal* elements. Man simply elaborated these according to the needs of his growing science. Man made them what they are today—and on occasion, *unmade* them. You remember the havoc Mendelyeev created with his periodic law. He declared that the elements had to follow valence sequences of increasing weight, and when they didn't, he insisted his law was right and that the atomic weights were wrong. He must have had Stas and Berzelius whirling in their graves, because they had worked out the 'erroneous' atomic weights with marvelous precision. The odd thing was, when the weights were rechecked, they fitted the Mendelyeev table. But that wasn't all. The old rascal pointed out vacant spots in his table and maintained that there were more elements yet to be discovered. He even predicted what properties they'd have. He was too modest. I state that Nilson, Winkler, and de Boisbaudran merely *discovered* scandium, germanium, and gallium; Mendelyeev *created* them, out of the original tetraelemental stuff."

E leaned forward. "That's a bit strong. Tell me, if man has changed the elements and the cosmos to suit his convenience, what was the cosmos like before man came on the scene?"

"There wasn't any," answered Prentiss. "Remember, by definition, 'cosmos' or 'reality' is simply man's version of the ultimate *noumenal* universe. The 'cosmos' arrives and departs with the mind of man. Consequently, the earth—as such—didn't even exist before the advent of man."

"But the evidence of the rocks . . ." protested E. "Pressures applied over millions, even billions of years, were needed to form them, unless you postulate an omnipotent God who called them into existence as of yesterday."

"I postulate only the omnipotent human mind," said Prentiss. "In the seventeenth century, Hooke, Ray, Woodward, to name a few, studied chalk, gravel, marble, and even coal, without finding anything inconsistent with results to be expected from the Noachian Flood. But now that we've made up our minds that the earth is older, the rocks *seem* older, too."

"But how about evolution?" demanded Burchard. "Surely that wasn't a matter of a few centuries?"

"Really?" replied Prentiss. "Again, why assume that that the facts are any more recent than the theory? The evidence is all the other way. Aristotle was a magnificent experimental biologist, and he was convinced that life could be created spontaneously. Before the time of Darwin there was no need for the various species to evolve, because they sprang into being from inanimate matter. As late as the eighteenth century, Needham, using a microscope, reported that he saw microbe life arise spontaneously out of sterile culture media. These abiogeneticists were, of course, discredited and their work found to be irreproducible, but only *after* it became evident that the then abiogenetic facts were going to run inconsistent with later 'facts' flowing from advancing biologic theory."

"Then," said Goring, "assuming purely for the sake of argument that man has altered the original *noumena* into our present reality, just what danger do you think Luce represents to that reality? How could he do anything about it, even if he wanted to? Just what is he up to?"

"Broadly stated," said Prentiss, "Luce intends to destroy the Einsteinian universe."

Burchard frowned and shook his head. "Not so fast. In the first place, how can anyone presume to destroy this planet, much less the whole universe? And why do you say the 'Einsteinian' universe? The universe by any other name is still the universe, isn't it?"

"What Dr. Prentiss means," explained E, "is that Luce wants to revise completely and finally our present comprehension of the universe, which presently happens to be the Einsteinian version, in the expectation that the final version would be the true one—and comprehensible only to Luce and perhaps a few other ontologic experts."

"I don't see it," said Dobbs irritably. "Apparently this Luce contemplates nothing more than publication of a new scientific theory. How can that be bad? A mere theory can't hurt anybody—especially if only two or three people understand it."

"You—and two billion others," said Prentiss softly, "think that 'reality' cannot be affected by any theory that seems to change it—that it is optional with you to accept or reject the theory. In the past that was true. If the Ptolemaics wanted a geocentric universe, they ignored Copernicus. If the four-dimensional continuum of Einstein and Minkowsky seemed incomprehensible to the Newtonian school they dismissed it, and the planets continued to revolve substantially as Newton predicted. But this is different.

"For the first time we are faced with the probability that the promulgation of a theory is going to *force* an ungraspable reality upon our minds. It will not be optional."

"Well," said Burchard, "If by 'promulgation of a theory' you mean something like the application of the quantum theory and relativity to the production of atomic energy, which of course has changed the shape of civilization in the past generation, whether the individual liked it or not, then I can understand you. But if you mean that Luce is going to make one little experiment that may confirm some new theory or other, and *ipso facto* and instantaneously reality is going to turn topsy turvy, why I say it's nonsense."

"Would anyone," said Prentiss quietly, "care to guess what would happen if Luce were able to destroy a photon?"

Goring laughed shortly. "The question doesn't make sense. The mass-energy entity whose three-dimensional profile we call a photon is indestructible."

"But if you *could* destroy it?" insisted Prentiss. "What would the universe be like afterward?"

"What difference would it make?" demanded Dobbs. "One photon more or less?"

"Plenty," said Goring. "According to the Einstein theory, every particle of matter-energy has a gravitational potential, lambda, and it can be calculated that the total lambdas are precisely sufficent to keep our four-dimensional continuum from closing back on itself. Take one lambda away—my heavens! The universe would split wide open!"

"Exactly," said Prentiss. "Instead of a continuum, our 'reality' would become a disconnected melange of three-dimensional objects. Time, if it existed, wouldn't bear any relation to spatial things. Only an ontologic expert might be able to synthesize any sense out of such a 'reality.' "

"Well," said Dobbs, "I wouldn't worry too much. I don't think anybody's ever going to destroy a photon." He snickered. "You have to catch one first!"

"Luce can catch one," said Prentiss calmly. "And he can destroy it. At this moment some unimaginable post-Einsteinian universe lies in the palm of his hand. Final, true reality, perhaps. But we aren't ready for it. Kant, perhaps, or *homo superior,* but not the general run of *h. sapiens.* We wouldn't be able to escape our conditioning. We'd be stopped cold."

He stopped. Without looking at Goring, he knew he had convinced the man. Prentiss sagged with visible relief. It was time for a vote. He must strike before Speer and Goring could change their minds.

"Madame"—he shot a questioning glance at the woman—"at any moment my men are going to report that they've located Luce. I must be ready to issue the order for his execution, if in fact the staff believes such disposition proper. I call for a vote of officers!"

"Granted," said E instantly. "Will those in favor of destroying Luce on sight raise their right hands?"

Prentiss and Goring made the required signal.

Speer was silent.

Prentiss felt his heart sinking. Had he made a gross error of judgment?

"I vote against this murder," declared Dobbs. "That's what it is, pure murder."

"I agree with Dobbs," said Burchard shortly.

All eyes were on the psychologist. "I presume you'll join us, Dr. Speer?" demanded Dobbs sternly.

"Count me out, gentlemen. I'd never interfere with anything so inevitable as the destiny of man. All of you are overlooking a fundamental facet of human nature—man's insatiable hunger for change, novelty—for anything different from what he already has. Prentiss himself states that whenever man grows discontented with his present reality, he starts elaborating it, and the devil take the hindmost. Luce but symbolizes the evil genius of our race—and I mean both our species and the race toward intertwined godhood and destruction. Once born, however, symbols are immortal. It's far too late now to start killing Luce. It was too late when the first man tasted the first apple.

"Furthermore, I think Prentiss greatly overestimates the scope of Luce's pending victory over the rest of mankind. Suppose Luce is actually successful in clearing space and time and suspending the world in the temporal stasis of its present irreality. Suppose he and a few ontologic experts pass on into the ultimate, true reality. How long do you think they can resist the temptation to alter it? If Prentiss is right, eventually they or their descendants will be living in a cosmos as intricate and unpleasant as the one they left, while we, for all practical purposes, will be pleasantly dead.

"No, gentlemen, I won't vote either way."

"Then it is my privilege to break the tie," said E coolly. "I vote for death. Save your remonstrances, Dr. Dobbs. It's after midnight. This meeting is adjourned."

She stood up in abrupt dismissal, and the men were soon filing from the room.

E left the table and walked toward the windows on the far side of the room. Prentiss hesitated a moment, but made no effort to leave.

E called over her shoulder, "You, too, Prentiss."

The door closed behind Speer, the last of the group, save Prentiss.

Prentiss walked up behind E.

She gave no sign of awareness.

Six feet away, the man stopped and studied her.

Sitting, walking, standing, she was lovely. Mentally he compared her to Velasquez' Venus. There was the same slender exquisite proportion of thigh, hip, and bust. And he knew she was completely aware of her own beauty, and further, must be aware of his present appreciative scrutiny.

Then her shoulders sagged suddenly, and her voice seemed very tired when she spoke. "So you're still here, Prentiss. Do you believe in intuition?"

"Not often."

"Speer was right. He's always right. Luce will succeed." She dropped her arms to her sides and turned.

"Then may I reiterate, my dear, marry me and let's forget the control of knowledge for a few months."

"Completely out of the question, Prentiss. Our natures are incompatible. You're incorrigibly curious, and I'm incorrigibly, even neurotically, conservative. Besides, how can you even think about such things when we've got to stop Luce?"

His reply was interrupted by the shrilling of the intercom: "Calling Mr. Prentiss. Crush calling Mr. Prentiss. Luce located. Crush calling."

CHAPTER VI
Impending Chaos

With his pencil Crush pointed to a shaded area of the map. "This is Luce's Snake-Eyes estate, the famous game preserve and zoo. Somewhere in the center—about here, I think—is a stone cottage. A moving van unloaded some lab equipment there this morning."

"Mr. Prentiss," said E, "how long do you think it will take him to install what he needs for that one experiment?"

The ontologist answered from across the map table, "I can't be sure. I still have no idea of what he's going to try, except that I'm reasonably certain it must be done in absolute darkness. Checking his instruments will require but a few minutes at most."

The woman began pacing the floor nervously. "I knew it. We can't stop him. We have no time."

"Oh, I don't know," said Prentiss. "How about that stone cottage, Crush? Is it pretty old?"

"Dates from the eighteenth century, sir."

"There's your answer," said Prentiss. "It's probably full of holes where the mortar's fallen out. For total darkness he'll have to wait until moonset."

"That's three thirty-four a.m., sir," said Crush.

"We've time for an arrest," said E.

Crush looked dubious. "It's more complicated than that, Madame. Snake-Eyes is fortified to withstand a small army. Luce could hold hold off any force the Bureau could muster for at least twenty-four hours."

"One atom egg, well done," suggested Prentiss.

"That's the best answer, of course," agreed E. "But you know as well as I what the reaction of Congress would be to such extreme measures. There would be an investigation. The Bureau would be abolished, and all persons responsible for such an expedient would face life imprisonment, perhaps death." She was silent for a moment, then sighed and said: "So be it. If there is no alternative, I shall order the bomb dropped."

"There may be another way," said Prentiss.

"Indeed?"

"Granted an army couldn't get through. One man might. And if he made it, you could call off your bomb."

E exhaled a slow cloud of smoke and studied the glowing tip of her cigarette. Finally she turned and looked into the eyes of the ontologist for the first time since the beginning of the conference. "*You* can't go."

"Who, then?"

Her eyes dropped. "You're right, of course. But the bomb still falls if you don't get through. It's got to be that way. Do you understand that?"

Prentiss laughed. "I understand."

He addressed his aide. "Crush, I'll leave the details up to you, bomb and all. We'll rendezvous at these coordinates"—he pointed to the map—"at three sharp. It's after one now. You'd better get started."

"Yes, sir," wheezed Crush, and scurried out of the room.

As the door closed, Prentiss turned to E. "Beginning tomorrow afternoon— or rather, *this* afternoon, after I finish with Luce, I want six months off."

"Granted," murmured E.

"I want you to come with me. I want to find out just what this thing is be- tween us. Just the two of us. It may take a little time."

E smiled crookedly. "If we're both still alive at three thirty-five, and such a thing as a month exists, and you still want me to spend six of them with you, I'll do it. And in return you can do something for me."

"What?"

"You, even above Luce, stand the best chance of adjusting to final reality if Luce is successful in destroying a photon. I'm a border-line case. I'm going to need all the help you can give me, if and when the time comes. Will you remember that?"

"I'll remember," Prentiss said.

At 3 a.m. he joined Crush.

"There are at least seven infra-red scanners in the grounds, sir," said Crush, "not to mention an intricate network of photo relays. And then the wire fence around the lab, with the big cats inside. He must have turned the whole zoo loose." The little man reluctantly helped Prentiss into his infra-red-absorbing coveralls. "You weren't meant for tiger fodder, sir. Better call it off."

Prentiss zipped up his visor and grimaced out into the moonlit dimness of the apple orchard. "You'll take care of the photocell network?"

"Certainly, sir. He's using u.v.-sensitive cells. We'll blanket the area with a u.v.- spot at three-ten."

Prentiss strained his ears, but couldn't hear the 'copter that woud carry the u.v.-searchlight—and the bomb.

"It'll be here, sir," Crush assured him. "It won't make any noise, anyhow. What you ought to be worrying about are those wild beasts."

The investigator sniffed at the night air. "Darn little breeze."

"Yeah," gasped Crush. "And variable at that, sir. You can't count on going in up-wind. You want us to create a diversion at one end of the grounds to attract the animals?"

"We don't dare. If necessary, I'll open the aerosol capsule of formaldehyde." He held out his hand. "Good-by, Crush."

His asthmatic assistant shook the extended hand with vigorous sincerity. "Good luck, sir. And don't forget the bomb. We'll have to drop it at three thirty-four sharp."

But Prentiss had vanished into the leafy darkness.

A little later he was studying the luminous figures on his watch. The u.v.-blanket was presumably on. All he had to be careful about in the next forty seconds was a direct collision with a photocell post.

But Crush's survey party had mapped well. He reached the barbed fencing uneventfully, with seconds to spare. He listened, a moment, and then in practiced silence eased his lithe body high up and over.

The breeze, which a moment before had been in his face, now died away, and the night air hung about him in dark lifeless curtains.

From the stone building a scant two hundred yards ahead, a chink of light peeped out.

Prentiss drew his silenced pistol and began moving forward with swift caution, taking care to place his heel to ground before the toe, and feeling out the character of the ground with the thin soles of his sneakers before each step. A snapping twig might hurl a slavering wild beast at his throat.

He stopped motionless in midstride.

From a thicket several yards to his right came an ominous snuffing, followed by a low snarl.

His mouth went suddenly dry as he strained his ears and turned his head slowly toward the sound.

And then there came the reverberations of something heavy, hurtling toward him.

He whipped his weapon around and waited in a tense crouch, not daring to send a wild, singing bullet across the sward.

The great cat was almost upon him before he fired, and then the faint cough of the stumbling, stricken animal seemed louder than his muffled shot.

Breathing hard, Prentiss stepped away from the dying beast, evidently a panther, and listened for a long time before resuming his march on the cottage. Luce's extraordinary measures to exclude intruders but confirmed his suspicions: Tonight was the last night that the professor could be stopped. He blinked the stinging sweat from his eyes and glanced at his watch. It was 3:15.

Apparently the other animals had not heard him. He stood up to resume his advance, and to his utter relief found that the wind had shifted almost directly into his face and was blowing steadily.

In another three minutes he was standing at the massive door of the building, running practiced fingers over the great iron hinges and lock. Undoubtedly the thing was going to squeak; there was no time to apply oil and wait for it to soak in. The lock could be easily picked.

And the squeaking of a rusty hinge was probably immaterial. A cunning operator like Luce would undoubtedly have wired an alarm into it. He just couldn't believe Crush's report to the contrary.

But he couldn't stand here.

There was only one way to get inside quickly, and alive.

Chuckling at his own madness, Prentiss began to pound on the door.

He could visualize the blinking out of the slit of light above his head, and knew that, somewhere within the building, two flame-lit eyes were studying him in an infra-red scanner.

Prentiss tried simultaneously to listen to the muffled squeaking of the rats beyond the great door and to the swift, padding approach of something big behind him.

"Luce," he cried. "It's Prentiss! Let me in!"

A latch slid somewhere; the door eased inward. The investigator threw his gun rearward at a pair of bounding eyes, laced his fingers over his head, and stumbled into more darkness.

Despite the protection of his hands, the terrific blow of the blackjack on his temple almost knocked him out.

He closed his eyes, crumpled carefully to the floor, and noted with satisfaction that his wrists were being tied behind his back. As he had anticipated, it was a clumsy job, even without his imperceptible "assistance." Long fingers ran over his body in a search for more weapons.

Then he felt the sting of a hypodermic needle in his biceps.

The lights came on.

He struggled feebly, emitted a plausible groan, and tried to sit up.

From far above, the strange face of Dr. Luce looked down at him, illuminated, it seemed to Prentiss, by some unhallowed inner fire.

"What time is it?" asked Prentiss.

"Approximately three-twenty."

"*Hm.* Your kittens gave me quite a reception, my dear professor."

"As befits an uncooperative meddler."

"Well, what are you going to do with me?"

"Kill you."

Luce pulled a pistol from his coat pocket. Prentiss wet his lips. During his ten years with the Bureau, he had never had to deal with anyone quite like Luce. The gaunt man personified megalomania on a scale beyond anything the investigator had previously encountered—or imagined possible.

And, he realized with a shiver, Luce was very probably justified in his prospects (not delusions!) of grandeur.

With growing alarm he watched Luce snap off the safety lock of the pistol.

There were two possible chances of surviving more than a few seconds.

Luce's index finger began to tense around the trigger.

One of those chances was to appeal to Luce's megalomania, treating him as a human being. Tell him, "I know you won't kill me until you've had a chance to gloat over me—to tell me, the inventor of ontologic synthesis, how you found a practical application of it."

No good. Too obvious to one of Luce's intelligence.

The approach must be to a demi-god, in humility. Oddly enough his curiosity *was* tinged with respect. Luce *did* have something.

Prentiss licked his lips again and said hurriedly: "I must die, then. But could you show me—is it asking too much to show me, just how you propose to 'go through'?"

The gun lowered a fraction of an inch. Luce eyed the doomed man suspiciously.

"Would you, please?" continued Prentiss. His voice was dry, cracking. "Ever since I discovered that new realities could be synthesized, I've wondered whether *homo sapiens* was capable of finding a practical device for uncovering the true reality. And all who've worked on it have insisted that only a brain but little below the angels was capable of such an achievement." He coughed apologetically. "It is difficult to believe that a mere mortal has really accomplished what you claim—and yet, there's something about you . . ." His voice trailed off, and he laughed deprecatingly.

Luce bit; he thrust the gun back into his coat pocket. "So you know when you're licked," he sneered. "Well, I'll let you live a moment longer."

He stepped back and pulled aside a black screen. "Has the inimitable ontologist the wit to understand this?"

Within a few seconds of his introduction to the instrument everything was painfully clear. Prentiss now abandoned any remote hope that either Luce's method or apparatus would prove faulty. Both the vacuum-glassed machinery and the idea behind it were perfect.

Basically, the supplementary unit, which he now saw for the first time, consisted of a sodium-vapor light bulb, blacked out except for one tiny transparent spot. Ahead of the little window was a series of what must be hundreds of black discs mounted on a common axis. Each disc bore a slender radial slot. And though he could not trace all the gearing, Prentiss knew that the discs were geared to permit one and only one fleeting photon of yellow light to emerge at the end of the disc series, where it would pass through a Kerr electro-optic field and be polarized.

That photon would then travel one centimeter to that fabulous Nicol prism, one surface of which had been machined flat to a molecule's thickness. That surface was turned by means of an equally marvelous goniometer to meet the oncoming photon at an angle of exactly 45 degrees. And then would come chaos.

The cool voice of E sounded in his ear receptor. "Prentiss, it's three-thirty. If you understand the apparatus, and find it dangerous, will you so signify? If possible, describe it for the tapes."

"I understand your apparatus perfectly," said Prentiss.

Luce grunted, half irritated, half curious.

Prentiss continued hurriedly, "Shall I tell you how you decided upon this specific apparatus?"

"If you think you can."

"You have undoubtedly seen the sun reflect from the surface of the sea."

Luce nodded.

"But the fish beneath the surface see the sun, too," continued Prentiss. "Some of the photons are reflected and reach you, and some are refracted and reach the fish. But, for a given wave length, the photons are identical. Why should one be absorbed and another reflected?"

"You're on the right track," admitted Luce, "but couldn't you account for their behavior by Jordan's law?"

"Statistically, yes. Individually, no. In nineteen thirty-four Jordan showed that a beam of polarized light splits up when it hits a Nicol prism. He proved that when the prism forms an angle, alpha, with the plane of polarization of the prism, a fraction of the light equal to $\cos^2$ alpha passes through the prism, and the remainder, $\sin^2$ alpha, is reflected. For example, if alpha is 60 degrees, three-fourths of the photons are reflected and one-fourth are refracted. But note that Jordan's law applied only to streams of photons, and you're dealing with a single photon, to which you're presenting an angle of exactly 45°. And how does a single photon make up its mind—or the photonic equivalent of a mind—when the probability of reflecting is exactly equal to the probability of refracting? Of course, if our photon is but one little mote along with billions of others, the whole comprising a light beam, we can visualize orders left for him by a sort of statistical traffic keeper stationed somewhere in the beam. A member of a beam, it may be presumed, has a pretty good idea of how many of his brothers have already reflected, and how many refracted, and hence knows which he must do."

"But suppose our single photon isn't in a beam at all?" said Luce.

"Your apparatus," said Prentiss, "is going to provide just such a photon. And I think it will be a highly confused little photon, just as your experimental rat was, that night not so long ago. I think it was Schrödinger who said that these physical particles were startlingly human in many of their aspects. Yes, your photon will be given a choice of equal probability. Shall he reflect? Shall he refract? The chances are 50 percent for either choice. He will have no reason for selecting one in preference to the other. There will have been no swarm of preceding photons to set up a traffic guide for him. He'll be puzzled; and trying to meet a situation for which he has no proper response, he'll slow down. And when he does, he'll cease to be a photon, which must travel at the speed of light or cease to exist. Like your rat, like many human beings, he solves the unsolvable by disintegrating."

Luce said: "And when it disintegrates, there disappears one of the lambdas that hold together the Einstein space-time continuum. And when *that* goes, what's left can be only final reality untainted by theory or imagination. Do you see any flaw in my plan?"

CHAPTER VII
New World

Tugging with subtle quickness on the cords that bound him, Prentiss knew there was no flaw in the man's reasoning, and that every human being on earth was now living on borrowed time.

He could think of no way to stop him; there remained only the bare threat of the bomb.

He said tersely: "If you don't submit to peaceable arrest within a few seconds, an atom bomb is going to be dropped on this area."

Sweat was getting into his eyes again, and he winked rapidly.

Luce's dark features convulsed, hung limp, then coalesced into a harsh grin. "She'll be too late," he said with grim good humor. "Her ancestors tried for centuries to thwart mine. But we were successful—always. Tonight I succeed again and for all time."

Prentiss had one hand free.

In seconds he would be at the man's throat. He worked with quiet fury at the loops around his bound wrist.

Again E's voice in his ear receptor. "I had to do it!" The tones were strangely sad, self-accusing, remorseful.

Had to do *what?*

And his dazed mind was trying to digest the fact that E had just destroyed him. She was continuing. "The bomb was dropped ten seconds ago." She was almost pleading, and her words were running together. "You were helpless; you couldn't kill him. I had a sudden premonition of what the world would be like— afterward—even for those who go through. Forgive me."

Almost mechanically he resumed his fumbling with the cord.

Luce looked up. "What's that?"

"What?" asked Prentiss dully. "I don't hear anything."

"Of course you do! Listen!"

The wrist came free.

Several things happened.

That faraway shriek in the skies grew into a howling crescendo of destruction.

As one man Prentiss and Luce leaped toward the activator switches. Luce got there first—an infinitesimal fraction of time before the walls were completely disintegrated.

There was a brief, soundless interval of utter blackness.

And then it seemed to Prentiss that a titanic stone wall crashed into his brain, and held him, mute, immobile.

But he was not dead.

For the name of this armored, stunning wall was not the bomb, but Time itself.

He knew in a brief flash of insight, that for sentient, thinking beings, Time had suddenly become a barricade rather than an endless road.

The exploding bomb—the caving cottage walls—were hanging, somewhere, frozen fast in an immutable, eternal stasis.

Luce had separated this fleeting unseen dimension from the creatures and things that had flowed along it. There is no existence without change along a temporal continuum. And now the continuum had been shattered.

Was this, then, the fate of all tangible things—of all humanity?

Were none of them—not even the two or three who understood advanced ontology—to get through?

There was nothing but a black, eerie silence all around.

His senses were useless.

He even doubted he had any senses.

So far as he could tell he was nothing but an intelligence, floating in space. But he couldn't even be sure of *that*. Intelligence—space—they weren't necessarily the same now as before.

All that he knew for sure was that he doubted. He doubted everything except the fact of doubting.

Shades of Descartes!

To doubt is to think!

Ergo sum!

I exist.

Instantly he was wary. He existed, but not necessarily as Adam Prentiss Rogers. For the *noumenon* of Adam Prentiss Rogers might be—whom?

But he was safe. He was going to get through.

Relax, be resilient, he urged his whirling brain. You're on the verge of something marvelous.

It seemed that he could almost hear himself talk, and he was glad. A voiceless final reality would have been unbearable.

He essayed a tentative whisper:

"E!"

From somewhere far away a woman whimpered.

He cried eagerly into the blackness, "Is that you?"

Something unintelligible and strangely frightening answered him.

"Don't try to hold on to yourself," he cried. "Just let yourself go! Remember, you won't be E any more, but the *noumenon*, the essence of E. Unless you change enough to permit your *noumenon* to take over your old identity, you'll have to stay behind."

There was a groan. "But I'm *me!*"

"But you *aren't*—not really," he pleaded quickly. "You're just an aspect of a larger, symbolical *you*—the *noumenon* of E. It's yours for the asking. You have only to hold out your hand to grasp the shape of final reality. And you *must*, or cease to exist!"

A wail: "But what will happen to my body?"

The ontologist almost laughed. "I wouldn't know; but if it changes, I'll be sorrier than you!"

There was a silence.

"E!" he called.

No answer.

"E! Did you get through? *E!*"

The empty echoes skirled between the confines of his narrow blackness.

Had the woman lost even her struggling interstitial existence? Whenever, whatever, or wherever she now was, he could no longer detect.

Somehow, if it had ever come to this, he had counted on her being with him—just the two of them.

In stunned uneasy wonder he considered what his existence was going to be like from now on.

And what about Luce?

Had the demonic professor possessed sufficient mental elasticity to slip through? And if so, just what was the professorial *noumenon*—the real Luce—like?

He'd soon know.

The ontologist relaxed again, and began floating through a dreamy patch of light and darkness. A pale glow began gradually to form about his eyes, and shadowy things began to form, dissolve, and reform.

He felt a great rush of gratitude. At least the shape of final reality was to be visible.

And then, at about the spot where Luce had stood, he saw the Eyes—two tiny red flames, transfixing him with unfathomable fury.

The same eyes that had burned into his that night of his first search!

Luce had got through—but wait!

An unholy aura was playing about the sinuous shadow that contained the jeweled flames. Those eyes were brilliant, horrid facets of hate in the head of a huge, coiling serpent thing! Snake-Eyes!

In mounting awe and fear the ontologist understood that Luce had not got through—as Luce. That the *noumenon*, the essence, of Luce—was nothing human. That Luce, the bearer of light, aspirant to godhood, was not just Luce!

By the faint light he began shrinking away from the coiled horror, and in the act saw that *he,* at least, still had a human body. He knew this, because he was completely nude.

He was still human, and the snake-creature wasn't—and therefore never had been.

Then he noticed that the stone cottage was gone, and that a pink glow was coming from the east.

He crashed into a tree before he had gone a dozen steps.

Yesterday, there had been no trees within three hundred yards of the cottage.

But that made sense, for there was no cottage any more, and no yesterday. Crush ought to be waiting somewhere out here—except that Crush hadn't got through, and hence didn't really exist.

He went around the tree. It obscured his view of the snake-creature for a moment, and when he tried to find it again, it was gone.

He was glad for the momentary relief, and began looking about him in the half-light. He took a deep breath.

The animals, if they still existed, had vanished with the coming of dawn. The grassy, flower-dotted swards scintillated like emeralds in the early morning haze. From somewhere came the babble of running water.

Meta-universe, by whatever name you called it, was beautiful, like a gorgeous garden. What a pity he must live and die here alone, with nothing but a lot of animals for company. He'd willingly give an arm, or at least a rib, if—

"Adam Prentiss! *Adam!*"

He whirled and stared toward the orchard in elated disbelief.

"E! *Eve!*"

She'd got through!

The whole world, and just the two of them!

His heart was pounding ecstatically as he began to run lithely upwind.

And they'd keep it this way, simple and sweet, forever, and their children after then. To hell with science and progress! (Well, within practical limits, of course.)

As he ran, there rippled about his quivering nostrils the seductive scent of apple blossoms.

THE CHESSPLAYERS

Now please understand this. I'm not saying that all chessplayers are lunatics. But I do claim that chronic chessplaying affects a man.

Let me tell you about the K Street Chess Club, of which I was once treasurer.

Our membership roll claimed a senator, the leader of a large labor union, the president of the A. & W. Railroad, and a few other big shots. But it seemed the more important they were *outside,* the rottener they were as chessplayers.

The senator and the rail magnate didn't know the Ruy Lopez from the Queen's Gambit, so of course they could only play the other fish, or hang around wistfully watching the games of the Class A players and wishing that they, too, amounted to something.

The club's champion was Bobby Baker, a little boy in the fourth grade at the Pestalozzi-Borstal Boarding School. Several of his end game compositions had been published in *Chess Review* and *Shakhmatny Russkji Zhurnal* before he could talk plainly.

Our second best was Pete Summers, a clerk for the A. & W. Railroad. He was the author of two very famous chess books. One book proved that white can always win, and the other proved that black can always draw. As you might suspect, the gap separating him from the president of his railroad was abysmal indeed.

The show position was held by Jim Bradley, a chronic idler whose dues were paid by his wife. The club's admiration for him was profound.

But experts don't make a club. You have to have some guiding spirit, a fairly good player, with a knack for organization and a true knowledge of values.

Such a gem we had in our secretary, Nottingham Jones.

It was really my interest in Nottingham that led me to join the K Street Chess Club. I wanted to see if he was an exception, or whether they were all alike.

After I tell you about their encounter with Zeno, you can judge for yourself.

In his unreal life Nottingham Jones was a statistician in a government bureau. He worked at a desk in a big room with many other desks, including mine, and he performed his duties blankly and without conscious effort. Many an afternoon, after the quitting bell had rung and I had strolled over to discuss club finances with him, he would be astonished to discover that he had already gone to work and had turned out a creditable stack of forms.

I suppose that it was during these hours of his quasi-existence that the invisible Nottingham conceived those numerous events that had made him famous as a chess club emcee throughout the United States.

For it was Nottingham who organized the famous American-Soviet cable matches (in which the U.S. team had been so soundly trounced), refereed numerous U.S. match championships, and launched a dozen brilliant but impecunious foreign chess masters on exhibition tours in a hundred chess clubs from New York to Los Angeles.

But the achievements of which he was proudest were his bishop-knight tournaments.

Now the bishop is supposed to be slightly stronger than the knight, and this evaluation has become so ingrained in chess thinking today that no player will voluntarily exchange a bishop for an enemy knight. He may squander his life's savings on phony stock, talk back to traffic cops, and forget his wedding anniversary, but never, never, *never* will he exchange a bishop for a knight.

Nottingham suspected this fixation to be ill-founded; he had the idea that the knight was just as strong as the bishop, and to prove his point he held numerous intramural tournaments in the K Street Club, in which one player used six pawns and a bishop against the six pawns and a knight of his opponent.

Jones never did make up his mind as to whether the bishop was stronger than the knight, but at the end of a couple of years he did know that the K Street Club had more bishop-knight experts than any other club in the United States.

And it then occurred to him that American chess had a beautiful means of redeeming itself from its resounding defeat at the hands of the Russian cable team.

He sent his challenge to Stalin himself—the K Street Chess Club versus All the Russians—a dozen boards of bishop-knight games, to be played by cable.

The Soviet Recreation Bureau sent the customary six curt rejections and then promptly accepted.

And this leads us back to one afternoon at 5 o'clock when Nottingham Jones looked up from his desk and seemed startled to find me standing there.

"Don't get up yet," I said. "This is something you ought to take sitting down."

He stared at me owlishly. "Is the year's rent due again so soon?"

"Next week. This is something else."

"Oh?"

"A professor friend of mine," I said, "who lives in the garret over my apartment, wants to play the whole club at one sitting—a simultaneous exhibition."

"A simul, eh? Pretty good, is he?"

"It isn't exactly the professor who wants to play. It's really a friend of his."

"Is *he* good?"

"The professor says so. But that isn't exactly the point. To make it short, this professor, Dr. Schmidt, owns a pet rat. He wants the rat to play." I added: "And for the usual simul fee. The professor needs money. In fact, if he doesn't get a steady job pretty soon he may be deported."

Nottingham looked dubious. "I don't see how we can help him. Did you say *rat?*"

"I did."

"A chessplaying rat? A four-legged one?"

"Right. Quite a drawing card for the club, eh?"

Nottingham shrugged his shoulders. "We learn something every day. Will you believe it, I never heard they cared for the game. Women don't. However, I once read about an educated horse . . . I suppose he's well known in Europe?"

"Very likely," I said. "The professor specializes in comparative psychology."

Nottingham shook his head impatiently. "I don't mean the professor. I'm talking about the rat. What's his name, anyway?"

"Zeno."

"Never heard of him. What's his tournament score?"

"I don't think he ever played in any tournaments. The professor taught him the game in a concentration camp. How good he is I don't know, except that he can give the professor rook odds."

Nottingham smiled pityingly. "I can give you rook odds, but I'm not good enough to throw a simul."

A great light burst over me. "Hey, wait a minute. You're completely overlooking the fantastic fact that Zeno is a—"

"The only pertinent question," interrupted Nottingham, "is whether he's really in the *master* class. We've got half a dozen players in the club who can throw an 'inside' simul for free, but when we hire an outsider and charge the members a dollar each to play him, he's got to be good enough to tackle *our* best. And when the whole club's in training for the bishop-knight cable match with the Russians next month, I can't have them relaxing over a mediocre simul."

"But you're missing the whole point—"

"—which is, this Zeno needs money and you want me to throw a simul to help him. But I just can't do it. I have a duty to the members to maintain a high standard."

"But Zeno is a rat. He learned to play chess in a concentration camp. He—"

"That doesn't necessarily make him a good player."

It was all cockeyed. My voice trailed off. "Well, somehow it seemed like a good idea."

Nottingham saw that he had let me down too hard. "If you want to, you might arrange a game between Zeno and one of our top players—say Jim Bradley. He has lots of time. If Jim says Zeno is good enough for a simul, we'll give him a simul."

So I invited Jim Bradley and the professor, including Zeno, to my apartment the next evening.

I had seen Zeno before, but that was when I thought he was just an ordinary pet rat. Viewed as a chessmaster he seemed to be a completely different creature. Both Jim and I studied him closely when the professor pulled him out of his coat pocket and placed him on the chess table.

You could tell, just by looking at the little animal, from the way his beady black eyes shone and the alert way he carried his head, that here was a super-rat, an Einstein among rodents.

"Chust let him get his bearings," said the professor, as he fixed a little piece of cheese to Bradley's king with a thumb tack. "And don't worry, he will make a good showing."

Zeno pitter-pattered around the board, sniffed with a bored delicacy at both his and Bradley's chess pieces, twitched his nose at Bradley's cheese-crowned king, and gave the impression that the only reason he didn't yawn was that he was too well bred. He returned to his side of the board and waited for Bradley to move.

Jim blinked, shook himself, and finally pushed his queen pawn two squares.

Zeno minced out, picked up his own queen pawn between his teeth, and moved it forward two squares. Then Jim moved out his queen bishop pawn, and the game was under way, a conventional Queen's Gambit Declined.

I got the professor off in a corner. "How did you teach him to play? You never did tell me."

"Was easy. Tied each chessman in succession to body and let Zeno run simple maze on the chessboard composed of moves of chessman, until reached king and got piece of bread stuck on crown. Next, ve—one moment, please."

We both looked at the board. Zeno had knocked over Jim's king and was tapping with his dainty forefoot in front of the fallen monarch.

Jim was counting the taps with silent lips. "He's announcing a mate in thirteen. And he's right."

Zeno was already nibbling at the little piece of cheese fixed to Jim's king.

When I reported the result to Nottingham the next day, he agreed to hold a simultaneous exhibition for Zeno. Since Zeno was an unknown, with no reputation and no drawing power, Jones naturally didn't notify the local papers, but merely sent post cards to the club members.

On the night of the simul Nottingham set up 25 chess tables in an approximate circle around the club room. Here and there the professor pushed the tables a little closer together so that Zeno could jump easily from one to the other as he made his rounds. Then the professor made a circuit of all the tables and tacked a little piece of cheese to each king.

After that he mopped at his face, stepped outside the circle, and Zeno started his rounds.

And then we hit a snag.

A slow gray man emerged from a little group of spectators and approached the professor.

"Dr. Hans Schmidt?" he asked.

"Ya," said the professor, a little nervously. "I mean, yes sir."

The gray man pulled out his pocketbook and flashed something at the professor. "Immigration service. Do you have in your possession a renewed immigration visa?"

The professor wet his lips and shook his head wordlessly.

The other continued, "According to our records you don't have a job, haven't paid your rent for a month, and your credit has run out at the local delicatessen. I'm afraid I'll have to ask you to come along with me."

"You mean—*deportation?*"

"How do I know? Maybe, maybe not."

The professor looked as though a steam roller had just passed over him. "So it comes," he whispered. "I knew I should not haf come out from hiding, but one needs money . . . ."

"Too bad," said the immigration man. "Of course, if you could post a $500 bond as surety for your self-support—"

"Had I $500, would I be behind at the delicatessen?"

"No, I guess not. That your hat and coat?"

The professor started sadly toward the coat-racks.

I grabbed at his sleeve.

"Now hold on," I said hurriedly. "Look, mister, in two hours Dr. Schmidt will have a contract for a 52-week exhibition tour. " I exclaimed to the professor: "Zeno will make you all the money you can spend! When the simul is over tonight, Nottingham Jones will recommend you to every chess club in the United States, Canada, and Mexico. Think of it! Zeno! History's only chess-playing rat!"

"Not so fast," said Nottingham, who had just walked up. "I've got to see how good this Zeno is before I back him."

"Don't worry," I said. "Why, the bare fact that he's a rat—"

The gray man interrupted. "You mean you want me to wait a couple of hours until we see whether the professor is going to get some sort of a contract?"

"That's right," I said eagerly. "After Zeno shows what he can do, the professor gets a chess exhibition tour."

The gray man was studying Zeno with distant distaste. "Well, okay. I'll wait."

The professor heaved a gigantic sigh and trotted off to watch his protégé.

"Say," said the gray man to me, "you people ought to keep a cat in this place. I was sure I saw a rat running around over there."

"That's Zeno," I said. "He's playing chess."

"Don't get sarcastic, Jack. I was just offering a suggestion." He wandered off to keep an eye on the professor.

The evening wore on, and the professor used up all his handkerchiefs and borrowed one of mine. But I couldn't see what he was worried about, because it was clear that Zeno was a marvel, right up there in the ranks of Lasker, Alekhine, and Botvinnik.

In every game, he entered into an orgy of complications. One by one his opponents teetered off the razor's edge, and had to resign. One by one the tables emptied, and the losers gathered around those who were still struggling. The clusters around Bobby Baker, Pete Summers, and Jim Bradley grew minute by minute.

But at the end of the second hour, when only the three club champions were still battling, I noticed that Zeno was slowing down.

"What's wrong, professor?" I whispered anxiously.

He groaned. "For supper he chenerally gets only two little pieces cheese."
And so far tonight Zeno had eaten twenty-three! He was so fat he could hardly waddle.

I groaned too, and thought of tiny stomach pumps.

We watched tensely as Zeno pulled himself slowly from Jim Bradley's board over to Pete Summers'. It seemed to take him an extraordinarily long time to analyze the position on Pete's board. At last he made his move and crawled across to Bobby Baker's table.

And it was there, chin resting on the pedestal of his king rook, that he collapsed into gentle rodent slumber.

The professor let out an almost inaudible but heart-rending moan.

"Don't just stand there!" I cried. "Wake him up!"

The professor prodded the little animal gingerly with his forefinger. "*Liebchen,*" he pleaded, "*wach' auf!*"

But Zeno just rolled comfortably over on his back.

A deathly silence had fallen over the room, and it was on account of this that we heard what we heard.

Zeno began to snore.

Everybody seemed to be looking in other directions when the professor lifted the little animal up and dropped him tenderly into his wrinkled coat pocket.

The gray man was the first to speak. "Well, Dr. Schmidt? No contract?"

"Don't be silly," I declared. "Of course he gets a tour. Nottingham, how soon can you get letters off to the other clubs?"

"But I really can't recommend him," demurred Nottingham. "After all, he defaulted three out of 25 games. He's only a *Kleinmeister*—not the kind of material to make a simul circuit."

"What if he *didn't* finish three measly games? He's a good player, all the same. All you have to do is say the word and every club secretary in North America will make a date with him—at an entrance fee of $5 per player. He'll take the country by storm!"

"I'm sorry," Nottingham said to the professor. "I have a certain standard, and your boy just doesn't make the grade."

The professor sighed. "*Ja, ich versteh'.*"

"But this is crazy!" My voice sounded a little louder than I had intended. "You fellows don't agree with Nottingham, do you? How about you, Jim?"

Jim Bradley shrugged his shoulders. "Hard to say just how good Zeno is. It would take a week of close analysis to say definitely who has the upper hand in *my* game. He's a pawn down, but he has a wonderful position."

"But Jim," I protested. "That isn't the point at all. Can't you see it? Think of the publicity . . . a chess-playing *rat . . . !*"

"I wouldn't know about his personal life," said Jim curtly.

"Fellows!" I said desperately. "Is this the way all of you feel? Can't enough of us stick together to pass a club resolution recommending Zeno for a simul circuit? How about you, Bobby?"

Bobby looked uncomfortable. "I think the school station wagon is waiting for me. I guess I ought to be getting back."

"Coming, doc?" asked the gray man.

"Yes," replied Dr. Schmidt heavily. "Good evening, chentlemen."

I just stood there, stunned.

"Here's Zeno's income for the evening, professor," said Nottingham, pressing an envelope into his hand. "I'm afraid it won't help much, though, especially since I didn't feel justified in charging the customary dollar fee."

The professor nodded, and in numb silence I watched him accompany the immigration officer to the doorway.

The professor and I versus the chessplayers. We had thrown our Sunday punches, but we hadn't even scratched their gambit.

Just then Pete Summers called out. "Hey, Dr. Schmidt!" He held up a sheet of paper covered with chess diagrams. "This fell out of your pocket when you were standing here."

The professor said something apologetic to the gray man and came back. *"Danke,"* he said, reaching for the paper. "Is part of a manuscript."

"A *chess* manuscript, professor?" I was grasping at straws now. "Are you writing a chess book?"

"Ya, I guess."

"Well, well," said Pete Summers, who was studying the sheet carefully. "The bishop against the knight, eh?"

"Ya. Now if you excuse me—"

"The bishop versus the knight?" shrilled Bobby Baker, who had trotted back to the tables.

"The bishop and knight?" muttered Nottingham Jones. He demanded abruptly: "Have you studied the problem long, professor?"

"Many months. In camp . . . in attic. And now manuscript has reached 2,000 pages, and we look for publisher."

"*We* . . . ?" My voice may have trembled a little, because both Nottingham and the professor turned and looked at me sharply. "Professor"—my words spilled out in a rush—"did Zeno write that book?"

"Who else?" answered the professor in wonder.

"I don't see how he could hold a pen," said Nottingham doubtfully.

"Not necessary," said the professor. "He made moves, and I wrote down." He added with wistful pride: "Zenchen is probably world's greatest living authority on bishop-knight."

The room was suddenly very still again. For an overlong moment the only sound was Zeno's muffled snoring spiraling up from the professor's pocket.

"Has he reached any conclusions?" breathed Nottingham.

The professor turned puzzled eyes to the intent faces about him. "Zeno believes conflict cannot be cheneralized. However, has discovered 78 positions in which bishop superior to knight and 24 positions in which knight is better. Obviously, player mit bishop must try—"

"—for one of the winning bishop positions, of course, and ditto for the knight," finished Nottingham. "That's an extremely valuable manuscript."

All this time I had been getting my first free breath of the evening. It felt good.

"It's too bad," I said casually, "that the professor can't stay here long enough for you sharks to study Zeno's book and pick up some pointers for the great bishop-knight cable match next month. It's too bad, too, that Zeno won't be here to take a board against the Russians. He'd give us a sure point on the score."

"Yeah," said Jim Bradley. "He would."

Nottingham shot a question at the professor. "Would Zeno be willing to rent the manuscript to us for a month?"

The professor was about to agree when I interrupted. "That would be rather difficult, Nottingham. Zeno doesn't know where he'll be at the end of the month. Furthermore, as treasurer for the club, let me inform you that after we pay the annual rent next week, the treasury will be as flat as a pancake."

Nottingham's face fell.

"Of course," I continued carefully, "if you were willing to underwrite a tour for Zeno, I imagine he'd be willing to lend it to you for nothing. And then the professor wouldn't have to be deported, and Zeno could stay and coach our team, as well as take a board in the cable match."

Neither the professor nor I breathed as we watched Nottingham struggling over that game of solitaire chess with his soul. But finally his owlish face gathered itself into an austere stubbornness. "I still can't recommend Zeno for a tour. I have my standards."

Several of the other players nodded gloomily.

"I'm scheduled to play against Kereslov," said Pete Summers, looking sadly at the sheet of manuscript. "But I agree with you, Nottingham."

I knew about Kereslov. The Moscow Club had been holding intramural bishop-knight tournaments every week for the past six months, and Kereslov had won nearly all of them.

"And I have to play Botvinnik," said Jim Bradley. He added feebly, "But you're right, Nottingham. We can't ethically underwrite a tour for Zeno."

Botvinnik was merely chess champion of the world.

"What a shame," I said. "Professor, I'm afraid we'll have to make a deal with the Soviet Recreation Bureau." It was just a sudden screwy inspiration. I still wonder whether I would have gone through with it if Nottingham hadn't said what he said next.

"Mister," he asked the immigration official, "you want $500 put up for Dr. Schmidt?"

"That's the customary bond."

Nottingham beamed at me. "We have more than that in the treasury, haven't we?"

"Sure. We have exactly $500.14, of which $500 is for rent. Don't look at me like that."

"The directors of this club," declared Nottingham sonorously, "hereby authorize you to draw a check for $500 payable to Dr. Schmidt."

"Are you cuckoo?" I yelped. "Where do you think I'm going to get another $500 for the rent? You lunatics will wind up playing your cable match in the middle of K Street!"

"This," said Nottingham coldly, "is the greatest work on chess since Murray's *History*. After we're through with it, I'm sure we can find a publisher for Zeno. Would you stand in the way of such a magnificent contribution to chess literature?"

Pete Summers chimed in accusingly. "Even if you can't be a friend to Zeno, you could at least think about the good of the club and of American chess. You're taking a very funny attitude about this."

"But of course you aren't a real chessplayer," said Bobby Baker sympathetically. "We never had a treasurer who was."

Nottingham sighed. "I guess it's about time to elect another treasurer."

"All right," I said bleakly. "I'm just wondering what I'm going to tell the landlord next week. He isn't a chessplayer either." I told the gray man, "Come over here to the desk, and I'll make out a check."

He frowned. "A check? From a bunch of chessplayers? Not on your life! Let's go, professor."

Just then a remarkable thing happened. One of our most minor members spoke up.

"I'm Senator Brown, one of Mr. Jones's *fellow chessplayers*. I'll endorse that check, if you like."

And then there was a popping noise and a button flew by my ear. I turned quickly to see a vast blast of smoke terminated by three perfect smoke rings. Our rail magnate tapped at his cigar. "I'm Johnson, of the A. & W. *We chessplayers* stick together on these matters. I'll endorse that check, too. And Nottingham, don't worry about the rent. The senator and I will take care of that."

I stifled an indignant gasp. *I* was the one worrying about the rent, not Nottingham. But of course I was beneath their notice. I wasn't a *chessplayer*.

The gray man shrugged his shoulders. "Okay, I'll take the bond and recommend an indefinite renewal."

Five minutes later I was standing outside the building gulping in the fresh cold air when the immigration officer walked past me toward his car.

"Goodnight," I said.

He ducked a little, then looked up. When he answered, he seemed to be talking more to himself than to me. "It was the funniest thing. You got the impression there was a little rat running around on those boards and moving the pieces with his teeth. But of course rats don't play chess. Just human beings." He peered at me through the dusk, as though trying to get things in focus. "There wasn't really a rat playing chess in there, was there?"

"No," I said. "There wasn't any rat in there. And no human beings, either. Just chessplayers."

When my daughter Shan was a little girl and just starting to go to school I noted that she was developing (copying?) many of her mother's mannerisms: a certain charming lift of the shoulder, a disapproving clenching of the jaws, a beautiful grin. What do we have here, I wondered. Who's who?

And so the story popped out of my Freudian toaster.

CHILD BY CHRONOS

You just lie there and listen. The sunshine will do you good, and anyhow the doctor said you weren't to do much talking.

I'll get to the point.

I have loved three men. The first was my mother's lover. The second was my husband. The third . . .

I'm going to tell you all about these three men—and me. I'm going to tell you some things that might send you back to the hospital.

Don't interrupt.

As a child I never knew my father. He was declared legally dead several months before I was born. They said he had gone hunting and had never returned. Theoretically you can't miss what you never had. Whoever said that didn't know me. I missed my lost father when I was a brat and when I was a gawky youngster in pigtails and when I was a young lady in a finishing school in Switzerland.

Mother made it worse. There was never any shortage of males when mother was around, but they wouldn't have anything to do with me. And that was her fault. Mother was gorgeous. Men couldn't stay away from her. By the time I was ten, I could tell what they were thinking when they looked at her. When I was twenty they were still looking at her in the same way. *That* was when she finally took a lover, and when I fled from her in hate and horror.

There's nothing remarkable about a daughter's hating her mother. It's just that I did more of it than usual. All the hate that I ever commanded, ever since I was in diapers, I saved, preserved, and vented on her. When I was an infant, so they said, I wouldn't nurse at her breast. Strictly a bottle baby. It was as though I had declared to the world that I hadn't been born in the way mortals are born and that this woman who professed to be my mother wasn't really. As you shall see, I wasn't entirely wrong.

I always had the insane feeling that everything she had really belonged to me and that she was keeping me from claiming my own.

Naturally, our tastes were identical. This identity of desire became more and more acute as I grew older. Whatever she had, I regarded as really mine, and generally tried to confiscate it. Particularly men. The irritating thing was that, even though mother never became serious about any of them (except the last one), they still couldn't see me. Except the last one.

163

Mother's willingness to turn over to me any and all of her gentlemen friends seemed to carry with it the unrelated but inevitable corollary, that none of them (with that one exception) had any desire to *be* turned over.

You're probably thinking that it was all a consequence of not having a father around, that I subconsciously substituted her current male for my missing father, and hence put claims on him equal to hers. You can explain it any way you want to. Anyway, except at the last, it always turned out the same. The more willing she was to get rid of him, the less willing he was to have anything to do with me.

But I never got mad at *them;* only at *her.* Sometimes, if the brush-off was particularly brusque, I wouldn't speak to her for days. Even the sight of her would make me sick to my stomach.

When I was seventeen, on the advice of her psychiatrist, she sent me to school in Switzerland. This psychiatrist said I had the worst Electra complex with the least grounds for it of any woman in medical history. He said he hoped that my father was really dead, because if he should ever turn up alive . . . Well, you could just see him rubbing the folds of his cerebrum in brisk anticipation.

However, the superficial reason they gave for sending me to Switzerland was to get an education. There I was, seventeen, and didn't even know the multiplication table. All I knew was what mother called "headline history." She had yanked me out of public school when I was in the second grade and had hired a flock of tutors to teach me about current events. Nothing but current events. Considering that she made her living by predicting current events before they became current, I suppose her approach was excusable. It was her method of execution that made the subject unutterably dull—then. Mother wouldn't stand for any of the modern methods of history teaching. No analysis of trends and integration of international developments for mother. My apologetic tutors were paid to see that I memorized every headline and caption in every *New York Times* printed since Counterpoint won the Preakness in 1957—which was even several months before I was born. That and nothing more. There were even a couple of memory experts thrown in, to wrap each daily pill in a sugar-coated mnemonic.

So, even if the real reason for sending me to Switzerland was not to get an education, I didn't care. I was glad to stop memorizing headlines.

But I'm getting ahead of my story.

One of the earliest memories of my childhood was a big party mother held at Skyridge, our country lodge. I was six years old. It was the night after James Roosevelt's re-election. Of all the public opinion diagnosticians, only mother had guessed right, and she and the top executives of the dozen-odd firms that retained her prophetic services congregated at Skyridge. I was supposed to be upstairs asleep, but the laughter and singing woke me up, and I came down and joined in. Nobody cared. Every time a man put his arm around mother and kissed her, I was there clutching at his coat pockets, howling, "He's *mine!*"

My technique altered as the years passed; my premise didn't.

Do you think it bothered her?

Ha!

The more I tried to take from her, the more amused she became. It wasn't a wry amusement. It gave her real belly laughs. How can you fight *that?* It just made me madder.

You might think I hadn't a shred of justice on my side. Actually, I did.

There was *one* thing that justified my hatred: she didn't really love me. I was her flesh and blood, but she didn't love me. Perhaps she was fond of me, in a lukewarm way, but her heart had no real love in it for me. And I knew it and hated her, and tried to take everything that was hers.

We must have seemed a strange pair. She never addressed me by my name, or even by a personal pronoun. She never even said such things as, "Dear, will you pass the toast?" Instead it was "May I have the toast?" It was as though she considered me a mere extension of herself, like another arm, which had no independent identity. It was galling.

Other girls could keep secrets from their mothers. I couldn't hide anything important from mine. The more I wanted to conceal something, the more certain she was to know it. That was another reason why I didn't mind being shipped off to Switzerland.

I'm sure she wasn't reading my mind. It wasn't telepathy. She couldn't guess phone numbers I had memorized, nor the names of the twenty-five boys on the county high school football team. Routine things like that generally didn't "get through." And telepathy wouldn't explain what happened the night my car turned over on the Sylvania Turnpike. The hands that helped pull me through the car window were hers. She had been parked by the roadside, waiting. No ambulance; just mother in her car. She had known where and when it would happen, and that I wouldn't be hurt.

After that night I was able to figure out all by myself that mother's business firm, Tomorrow, Inc., was based on something more than a knowledge of up-to-the-minute trends in economics, science, and politics.

But *what?*

I never asked her. I didn't think she would tell me, and I didn't want to give her the satisfaction of refusing an explanation. But perhaps that wasn't the only reason I didn't ask. I was also afraid to ask. Toward the end it was almost as though we had arrived at a tacit understanding that I was not to ask, because in good time I was going to find out without asking.

Tomorrow, Inc., made a great deal of money. Mother's success in predicting crucial public developments was uncanny. And she never guessed wrong. Naturally, her clients made even more money than she did, because they had more to invest initially. On her advice they plunged in the deeply depressed market two weeks before the Hague Conference arrived at the historic Concord of 1970. And it was mother who predicted the success of Bartell's neutronic-cerium experiments, in time for Cameron Associates to corner the world supply of monazite sand. And she was equally good at predicting Derby winners, Supreme Court decisions, elections, and that the fourth rocket to the moon would be the first successful one.

She was intelligent, but hardly in the genius class. Her knowledge of the business world was surprisingly limited. She never studied economics or extrapolated stock market curves. Tomorrow, Inc., didn't even have a news ticker in its swank New York office. And she was the highest paid woman in the United States in 1975.

In 1976, during the Christmas holidays, which I was spending with mother at Skyridge during my junior year at college, mother turned down a three-year contract with Lloyd's of London. I know this because I dug the papers out of the wastebasket after she tore them up. There were eight digits in the proposed annual salary. I knew she was making money, but not that kind. I called her to task.

"I can't take a three-year contract," she explained. "I can't even take a year's contract. Because I'm going to retire next month." She was looking away from me, out over the lodge balcony, into the wood. She couldn't see my expression. She murmured, "Did you know your mouth was open rather wide?"

"But you *can't* retire!" I clipped. And then I could have bitten my tongue off. My protest was an admission that I envied her and that I shone in her reflected fame. Well, she had probably known it anyhow. "All right," I continued sullenly. "You're going to retire. Where'll you go? What'll you do?"

"Why, I think I'll stay right here at Skyridge," she said blithely. "Just fixing up the place will keep me busy for a good many months. Take those rapids under the balcony, for instance. I think I'll just do away with them. Divert the stream, perhaps. I've grown a little tired of the sound of running water. And then there's all that dogwood out front. I've been considering cutting them all down and maybe putting in a landing field. You never know when a copter might come in handy. And then there's the matter of haystacks. I think we ought to have at least one somewhere on the place. Hay has such a nice smell, and they say it's so stimulating."

"Mother!"

Her brow knitted. "But where could I put a haystack?"

Just why she was using such a puerile method of baiting me I couldn't understand. "Why not in the ravine?" I said acidly. "It'll be dry after you divert the rapids. You'd be famous as the owner of the only ground-level haystack in New England."

She brightened immediately. "That's *it!* What a clever girl!"

"And what happens after you get him in the haystack?"

"Why, I guess I'll just keep him there."

"You *guess!*" I cried. (I'd finally trapped her!) "Don't you *know?*"

"I know only the things that are going to happen during the next six months—up until the stroke of midnight, June 3, 1977. As to what happens after that, I can't make any predictions."

"You mean you *won't.*"

"*Can't.* My retirement is not arbitrary."

I looked at her incredulously. "I don't understand. You mean—this ability—it's going to leave you—like *that?*" I snapped my fingers.

"Precisely,"

"But can't you stop it? Can't your psychiatrist do something?"

"Nobody could do anything for me even if I wanted him to. And I don't want to know what is going to happen after midnight, June 3."

With troubled eyes I studied her face.

At that moment, just as though she'd planned it, the clock began to chime, as if to remind me of our unwritten agreement not to probe into her strange gift.

The answer was only six months away. For the time being, I was willing to let it ride.

The epilog to our little conversation was this:

A couple of months later, after I was back at school in Zurich, a friend of mine wrote me (1) that the rapids had been diverted from the stream bed; (2) that just below the balcony the now dry ravine contained ten feet of fresh hay; (3) that the hay was rigged with electronic circuits to sound an alarm in the lodge if anyone went near it; (4) that the dogwood trees had been cut down; (5) that in their place stood a small landing field; (6) and that on the field there stood an ambulance copter, hired from a New York hospital, complete with pilot and interne.

"Anility," wrote my friend, "is supposed to develop early in some cases. You ought to come home."

I was having fun at school. I didn't want to come home. Anyway, if mother was losing her mind, there was nothing anybody could do. Furthermore, I didn't want to give up my plans for summering in Italy.

A month later, early in May, my friend wrote again.

It seems that the haystack alarm had gone off one night, two weeks previous, and mother and the servants had hurried down to find a bloody-faced one-eyed man crawling up the gravelly ravine bank. In one hand he was clutching an old pistol. According to reports, mother had the copter whisk him in to a New York hospital, where he still was. He was due to be discharged May 6. The next day, by my calculations.

There were details about how mother had redecorated two bedrooms at the lodge. I knew the bedrooms. They adjoined each other.

Even before I finished the letter I realized there was nothing the matter with mother's mind and never had been. That witch had foreseen all this.

The thing that *was* the matter, and which had apparently escaped everyone but me and mother, was that mother had finally fallen in love.

This was serious.

I canceled the remainder of the semester and the Italian tour and caught the first jet home. I didn't tell anyone I was coming.

So, when I paid off the taxi at the gatehouse, I was able to walk unannounced and unseen around the edge of the estate, and then cut in through the woods toward the ravine and lodge just beyond it.

The first thing I saw on emerging from the trees along the ravine bank was the famous bargain basement haystack. It was occupied.

The sun was shining, but it was early in May, and not particularly warm. Still, mother was wearing one of those new sun briefs that—well, you get the idea. I guess haystacks generate a lot of heat. Spontaneous combustion.

Mother was facing away from me, obstructing *his* one good eye. I hadn't made a sound, but I was suddenly aware of the fact that she had been expecting me and knew I was there.

She turned around, sat up, and smiled at me. "Hi there! Welcome home! Oh, excuse me, this is our good friend Doctor . . . ah . . . Brown. John Brown. Just call him Johnny." She picked a sliver of hay from her hair and flashed a grin at "Johnny."

I stared at them both in turn. Doctor Brown raised up on one elbow and returned my stare as amiably as the glaring black patch over his right eye would permit. "Hello, honey," he said gravely.

Then he and mother burst out laughing.

It was the queerest sound I'd ever heard. Just as though nothing on earth could ever again be important to either of them.

That summer I saw a lot of Johnny. Things got on an interesting basis very quickly. It wasn't long before he was giving me the kind of look that said, "I'd like to get involved—but . . . " And there he'd stop. Still, I figured that I was making more headway with him than I ever had with any of mother's previous friends.

Finally, though, his "thus far and no farther" response grew irritating. Then challenging. Then . . .

I guess it was being around him constantly, knowing that he and mother were the way they were, that made things turn out the way they did. In the process of trying to reel him in for closer inspection, I got pulled in myself. Eventually I became quite shameless about it. I began trying to get him off to myself at every opportunity.

We talked. But not about *him*. If he knew how he'd had his accident, and how he'd got here, he apparently never told anybody. At least he would never tell me.

We talked about magnetrons.

Don't look so surprised.

Like yourself he was an expert on magnetrons. I think he knew even more than you about magnetrons. And you thought you were the world's only expert, didn't you?

I pretended to listen to him, but I never understood more than the basic concepts—namely, that magnetrons were little entities sort of like electrons, sort of like gravitons, and sort of like I don't know what. But at least I grasped the idea that a magnetronic field could warp the flow of time, and that if you put an object in such a field, the results could be rather odd.

We talked a lot about magnetrons.

I planned our encounters hours, sometimes days, ahead. Quite early, I started borrowing mother's sun briefs. Later, at times when he *theoretically* wasn't around, I sunbathed *au naturel*. With no visible results except sunburn.

Toward the last I started sneaking out at night into the pines with my sleeping bag. I couldn't stand it, knowing where he probably was.

Not that I gave up.

He was building a magnetronic generator. The first in the world. I'd been helping him all one day to wire up some of his equipment.

He had torn down the balcony railing and was building his machine out on the balcony, right over the ravine. He could focus it, he said. I mean, there was a sort of "lens" effect in the magnetronic field, and he was supposed to be able to focus this field.

The queer thing was, that when he finally got the lens aligned, the focus was out in thin air, just beyond the edge of the balcony. Directly over the ravine. He didn't want anyone stumbling through the focus by accident.

And through this lens you could hear sounds.

The ravine had been dry for months, ever since mother had diverted the rapids. But now, coming through the lens, was this endless crash of water.

You could hear it all over the house.

The noise made me nervous. It seemed to subdue even *them*.

I didn't like that noise. I hauled my sleeping bag still farther into the pines. I could still hear it.

One night, a quarter of a mile from the house, I crawled out of my sleeping bag and started back toward the house. I was going to wake him up and ask him to turn the thing off.

At least, that was my excuse for returning. And it was perfectly true that I couldn't sleep.

I had it all figured out. Just how quietly I'd open his door, just how I'd tiptoe over to his bed. How I'd bend over him. How I'd put my hand on his chest and shake him, ever so gently.

Everything went as planned, up to a point.

There I was, leaning over his bed, peering through the dark at the blurry outlines of a prone figure.

I stretched out my hand.

It was not a male chest that I touched.

"What do you want?" mother whispered.

In the length of time it took me to get my breath back I decided that if *I* couldn't have him, *she* couldn't either. There comes a limit to all things. We were racing toward the showdown.

He always kept his old pistol on the table ledge, the one he'd brought with him. Soundlessly I reached for it and found it. I knew it was too dark for mother to see what I was now pointing toward her.

I had a clairvoyant awareness of my intent and its consequences. I even knew the place and the time. Murder was building up in Doctor John Brown's bedroom at Skyridge, and the time was five minutes of midnight, June 3, 1977.

"If that goes off," whispered mother calmly, "it'll probably awaken your father."

"My—*who?*" I gasped. The gun butt landed on my toe; I hardly knew I'd dropped it.

I heard what she'd said. But I suddenly realized it didn't make sense. They'd have told me long before, if it had been true. And he wouldn't have looked at me the way he did, day after day. She was lying.

She continued quietly: "Do you really want him?"

When one woman asks this question of another, it is ordinarily intended as an announcement of a property right, not a query, and the tone of voice ranges from subtle sardonicism to savage gloating.

But mother's voice was quiet and even.

"Yes!" I said harshly.

"Badly enough to have a child by him?"

I couldn't stop now. "Yes."

"Can you swim?"

"Yes," I parroted stupidly. It was obviously not a time for logic or coherence. There we were, two witches bargaining in life and death, while the bone of our contention slumbered soundly just beyond us.

She whispered: "Do you know when he is from?"

"You mean *where?*"

"*When.* He's from 1957. In 1957 he fell into a magnetronic field—into my 1977 haystack. The lens—out there—is focused—"

"—on 1957?" I breathed numbly.

"*Early* 1957," she corrected. "It's focused on a day a couple of months prior to the moment he fell into the lens. If you really want him, all you've got to do is jump through the lens, find him in 1957, and hang on to him. Don't let him fall into the magnetronic field."

I licked my lips. "And suppose he does, anyway?"

"I'll be waiting for him."

"But you already have him. If I should go back, how could I stop something that has already happened?"

"If you hold on to him in 1957, this particular stereochronic alternate of 1977 must collapse, just as though it never happened."

My head was whirling. "But, if I go back to 1957, how can I be sure of finding him in time? Suppose he's on safari in South Africa?"

"You'll find him, right here. He spent the spring and summer of 1957 here at Skyridge. The lodge has always been his property."

I couldn't see her eyes, but I knew they were laughing at me.

"The matter of a child," I said curtly. "What's that got to do with him?"

"Your only chance of holding him permanently," she said coolly, "is the child."

"*The* child?"

I couldn't make any sense out of it. I stopped trying.

For a full minute there was silence, backgrounded by the gentle rasp of Johnny's breathing and the singing water twenty years away.

I blinked my eyes rapidly.

I was going to have Johnny. I was going back to 1957. Suddenly I felt jaunty, exhilarated.

The hall clock began to chime midnight.

Within a few seconds, June 3, 1977 would pass into history. Mother would be washed up, a has-been, unable to predict even the weather.

I kicked off my slippers and pajamas. I gauged the distance across the balcony. My voice got away from me. "Mother!" I shrieked. "Give us one last prediction!"

Johnny snorted violently and struggled to sit up.

I launched my soaring dive into time. Mother's reply floated after me, through the lens, and I heard it in 1957.

"You didn't stop him."

His real name was James McCarren. He *was* a genuine Ph.D., though, a physics professor. Age, about 40. Had I expected him to be younger? He seemed older than "Johnny." And he had two good eyes. No patch.

He owned Skyridge, all right. Spent his summers there. Liked to hunt and fish between semesters.

And now, my friend, if you'll just relax a bit, I'll tell you what happened on the night of August 5, 1957.

I was leaning over the balcony, staring down at the red-lit tumult of the rapids, when I became aware that Jim was standing in the doorway behind me. I could feel his eyes sliding along my body.

I had been breathing deeply a moment before, trying to slow down the abnormal surging of my lungs, while simultaneously attempting to push Jim's pistol a little higher under my armpit. The cold steel made me shiver.

It was too bad. For during the past two months I had begun to love him in a most interesting way, though, of course, not in the much *more* interesting way I had loved Johnny. (A few weeks with mother can really change a man!) In 1957 Johnny—or Jim—was quaintly solicitous, oddly virginal. Almost fatherly. It was too bad that I was beginning to love him as Jim.

Still, there was mother's last prediction. I had thought about it a long time. So far as I could see, there was only one way to make sure he didn't "go through" to her.

"Come on out," I said, turning my face up to be kissed.

After he had released me, I said, "Do you realize it's been exactly two months since you fished me out of there?"

"The happiest months of my life," he said.

"And you still haven't asked me how I happened to be there—who I am— anything. You're certainly under no illusion that I gave that justice of the peace my right name?"

He grinned. "If I got too curious, you might vanish back into the whirlpool, like a water nymph."

It was really sad. I shrugged bitterly. "You and your magnetrons."

He started. "*What?* Where did you ever hear about magnetrons? I've never discussed them with anyone!"

"Right here. From you."

His mouth opened and closed slowly. "You're out of your mind!"

"I wish I were. That would make everything seem all right. For, after all, it's only after you get to thinking about it logically that you can understand how impossible it is. It's got to stop, though, and now is the time to stop it."

"Stop *what?*" he demanded.

"The way you and I keep jumping around in time. Especially you. If I don't stop you, you'll go through the lens, and mother will get you. It was her last prediction."

"Lens?" he gurgled.

"The machine. You know, the one with the magnetrons."

"Huh?"

"None of that exists yet, of course," I said, talking mostly to myself. "At least, not outside of your head. You won't build the generator until 1977."

"I can't get the parts now." His voice was numb.

"They'll be available in 1977, though."

"In 1977 . . . ?"

"Yes. After you build it in 1977, you'll focus it back to 1957, so that you *could* jump through, now, into 1977, that is. Only I'm not going to let you. When mother made her last prediction she couldn't have known to what lengths I'd go to stop you."

He passed his hand plaintively over his face. "But . . . but . . . even assuming you're from 1977, and even assuming I'll build a magnetronic generator in 1977, I can't just jump into 1977 and build it. I certainly can't move forward in time to 1977 through a magnetronic field that won't be generated and beamed backwards to 1957 until I arrive in 1977 and generate it. That's as silly as saying that the Pilgrims built the *Mayflower* at Plymouth Rock. And anyway, I'm a husband who'll soon be a father. I haven't the faintest intention of running out on my responsibilities."

"And yet," I said, "if the sequence proceeds normally, you will leave me . . . for *her*. Tonight you're my lawful husband, the father of our child to be. Then— bing! You're suddenly in 1977—wife-deserter, philanderer, and mother's lover. I won't let that happen. After all I've been through, I *won't* let her get you. My blood goes into a slow boil just thinking about her, smiling way up there in 1977, thinking how she got rid of me so she could eventually have you all to herself. And me in my condition." My voice broke in an artistic tremolo.

"I *could* age normally," he said. "I could simply wait until 1977 and *then* build the generator."

"You didn't, though—that is, I mean you *won't*. When I last saw you in 1977 you looked even younger than you do now. Maybe it was the patch."

He shrugged his shoulders. "If your presence *here* is a direct consequence of my presence *there*, then there's nothing either of us can do to change the sequence. I don't want to go through. And what could happen to force me through I can't even guess. But we've got to proceed on the assumption that I'll go, and you'll be left stranded. We've got to make plans. You'll need money. You'll probably have to sell Skyridge. Get a job, after the baby comes. How's your shorthand?"

"They'll use vodeographs in 1977," I muttered. "But don't you worry, you cheap two-timer. Even if you succeeded in running off to mother, the baby and I'll get along. As a starter, I'm going to put the rest of your bank account on Counterpoint to win the Preakness next Saturday. After that—"

But he had already switched to something else. "When you knew me in 1977, were we—ah—intimate?"

I snorted. "Depends on who 'we' includes."

"What? You mean . . . *I* . . . and your *mother* . . . *really* . . . ? He coughed and ran his finger around his collar. "There must be some simple explanation."

I just sneered at him.

He giggled. "Your mother—ah—in 1977—a good-looking woman, I gather?"

"A wrinkled, painted harridan," I said coldly. "Forty, if she's a day."

"Hmph! *I'm* forty, you know. Contrary to the adolescent view, it's the best time of life. You'll feel the same way about it in another twenty years."

"I suppose so," I said. "They'll be letting me out of the penitentiary about then."

He snapped his fingers suddenly. "I've got it! Fantastic!" He turned away and looked out over the balcony, like Cortez on his peak. "Fantastic, but it hangs together. Completely logical. Me. Your mother. You. The child. The magnetrons. The eternal cycle."

"This isn't making it easier for me," I said reproachfully. "The least you could do would be to remain sane until the end."

He whirled on me. "Do you know where *she* is—now—tonight?"

"No, and I spent two-thirds of our joint bank account trying to locate her. It's just as though she never existed."

His eyes got bigger and bigger. "No wonder you couldn't find her. You couldn't know."

"Know what?"

"Who your mother is."

I wanted to scream at him. "Oh," I said.

But he was off on another tangent. "But it's not entirely without precedent. When a cell divides, which of the resultant two cells is the mother? Which the daughter? The answer is, that the question itself is nonsense. And so with you. The cell divides in space; you divide in time. It's nonsense to ask which of you is mother, which is daughter."

I just stood there, blinking.

He rambled on. "Even so, why should I want to 'go through'? That's the only part that's not clear. Why should I deliberately skip twenty years of life with you? Who'd take care of you? How could you earn a living? But you must have. Because you didn't have to sell Skyridge. You stayed here. You educated *her*. But of course!" He smacked his fist into his palm.

"Simplest thing in the world," he howled happily. "Counterpoint at the Preakness. You'll become a professional predictor. Sports. Presidential elections. Supreme Court decisions. All in advance. You've got to *remember*. Train your ability to recall. Big money in it!"

My mouth was hanging open.

"Isn't that what happens?" he shouted.

"I know all the headlines already," I stammered. "Only that's the business *mother* started . . . predicting for a living . . ."

"Mother . . . mother . . . *mother!*" he mimicked. "By the great Chronos, child! Can't you face it? Does your mind refuse to accept the fact that you and your 'mother' and your unborn daughter are iden—"

I screamed, "No!"

I pulled out the pistol.

I raised it slowly, as though I had all the time in the world, and shot him through the head.

Even before he hit the floor I had grabbed his right hand and was flexing his fingers around the handle.

A moment later I was out the door and racing toward the garage.

I thought it would be best to "find" his body on returning from a shopping expedition in the village, where I had happened to pick up a couple of friends. The only thing wrong with this plan was that he wasn't there when I returned with my witnesses.

It was generally agreed that James McCarren had become lost in the woods while hunting. Poor fellow must have starved to death, they supposed. Neither he nor the pistol were ever found. A few months later he was declared legally dead, and I collected his insurance.

The coroner and the D.A. did give me a bad moment when they discovered some thin smudges of dried blood leading toward the edge of the balcony. But nothing turned up, of course, when they dragged the whirlpool. And when I informed them of my condition, their unvoiced suspicions turned to sympathy.

From then on, I had plenty of time to think. Particularly during the first lean months of Tomorrow, Inc., before I landed my first retainer.

And what I thought was this: what other woman ever had a man who loved her so much, even after she had shot him through the eye, that he would willingly drag himself after her, through twenty years, to claim her again, sight unseen?

The very least I could do was to drain the ravine and break your fall with this haystack.

Do you honestly like my new sun brief? The red and green checks go nicely with the yellow hay, don't they? Do you really want me to come over and sit by you? Oh, don't worry about interruptions. The servants are down in the village, and she won't come sneaking around through the woods for an hour yet . . . Ooooh, *Johnny!*

For ten years I had been very busy just being a patent attorney, and hadn't written anything. But now Shan was heading off to college, and I was looking at new expenses. Time to get back into the arena. Write what you know about, the experts say. So I wrote this little novelette about life in a patent department in a chemical laboratory. Plus ghosts . . . plus a demon . . . stuff that ordinarily would make John Campbell turn purple. But he took it anyway.

The locale is real. The lab is right up the road from where I live. The little woodlot, the stream, the stone desk (sinking slowly into the creek) are my own. The lilacs (now dead) were genuine Charles Joli's. (Wife Nell called them "Jolly Chollies.") How did she and Shan react to the story? They eventually forgave me. I think.

An Ornament
to His Profession

The world has different owners at sunrise . . . Even your own garden does not belong to you.

— Anne Lindbergh

Conrad Patrick reached over and shut off the alarm. The dream of soft flesh and dark hair faded into six o'clock of a Friday morning. Patrick lay there a moment, pushing Lilas out of his thoughts, keeping his mind dark with the room, his body numb.

To move was to accept wakefulness, and this was unthinkable, for wakefulness must lead to knowledge, and then the problem barbs would begin to do their ulcerous work in his brain. They would begin, one by one, until all were in hideous clamor. None of them seemed ever to get really solved, and getting rid of one didn't necessarily mean he had solved it. More often, getting rid of it just meant he had found some sort of neutralizing paralysis, or that he had once more increased his pain threshold.

Patrick got up heavily, found his robe and slippers, and stumbled into the bathroom, where he turned on the light and surveyed his face with overt distaste. It was a heavy, fleshy face, and the red hair and mustache were awry. He was not exactly thin, but not really fat, either. His cheeks and stomach showed the effects of myriad beers in convivial company. He considered these beers, these cheerful hours, one by one, going back, in a mirrored moment of wonder and gratitude. He considered what life would have been like without them, and as the realization hit, his forehead creased uneasily. He scowled, dashed water over his eyes, and reached for a towel.

"Patrick," he muttered to himself in the mirror, "it's Friday. Another day has begun, and still the Company hasn't found you out."

Patrick no longer knew exactly what he meant by this routine, which he had started some years before, when he was the newest chemical patent attorney with Hope Chemicals. He had first been a chemist, but not a very good one, and then, after he and Lilas had got married, he had gone to law school at night. After he got his LL.B. he had discovered, with more fatalism than dismay, that he was not a very good lawyer, either. Yet, all was by no means lost. He was accepted by Hope's Patent Department. And not just barely accepted; he was accepted as an excellent chemical patent attorney. He found this incredible, but he did not fight it. And finally, he deliberately masked his supposed deficiencies; when he was in the company of chemists, he spoke as a lawyer, and when with lawyers, he was a chemist. And when with the chemical patent lawyers, he didn't mind being just a fifty-fifty chemist-lawyer. They had his problem, too. It was like group therapy. Patent lawyers had a profound sympathy for each other.

From the beginning he had thrown himself into his work with zest. And now, with Lilas and the baby gone, his work was not just an opiate; it was a dire necessity.

He got the kettle boiling in the kitchen. There was now a pink glow in the east. He looked out the kitchen window and almost smiled. It was going to be a beautiful morning. He made the coffee quickly, four spoons of coffee powder in his pint mug, took the first bitter, exhilarating sip, tightened his robe about him, stepped out the kitchen door, and padded off down the garden path, holding his coffee mug carefully.

This, again, was all part of his morning routine. Today, of course, there was a special reason. Theoretically the house and grounds were ready and waiting for the little party tonight, but it would do no harm to take a look around, down by the pool.

The flagstone path lay down a grassy slope, and was lined with azaleas. He and Lilas had put them in together. At the foot of the slope was a tiny stream, fed mostly by a spring half a mile away, on his neighbor's property. In this little stream Patrick had contrived a series of pools by dint of fieldstone and mortar, slapped together with such indolence into the stream side that the result was a pleasing but entirely accidental naturalness. These little pools were bordered with water cress, cat-o'-nine-tails, arrowhead, water iris, and lovely things with names he could no longer remember. He and Lilas had splurged one summer and bought all manner of water plants by mail. They had got very muddy planting them, and they had sorrowed over those that had died the next spring or that the baby had happily yanked. And then suddenly everything had begun to grow like weeds, and in a wild way, it was all very pretty.

The path along the stream led toward a grassy sward. Patrick stopped on the path a moment, and listened. Yes, there it was, very faint, like a tinkling of tiny bells. He held his breath. Around the turn of the path, and so far invisible, was the bench. He and Lilas used to sit here, overlooking the lily pond. Only then, of course, it wasn't the lily pond, but the baby's wading pool. It was . . . how long ago? . . . that she had splashed in the pool and her baby delight had shattered the garden peace. And that was what he heard now. And he could hear Lilas' answering laughter. This had happened to him on many past mornings. To him, it was not a conjured thing; it was faint, very far away, but it was real.

He began to walk again, and rounded the bend in the path. But as soon as the pool and the bench came in view, the sounds stopped abruptly. He had tried to deal with the phenomenon logically. This led him to various alternative conclusions, neither of which he completely disbelieved: (a) he was subject to hallucinations; (b) Lilas and the baby were really there.

Patrick sighed and looked about him. Here, all within a few steps of each other, were the lily pool, the benches, the outdoor grill, and the arbor. The arbor was a simple structure, framed with two-by-fours, bordered with lilacs that had never bloomed, and which enclosed his "work table." This was a stone-stepped table with a drawer, which contained writing materials and a few scribbled pages.

He looked into the arbor. From somewhere up in the ceiling of honeysuckle there was a flutter of wings. Sparrows. The "room" seemed to concentrate the odor of grass clippings, fresh from yesterday's mowing. Patrick glanced over at the stone table, and permitted himself the habitual morning question: Would he have a few moments to work on his article? This was followed by a prompt companion thought: He was being stupid even to think about it. In three years he had not even finished the first chapter. And already the Court of Customs and Patent Appeals had wrought far-reaching revisions in the law of prior printed publication. Maybe he should pick another subject. An article he could do quickly, get into print quickly, before the Court could hand down a modifying decision. Somehow, there must be a way to get this thing off dead center. A top-flight professional in any field ought to publish. Not that he was really that good. Still, as Francis Bacon had said, a man owed a debt to his profession.

He opened the drawer and pulled out the sheaf of papers. But he knew that he wasn't going to work on it this morning. A breeze fluttered the sheets. His eye cast about for a paperweight and found the candle-bottle; a stub of candle sticking in the neck of a wine bottle, used when he sat here at night and did not want to use the floodlights. He put the bottle on the papers.

Glumly he accepted his first inadequacy of the day. No use trying to hold the others back. The line forms to the right. The magic was gone from the morning; so be it. Let them come. He finished off his coffee. In his own garden he was a match for all of them. He felt girded and armored.

They came.

One. His department was about to lose a secretary—Sullivan's Miss Willow. He hadn't told Sullivan. But maybe Sullivan knew already. Maybe even Miss Willow knew. These things always seemed to get around. He didn't mind interdepartmental promotions for the girls. He'd used it himself on occasion. But he didn't like the way Harvey Jayne was using company personnel policy to pressure him. And right now was a bad time to lose a secretary, with all those Neol cases to get out. As an army travels on its stomach, so his Patent Department traveled on its typewriters, or, more exactly, on the flying fingers of its stenographers as applied to the keys of those typewriters, "thereby to produce," as they say in patentese, a daily avalanche of specifications, amendments, appeals, contracts, and opinions.

He halfway saw an angle here. Maybe he could boomerang the whole thing back on Harvey Jayne. Have to be careful, though. Jayne was a vice-president.

Two, and getting worse. Jayne wanted publication clearance for the "Neol Technical Manual," and he wanted it today. It had to be cleared for legal form, proofread, and back to the printers tonight, because bright and early Monday morning twenty-five crisp and shining copies, smelling beautifully of printer's ink, had to be on that big table in the Directors' Room. Monday, the Board was going to vote on whether the company would build a six-million-dollar Neol plant.

Three, and still worse. John Fast, Neol pilot plant manager, wanted the Patent Department to write a very special contract. Consideration, soul of the party of the first part, in return for, inter alia, guarantee of success with Neol. It was impossible, and there was something horrid and sick in it, and yet Patrick was having the contract written by Sullivan, his contract expert, and in fact the first draft should be ready this morning. He was *not* going to refer Fast to the company psychiatrist. At least not yet. Maybe in two or three weeks, after Fast was through helping Sullivan get those new Neol cases on file in the Patent Office, he might casually mention this situation to the psychiatrist. Why did it always happen this way? Nobody could just go quietly insane without involving him. Forever and ever, people like John Fast sought him out, involved him, and laid their madness upon him, like a becoming mantle.

Fourth, and absolutely and unendurably the worst. The patent structure for the whole Neol process was in jeopardy. The basic patent application, bought by the company from an "outside" inventor two years before, was now known to Patrick, and to several of the senior attorneys in his department, to be a phony, a hoax, a thing discovered to have been created in ghastly jest—by a man in his own department. This was the thing that really got him. He could think of nothing, no way to deal with it. The jester, Paul Bleeker, was the son of Andy Bleeker, his old boss and good friend. (Did anybody have any real friends at this crazy place any more?) And that was really why he had come up with an answer. It would kill Andy if this got out. Certainly, he and both Bleekers would probably have to resign. After that there would come the slow, crushing hearings of the Committee on Disbarment.

Problems.

Was this why he couldn't write, why he couldn't even get started? He blinked, shook his head. Only then did he realize that he was still staring, unseeing, at the handwritten notes in front of him.

He leafed slowly through the scribblings. How long ago had he started the article? Months? Nearly three years ago, in fact. He had wanted to do something comprehensive, to attain some small measure of fame. This was the real reason lawyers wrote. Or was it? Some time soon, he'd have to re-examine this thing, lay bare his real motives. It was just barely conceivable it would be something quite unpleasant. He gave a last morose look at the title page, "The College Thesis as Prior Art in Chemical Patent Interferences," and put the papers back in the envelope. He just didn't know how to put this thing back on the rails. Fundamentally he must be just plain lazy.

But time was wasting. He looked at his wristwatch, put the papers back, closed the drawer, and walked out to the lily pond again.

It was in the same wet sparkle of sunlight that he remembered his baby daughter, splashing in naked glee that warm summer day so many months ago. Lilas had stood there and called the baby out of the pool to get dressed, for that fatal Saturday afternoon trip to the shopping center. And his daughter had climbed out of the pool, ignored the tiny terry cloth robe, and dashed dripping wet into her father's arms. At least her front got dried as he held her writhing wetness against his shirt, patting her dancing little bottom with the palm of his hand.

Slowly he sat down again. It must have been that sunbeam on the pool. It was going to be bad. He began to shudder. He wanted to scream. He bent over and buried his face in his hands. For a time he breathed in noisy rasps. Finally he stood up again, wiped his gray face on the sleeve of his robe, and started back up the garden path to the house. He would have to be on his way to the office. As soon as he got to the office, he would be all right.

> *'Tis all a Chequer-board of Nights and Days*
> *Where Destiny with Men for Pieces plays . . .*
> — Omar Khayyam

Patrick sometimes had the impression that he was just a pawn on Alec Cord's chessboard. Cord was always looking seven moves deep, and into a dozen alternate sequences. Patrick sighed. He had long suspected that they were all smarter than he was, certainly each doing his job better than Patrick could do it. It was only the trainees that he could really teach anything anymore, and even here he had to fight to find the time. Nothing about it made sense. The higher you rose in the company, the less you knew about anything, and the more you had to rely on the facts and appraisals developed by people under you. They could make a better patent search than he; they could write a better patent specification, and do it faster; they could draft better and more comprehensive infringement opinions. In a gloomy moment he had wondered whether it was the same way throughout the company, and if so, why had the company nevertheless grown into the Big Ten of the American chemical industry? But he never figured it out.

He looked up at his lieutenant. "I understand it was the crucial game, in the last round. If you beat Gadsen, you won the tournament, and if he beat you, he won."

"Didn't realize you followed the sports page, Con," said Alec Cord.

"Gadsen had white, and opened with the Ruy Lopez. You defended with Marshall's Counter Gambit. They gave the score in the paper. Somebody said it was identical, move for move, with a game between Marshall and Capablanca, in 1918, when Marshall first pulled his gambit on Capablanca."

"I wouldn't know."

"That's a surprise. They say you even had an article in *Chess Review* last year on the Marshall Counter Gambit."

Cord was silent. Patrick took a new tack. "Gadsen's that Examiner in Group 170, the one handling your Neol cases?"

"That's right."

"Including the basic case, the one we know now is the phony? The one our whole Neol plant depends on?"

"The very one."

"The one you would have given just about anything, even the Annual D.C. Chess Tournament, for Gadsen to allow?"

"All right, Con. But it's not what you think. I didn't throw the tournament. And Gadsen didn't throw the allowance. We didn't discuss it at all. I admit I let him win that game, but there wasn't any deal. It would have to occur to him, with no help from me, that there was something he owed me. He could have done it either way, and I'd have had no kick. Maybe he'd have given the allowance anyhow. In fact, for all you know, maybe he allowed the case despite the game, and not because of it."

"I won't argue the point, Alec. We may never know. Anyhow, the thing I came to see you about is this." He handed the other a legal-size sheet.

Cord's eyes widened. "An interference!"

"So maybe Gadsen allowed the claims just to set you up for an interference."

"Maybe. But not likely. If he were going to do that, he would have just sent the interference notice, this thing, without the allowance."

"Any ideas who the other party is?"

"Probably Du Santo. We've been picking up their foreign patents in the quick-issue countries, like Belgium. We'll know for sure after the inventors file their preliminary statements. Which brings me to the next question: How can we file a preliminary statement sworn to by a phony inventor who doesn't even exist?"

"I don't know. I want you to figure out something after we talk to Paul Bleeker."

"Take it from the beginning, Paul," said Patrick.

Paul Bleeker's face rippled with misery.

Cord said: "Maybe I'd better go."

"Stay put," said Patrick shortly. "Paul, you understand why we have to have Alec in on this. You're emotionally involved. You might not be able to do what has to be done. Alec has to listen to everything, so he and I together can plan what to do. You trust him, don't you?"

The young man nodded.

"It began as sort of a joke . . . ?" prompted Patrick.

"Yes, a joke," said Paul. "When I was a freshman in law school. Harvey Jayne and those others were teasing Dad. That was when Dad was still Director of the Research Division, before they promoted him."

The light was dawning. Patrick sat up. "They were teasing him about the Research Division?"

"Yes, then Mr. Jayne said Dad's Research Division was essential, but only to verify outside inventions he bought."

"So you decided to booby-trap Mr. Jayne?"

"Yes."

"You then wrote those patent attorneys in Washington?"

"Yes, I mailed them the examples for the patent application. They took them and changed them around a little bit, the same way we do here in the Patent Department. They added the standard gobbledygook at the front, and eight or ten claims at the back. They sent the final draft back to me for execution. The standard procedure. They sent me a bill for three hundred dollars. I paid that out of the money Mr. Jayne sent them, when he bought the invention. I still have the rest—four thousand and seven hundred dollars. I haven't spent any of it." He looked uncertainly at Patrick. "You won't tell Dad about this, will you?"

"Certainly not." Patrick looked at him with genuine curiosity. "But how were you able to make the oath? What notary would notarize the signature of 'Percy B. Shelley'?"

"Absolutely any, Con. They all just assume you are who you say you are, so long as you pay the fee."

Patrick was momentarily shaken. "But that's the whole idea of notarizing, to make the inventor swear he's truly the inventor, the person named in the oath."

Cord smiled faintly. "Not all notaries waive identification, Con."

"Well," said Patrick, "now we've committed perjury, sworn falsely to the United States Patent Office. So far, all they can do to you, Paul, besides disbarring you, followed by imprisonment in the Federal Penitentiary, is to strike your Shelley case from the files in the Patent Office."

The young man was silent.

Cord said: "Harvey Jayne bought the patent application only after he knew it worked. The whole thing depended on whether John Fast could reproduce it in the lab. Paul, how could you be so sure it would work?"

"If John did it right, it couldn't *not* work. I copied the examples right out of something in the library. Somebody's college thesis."

Patrick brightened. "Alec?"

Cord shook his head. "Nothing like that ever turned up in our literature searches. We hit the Dissertation Abstracts, all the way back to the beginning."

Patrick turned back to Paul Bleeker. "You'll have to tell us more about this thesis. What was the name of the student? We'd also like the name of the university, and the year. In fact, anything and everything you can remember."

"All I can remember is these runs, tucked away in the back pages. They didn't really seem pertinent to the main body of the thesis. Other than that, I can't remember anything."

"You must have seen the title page," pressed Patrick.

"I guess so."

"You could identify it if you saw the thesis again?"

"Sure, but it's gone."

"Gone?"

"The library just had it on loan. They have hundreds come in, this way. Our people keep them a while, then send them back. You know the procedure."

"There must be some record."

Cord shook his head. "We've checked all the inter-library loans for the past five years. We found nothing. If Paul's memory is correct on the facts, that it *was* within the last five years, and the library *did* have it on loan, we are led to the conclusion that the thesis was done by somebody here at Hope, and lent on a personal basis to the library, without any formal record."

Patrick groaned. "Our own inventor, here all the time? That's all we need. He'll scream. He'll take it to court. We've got to find him first, before he finds us." He turned to Cord. "Alec, add it all up for us, will you?"

"It admits of precise calculation," said Cord, "in the manner of a chess combination. There are two primary variations. Each of these has several main subvariations. None of them is really difficult. The only problem is to recognize that our tactics are absolutely controlled, move by move, by events as they develop."

Patrick raised his hand. "Not so fast. Let's take the main angles. The primary variations."

"First primary. We do nothing. If we're senior party in the interference, this means we take no testimony, but rely purely on our filing date. Chances: better than even. If we're junior party, we lose hands down.

"Second primary. We fight. Firstly, this gives subvariant A. With Paul's help we find the real inventor. We buy his invention from him, and, if he hasn't already published, we file a good and true application for him. We enter a motion to substitute the new case for Paul's case, and then we expressly abandon Paul's case. If this inventor actually has published in the way Paul remembers, this gives subvariant B. We find that thesis, then we move to dissolve the interference, contending that the sole count is unpatentable over the disclosures in the thesis."

Patrick twisted his mustache nervously. "However you state it, we wind up with no chance of a patent. Maybe we can live with that. Perhaps we can forgo a patent-based monopoly. But there's one thing we *must* have—and that's the right to build the plant, free and clear from interference or infringement of anybody else's patent. Can we tell the Board we have that right? The Board wants to know. They're going to vote on it Monday. And I don't think we can tell them anything . . . not yet. The economics and market are there. Everything hangs on the patent situation. Bleeker says the vote will be to build, if the patent picture is clear. We're holding the whole thing up in our shop right here." He turned back to Cord. "Alec, take it from the college thesis. Run the variations off from that."

"Variation One," said Cord, "the thesis is a good reference. This means it adequately describes the invention, that it was at least typewritten, that it was placed on the shelves at the University Library, available to all who might ask for it, and that all of this was done more than one year before either Paul or his opponent filed their respective cases. This would support the motion to dissolve. Both parties would lose, and neither would get a patent, fraudulent or otherwise. With no basic patent to be infringed, it follows that anybody could build a Neol plant. Paul's application would be given a prompt final rejection and would be transferred to the abandoned files in the Patent Office. Then it would lie buried until destroyed under the twenty-year rule. Nobody would ever learn about it.

"Variation Two. The thesis for some reason is not citable as a good, sufficient, and competent reference under the Patent Office rules. For example, we might not find it in time, or if we do find it, it might really present substantial differences from Paul's disclosure. Even if we are senior party, we will not be able to negotiate a settlement of the interference without grave danger of discovery of what Paul did. If we turn out to be junior party, it's even more certain we can't settle the interference, but there's actually less risk of being found out, if only because the opposition won't talk to us."

Patrick's mouth dropped. "All right. We always come back to the thesis. We've got to find it. If we find it, we can build a Neol plant. If we can't find it, we can't build a plant, and even worse things will probably happen to a number of people in this company." He turned to Cord. "Have you and Paul exhausted every possibility, every lead?"

Cord nodded glumly. Paul Bleeker bent over and put his face in his hands.

Patrick sighed. He thought, "I'll have to do it the hard way. Tonight." He said, "Paul, you'll be over tonight, won't you?"

"Yes, Con."

"Thanks, fellows. Paul, would you ask Sullivan to come in?"

He must needes goe whom the devill doth drive.
— John Heywood

Patrick smiled at Sullivan. "Good morning, Mike. How are those Neol cases coming?"

"We're in good shape. John Fast and I will need a couple of more weeks, though. It's a whole series of cases. Covers the catalysts, the whole pilot-plant set up, the vapor phase job, everything. John and I get together every morning and dictate this stuff to Willow. She types her notes in the afternoon. Except that as of now she's about a week behind in transcription. If she left right now, the Neol patent cases would be in quite a hole."

Patrick met Sullivan's studied gaze noncommittally. "He knows," he thought. "They all know about Willow." He said easily, "I guess you're right. How about John? Will he stick with your program?"

Sullivan shrugged his shoulders. "He'd better. We need him. But, like I said, he needs us, too. And he insisted that you approve the contract. Do you want to see it?"

Patrick shifted uncomfortably. "It's nearly ten o'clock. He'll be here in a minute. You can read it to both of us, then."

Sullivan smiled. "You're getting off easy."

Patrick said, "I know what you're thinking, Mike. And you're right. We *are* going to turn him over to the psychiatrist. But not just yet. Not until you get these last three Neol disclosures written up. Another couple of weeks won't hurt him."

Sullivan's smile deepened.

Patrick said, "Medically, it certainly can't hurt to humor him."

Sullivan laughed. "Con, you're a sham, a fraud, and a hypocrite. Preserve him long enough for him to file his cases, then let him drop dead."

Patrick bridled. "That's putting it a little strong. If I thought for a moment . . ."

"Oh, come off it, Con. We're all on edge with this thing. Anyhow, you can take comfort in the thought that the Patent Department has simply ground out one more contract, one out of a hundred a year, doing their daily hacking, what they are paid to do, and therefore what they rejoice in doing. If you look at it that way, you have served your client to the very best of your ability, and at night you can sleep with sound conscience."

Patrick growled, "If I didn't need you—"

Sullivan held up his hand. "Speak of the devil—"

"Come in," called Patrick.

John Fast entered the room. He was an average looking man, average size, of an average grayness. His face was almost without expression, perhaps a little sad. There was something unnerving in his eyes. They were acquainted with—

"Horror?" thought Patrick, wondering. No. That was too simple. John Fast was acquainted with the sub-elements of horror, with the building stones of terror, and with the unrest of darkness. And this was the man whom he would need tonight. "Hello, John," he said genially. "I hear your Neol cases are going a mile a minute."

"Going nicely, Con, thanks." Fast looked at Sullivan, then back at Patrick. "Is my contract ready?"

"Contract? Yes, of course, the contract. Mike and I have been going over it. Before we read it to you, though, we'd like to make sure we've covered everything. Now Mike here has heard your story, but I haven't. I'd like to hear it from you, straight, exactly the way it happened."

"It's a long story, Con."

"We've got lots of time."

"All right, then." Fast took a deep breath; his eyes grew distant. "I think it began with the ozonator. You know what ozone smells like? It's sharp, electric. In certain concentrations it's hard to distinguish from chlorine or sulfur dioxide. You know how the Bible talks about brimstone? Brimstone is sulfur, but there wasn't any sulfur in Palestine. The old prophets were just trying to identify an odor that was there long before they learned about sulfur. This creature moves in an atmosphere of ozone. He moves around in time and space, and to do this he applies an electrical field on the space-time continuum. Ozone is sort of a by-product, the same as when you run an electric motor. So this thing moves around in a fog of ozone. Not only that, ozone seems to attract him, the way nectar attracts bees.

"For a long time I didn't really realize he was around. And then last week I met him. It might have been an accident. But with all this Freudian theory, maybe there's no such thing as an accident. Maybe, on a subconscious level, I did it deliberately. Anyhow, you know we have a big structural formula of pentacyclopropane drawn in white paint on the floor of the pilot plant. This makes a star, with the methylene groups as the five points. It is also a pentagram—a starlike geometric design used in certain . . . rituals. Within the history of the United States, people have been burnt for making a pentagram. The stage was set. Just one more thing was needed: the Lord's Prayer recited backwards. This was provided. I'm a steady churchgoer. Bible class on Sunday mornings. Last Sunday I took my office tape recorder to Bible class. Yes, we said the Lord's Prayer. It was still on the tape when I was going to dictate my monthly progress report. I rewound the tape, so there it was, everything going backwards on audio. I was inside the pentagram. And suddenly, there—it—was, on the other side. I was so scared I was petrified. I wasn't surprised. Just scared. Maybe that means I knew what I was doing. So we stared at each other. Except I wasn't sure what I was staring at. But it was definitely a shape, with arms, head, eyes . . ."

"You were tired," said Patrick. "You know how fatigue can induce hallucinations."

"It's not that simple, Con. There—*was*—there *is*—something there, some kind of elemental force, It's a being, an intelligent being. And powerful, in strange ways. It can . . . alter the laws of chemistry and physics. I got it to increase the yield of terpineol—'Neol'. At first, by about ten per cent. Then another ten per cent. It was easy. And then last night we started up the pilot plant. We ran the C-10 through first, cold, just to flush the lines and check the flowmeters. We got the ozonator tied in about midnight. Now you understand the ozone won't start reacting with the C-10 until you hit about one sixty F., and we'd planned to turn steam into the jacket after the ozone concentration had built up to about five per cent. But the reactor began to warm up. It hit one sixty in a matter of seconds. The two technicians on shift were scared. They ran over behind the explosion mat. I stayed put. I knew what was going on. *He* was doing it. I wanted to know how far he could push it. I shunted the C-10 through the flowmeter. I switched in the product receiver. It took about thirty minutes to feed one pound mole of C-10 . . . exactly one hundred and thirty pounds. I shut everything off. I had been watching the product scales all along, so I knew what it was going to be. It was one hundred fifty-four pounds, one pound mole of Neol, exactly. Yield: one hundred per cent of theory.

"They came out from behind the mats, then. They looked at the graphs. Nobody believed the graphs. They looked for a weighing error. They knew it couldn't happen. So I told them to check the meters. The meters were all right. I knew there was nothing wrong with the meters. Then we started another run. The reaction didn't start cold this time. So we turned the steam into the jacket. That was supposed to start the reaction. We usually start getting terpineol in the receiver at about one sixty. We watched it for a good hour. Not a drop of product. Just C-10 going in, C-10 coming out. We couldn't explain it. We were making ozone. The ozonator was O.K. We had the right concentration of C-10, the right temperature, mole ratio, space velocity, everything was right. But not a grain of terpineol was coming out. *He* wanted to *show* me, you understand, that he could control it either way. But he was going to leave it up to me which way it went. I didn't want to decide right then. I didn't know what to do. Just then I didn't even know how I could tell him, if I did decide. So we simply shut down and knocked off.

"I went home, but I couldn't sleep. I tried to think it through. And I guess I did think it through. This *being* can put me through. With him on my side I can do anything. There's no position in this corporation I couldn't have. And *that* would just be a starter. I don't know where the end would be. So I want to make the deal. I know exactly what I want. And what *he* wants. He wants, well, he wants *me*. Not my body, really, or anything like that. It's more like something mental. He wants to take it from me a little at a time, like a parasitical drain. But it wouldn't affect me physically or mentally. In fact, I'd get sharper all the time. And whatever it is, it would go so slowly, day-by-day, that I wouldn't notice it. This goes on for years. I'll even have a normal life expectancy. When he's got all of it, I'll die. And that's the deal. The next thing is to get it down on paper. Something he and I can both sign. A binding contract. It doesn't matter whether you believe he exists. Call him the Devil if you like. And call the thing I'm giving him, my soul. A lot of people who believe in God don't believe the Devil exists. And some of them don't believe in souls, either. Although, as I said, it isn't really that simple."

There was a long silence.

"The contract?" prompted Fast.

Patrick nodded, as in a dream, to Sullivan.

Sullivan began: "This Agreement, made as of this blank day of blank, in the year of our Lord—"

"Not 'of our Lord'," said Fast.

"Quite so," said Sullivan. "I'll fix that." He continued: ". . . By and between John Fast, hereinafter sometimes referred to as 'Fast', and His Satanic Majesty, hereinafter sometimes referred to as 'The Devil', Witnesseth: Whereas Fast is desirous of certain improvements in his present circumstances; and Whereas The Devil is able to cause and bring about said improvements; now therefore, in consideration of the mutual promises herein contained, and for other good and valuable consideration, the receipt of which is hereby acknowledged, the parties agree as follows: Article One. The Devil shall promptly cause the Hope Chemical Company to erect a plant for the production of terpineol, hereinafter referred to as 'Neol', and to make Fast the manager thereof. The Devil shall, with all deliberate speed, cause Fast to become a world-famous chemist, rich, respected, and to win at least two Nobel prizes. Without limiting the generality of the foregoing, The Devil will immediately enter upon the performance, and will continue same, for the full term of this Agreement, of every obligation set forth on Exhibit A, annexed hereto, and incorporated by reference herein."

Sullivan looked up at Fast. "You wrote out the list?"

"Right here."

"Mark it 'Exhibit A'," said Sullivan. He continued. "Article Two. Fast hereby assigns, grants, conveys, sets over, and transfers all his right, title, and interest in and to his soul, to the said Devil, on the death of Fast; provided, however, that Fast shall live until the age of seventy, and that during said period The Devil shall have met faithfully, and in a good and workmanlike manner, all his obligations, both general and specific, as above set forth."

Patrick nodded. "That's fine."

"We had to change some of our 'boiler-plate' clauses," said Sullivan. "Others we had to leave out altogether. For example, we thought it best to omit completely the 'Force Majeure' clause, whereby the Devil is relieved from his obligation to perform, if prevented by an Act of God, but can nevertheless require you to perform, that is, give up your soul!"

"Logical," agreed Fast.

"And we had to change the 'construction and validity' clause. Ordinarily we provide that our contracts shall be construed, and their validity determined, under the laws of the State of New York. However, we think that under New York law, the contract might be held invalid, as having an immoral object, and hence unenforceable by either side. So we changed it to Hawaiian law."

"Yes," said Fast. "It's all ready to sign, then?"

"Right there, there're lines for the signatures of both, ah, parties," said Sullivan. "Are we to understand, John, that the Devil will actually affix his signature to this document, in real pen and ink?"

"I sign in blood," said Fast calmly. "How *he* signs, I'm not really sure. All I know is, he'll do something, maybe make a special appearance, to let me know that he accepts."

"I see," said Patrick. (He saw nothing.) He asked curiously, "But why do you think you need the Devil? An energetic man with a solid technical background and a high I.Q. in a big, growing chemical company doesn't need assistance such as this."

Fast looked at him in surprise. "Coming from you, Con, that's a very strange question."

"How is that?"

"I accept aid from any source, because I am totally committed. But so are you, and therefore, you, too, will accept assistance without asking the cost, or to whom the payment will be made."

Patrick felt a flurry of confusion. "And to what am I totally committed?"

"To your patents. Did you not know?"

Patrick had to think about this. Finally, he shook his head, not in denial, but to admit incomprehension. "Well," he defended, "it's my job."

Fast's mouth, immobile and cryptic as the Mona Lisa's, seemed almost to smile. "Yes, but only because you have contracted for it. So you see, what I have done is not a particularly strange thing. You . . . everyone . . . has entered into his own private contract, with something. My only difference is that I have put mine in writing. This does not necessarily mean that I am more honest than you. Perhaps I am merely more perceptive.

"True, my deal is with the Devil. But is that immoral? Morality is relative. *My* action, *my* way of life, has to be evaluated against the background of *your* action, and *your* way of life. You think me immoral, if not insane. Yet you wrote this contract for me. Why? Because you want to keep me happy. And why do you want to keep me happy? So that I'll keep your patents coming. Therefore you've made your own contract—with your patents. You resolve all questions of sin, virtue, and morality in light of the effect on your patents. With you, nothing can be sinful—even an assignment to hell—if it helps your terpineol patents. Before you judge my contract, take a look at your own."

Patrick stared at the gray man. Finally he smiled uneasily. "Whatever you say, John."

"And now I'll do *you* a favor, Con. Change the name."

"Change what name?"

"Neol. It's wrong."

"What's wrong with it?"

"The sound; wrong altogether. If you should ever have to . . . call . . . anyone with it, it wouldn't do it. Also, you ought to have five letters, exactly, one letter for each point of the pentagram. Correct symbology is essential."

"Whom would I be calling?" said Patrick. "And why?"

"You know . . . for your patents."

Patrick looked blank, then frowned, then finally he smiled. "All right, John. Whether or not you're a mystic, I'll give you 'x-plus', for mystification."

After Fast had gone, Patrick and Sullivan stared at each other.

"Do *you* believe any of that?" said Patrick.

"I believe he *thinks* he saw something. A kind of self-hypnosis."

"How about the yield? You know one hundred per cent of theory is impossible."

"No, Con, I don't know that. And neither do you. Within experimental errors, he may well have got one hundred per cent. And even if he didn't, he really might have got fairly close to it. A pilot plant always does much better than a bench-scale unit. You just naturally expect the yield to be high. All the variables are optimized, easily controlled."

"So you think he just hypnotized himself into seeing the Devil?"

"Why not? Actually, he's an accomplished amateur hypnotist. I'm told he is quite a parlor performer, if you can catch him."

"I know. He'll be at the party tonight, for something like that. But he's wrong about me. I'm *not* totally committed to my patents. It's my job, the same as it's your job. John Fast doesn't know what he's saying."

Sullivan's eyes twinkled wickedly. "You're absolutely right, Con. There are *some* things you would not resort to, even to save the Neol patent position. You would *not* sell your own grandmother into white slavery even if it would win the interference and solve the whole problem." He, paused, then added maliciously, "Would you, Con?"

Patrick snorted. "Don't tempt me!"

"Are you going to change the name?" asked Sullivan.

" 'Neol'?"

"You know what I mean."

"Well, maybe. There's nothing really wrong with 'Neol'."

"Except that John Fast thinks it's wrong."

". . . Without saying how to make it right," added Patrick. "I want to think about it. And I might change it, just to be ornery."

> *That which we call a rose*
> *By any other name would smell as sweet.*
> — Shakespeare

Patrick sat in his office, looking at the proofs of the "Neol Technical Manual," and thinking hard. This was Harvey Jayne's Manual, and Jayne was trying to steal Miss Willow. But Jayne needed Patent Department clearance for his Manual. Right away, this suggested possibilities. This morning, he had it nearly figured. And then John Fast had decided the name was wrong. And what difference did it make to John Fast? He wasn't even going to ask, because tonight he was going to need the man.

But *could* he change the name? How sacred was this Manual to Jayne? Patrick considered the matter.

He knew, certainly, that a technical manual prepared and published by an American chemical giant was like nothing else in the world of books. It was the strange child of the mating of the laboratory with Madison Avenue, midwifed by the corporate public relations committee. It told all. It was rich in history, process descriptions, flow sheets, rotogravures, chemical equations, and nomographs. It was comprehensive, and its back pages were filled with thousands of arrogant footnotes. The stockholders of Hope Chemical were given the impression that the sole function of the "Neol Technical Manual" was to incite an unendurable craving for Neol in the hearts of purchasing agents throughout the country. But Patrick knew that the compiler privately harbored other motives. For that man, Harvey Jayne, it represented an opportunity for creativity that comes only when the company builds a new plant; it could not happen to Jayne twice in one lifetime.

In this manual, Harvey Jayne would have a ready-made solace for whatever disasters might lie ahead. His wife might on occasion fail to recognize his greatness; his son might fail in school; he might, alas, even be laterally transferred within the company. Yet, withal, his faith in himself would be restored, and the blood brought back into his cheeks, when he gets out his old Technical Manual, to read a little in it, to fondle its worn covers, and to look at the pictures. So doing, Harvey Jayne might murmur, with tears in his eyes, as did Jonathan Swift, re-reading *Gulliver's Travels,* "God, what genius!"

So, thought Patrick, this volume will be cherished forever by Harvey Jayne. He will keep it in his office bookcase, with a spare in his den at home. When he transfers, it will be carefully packed. Years later, for presentation at his retirement dinner, his lieutenants will borrow his last copy from his wife, or perhaps steal one from the company library. They will have it bound in the company colors, blue and gold; and the chairman of the board, the president, and numerous fellow vice-presidents will autograph its pages.

Now, brooded Patrick, the whole of this immense and immemorial undertaking, this monster, this Manual, centers around the product trademark, which is as essential to it as the proton to the atom, the protoplasmic nucleus to the growing cell. The Manual is known by this name. Once thus baptized, the name is sacred. And to deny this book its name, to suggest that its name is wrong, that it should have another name, is to invite the visitation of the Furies, for this is desecration, a charge so sinister that it must rank with defamation of motherhood, or with being against J. Edgar Hoover.

Yes, there were possibilities. For personal disaster. He could not change the name of the Manual. And yet he was going to. Why? he wondered. Why am I going to do this? I am as crocked as John Fast. His mind floundered, searching. I have to fight Harvey Jayne, that's why. No. That's not why. It's something else. John Fast said the name was wrong. The new name should have five letters. He tugged briefly at his mustache, then leaned over to the intercom.

> *Books cannot always please.*
> — George Crabbe

"Con," said Cord, "it's not really bad. A few editorial changes should do the job."

Patrick's face was a blank. "How about 'Neol'?"

"It's clear. The closest thing is 'Neolan', registered for textiles."

Patrick brightened. "Clear? It's a clear case of infringement!"

Cord stared at him. "What . . . what did you say?"

"I said it infringes. And I hasten to add, Cord, my boy, that you look quite strange, with your mouth open." He reached for the phone and dialed Jayne.

"Oh, hi there, Harvey . . . No, I didn't call to protest about Miss Willow. We're really grateful you can do something for her, Harvey. Her place is with you, Harvey. On one condition . . . It's this, Harvey, that you double her raise. She's worth every bit of it. Good, Harvey, splendid you see it our way . . . Tech Manual, Harvey? Yes, we're looking at it right now. No, Harvey, I'm afraid we can't do that. There's a very close prior registration that will probably kill Neol as a trademark. No, Harvey, please get that out of your head. Miss Willow has nothing to do with it. She will transfer with our very best wishes . . . That is indeed your privilege, Harvey. If you want to present the Manual to the Board on Monday morning without Patent Department clearance, go right ahead. It would, of course, be my duty to give Andrew Bleeker a memo itemizing my objections, absolving the Patent Department of all responsibility for the content of the Manual. There will be carbons, of course, to . . . You will? Why, that's fine, Harvey." He hung up. "He's coming over."

"I'm amazed," said Cord dryly.

"Keep your fingers crossed on Willow."

"But you said the louse could have her, with a double raise," said Cord.

"Alec, you wouldn't believe me if I told you what is about to happen. So I won't waste time. We have only a few minutes before Harvey is due to show. So—*Cord.*"

"Yes, Con?"

"I didn't address you. I merely stated your name. It turns crisply from the tongue, like honest bacon in the griddle. A fine name. Cord, Cord, Cord. A good word to say. Here, I'll write it, too. Flows easily on paper. Cord looks good. Listens good. Charming. A man's name is the best thing about him. Like Narcissus. Hello there, you beautiful name!"

Cord flushed red. "Con, for goodness' sake. It isn't at all remarkable!"

"Yes, my boy, it is . . . to you." He leered at his lieutenant. "A man's name is his most enchanting possession. For you, for me, for Harvey Jayne, for anybody."

"So?"

"That's how we find a substitute for Neol. We will derive us a new word, from 'Jayne'. Harvey will find it irresistible. And it will be a good trademark. Think of the trouble American Cyanamid had, trying to find a trademark for their acrylic fiber. They finally named it after the project leader, Arthur Cresswell. They called it 'Creslan'. And Cluett-Peabody, naming their 'Sanforize' process for preshrunk fabric after the inventor, Sanford. And think of how many of Willard Dow's products are 'Dow' something or other, 'Dowicide', for example. And look at Monsanto's 'Santowax', 'Santowhite', 'Santomerse'. And Du Ponts 'Duponol', and W. R. Grace's 'Grex' polyethylene. So we'll name our terpineol after Harvey Jayne. 'Jayne-ol'. Of course not exactly 'Jayne-ol'. We'll have to fix it so he won't recognize it. Some phonetic equivalent."

"He'll recognize it, Con. It'll just make him madder."

"No, I don't think he will. A man has a selfish complex on his own name. He loves it, and he doesn't want other people to have it. He has trouble remembering people who have similar names. So if we do this right, he won't recognize it when he hears it. It'll fascinate him, but he won't understand why. He'll approve it on the spot. But first, we'll have to work him over, soften him up a little. So listen carefully as to what you have to do."

"Harvey," said Patrick, "you're making us revise our company leaflet on trademarks."

"I didn't know you had one," said Harvey Jayne suspiciously.

"It lists everything that shouldn't be done—all possible error. At least it *did*. Now, you've added a few more. We'll have to revise."

"This brochure. You wouldn't happen to have a copy—"

Patrick handed him the leaflet. "Brand-new edition, just off the press this afternoon."

Jayne read slowly. " 'The trademark should be capitalized, and preferably set in distinctive type. If the trademark is registered in the United States Patent Office, follow it with the registration symbol, ®. If no application for registration has been filed, or, if filed, not yet granted, then use an asterisk after the trademark, with footnote identification. Hope Chemical Company's trademark for . . . '." He looked up. "I'm not sure I follow your reasoning on this particular point. For example, I didn't capitalize 'neol'. I don't care whether it's capitalized or not. And I didn't say 'trademark' every time I said 'neol'. I just said plain old neol. I want it to become so familiar to our customers that they'll think of it as a household word."

Patrick shook his head sadly. "Harvey, I understand your viewpoint, and I deeply sympathize. Such charity and philanthropy are all too infrequent in this hatchet-hearted corporation."

"Charity? Philanthropy?"

"Yes. Really touching. Gets me, *here*." Patrick struck his fist to his chest. "You want to give the trademark to the general public, including our competitors. Come one, come all, anybody can use this name, which isn't a trademark any more, because Harvey doesn't want it spelled with a capital."

"I don't see how spelling it lowercase prevents it from being a trademark."

"It converts it into the *thing itself.* Remember 'cellophane'? It used to be Du Pont's trademark for transparent wrappings, and it was spelled with a capital 'C'. And then it became so well known that the newspapers and magazines began spelling it lower case; and they never mentioned it was Du Pont's brand of anything, because everybody by that time thought of cellophane only as the transparent wrapping itself. It had become the common name of the thing itself: it had become *generic.* Now anybody can sell his own transparent wrapping and call it 'cellophane'. Cellophane has now joined the list of irresistible trademarks that are wide open to the public: shredded wheat, mineral oil, linoleum, escalator, aspirin, milk-of-magnesia."

"Anything else wrong?"

"Several other points. On the title page, you ought to say 'Copyright, Hope Chemical Company'."

"But how can I say 'Copyright' before we publish? I thought you just said you couldn't do that. You said we couldn't say Neol was registered."

"I won't try to explain it, Harvey. That's the way it has worked out historically."

"Anything else?"

"We don't like your trademark, 'Neol'," said Patrick. "We think it infringes at least one mark already registered. Besides which, it's a weak mark, made up of weak syllables."

"What . . . what are you saying?" sputtered Jayne. "There's nothing wrong with 'Neol'. How can it be weak?"

"Look at it this way," said Patrick smoothly. "Fashions in trademarks come and go, like women's hats. At the moment, the ad people are conditioned to think in terms of certain well-worn prefixes and suffixes. The suffix is supposed to classify the product as a liquid, a solid, a plastic, a synthetic fiber, a flooring compound, soap, deodorant, toothpaste, and so on. True, they have their differences, but these are minuscule. The pack of them are so much alike you'd take them for a children's *a capella* choir."

"That's probably true for most trademarks," said Harvey Jayne smugly, "but not for 'Neol'. 'Neol' was selected by our computer, which was programmed to synthesize words from certain mellifluous-sounding syllables, and to discard everything harsh. And not only that, but to present a final list of one hundred names graded according to final audial acceptance. 'Neol' headed the list."

Patrick shook his head pityingly. "Look, Harvey, when you use a computer, you've got two-and-a-half strikes against you from the start. In the first place, the only marks the computer can grind out will be made up of these forbidden syllables we've already ruled out. And secondly, no computer can zero in on the gray area between the legally acceptable 'suggestive' marks and the legally unacceptable 'descriptive' marks. Even the courts have a hard time with this concept. To demonstrate this, we are going to decomputerize 'Neol' for you."

"De . . . computerize . . . ?"

"Yes, our decomputer takes a computerized trademark and tells us whether it's too close to known marks or names to be registrable."

"May I see it, this decomputer?"

"You could, but that won't be necessary. It's so simple, I'll just describe it to you briefly. It consists of two cylinders, rotating on the same shaft, one next to the other. On the left cylinder we have prefixes; on the right, suffixes. All our syllables were compiled from trademarks in the chemical and plastics fields. When a new trademark comes in, we break it down into syllables and see if it's in our decomputer. If it's not here, we search it in the Trademark Division of the Patent Office, in Washington."

"What syllables do you have on your, ah, decomputer?" said Jayne uneasily.

"Really only the extremely common ones. For prefixes, things like 'ray', 'hy', 'no', 'ko', 'kor', 'di', 'so', 'ro', the 'par-per-pro' set, 'vel', 'var', and of course, 'neo'."

"Neo, you said?"

"Yes, 'neo', which is simply the Greek variant of 'new', which again frequently comes out as 'nu', or in the Latin form, 'novo'."

"And I presume 'ol' is among your proscribed suffixes?" demanded Jayne bitterly.

"Yes, that's 'ol', from Latin, 'oleum', oil. So that gives us 'Neol', or 'new oil'."

Jayne frowned and looked at his notes. "Well, how about 'Neolan'? Or do you have 'lan' in your suffixes, too?"

"Yes, indeed. But there again, we consider 'lan' as a species of the 'on' family, from 'rayon', of course. Between vowels, 'on' takes a consonant, so you would come out with 'lin', 'lan', 'lon', and so you have 'neolan'."

Jayne threw up his hands. "Well, then, you fellows just do whatever you have to do, to fix this. Say the right words over it. Do your legal mumbo jumbo."

Patrick studied Jayne quietly for a moment. "Harvey. I'm going to do something I shouldn't. I'll clear a trademark—no, not Neol. Some other mark."

Jayne looked dubious. "*We* would have to originate it. Our ad people have to screen these things. All kinds of image and audio requirements."

"Impossible, Harvey. This is not a job for the agency. All they can do is put together syllables to skirt along the fringes of what they think your customers will almost but not quite recognize. The way they draw up those lists, they practically guarantee their mark will be weak. Leave them out of this. I'll give you a mark I will guarantee *you* will like and that will not infringe any existing mark."

"But if it isn't on my list, how can you be so sure I'll like it?"

Patrick smiled. "We've never lost a customer."

"Probably it will be very similar to a trademark on my list."

Patrick picked up the list and scanned it briefly. "No, I think not. But we're wasting time. Let's move on to the next item."

"Next item?"

"Payment."

"Charge my department."

"You don't quite understand, Harvey. Let's go over it again. I'm promising you a clean, desirable trademark. I'm giving you a guarantee—on something that as yet doesn't even exist. I don't have to do it. This is above and beyond the call of duty. A big favor to you."

"So?"

"If the company gets sued, you're in the clear, but it's a black eye for me. They'll say Hope needs a younger man in their Patent Department. Patrick is slipping. And then the next time it happens, I'm out on my ear. So I'm taking a chance, and I want payment."

Jayne was suspicious. "Like what?"

"We need not be crass. You could offer a prize for a suitable mark."

"And *you* would win it?"

"The Patent Department would win it."

"Go on," said Jayne acidly.

"The prize couldn't be money."

"I can see that. As you say, crass. How about wall-to-wall carpeting?"

"No."

"A conference room . . ."

"Not that, either."

"Electric typewriters . . ."

"Not exactly what I had in mind."

"Then what *do* you want?"

Patrick leaned over and murmured, "Willow."

Jayne was silent for a moment. Finally he said, "I don't know what to say. It's cheap, shoddy, not in character with you, Con. Furthermore, I don't make the rules. This promotion program is a company policy. It's not anything you or I have anything to do with. I need a secretary. I have a vacancy. I either fill it by promoting a girl from the lab, or I go outside. I think it's a good policy."

"So do I," said Patrick morosely. "I hate to do this."

"You don't have to do it. In fact, you're being absolutely unreasonable. If you insist on doing this to me, I'll have to take it up with Andrew Bleeker."

"If you do that, you could get me in trouble."

"As you say, I would hate to have to do it."

"At the same time, you will also have to mention to Bleeker that you couldn't get the Manual out in time for the Board. You won't have to tell him why, though. He'll be first on my list of carbons of my trademark infringement report to you. He will not be happy."

The room became very quiet. The pale drift of typewriters ebbed and flowed in the outer bays.

Jayne's restraint was massive. "You win."

"Thank you, Harvey. And now, just so we won't have any misunderstandings, when Miss Willow comes back to us from having been your secretary, she'll keep her double raise?"

"I thought that she was never leaving you. How can she come back to you?"

"It's all over the place, Harvey, that she's being transferred to you. If we kept her here, she'd be entitled to think that we cheated her out of a raise. So we have to get her transferred to you on the books, get her double raise, and then transferred back to us on the books. Physically, of course, there would seem to be no reason for her to transfer . . . that is, clean out her desk, or anything like that."

"So that not only I don't get a secretary, Willow gets two raises."

"But you get a clean bill of health for your Manual."

"And a good trademark?"

"Absolutely." Patrick was solemn. "We can pick one here and now. We guarantee we can get the trademark application on file this afternoon. All we need is a more exotic name—one not made out of these garden variety building units. A really *beautiful* name."

Cord picked up the cue. "How about some foreign words that mean 'beautiful'?"

"Well, there's a thought. Harvey, what do you think?"

Jayne shrugged his shoulders. "Like what?"

"*Pulchra*—Latin for 'pretty'," said Cord.

"Hard to do anything with it," said Patrick. "What else?"

"*Kallos*—'beautiful' in Greek."

Patrick looked doubtful.

"*Bel?*" said Cord.

"That's a little better. What is it in Italian?"

"*Bella.*"

"Still not quite right," said Patrick.

"You could take a big jump. 'Beautiful' in German is *schön*. You'd have to Anglicize the accent a little, give it a long 'a'."

"Ah yes. 'Shane'. *Shane!*" Patrick's eyes lit up. "I really like that. Harvey?"

"Not bad. Shane. Hm-m-m. Yes, I must admit, there's something about it. Something tantalizing."

"I hear it, too, Harvey."

Cord's eyes rolled upward briefly.

"How long will it take to search it out in the Washington trademarks?" demanded Jayne.

"We can do it this afternoon. My man will call in, any minute now, and we'll tell him to go ahead."

"I'll take it," said Jayne.

"Good enough. If it's clear in the Trademark Division, we'll get the application on file this afternoon."

Jayne looked surprised. "You'll have to have labels made up. Then you'll have to make a bona fide sale in interstate commerce. And then have the trademark application executed by Andy Bleeker. I don't think you can do all that in three hours. And I won't pay off on a phony."

"Of course not." Patrick smiled angelically as the other left.

In the early afternoon Patrick walked across the court to the terpineol pilot plant and into the cramped dusty office of John Fast. As he stepped inside, his eyes were drawn immediately across the cubicle, beyond Fast's desk, to a large painting, in black and white, hanging on the wall behind Fast. He poised at the doorway, slackjawed, staring at this . . . thing.

Within the plain black frame were two figures, one large, and, in front, a smaller. The outlines of the larger figure seemed initially luminous, hazy, then, even as he squinted, perplexed and uneasy, the lines seemed to crystallize, and suddenly a face took form, with eyes, a mouth, and arms. The arms were reaching out, enfolding the figure in front, a man wearing a medieval velvet robe and feathered beret.

Unaccountably, Patrick shivered. His eyes dropped, and found themselves locked with those of John Fast, unquestioning, waiting.

Fast murmured, "It is an oversize reproduction of Harry Clarke's pen-and-ink drawing, the end-piece of Bayard Taylor's translation of Goethe."

"What is it?" blurted Patrick.

"Mephistopheles, taking Faust," said John Fast.

Patrick took a deep breath and got his voice under control. "Very effective." He paused. "John, I'm here to ask a favor."

Fast was silent.

"I understand you have a certain skill in the art of hypnosis."

Fast's great dark eyes washed like tides at Patrick. "That's not quite the right word. But perhaps the result is similar."

"I'll come to the point. All this is highly confidential. Our basic terpineol patent application is in interference in the Patent Office. We intend to dissolve the interference by a motion contending that the interference count is unpatentable over the prior art. This prior art is a college thesis. The problem is, Paul Bleeker is the only one who has seen the thesis, and he can't remember anything about it. Is it possible for him to remember, under hypnosis?"

"It's possible," said Fast, "but by no means a certainty."

"But isn't it true that everyone records, somewhere on his cerebrum, everything he has ever experienced?"

"Possibly. But that doesn't necessarily mean we can remember it all. Recall is a complicated process. The theory in fashion today is the 'see-all-forget-nearly-all' theory. In this one, every bit of incoming sensation is recorded and filed away in your subconscious. But to bring it up again, you not only have to call for it, you also have to walk it out, holding it by the hand, chopping along with a mental machete to clear away all the subconscious blocks along its path. Persistence will turn up many a forgotten item in this way. But if it's quite old, there may be so many blocks that it will never be able to penetrate the conscious mind. In this case you have to get down there with it, in your far subconscious—take a good look at it, and then holler out to somebody what you see. Hypnosis is the accepted procedure. In the hands of an expert, all kinds of oddities can be turned up in this way: stimuli the subject barely had time to receive; or things, which if recalled on a conscious level, would be intolerable."

"I want you to try it on Paul Bleeker tonight."

Fast hesitated a moment. "I gather you renamed 'Neol'?"

Patrick's eyebrows arched. "Yes. How did you know?"

"It was best for your patents, and you always do what's best for your patents."

" 'Neol' was a poor trademark," said Patrick doggedly. "That was the only reason we changed."

"What is the new name?" asked Fast

And now Patrick hesitated. He found himself unwilling to answer this question. Suddenly, he almost disliked John Fast. He shook himself. " 'Shane'," he said curtly.

Tiny iridescent lights seemed to sparkle from somewhere deep in the eyes of the other.

"Well?" demanded Patrick.

"Exquisite," mumured Fast. "I will do this thing for you. It may involve something more than hypnotism. You understand that, don't you?"

"Of course."

"No, you don't. You can't, at least not yet. But no matter. If Paul is willing, I will do it for you anyway. Since you are totally committed, it cannot be otherwise."

> *Those who have lost an infant are never, as it were, without an infant child. They are the only persons who, in one sense, retain it always.*
>
> — Leigh Hunt

Andrew Bleeker swung his swivel chair slowly back and forth as he motioned to the two chairs nearest his desk.

Patrick said cheerfully, "Good afternoon, Andy."

Harvey Jayne grunted. He was not cheerful.

Bleeker's eyes flickered broodingly at Patrick's face. He had a horror of these nasty internecine arguments. Patrick beamed back, and Bleeker sighed. "I'll come to the point, Con. There seems to be some question about the way you handled Harvey's Neol Manual."

"Really? I realize I wasn't able to satisfy him completely, but I didn't think he felt strongly enough about it to take it to the head office."

"What was the problem, Con?"

Harvey rose out of his chair. "Andy, let *me* state—"

"Con?" said Bleeker quietly.

"I sort of blackmailed him, Andy. I pressured him into giving one of our secretaries a double raise, out of *his* budget. In return I got him a good trademark, made an infringement search on it, and got the trademark application on file in the Patent Office, all within four hours. He still has time to get his brochure proofs corrected and back to the printers tonight. But it isn't the Neol Manual anymore. We changed the trademark to 'Shane'."

" 'Shane'?"

"Harvey picked it out, all by himself."

"You don't say," murmured Bleeker.

"The name is all right," grumbled Jayne. "It's the trademark *application* I'm protesting. It's a fraud, a phony. Andy, you perjured yourself when you made oath that the company had used the trademark in commerce. The mark didn't even exist until a few hours ago, and I know for a fact our shipping department hasn't mailed out anything labeled 'Shane' across a state line. It has to be interstate commerce, you know. But there hasn't been any shipment at all. Not one of the packages has left the Patent Department. I just checked."

Bleeker hunched his shoulders and began to swing his chair in slow oscillations. "Con?"

"He has the facts very nearly straight, Andy, but his inference is wrong. There was no fraud. When you signed the declaration, you did not commit perjury."

"But doesn't the form say that the goods have been shipped in interstate commerce? Didn't I sign something to that effect?"

"The trademark application simply asks for the date of first use in commerce. The statute defines commerce as that commerce regulated by Congress. *That's* been settled for over a hundred and fifty years. Congress controls commerce between the states and territories, commerce between the United States and foreign countries, and commerce with the Indian tribes."

"But we didn't ship in interstate commerce," said Jayne.

"That's right," said Patrick.

"Nor in foreign commerce?" asked Bleeker.

"No, Andy."

"That leaves—"

"The Indians," said Patrick.

"Apaches," said Jayne acidly, "disguised as patent attorneys."

"Not exactly Apaches, Harvey," said Patrick. "But we do have a lawful representative of the Sioux tribe, duly accredited to the Bureau of Indian Affairs in Washington. Commerce is with the Sioux, through their representative. A sale to her is a sale to the tribe. If you checked on the packages, you probably noticed that one was on her desk."

"*Her* desk," rasped Jayne. "This . . . Indian . . . *you mean*—"

"Miss Green Willow, late of the Sioux reservation? Of course. Drives a hard bargain. We finally settled on fifteen cents for the gallon jug of terpineol. Her people back in Wyoming will make it into soap for the tourists."

Bleeker seemed suddenly to have problems with his face, and this was detectable largely by the efforts he was making to freeze his mouth in an expression of polite inquiry. Then his cheeks turned crimson, his stomach jumped, and he hastily swiveled his chair away from his visitors.

There was a long silence. Jayne looked from Bleeker's back to Patrick's earnest innocence. He was bewildered.

Finally Bleeker's chair swung around again. His eyes looked watery, but his voice was under control. "Harvey, can't we be satisfied to leave it this way?"

Jayne stood up. "Whatever you say, Andy." He refused to look at Patrick.

Bleeker smiled. "Well, gentlemen."

Jayne walked stiffly out the door. Patrick started to follow.

"Just a minute, Con," said Bleeker. He motioned Patrick back inside. "Close the door."

"Yes, Andy?"

Bleeker grinned. "One day, Con, they'll get you. They'll nail you to the wall. They'll hang you up by the thumbs. You have got to stop this. Is Willow really an Indian?"

"Certainly, she is." Patrick was plaintive. "Doesn't *any*body trust me? The arrangement is legal."

"Of course, of course," soothed Bleeker. "I was just thinking, how convenient to have your own Indian when you need a quick trademark registration. It's like having a notary public in your office."

"All our secretaries are notaries," said Patrick, puzzled.

Bleeker sighed. "Of course. They would be. I stepped into that one, didn't I?"

"What?"

"Never mind." Bleeker's chair began its slow rhythm again. "How's that chess player getting along? Alec Cord?"

"He made second place in the D.C. Annual."

"He's still not in your league, though, Con. Nobody, absolutely nobody, can equal your brand of chess."

Patrick squirmed. "I don't even know the moves, Andy."

"And your contract man, Sullivan? Can he write as good a contract as you?"

"Much better," said Patrick.

"Did he write the contract that bound you to the Hope Patent Department?"

"What do you mean, Andy?"

"Oh, never mind. I don't know what I mean. I don't think I'll ever understand you patent fellows. Take Paul. Chemists become lawyers; lawyers never become chemists. Paul can't—or won't—explain it. There's probably something profound in this, but I've never been able to unravel it. Does it mean chemists have the intellect and energy to rise to advocacy, but that lawyers could never rise further into the realm of science? Or does it mean that the law is the best of all professions, that once in the law, other disciplines are attainted?"

Bleeker's chair began to swivel slowly again. Patrick knew what was coming. He got everything under control.

"How *is* Paul the patent lawyer?" asked Bleeker.

"A competent man," said Patrick carefully. "We're glad you sent him around to us."

Bleeker was almost defensive. "You know why I did it, Con. There's nobody else in the company I could trust to make him toe the mark. Really make him. You know what I mean."

"Sure, Andy, I know. He's a bright kid. I would have hired him anyway. Quit worrying about him. Just let him do a good job, day by day. Same as I did when I worked for you."

"I worked you hard, Con. Make Paul work hard."

"He works hard, Andy."

"And there's one more thing, Con. You switched trademarks. Neol to . . . Shane, you said?"

"That's right. Neol is a poor trademark. Shane is better."

"That's another thing Jayne is going to hold against you, Con. Switching marks on his cherished Manual."

"It isn't really that bad, Andy." Patrick marveled at the older man's technique. At no time during the conversation had Bleeker asked Patrick whether the Patent Department was going to approve the terpineol plant, nor in fact had he asked him anything at all about the terpineol patent situation, even though they both knew this was vital to Bleeker's future in the company. And yet the questions and the pressure were there, all the same, and the questions were being asked by their very obvious omission. Patrick decided to meet the matter with directness. He said simply: "We haven't completely resolved the patent problem, Andy. But we certainly hope to have the answer for you well before the Board meeting Monday morning. With luck, we may even have it tonight."

Bleeker murmured absently, "That's fine, Con."

Patrick started to get up, but Bleeker stopped him with a gesture.

"Shane," said Bleeker thoughtfully. "Very curious." His eyes became contemplative. "Perhaps you never realized it, Con, but we regarded your wife as an outstanding scientist. *You* were wise, however, to take up law in night school."

Patrick nodded, wondering.

"We got interested in her," continued Bleeker, "when she was just finishing up her master's degree at State. I think we still have her thesis around somewhere. Old Rohberg made a special trip to drive her up for her interview. She was so pretty, I made her an offer on the spot. My only error was in turning her over to you for the standard lab tour. You louse."

Patrick smiled, his face warmly reminiscent.

Bleeker studied the other man carefully. "What was the name of your little girl?"

"Shan."

"Odd name."

"Lilas picked it. It's short for *'chandelle'*, French for 'candle'. Lilas was French, you know. Lilas Blanc. White lilac. And Shan was our little candle. The wallpaper in the nursery was designed with a candle print. The lights above her crib were artificial candles. We painted fluorescent candles inside her crib. She would pat them every night before I tucked her in."

Bleeker cleared his throat. "Con, sooner or later somebody's going to tell Harvey Jayne that you renamed Neol after your baby daughter."

Patrick didn't get it. He stared back, stupidly. "After . . . Shan?"

"Well, didn't you? Shan . . . Shane . . . ?"

Patrick felt his insides collapsing. "But I didn't . . ." he blurted. "It didn't occur to me." Then his mouth twisted into a lopsided smile. "At least, consciously. But there it is, isn't it? So maybe you're right, Andy. I really walked into that one. There I was, telling Cord that Jayne's mental blocks wouldn't let him see why he liked Shane. The same rule applied to me, although I don't want my daughter's name on terpineol, plastered on tank cars, warehouses, stationery, magazine ads. Too late now. Botched the whole thing."

Bleeker regarded him gravely. "Con, how long has it been now, since the . . . accident?"

"Three years."

"You're still a young man, Con. Relatively speaking. Our young ladies think it's about time you got back into circulation."

"You might be right, Andy."

Bleeker coughed. "You're just being agreeable to avoid an argument. Believe me, Con, it's one thing to remember the dead. It's an altogether different thing to have your every waking thought controlled by your memories. You ought to get away from that place."

Patrick was shocked. "Move? From the garden? The house? It has our bedroom. Shan's room. How about Lilas? How about Shan? They're *buried* there. Their ashes—"

"Ashes?"

"They were cremated. Lilas wanted it that way. I spread the ashes in the lilacs."

The older man looked at him with compassion. "Then release *them*, Con. *Let them go!*"

"I *can't*, Andy." Patrick's face twisted. "They're all I have. Can't you understand?"

"I guess I do, Con. I guess I do. I'm sorry. None of my business, really."

> *On this night of all nights in the year,*
> *Ah, what demon has tempted me here?*
> — Edgar Allan Poe, "Ulalume"

The evening was warm, and along about ten o'clock the party drifted down into the garden.

Patrick, as usual drinking only beer, was, for all practical purposes, cold sober, a condition that enhanced rather than alleviated an unexplainable and growing sense of anxiety. The nearness of the lilacs, usually a thing of nostalgic pleasure, somehow contributed to his edginess. He was startled to note that several clusters were on the verge of opening. He started to call Cord's attention to this, then thought better of it. And then he wondered, "Why didn't I? What's the matter with me? What's going on?"

The group was in the arbor now. He would have to get on with it, the reason why they were all here. Paul Bleeker and John Fast knew what they were supposed to do. All he had to do was to ask them to start. Paul was already seated at the stone table. As he watched, Paul pulled the table drawer out in an idle exploratory gesture.

"My notes for a patent law article I started . . . a couple of years ago," said Patrick wryly. "I just can't seem to get back to it."

"Then perhaps you should be thankful," said Fast.

"What do you mean?"

"A professional man writes for a variety of reasons," said Fast. "I'm working now on my 'Encyclopedia of Oxidative Reactions.' I know why I'm writing it. And I know why you're not writing, Con. It's because life has been kind to you. Let it stay that way."

Paul Bleeker broke in. "You say a professional man writes for a variety of reasons, John. Name one. Why do you write?"

Fast's dark eyes turned on Paul Bleeker. "You have heard it said, a man owes a debt to his profession. This may be true. But no professional man pays his debt by writing for the profession. If he is an independent, say a consulting engineer, or a partner in a law firm, or a history professor in a big university, he publishes because it's part of his job to advertise himself and his establishment. There's very little money in it *per se*. If he's a rising young man in a corporate research or corporate law department, he writes for the reputation. It helps him move up. If his own company doesn't recognize him, their competitors will. But if he's already at the top of his department in his company, he has none of these incentives. But he doesn't need them. If such a man writes, he has behind him the strongest force known to the human mind."

"And what might that be?"

"Guilt," said Fast quietly. "He writes to hide from the things he has done in the name of his profession. It gives him a protective cocoon to burrow into. A smoke screen to hide behind."

"In the name of the patent system," said Patrick firmly, "I've committed every crime known to man. And still I can't get started."

"You've done very little, really," said Fast in his nearly inaudible monotone. "But when you really have done something, you'll know it. You won't have to wonder or conjecture. Then, you'll begin to write. It'll come instantly. No floundering. No lost motion. You'll leap to it. The words, pages, and chapters will pour out in a torrent. It will be your salvation, your sure escape."

They stared at him. Cord laughed nervously. "So why do *you* write, John? What is your unspeakable crime?"

Fast turned his great black eyes on the other, almost unseeing. "I cannot tell you, my friend. And you wouldn't believe me if I did tell you. Anyhow, it can never happen to you." He looked away to Patrick. "But to you, Con, it could happen. And it could happen soon. Tonight. In this place."

Patrick laughed shakily. "Well, now, John. You know how careful I am. Nothing is going to happen to me. It's spare time I need to start writing, not penitence."

Fast looked at him gravely. "You do not weep. You smile. Before the Nazarene called Lazarus up, He wept." His toneless eyes seemed almost sad. "How can I explain this to you. Then let it be done. I have placed the Shane Manual at the five angles of the pentagram. I think they are waiting."

"They?" stammered Patrick. "Oh yes, of course. The fellows. Perhaps we should begin."

"What's that smell?" called Sullivan.

"It's a terpineol," said Fast, sniffing a moment. "Like 'Shane'. Maybe a mixture of alpha and gamma terpineols." He snapped his fingers. "Of course!"

"Of course . . . *what?*" said Patrick. His voice was under control, but he felt his armpits sweating copiously.

"The mixture . . . very correctly balanced, I'd say. Just right for synthetic oil of lilac."

Patrick was struck dumb.

"That's very odd," said Sullivan. "Con's lilacs are not open yet."

"The odor must be coming from somewhere."

"Maybe we're all tired," said Cord. "Breeds hallucinations, you know."

Patrick looked at him in wonder.

"It's hard to convince anybody that odor can have a supra-chemical source," said Fast.

Cord laughed incredulously. "You mean there's something out there that is synthesizing oil of lilac . . . or Shane . . . or whatever it is?"

"We are so accustomed to thinking of the impact of odors *on* people that we don't think too much about the creation of odors *by* people. Actually, of course, everyone has his characteristic scent, and it's generally not unpleasant, at least under conditions of reasonable cleanliness. In this, man is not really basically different from the other animals. But man—or rather, a certain few extraordinary people—seem to have the ability, quite possibly involuntary, of evoking odors that could not possibly have come from the human sweat gland."

"Evoking?" said Sullivan.

"No other word seems to describe the phenomenon. Chemically speaking, in the sense of detectable air-borne molecules dissolving in the olfactory mucosa, the presence of odor is indeed arguable. On the other hand, in the strictly neuro-psychic sense, that an 'odor' response has been received in the cerebrum, there can be no real doubt. The phenomenon has been reported and corroborated by entire groups. The 'odor of sanctity' of certain saints and mystics seems to fall in this category. Thomas Aquinas radiated the scent of male frankincense. Saint John of the Cross had a strong odor of lilies. When the tomb of Saint Theresa of Avila—the 'great' Theresa—was opened in 1583, the scent of violets gushed out. And more recently, the odor of roses has been associated with Saint Theresa of Lisieux—the 'little' Theresa." He looked at Patrick. "I think—everyone is ready."

Patrick wiped his face with his handkerchief. "Go ahead," he said hoarsely.

Ma chandelle est morte . . .
— French Nursery Rhyme

Paul Bleeker was seated in the iron chair at the stone table. John Fast faced him, from one side. The others stood behind Paul.

"You are in a long dark tunnel," said John Fast quietly. "Just now everything is pitch black. But your eyes are beginning to adjust."

There was absolute silence. Then Fast's voice droned on. "In a little while, far ahead of you, you will be able to see the tunnel opening. It will be a tiny disk of light. When you see this little light, I want you to nod your head gently."

From far down stream drifted the plaintive call of a whippoorwill.

Paul Bleeker's eyes were heavy, glazed. His stony slump in the iron chair was broken only by his slow rhythmic breathing.

"You now see the little light—the mouth of the tunnel," monotoned Fast. "Nod your head."

"Candle," whispered Paul.

Patrick started, then recovered himself instantly.

Fast picked it up smoothly. "Watch the candle," he said. "Soon it will start to move toward you. It is beginning to move."

"Closer," murmured Paul.

In a flash of feverish ingenuity Patrick stepped forward, seized the wine bottle and its stub of candle from the stone table, struck his lighter, then lit the candle. He replaced the bottle on the table front. The flame wavered a moment, then flickered up. Patrick stole a glance at Paul's face. It was frozen, impassive.

Fast continued gravely: "Soon you will have enough light to see that you are sitting at your desk in the library. In a moment you will see the piles of books on the tables near by. There are several books on your desk. There's a big book just in front of you. Now the candle is close enough."

"Close," murmured Paul.

The hair on Patrick's scalp was rising. The odor of lilacs was stifling. And he then noticed that the lilacs were opening, all around him. He somehow realized that lilacs do not bloom in minutes. It was a botanical impossibility. He could almost hear the tender calyxes folding back.

Fast continued, "You are opening the front cover. You are looking at the title page. It is typewritten. It is a thesis. You are able to read everything. You can see the name clearly. The name of the student is—"

Patrick heard gasps behind him, and his eyes suddenly came into focus. Beyond Paul, on the far edge of the stone table, beyond the candle, he saw the two figures. They were wavering, silent, indistinct, but they were there. The larger one would just about reach his chin. The eyes of the small one came barely to the table edge.

He wanted to scream, but nothing would come out of his throat.

The taller figure was leaning over the table towards Paul, and she was holding something . . . an open book. But neither figure was looking at Paul. Both of them were looking at him. He knew them.

In this frozen moment his nose twitched. The scent of lilacs wavered, then was suddenly smothered by something sharp, acrid. Patrick recognized it, without thinking. It was ozone. And as if in confirmation of its olfactory trademark, a luminous . . . thing . . . was taking shape behind the two figures. Suddenly it acquired a face, then eyes. Then arms, reaching out, encircling.

Patrick had a horrid, instantaneous flash of recognition. The portrait in John Fast's office. Mephistopheles taking Faust.

"The name of the student is Lilas Blanc," said Paul Bleeker metallically. "State U—"

"Oh, God, *NO!*" screamed Patrick.

The candle blew out instantly. Paul struggled in his chair. "Hey, what . . . where?" He knocked the chair over getting up.

The voices rose up around Patrick in the darkness.

He dropped in a groaning heap on the grass. "Lilas, Shan, forgive me. I didn't know." But he must have known. All along.

And now his mind began to swing like a pendulum, faster and faster, finally oscillating in a weird rhythm of patterns so bewildering and contradictory that he could hardly follow them. His mind said to him, they escaped. It said to him, they did not escape. It said to him, they were there. It said, nothing was there. And then it started again. His throat constricted, his teeth bit the turf, and by brazen command his thoughts slowed their wounded flailing. He ceased to ask, to wonder. And finally he refused to think at all.

He heard Cord's firm voice. Somebody found the light switch. There were querulous whispers. And then there was something on his back. Some of them had dropped their jackets on him. A man's hand lingered briefly on his shoulder. It was a gentle, even affectionate gesture, and he recognized the touch as that of a man accustomed to tucking small children into their beds at night. He had used the same touch, many times, and long ago.

And now the sound of footsteps fading. And then, motors starting. And finally nothing, just the splash of the little falls, the crickets, and far away, the whippoorwill.

He did not want to move. He wanted only never to have been born.

He closed his eyes, and sleep locked him in.

> *I hold every man a debtor to his profession; from the which, as men of course do seek to receive countenance and profit, so ought they of duty to endeavor themselves by way of amends to be a help and ornament thereunto.*
>
> — Francis Bacon,
> Preface to Maxims of the Law

It was early morning, and with the pink of dawn on his cheek, waking was instantaneous. His mind was clear and serene as he threw the jackets aside and got to his feet. He rubbed his eyes, stretched with enormous gusto, and walked over to the lily pond. A green frog was sitting on a pad of the yellow lotus, but jumped in as Patrick bent over to splash water on his face. He dried his face on his shirttail, which was flopping out over his belt.

The sun was now barely over the little hill, and a shaft of light was slicing into the pond. Patrick considered this phenomenon briefly, then peered into the bottom of the pool for the refracted beam. There was some kind of rule of optics—law of sines. Somebody's law. Check into it. Meanwhile, there was work to be done. Important work.

He walked into the arbor, picked up the overturned iron chair, sat down at the stone table, and pulled a pencil and paper pad out of the drawer. After a moment, he began to write; slowly, at first.

"Ex parte Gulliksen revisited. The typewritten college thesis as a prior printed publication. This decision from the Patent Office Board of Appeals in . . ."

Then faster and faster. ". . . essential, of course, that the thesis be available to the public. This requirement is satisfied by . . ."

Now, he was writing furiously, and the pages were accumulating.

He was going to make it. Just a question of staying with it, now, and it would give him complete protection. No need to worry about what to work on *after* this article, either. He knew he could turn out a text. No trouble at all. Or even an encyclopedia. Patrick, "Chemical Patent Practice," four volumes. He could see it now. Red vinyl covers, gilt lettering.

The stack of sheets torn from his pad was now quite bulky. He pushed the pile to the table corner, and in so doing knocked the bottle and candle unheeding to the ground and into the withering lilacs. Already he could visualize his "Preface to the First Edition." It should be something special, based perhaps on a precisely apt quotation. What was that thing from Bacon? He frowned, puzzled. No. There was something not quite right about *that*. But never mind. Plenty of others. Somehow, somewhere, there would be a word for him.

THE ALCHEMIST

Andrew Bleeker, research director of Hope Chemicals, had more than once referred to his laboratory as "the soap opera," "the sideshow," or "the country club." He took instant umbrage, however, if anyone else ventured any jesting synonyms for his group of some five hundred people in the cluster of red brick buildings at Camelot, Virginia. Ordinarily, therefore, he would have been mildly incensed when Conrad Patrick, the Hope patent director, stuck his head in the door and told him that a three-ring circus was about to start down in Silicon Compounds, with Pierre Celsus in the center ring. But the circumstances were not ordinary. For the past two days, at the request of the United States government—which, the Chairman of the Board had bluntly reminded him, was Hope's biggest single customer—Bleeker had been turning the lab inside out for the benefit of Alexei Sasanov, Minister of Technology for the People's Republic, and for the past several hours had listened patiently to a comparison of decadent American chemical research and burgeoning socialistic research. The interruption offered a chance of respite, and his heart leaped. Nevertheless, appearances had to be maintained.

"What's Celsus up to?" he growled.

"He's going to try to start the silamine unit," said Patrick.

Bleeker's voice rose sharply. "Silicon Compounds has been trying to start that crazy thing for two months. I told them yesterday to junk the project. It's *dead*."

Patrick laughed. "Old projects never die. They just smell that way."

Bleeker snorted. "How does Celsus intend to do it?"

"He wants to try to synthesize *one* molecule of silamine in the reactor. He says the reaction should be autocatalytic, and once seeded, the fluidizer will start making more silamine. There'll be a little picric acid in the receiver, which ought to throw down a yellow silamine picrate within seconds, if it works."

"But that's idiotic! How can he *seed* the reactor with one molecule of silamine when not one single molecule of silamine exists anywhere on earth?"

Bleeker's distinguished visitor spoke up. "I quite agree with Mr. Bleeker." On the face of a less complicated man, the faint smile that played briefly about Sasanov's mouth might have been interpreted as a sneer. "It is a technical impossibility. Our central laboratories in Czezhlo have spent hundreds of thousands of rubles attempting to synthesize silamine. We want it as an intermediate for heat-resistant silicon polymers for missile coatings. We offered great incentives for success."

"And penalized failures?" murmured Bleeker.

Sasanov shrugged delicately. "The point is, where the most efficient, the most dedicated laboratory in the world has failed, it is hardly likely that a commercial American laboratory can succeed."

Patrick felt his red moustache bristling. He ignored the warning in Bleeker's eyes. "Would you care to make a small wager?"

Sasanov turned to Bleeker. "It is permitted?"

It was Bleeker's turn to shrug. "You have diplomatic immunity, Mr. Sasanov."

"So. A small wager then. If you make any silamine, the People's Republic will give Hope Chemicals a contract for a plant design, with a handsome running royalty for every pound of silamine we make."

"At twenty-five cents a pound," said Bleeker quickly.

Sasanov thought a moment. "Exorbitant, of course. But agreed."

"This will have to be approved by Hope management," said Bleeker carefully. "We've heard complaints, you know, about the . . . ah . . . slow royalty payments to other American firms who have designed plants for your country in the past."

Sasanov spread his hands expressively. "Vicious lies. Surely you trust the People's Republic?"

Bleeker coughed.

"This contract isn't much of a stake," objected Patrick. "That's between your government and the Hope corporation, not between you and me."

"Readily remedied," smiled Sasanov. "What is the classic consideration in your English common law? A peppercorn, isn't it? Well then, I offer the contract and a jug of vodka, to be sent direct to you here at the lab, if I lose."

"Against the rules," said Bleeker. "Spiritous liquors can't be brought into the lab."

"Make it sweet cider," said Patrick.

"Certainly, sweet cider," said Sasanov. "The best in the world. Cider from your Winchester apples is a poor thing in comparison."

Bleeker set his jaw. "All right, your stake is a contract and a jug of cider. What's *our* stake?"

"*Our* stake, Mr. Bleeker? I think Mr. Patrick suggested the wager. The matter is, therefore, between him and me. And Mr. Patrick can readily provide his stake."

"Such as what," demanded Patrick,

"Your desk."

"My . . . desk?" repeated Patrick stupidly.

"You don't have to do this, Con," said Bleeker quietly.

"Well, I don't know . . ." As Patrick considered the matter, his throat began to contract. His desk was a "rolltop," over a hundred years old, and one of the few remaining in the country that had never been used by Abraham Lincoln. It had caught his eye when browsing through the junk shops of Washington, and its entire panorama of possibilities opened up to him instantly. He bought it on the spot. He himself had carefully removed the ancient peeling finish by dint of solvent, scraper, and sandpaper, and had then slowly refinished it over a period of months. Finally he had moved it to his office at the lab. The pigeonholes were semi-filled with rolled documents, bound with genuine red tape that his London patent associates had found for him. He had patinated the papers with a light layer of dust recovered from his vacuum cleaner. His intercom and dictating machine were installed in the side drawers, and a tiny refrigerator in the lower left-hand cabinet. A kerosene reading lamp—converted to fluorescent in the Hope maintenance shop—sat on the upper deck of the desk, and a brass cuspidor gleamed in the lower right-hand cabinet. As a final touch, he had captured and imprisoned one small, bewildered spider, who, after a shrug of its arachnid shoulders, had gallantly garlanded a few of the more remote pigeonholes with sterile, dust-gathering strands.

For a time, Patrick's rolltop had been the talk of the lab; soon after its arrival dozens of people found it suddenly necessary to confer with Patrick on all kinds of patent problems. And now, even after the fine edge of novelty was gone, Hope people visiting from out of town still came in to see it. More importantly, as Patrick now realized with a chill, Comrade Sasanov, after his introduction to the patent director on the first day of his visit, had since dropped in to Patrick's office several times, for no apparent reason, and had stared thoughtfully at the desk.

There was no comparison between his desk and a jug of cider.

Still, a man had to have faith. And he had faith in Pierre Celsus.

"It's a bet," said Patrick.

The three men pushed their way through the spectators surrounding Pierre Celsus and the silamine setup.

Celsus, a slight nervous figure, largely hidden in an unlaundered lab coat, was evidently finishing up his preparations. He checked the fluidizer, which was a two-inch-diameter glass tube about one-third full of silica gel, then the Variac control on the resistance heater wound around the tube, then the ammonia inlet at the bottom of the fluidizer, then the glassware leading to the condenser—a two-neck glass flask venting to the hood. Finally he turned on the ammonia pre-heater and slowly opened the flow meter. The silica gel in the column shuddered slightly as a "bubble" of ammonia vapor forced its way up through the bed. Celsus opened the ammonia valve wider and turned up the pre-heater further, his eyes flickering from the column to the thermocouple readers and the flow meter and back again. Not once did he look at the collector, where the ammonia flowing into the flask was already sucking the water back, with intermittent gurgles, into the gas beaker. Finally he seemed satisfied. He stopped adjusting things and stood back a moment.

Patrick heard strange sounds. Celsus was muttering in a queer rhythm.

The room grew instantly still.

Patrick realized that the man was *chanting . . . to the equipment.* The patent director tugged at his red moustache uneasily. Goose pimples began to flow in waves over the nape of his neck.

Celsus now donned a pair of white asbestos gloves and stroked the fluidizer column as he sang.

Bleeker and Sasanov exchanged glances. Sasanov looked faintly bewildered. Bleeker felt the same way, but was determined not to let it show.

Patrick looked about him. There were at least fifteen people there—group leaders and senior chemists, mostly. A couple of people from his own department were there: Alec Cord and one of the women attorneys, Marguerite French.

They were both completely oblivious to him. Marguerite was moving her eyes continuously back and forth between Celsus and something metallic she held in her hand. Patrick recognized it with a start. It was a stopwatch.

It then occurred to Patrick that there was something strangely familiar in Celsus' urgent intonations, and in the manner in which he stroked and caressed the equipment. But he couldn't quite identify it.

Suddenly Celsus stepped back, right arm raised, and cried: "Silamine! Exist!" And instantly Patrick had it. Celsus was like a "hot" gambler who had just thrown the dice.

Silent seconds passed, broken only by the shuffle of shoes as Bleeker and Sasanov edged in closer to the bench.

Patrick stole a glance at Marguerite French, who was leaning forward as though hypnotized by the bubbling liquor in the collection flask. Suddenly a yellow cloud appeared in the flask, and Marguerite's arm jerked. Patrick knew she had pushed the timer on her watch. She looked down at the watch, and her face began to turn white. Patrick, concerned, started over to her, but just then, Bond, Silicon Compounds Group Leader, called out: "That's enough! Let's take a sample for infrared!"

"Go ahead, Prufrock," said Celsus.

A. Prufrock Prentice, Celsus' technician, who until now had been hovering in the background, now stepped forward, removed the vent assembly in the collector with a swift expert gesture, and drew out a few cc. of the slurry with a pipette. He dropped the sample into a bottle and then disappeared out the door.

Patrick forgot momentarily about Marguerite French. He turned to the bemused Sasanov with a grin. "Efficient, aren't they? We'll know in a minute what it is."

Sasanov shook his head. "How can it be efficient when they were ordered not to do it?"

"You've got a point, Comrade," grumped Bleeker. "You don't see them stumbling all over themselves on a *scheduled* run."

"Of course not, Andy," smiled Patrick. "But this was a *bootleg* run. You ought to institute a required schedule of bootlegs."

"Bootlegs?" queried Sasanov. "What are these bootlegs, please?"

"Just a decadent American laboratory custom, Comrade. When you have orders to stop trying, but you know it will work if you try one more time, then you just go ahead and do it. Sneaky, isn't it?"

Sasanov sniffed.

Patrick was in high spirits. He looked about for Marguerite. She had disappeared. That surprised him. After all that business with the watch, didn't she really want to know whether Celsus had made it? Or—the thought hit him hard—was she so sure he *had* made it, that there was no point in staying for the i.r. report?

The phone rang. Bond grabbed it. The conversation was brief. Bond replaced the phone and turned around, his eyes searching the room. "Where's Pierre?" he demanded.

But Celsus, too, had gone.

"Was it silamine?" called Patrick. He turned to face Sasanov.

"It was silamine," said Bond.

Sasanov's face was a mask. He bowed low to Patrick. "I will send the contract and the cider, as soon as I arrive at the chancellery in Czezhlo. And now, if you will excuse me, I have a plane to catch."

The lab was the slave of fad and fashion, and news of a new discovery flashed through the bays faster than the speed of light and with an audience saturation that dwarfed Bleeker's Management Bulletins. A new catalyst discovered in Inorganics in the morning was likely to be warming up in the test tubes in Polymer that afternoon. A new herbicide found effective in the Biology Bay in the afternoon would probably be followed up by a new synthesis in Organics the next morning. Currently, however, thanks to Pierre Celsus, the rage had now become that lovely child of the petroleum refinery, the fluidized reaction, in which hot gases having composition A streamed up through a turbulent mass of tiny catalyst particles, while simultaneously suspending that mass, to emerge at the top of the bed with composition B.

During the entire previous year, there had not been a single fluidized experiment at Hope. But within the hour following Celsus' silamine run, Group Leaders were holding conferences behind closed doors with their chief assistants as to how to reconstruct the chemistry of tried and true reactions so as to make them amenable to fluidization. Overnight the senior chemists were talking knowledgeably of "slide valves," "strippers," "regenerators," "standpipes," and "suspensoid"; and within a very few days they would go on to "bed viscosity," "Nusselt number," and "voidage at incipient slugging." The Library was promptly stripped of all books remotely touching on fluidization, and even the "F" volume in the sacrosanct *Kirk-Othmer Encyclopedia* disappeared from the reference shelves for several days. Miss Addie, the librarian, posted stern notices on all bulletin boards. Overnight, the volume was returned, sheepishly, by Andrew Bleeker.

Bleeker didn't fight the new trend. He knew it would do no good, and besides, the new thinking both intrigued and amused him. It intrigued him because it was a new and potentially useful approach, not only for a silamine design, but also for a number of other research problems of long standing. It amused him because he knew from long experience that a number of project shifts would now be inevitable. Programs on supersonic reaction initiation, free radical mechanisms, photocatalysis, and selective adsorption would be quietly, even surreptitiously, phased out. In some ways, his people reminded him of a cohesive group of teen-agers, with the same compulsion to conform in dress, thought, and behavior. The minority that he would force to continue on their old projects would probably be apologetic to the lucky ones launching into the new fluidized techniques. Bootleg runs meanwhile would become the order of the day, with glassware fluidizers of all shapes and sizes springing up all over the lab like wildflowers in May. He made a mental note to contact the Budget Committee immediately for a decent bench unit. He had a good excuse. Sasanov had already opened negotiations from Czezhlo. They'd be needing some good bench equipment in a matter of days.

In fact, to handle the expected volume of requests for bench runs, he might need as many as three columns—stainless steel, of course, twelve feet high, and heavy. They'd need a basement foundation. There was just the place for them, downstairs in Building V. He'd call it the Fluidizer Bay.

Two days later the Safety Committee investigated a minor explosion in Silicon Compounds. There was no damage, beyond a wrecked hot plate, and nobody was hurt. As the Committee noted in their written report to Andrew Bleeker, the explosion was the expected result of an experiment by Pierre Celsus, done in the hood behind shatterproof glass, all in approved and careful fashion. One gram of fulminate had been heated on the hot plate to 145° C., then detonated—by touching it with a feathertip.

Explosions, controlled or otherwise, made Bleeker uneasy. He called Bond on the phone. "What fulminate was it?" he demanded.

"I don't know," said Bond candidly.

"Find out," said Bleeker.

The group leader called back in a few minutes. "It was gold fulminate." He sounded uncertain. "It's not a true fulminate, not a salt of fulminic acid. It's made by reacting auric oxide, water, and ammonia. When dry, it's highly unstable . . . detonates by light friction."

"Why was Celsus working with it? How does it relate to anything in the silamine program?"

Bond coughed. "I asked Celsus about that—"

"And?"

"It has something to do with a new silamine catalyst." Bond sounded defensive.

Bleeker started. "Good heavens! Gold fulminate . . . a *catalyst?*"

"I don't think so. But I'm not really sure. As Celsus explained it, the real catalyst won't be gold, but rather one of the rare earth oxides. Terbium, I think. I know this sounds rather strange, Andy. It's probably my fault for not understanding Celsus." Bond's voice trailed away unhappily. "Sometimes, it's difficult to communicate with him."

Bleeker paused. Finally he said, "Let me know if you find out anything further."

After he replaced the phone, Bleeker began swinging his chair in slow oscillations, eyes narrowed and brows knotted. "Nobody," he thought grimly, "ever tells me anything." He swung around toward the window. "And why? Because nobody in this lab ever tells anybody anything. And it's getting worse every day. No organization. Maybe Sasanov was right." He swung back around and stared through his open office door. As he peered, he caught a serio-comic vision of the lights going out, one by one, all over the lab. He suppressed a shiver.

From test tube to commercial plant at Hope Chemicals classically proceeded through four well-defined steps. Step one was "in glass"—generally with a glass one-liter reaction vessel with a train of glass accessories, all stock equipment, with parts out of the cupboard. Celsus' first silamine run had been "in glass." Step two was the "bench unit." Nearly all parts were metal, and many were specially designed or ordered out of the special chemical apparatus catalogs. The bench unit was supposed to "prove out" and "optimize" the glass setup. The pilot plant was next. From its operation the engineers were able to draw up thermodynamic data and could analyze feed, recycle, purification, and effluent streams, all of which were absolutely essential in designing a commercial plant, which was the fourth and final step. Each of these steps was vital, and none could safely be omitted. They were like links in a chain. If one failed, the whole sequence of events came to an abrupt halt, never to be revived. Although each phase was essential, everyone at the lab, from Bleeker on down, knew very well that one certain phase was more essential than the others. For sad history had shown that if a project were going to die, it nearly always picked the bench unit for its coffin.

In his Monthly Project Report on his work "in glass," the less experienced chemist might report loftily that, although yields in glass were perhaps a little low, they could be expected to improve with the adequate temperature control available in a bench unit; or that by-product contamination would not be a problem in a bench unit, where a purge would operate continuously. And then the bench unit would be built, and he would have to eat his predictions on a stainless steel platter. So chemists at Hope were generally quite chary of predicting the performance of a projected bench unit. At best, they would answer Andrew Bleeker's inquiries with, "It seems to have a good chance." "Certainly worth a try." "Something similar worked at Du Pont."

Bleeker complained about it to Patrick. "Weasel words! Nothing but weasel words! You'd think they were a bunch of patent lawyers."

Patrick grinned slyly. "Not all of them. Look up Celsus' Project Report on Silamine."

Bleeker did. His eyes nearly fell out of his head.

He read: "Yields were poor in glass because the process was necessarily limited by the heat input. The reaction is extremely endothermic, requiring a thermal outlay heretofore attainable only in nuclear reactions. In the existing setup the necessary heat cannot be supplied through the reactor walls because of the low heat transfer coefficient available for a fluidized system. The same difficulty applies with respect to internal heaters. Nor can the requisite heat be supplied by pre-heating the ammonia, since NH_3 cracks back to N_2 and H_2 at 600–700° C. The only way to provide the necessary heat is to create it *in situ* on the silica gel particles. This may readily be done by adding terbium oxide with a little xerion to the silica. This system will, in fact, create a substantial thermal excess, requiring a cooling jacket on the reactor. At the end of the run—disappearance of terbium—spent catalyst, while still wet, must be immediately discharged into alkahest. Yield of silamine, based on SiO_2, should be substantially quantitative."

Bleeker shook his head vigorously, like a dog shedding water. He studied the report again, as if hoping the words would rearrange into sentences he could understand. But there wasn't any change.

The Research Director reflected a moment. Should he ask Celsus to report and explain? Celsus, being a senior chemist, had no group leader, and instead reported directly to him, Bleeker. Yet, somehow, he felt that any such conference could only lead to further confusion. But now a crafty thought occurred to him.

The Patent Department. It was the job of the patent attorneys to understand these new inventions. They were supposed to file on important cases within a few days after the thing had been reduced to practice. The application had to explain the invention in intelligible terms, or else the Patent Office in Washington would rule the disclosure fatally defective. There was certainly no dishonor in asking the attorney in charge of this invention to step into his office and explain Celsus' report. It would be like the judge in a trial asking the court reporter to repeat some testimony the judge had missed. And no need to bother Con Patrick.

He buzzed his secretary: "Miss Sally, look at the Patent Department organization chart and get hold of the attorney responsible for Pierre Celsus' work. But don't bother Mr. Patrick."

As events developed, this was a mistake. While the Patent Department organization chart clearly showed that Alec Cord handled the inventive affairs of Pierre Celsus, Cord happily informed Miss Sally that all that had changed. Somebody else was now responsible. Additional phone calls established the apparent fact that, for the moment, at least, nobody was writing cases for Celsus.

This puzzled Bleeker. He knew that Patrick loved order, organization, and the predictable flow of life, and that when Patrick had taken the Patent Department of Hope Chemicals, he had drawn an organization chart to define precisely the areas of contact of each of his attorneys with each group in the Research Division.

This was all very true; in fact, during the early days Patrick had kept the chart current, showing every assignment change. But Patrick had been in office less than a year when the Nitrogen Group had their breakthrough in acrylonitrile, and it had been necessary for him to reshuffle all Patent Department assignments drastically until he could get the Nitrogen docket back to normal. While the dust was settling, Research formed the new Polymer Group, and the Budget Committee—after much muttering and review of Patent Department efficiency—finally let Patrick hire two new attorneys for the new Group. Meanwhile, Foams and Fibers were screaming, so one of the new polymer attorneys was assigned to them. And then Nitrogen insisted that Cord be assigned to them permanently, because he was the only man in the lab who could beat Dr. Fast at the chessboard—it being well known that Fast would talk about his inventions only in a losing position. The second new polymer man got clewed in to Mining and Metallurgy on an emergency job when it was discovered that he had worked summers on a barytes washer in Missouri. When he finished the emergency case, M & M refused to release him.

And that was when Patrick stopped revising the chart. From then on he kept everything in his head, like a general in the midst of shifting battle lines. He developed an exquisite facility in matching attorney to project, project to attorney, attorney to inventor. His manning assignments never failed. Except for Pierre Celsus. Nobody could understand Celsus. His few cases had been written personally by Patrick.

Bleeker discovered all this in slow fragments. Then he put in a call for Patrick.

After ten minutes in Bleeker's office, Patrick finally convinced him he knew no more about silamine than the research director. Following which, point by point, sentence by sentence, they went through the Project Report together.

"And listen to this," groaned Bleeker. "He's proposing some kind of dispersant for the residual silica."

"Why would he need a dispersant?" asked Patrick. "Why not just flush it direct to solids disposal?"

"I haven't the faintest idea. But that's not my point. Listen to what's in it:

> Vitriolated tartar
> Butter of antimony
> Libavius' fuming liquor
> Sal mirabile
> Magnesia nigra . . .

And the whole thing, he calls"—Bleeker looked at the report—"the *alkahest*." He looked up helplessly at Patrick. "*What* is the man *talking* about?"

"Alkahest?" Patrick looked troubled.

"Maybe I'm not pronouncing it right."

"No, you had it right. Except—I thought . . ."

"You thought what?"

"The term hasn't been used in earnest in over five hundred years. It's an alchemical term. It means 'universal solvent.' It dissolves anything you put in it."

"Alchemical? Solvent?" Bleeker looked blank.

"It might really dissolve the silica," ventured Patrick. "Although I can't see any reason why it would be necessary, technically."

"Alchemy . . ." muttered Bleeker. "What century does he think this is?" His chair began to swing slowly. "That man needs help. He ought to see Siegfried Walters."

"I understand he's been in therapy with Walters for some months," said Patrick. He added quietly: "Does this mean you won't approve the bench run?"

"No. It doesn't mean that. I'm going to approve it. In fact, the Board of Directors insists that we develop a process we can sell to the People's Republic. That twenty-five-cent royalty has them hypnotized. Anyhow, the new Fluidizer Bay will be finished in a few days. The runs can start then. Put one of your best men on it. If it works, get a case on file as soon as you get that madman translated into basic English."

"Of course, Andy."

"And now," said Bleeker, "what do I do with Celsus?"

"Nothing," said Patrick. "Leave him alone. Maybe you and I don't have what it takes to understand him."

"Nor does anyone else," declared Bleeker. "And that's the whole problem. Any chemist in corporate research has got to be one hundred per cent clear to the rank and file that have to translate him into a tonnage plant. His thinking has to be something our run-of-the-mill people can take and break down into its elements, its unit processes."

"I think he's some kind of a genius," said Patrick stubbornly.

"Maybe he is, but in this business, his kind of genius is not an asset, it's a disaster. What happens when he explains something? Do you understand it? You do not. I don't understand it. Nobody understands it. A few days ago he made the silamine process work for the first time. Four separate teams had already given up. And how does he explain it?"

"He just needed one seed molecule to initiate it," said Patrick. He added, quickly, "And don't ask me where he got it."

"But I *will* ask you. Where *did* he get it—a thing that had never before existed?"

Patrick shrugged his shoulders helplessly.

"Maybe you're right," said Bleeker thoughtfully. "Perhaps we're not mentally equipped to understand him. Perhaps we should examine our own capacity for comprehension of novel technology. It's like Willard Gibbs and the phase rule. He published in 1876, but nobody in America was capable of understanding him until Ostwald explained him in German. For a long time, if you couldn't read German, you couldn't understand the phase rule. Is something like that happening here? Maybe *we* can't be communicated with. Maybe *we* need to be examined. There are firms that do that, you know—management evaluation firms . . . research evaluation firms."

Patrick nodded absently. "Suppose he has something the rest of us don't have— but we just won't let him use it. We don't know *how* to listen to him.. We see him as a freak. Are *we* freaks to him?"

"But *alkahest*, Con, *really*. I suppose next we'll get a Project Proposal for making gold." He shook his head. "All I remember about alchemy was my undergraduate course in History of Chemistry, at State U. Frederick of Würtzburg reserved a place of distinction, a position of great elevation, for each and every alchemist who visited the realm."

"What was that?" asked Patrick.

Bleaker said grimly: "The highest gallows in all Europe."

When Patrick had gone, Bleeker sat swiveling slowly at his desk for a long time. Was Sasanov right? Maybe the lab *was* a little disorganized. *Something* was wrong, out-of-joint. Was it Celsus? The administration?

Bleeker prided himself on knowing everything that went on in his laboratory. (He almost did know.) He knew who was coming up with the ideas that might be commercial five or ten years from now. He knew the misfit who would have to be reshuffled. But no matter how bad the incompatibility, in the past his operations were big enough to find something which, if it did not completely match the talents of the transferee, at least kept him at something useful to the company and to himself.

But now, for the first time in thirty years, he felt truly baffled. Sasanov, he suspected, would never encounter this problem, or, if he did, it would be solved with prompt and drastic measures.

Bleeker chose a different way, gentler, but equally definitive.

He buzzed his secretary. "Miss Sally, get me Arnold Gruen, Gruen Associates," he said grimly.

Later, he explained it all to Patrick.

"Gruen Associates is unique in several respects. They're the oldest in the business, for one thing. For another, right now they're the only management-survey group equipped to look at research labs, although I dare say it's just a question of time before they lose *that* monopoly, what with so many billion dollars being spent on research in this country every year."

"Gruen is unique, you were saying?" nudged Patrick gently.

"I was explaining that," said Bleeker testily. "Well, Gruen brought in another outfit to study them, show them how they could tighten up their analysis techniques, rely on smaller samples, reduce study time and the overall cost of their surveys. Sort of like a psychiatrist getting himself psychoanalyzed, so he'll be a better doctor. Well, Gruen had this done to *them,* and they seem to be the only *surveyed* surveyors in the business. That's how they developed their 'Unit Profile', where they pick one man who has nearly all the faults of the research laboratory they're trying to correct."

"But wouldn't it be *still* better," said Patrick blandly, "if we could be surveyed by a group who had been straightened out by Gruen? Then we'd be surveyed by a *surveyed* surveyed group. Hope uses only the very best, you know."

"The point came up." Bleeker was equally bland. "But good sense prevailed."

Both men were silent a moment. Each seemed to be waiting for the other to speak. Patrick knew then that the same thought must be on Bleeker's mind. So Patrick, being the junior, said it. "What happens when they find Pierre Celsus?"

The first session with Gruen Associates took place in the Executive Dining Room, an intimate, expensively appointed room down the hall from the large lab cafeteria.

Patrick had long ago noted that Bleeker liked to conduct important discussions at the luncheon table. The theory was that Yankee pot roast following cocktails loosened a man's tongue and evoked basic truths, or at least turned up any latent disagreements, all of which might require excessive time and money to discover in other ways. Furthermore it was the simplest and quickest way to get to call a man by his first name, and everybody agreed this helped communication and delayed the development of paralyzing differences of viewpoint. But whatever the reasons, Patrick always liked a good meal with experts in their own fields.

While coffee was being poured, they finally got down to business.

"I want to make one thing clear," said Bleeker. "This is not a criticism of anyone, except possibly myself. Arnold Gruen and his people are here to determine whether I can improve the operation of the lab. Arnold's staff, Joe and Ben, here, will come in, starting tomorrow, and they'll be talking to a number of us. They'll talk to all our group leaders and to a number of our chemists and technicians at all levels. They'll make appointments ahead of time. Work them in, somehow. Within a few weeks, Arnold will put together a report, and then I'll decide whether we ought to change some of our procedures. Arnold, perhaps you can explain the mechanics of your survey, exactly what you intend to accomplish, and how you will do it."

"Of course, Andy. It's really quite simple. We at Gruen have one basic objective—increasing the dividend to the shareholders. We continue to exist because we have been able to help our clients meet this objective. Now, there's a fundamental corollary to our main objective, and that is, that industrial research, such as you have here at Hope, exists for the sole purpose of making money for the company, and to make this money as quickly as possible. To accomplish this, every man in the lab must recognize that he is part of a *team*. No man in a modern laboratory can work alone. He must recognize roadblocks instantly, and call in help immediately. He must be able to analyze and explain, or his project will bog down. He must *communicate*. That's the key word: *communicate*. And it must be *instant*." He turned to Patrick. "Con, your department has a vital function in all this. The life of a United States patent is seventeen years. Our studies show that, up until recent years, only the last five to seven years of a typical patent are of any use in protecting a basic new invention. Why? Because it so often takes ten to twelve years to proceed from the first experimental work to the first commercial plant. One of our aims is to cut this idle patent time. We do this by cutting the development phase to three years." Gruen took a sip of coffee and smiled. "Do I hear incredulous murmurs? I repeat: three years. It can be done. And it's all in *communication*. Everybody knows what everybody else is doing. Problems will be recognized instantly. But here I am, still talking in generalities." He turned to Kober. "Ben, will you explain what you and Joe Marel are going to do, starting tomorrow?"

"Certainly, Arnold. My function—and Joe's—is to interview some of your key people. We've already drawn up a list. This was based on a study of several hundred project reports written by approximately fifty different bench chemists, senior chemists, and group leaders. Con, we'll include one man in the Patent Department, probably you. We will interview each of these people. As a result of these interviews we will develop a further sampling of six or eight chemists who offer most in the way of a challenge to the Gruen technique. We will then hope to be able to boil this list down to one man. This man, if our survey is valid, will constitute a walking summary of all that we hope to recommend be corrected here."

Arnold Gruen looked over at Patrick. "You lawyers have your 'reasonable man'. We are looking for the 'unreasonable man': a compendium of errors—our Unit Profile."

"Profile?" asked Patrick. "You mean something like the Bernreuter or Thurstone personality profiles for executives?"

"Something like that," said Gruen. "Except that the Bernreuter profile provides a *positive* model for the up-and-coming executives of our large mail order houses—a real inspiration, too, if I may say so!—whereas the Gruen profile is *negative*. When we establish it, we offer it to the client as something to be shunned by all right-thinking employees. Another difference is, the Gruen profile is personified; it is drawn from one actual man, a case history. In fact, our main effort in the study is to find that man." He nodded toward Bleeker. "And when we find him, our bill for services will follow shortly."

Patrick was eternally amazed by his women attorneys. Marguerite French was a case in point. Hired fresh out of State U. with straight A's in chemistry, he had first put her on novelty searches in the Patent Office in Washington. She had picked up the patter almost overnight. ("I'll be in the stacks tomorrow, Mr. Patrick, flipping the bundles for that new polymer." But when she dictated her search report, she had the good sense to call it "information retrieval.") She soon knew the Patent Office Search Manual by heart, and better still, most of the chemical patent examiners on a first-name basis. They told her what subs to check in the Search Room and pointed out unofficial "shoes" in their own offices that cut her search time to a minimum. Examiners had been known to hover over her shoulder, helping her through their soft copies, to find a "dead reference."

A couple of years after hiring her, Patrick learned by accident that she had passed the Patent Agent's exam—the dreaded Patent Bar—on her first try (Patrick had failed it the first time) and was halfway through law school at night. That was when Patrick started her on writing patent applications. In good time she had finished law school and had become a full-fledged attorney, in most respects as good as any of his men. And in one particular respect she excelled any man in the department. This was her ability to work with certain of the more refractory male chemists. Whatever their inability to write an intelligible project report, she somehow was able to analyze, define, and summarize the most involved reactions that any of them ever brought forth. When working with her, they suddenly became expressive, articulate, even voluble. ("Maybe they're all in love with her," mused Patrick. But that was too simple. "She's a kid sister to them," he thought once. No, that wasn't it, either. "She appreciates them." Yes, he felt he was getting warm.)

Well, no matter what it was, he had made up his mind as to who was to be assigned to Pierre Celsus. If Celsus could be persuaded to talk to anyone, he would talk to Marguerite French.

Patrick drew the structural formula on his office blackboard. "Silamine. As you probably know, Celsus' new synthesis is somewhat analogous to the commercial process for making urea from ammonia and carbon dioxide, except that we use SiO_2, instead of CO_2. In other words, we react ammonia and silica, and we get silamine and by-product water."

"It's strange that it should react at all," said Marguerite. "Silica is one of the most unreactive oxides known."

Patrick smiled. "That's the general impression, all right, and that's why we think we may have something patentable. Actually, we don't use plain old silica sand—the low surface area makes it too inactive. We use an extremely porous, high-surface-area silica, five thousand square meters per gram. That means a thimbleful—if you could spread it out—would cover two or three football fields. And this means that it is thousands of times as reactive as sand, because a given weight of high-surface-area silica can make contact with thousands more ammonia molecules than plain sand."

"I gather there's more to it than that. Certainly ammonia and high-surface-area silica have been brought together before without making silamine."

"Yes, Marguerite, as you very well know, there's more to it than that. Firstly, the silica contains a new catalyst, terbium oxide, one of the rare earths. Celsus proposed this after his first successful run, back in Silicon Compounds." He looked at her. "You were there."

She replied noncommitally. "Yes, I was there."

Patrick sighed. She was not going to volunteer anything about the stopwatch. In a little while, he'd have to ask her.

He continued. "Next, Celsus adds a thing he calls 'xerion'."

" 'Xerion'?"

"Don't ask me what it is. Some kind of co-catalyst, I think. It's your job to find out. Celsus contends his new system provides extremely high temperatures right in the fluidizers, so much heat, in fact, that the columns have to be cooled. He cools by heat-exchanging with incoming liquid ammonia, which goes next to the base of the columns, where it serves as both reaction gas and suspending medium for the silica gel."

"What happens to the by-product water?"

"Some gets stripped out with silamine product, but some stays on the silica. Celsus seems to think it's very important that some stay on the silica. He wants the silica to be 'wet' throughout the reaction. I don't know why. Again, this is something you should ask him about. Also, he runs the residual silica into a tank of something he calls 'alkahest'—some kind of solvent or dispersant. Find out why the stuff can't simply be dried and carted off to waste. Is it dangerous, or what?"

Marguerite looked up from her notebook. "There's still one very basic thing I don't understand. This terbium-xerion thing . . . how does the combination make heat?"

Patrick shrugged his shoulders helplessly. "You'll have to ask Celsus."

"Do you think he will tell me any of this?"

"I don't know, Marguerite."

"What about his Project Reports?"

"He's made several. They're all different. But don't try to reconcile them; it's impossible. So it boils down to this: Celsus knows, or thinks he knows, how to make the thing work. But he hasn't been able so far to explain it to his own people. This is where you come in. Defining technical data is your job, as a patent attorney. You're better at it than his brother chemists. Also, you'll bring a new outlook."

Marguerite French closed her notebook. "Is that about it?"

"One more thing." Patrick eyed her speculatively. "The other morning, at that first silamine run, you had a stopwatch. What was all that about?"

The girl hesitated. "I don't think you will believe me."

"Tell me anyway."

"I timed the reaction. With the stopwatch. All I had to do was calculate the space velocity of the ammonia. From this you get the time it took to move the first silamine product from the reactor to the collector, where it immediately gave the picrate test. This was 38.6 seconds. When Pierre called on the silamine to exist, I started the watch. When the picrate showed, I stopped it." She opened her purse. "I've been carrying it around—it's still stopped. I don't know what to do with it. Suppose you keep it a while." She handed the watch to Patrick. He took it dubiously. It read 38.5 seconds. Experimental error? Not, he suspected, Pierre Celsus'.

"I think it was telekinesis," said Marguerite.

Patrick studied the girl with widened eyes. Her face was pale, but she was staring back defiantly. The man tugged at his moustache, his brows creasing. He remembered Celsus' behavior at that now notoriously successful run, crooning, whispering, exhorting, caressing the flask. Like a "hot" gambler talking to the dice. And then the throw. Some gamblers were supposed to have this power, this control of inanimate matter. TK. Psi.

He said hoarsely, "Is it possible?"

"I think it is. With some chemists. Pierre isn't the first. He won't be the last. If he's different, it's only because he can do it better, and because he *knows* what he can do."

Patrick's mind raced ahead. The implications . . . were staggering. He suppressed a shiver. "But that isn't chemistry. It isn't science. It may even be against the law."

"It was the *first* chemistry," said the girl curtly. "It is alchemy."

"Now wait just a minute," protested Patrick, struggling back to firmer ground. "If Celsus were a real genuine alchemist, he'd be making gold, wouldn't he? Is he making gold? Of course he's not. But again, suppose he could make gold, how would you explain it to the United States Mint and the F.B.I.?"

"You miss the point entirely," said the girl. "He's not trying to convince anybody he's an alchemist. It's the other way around. He's trying to *hide* it. He wants to be just a plain ordinary twentieth-century chemist. If he could make gold, he'd keep it a secret. So it's pointless to argue that since he hasn't made any gold, he's not an alchemist. The alchemist uses his powers to supply the requirements of his patron. In the fifteenth century, the big requirement was gold. In a modern laboratory, it could be anything from plastics to lasers to silamine. And finally, what's so wonderful about gold? Today dozens of fine chemicals sell at more per ounce than gold."

The man groaned. "But the patent application . . . what will the Patent Office do when we file an application on an alchemical process? And how will the main claim read? Can we say, 'In the process of reacting silica and ammonia to form silamine, the improvement comprising telekinetically first forming one molecule of silamine, thereby to autocatalyze the reaction'? How is that going to sound to the Examiners in Class 23?"

"It is sufficient if those skilled in the art can reproduce the invention," said Marguerite. "Maybe that means other alchemists."

Patrick fought for control over the gurgle rising in his throat. "Others? God forbid!"

The girl waited in quiet sympathy.

At last Patrick said lamely "Well . . . see what you can do—"

When Marguerite had gone, Patrick sat staring at the pigeonholes of his desk and tugging glumly at his moustache. There wasn't anything he could do. He couldn't go in to Andrew Bleeker and say, "Andy, your man Celsus has TK. He's a psi. And that's why he got silamine, and that's why his processes are not reproducible." Patrick shook his head sadly, remembering what Bleeker had said to the applicant from California who claimed he had seen a flying saucer.

The intercom shattered his musings. Joe Marel of Gruen wanted to interview him.

Joe Marel stared at the rolltop desk for several seconds.

Patrick said finally, "You wanted to review some Patent Department procedures, you said."

"Oh, of course. Forgive me for staring. I've never seen anything quite like it—the desk, I mean."

"Biggest phony in the lab," said Patrick genially.

"I wouldn't know. Well, suppose we start with your infringement opinion on the new silamine process."

"Certainly."

"You say here, 'This patent does not present a serious risk of infringement.' Do you mean it is not infringed?"

"Not exactly. No one can predict with certainty what the courts will do with a given patent. It's always a guess. We simply try to assess the degree of risk."

Marel looked at him curiously. "You mean, then, it's *probably* not infringed?"

"In a sense, yes. But bear in mind, it's not a thing that admits of calculating percentages."

"But I gather that when your management reads that, they will understand that the patent situation is in the clear?"

"Well, not inevitably, and not necessarily. But it very well *could* have that effect."

Marel was silent a moment. He ran his finger around his collar, then continued. "Well, then, you go on to say, about another patent, 'At the appellate level, the defense of patent invalidity would probably be affirmed.' Does that mean the patent is invalid?"

"No, here again we simply try to crystal ball what the courts will do with a given patent question. No lawyer can advise his client whether a patent is valid or invalid. Only the courts can do that. If the courts have not spoken, then at best the lawyer can only state how he thinks the courts would rule, if and when they should get the question. And you realize, of course, that the courts in different federal circuits could come up with different answers. The patent could be held invalid in Maine, but valid and infringed in California. And then there are other reasons we might not want to come right out and say a patent is invalid. For example, some day we might buy the patent, and then we might want to continue the litigation, except that we'd now be on the other side."

Marel blinked his eyes rapidly. At last he said: "Then why not just pick up the phone and tell whoever in management wants to know? Why have a written opinion at all?"

"Oh, there has to be a written opinion—something for dozens of people in Hope management to look at, as well as people outside. The banks and insurance companies that provide the financing for the proposed new plant—*their* lawyers want to see the patent opinion. Now, lawyers have their own special language when they talk to each other. They never say 'yes' or 'no.' If our lender's lawyer gets an opinion that says 'yes' or 'no,' he might regard it as incompetent, and then we might not get the financing. The same thing is true for our own sub-licensing. When we sell the process for use in England or West Germany or Japan, or wherever it may be, we have found that *their* lawyers place more confidence in one of my twenty-page opinions than in a categorical clearance from the President of Hope Chemicals."

"I see. I mean, I *think* I see. You mean you can't just say 'yes' or 'no' . . . ?"

"Exactly," said Patrick. "Too deceptive, by far. Wouldn't be cricket." He became expansive. " 'Yes' and 'no' are the two most dangerous words in the English language. Each inherently means something that is by definition impossible. Each, as ordinarily used, is accompanied by a protective cloud of implied qualifying conditional clauses. Problems arise when the speaker and his listener fail to achieve a coincidence in qualifications implied and qualifications inferred."

Marel shifted nervously.

Patrick continued, "Now that you are studying patent opinions, perhaps a little basic theory is in order. To start with, what is the object of a good patent opinion?"

"Tell me," said Marel.

"The object is," said Patrick, "that the opinion turn out to be correct, no matter what happens after it is written. Is the company sued for infringement? The opinion says this is a possibility. Do we lose the suit? We said that our chances were better than even. They were, but we provided for the possibility of loss, because 'better than even' *could* mean only fifty-one percent—in other words, we should expect to lose nearly half of such cases. But then we take a final appeal, and win. In the opinion we find our conclusions apply to decisions at the appellate level. And of course, there's a strong suggestion in the opinion that we settle on a reasonable basis if we get into real trouble."

Marel stared at the patent director in fascination.

Patrick continued smoothly, "In other words, as history unfolds, day by day, and month by month, you should be able to reread the opinion and find that nothing in it is inconsistent with subsequent events. In this sense, it should resemble a prophecy out of Nostradamus, which becomes completely clear only *after* the occurrence of the prophesied event."

"I guess that's why most people find a patent opinion hard to read," said Marel.

"Granted," said Patrick. "However, let us not confuse readability with clarity. Actually, there's generally an inverse relationship: the more readable, the less precise; a real literary masterpiece is so honeycombed with ambiguities as to be incomprehensible. Take Coleridge's 'Kubla Khan'. Would you consider that a masterpiece?"

"Certainly."

"But can you tell me where the dome was going to be built?"

"The dome? Oh yes, the pleasure dome. How does the thing go?" Patrick quoted from memory:

> " 'In Xanadu did Kubla Khan
> A stately pleasure-dome decree:
> Where Alph, the sacred river, ran
> Through caverns measureless to man
> Down to a sunless sea.'

"Now, then," said Patrick, where was the dome to be built?"

"In Xanadu," said Marel.

"Then where was Kubla Khan when he decreed the dome?"

"Oh. In Xanadu? I see the problem. Well, then the dome must have been on the Alph River."

"It's a long river. Where on the river? In the caverns?"

"I shouldn't think so."

"Nor on the shores of that sunless sea?"

"Probably not."

"You see my point, Joe. In the arts, when a thing is incomprehensible, it helps it to be a masterpiece. But not in the law. If a lawyer had written 'Kubla Khan', these ambiguities would never have cropped up. He would have made the thing crystal-clear."

"No doubt," smiled Marel. "Con, what does Andy Bleeker do when he gets your patent opinions? Say, like this silamine opinion?"

Patrick looked at Marel carefully. He said: "You raise a very interesting point. He's a very busy man, you know . . . excuse me, I think this is Bleeker on the intercom. No, don't leave." He flipped the switch. "Yes, Andy?"

Bleeker's voice came in strongly. "Con, this silamine opinion . . . I don't know when I'll get time to go over it thoroughly. Just tell me whether we're clear or not."

"We're clear, Andy."

"That's what I thought. Thanks, Con."

The intercom went off. Patrick looked at Marel. "It was a masterpiece," he said coolly.

An hour after Marel left Patrick, the patent director got another call from Bleeker.

"Con, I thought you'd be interested. Marel and Kober are sitting here with me. They think they've found their man for the Profile."

"So soon? I didn't realize they'd already interviewed Celsus."

"They haven't. But they see no need to continue the study."

"Why that's fine . . . I guess." Patrick was puzzled. "Who is he?"

He heard Bleeker exhale slowly.

"It's confidential. However, Con, I'm suggesting to Kober and Marel that they skip the patent department in their survey."

"I'm sorry to hear it, Andy. We'd hoped to get a lot of help from them."

"It could run into a lot of time and money," said Bleeker. "Also, I'm not sure they have the necessary background to study . . . a patent man."

"That's a shame," said Patrick. "I liked Marel."

"He likes you, too, Con. In fact, you . . . ah . . . fascinate him." Bleeker's voice seemed to lose strength.

"Will you explain to me, Pierre, why you use so many words that are not in the dictionary?"

Celsus looked at Marguerite in surprise. "Not in the dictionary? Such as what?"

"Such as 'xerion'."

"Hm-m-m. Let's see." Chin in hand, Celsus studied the volumes in his little book case. "Let's try this one." He pulled down a worn, leather-clad tome and opened it carefully. The pages seemed yellow and brittle, and many had evidently been patched with transparent tape. "Doesn't seem to be here." He flipped back several pages. "Let's try it by the modern name, 'elixir'. Ah, just as I thought. 'Elixir' is from 'al iksir', Arabic, and 'iksir' is from 'xerion', Greek. That's the Alexandrine Greeks, of course, and I'm sure *they* got it from the Egyptians." He looked up brightly. "So 'xerion' is the same as 'elixir'. I'd forgotten they'd changed over, after Avicenna."

"May I see the book?"

"Sure." He handed it over.

"Alchemyia collecta," read Marguerite, looking at the frontispiece. "By Andreas Livau." Her eyes widened. "It was printed in 1895 . . . and it's all in Latin."

"Why, yes. One of the old standards. Still very useful, though."

"It must be worth a lot of money." She handed it back slowly. "Now we're down to 'elixir', at any rate. What's 'elixir', Pierre?"

"Why, I thought every chemist knew *that*, Marguerite. 'Elixir' is the exactly correct union of the four elements: the body—as represented by copper and lead; the spirit—as represented by mercury; the male element; and the female element. Some of the philosophers added gold, but I think that rather begs the question, doesn't it?" He looked at her expectantly.

"Pierre, you're making me feel very stupid. What does it *do?*"

"Why, it causes the reaction, of course."

"You mean it's the catalyst?"

"Well, not exactly. It would be more accurate to say it causes the silicon and terbium to react to provide the necessary reaction heat. The atomic number of silicon is fourteen, terbium is sixty-five. Add them together, and what do you get?"

"Seventy-nine?"

"Quite right. Terbium, at sixty-five, is only fair. It's not even a prime. Seventy-nine is perfect. It's a prime, a favorite of Pythagoras, and even though it's a rather low isotope, it's a sure thing for quantitative yields of silamine. Does that clear it up?"

The girl sighed.

"I like talking to you, Marguerite," said the man. "I'm glad Con Patrick has finally got a patent attorney who can understand real chemistry."

Marguerite looked at him quizzically. "Pierre, I'm glad you like me, because I like you, too." She measured her words carefully. "Would you come over to my apartment for supper some evening?"

The man looked at her in amazement.

The girl continued hurriedly. "I'm a wonderful cook. We could talk and play records. But you don't have to, of course . . ."

"Oh, no—it's a wonderful idea. I've never been to . . . I mean, I never had an invitation before . . . What I mean, is, I'd love to. When?"

"How about tomorrow evening?"

"But that's the first shift run on silamine."

"Did they ask you to be there?"

"No, but I think I ought to be."

"Pierre, there's a rumor going around. Ben Kober is trying to persuade Mr. Bleeker to let him make that first run, all by himself."

The man frowned. "You mean . . . they don't want me to be there at all?"

"They don't mean it that way, Pierre. They don't mean to slight you. Ben simply wants to check out the process. He wants Analytical to stay open all night, for sample analysis."

Celsus caught his breath. "Samples of what?"

"Why, silamine product, I suppose. Is anything wrong?"

"No, not if that's all they're doing." He exhaled slowly.

"There's no danger in any of it, is there?" insisted the girl.

"Not if they follow the flow sheet."

"I'm sure that's exactly what they intend to do. See you tomorrow night?"

"Sure thing."

The next day Patrick got another call from Bleeker, this time to report to Bleeker's office, to review a problem with Ben Kober of Gruen.

As was his way with anything unpleasant, Bleeker got to the point at once. "Con, the Gruen people"—he nodded toward Kober—"have made a tentative selection for their Unit Profile. This time I agree with them."

Patrick pulled out his meerschaum, filled it expertly from his pocket pouch, and fired up. He puffed and waited. He did not intend to make it easier for the older man.

Bleeker took this all in. He smiled faintly. "It's Celsus."

"But tentative?" said Patrick.

Kober answered. "We're pretty sure. But we want to do one more thing. We want to take one of his projects and make it work all by ourselves, simply by following his written instructions. He will not be present."

"Have you picked a project?" asked Patrick quietly.

Kober looked at Bleeker.

"There's really only one," said the research director. "Silamine."

"In the new Fluidizer Bay?" asked Patrick.

"Yes."

"How am I involved?"

"Your man in the patent department and Ben Kober will both be trying to develop the identical information. Each will be trying to extract from Celsus the explanation of the silamine reaction. But there's a basic difference. Your man—"

"Marguerite French," murmured Patrick.

"Ah, yes, Miss French. Good man. Well, she'll be talking to Celsus on the theory he can and will explain the process. Kober will be talking to Celsus on the theory Celsus can't or won't explain anything. Each will be a check on the other. Both cannot be right."

Patrick groaned inwardly. He could not say it, and yet it had to be said, here, now, before this thing got out of hand. "Just suppose it's something not in the books—something Celsus can do but can't explain to anyone else how to do."

"Like what?" said Kober.

"Like telekinesis!" blurted Patrick. "Psi . . ." He blushed easily, and he realized with hellish discomfort that he was blushing now.

Kober stared at him in unabashed amazement.

Bleeker swiveled mercifully around and looked through the office window.

Kober gave a short embarrassed laugh. "I don't think you need me anymore. If you'll excuse me . . ." He left quickly.

Bleeker turned back to the patent director. He began swiveling in slow unease. "Con, I appreciate your telling me your views, especially in front of Kober." The monotonous oscillations continued. "However, please understand me. I cannot accept psi as an explanation. That's as bad as alchemy; we've been through all that. To put the matter even stronger: even if what you say is true, I couldn't accept it as any part of our normal research effort. Maybe psi is all right for esoteric seminars at the universities, where they don't really bother anybody. But it is *not* all right in a modern chemical laboratory. How could we put twenty million dollars in a silamine plant, when start-up depended on the availability of Pierre Celsus? And suppose we went through with this plant design and license with the People's Republic? Could we give plant guarantees? What if we truly did have to have some hocus-pocus from Celsus to get the plant on stream? Are we sure we could deliver Celsus on twenty-four hours' notice? And if we couldn't, would we be protected in our Force Majeure clause? Is Celsus an Act of God that relieves Hope of liability?" Bleeker leaned forward and looked at Patrick earnestly. "Con, this is madness. Don't even *think* about it anymore. It *can't* be psi."

"It *has* to be," insisted Patrick. "It was impossible, until he made it work."

The research director stared hard at Patrick. He said finally, "All right, let's assume that he *can* make just about anything work. Let's assume that he can even make an impossible reaction go, because he wills that it shall go. (Not that I believe it, not for a moment!) Let's say he can upset every known law of chemistry. Yet, if he alone can make it work, what good is it to the company? He can never explain it to the Engineering Department. You could never build a commercial plant based on his data. That's why Kober wants to conduct the new silamine process in the Fluidizer Bay personally."

Patrick sighed and got up. "Maybe you're right."

"Where are you going?"

"To see our psychiatrist."

"We all need it. Wish I had the time."

Patrick smiled.

Siegfried Walters was "free-associating." Inventors. Very few. Why does a man invent? *How* does he invent? There's an element of play in it. The best of them don't really seem to care whether it works or not. Indifferent. Barely one real inventor in a hundred. Steinmetz. White's *Organization Man* explained all this. I could do a paper with figures. Statistics. One man starts it all. Study him. Pick one man. The oddest. Pierre Celsus. Bleeker has this study going. This Gruen outfit. Profile. How long would it take them to find Celsus? And what will they do with a fistful of mercury?

His reverie was broken by the intercom. Conrad Patrick was waiting in the anteroom.

Walters chose his words carefully. "Con, you realize that I may not be able to tell you what you want to know. I cannot discuss confidential matters."

"Relax, Siegfried. I'm not going to let you get called up before the Ethics Committee. I just need a few nonconfidential facts about Pierre. I've assigned one of my women attorneys to him, and now I'm wondering if I did the right thing."

"How can I help you?"

"Is he dangerous?"

"No. At least not in the sense that he would pick up a wrench and start swinging. He has no wish to hurt—conscious or subconscious. Quite the contrary. He has been most helpful—to me, at least. In fact, our doctor-patient relationship has become somewhat . . ." The psychiatrist hesitated.

"Somewhat *what?*" demanded Patrick.

But Walters was silent.

Frustrated, Patrick tried another tack. "Well, is he sane?"

"Sane? For him, that question is either irrelevant or wrong. Were William Blake and Beethoven and Buddha sane? Is a Chopin nocturne? Consider the falcon, the tiger, the temple at Karnak, and a moonbeam on a field of snow. Are these things sane?" His head jerked as though to squelch Patrick's snort of impatience. "The point is, Con, all these things, these people, these creatures, are the best of their kind. Perfect. Unique. Standards of comparison that work for other things are meaningless for them. And you ask whether Pierre Celsus is sane."

"That still is the question," said Patrick grimly.

"Well, then, he's not sane. But not insane, either. Maybe the best word—and not really a good one—is *un*sane."

Patrick shook his head in helpless frustration.

"Take this study by Gruen," continued Walters. "They are trying to pick this one man, to summarize all that is wrong with this lab. But suppose that he also summarizes all that is right at Hope? Suppose that he adds up all the magic and mystery of chemistry—the control of mind over matter . . . sixty centuries of reacting things and coming out with other things?" He paused, searching for the phrases that would explain Pierre Celsus to the patent director. "Do you remember H. G. Wells' short story 'In the Country of the Blind'?"

" 'In the country of the blind, the one-eyed man is king'?"

"That's just the point. He wasn't. Being sighted, he was regarded as a freak. When he talked about 'seeing', they thought he was crazy. They felt sorry for him. To cure him so that he could be a fit member of the community, they blinded him. If we're not careful, we might do the same to Pierre Celsus."

There was a pause. Patrick cleared his throat and studied the psychiatrist a moment. "Siegfried, I know this sounds crazy, but have you ever detected anything . . . unusual . . . I mean, really extraordinary . . ." He realized he must sound very strange. "Like—"

"Psi?" asked Walters quietly.

Patrick started.

Walters seemed almost relieved. "You do know, don't you? I wonder how." He took a deep breath. "I'm going to stretch medical ethics just a trifle, Con. Since one of your patent people will be working closely with Pierre, I think you are entitled to know something further about him—something you don't even know to ask about." He got up and walked over to the tape recorder. "Pierre and I make tapes. We do this every session, once a week. The theory is, the patient can replay the tape at leisure to reinforce his therapy. Except replay isn't the right word. Not the right word at all. Because some of the material on these tapes, the recent ones, was never spoken during the analysis."

Patrick was silent, expectant. Walters became almost pleading. "Do you understand what I have just told you?"

"I *guess* so," said the attorney hesitantly. "But there must be some logical explanation. Did somebody dub in something on the tape afterward?"

"That's what I thought, too, the first time it happened. The second time, I knew it was the right tape, even though I knew that what was on it was impossible."

"What *was* on it?"

"The *real* stream of consciousness. *The real thing,* mind you."

"What's so unusual about that? Isn't that the standard procedure?"

Walters leaned forward anxiously, as though it were essential to his own sanity that Patrick understand him. "Let me explain. We talk about the 'stream of consciousness'. It's a great tool in analysis. When a patient starts to think out loud, his thoughts soon wander to topics closely connected with the experiences buried in his subconscious, the things causing his neurosis. The patient puts up road signs, as it were, to guide the analyst. Now, you will have to appreciate that in this oral free association, the patient's tongue is hopelessly outdistanced by his mind, which is racing ahead a mile a minute, hearing sounds, seeing and feeling things, and his tongue has to pick and choose out of this kaleidoscope of sensation a few meager, widely spaced scraps to pass along to the analyst. So a great deal is lost when the stream of consciousness passes through the speech bottleneck. I complained about this to Pierre in one of our early sessions. He . . . ah . . . solved the problem."

"Siegfried," said Patrick, "are you trying to tell me that Celsus is telekinetically imposing his thoughts on tape?"

The two men stared dumbly at each other. Patrick waited for the psychiatrist to say yes, to nod. But there was no gesture. In silence Walters picked up a spool of tape and put it on the recorder. Instantly the room was full of sound. There were cries, tense voices. Patrick looked at Walters.

"You'd have to be a doctor to recognize what's going on there," said the other. "A baby is being born."

"Incredible," breathed Patrick.

"You think *that's* incredible?" said Walters, almost pensively. "Then listen to *this*." He put on a second tape, ran it soundlessly for a few seconds, then turned up the volume.

Patrick leaned forward.

Something rhythmic was coming from the speaker. ". . .Thub-lub . . . thub-lub . . . thub-lub . . ."

Walters snapped off the recorder. "Recognize *that?*"

Patrick shook his head in wonder.

"It's a heartbeat," said Walters quietly.

"Heartbeat? Whose heartbeat?"

"My mother's."

"Your . . . *mother's?*" Patrick's jaw dropped. "You mean, *your* mother's?"

"Of course. Whom did you think I've been talking about? It's *my* stream of consciousness. It's *my* prenatal recall. Remarkable, isn't it? Even Freud couldn't recall farther back than age three. Pierre has been helping me. He puts this beam—sort of a psi laser—on my cerebral cortex, and then reflects and focuses it on the tape."

Patrick gulped. "I see. Then when you said doctor-patient confidence, you meant that the *doctor* was—"

"Con," said Walters, looking at his watch, "you'll have to excuse me. I have an appointment."

As Patrick left, he met Pierre Celsus coming in.

"Well, Sieg, how are we today?" cried Celsus cheerily.

"You're late," said Walters petulantly.

"I was tied up on silamine." He smiled contritely. "Sorry."

"Well, let's get started," said Walters.

Celsus nodded gravely and sat down in the big leather chair in back of the couch. Walters walked over to the couch, where he lay down and crossed his fingers behind his head.

"I hope you've reconsidered what you threatened to do at our last session," said Celsus.

"No, Pierre. My mind's made up. I'm going back to Vienna for a long refresher course. I'll be gone several months. You've given me a terrible inferiority complex. In fact, I think I may be on the verge of total breakdown. They didn't teach psi at the University. They didn't prepare me for people like you. They let me down." His voice trembled. "I'm no good to myself, my patients, or to anybody."

"They didn't know," soothed Celsus. "It couldn't be helped. Psi wasn't accepted when you went to med school. I guess it still isn't. But you can't blame yourself. There's nobody to blame."

Walters' face twisted around. "You're not putting this on tape. You *know* I have to reinforce my therapy by replaying these tapes."

"Of course, Sieg. Right away."

There was a click from Walters' desk, followed by the almost inaudible whirring of the tape recorder turntable. Celsus had not moved from his chair.

"That's better," said Walters, mollified. He closed his eyes. "I've looked you up, you know . . . your kind. It's quite a story.

"Ten centuries ago the best metal workers were respected dealers in the black arts. That's where the *black* smith got his name. An oath taken on his anvil was sacred, and binding in the courts. In China, only the priests were permitted to work copper and bronze, because everyone understood that extra-human help was necessary. But this is all gone. Nowadays, when anything impossible happens in a chemical laboratory, science always assumes there's a perfectly good reason, and generally they're able to find some sort of way to reproduce the impossibility. They overlook the fact that before it was first done, it was often truly impossible. They overlook the nature of the man who caused it to happen that first impossible time. Often the man himself doesn't understand how he did it. He would resist knowing. Even those who have psi often refuse to believe it. Take Carothers and nylon, Bell and the telephone, De Forest and the triode, Röntgen and X rays, Goodyear and rubber. They did these things, and later, much later, their successors figured out why the thing worked. They want you to explain why silamine works. But you can't. At least, not in terms that would make sense to Andrew Bleeker and Arnold Gruen.

"This Gruen thing. They're going to find you, you know."

"Yes, I know." The response came from the speaker on the tape recorder.

"You don't seem to be worried. Do you know what's going to happen?"

"Some of it," said the recorder, "but I don't know where or when."

"What will it be like?"

There was a silence. And then, as if to answer him, there came sounds from the speaker that the psychiatrist could barely make out. He sat up slowly, heavily, as though wakening from a dream. He was alone in the room. The impression grew on him that he had been alone for some time. He stared at the tape recorder, and now he understood the sounds. It was music. It was beautiful. He slowly recognized it. Bach's "Sheep May Safely Graze." And then other sounds began to emerge through the music in eerie counterpoint. He recognized the intrusive, incessant ringing of a telephone. Then an automobile horn. Then a woman's scream. And then there was a click, and the recorder stopped. Siegfried Walters pressed his hands to his face and groaned. "Oh, Freud, how could you have missed it!"

It was nearly midnight.

They sat on the sofa in Marguerite's tiny parlor, leaning back, and listening to Bach. It came to its lovely dreaming end, and continued to float in the silence.

Finally Pierre Celsus said quietly, "What do you want of me, Marguerite?"

"I want to be your friend."

"Always before, when somebody wanted to be my friend, he really wanted something else."

"I know, Pierre. I once hoped you would explain—*really* explain—your silamine process to me." Her voice became morose. "But I gave up. I don't care anymore."

"But we've been through all that, Marguerite," he said patiently. "The reaction needs heat in an amount available only in a nuclear process. So we provide that. The terbium reacts with the silicon. The atomic number of silicon is fourteen. Terbium is sixty-five. To make them react, we simply feed in a little xerion. It doesn't react all at once; it's continuous—over several hours. This gives the necessary BTUs over the required reaction period. In fact we get a little *too* much heat. That's why we have to cool the fluidizer column. We cool it with liquid ammonia, which we heat exchange from the hot column. This vaporizes the ammonia, so we just use the resulting vapor ammonia as the combination fluidizing and reaction vapor. The vapor ammonia reacts with the suspended silica particles, and out comes silamine. But you know all that. Why do you want to hear it again?"

The girl was puzzled. "You mean, the terbium oxide *really* reacts with the silica?"

"Of course. The xerion, or elixir, causes it. Some centuries ago, it was a very well known catalyst for this kind of reaction."

"I don't think it's in *Gmelin*."

"No, I suppose not. But of course *Gmelin* is concerned only with chemical reactions. There's nothing nuclear in the *Handbuch*."

"Nuclear . . . ?"

"Of course. How else could you get the necessary heat?" He looked at his watch. "Kober ought to be finishing the first silamine run right now. You're sure he isn't changing anything?"

"Not really. I think he plans to collect the catalyst, after the run, to analyze it."

The man started. "What do you mean, collect it? He's supposed to discharge it into the alkahest."

"Why, Pierre, I'm sure I don't know. Can't he simply ladle out a sample from the alkahest?"

The man's voice was suddenly harsh. "The alkahest will dissolve anything he dips into it. And *then* what will he try?"

As she watched, the blood drained slowly from his face. Yet, when he spoke, his voice was controlled, almost resigned. "I have to go now, Marguerite."

Troubled, she did not try to stop him.

But after she heard his car drive away from the front of the apartment building, she began to worry in earnest. She had a premonition that something terrible was going to happen. But what? In fact, what *was* happening? What was going on, down at the lab, right now? Why did the process work at all? What was terbium plus silicon? Suppose you added their atomic numbers? What was sixty-five plus fourteen? Seventy-nine. And what element was number seventy-nine? It could be . . . but it couldn't be . . . She jumped up, ran over to her bookcase.

Ephraim would have it. She flipped through the pages. There it was, "Gold, atomic number 79." Pierre Celsus was making gold. *That* was his nuclear reaction, his source of tremendous heat. The wisdom of the ages applied to making silamine in the twentieth century. And if gold were really there, it was there as auric oxide. And auric oxide, ammonia, and water would react to form—gold fulminate.

She whirled, seized the phone, and dialed rapidly.

Marguerite's voice was low, urgent. "Ben? Ben Kober?"

"Yes? Who is it?"

"Ben, this is Marguerite French. I want you to listen carefully."

"I can't talk now, Marguerite. The silamine yield was twice what we expected. The collector overflowed, and I had to shut down. I'm still mopping up." Kober sounded irritable, impatient. "Marguerite, I'll have to call you back."

"No, Ben! This is extremely important. Just tell me this: Are you running the spent catalyst into the alkahest—all of it?"

"No, I'm not. That alkahest stuff is—crazy. I tried to ladle some spent catalyst out of it with an iron dipper, and the whole dipper dissolved. Anything that goes into that alkahest is *gone*. The only way to collect a sample of catalyst is to dry it with hot air, *in situ*, in the fluidizer columns. Which is what I'm doing now. And as soon as it's dry, I'm going to take samples for analysis."

"That's what I thought. Ben, you must get everyone out of the Fluidizer Bay, instantly."

"There's no one else here."

"Then get out, yourself. Don't even wait to cut the switches."

"And why should I get out?"

"The catalyst is going to blow."

She heard Kober's curt chuckle. "You don't say. This is just plain silica, Marguerite. Sand."

"It is *not*. If I tried to explain, it wouldn't make any sense to you."

"Try me."

"Some . . . gold . . . has got into the fluidizers. This has reacted with the ammonia. The whole unit has been working with gold fulminate coating the silica. The fulminate was harmless, because it was wet with by-product water, and Pierre intended that it all be dumped into the alkahest, where it would—disappear. But now you're drying it in the fluidizers. As soon as it's dry, it will explode."

"Gold . . . fulminate—?" said Kober slowly.

Marguerite continued with a sense of desperate futility. "Yes. You get it when you react auric oxide with ammonia and water. When it's hot, it detonates by friction. Your drying conditions are perfect."

"Marguerite, have you been drinking?"

"No, Ben. Just a couple before dinner. That was hours ago."

"You had dinner alone?"

"With Pierre."

"Now, Marguerite, let's consider this thing calmly. I don't know what nonsense Celsus has been feeding you. But believe me, there's not a trace of gold in the whole silamine system. We analyzed everything that went in, and I've been here from the beginning. Celsus is just trying to queer the whole run, because he wasn't asked to supervise it."

"No, Ben, it isn't that way at all. I know there was no gold in the catalyst in the beginning. *But there is now.*"

"Impossible. The seals on the fluidizer and the feeder are still intact. There's absolutely no way for anything, gold, silver, or your fine pea soup to get into the reactor."

Marguerite felt her slight body begin to shake. She took a big breath, then exhaled slowly. When she spoke again, her voice was quiet, with the calm of fatalism. "Pierre did it. By a technique that neither you nor I could possibly understand. There is reason to think that he is an . . . alchemist. You know . . . philosopher's stone . . . xerion . . . alkahest . . . universal solvent . . . the whole bit. He can create gold on the silica—*out* of the silica. That's what provides the heat."

Kober said curtly, "I must say, Marguerite, this is the last thing I'd expect to hear from one of your standing in this company. What are you trying to do to our survey?" He continued with mounting bitterness. "The patent department stands to gain as much from our study as any group in the lab. I know Gruen has enemies. We expect that. But not at your level. You can be sure Bleeker will be told."

There was a click.

"Ben!" screamed the girl. Instantly, she dialed back. She listened to the ring for a moment, and then there was another click. "Ben? Ben?" There was no answer, and she finally realized that Kober must have taken the phone off the cradle. And that meant her own phone was dead. She could not call Patrick.

Within seconds Marguerite had pulled on her coat and was running downstairs to her car. Patrick. Kober would listen to Patrick. And fortunately Patrick's house was on the way to the lab.

In five minutes she was simultaneously jabbing at Patrick's doorbell and pounding on the door. The lights came on after what seemed forever, and Patrick stumbled downstairs, pulling ineffectually at the sleeves of his robe, red hair and moustache awry. "I'm coming, I'm coming," he called hoarsely. "Marguerite, what in the world!"

She had a momentary impulse to dump the whole thing in Patrick's lap and then collapse. But suppose *he* didn't believe her either? What then? She couldn't take the chance. There was only one way to do it.

She said quickly: "Emergency at the lab. Where's your phone?"

Patrick was already moving into the study. "This way."

"Call the night watchman. Tell him to call an ambulance. And tell him to stay away from the Fluidizer Bay. Then you follow me down."

"I'll be right behind you, Marguerite. Don't take any unnecessary—"

But the front door had already slammed behind the girl.

Marguerite's ride down Route 29 to the lab had a vague, dreamlike quality. At eighty miles an hour, the car seemed floating lazily. Ridiculous irrelevancies flitted through her mind. It can't be happening. Not now. Not today. Not in the twentieth century. Perhaps it would be all right in some dark thirteenth-century cellar, but not at the Research Laboratory of Hope Chemical Corporation, organized and existing under the laws of the State of Delaware, United States of America, and having a principal place of business at Camelot, Virginia.

Somewhere behind her she heard a siren howling, and her eye caught a blinking red light in her rear-view mirror. Ambulance? No, patrol car. She laughed soundlessly and turned up the drive into the lab grounds. As she did so, she saw ahead of her another car already far up in the drive, already drawing to a halt at the first of the buildings. In a moment of dark prescience, Marguerite knew it had to be the little red compact of Pierre Celsus. And it was plainly Celsus who ran into the building.

Marguerite honked her horn savagely. Then she screamed, "Pierre! Pierre!" It was useless. She pulled in behind the other car, brakes screeching, and ran in through the lobby, then dashed down the corridor toward the Fluidizer Bay. As she burst through the swinging doors of the Bay, she thought she was in time. Celsus and Kober were struggling on the floor by the silamine control panel. Each of the three fluidizer columns was gleaming peacefully under the bright fluorescent lights.

She saw Celsus break away, reaching for the switches.

Then the first column exploded.

The blast, projecting outward, for a microsecond bathed Celsus in an iridescent spray, outlining his shadow on the gray-painted concrete block wall behind him.

In that moment a great wind lifted the girl, almost gently. She closed her eyes by reflex, and wondered whether her back would be broken when she was hurled through the doors behind her. But she did not touch the doors, because they were burst from their hinges even before she was thrown through the doorway. Then there was a second blast, and something massive whistled over her head while she was still in the air. The third blast was complete before she stopped skidding down the hall. All three fluidizers had blown in sequence. She picked herself up and ran back to the doorway, where Kober passed her, staggering, coughing, face bleeding.

Inside, Celsus lay face down in the wreckage of the silamine unit. In the bay, a merciful pall of dust swirled slowly, and nothing was recognizable.

She gathered her crumbling wits and stumbled down the stairs to the body, lying small and rumpled on the concrete floor. She knelt down, thrust her hands gently under the armpits, and began to drag the body slowly toward the stairs. She was met halfway by Patrick, who seemed to have materialized from nowhere. Together they got Celsus into the hall. He was unconscious, but breathing regularly, and no bones seemed broken. By now they had been joined by Kober, the night watchman, a state trooper, and two ambulance attendants.

Celsus, amid groans, tried to sit up. Patrick peremptorily pushed him back down. Then, as Patrick straightened up, he looked back into the Bay. He pointed, wordless. Marguerite stared with him.

The dust was settling, and as it settled it was changing color. It went through the spectrum. It was pink. Then it was blue. Then purple, brown, black. The emergency lights were turning green, and Marguerite knew that this had to be so, because gold was translucent in thin sections and transmitted green light.

The aluminum blinds just beyond the fluidizers were momentarily purple, with the instant formation of gold-aluminum alloy, and even as she watched, the color was changing to a more golden luster. Even the iron stair guard was changing, the blue of the ferro-gold creeping rapidly up toward them. And then the shift of colors slowly ceased, and an aureate patina lay everywhere. Marguerite knew then that every piece of exposed metal in the bay, from the wrecked fluidizers to the sink fittings, was Midas-stricken.

And then Patrick pointed again, this time across the great room, toward the opposite wall. On that wall was the shadow of a man, blast-written, one arm raised to them in eternal greeting, a gray silhouette stenciled within a scintillating sheet of golden particles embedded in concrete, a chiaroscuro of darkness and shining promise, a thing to measure them forever.

"What it is?" whispered Celsus.

With awe, Patrick replied, "Your profile."

The Staff Room, used regularly by Bleeker for the monthly meetings of his department heads, was kept on a continuing standby basis by Miss Sally for instant emergency use. To ensure this condition of perpetual preparedness, she had made it clear to her boss and his lieutenants that the pencils, tablets, and ash trays in front of each chair were there solely for purposes of state and were never to be touched. Patrick, who felt naked and insecure without his meerschaum, met the ashtray problem by hiding several in an old briefcase in the drawer of the big conference table. The conferees, of course, took notes, if any, on paper they brought with them. Bleeker sometimes assigned to one man, generally Henry Pfennig, the comptroller, the task of "writing up" the meeting for circulation to all participants, after checking the draft with Bleeker, who occasionally added a few comments, which, although never said in conference, should, on his due reflection, have been said. And sometimes he struck passages—his own and those of others—which he felt were inconsistent with conclusions reached after the conference.

Except for Bleeker, the seating at Bleeker's conferences was a matter of subconscious choice. Bleeker always sat at the head of the long table, like the captain at the helm. From there on, the seating varied, depending on the type of meeting expected. If it were rumored that Bleeker was going to read a letter of praise from the Board of Directors for accomplishments of the past year, all the chairs close to the head of the table were likely to be occupied. And contrariwise, if the meeting were rumored to deal with matters of budget cutting, then the staff shrank to the far end of the table in an anxious cluster.

This morning, of course, as everyone knew, the conference sat as a court of inquiry, and from this fact the proper seating emerged. Patrick, as counsel for the defense, took the end of the table opposite from Bleeker, the judge-prosecutor. The defendants, Celsus and Prentice, took seats together, alone on one side of the table, and opposite them, Gruen, Kober, Bond, Pfennig, and Marvin—of Personnel—formed the jury.

Pierre Celsus stole uneasy glances at the unsmiling faces opposite him. He sighed and dropped his eyes. He knew he had sinned chemically. Because of him, three people might have been killed. His process had demolished equipment worth many thousands of dollars. The project had been set back by several weeks. Now, in fact, silamine might never reach the pilot plant stage.

Initiative, he had been told, was valued at Hope, but, he suspected, not when it resulted in disaster. That was when they stopped talking about brilliant break-throughs, and started talking about sheer crass sophomoric stupidity. There was no use in trying to explain anything. Those few who accepted his talent required no explanations; to those who did not accept psi, no explanation was possible.

He knew he was through at Hope. He wouldn't mind being fired, except for Marguerite. He was going to miss Marguerite. He slumped miserably down into his chair. Prentice looked at him for a moment and then did the same.

Bleeker looked slowly around the table. "I think you all know why we are here. Last night's explosion merely brought matters to a head. Apparently this situation has existed for some time, and with certain exceptions"—he nodded gravely to Patrick—"we have been too blind to see what has been going on. I have asked all of you here to help me decide on a course of action. And Pierre, I'll start with you. Do you really have this power, psi, or whatever it's called?"

"Yes, Mr. Bleeker, I guess I do."

"And Prentice, he has it, too?"

"He has it, too, but I'm still teaching him how to control it."

"Perhaps both of you could use a little more instruction," said Bleeker dryly.

"Kober shouldn't have tried to dry the catalyst," said Celsus shortly.

"I don't hold him blameless," said Bleeker. "But the question is, what do we do about it? I take it, Pierre, this is by no means the first time you have used psi in our research?"

"That's right, sir. Only, this is the first time we got caught."

Bond asked curiously, "What were the other times?"

"Different times. Certain processes required high exotherms, and we provided the heat the same way that we did for silamine, by nuclear reactions in which we made gold *in situ*. And then we got rid of the gold in various ways."

"How do you mean, various ways?" asked Bleeker.

"Well, last year we ran the effluent into a tank of ferrous sulfate-sodium hypo-phosphite. The iron came out as metallic iron, of course, and then immediately alloyed with the gold, to give crystals of green iron-gold alloy. It sat around in the solids-disposal vat, near the parking lot, for several weeks before it was hauled away. Mr. Pfennig used to toss his cigarette butts into it, coming to work every morning. Another time we hid the gold as nice purple crystals of aluminum-gold alloy. Nobody noticed, because everybody thinks that gold is gold-colored."

"Why did you switch over to alkahest, in the silamine process?" asked Bleeker. "Why didn't you figure out another way to 'hide' the spent catalyst?"

"We were afraid there would be too much catalyst to hide. We needed some-thing that would absorb hundreds, even thousands of pounds of spent catalyst. It had to be the alkahest."

Pfennig turned his cold blue eyes on Celsus. "Gold is worth thirty-five dollars an ounce. How many ounces, all told, did you throw away?"

Celsus studied the ceiling. "Well, from the beginning, I guess there was a total of about three or four hundred."

Pfennig's eyes widened. "Four hundred ounces? That's fourteen hundred dollars!"

"No, Mr. Pfennig. I meant four hundred pounds. Twelve ounces to the pound, troy weight."

"But that's"—his voice rose in a horrified shriek—"one hundred sixty-eight thousand dollars!"

"Spare us the arithmetic, Henry," said Patrick. He turned to Celsus. "About the silamine unit. You started it with psi. You heated it with nuclear psi. Could you shut it down with psi?"

Celsus and Prentice exchanged glances. Celsus rubbed his chin. "In the sense you mean, I think the answer is 'yes'."

"Without blowing up the plant, I mean," said Patrick hastily.

"Of course."

Patrick relaxed back into his chair, fired up his meerschaum, and smiled across at Bleeker as though to say, "Your witness."

"I don't see your point, Con," said Bleeker impatiently. "Who cares whether he can *stop* it? I think we'd better go on to the technology of the operational process. Pierre, about this alkahest: Is this a true universal solvent?"

Celsus shrugged his shoulders. "I think so."

"Then why," demanded Kober triumphantly, "doesn't it dissolve the vessel that contains it?"

Celsus looked at Prentice. The latter grinned, then replied, "That's easy. The solvent isn't in direct contact with the container. Also, I don't believe the solvent action is really chemical."

"You don't *believe!*" sneered Kober. "You admit you don't know?"

"That's right. We think it's more—mental-electrical. To activate it, we have to set up these encephalographic oscillations. In fact, we think that anything that goes into the alkahest truly disappears—dematerializes. Now, if we had a companion psi field, we might make it remateria . . ."

"I believe that's enough for now," said Bleeker quietly. "Pierre, would you and Prufrock be good enough to wait in the anteroom? I'd like to discuss this further with the rest of the group."

After the two had gone, Bleeker looked around the table. "And now, I want some constructive suggestions."

"The answer's obvious, Andy," said Pfennig. "These men are dangerous. They've destroyed equipment, nearly killed a couple of people, fouled up orderly administrative processes, and driven our psychiatrist crazy. We'll have to let them go."

Bleeker looked thoughtful. He glanced over at Bond. "Jim?"

The Silicon Group Leader spoke with slow dignity. "I've been with this company ever since I got out of graduate school. When I arrived here, the lab was one wooden shack in the middle of a corn field. Our pilot plant was an old bathtub. I watched the first brick building go up. I've spent my professional life watching Hope Chemicals grow into the giant it is today, and I like to think I've done my share to help it grow. We did this by science, by ordered imagination. And we can keep doing it. We don't need magic or chicanery. Are you going to let these men louse up a generation of Hope chemistry? In fact, will you let them destroy several centuries of genuine science? Are we to return to the Dark Ages? And suppose we branch out into alchemical processes—do you think it will end there? What lies beyond alchemy?" Bond's mouth wrenched bitterly. "Can't you see what will happen? This means the breakdown of modern chemistry. It's like Einstein and the collapse of classical physics, except this will be worse—much, much worse."

Bleeker winced. "You brought out a number of interesting points." He turned to Gruen. "Arnold, how does our consultant say?"

"Even if it's all true, what Celsus claims, this talent, which I very much doubt, I suggest that you wait a while. Let some of the smaller, irresponsible chemical companies make fools of themselves. Of course, in the remote event it works, then Hope can always pick it up."

"I see. Dave?" Bleeker nodded to Marvin of Personnel.

"Insane," muttered Marvin. "If any rumor of this thing leaks out, we'll never get another serious job applicant—just kooks."

"And now, Con," said Bleeker. "It's your turn. What's the legal viewpoint?"

"I've looked into a number of points," said Patrick, "but I'm sure I haven't caught everything. Our corporate charter is silent on alchemy. It says generally, though, that we can engage in any lawful activity in the chemical field. The early Virginia laws against witchcraft and magic were repealed in the eighteenth century, during the Williamsburg days, and I believe we could argue that any implied restrictions against alchemy were abolished at the same time. At the national level, though, there may be a problem on alchemical gold-making as such. Nuclear processes belong by law to the Atomic Energy Commission. If word got out, the United States government might seize Celsus and Prentice by eminent domain. Furthermore, aside from a little jewelry use, the only real market for gold is the United States Mint. We seem to be clear, though, on all other alchemical processes, such as silamine."

"Can we take out patents on these processes?" asked Bond heavily.

"No. Not at present. There are no specific statutes permitting psi patents. Also, the United States Supreme Court held in Halliburton v. Walker that a patent claiming a mental step is invalid. This is a gap in our patent statutes that can be overcome only by legislation specifically aimed at psi patents, just as the Plant Patent Statute was enacted in 1930 to protect certain new varieties of plants. But I'm not sure we want psi patent legislation. Not yet, anyhow."

Bleeker looked at him curiously. "If we can't get patent protection, what's to stop Celsus from leaving us and setting up a competitor in the silamine business?"

"Any court in the country would give us an injunction against that," said Patrick. "His employment contract with Hope says that we own all processes he developed here, and requires that he won't disclose our processes to any subsequent employer. On the other hand, if we make life attractive for him here, why would he want to leave?"

"You mean," said Bleeker, "have him *deliberately* develop more psi processes?"

"Certainly, and hold them all as trade secrets. Exploiting psi techniques as trade secrets will have many advantages over our normal patent procedures. In the first place, you don't have to worry about infringing adverse psi patents. There aren't any. Secondly, most foreign countries can force you to grant a license under your foreign patents. We'd never have to worry about that. With psi, we can always pick our own licensees. Thirdly, all patents finally expire. But a psi technique need never expire."

Bleeker leaned forward and peered keenly at Patrick. "Let's get specific. Suppose we license silamine to the People's Republic at a running royalty. How do we enforce payment?"

"They pay or Celsus shuts them down," said Patrick simply.

Bleeker studied the blank pad in front of him. His face held no expression, but his mind was racing, searching. The answer was here, if he could only put his finger on it.

"Besides our own plant," continued Patrick quietly, "we would have licensees in all civilized countries. But of course," he shrugged, "it's only money."

Bleeker stared at him with widening eyes. "Money . . ." he whispered. And suddenly he saw the solution . . . the answer . . . the way out. And with this came a shocking, awesome insight into those glacial faces in Richmond, with their rimless spectacles: the Hope Board of Directors. They had put him here, knowing that when this moment arrived, he, and he alone, would know what to do, and would be worthy of their trust, and of the fabulous salary they paid him. It made a man very humble. And yet, it was so easy, and so obvious, at least to him. He felt almost sorry for his department heads, with their routine minds, thinking only of patents, of personnel, of run-of-the-mill research problems, and of the ordered progress of science.

"Arnold," said Bleeker to Gruen, "before we get too far with this, I want to thank you on behalf of Hope. Without your survey, we might never have discovered this potential hidden in our midst."

Gruen was puzzled, but took it in stride. He had not reached his present eminence by rejecting undeserved credits. "We simply did our duty," he said with noncommittal modesty. That, he thought, would take care of most anything.

Ben Kober stared in bemused silence, first at the research director, then at Gruen.

"Does this mean," demanded Pfennig with painful perception, "that Celsus and Prentice stay?"

Bleeker nodded. "Of course they stay. But that's just the start. Call them both back in, will you, Henry, and let's get this thing organized."

The two men came back in hesitantly, looking scared.

"Gentlemen, be seated," said Bleeker genially. "Pierre, I think you'll be delighted to know that we're going to set up a group for you, a psi group, devoted exclusively to alchemy. You can work on anything you like, so long as it's a money-maker, of course."

Celsus slowly relaxed. "Why, that's wonderful. However, I wonder if you could make it retroactive to last month, when the moon was in Aries?"

"Astrology!" cried Pfennig. "What incredible impertinence!"

Bleeker held up his hand. "The auspices were at their maximum then?" he asked Celsus gravely.

"Yes, sir."

"Call me Andy, Pierre."

"Yes, Andy."

"So be it. Now, Pierre, everything should have a name. What shall we call your new group?"

Celsus looked doubtful. "Most anything. 'Special Projects' . . . ?"

"Too tame," said Bleeker. "How about the 'Alchemical Group'?"

"Andy!" cried Dave Marvin. "The Board of Directors will think you're crazy!"

"Crazy, Dave? If it makes money, it can't be crazy. That's a contradiction in terms. Anyhow, if the Board notices it at all, they'll think it's just another promotion gimmick of our Madison Avenue ad agency. You know, like 'miracle plastics', 'miracle cigarette filters', 'miracle detergents', except that they'll be pleased that we're not using a tired, overworked word like 'miracle'."

"They'll find out sooner or later," said Bond sourly.

"I know. But by then the silamine contract with the People's Republic will be making so much money they won't care what we call it."

"With that name, we'll be tipping our hand to the competition," demurred Marvin.

"The industry may eventually find out," conceded Bleeker. "But at least this will delay the discovery. This way, they'll think we're joking. Everybody knows there's no such thing as alchemy. But if we called it 'Special Projects', they'd have spies in here overnight. Our best camouflage is to be wide open. Business as usual. So we have a name." Bleeker leaned back. He was enjoying himself immensely. "And when we sign that People's Republic contract, we'll automatically have to spend ten per cent of the receipts on supporting research. So now let's staff the new group and give this thing some functional structure." He looked across to Celsus. "Pierre, you'll need an Assistant Group Leader. Anyone in mind?"

"Well, Prufrock and I have worked together—"

"Oh no!" groaned Pfennig.

Patrick shot a warning glance at the comptroller. "Don't say it, Henry," he said quietly.

"I will say it! A. P. Prentice—*the sorcerer's apprentice!*"

Bleeker looked at him thoughtfully. "Well, there's an idea. 'Sorcerer's Apprentice'. Hm-m-m. Perhaps we should use *that* as the title, instead of 'Assistant Group Leader.' It goes nicely with the alchemical motif. Is that all right with you, Prufrock?"

"It's fine with me," said Prentice. "I never had *any* title before. Can I use it when signing mail?"

"Certainly. Now, then, let's go on. Hope has big insurance policies on the lives of its key executives, payable to Hope, of course. Henry, we'll need something like that for our people in the Alchemical Group, something similar to a violinist insuring his hands. Only here, we're covering loss of psi."

"I'll try Lloyd's of London," said Pfennig. He added cynically, "The premium should be fairly cheap, if we tell them it's for continuance of *existing* talent."

"Fine," said Bleeker. "Now, the new group will need some technicians. Dave Marvin can take another look around here, for talent. And also, Dave, will you line up a good body-snatching technique for locating psi talent in the colleges . . . and among our competitors. When we set up our job application booths at the A.C.S. conventions, include some way to catch the psi's."

Marvin looked dubious. "We stopped the A.C.S. job booth months ago. As you may recall, Con, we borrowed your Miss French to take the applications. Very attractive young lady. And we got more applications from our own lab than we did from the competition."

"Try her again," said Bleeker. "At least, this way maybe she can detect some talent in our own applicants. Now then, for the universities. We ought to sponsor some graduate research. Two or three fellowships to start. Pierre, any ideas?"

"Oh, there's plenty of projects. Psi-rearrangement of plant chromosomes for better crops. And Prufrock could use some blue sky research on the operation of the alkahest."

"Sounds good," said Bleeker. "How about placing them with Duke University? They've done a lot of work on psi phenomena."

Patrick frowned. "I don't know. Duke is too ivory tower for my taste. They've been in this field for thirty years, and never made a nickel on it."

"All right," said Bleeker, "we'll try a school with a more realistic approach."

"How about the University of Transylvania?" said Bond acidly.

"Just the thing," said Bleeker. "And that'll give us an objective foreign viewpoint, too."

"Also," said Celsus, "we ought to place a project on psi-control of Maxwell's Demon, for our thermodynamic studies."

"For that one," said Bond wearily, "Texas Christian University."

Bleeker beamed at him. "The very thing!" He studied his notes. "Consultants. We ought to have a couple of top-flight men."

"We need a good astrologer," said Celsus.

"Fine. Get some names. I'll go over them with you. Any others?"

"I've been corresponding with a man in Trinidad . . . a *houngan*."

"That's voodoo!" hissed Pfennig. "And it's outlawed there."

"The government of Trinidad is squarely behind its new chemical industry," said Bleeker smoothly. "I'm sure they would help us in making the necessary arrangements for a bona-fide chemical consultant, such as Pierre's friend."

"We'll also need a computer expert," said Celsus, "at least one, for programming our machine translators."

"What for?" demanded Kober.

"It's for the incantations for our foreign licensees," explained Celsus. "For example, English won't work for the People's Republic plant in Czezhlo, and I don't know whether we could trust an interpreter."

"Agreed," said Bleeker. "One computerman. Now, we'll need a trademark for silamine. Any ideas?"

" 'Psilamine'," said Patrick, sounding the 'p.'

"Will the Patent Office register that?" demanded Bleeker. "Isn't it descriptive?"

"Is the Patent Office going to believe it's made with psi?" countered Patrick.

"I suppose not. Very well, then, 'Psilamine' it is."

Patrick broke in. "The new group should include a Trade Secret Officer, to work on psi inventions in liaison with my own department. He could take quite a load off us."

Bleeker looked at Patrick blankly. It was incomprehensible that Patrick should recommend that the function of the Hope Patent Department be diminished in favor of a competing group. As Patrick continued, however, Bleeker relaxed.

"Marguerite French is the obvious candidate for the job," said Patrick. "And, of course, I'll need an additional man in *my* group to work with her, besides another attorney to replace her."

"Seems reasonable," said Bleeker. At least, he thought, it fits the pattern. Whenever we figure out how to eliminate one man, we find we need two more to replace him. He sighed. "All this is going to cost a lot of money. So let's start making that money. Con, if you will blue-back a couple of execution copies, I think we can sign that contract with the People's Republic."

So the world's first commercial silamine plant was built. The day it went on stream Comrade Sasanov dedicated the plant to the People's Republic in an elaborate ceremony, with ribbon cutting, valve turning, and Pierre Celsus standing beside the machine translator awaiting the signal to start the punched-tape incantation.

Three months later Pfennig telephoned Bleeker. "The first royalty check is now one week overdue."

This struck a chill to Bleeker's heart, but he kept his voice assured and cheerful. "Don't worry about it, Henry. I'll cable Sasanov."

The cables—and there were finally three—brought no response. Bleeker then telephoned the chancellery at Czezhlo. He got as far as the second assistant secretary. Comrade Sasanov was unavailable.

"Then give His Excellency a message," said Bleeker in clipped fury. "We are going to close down your plant."

Across six thousand miles, he heard a polite purr: "How very droll, Mr. Bleeker! When, exactly, do you plan to shut down our plant?"

Bleeker thought wildly. Had he stepped into something? Still, Celsus had assured him he could, if necessary, shut the plant down. "Next Friday," he grated. "At midnight, Czezhlo time. And it will stay down until we get that check. Tell Sasanov."

A chuckle squeaked, back through the static. "I shall, Mr. Bleeker, I shall indeed."

Even as he was hanging the phone up, Bleeker realized that he had violated the basic rule of leadership: he had made an emotional decision. Even worse, he would now have to call on his assistants to bail him out, and he hadn't the faintest idea how, or whether, they could do it.

Ordinarily Bleeker knew how far his people could be led, cajoled, threatened, coaxed, and pushed. He knew their inner resources, hidden strengths, latent ingenuities, better than they themselves.

But psi was different. He knew he didn't have the "feel," the insight, and the understanding that would surely bring forth the necessary team effort to solve the Sasanov problem. It would be like trying to conduct the lab symphony orchestra in an evening of Beethoven, when he couldn't even read music.

He glared bitterly across the room at the model of the silamine plant sitting on his credenza. The model had been painstakingly contrived in the lab maintenance shop. It had first been exhibited to the Board of Directors, and later, by special recommendation of the Hope President, it had sat in glory on a dais at the annual stockholders' meeting in Richmond.

A dozen times in the past few months Bleeker had caught himself daydreaming in the direction of the model. The scene of his visions varied, but generally it was the bar of the Chemists Club in New York. He was seated there over cocktails with a couple of old friends, research directors with Hope's competitors, basking in their eager, envious inquiries as to how he had pulled off that fabulous silamine license with the People's Republic. He could see himself smiling in poorly-simulated self-deprecation. "Seems like magic to us, too." That's all he would tell them. And now the vision was fizzling out. If Sasanov refused to pay royalties, Bleeker would never dare show his face in the Chemists Club again.

Just now the model was gleaming at him in minuscule mockery.

He took a deep breath and buzzed his secretary. "Miss Sally, get me Mr. Celsus."

Bleeker looked gravely from the silamine plant model occupying the center of the conference table to the surrounding faces. "I want to thank all of you for coming, especially you, Dr. Dessaline. We apologize for the short notice."

The dusky *houngan* from Trinidad nodded inscrutably.

Bleeker continued. "As you all know, this is a real emergency." He looked at his watch impatiently. "Does anyone know where Con Patrick is?"

"He's on his way from the airport," said Celsus evasively. "He'll be here in a few minutes."

Bleeker sighed. Give a man a title, and the first thing you know he starts wearing a clean lab coat: next, he wears a suit, and the jacket matches his pants. But Celsus had not stopped there. He was now wearing a vest. He had obviously hired another very important—and very expensive—consultant. Patrick was probably bringing him in from the airport.

"We'll have to go ahead without Patrick," said Bleeker. "It's already five o'clock—eleven p.m. Czezhlo time. If we're going to accomplish anything, we have barely an hour. Pierre, what can we do?"

"I've reviewed the background with Dr. Dessaline," said Celsus. "We both agree on the basic approach. We must put a temporary hex on the Czezhlo plant."

"What does that involve?" asked Bleeker, curiosity breaking through his gloom.

"The principle of malediction is quite simple," said Dr. Dessaline. "The condemnation recital requires no set words. If it is sincere, if it comes from the heart, that is enough. Promptly following the incantation, the denunciator sticks the pin in the effigy—the doll, if you will. The entity represented by the doll instantly falls into a swoon and recovers only when the pin is removed."

"Doll?" said Bleeker apprehensively. "Of Sasanov?"

Dr. Dessaline smiled thinly. "Nothing so sophomoric, Mr. Bleeker. The doll we mean is this model of the plant, which Mr. Celsus brought in from your office just for this purpose. For a pin we can use almost anything—a knife, a ruler . . . this letter opener will do."

"I see," said Bleeker. He turned to Celsus. "*You* are going to perform this hex, I presume?"

"No, Mr. Bleeker!" said Dessaline quickly. "Not Mr. Celsus. You must not ask him to curse his own child! Even if he should try, out of loyalty to you, it probably would not be completely effective, because he could not possibly be sincere at the necessary subconscious level."

"Well, then," said Bleeker grimly, "who *is* going to do it? *You,* Dr. Dessaline?"

The *houngan* sighed. "I could do it, but I would need time for the necessary preparations, and I would have to collect suitable assistants, with specially tuned drums. This could be done only back in Port-of-Spain, and would mean a delay of several days. The dramatic effect of calling the exact time would be lost. Sasanov would not be sure that the shutdown was your direct act."

"Am I to understand, then," said Bleeker slowly, "that *nobody* can do *anything,* here and now?"

"We intend to try, Andy." Celsus studied his superior hesitantly. "I hope the budget will stand one more consultant?"

"I suppose so." Bleeker turned to Pfennig. "Henry, how much is this hex going to cost?"

The comptroller adjusted his pince-nez and studied his accounting sheets. "Depends on whether we charge it out as a normal operating expense, or whether we have to amortize it as a capital expense resulting from the transfer of assets held more than six months." He cleared his throat. "I must confess, I've had trouble in getting a clear answer from the Internal Revenue people—"

"Never mind," said Bleeker hastily. "If we really have to have another consultant for the hex, we can't bother about the expense."

"We need someone with unusual qualifications, Andy," said Arnold Gruen. "We have analyzed his profile. As a minimum, he must be a physical chemist with an international reputation. He must be a man of convictions, and not given to delicate nuances in his pronouncements."

(How curious, thought Bleeker. Not so many months ago, I had to ram the Alchemical Group down their throats. Now they are all telling me how it ought to be run.)

"To sum up," concluded Gruen, "he must be a scientific man of letters, sincere, yet eloquent in extemporaneous scientific discourse."

"This is all very fine," said Bleeker, "but where will you find such a man within the hour remaining to us?"

The door burst open.

Patrick and a stranger entered.

"Gentlemen," announced Patrick triumphantly, "Professor Max Klapproth!"

As a man, the group stood up. Patrick made the introductions.

Bleeker studied the newcomer with interest. Professor Klapproth was a big man with a shaven skull, penetrating blue eyes, and an inquisitive tetrahedral nose. Bleeker had never before met him, but knew him by reputation.

Professor Klapproth's texts on physical chemistry had been standards in American universities for a quarter of a century. His research and publications in heat transfer, catalysis, and vapor phase reactions were classics, and his work on reaction rates had won him a Nobel prize. All of this he had done with a purity, logic, and economy of concept that was at once the inspiration and despair of his following throughout the world. He had turned down innumerable offers from industry, but freely accepted consulting assignments, on the theory that when he worked for everyone, he need not curb his tongue for anyone. Despite his outspoken independence, and despite the fact that he charged by the hour the fees asked by most other consultants by the day, he was in such demand that he was able to select assignments that really interested him. He delighted in going over a flow sheet for a few minutes and then pointing out to the dismayed client errors in design that would require hundreds of thousands of dollars to correct. He stood for no nonsense. There was an apocryphal story that he had dismissed a graduate student who had proposed as his Ph.D. thesis, "Free Will Aspects of Brownian Motion."

Yes, thought Bleeker, the boys have chosen well. He felt a warm glow begin to diffuse through his chest. For the first time in three days, he relaxed.

Patrick motioned Klapproth to a chair.

"I don't think I'll be here long enough to sit down, Mr. Patrick," said Klapproth curtly. He looked at his watch. "I hope to be on the next plane to Kennedy Airport."

Celsus glanced at the wall clock and smiled. "We'll have you on that plane, Professor Klapproth."

"Is that the plant model?" demanded Klapproth, pointing at the table.

"Yes." Dessaline handed the letter opener to the professor.

"And you want my opinion as to whether it will work?"

"Yes," said Bleeker.

"It can't possibly work," said Klapproth. "I went over the flow sheet thoroughly with Mr. Patrick as he drove me out from the airport. Someone is trying to make a fool out of you, Mr. Bleeker. You got hold of me just in time." He tapped the model fluidizer with the tip of the letter opener. "You'll need a fantastic heat input here—a BTU requirement that you could obtain only in a semi-nuclear reaction. But instead of heating, you *cool* the reaction. Also, you plan to dead-end spent catalyst continuously into *this* vessel"—he tapped the alkahest container—"which will certainly overflow within a few hours. And another thing. Your reagents . . . xerion . . . alkahest . . . there are no such things. And finally, by your own admission, no silamine process can operate without being autocatalyzed by at least one molecule of preexisting silamine. Which is a contradiction in terms . . . an insuperable paradox."

"Might not all these problems be overcome by the proper application of psi?" asked Patrick innocently.

". . . *Psi?*" Klapproth stared at the patent director in open amazement. Then his face, forehead, and scalp slowly turned red. "Gentlemen!" he sputtered. "What do you take me for!"

"Mr. Patrick," said Bleeker soothingly—while carefully avoiding Patrick's indignant eyes—"is our patent attorney."

"Oh, of course," said Klapproth coldly. "I forgot." He looked about him suspiciously. No one seemed to be disconcerted or chagrined. One or two seemed actually pleased.

Celsus broke in hurriedly. "We have to watch our timing very carefully now. Would you say, Professor Klapproth, that any silamine plant represented by this model probably would not work?"

"It could not possibly work," snorted Klapproth. "And when I say a thing is impossible, IT'S IMPOSSIBLE!"

"Completely hopeless, would you say," prodded Patrick.

"Worthless, futile, useless . . ." echoed Klapproth.

"Ridiculous?" murmured Dessaline.

"And stupid, idiotic, feckless, moronic, otiose," boomed Klapproth.

Patrick stared at the man, transfixed by awe and admiration. Mark Twain, he thought, had not been more eloquent in his mule-skinner days.

But Klapproth had not finished. "A pixilated pile of junk . . . a raffish refugee from a scrap heap . . . a haphazard heap of hare-brained hardware . . ."

"It's midnight in Czezhlo!" whispered Bleeker.

"Through the heart!" cried Dr. Dessaline.

Professor Klapproth plunged the letter opener into the vitals of the model. And then immediately jumped back in horror. "Mr. Bleeker," he gasped, "I don't know what came over me! I got carried away . . ." He leaned over to pull the knife out.

Dessaline seized his wrist. "Not just yet, Professor."

"But—"

"No. We stick the pin in the doll. Now we wait. I think we do not wait very long."

"Wait? For what? What is this all about?"

"Dr. Dessaline means we are now waiting for a transatlantic telephone call," said Bleeker. "But we don't know how long it will take. Con, maybe you'd better take Professor Klapproth on to the airport."

Klapproth looked uncertainly at the faces around the table. He finally picked up his hat. It was clear that he considered himself among madmen. "Telephone call?" he muttered to Patrick.

"Yes, a Mr. Sasanov, in Czezhlo," explained Patrick. "Just now, you put a curse on his silamine plant, and Mr. Sasanov is going to call Mr. Bleeker and tell him he'll pay up his back royalties, and then he'll ask Mr. Bleeker to get the plant started again."

The visitor stepped back uneasily. "Don't bother about me, Mr. Patrick. I'll get a taxi at the desk."

The phone rang. Bleeker picked it up. "Yes, operator, Bleeker here. By all means, put him on. Comrade Sasanov, what a delightful surprise!"

In the excitement no one noticed Professor Klapproth's flight.

THE MILLION YEAR PATENT

Bryan Burke pushed aside his physics book and his slide rule and turned to his father. "How do I go about getting a patent?"

"What on?" said Jim Burke from behind his news tapes.

"Space travel—at speeds faster than light."

"Unpatentable, my boy. Nothing can move faster than light. Einstein settled that centuries ago."

"Einstein was wrong."

"Can you prove it?"

"I think so. All you need is two ships, each traveling toward the other at a speed of more than one-half the speed of light. According to Einstein, all motion is relative. So you can imagine that either ship has zero motion, and the other has all the motion."

"True, I *think*. But where will you find two such ships?"

"It says here in the shipping news, that *Electra,* in dock on Joro, sixth planet of Sirius, will convert to your new Burke drive while taking on cargo and passengers, and then take off for Earth. It also mentions that *Thor,* of Alpha Centauri, will convert to Burke, and drive for Earth. I've just plotted the courses of both ships as part of my homework in Astrogation. Both ships will land here at Washington Terminal on the same day and at practically the same hour, three years from now . . ."

". . . and with my new drive," said Jim, "each ship would have a velocity of six-tenths the speed of light toward Terra, and a total of 1.2 times the speed of light toward each other. Very interesting, and somehow, of course, impossible."

Bryan's face fell.

"Oh well," said Jim, "at least I'll get you a date with Jack Lane. He's a patent attorney who handles some of my private inventions, outside my research at Pan-Stellar."

The boy brightened. "Just one more question. How long would the patent last?"

"Seventeen years, I suppose."

"I know *that*. I mean, how do you calculate those seventeen years on a ship moving at a substantial fraction of the speed of light? Remember, time slows down on an accelerating body. Seventeen years Earth time might be only five or ten years, ship time."

Jim shrugged. "Nice legal point. Maybe your patent—if you ever get it—would still be in force on such a ship, after seventeen years of Earth time. It would depend on whether ship time is legal time. That's one for Jack Lane. What difference does it make?"

"Maybe none," said Bryan thoughtfully.

And so the patent application was filed, and Jim Burke pretty much forgot about it.

During this time, *Electra* and *Thor* continued to gather speed. They peaked out at 0.6 *c* on schedule, and toward the end of the third year, they began the long deceleration toward Sol.

And then came the explosion in the research laboratories of Pan-Stellar, which nearly killed Jim Burke, and following which he was hauled off to Washington Central Hospital.

And then there came, during the next months, with a certain horrid rhythm, additional unpleasant events. These included a series of operations on Jim Burke, which finally established that he was probably going to live; but that radiation side effects would prevent competent use of his optic nerves; that all his money was gone; and that Pan-Stellar deeply sympathized, but that the Burkes could not expect any financial help.

In fact, Pan-Stellar sent out their special representative to see Jim and to explain exactly how things stood between Pan-Stellar and Jim Burke. They sent Mr. Slicer.

T. Elliott Slicer, Esq., Chief of the Accident and Claims Section at Pan-Stellar, thought of himself as a kind man. This particular term, however, was rarely foremost in the list of adjectives that other people used when referring to him. Nevertheless (or possibly, therefore) his superiors considered him a brilliant adjuster, whose technique had saved the Line millions of talers. Rather often, when lawyers were contacted to handle accident claims against the Line, they turned down the case when they learned Slicer was on the other end.

Mr. Slicer smiled a lot, and he was smiling when he walked into the hospital room and introduced himself to Jim Burke, who held out his hand. Mr. Slicer put a piece of paper in it and said, "Since you cannot read, Mr. Burke, I will tell you what it is. It is a copy of our complaint, which I have just filed in the Hall of Justice."

"Huh?"

"In summary, Mr. Burke, Pan-Stellar holds you personally responsible for the damage to the new experimental drive and to the building, plus incidentals including the resulting delay in the drive research program."

"But . . . but . . ."

"The claim is in the amount of four hundred eighty-three thousand talers," said Mr. Slicer.

It finally sank in, and Jim began to react. "You've got it all mixed up! I'm here because of what I was doing for Pan-Stellar. Pan-Stellar owes *me!*"

Mr. Slicer smiled kindly. "I hope you will retain competent counsel, Mr. Burke, who can help you correct these odd misconceptions."

"But my insurance . . . terminal pay . . . pension . . . disability . . . ?"

Mr. Slicer grinned. "We have deducted these, of course, Mr. Burke, from the gross amount of the damage you have done to the laboratory. Our claim represents our net loss, after all deductions. We are fair."

Jim Burke was silent.

Mr. Slicer pursed his lips, then continued. "You have a magnificent reputation with the Line, Mr. Burke. I am informed that you invented the basic drive now being installed in the newer ships. The Line has asked me to take this into consideration, and I will. Under the circumstances, we are willing to drop our suit if you will waive all claims, past, present, and future, against Pan-Stellar. I have the waiver, here."

Jim Burke heard the rustle of paper.

"Couldn't you throw in a small pension?" he asked in a low voice.

"I'm afraid not, Mr. Burke."

"Something for my son's college education?"

"Quite out of the question."

"My hospital bill?"

"My dear Mr. Burke. Are you being deliberately difficult? Well, never mind. Perhaps I can help you see things our way, after our next legal step. It distresses me to inform you that I shall have to attach all your property, real and personal, including your house, your cars, furniture, books, instruments . . . everything."

"Why should that distress, you, Mr. Slicer?" Jim was genuinely curious.

"Because the expenses of attachment are not taxable to the defendant, but must be borne by Pan-Stellar."

"My heart goes out to the Line," murmured Jim.

"I'll leave the waiver on the night table," said Mr. Slicer cheerfully.

A week after Mr. Slicer's visit, Margie Burke and Bryan were walking behind Jim's exercise chair in the sunshine room at the hospital. Margie was trying to explain it all to Bryan. "The Line won't pay anything. Mr. Lane has had it out with their lawyers."

Jim Burke said something so quietly that Bryan did not quite get it; the hair on his neck rose nevertheless.

Margie Burke continued. "Mr. Lane says he is going to see Mr. Slicer again next week. He thinks Mr. Slicer might still call off the damage suit against your father and give us a little money, if we coax and plead a little. It's the custom in the big Lines to give a small income to permanently injured employees."

"Will there be enough money for my patent application, too?" asked Bryan.

"I'm afraid not," said his mother.

"Just a minute," said Jim. He sensed an interesting possibility, even though he was not sure just how he could use it. "What's the latest on your patent?"

"Mr. Lane says the Patent Office has sent another rejection. He says the Patent Examiner doesn't believe the invention can work, and that to continue prosecution, we will have to submit actual proof that two space ships have moved toward each other at a speed greater than the speed of light. But I think we can provide the proof pretty soon."

"How's that?"

"It just happens that Dr. Talix is on the *Electra*, due to arrive next week here at Washington Terminal. And this new drug, *kae* extract, that they want Dr. Talix to try on your eyes, is due to arrive on *Thor*, all on the same day, maybe the same hour. You can calculate the distances from Sirius and Alpha Centauri, and the time in flight, and by simple arithmetic you can get a velocity of 0.6 *c* for each ship toward Sol. So the ships would have to have a net approach velocity toward each other of 1.2 times the speed of light."

"Ah, yes," mused Jim. "I remember now. Very curious, and very impossible. Things just can't move faster than light, whether they're moving towards themselves or towards Sol or a third-party observer. Or can they? Could Einstein be wrong?" He was silent for a long time. "It's curious to think, isn't it, that if you *are* right, and if you *do* get a patent, the Line will soon be infringing it with every pair of ships moving toward each other along the same vector, where each of the ships has an average speed over one-half *c*."

"And that's also true if the ships are going *away* from each other," said Bryan. "They'd start infringing soon after they left the same space port."

"Margie," said Jim, "get hold of Jack Lane again."

"What for?"

"I want him to go down to the Patent Office with Bryan. I want him to get this patent issued, and then I want him to file a counterclaim against Pan-Stellar."

"Counterclaim?"

"For one million talers, for patent infringement."

Patent Examiner Honaire addressed his two visitors with care and precision. This was in accordance with the Terran Patent Office rule that all interviews be entered into the computers for instant evaluation in the prompt determination of patentability. "The Application Branch," said Honaire, "had a problem the day this application was received. As I'm sure you are aware, Mr. Lane, there is a very ancient rule, dating back to the first century of operation of the old United States Patent Office, that if the application clearly calls for a mode of operation that violates a law of nature, this would be called to the attention of the applicant, with an offer to return his application fee. If the applicant refused the offer, we would take his money and then demand a working model. That generally ended the matter. But we couldn't apply that rule here. In the first place, the Solicitor's Computer gave us a ruling that Einstein's Theory of Relativity wasn't a law of nature, but only a hypothesis. So when Einstein said that an object couldn't move at a velocity greater than the speed of light, he was simply stating a consequence of his theory. Therefore we have accepted your fee, and we have duly examined your application, and we will let you try to prove Einstein wrong."

"That seems fair," said Bryan.

"Yes, indeed," said Jack Lane.

"Now, then," continued Honaire, "let us get to the heart of the matter. In your working example, you mention two ships, *Electra* and *Thor*. You concede that, as observed from the Earth, the velocity of each ship with respect to the Earth will never exceed the speed of light. On the other hand, what is the velocity of each ship as measured by the other? In neither ship will there be any apparent motion to the occupants of that ship. On the contrary, the other ship will appear to have all the motion, and will further appear to be approaching the observing ship at the combined velocities of the two ships, which, in the case suggested in your latest amendment, for *Electra* and *Thor,* is alleged to be 0.6 plus 0.6, or 1.2 times the speed of light. You contend that the gap will therefore be closing at a rate greater than the speed of light. The position of the Office is that this is quite impossible in view of Einstein's Theory."

"And my client, of course, respectfully traverses," said Lane, looking at his watch. "*Electra* and *Thor* should be arriving at the Washington Terminal any minute now. If they come in on schedule, Einstein and the Patent Office are wrong. It's as simple as that!"

"Not quite, Mr. Lane. Perhaps I should have explained earlier another unusual aspect of this case. The Einstein Theory is integrally programmed into all Patent Office computers. For this reason we can rely on our computers only in limited areas in examining an application predicated on the proposition that the Theory itself is wrong. This requires that all essential features of patentability be developed personally by the Examining Corps. Indeed, the Commissioner of Patents himself has taken a personal interest in this application. This is, of course, on account of the fact that the patent, if granted, could be expected to cover a large segment of the interstellar traffic of the Cluster. The Commissioner has advised further that proof of operability of a most clear and convincing character will be required. The reason is, obviously, that operability, if established, will necessarily refute Einstein's Theory, a theory which has been accepted as axiomatic for several hundred years. The Commissioner therefore requires that any demonstration adduced in support of operability be witnessed by himself in person."

Lane rose from his seat in protest. "But that would require that we arrange for the Commissioner to be at the Terminal when two specific ships arrive simultaneously! We have no other way to prove operability. And it will take weeks of negotiations with the space lines, not to mention the problems of getting hold of the Commissioner on a split-second schedule!"

"I appreciate the difficulties inherent in your position," agreed Honaire gravely. "Unfortunately, in view of the interest of the Commissioner, I'm afraid I must adhere to the proof requirements as I have stated them. You can, of course, appeal my decision to the courts."

"No," said Lane glumly. "We don't have time for that. We need the patent now."

Honaire glanced at the clock on the wall behind his visitors, then studied Bryan for a moment. "Then I would recommend," he said enigmatically, "that we defer the question of operability for the time being, and proceed to the issue of aggregation raised in the latest Office action."

Bryan studied his copy of the Office action. "What's 'aggregation'?"

" 'Aggregation'," said Honaire, "means that each of the elements of the invention contributes merely what it would do anyway, if the other elements were not there. Aggregation is unpatentable because it is obvious to one skilled in the art. The instant rejection on aggregation is based on the facts that each ship carries its own load, makes its own schedule, and travels at its own 0.6 c, quite independently of the other. The total system is therefore aggregative, and hence unpatentable."

"We traverse," said Lane. "In fact, we rely on aggregation to prove patentability. *Our* aggregation is unobvious!"

Honaire blinked. "How can aggregation ever be unobvious? It's a contradiction in terms."

"Let me explain," said Lane. "Normally, when you add 2 and 2 you expect to get 4; and so, when you *do* get 4, that's aggregation. It's obvious, and unpatentable. But if you got 3 or 5, that could not possibly be aggregation, and therefore it might be patentable invention. Well, our situation is exactly the reverse. When *we* add 0.6 and 0.6, we do *not* expect to get 1.2, but rather a value somewhat less than 1.0. So when we actually do add 0.6 and 0.6 and get 1.2, that *is* unexpected. In other words, it's the very fact that we *do* get aggregation that is unexpected, and therefore unobvious, and therefore patentable."

"A novel concept, indeed." Honaire was thoughtful. "And it reduces still further the area of logic circuits in our computers available for interim findings of law and fact in this application."

"It would appear, then," said Lane, "that the question of aggregation rests entirely within the personal discretion of the Examiner. We formally request a ruling."

"I accept the personal jurisdiction of the issue," said Honaire coolly. "Nevertheless I shall retain the rejection on aggregation until a suitable showing of operability is made." He looked across at the clock. "By your calculations, *Electra* and *Thor* should be landing in about ten minutes?"

Lane shrugged his shoulders. "And the Commissioner is probably out playing golf. Shall we proceed to the rejection on art?"

Honaire smiled. "Very well. We have a rejection on the prior art, based on counsel's own statements made in prior prosecution of record, to the effect that *Electra* and *Thor,* taken together, are examples of operability and utility of the invention. But in view of *Electra-Thor,* how can the instant invention be *novel?*"

"It's novel because this application was filed three years ago, before either *Electra* or *Thor* reached 0.6 c," said Lane. "In other words, the *Electra-Thor* system, considered as a supra-c system, isn't prior art simply because it isn't *prior.*"

Honaire nodded. "We agree. That particular rejection will be withdrawn. We can now proceed to the formal objections."

"He means objections to the language of the claims," Lane explained to Bryan.
"Quite right," said Honaire. "Your main claim simply says 'Space travel at speeds greater than the velocity of light.' The claim would cover all motion in excess of light, regardless of how it is accomplished."

"But that's what I invented," said Bryan. "Why can't I claim it?"

"You invented *one* method of moving at speeds greater than light," said Honaire. "Your method requires two vessels, each moving at a speed greater than 0.5 *c*. Later on, if someone else can invent another way to cause a vessel to move at a speed greater than the speed of light, independent of a second vessel, your patent ought not to cover such subsequent invention."

"Suppose we amend to recite two ships," said Lane, "each having a velocity greater than 0.5 *c*, and having a net velocity with respect to each other exceeding *c*?"

"Still too broad," said Honaire. "In your invention, as described in your application, both ships are *accelerated* until they reach 0.6 *c*."

"We will further amend," said Lane, "to recite that each ship is accelerated to a velocity of at least 0.6 *c*."

"Seems reasonable," said Honaire, making interlineations in his file. "Would you please read the proposed claims into the record?"

Lane dictated briefly, then looked up at Honaire expectantly.

"The revised claims meet all objections in phraseology," said Honaire, looking at the clock. "This leaves only the issues of aggregation and operability, which we are forced to postpone until—"

The audio buzzed.

"Ah!" said Honaire. "Perhaps *this* is what we have been waiting for." He flipped the incoming button.

A crisp voice crackled through. "Honaire!"

"Yes, sir!"

"Both ships came in on schedule. Incidentally, I have both Dr. Talix and the *kae* in my private car, and we are headed for the hospital. You might so inform the applicant."

"He's going to see Dad!" exclaimed Bryan. "Who is he?"

Jack Lane was shaken. "*That* was the Commissioner of Patents." His voice gradually came back. He asked Honaire: "I gather that the Commissioner witnessed the arrival of the ships with his own eyes?"

Honaire smiled. "Yes. So the Office must withdraw the rejections on inoperability and aggregation."

"And you'll allow the claims?" Lane's voice had an edge of unbelief.

Honaire was calm. "I am pleased to inform you, Mr. Lane, that, as presently advised, all objections and rejections in this application have been met, and in accordance with the Statutes and the authority vested in me by the Commissioner of Patents, I do now grant the patent."

Bryan started to cheer, then remembered where he was. Instead, he jumped up, whirled around twice, and sat down again. "You mean *right now?*"

"Yes, right now," said Honaire. "In ancient times, it took at least six weeks after allowance, to issue the patent. Now, of course, with computers, we can deliver the sealed document within a few minutes—and *here it is.*" A gold-sealed document emerged from a slot on the top of his desk, and he handed it to Bryan. And at that instant the room was plunged in darkness.

"What's the matter?" whispered Bryan.

Honaire laughed wryly. "I think I can explain. When a patent is granted, it is automatically abstracted and integrated into our computers, so as to constitute a reference against any future patent application for a similar invention. Simultaneously, all points of law involved are programmed into the computers in the Solicitor's office. These operations necessarily require our computers to accept and digest data on the Einstein Theory, and on the law of aggregation, that they 'know' are wrong. Their circuits probably couldn't handle the conflict. My guess is, that all the computers involved are temporarily out of commission— nervous breakdowns, if you will." He sighed. "And *my* office lights are out because our government, always economy conscious, has wired our computers and office lights on a common circuit. But if you will bear with us, the current balancers will take care of the problem in a moment. Ah, here come the lights again."

"Then we'd better leave before we cause any further difficulty." Lane shook hands with Honaire. "The courtesies of the Office are greatly appreciated," he said formally. But he was grinning from ear to ear.

Honaire played it dead-pan. "We serve the Cluster." His eyes flickered, and he turned to Bryan. "There is just one final requirement."

Bryan's heart skipped a beat. "Sir?"

"May I have the autograph of the boy who blew the fuse at the Patent Office?"

They found Jim Burke waiting for them impatiently in his room at the hospital. "You missed all the excitement," he said from behind his bandages. "Some government fellow collected Dr. Talix and the *kae* at the port and brought them here together. Talix has just finished giving me my first treatment."

"Can you see yet?" demanded Bryan eagerly.

"Well, of course not, not yet. Even if it works, it'll take weeks. But enough about me. You got the patent?"

"Yes," said Lane.

"So now you can file the counterclaim and preliminary injunction against the Line?"

"Both are now on record. We stopped by the Hall of Justice."

"What's our next step?"

"We wait. Slicer is certainly going to put out feelers for settlement. When he comes around again, we'll have to be ready to talk to him about a license under the patent . . ."

"I am here," said Mr. Slicer warmly, "because of my continuing deep concern about Mr. Burke. All of you will be delighted to learn that I have been able to persuade Pan-Stellar to offer a generous disability pension to Mr. Burke."

"How much?" asked Jim.

"One hundred and twenty-five talers a month," said Mr. Slicer kindly.

Jim Burke began a slow rhythmic gurgling.

"Mr. Slicer," said Lane patiently, "we know you mean well, but owing to my client's facial bandages, it is painful for him to laugh."

Slicer stared at Jack Lane suspiciously. "I wasn't trying to be humorous. My motives are entirely humane—"

"I'm sure they are," smiled Lane. "And of course our counterclaim for patent infringement has nothing to do with your presence here. So if your tactics require that you spend the first fifteen minutes telling us that our patent is worthless and that we ought to settle for a monthly payment of one hundred and twenty-five talers, you go right ahead. But we may smile."

Slicer studied the three uneasily; then he shrugged his shoulders. "Well, frankly, now that you mention it, I *don't* think much of your patent. But it would take a long and expensive fight in the courts to find out where we stood. For this reason, we are willing to buy in, if the price is right. But the figure in your counterclaim, one cent per ton, seems high."

"What rate did you have in mind?" said Lane carefully.

"Something like, say, one-tenth of a cent."

"Too low."

Slicer was no longer smiling. "I don't think your patent will stand up in court."

"We'll soon know, won't we?" said Lane genially. "Since patent infringement is a counterclaim in Pan-Stellar vs. Burke, the question of whether my client must reimburse the Line for the explosion will be decided by the same jury that decides whether the Line infringes the patent issued to this man's son—this same bright young lad, who, with tears running down his cheeks, helped carry his father's stretcher down in front of the jury box."

Slicer patted his forehead with his handkerchief. "Mr. Lane, we seem to be constantly misunderstanding each other. What are your minimum terms?"

"One-quarter cent per ton royalty, non-exclusive. Exclusive is half-a-cent per ton."

"If we were exclusive, could we sub-license the other lines and keep the income?"

"You can," said Lane, "if you will take the responsibility for policing the patent and financing all litigation."

"Seems reasonable."

"But before we get too far along," said Lane, "let me mention that we will require a substantial lump-sum down payment."

"Ah, the down payment. How much?"

Bryan said: "One million talers." Then he held his breath.

"Make it a quarter million," said Slicer.

"That's not enough," said Bryan. "Remember, Mr. Slicer, we have to get enough to pay the Line your claim of 483,000 talers. But we'll come down a little, to 966,000 talers. Then we could pay your claim and still have 483,000 talers left over."

Slicer glared at Bryan. "Which, by some strange coincidence, is exactly what we were suing your father for!" His eyes rolled upward. "Never in my entire professional career have I dealt with such unreasonable people."

"Then maybe there's another way, Mr. Slicer," said Bryan carefully. "But first, a question for our lawyer. Mr. Lane, is ship time legal time? I mean, can you write a patent license where something happens by ship time?"

Jim Burke leaned forward suddenly.

"Yes, of course," said Lane, looking puzzled.

"What difference does it make?" sniffed Slicer. "The patent expires in seventeen years, no matter how you calculate it. Earth time, ship time, it's all the same. After seventeen years, your royalties stop."

"Then we're pretty close to agreement," said Jim quickly. "If the Line will waive its claim against me, I'll waive the down payment. On one condition."

"Which is?"

"The seventeen-year period will be determined by the chronometers of ships operating under the patent claims."

Slicer studied the three. "There's something here I can't quite put my finger on." He rubbed his chin thoughtfully. "All right, it's a deal. I'll send the contract over within the hour." And now he was smiling again. He smiled his warmest, kindliest smile. "Master Bryan, you have no idea just how much money the Line is going to make from this license."

Bryan smiled back. "No, sir. But then, the Line doesn't know for how long it's going to be paying the Burkes."

One year later Jim Burke drove Jack Lane, Bryan, and Margie out to the dedication ceremonies for the new Burke Research Laboratories.

"I still don't like it," said Margie. "Putting all our patent money into those buildings and that funny equipment. It'll take years before you get enough clients to break even. You'll overwork. And you know what Dr. Talix says about not tiring your eyes. Also, I'm sure the patent royalties won't go on forever."

"Now *there* is a curious point," soothed Jim. "Because, for practical purposes, the patent royalties *will* go on forever."

"Are you out of your mind? The patent expires in seventeen years." She turned to Lane. "Doesn't it, Jack?"

Lane chuckled. "It does, but it all depends where the seventeen-year period is taking place. Bryan gets the credit for this gimmick, so why don't we let him explain it?"

"It was the last thing we talked about, with that nice Mr. Slicer," said Bryan. "We got him to agree to keep paying the royalties as long as the patent was in force, as determined by ship time."

"Well?" said Margie.

"Don't you see, dear?" said Jim. "Everything on a ship under acceleration slows down, including clocks. The faster the ship, the slower the clock. But, as long as Pan-Stellar ship-pairs are arriving or departing at high speeds during the remaining sixteen years of the patent *on their clocks,* they are accruing royalty under the patent, no matter whether the patent has long since expired by local time here in Washington. So when the patent expires in sixteen more years, Earth time, there will be hundreds of Line ships in deep space with clocks that register only a two-year lapse. The patent will still be in force on those ships, and we collect our royalties on them, even though some of them won't be back for twenty or thirty years, Earth time."

"And that's just a starter," said Bryan. "Right now, Pan-Stellar is provisioning nearly fifty ships for the first attempts at several of the nearer globular clusters. The round trip will take nearly a hundred years, Earth time, but their clocks will show a time lapse of only about seven years."

"*Those* royalties should take care of our grandchildren comfortably," said Jim Burke.

"And that isn't all," said Bryan. "Pan-Stellar is building ships to try for the Magellanic Clouds. The round trip is about 40,000 light years, Earth time, but the ships' clocks will show only about ten years lapse, well within the patent."

"And next will be the nearer galaxies," said Lane. "M-31 in Andromeda is nearly a million light years away, but, calculating ship time by the Einstein Theory, the round trip will be less than seventeen years for the people on the ships."

"But what kind of patent is it," wondered Margie Burke plaintively, "if you got it in the first place only because Einstein was *wrong,* and then you make it last for a million years because Einstein is right? Don't you have to be consistent?"

Lane laughed. "Not in the patent game. But don't worry about Einstein. He would understand. After all, he was a patent examiner in ancient Switzerland!"

A letter from John Campbell started this one. Could I write a story involving psi and the U.S. Supreme Court? So I did. But he sent it back. "This is serious," he complained. "Make it funny."

I didn't reply. I sent it to Damon Knight, who took it for Orbit, *which paid better anyway.*

While working on this Nell and I used to experiment with telepathy. We would sit in different rooms, one draws something, the other draws something. Do the pictures match? Very frequently they did. Probably a psychologist would say it was perfectly normal—we were "close"—whatever that means.

PROBABLE CAUSE

The right of the people to be secure in their persons, houses, papers, and effects, against unreasonable searches and seizures, shall not be violated, and no Warrants shall issue, but upon probable cause . . .
Nor shall any person be compelled to be a witness against himself . . .

— Constitution of the United States,
excerpts, Fourth and Fifth Amendments

Benjamin Edmonds turned the film advance knob on the self-developing camera in slow rhythmic motions of hand and wrist. When the mechanism locked, he placed the camera on its side next to the bronze casting on the wall table. He flipped off the ceiling light and turned on the faint red darkroom lamp over the developing trays. He sat for a moment, studying the casting and waiting for his eyes to adjust to the near darkness.

The replica was a plain, almost homely thing: a hand clasping a piece of broomstick. Even after a century and a quarter it still radiated the immense strength and suprahuman compassion of its great model, and it would surely help to waken the distant sleeping shadows. Edmonds laid his own big hand over it softly; the metal seemed oddly warm.

It was time to begin.

He turned off the red light and let the blackness flow over him.

The images began almost immediately. At first they flickered vaguely, seemingly trapped within the plane of his eyelids. Then they gathered clarity and stereoscopic dimension, and moved out, and away. They were real, and he was there, in the crowded theater, looking up at the flag-draped presidential box, occupied by the three smaller figures and the tall bearded man in the rocking chair. And now, from behind, a fifth. The arm surely rising. The deadly glint of

261

metal. The shot. The man leaping out of the box to the stage below. And pandemonium. Fluttering scenes. They were carrying the tall man across the street in the wavering paschal moonlight. And finally, in that far time, Edmonds permitted the strange hours to pass, until the right moment came, and the right image came.

It was the critical instant. This last scene, this static vision in time, must now be captured on the emulsion waiting inside the camera. As always, the mental process of transfer was sharp, burning. And then it was done.

He stood up and turned on the ceiling light again. He was breathing heavily. He felt cold, but his face was dripping with sweat. He pushed the bronze casting aside, rubbed at his eyes with a couple of paper towels, then pulled the film out of the camera. He studied the positive print briefly, but with approval. He rubbed the negative carefully with a hypo-stick and placed it between the carrier plates of the enlarger.

Why, of all the transcendent possibilities, did he think Helen would want this simple thing of hands? Why not the gangling young man, brooding at the grave of Ann Rutledge? Or the poignant farewell from the rear of the train just before it pulled out of Springfield? No, none of these. For Helen Nord, it had to be the hands.

For a bachelor in his fifties, thought Edmonds, I am a fool. And if Helen only knew what I have been doing here, she would certainly agree. I'm worse than Tom Sawyer, walking the picket fence to show off in front of his young lady friend.

He smiled wryly as he turned off the ceiling light once more and reached for the 8X11 bromide paper.

The secretary in the outer office looked up from her typewriter and smiled. "Good morning, Madam Nord. The Justice is expecting you. Please go right in."

"Thank you." Mrs. Nord returned the smile and walked through into the inner office.

Benjamin Edmonds stood up gravely and motioned her to the chair by the great oak desk.

Helen Strachey Nord of Virginia, once known only as the widow of John Nord and the mother of three sons (all now launched in professional careers) was a handsome woman in her late forties. The tragic death of John Nord in the first Mars landings had brought her initially to the public eye, but her own remarkable abilities had kept her there. After working several years at NASA and taking her law degree at night, she had been appointed to the U.S.-Soviet Arbitration Commission to settle the Lunar Disputes of the late seventies. War had been averted. She was the obvious choice for the next appointment of a United States delegate to the U.N. And finally, when old Justice Fauquier died, President Cromway submitted her name to the Senate as the first female Justice of the United States Supreme Court. The ensuing senatorial debates and hearings made the long forgotten Cardozo and Black appointments seem exercises in benevolence. But for Cromway's assassination, she would never have made it. As a courtesy to the late President, enough votes were collected. Just barely.

How strange, thought Edmonds, that this woman, who has known passion, and who has nourished three fine sons, can yet bring such intricate insights into bankruptcy, space law, admiralty . . . the whole gamut. He said: "Glad you could drop by, Helen. I have something for you." He opened the attaché case, took the picture out, and handed it to her. "It's only an eight by eleven, but if you like it I can make you a bigger blowup for framing."

The woman walked over to the window and studied the picture.

Edmonds asked: "Do you know what it is?"

"Yes—that is, I know what it would be, if it were possible. The hand of Charles Leale holding the hand of the dying Lincoln in the dawn hours of April fifteenth, eighteen sixty-five." She looked back at him, pondering. "But it can't be, because I also know that no photographs were taken. Not on that terrible night. But no matter. It is superb." She continued, sorting it out in her own mind. "It was the crowning, exquisite irony of the Civil War. You know the story, of course. Dr. Leale was a young army surgeon. He had come to Ford's Theatre that night just to see Lincoln. It was the great ambition of his young life to shake the hand of the President, but he scarcely dared hope for this. And so he was the first doctor in the presidential box after Booth leaped down to the stage. Leale had the President moved across the street, and endured the last hours with him. And, it being his army experience that a dying man will sometimes regain consciousness in the moments just before the end, and wanting Lincoln to know he was among friends, he came around to his right side, and took him by the hand, with the tip of the forefinger on the fading pulse, just as you see here." She looked back at Edmonds thoughtfully. "It is certainly pertinent, considering the case we'll have at conference today."

His eyes searched her face uneasily. "Poor timing, wasn't it? I'm truly sorry. But you'll have to learn not to let a case get to you, Helen. Not even *Tyson* v. *New York*. Especially not *Tyson*."

"Ben, do *you* think Frank Tyson shot President Cromway?"

"What *I* think about it personally is irrelevant. I can think about it only as a judge. And being a judge, even on this Court, is a job like any other. We get paid for interpreting laws made by other people. Our personal feelings of right and wrong are supposed to be irrelevant." How could he explain to her that he himself had never learned how to deal with that bitterest judicial duty—to decide whether a man lives or dies—and that he was reconciled to the knowledge he would never learn how to deal with it? He had never understood the rationale of capital punishment. After a history of six thousand years, it did not deter murders that led to further capital punishment. Maybe it had reduced the number? There was no way to tell. There was no control experiment. He shrugged. "The only thing that you and I and our seven brothers will have to think about is whether New York violated Tyson's constitutional rights in convicting him. As a Lincolnian, you must appreciate that."

"I know. Poor Dr. Mudd—his only crime was to set the broken leg of a stranger—who later turned out to be John Wilkes Booth. For which he was sentenced to life imprisonment."

"And Mrs. Surratt, in whose house the conspirators met."

"Yes. Even when the hangman pulled the black bag over her head, she did not understand."

They both looked around. Edmonds' secretary was standing in the doorway. "Excuse me, sir. The five-minute buzzer."

Edmonds nodded.

Helen Nord took a last puzzled look at the photograph before she put it away in her briefcase. Edmonds followed her out into the corridor.

> *Subtler and more far-reaching means of invading privacy have become available to the government. The progress of science in furnishing the government with means of espionage is not likely to stop with wiretapping. Ways may someday be developed by which the government, without removing papers from secret drawers, can reproduce them in court, and by which it will be enabled to expose to a jury the most intimate occurrences of the home. Advances in the psychic and related sciences may bring means of exploring unexpressed beliefs, thoughts, and emotions.*
>
> —Justice Brandeis, dissenting in
> *Olmstead* v. *United States* (1928)

At his first Friday conference, Edmonds had thought the custom rather silly: each of the nine justices of the United States Supreme Court, the most prestigious body in the world, had to shake hands with the eight others before they could take their seats around the long table. But now, after several years on the high court, he could understand why Chief Justice Fuller had instituted the practice nearly a hundred years ago. It softened long-standing frictions and differences that might otherwise prevent nine totally divergent minds from meshing together as a court. He thought wryly of analogies from the ring: "Shake hands and come out fighting." Thirty-six handshakes. It was possible now, at eleven o'clock in the morning. When they adjourned at six, it might not be.

And now they took their places around the long black table, Chief Justice Shelley Pendleton at the south end, Senior Associate Justice Oliver Godwin at the north end, and the other associate justices, in order of seniority, around the sides. The great John Marshall gave them his blessing from his portrait over the ornate marble fireplace.

The face of Chief Justice Shelley Pendleton was a paradox—almost ugly in its craggy, masklike impassivity, yet capable of dissolving into a strangely beautiful humanity, warm, humorous, even humble. It was whispered that he had retired to his office and wept after his first affirmation of a death penalty, and that the widow was still receiving a pension from the manager of his immense personal estate. Before his appointment, he had been a well-known figure on Wall Street. Edmonds admired the man. He found it incredible that such lucid opinions could flow from such a complicated intellect. It used to bother him, until he finally concluded that the Chief Justice considered *all* possible angles, sifted out the major controlling aspects, weighed them against each other in a multi-dimensional balance, and accepted the answer. The Pendleton technique involved all factors of legal precedent . . . *stare decisis* . . . logic . . . the common law . . . social needs . . .and a fine prophetic grasp of the impact of a given decision on future similar cases. Marshall had been a constitutionalist, Holmes a historian, Brandeis a sociologist, Cardozo a liberal, and Warren a humanist—but Pendleton was none of these; for he was all.

The Chief Justice spoke rapidly and concisely. "The first case on our agenda is *Frank Tyson, petitioner, v. New York*. Petition for certiorari to the Court of Appeals of New York. All of you know what this one is about, so I need restate the facts but briefly. Tyson was indicted, tried, and convicted of killing our late President Cromway in the entrance of the United Nations Building, with one bullet from a telescopic-sighted rifle, from a window in an empty room in a nearby building. Tyson's palm-print was found on the rifle, and ballistics tests showed that the bullet taken from the President's body was fired from the rifle. An elevator operator named Philip Dopher testified that he saw Tyson leave the room, carrying something, and hurry down the stairs. Tyson, a porter in the building, contends that he was supervising a shipment of files to a warehouse for storage, that he heard a shot in the empty room, went in to investigate, found the rifle, picked it up, then looked out the window, took in the scene instantly, and realized that he was holding the weapon that had just killed a President of the United States. He panicked, thinking only to get rid of the rifle. He ran down the side stairs with it and hid it, unobserved, in a crate of files standing by the freight elevator. Seconds later, the movers took the crate down the elevator to the van waiting on the other side of the building. And there, in that warehouse, it was eventually found."

He paused and looked around at the intent faces.

"Thus far, the case does not present a federal question. I want you to ignore the enormity of the crime and the fact that a President of the United States was murdered. All of us knew him personally, and we all have an abiding respect and affection for his memory; some of us are here by his appointment. These aspects standing alone cannot possibly warrant our review. The sole issue of relevance to us, and indeed, the sole ground urged as basis for reversal, is the alleged violation of the Fourth Amendment to the Constitution by officers of the State of New York, in that their warrant to search the warehouse was not issued 'upon probable cause.' Specifically, petitioner contends that the officers hired a clairvoyant, one Dr. Drago, to read petitioner's mind, without his consent, thereby to visualize the location of the rifle, and that the New York magistrate issued the warrant to search the warehouse on this so-called information, and on nothing else. The primary question therefore seems to be, can clairvoyance adequately substitute for the routine and legally sufficient visual and aural observations as basis for a sworn statement on which a search warrant may validly issue? If we accept this as the heart of the matter, we may have to consider ancillary questions. For example, is there actually such a thing as clairvoyance? If we can satisfy ourselves here and now that there is not, then we would of course have some basis for deciding that the warrant was not issued on probable cause: and Tyson might be freed. On the other hand, if we can decide here and now that clairvoyance does exist, we have no escape from the next question: Was the exercise of this power an unconstitutional invasion of Tyson's right of privacy? If it was not, then he was properly convicted. But if it was an improper invasion, then of course the evidence developed by it—the rifle, and his fingerprints on the rifle—would be inadmissible under the Fifth Amendment, and again he would go free."

He shifted restlessly in his chair. "There is more. Mrs. Nord, will you please step to the door and ask the marshal to bring in Exhibit Q?"

For over a century, no clerks, messengers, or secretaries had been permitted in the room during conference. The duty of doorman fell to the juniormost appointee.

Helen Nord stepped to the door, waited until the marshal and his assistant had placed the object on the felt pad in the center of the great table, and closed the door after they left.

"As you know," resumed the Chief Justice, "this is *the* safe. And you know what it is said to contain. During Tyson's trial, the so-called clairvoyant, Dr. Drago, testified that he had placed a suitably cushioned auto-developing camera inside, then locked the safe, and delivered it into the custody of the trial court—but without the combination. So far as the record goes, Drago is the only one who knows the combination. If we grant certiorari, he will provide the combination. In fact, he is waiting in my outer office at the moment. He refuses to give the combination to anyone but me. But back to the facts. At the trial, New York put Drago on the stand to prove the existence of clairvoyance, and hence that the warrant was validly issued. Drago testified that his clairvoyant power—he called it 'psi'—was erratic, that it comes and goes, and could not always be called up at will. But he said he could prove it existed. He then predicted, over petitioner's objection, that New York would convict Tyson, that we would grant certiorari, and that the majority of us would reverse Tyson's conviction, holding that the warrant was not issued upon probable cause. He further predicted that most of us would deny the existence of psi. His proof to the contrary is supposed to be inside Exhibit Q, which we are invited to open after handing down our predicted decision."

"What colossal impertinence!" roared Oliver Godwin. His white handlebar mustache trembled indignantly.

"Mr. Godwin," said Justice Roland Burke coldly, "since the days of John Marshall it has been the custom at these conferences that each of us will be heard in turn without interruption, starting with the Chief Justice and proceeding down the line in order of seniority. I will ask you to await your turn."

The hard blue eyes of the Senior Associate Justice crackled. He said gravely, "Sorry, Roly. Sometimes I forget you're no longer barely passing my course in torts, back at Harvard Law. Ah, what a time you had with proximate cause, and those prolix, tautological so-called briefs. In fact, you still do. You used nearly fifty words just to tell me to shut up."

The ample cheeks of Justice Burke turned pink. "I'd resent that, if you weren't a senile old man, who should have retired long ago." He concluded primly, "You confuse tautology with logic."

Godwin grinned evilly. "Do I? 'Senile' is from *senex,* Latin for 'old man.' I'm an 'old-man old man.' " He laughed. "Well, perhaps I am. But age is a relative thing, Roly. If you leave me out, the average age on this court would be about sixty. And you're well over *that.* If it weren't for me, Roly, *you'd* be an old man."

Pendleton's mouth twitched faintly. "If we can defer the actuarial comparisons for a moment, I think I can finish. I don't want us to grant certiorari and then find we have to decide whether there is or is not such a thing as psi. And I want to ignore Exhibit Q altogether. Its contents—or at least the eventual contents of the camera—if any—are not of record. Drago's insistence to the contrary, we can give it no consideration. Certainly, we cannot open it. Another point: petitioner urges an analogy to wiretapping. What has been done to him, if clairvoyance was in fact used, he calls 'clairtapping.' We have held that evidence obtained by wiretapping or by any other unlawful means is inadmissible, in both federal and state courts. *Mapp* v. *Ohio, Berger* v. *New York.* The contention is therefore made that 'clairtapping' is a violation of privacy as bad as, if not worse than, wiretapping, and that evidence so obtained must be similarly excluded. I think that there is merit in this contention. In summary, if the rifle was located by clairvoyance, the search may well have been unconstitutional in analogy to wiretapping. If clairvoyance does not exist, then there was no basis on which a valid warrant could have issued at all. Thus there is a possibility that we could decide the case without deciding anything about psi." He paused and looked down the table. "Mr. Godwin, I yield to you."

"Thank you, Shelley. It was about time. Several things bother me. *Can* we decide on the merits without deciding about psi? It's rather like that Kidd will case in Arizona, back in the sixties, where the testator gave all his money to anybody who could prove the existence of the soul. The judge *had* to decide whether human beings have souls. Pity we didn't grant cert on that one. Always wondered whether I'd get a soul out of a 5-4 decision. Sorry, brothers—and sister. An old man likes to ramble. So I'll just ask a question: why don't we just open that safe right now and see what's on the film? Might save a lot of argument and embarrassment later on."

"You read the testimony," said Pendleton. "At the moment there's supposed to be nothing on the film."

"Then what in tarnation is the good of it?"

"Some kind of image—and don't ask me what—is eventually supposed to appear on it."

"When?"

"On Decision Day."

The Senior Associate Justice snorted. "You expect us to believe that?"

"No."

"I should think not. Let's get back to reality. As I view this thing, we're on the horns of a real dilemma. If we take the case and reverse Tyson's conviction because there was an unconstitutional invasion of privacy, then we have probably ruled that clairvoyance is a real and functional phenomenon. Science arises in anguish. On the other hand, if we rule that clairvoyance doesn't exist, and that, therefore, there was no invasion of privacy, then the bleeding-heart liberals arise in howling dismay at the official blessing we have now given police use of clairvoyance. Who needs wiretaps anymore? Psi is easier, and the cops will be welcome to use all the psi techniques they can dig up: telepathy, clairvoyance, hexing, prekenners . . ."

"What's a 'prekenner,' Judge?" asked Edmonds, fascinated.

"Somebody who *previously kens* what's going to happen, so as to set up police traps to catch criminals in the act. I just made up the word. But if Roly can use two words when he means one, surely I can use one word when I mean two. That's all I wanted to say. You take it, Roly."

"Thank you, Mr. Godwin," said Burke coldly. He paused a moment, looking at the chandeliers overhead, as though simplifying and tailoring his thoughts for certain of the less disciplined minds around him.

Edmonds awaited the dissertation with interest. Somehow, of course, it would turn on logic.

In Burke's early days as a judge on the New Jersey bench, Frankfurter had been his model. But this had changed over the years. Burke (like Cervantes) had finally recognized that every man was the product of his own work. But where Cervantes had been content to permit the process to operate subconsciously, Burke went to the final logical limit. He found in his own past works his best inspiration. As he shaved in the morning, he listened to tapes of his previous decisions. And he listened to the same tapes in his car as he drove to court, and at night put himself to sleep with them.

He had founded the Burke Chair in Logic at Harvard. His famous text, *Logic in Appellate Decisions* (dedicated to himself) consisted largely of annotated excerpts from his own decisions. He was both ignorant of and indifferent to what others thought of his magnificent narcissism. In fact, he considered himself modest, and sought out situations where his modesty might be displayed, noticed, and commented on. Roland Burke's long love affair with himself had not dimmed with the passing of time: it was a serene thing, unmarred by lovers' quarrels. He had no portraits hanging in his office; only mirrors.

Edmonds sometimes wondered at his own reaction to Burke. Far from feeling contempt or derision, he found he envied the famous jurist's confident, self-centered, doubt-free integration into his codified environment, and his system of logic that so easily resolved all questions into black and white, with no plaguing shades of gray left over.

"Psi," began Burke, "is hogwash—illogical by its very definition. Yet, as I shall demonstrate, logic requires that we take the case. There are only two possibilities: a) to deny the petition, and b) to grant. If we deny, this sets a precedent that the Supreme Court will refuse to review constitutional questions involving psi. Our refusal would be interpreted by the lower courts as endorsing warrants issuing on clairvoyant information. Such a consequence is clearly unthinkable. This leaves us, therefore, only with the second alternate, b), to grant. Logically, we must grant."

"*Quod erat demonstrandum,*" murmured Godwin.

Burke ignored him loftily.

"Thank you, Mr. Burke," said the Chief Justice. "Mr. Moore?"

Nicholas Moore of Louisiana spoke with a soft drawl. "I disagree. This is not the kind of case this court should take. Even if there *is* a federal question—which I doubt—we can turn it down. Since the revision of the Judiciary Act in the twenties, we have been free to turn down practically any case we wish—excepting issues between the states, or the states and the United States government. It's a question of policy. We can handle no more than a hundred to a hundred fifty cases a year—less than ten percent of the appeals that come to us. Our every decision should throw light on some current judicial problem and state principles for the guidance of the lower courts in thousands of similar cases. We did this with the wiretapping cases, the desegregation cases, the school-prayer cases. But how many cases involving this psi thing are currently pending in the lower courts? None at all, that I've heard about."

"Mr. Blandford?"

"I agree with Moore," said the Massachusetts justice thoughtfully. "We took considerable interest in this kind of thing in Salem three hundred years ago. We burned people at the stake for less. We weren't too sure about God, but we certainly believed in the Devil. I hope this isn't evidence of a trend. We're not an ecclesiastical court of the Middle Ages. We can't go back. I don't think we should get involved. No, never again."

"Thank you. Mr. Lovsky?"

Justice Lovsky stared suspiciously at the safe. "The whole thing smells. But I agree with Mr. Burke, *supra*. We ought to take it. If we deny the cert, you'll have every J.P. in the country issuing warrants on psi. *Cf.* Godwin. It's a return to the general warrants of eighteenth-century Britain, *q.v.* We had a little revolution about *that*. Madison, *Federalist Papers*. The Bill of Rights, Madison, *op. cit.,* would be down the drain. In a few years we'll get a hundred petes for cert on the same point. *Ibid.* The time to stop it is now."

"Mr. Randolph?"

Justice Randolph spoke on all occasions with slow incision, as though dictating, direct to the stone cutter, immortal inscriptions for the entablature of a majestic new federal building. He clipped:

• CONSTITVTIONAL •QVESTION •

and then was gloomy because the first word, under the circumstances, was possibly superfluous. His law clerks always conferred with those of Justice Lovsky, fitting, with consummate artistry, Lovsky's footnotes to Randolph's headnotes. The result read like pages in *Corpus Juris Tertium*. This procedure required that the justices always agree; they found this a small price to pay for the exquisite result.

"Mr. Edmonds?"

"Isn't it a strange coincidence? Here we are in the opening months of nineteen eighty-four." He tossed a book on the table. "It's Orwell's *Nineteen Eighty-Four*— the ultimate regimented state. All citizens under police surveillance twenty-four hours a day. No privacy at any time. The police have even installed closed-circuit TV in homes and apartments. When this book was popular, forty years ago, many people laughed. It was absurd. It couldn't happen in America. Well, it *has* happened. It's here now—except clairtapping is even worse than spy TV. It penetrates the privacy of our minds. We must deny its use to the police."

"You sound as though you really believe in this stuff," said Godwin.

Edmonds shrugged.

"Thank you, Mr. Edmonds. Madam Nord?"

"*My* argument for granting certiorari will, I think, seem totally incompetent and irrelevant to most of you. And I expect that my distinguished brother, the Senior Associate Justice, may have a stroke. In a word, I think Tyson is innocent. Also, I think we ought to open the safe."

There was an embarrassed silence.

Then came Oliver Godwin's stage whisper: "Don't knock it, boys. Never forget, we're the only high court in the world with our own Madam."

Helen Nord led the laughter.

The Chief Justice rapped the table with his knuckles. "We will vote. Madam Nord?"

"To grant."

The vote went backwards, in inverse order of seniority. The theory, which seemed utterly fallacious to Edmonds, was that the junior justices would thereby not be influenced by their seniors. In this group, he thought, nobody influences anybody. Nine sovereign independent republics.

"Mr. Edmonds?"

"Grant."

Two more votes were needed.

"Mr. Randolph?"

• GRANT •

"Mr. Lovsky?"

"To grant."

"That's it. And now we can accept the combination to the safe. Madam Nord, will you please ask the deputy to summon Dr. Drago?"

"Most irregular," grumbled Justice Burke.

"Possibly," admitted Pendleton. "But at least it's by stipulation of counsel. All we permit him to do is hand me the combination in a sealed envelope. We ask him nothing, and we must silence him if he attempts to speak. Ah, here they come."

Edmonds was mildly surprised. Drago was a tall, dignified young man with smooth, pale cheeks. He might have been the desk clerk at the local YMCA, or a bank teller, or a deacon at Edmonds' own church.

Drago's eyes opened a little wider as he exchanged glances with Edmonds. And then his searching stare passed quickly around the table, next resting momentarily on Helen Nord . . . then Moore . . . Blandford . . . Godwin . . . and finally Pendleton. His mouth opened slightly, as though he were whispering to himself. Edmonds strained to hear. Was it, "Oh no"? He could not be sure.

Pendleton said gently, "We thank you for coming, Dr. Drago. I am Pendleton. I understand you wish to give me the combination to the safe."

Like an automaton, Drago walked to the end of the table, and without a word handed the envelope to the Chief Justice.

Edmonds was leaning forward intently. There was suddenly something very strange about Drago's face. The cheeks were no longer smooth. And the man's hair . . . seemed *bushier*. And then Edmonds knew: Drago's face and scalp were rough with goose bumps. The thought sent a chill along his own spine. He looked rapidly around the table. No one else had noticed.

But *why?* And *what*, in this, the law's inmost, most austere sanctum, could possibly terrify any man, be he clairvoyant or not? He watched uneasily as Helen Nord led Drago outside and closed the door behind him. It required an effort of will to return to the business at hand.

Pendleton was dictating into the transcriber: "Frank Tyson, petitioner, *v.* New York. Petition for writ of certiorari to the Court of Appeals of New York, granted, limited to the single question presented by the petition as follows: 1. Whether the search warrant used by the State Officers in the instant case violated the Fourth Amendment to the United States Constitution in that said warrant was not founded upon probable cause."

> *Eavesdroppers, or such as listen under walls or windows, or the eaves of a house, to hearken after discourse, and thereupon to frame slanderous and mischievous tales, are a common nuisance and presentable at the court-leet.*
> —Blackstone, *Commentaries*

Edmonds paused at the door to Godwin's office, and, as was his habit, stared across at the portrait of Laura Godwin hanging on the opposite wall.

The room was full of reminders of the old justice's dead wife. Actually, three portraits of Laura hung from the walls. The last, the one that now held Edmonds, was a brilliant, haunting thing, painted by the younger Wyeth just before her last illness. It still showed the elfin eyes that had conquered presidents. On her right wrist she wore Godwin's wedding gift, a bracelet of green laurel leaves, clustered with pink pearls representing the little flowers. In death, as in life, the great court left her unawed, and she looked out upon the justices, individually and collectively, with the tolerant respect due precocious children.

Godwin sought out anything that spoke her name. On a stand by the window grew a tiny bonsai laurel, a *Kalmia latifolia* transplanted from the Blue Ridge Mountains. Like the ancients, Godwin believed that this living symbol of his wife had the power to ward off lightning and similar disasters.

In the burdened bookshelves behind his desk was an illustrated edition of Petrarch. Godwin had learned Italian just to be able to read of the poet's Laura in the original. Next to Petrarch was a volume of Goethe's poems. Edmonds had once pulled it out, and it had fallen open automatically to the marvelous *Mignon: "Die Myrte still und hoch der Lorbeer steht.* The myrtle silent, and high the laurel stands."

The clock on the fireplace mantel had been stopped years ago, at the moment of Laura's death. Godwin had never since permitted it to be wound. On his credenza sat a small silver casket engraved in laurel leaves. Edmonds knew its contents: a shining black plastic ink-blot; a box of matches that would not light; a deceptive fiberglass cigar; a cement egg—all paraphernalia that Laura had used in years past in perpetrating her famous April Fool jokes on her famous husband.

The room seemed warm to Edmonds. A log fire was burning with steady cheerfulness in the handsome fireplace. He knew that Godwin's chief secretary got to the office thirty minutes early to start the fire, after the old man had once complained of being cold.

"Ben! Come in, my boy." Oliver Godwin peered up at Edmonds from behind the stacks of books, files, and documents cluttering his big oak desk. "We'll have a full house at argument today. Have you seen the headlines? Here's the *Daily News:* High Court Hears Mindreading Case. And the *Post:* Assassination Case to Supreme Court. And the *Star:* Supreme Court Questions Tyson Evidence. Well, I think we're ready for 'em. I've dug up a little wiretap chronology. History, dear boy, that's the modern touchstone. Bah! Holmes said it first, nearly a hundred years ago. 'One page of history is worth a volume of logic.' " His hands began fluttering like pink mice through the debris covering his desk. "Strange, very strange. I had it here just yesterday, right next to the nineteen eighty-three *Annual Index.*"

Edmonds had seen this a hundred times. It always fascinated him. He knew that Godwin made valiant efforts to keep all his papers and files on his desk. Godwin never knowingly filed anything. And although his desk was the largest in the Marble Palace, it had become buried years ago, soon after his appointment to the Court. Thereafter, the heaps could grow only vertically. Still, legend stated that the system had actually worked in the early years. Nothing could possibly get lost; it had to be there, somewhere. And knowing that it was there, Godwin did not mind digging until he found it. He developed the skill, intuition, and patience of a trained geologist in excavating for the exact stratum. Stooping, he could peer at the side of a stack of papers and read them, edgewise, as an archaeologist would read tree-rings, or varve-layers in an ancient lakeside. At one time, Edmonds had wondered whether Godwin would be driven to rediscover carbon-dating. But then came the day when Godwin had mislaid his famous dissent in the double jeopardy case. Laura Godwin had to drive in with his "house copy," just at robing time. And then and there she had forced his clerks and secretaries to swear an oath in blood, the old man's wrath notwithstanding, that they would start a decent filing system.

And now Godwin pounded the stacks on his desk and shouted through the rising clouds of dust: "GUS!" Although monosyllabic, it was a long, wailing cry, fully orchestrated, a blend of supplication, outrage, entreaty, and indignation.

His senior law clerk, Miss Augusta Eubanks, a lady of indeterminate years, walked in quietly, holding a paper cup in each hand and a file under her arm. "The Tyson file, Mr. Godwin?"

"What else?" he roared. "I'll bet it was lost in that metal junkheap you keep out there to curse and torment my declining years. Well, hand it over!"

"First, your pills, Mr. Godwin. And we will not have a scene in front of Mr. Edmonds."

Edmonds took all of this philosophically. He happened to know that Laura Godwin had called Augusta to her deathbed and had extracted her promise to stay with the judge until he retired. He also knew that the old gentleman had set up a sizable trust in Augusta's name.

The old man meekly tossed down the pills and water. She gave him the file.

"You have to be firm with them," he whispered as she left. "Patient, but firm. *They're* the ones the Senate ought to confirm. They think they run the place. And maybe they do." He flipped the folder open. "Ah, here we are. First wiretapping, California, eighteen sixty-two, after they strung the telegraph across the Rockies. And California was the first state to make wiretapping a crime. But General Jeb Stuart of the Confederate cavalry couldn't care less. He had his own personal wiretapper in the field. Doesn't say how they did it. Shunt tap, maybe. And then Alexander Graham Bell invented the telephone in eighteen seventy-six, and the real fun began. The New York police had already been actively tapping for several years when the first tapping litigation hit the courts and the newspapers, in eighteen ninety-five. And here's a note on the nineteen twenty-eight Supreme Court case, *Olmstead* v. *United States*. The feds tapped the phone of four indignant rum runners." He leaned back in happy contemplation. "Prohibition, Ben. Before you were born. Everyone had his personal bootlegger. Speakeasies. The eye at the peephole. The raids. But the bathtub gin—ugh! That's why they smuggled it in."

"So what happened to the four rum runners?"

"The Supreme Court said their constitutional rights hadn't been violated by the wiretap, and that the evidence obtained by tapping was admissible. Holmes dissented, of course. 'A dirty business . . . the government played an ignoble part.' And do you know, it took us thirty years, but we gradually came around to Holmes's view. Ten years after *Olmstead,* in *Nardone* v. *United States,* we conceded that maybe Holmes was partly right, but only for evidence offered in federal courts. We still didn't think the Fourth and Fifth Amendments applied to the state courts. And then finally, in *Mapp* v. *Ohio,* we extended the doctrine to apply to the states. In those early days, when we finally did get around to finding a few instances of illegal wiretapping, we made it turn on trespass. Some of the early distinctions were fabulous. If you drilled a hole in a wall and pushed a mike through, that was trespass, and it was illegal. But merely hanging a mike on the outside of the wall was still okay. And if you drove a spike mike into the wall, it was legal if it didn't go all the way through, provided it didn't touch a ventilating duct. But of course all these nice distinctions are buried in the footnotes now. Today, any kind of electronic pickup is illegal, and evidence obtained by wiretapping can be excluded in any court in the country, even if the cops wiretapped by a court order. *Berger* v. *New York*. But do you think our rulings have stopped wiretapping?"

"I'm sure they haven't."

"Indeed not, my boy. In fact, we redoubled it. The police now have to wiretap twice as much to get evidence that they can prove they didn't get by wiretapping. And telephone wiretapping is the simplest trick in the world. Ex-employees of big city phone companies do it best. They call a clerk in the repair section and ask for the terminal box and location of the 'pairs'—the two electrodes for a specific telephone. There're several pairs in each terminal box, in a nearby underground utility conduit. They run a line from the pairs, attach a hand-set, and they're in business. They might run a dozen lines from a dozen different terminal boxes to an empty room in a nearby building, and have one man monitor all the lines, with automatic tape recorders that start whenever a number is dialed. I think at one time or another every important phone in Washington has been tapped."

"Surely not *our* phones."

"Of course, my boy. We were tapped liberally in nineteen thirty-five and thirty-six, in the *Ashwander* v. *T.V.A.* case. And maybe at other times that we never found out about."

"Holmes was right. It *is* a dirty business."

Godwin was thoughtful. "Dirty, ignoble . . . but very possibly necessary. Three-quarters of the racketeers and dope peddlers convicted in New York before the Berger case were caught with wiretapping. Ben, I just don't know. Surely there are instances where it is justified, say to recover a kidnapped child, or to save the life of an innocent man. Maybe we're going to have to figure out a way to let the police keep up with the criminal. Telephone tapping is passé, anyhow. The criminals are afraid to use a telephone. The police use bugs, hidden mikes, parabolic microphone pickups, light beams reflected from a windowpane vibrating from voices in the room."

Edmonds looked toward the window, and beyond to the white dreary innocence of the Library of Congress. "Do you think somebody out there is reading *your* window?"

"Who knows?" said Godwin genially. "The point is, you can't find the heading 'Wiretapping' in the *Index to Legal Periodicals* anymore. They started grouping everything under 'Eavesdropping' long ago—a broader term, of course. I imagine the rash of law journal articles that *Tyson* will generate will all show up under 'Eavesdropping,' not 'Clairvoyance' or 'Psi.' And we'll be back to the old common law misdemeanor. A dirty business? I suppose. But let's fit our reports together. What did your clerk turn up on clairvoyance?"

"Very little. Only two cases, in fact—both criminal." Edmonds opened his file. "Here's *Delon* v. *Massachusetts,* nineteen fourteen. A so-called clairvoyant was arrested for practicing medicine without a license. It seems she went into a trance, and the spirits gave her the diagnosis and what medicine to prescribe. She had a license to practice clairvoyance, but not to practice medicine. Went to jail."

"Seems reasonable. What's the other case?"

"*New York* v. *MacDonald,* eighteen ninety-six. MacDonald was absolutely identified as a would-be burglar in an apartment on Second Avenue in Manhattan. But he produced several hundred alibi witnesses who swore that at that very moment, he was on the stage of a Brooklyn theater, under hypnosis by the famous Professor Wein. The professor explained to the court that MacDonald's astral projection had simply got loose temporarily and had unwittingly materialized miles away in Manhattan. The judge let MacDonald off with a warning not to get hypnotized, ever again. But there's the bell. Time to robe."

They walked around to the robing corridor together.

> *The last demand upon him—to make some forecast of the consequences of his action—is perhaps the heaviest. To pierce the curtain of the future, to give shape and visage to mysteries still in the womb of time, is the gift of imagination. It requires poetic sensibilities with which judges are rarely endowed and which their education does not normally develop.*
>
> —Justice Felix Frankfurter

Lawyers on a Supreme Court case for the first (and generally the only) time describe the experience in hushed tones. They compare the long walk up the marble steps and through the towering white columns as a thing of horror, like mounting the guillotine, and the wait in the great boxlike courtroom until their case is called, a refinement of hell. And to wear tails, rented the day before from a Washington haberdashery, uncomfortable and occasionally not a perfect fit, when before they have never even worn a tux, with the certain knowledge that every mouth in the packed room is curled in scorn at their naivete and gaucherie, is an experience not voluntarily repeated.

It is thus for the petitioner's lawyer, even though he knows that over half the cases heard by the high court result in reversals in his favor. And it is even worse for the attorney for the state. He is full of gloomy forebodings. Back home, with all the power of his state behind him, he got a conviction. Here, he has to start all over again. And now immense forces are arrayed against him. The tables are turned. He is now the defendant.

Guy Winters, Assistant Attorney General for the State of New York, ran his finger halfway around his collar, then folded his hands self-consciously on the table in front of him. His eye wandered over the long bench of Honduras mahogany, extending almost the width of the courtroom, and then one by one to the nine faces behind it, and finally to the back of his opponent, Walter Sickles, representing Frank Tyson. Sickles was already at the lectern and was about to begin.

Edmonds was not surprised to find the courtroom packed. Some of these people, he guessed, had stood in line all night to get in. A triple quota of reporters was present. The oldtimers of the press could frequently forecast how the vote would go just by listening to the questions asked by the justices. He wished he could do as well.

From the lectern that stood squarely in front of Chief Justice Pendleton, Sickles began his presentation, slowly, in a low voice, without notes. He was glad of the microphone on the lectern, but hoped it would not pick up the knocking of his knees. As in a dream, he heard his own voice echoing back from the maroon drapes behind the great bench. "My client stands convicted of murder, on evidence improperly admitted, in that it was obtained in violation of his constitutional rights."

"You refer to the rifle, with Tyson's palm-print?" demanded Justice Godwin.

Sickles groaned inwardly. Not ten seconds at the lectern, and the questions had begun. "Yes, Your Honor."

"You admit the ballistics tests?"

"Yes, Your Honor."

"And that this evidence was obtained by search warrant giving the warehouse address and where the rifle would be found in it?"

"Yes, Your Honor, but—"

"But what, Mr. Sickles? Proceed." Godwin's mustache twitched grimly as he leaned back.

"The warrant was not issued upon probable cause."

"The information was not sworn to?"

"Oh, it was sworn to. But the officer who gave the sworn information admits he obtained it from one Dr. Drago, who admitted that he obtained it by his own personal clairvoyance."

"You don't believe there's such a thing?" demanded Justice Burke.

Oliver Godwin said calmly, "Don't answer that, sonny." He turned a bland face to his outraged colleague. "Relax, Mr. Burke. What counsel thinks personally is irrelevant."

Sickles sighed. If he were back in Brooklyn, he would be comfortably leaning back in his old wooden swivel chair, dictating during coffee break. He said, "I'd like to answer that this way, Your Honor. If there is such a thing, then it's the same as wiretapping. Maybe worse. And any evidence obtained by its use cannot justify a warrant. The circumstances of the issuance can be examined in court. This court has so ruled. And if the warrant issues wrongfully, the evidence obtained with the warrant is inadmissible, the same as if it had been obtained by wiretapping. Clairtapping . . . wiretapping . . . the legal consequences should be the same."

"There's no other evidence of Tyson's guilt?" asked Helen Nord.

"Not much, Your Honor. Just that of Dopher, the elevator operator. He testified he saw Tyson leaving the empty office, carrying an object in front of him. That alone is not enough to convict Tyson. His life or death depends on the admissibility of the rifle."

"Dr. Drago testified that clairvoyance is a fact?" asked Pendleton.

"He did, but he didn't offer proof beyond the bare statement, which was merely his own opinion."

"How about the camera in the safe, and Drago's predictions?" asked Edmonds.

"The contents of the safe are not actually in evidence, Your Honor. And as for his predictions . . . their value depends on the decision of this court. They have no present probative value."

"He predicted we'd grant the certiorari?" pressed Edmonds.

"He did, but—"

"And that we'd hold the warrant invalid, and reverse?"

"That is my expectation and hope, Your Honor."

"So that, if he turns out to be right, doesn't that prove clairvoyance, and would it not therefore follow that the warrant was in fact valid?"

"That involves a hopeless paradox, Your Honor. Anyhow, every case that is decided here is won by somebody, without benefit of clairvoyance."

Edmonds smiled. He had been thinking the same thing himself, but he wanted Sickles to make the point in open court.

"He! he!" Godwin slapped the bench with his open palm. "Well said, young man."

Sickles bowed to the aged justice—and wondered how many votes he had just lost.

"Mr. Sickles," said Helen Nord, "do you know what is in the safe—on the camera film, I mean?"

"No, Your Honor. I'm interested, of course. It may be nothing at all. But whatever it is, it can have no relevance in these proceedings."

"Suppose, Mr. Sickles," said the Chief Justice, "that it shows the face of the assassin?"

Sickles looked up at the great man in astonishment, then shrugged. "And who *is* the assassin, Your Honor? How would face and deed be connected? But I respectfully submit that the camera and its contents, whether present or prospective, are moot. Exhibit Q simply is not in evidence."

"Yes, that's true."

"Can electromagnetic radiation penetrate that safe?" asked Helen Nord.

"Quite impossible, Your Honor. The walls are one-inch steel and form a perfect Faraday box."

"So that, if psi does exist, and is a form of electromagnetic radiation, it would not be possible to penetrate the steel shell and affect the photographic emulsion in any way?"

"That's right, Your Honor."

"Then," asked Pendleton, "if we open the safe, and find the film activated, wouldn't this prove that psi is not a violation of Section six-oh-five of the Federal Communications Act, and hence that you have no benefit under *Nardone* v. *United States?*"

"That would seem to follow, Your Honor," said Sickles unhappily. He realized that he was being given the "treatment." The court frequently, at argument, forced both sides to admit they were in the wrong; then neither could complain if he lost. But he was not ready to admit defeat. "If the court please, I'd like to elaborate a little further on the constitutional question. I respectfully remind this court that under the British common law, before this country had a constitution, it was lawful to extract testimony on the rack. Farfetched, Your Honors? Similar things have happened here, and not too long ago. Your Honors will recall the case of *Rochin* v. *California,* in which the police used a stomach pump to recover the 'evidence,' two capsules of narcotics, from Rochin's stomach. After lengthy appeals, it was finally held that Rochin's constitutional rights had been violated, and the exhibits were ruled inadmissible. Now, if a man's stomach is sacred, how much more so his mind!"

"But surely Tyson does not contend that his body is inviolate from the police for all purposes?" demanded Justice Blandford. "Surely they can still fingerprint him, measure him, take his picture, record his voiceprint, and test his blood and breath for alcohol, and do it all without his consent?"

"Well, yes, Your Honor."

"Then how does clairvoyance differ?"

"It's the degree of privacy. The attributes that Your Honor has just mentioned, fingerprinting and so on, well, these are pretty well exposed to the public anyhow. But a man's thoughts are not. If Americans lose their right to have private thoughts, freedom is gone."

Edmonds found himself nodding in agreement.

"But you contend there is no such thing as clairvoyance," said Justice Burke. "How, then, this concern for privacy of thought?"

Sickles grinned crookedly. "Until this court rules that psi is nonexistent, I have to argue in the alternate: psi doesn't exist; but if it does, it was used in violation of Tyson's constitutional rights."

"Yes," agreed Burke. "Quite logical."

Sickles looked down at his wristwatch. He was done. There was no room in him to wonder whether he had saved a man's life. He felt only relief. He looked up at the Chief Justice. "I have nothing more, Your Honors."

"Thank you, Mr. Sickles. May we hear now from New York?"

Guy Winters took a deep breath and walked to the lectern, where he pulled off his watch and laid down a sheaf of notes. His eyes swept the faces at the bench without seeing them. He was tense, nervous. But he had rehearsed for hours, and knew exactly what he wanted to say—if they would let him.

"May it please the court, one issue alone is involved in this case—the question on which certiorari was granted, namely, whether the warrant was invalidly issued as based on clairvoyant information." He took another deep breath and wished he could do something about the perspiration soaking his armpits. "It is the position of New York that clairvoyance does exist, and that, although the state police did not explain that the information was obtained in this way, the magistrate, had he known, would necessarily have issued the warrant; and if this be so, the warrant was valid under the Fourth Amendment, the rifle was admissible under the Fifth, and Tyson's conviction must stand.

"The record below, through the testimony of Dr. Drago, is replete with a documentation of American psi, even to the very beginnings of history on this continent. With the court's indulgence, I'd like to digress for just a moment to present this historical background.

"As far as North America is concerned, historical psi began with the Aztec chief, Quetzalcoatl. When he was forced to abdicate the Aztec throne in ten nineteen, he predicted that in exactly five hundred years he would return in full war panoply and reclaim his dominions. That was why—in fifteen nineteen—the Aztec emperor Moctezuma was too paralyzed to act, when Hernando Cortes arrived at the gates of the Aztec capital.

"And psi is an integral part of the history of the United States. Many famous Americans were involved at one time or another with psi. In fact, we might reasonably infer that their psi abilities contributed to their fame. Their names include some of our best known writers, artists, politicians, poets, and religious leaders. One could turn to the *Index of American Biography* almost at random. Edgar Allan Poe said he did not know the meaning of *Ulalume,* the poem that describes a man wandering down a misty cypress-lined path, in the month of October, to the crypt where his wife lay buried. We can well understand his mental block. October, of course, was the month, a few years later, in which Poe followed *his* wife to the grave.

"And Sam Clemens—Mark Twain—dreamed he saw his brother Henry dead of a steamboat accident, lying in a metal casket, and that on his breast was a spray of white flowers centered with a single red rose. When he found him in Memphis, his brother was dying of injuries received in the explosion of the boilers of a river boat, the *Philadelphia.* On the fourth day, his brother died, and was placed in a metal casket. As Sam looked on, grieving, a lady walked up and placed flowers on the boy's chest. It was a spray of white blooms, and in the center was a single red rose. I might add that this final detailed touch, completing the dream, or vision, or hallucination, if you like, is quite common."

Pendleton broke in. "My question is perhaps not completely relevant, but I am curious. Is there any reason to believe that there is a psi on this court?"

Edmonds started, but continued to look at the assistant attorney general.

"I don't know for sure, Your Honor," said Winters. "But I think it likely, simply as a matter of statistical probability, that there are at least three psi's on this honorable court. And probably more." He stood there calmly as several of the justices leaned forward suddenly. There was a buzzing rustle in the crowded room behind him.

The Chief Justice rapped the gavel sharply. "Would you explain that, please?"

"Certainly, Your Honor. It's pretty difficult, of course, to take a census of psi's, although it's something the Bureau of the Census really ought to include in nineteen ninety. But fairly large samples have been made in the past. The English Society for Psychical Research canvassed seventeen thousand people in eighteen eighty, and ten percent reported that they had had psi experiences. The Boston Society for Psychical Research made a similar survey in nineteen twenty-five, and that time twenty percent reported psi experiences. In nineteen sixty-six, one hundred and fifteen students of Aberdeen University were similarly sampled. Thirty percent acknowledged a personal psi experience. The psi percentage of the population is certainly growing, but the rate is hard to determine. We may nevertheless estimate that at least thirty percent of this court is gifted in some phase of psi. And thirty percent of nine is about three. And, having regard to growth rate, and—forgive me, Your Honors—the fact that psi correlates strongly with intelligence, culture, and mental activity, one might reasonably expect to find four, possibly even five, psi's on the court."

"Incredible!" breathed the Chief Justice.

"Permit me to disagree, Your Honor. Many of us have some degree of psi, but are not consciously aware of it. Consider the studies of William E. Cox on train wrecks some years ago. He proved that the number of passengers on a train involved in a wreck was generally substantially less than the number for the same train the day before, or two, three, or four weeks before. He concluded that the missing passengers somehow had a 'hunch' about the impending wreck, and simply didn't make the trip. If they were Pullman passengers, they simply canceled the reservation."

Justice Blandford leaned forward. "That's curious indeed, Mr. Winters. It so happens I canceled a plane reservation to Miami tonight. Does that mean I'm clairvoyant?"

"I trust not, Your Honor. I mean, considering the circumstances, and the other lives involved. I merely make the point that psi is a generalized American experience, so common in fact that science must take notice, even though its possessors do not."

"I would go further than the Chief Justice," said Justice Burke. "This is not only incredible; it is absurd. Be that as it may, I think we are digressing."

"Yes, Your Honor. I was about to mention psi politicians. Lincoln is the prime example. He experienced autoscopy in eighteen sixty, shortly before he left Springfield, Illinois, for Washington."

"Autoscopy?" said Helen Nord.

"It simply means seeing oneself. Lying on the horsehair sofa in his home in Springfield, he saw two images, one firm, one vague, in the mirror across the room, which was not positioned to reflect any image of him. He correctly understood that the strong image meant that he would serve out his first term, and that the weaker image meant he would die in his second term. And in the first days of April, eighteen sixty-five, he had his famous dream of his own mourner-lined catafalque lying in the East Room of the White House. 'The President has been killed by an assassin,' they told him in the dream. And he knew, at least subconsciously, when it would be. Every night previous, when he dismissed his guard, he had said 'Good-night, Crook.' But on *that* night, Good Friday, April fourteenth, as he left for Ford's Theatre, he said, '*Goodbye*, Crook.'

"And Chauncey Depew was another psi politician. We all know how Coleridge 'saw' the lines of "Kubla Khan" as he came out of an opium dream, and was busily writing them down when interrupted by a 'person from Porlock.' But how many of us know that Depew's speech nominating Colonel Theodore Roosevelt for governor of New York was similarly pre-recorded? He had a vision of the nominating convention, and of himself making the speech, while sitting on the front porch of his home on the Hudson. The vision faded, but the speech remained vivid in his mind, and he quickly wrote it down. And so Theodore Roosevelt was launched into national politics—by psi."

From time to time during this interplay Edmonds had glanced down the bench where Oliver Godwin was busy taking notes. Godwin, he knew, had the remarkable faculty of abstracting and summing up a case during argument. He would turn his notebook over to Augusta Eubanks, who would flesh out the skeleton outline, cite the proper controlling decisions, and revise some of the old gentleman's language. (Augusta would write, "This is indeed a novel proposition, and one for which counsel urges no precedent in our judicial history," instead of Godwin's simpler "Sheep-dip.")

In a moment, Godwin would close his notebook and very likely doze off. Edmonds sighed.

"Let's get back to the camera," said Pendleton. "How can a camera inside a safe take a picture?"

"The technique is well established," said Winters. "Peter Hurkos in Holland and Ted Serios in this country were able to cause images to appear on film in a Polaroid camera. Fukurai and his associates in Japan did substantially the same thing, but caused Japanese ideograms to appear on the emulsion. Although the initial chemical mechanism within the emulsion is obscure, the subsequent steps of developing the latent silver image, fixing with hypo, and using the resultant negative to make positive prints or enlargements are the same as in conventional photography. One can only speculate as to how the sheer force of will, operating at a distance, could make certain molecules of silver bromide sensitive to the photographic developer, while leaving others unaffected."

Edmonds' temples were beginning to throb. He was glad when Burke interrupted.

"Tell me, counselor, why don't these clairvoyants play the ponies, or break the bank at Monte Carlo, or get rich in the stock market?"

"Apparently many do, Your Honor. But of course they would not publicize it."

Pendleton frowned. "My background in Wall Street is no secret. Are you suggesting that I am a psi?"

"I suggest nothing, Your Honor. But perhaps you will agree, on the other hand, that your success is not inconsistent with the possibility."

"Hmph."

"If all these psi's have this power," demanded Burke, "why didn't they warn President Cromway in the first place?"

"Several claim they did. The data are still coming in. It's quite similar to the warnings attempted for Kennedy's benefit in nineteen sixty-two, by Jeane Dixon, John Pendragon, Helen Greenwood, and even Billy Graham. Jeane Dixon even named the day and the hour—and from fifteen hundred miles away."

"Even if all you say is true," said Edmonds bluntly, "you have offered nothing to prove that the particular clairvoyance in issue was used lawfully."

"I believe I can satisfy Your Honor on that point. If the court please, I would like at this time to place psi in its proper perspective in police technique. For it *is* a police technique, quite modern, but as useful in its way as the Bertillon measurement system, the Henry fingerprint system, the Keeler polygraph, radar for speeding, alcohol detection in the breath and bloodstream, spectroscopic analysis of dust, ballistics, blood analysis, differentation by blood groups, voiceprinting, and many others. Many police departments in Europe, and in Holland especially, use clairvoyants routinely. Professor W. H. C. Tenhaeff at one time maintained a whole team of 'paragnosts' for assistance to the Dutch police. And they are used in this country much more often than is generally realized. For example, Gerard Croiset, the Dutch clairvoyant, told the FBI in nineteen sixty-four where the bodies of three civil-rights workers would be found in Mississippi. And the equally famous Dutch clairvoyant, Peter Hurkos, assisted materially in the Boston Strangler case."

"But Hurkos failed on the Jackson case, in Virginia?" demanded Edmonds.

"The results were inconclusive, Your Honor. But these are not the only examples. Some years ago, a policeman in Grosse Pointe Woods, Michigan, was found to have the knack of locating the criminals before the crime had even been reported to the police."

"What *is* clairvoyance, Mr. Winters?" asked Pendleton.

The assistant attorney general shook his head. "I don't know, Your Honor. Even clairvoyants themselves don't know. I mean, they know when it happens to them, but they don't know *how* it happens. Clairvoyance, of course, is just one well-defined variety of psi experience. There are several others."

"Would you explain that?"

"Certainly. Clairvoyance is a unilateral extrasensory phenomenon. Only one person is involved—the percipient. He perceives a visual or aural experience taking place at a different time or place. Telepathy requires at least two people, a sender and a receiver. Telekinesis is the mental ability to control the motion of matter. Gamblers have it frequently with dice. Radiesthesia is a special kind of psi."

"Radi-*what?*" demanded Justice Moore.

"Radiesthesia, your honor. The lay word is dowsing—for the location of water with a forked hazel wand."

"Nonsense, Mr. Winters. Dowsing is dowsing. Nothing supernatural about it. Back in Louisiana my father was the village dowser. I've dabbled in it a little myself."

"I'm no expert, Your Honor. But I understand that at least five Nobel prize winners consider radi— dowsing, that is, a valid form of psi."

Edmonds stole a glance down at Godwin. The old man's head was propped in his cupped hand and his eyes were closed. Pendleton had better hurry up.

The Chief Justice interrupted. "We seem to have taken you somewhat over your allotted time with our questions, Mr. Winters. In fairness to opposing counsel, and since our two-thirty adjournment is nearly at hand, I will ask that you draw to a close."

"This concludes the case for New York, your honor."

"Thank you. We stand adjourned." He stood up.

The clerk began his intonation: "All rise . . ."

That judges of important causes should hold office for life is not a good thing, for the mind grows old as well as the body.
—Aristotle

In the robing hall Helen Nord took Godwin by the arm. "I'm having some friends over tonight. We want you to come. Ben can pick you up."

"Thank you, my dear. But I don't know. I'd just be in the way. It's disgraceful to be old. You know what they say. Tired old man. Helen, I know I should retire, and I'm going to. But I don't want Roly Burke to think he's forcing anything. Actually, my resignation is already written. I will send it to the President the day we decide *Tyson*."

"No!"

"Yes. Oh, I'm not truly senile. Not yet. With a little help from Gus I can still crank out a passable decision. But I'm tired, Helen. Tired." His mustache drooped. "That's the only reason. I've told Ben, and now you. Later, I'll tell Pendleton. Until then, this is all in confidence."

"Of course."

"And no fuss and feathers at the end. No stupid sentimental retirement banquet. No idiotic gold watch, no initialed attaché case, no desk set. Maybe just a photograph of something familiar with a farewell card that all of you can sign. I would treasure it."

"However you want it."

He stood silent a moment, thinking. "Your party. I miss Laura's parties. All the old friends are gone. Ah, the times we used to have in Georgetown. Till four, five in the morning. I wish Laura could have known you. She would have liked you." His face clouded.

"You can turn in any time. You know where the guest room is."

He brightened. "In that case, I think I'll come." He put his arm around her shoulders and tried for his best leer. "Just down the hall from your bedroom."

"And what's a mere eighty-five years between friends?"

"That's *my* line, you forward wench!"

> *These judges, you will infer, must have something of the creative artist in them; they must have antennae registering feeling and judgment beyond logical, let alone quantitative proof.*
> —Justice Felix Frankfurter

Helen Nord lived on a two-hundred-acre farm near Port Royal, Virginia, an hour's drive to the Court by superhighway. Washington had been born nearby. Grant and Lee had struggled here, and Private Corbett had shot John Wilkes Booth in a burning barn a few miles away. She had inherited the land from her Strachey ancestors, and John Nord had designed the big house himself. Her sons had been born and raised here, and now they were grown and gone. She was grateful now for other interests, other ties. A steady stream of her brother justices and their wives attended her dinners and weekend parties. Of course, she rarely had them all out together. The air was strained when Burke and Godwin were merely in the same room. Tonight was the "Godwin" group, namely those whom the old gentleman could insult without offense.

The ladies of the court had accepted her instantly as the lawful successor of Laura Godwin, and felt their own somewhat anonymous status enhanced by direct representation of their sex on the high bench. Millie Pendleton explained it to her. "Laura used to say Washington was full of famous men and the women they married when they were young. But at least we now have a friend in court."

Just now Helen was leading a group down the garden path behind the house. Godwin left the path and walked over to the great oak tree. Its dead leaves from the previous year were still frozen to its branches. The others waited. He called back, "You're sure you don't mind?"

"I don't mind. But don't hurt yourself."

"Hah!" He kicked the tree trunk savagely, then danced for a moment. A forlorn dead leaf floated down and hung in his mustache. He flicked it off indignantly. As he rejoined the group, he explained matter-of-factly, "I was born in Manhattan, in a hospital next to the old Third Avenue El, in the days when they still used those wonderful steam locomotives. Laura loved the country, but I hate it, with its pure air and the crickets raising cain at night. So Helen lets me kick a tree when I come out here." (They had all seen this many times before.) "Now let's get on to this well."

Helen Nord laughed. "It's right over here, Judge." She led them to a pit some five feet in diameter, edged with a couple of layers of loose cinder blocks, then called back to Moore. "Nick, there's your well." She pointed to a length of pipe extending up from the pit. "We put the casing in today. The driller hit water at fifty feet—forty gallons a minute. He brought the county agent and the state geologist out. They just looked at it and shook their heads. The geologist had already proved from his maps it was impossible."

"But why all the excitement about a water-well?" demanded Godwin. "The way you're carrying on, anybody would think you had struck oil."

"When you're on a farm, twenty miles from a city main, water can be more important than oil. But the point I'm making is, Nick Moore showed me where to drill. That was after I had brought in three dry holes, one of them at a hundred twenty feet. Isn't that right, Nick?"

Moore grinned. "Right."

"What are you getting at?" asked Mrs. Pendleton.

"He did it by dowsing."

"No! Water-witching? But I thought that was an old wives' tale."

"It's real. Many people can do it. Actually, it's a recognized form of psi. At argument today we learned it has a fancy scientific name: radiesthesia."

"Fantastic!" breathed Millie Pendleton.

"We'd better be getting back."

"Bill," said Mrs. Blandford, "why do you keep looking up at the sky?"

"No reason at all, dear," said Blandford lamely. "Just thinking about the flight to Miami I canceled."

"I'm glad you did. You can go next week. This is much nicer."

"The farm is directly under the flight line from National Airport to Miami," said Helen Nord quietly. "We always see it out here. It seems to be late this evening."

After dinner she led them back into the parlor. Ben Edmonds followed with a tray of cigars and liqueurs.

When they were all settled, their hostess began, almost hesitantly: "I want to tell you a story, and then I am going to ask a question of each of you. This has a bearing on the Tyson case. To start, I think there is something about me all of you should know. Mr. Winters, at argument today, hinted very strongly that there were probably three or four psi's on the court. I don't know for sure, but I think I may be one of them. I do know that I have had at least one psi experience. I've even wondered whether I should disqualify myself on the Tyson case. At any rate, I'd like to tell you about it. It took place when my husband died in the first manned Mars flight. It was two-ten on a warm August morning when he lasered back to Orbit Central that the retro rockets wouldn't fire. They analyzed the trouble almost instantly. There was a relay malfunction. They lasered back and told him how to fix it. And he did fix it. And then the retros did fire. But it had taken three minutes for his message to travel thirty-five million miles to Earth, and another three minutes back to Mars. Six minutes was too long. He was barely eight hundred miles above the planet when the retros worked, and he was traveling over four thousand miles an hour. He hit ground at one thousand miles an hour. The ship—everything in it—simply vaporized. The point I wish to make is, when he pressed the retro button at two-ten, and nothing happened, I *knew*. And I knew at two-ten. Orbit Central didn't know until they actually received his call, at two-thirteen. I was with him all the way down. He talked to me." She looked over at Edmonds, almost curiously. "We held hands. And then I died with him. Except, of course, here I am. Some of the other astronaut wives have had similar experiences. Mine didn't surprise the medical people at NASA. In fact, they not only didn't tell me I was crazy—they put me to work in the Parapsychology Section. They were trying to develop psi as an alternate to laser communication, to avoid the time lag of six minutes for a round-trip message, or even to substitute completely in case of laser failure. Actually, there's nothing new about the principle. The Dutch psi Croiset had already demonstrated that engine defects can be diagnosed across the Atlantic Ocean by clairvoyance. Distance is no difficulty."

She paused and looked around at her guests. Mrs. Pendleton had drawn her chair closer and was sitting on the edge of the cushion. Moore's pipe had long since gone out. Ben Edmonds watched her with impassive eyes.

"It must have been a terrible experience," said Pendleton gravely. "But I'm glad you told us about it. It is indeed pertinent to the Tyson issue, especially on the question of psi transmission. But forgive me, Helen, I don't believe you were finished."

"I just wanted all of you to understand. For me, as an individual, psi exists. I agree with Mr. Winters that psi is a common human experience, that most people have had a psi experience of some type, and that the members of the Court eminently qualify. On the other hand, a certain stigma seems to attach to psi, and the higher our standing in our society, the more reluctant we are to admit our psi experiences or ability. So we will try this one by secret ballot. Ben, would you pass around pencils and paper? I would like each of you to write 'yes' if you have ever had a psi experience, or 'no' if you have not. Ben will collect the votes in this vase."

Godwin grumbled. "Woman, I'm old, but I'm not crazy. It's a silly game, and I won't play."

"No matter. Seven votes should tell us something." She picked the pieces of paper out of the vase. "Five yeses, two noes. You all know how I voted. So, not counting the judge, four of you have had a psi experience, and two have not. Messrs. Pendleton and Blandford are negative, I would assume. The majority vote seems to indicate that psi is a rather recurrent thread in the fabric of our daily lives. It's not something weird or strange, unless we make it so."

"Very dramatic, Helen," said Moore. "But if you believe in psi so strongly, doesn't it follow the search and seizure in *Tyson* was constitutional, and that he was lawfully convicted?"

"Of course not! I've already explained that. My intuition, my own psi, if you will, tells me Tyson is innocent. So I'm going to vote for reversal."

"You tell 'em, Helen," said Mrs. Pendleton firmly.

Their hostess leaned over and touched Edmonds on the sleeve. She pointed to Godwin, who was slumped in the deep maternal upholstery of the chair. His eyes were closed, and his outsize mustache ends vibrated with slow rhythm.

Edmonds got up softly, picked up the justice with hypnotic gentleness, as though the old man were a child, and with his burden held loosely against his chest, walked quietly toward the stairs.

The guests watched this in fascination. Mrs. Pendleton tried to catch the eye of Helen Nord, but Helen simply put her finger to her lips. Finally the muffled measured sound of steps died away above them.

Moore shook his head in wonder. "If anyone else tried that, the old gentleman would go through the ceiling."

"What a man," murmured Pendleton. "What are you waiting for, Helen?"

"He's never asked me," said Helen Nord shortly. "Millie, will you help me with the coffee?"

The maid had already turned back the bed. Edmonds put a hand under Godwin's head and laid the old man down on the waiting sheets. Then he eased off the shoes, loosened the belt, and pulled up the coverlet. He then realized that Godwin was awake and watching him.

"Sit down, Ben. When are you going to pop the question to little Nell?"

"I don't know. Maybe never. She can't forget—him. And I have a personal problem. Anyhow, maybe we are both too old."

"Of course she still thinks of him. She ought to. But life goes on. Memories should be a garden, not a prison. Talk to the three boys. Get them on your side. Be firm with her. Oh, you are both so stupid. My last twenty years with Laura were the best of all. April Fool's Day coming up soon. She loved it. Laura . . . Laura . . ." He seemed to drift off.

Whenever Godwin spoke of his dead wife in this intimate, carefree way, Edmonds felt, on some deep subsensory level, an emptiness akin to despair in the old man. His chest tightened. Does Helen still feel this way about John Nord? What is this sweet hell called love? Can no end come?

He pulled the blanket up about the old man's shoulders and tiptoed toward the door.

"Where's my teddy bear?" mumbled Godwin.

"Go to the devil," growled Edmonds.

Even as he left the hallway and re-entered the living room, he knew something was wrong.

Everyone was facing away from him, toward the open door of the study across the room. In that doorway stood Helen Nord's maid, holding the phone, one hand over the mouthpiece.

"What is it, Mary?" said Mrs. Nord quietly.

"It's your messenger, mum, calling from National Airport. He said to tell you Flight Sixty-seven to Miami crashed on takeoff. He could just now get to a telephone."

"Thank you, Mary. Tell him he can go home now." Helen Nord turned somberly to Blandford, who was standing, staring rigidly at her.

Mrs. Blandford gasped and sat down. "*That* plane!"

"Yes. I think Bill had a hunch he shouldn't take it."

"But that . . . that means," stammered Blandford, "I . . . I'm a . . ."

Helen Nord simply nodded. "Yes, Bill, you are. Join the club."

> *Judges are apt to be naif, simple-minded men, and they need something of Mephistopheles.*
> —Justice Oliver Wendell Holmes

It was late Thursday night, and Shelley Pendleton was alone in his office, and pacing.

Already he knew how the *Tyson* vote would go at conference tomorrow. Five to reverse, four to affirm. He'd be with the majority. Another five–four; and on a case like this! The newspapers, the editorial writers—the whole country would say that even the Supreme Court didn't know whether Tyson was innocent or guilty. And it was actually going to be worse than that. Burke, for instance, would vote to reverse, because psi was illogical. Godwin didn't believe in it, either, but would affirm. And Helen Nord, because she believed in her own psi (but not in Drago's!), would vote to reverse.

Women. *Sui generis.* On occasion incomprehensible. Yet indispensable. He could hardly complain: by ancient rumor, Laura Godwin had won his appointment by cheating in a poker game with the President's judiciary advisors.

There would be no sanity in the *Tyson* decision. And the public outcry would far dwarf the reaction to the Warren Report of the sixties. For the honor of the Court, he could not let it happen. And just how was he going to prevent it?

He resumed pacing and thinking. Had Tyson really pulled the trigger? Helen Nord seemed so certain he was innocent. Women and their intuition. But suppose she's right? (And I'll have to grant the validity of her psi experience with John Nord.) Can this Court intervene, *sua sponte,* to prove it? Certainly not. But can *I?* I have hunches, too. I've always had hunches. Made my money that way. Does this make me a psi? Maybe. I don't know. God! What a crew. Nord. Moore and his dowsing. Blandford and that plane to Miami . . . And what about Edmonds and those impossible photos? Is it actually conceivable that a human intellect can reach into the past and put what he sees on a camera film? Serios did it, and that Japanese fellow. It all begins to make sense. Edmonds is probably the worst of them. And if there will be no image on the film until Decision Day, how does it get there? What are the rules? Can one psi have a hunch about another psi? There's only one way to find out. And to find out, I will have to do a thing which, if done by one of my brother justices, would merit my strongest censure.

He stopped his slow striding and glared at the phone. He knew now that he would have no peace until he acted. In sudden resolution he seized the phone and dialed a number.

"Evans? Pendleton. I have a very delicate matter I want you to handle, very confidential. You've heard of Philip Dopher? Yes, *that* one—elevator operator in *that* building. I want you to find him and give him a thousand dollars. Tell him it's expenses to hear the *Tyson* opinion firsthand. He'll have to be here every Monday until we hand it down. It'll take several weeks. My guess is about April First. Tell him he gets another thousand on Decision Day. But he's got to be in court then to get it. Make up something. Tell him it's sponsored by the Sons of Justice. Tell him anything. Just get him here. No, Evans, I can't talk about it. It's just a hunch. Oh, one more thing, bring him in the first day yourself, and show him where he has to sit—well up front, where Ben Edmonds can see him easily."

> *Tweedledee: If it were so, it would be; but as it isn't, it ain't. That's logic.*
>
> —Lewis Carroll, *Through the Looking Glass*

It was Friday Conference again.

"We have been discussing *Tyson* now for over two hours. Agreement seems impossible." The voice of the Chief Justice was measured, controlled. But Edmonds thought he detected a note of grim amusement. His other colleagues, in contrast, seemed morose, almost sullen, as though only now they realized certain impossible aspects of their task. Pendleton continued as though in brooding monologue. "We must make an end and vote, even though it but defines our differences. I will begin by summarizing my own position. If clairvoyance does not exist, then clearly the warrant was invalid, and we must reverse New York. But I cannot reach that conclusion. There are too many documented cases of clairvoyance. Yet it is admittedly erratic, cannot be called up at will, and generally requires verification by the normal senses. Its most fervid proponents do not claim that it has the certainty of ordinary seeing and hearing. Any magistrate called upon to issue a psi warrant would certainly be entitled, perhaps even *required,* to look into the antecedents and previous record of the psi-informant. Some psi's of international reputation and long histories of demonstrated police success might be sufficiently reliable to support a warrant if there were no other fault in the arrangement. But unfortunately for this argument, I think there *is* a fault, and a grave one. Granted this is not wiretapping. Neither the electric current nor electromagnetic radiation is demonstrably involved in psi transmission. A Faraday cage shuts out electromagnetic radiation but cannot shut out psi. Absent interception and publication of an electrically generated message, Section six-oh-five of the Federal Communications Act has not been violated. So our long line of wiretapping cases—*as such*—is not directly controlling. And yet an invasion of privacy has occurred in a depth that far surpasses wiretapping. The intrusiveness, and the breach of privacy, goes far beyond the sounds and sights available to bugging and spy TV. Our very thoughts are laid bare. It's worse than truth serum: we needn't even be present to have it done to us. I think Tyson's constitutional rights were invaded. I think we should reverse. And now I'm done. Mr. Godwin?"

"I agree up to a point. The problem as I see it turns on whether this particular bit of clairvoyance involved reading Tyson's mind, that is, assuming there's such a thing as clairvoyance in the first place—which I very much doubt. I don't see how Tyson could have known exactly where the movers had put that particular box in the warehouse. Or even if he did know, we haven't been shown that it was Tyson's mind that was read. For all we know, the clairvoyant might have read the warehouseman's mind. Or nobody's mind. Tyson's privacy wasn't invaded unless his mind was read, and I just don't think it was read, whether or not psi is for real. But my main point is, we shouldn't interfere. These are very complex procedural matters better left to the state courts. Look at it this way. If a person is indicted for murder, the determination of his guilt or innocence should not be considered as a sporting event, to be governed by the Marquis of Queensberry Rules, but by a practical and actual determination of the guilt of the indictee, with the state, in order to prevail, being required to establish guilt beyond any reasonable doubt. In my view the State of New York has fully discharged its burden. Psi isn't even relevant. Roly?"

"Psi certainly *is* relevant, Mr. Godwin," said Burke calmly. "It's the sole question certified."

"I didn't vote to grant certiorari," said Godwin bluntly. "But now that we have the case, I can decide on any basis I like."

"Most illogical," snorted Burke. "But no matter." He turned to Helen Nord. "You say you believe in psi?"

"Yes."

"And also in logic?"

"Yes, at least as long as it makes sense."

The rotund justice looked over at her sharply. She returned his look with expectant interest. He knotted his jaw muscles and continued. "Logic by definition is that which makes sense: nothing more, nothing less. No miracles. No supernatural hocus-pocus. Everything that takes place, every event, every effect, is logically caused by something, something which preceded it in time, and which provided the physico-chemical causative chain that resulted in the effect. These premises are the foundations of our intellectual existence. Psi violates them. Therefore psi is false; it does not exist.

290 C<small>HARLES</small> L. H<small>ARNESS</small>

"I'm not very bright at logic," said Godwin, "but why can't you turn it around the other way? Psi exists: therefore the foundations of our intellectual existence are false."

"Just what I might have expected from you, Brother Godwin. You are using the conclusion to destroy the premise. The mental effort required for logical thinking is quite beyond a party of your years, I'm afraid."

Godwin sat up straight. His mustache began to twitch. Helen Nord broke in hurriedly. "All that sounds very complicated."

"Perhaps so, perhaps so," conceded Burke, "at least to those unaccustomed to disciplined cogitative processes." He touched his fingertips together and considered the matter. "Perhaps we can benefit from an example, taken from a sub-species of logic known as operationalism. So. If a loaded gun is pointed at my heart, the trigger is pulled, and the bullet proceeds toward me in a straight line, I would certainly be killed, would I not?"

"Of course."

"My death is the effect of the bullet in motion?"

"Agreed."

"And the bullet in motion is the effect of the pressure of the hot gases within the barrel of the gun?"

"Yes."

"And the gases are the effect of the ignition of the gunpowder by the primer, in turn the effect of the firing pin striking the primer cap?"

"Certainly."

"And the movement of the firing pin is caused by the trigger pull, in turn the effect of the squeeze of the gunman's finger?"

"True."

"So we have a complete chain of cause and effect?"

"Yes."

"And it is logical to assume that every effect must have some identifiable cause? Nothing happens without a specific cause?"

"It may be logical. But there may be a reasonable doubt as to whether the rules of logic apply to psi. Psi seems to operate without any cause-effect linkage. For example, if psi takes over, your bullet might vanish in midair."

Burke sighed. "I give up. I absolutely give up."

Pendleton hid a grin.

Godwin leaned forward querulously. "Are we to understand, Roly, that in *this* case you are trying to get by on *logic?*"

The insinuation was insidious; it implied that Burke's analysis was superficial; and indeed, that the justice had not devoted the necessary time and study to grasp all the fine points of the case.

Burke's face turned slowly pink. He glared back at Godwin. "I would like you to understand exactly that. Law has no other basis."

But it was no good. The others were looking at him almost sympathetically. Who are they to judge me, he thought bitterly. Logic is . . . logic!

Pendleton cleared his throat. "We'll have to go on. Mr. Moore?"

"I agree with our brother Godwin. You call it clairvoyance. If that's what it is, nobody's mind was read. By definition, clairvoyance excludes telepathic cognition of the mental activities of another person. And if nobody's mind was read, there was no invasion of privacy protected by the Fourth. I would affirm."

"Mr. Blandford?"

"In my view the evidence shows clairvoyance exists, but it also shows it is erratic, often not available on call, generally not reproducible, so I feel that clairvoyance is too unscientific for use as 'probable cause.' Reverse."

"Mr. Lovsky?"

"I agree with Burke, *supra,* that clairvoyance is an impossibility. But I don't agree that it must follow that the warrant was improperly issued. The warrant was duly sworn. It pinpointed what was to be searched, and the rifle was in fact found, exactly as described on the information. Pendleton *contra,* I would affirm. *Cf.* Godwin, *id.*"

"Mr. Randolph?"

• CONCVR •

"Mr. Edmonds?"

"Personally, I believe in psi. But I don't think it should be used as a police technique without the consent of the suspect, and any evidence thus discovered should be inadmissible. Reverse."

"Madam Nord?"

"I, too, believe in psi. And I think the warrant was valid and the rifle admissible. But I would reverse. Tyson didn't do it."

Pendleton took a deep breath. "*Why* do you think he didn't do it?"

She looked back defiantly. "*Because,* that's why."

Pendleton exhaled slowly, then smiled at her reassuringly. "Quite all right. So be it. Let me sum up. We have five to reverse, four to affirm. And in neither the majority nor the dissent do we have the slightest unanimity of rationale." He studied his notes. "Madam Nord, you're up next on the opinion list. Will you please draft the majority opinion? With the variation of views, and especially considering your own, your task will be cut out for you."

"I'll do my best," said Helen Nord. "In fact, in the interests of reconciliation of divergent views, I'll even go along with the rationale of the majority—that either psi doesn't exist, or if it does, the psi-based search warrant was defective."

"Yes?" said Pendleton, surprised.

"On one condition."

"Such as what?" demanded Burke suspiciously.

"That we open the safe on Decision Day."

"Preposterous!" cried Burke. "Exhibit Q was never properly admitted into evidence, and even if it had been, the question of its probative value would be within the exclusive jurisdiction of the trial court. The Supreme Court of the United States never decides facts except in rare cases of original jurisdiction!"

"Then I'll file a specially concurring opinion to reverse on the plain and simple ground I don't think Tyson is guilty!"

Godwin chuckled. "And she'd do it, too!"

"If I might make a suggestion," said Pendleton, with an enigmatic smile, "we could order the safe opened after handing down both the majority and dissent. It could of course have no bearing on our decision as then rendered, but both Tyson and New York could use it, if they choose, and if its contents truly merit it, as basis for rehearing. Mrs. Nord? Gentlemen? Then it's agreed.

"Just one more point. Despite the gravity of the case, we have a duty to the defendant and to the country to act as promptly as possible. Hopefully, we can hand down the decision on April First."

> *When the penalty is death, we are tempted to strain the evidence and even the law in order to give a doubtfully condemned man another chance.*
> —Justice Robert H. Jackson

It was Monday, April 1, Decision Day, in the Marble Palace.

Practically every appellate court in the country—saving only the United States Supreme Court—distributes printed or typewritten copies of its decisions to its litigants as the sole means of stating the outcome of the case. But from time immemorial the Supreme Court—the only appellate court with its very own printing shop on the premises—had "handed down" its decisions orally. And "orally" means whatever the delivering justice chooses it to mean. It might mean reading an entire ninety-page opinion—a favorite tactic of Justice Lovsky; or it might mean a very brief oral summary of the salient law and facts, after the manner of Justice Randolph. Or, as in the case of Justice Burke, it would start out as a summary and develop, willy-nilly, into a profound exposition of logic-in-law, through the historical framework of the Justinian Code, the Magna Carta, Coke, Comyn's *Digest,* the Constitutional Convention, the probable (corroborative) views of John Marshall, and would inevitably conclude with appropriate selections from Burke's *Logic in Appellate Decisions.* The law students of George Washington and Georgetown Universities might have to get the printed decision to discover who had won, but all agreed it was an enthralling experience.

After he was seated, Edmonds surreptitiously searched the first row of the pewlike red-cushioned seats and found there the face he had noted on previous Mondays, and the face he did not want to find: a bald man, burly, bearded, his eyes a study in controlled, violent cunning. Edmonds moaned inaudibly. Let this pass. But it would not pass. Everything was here, waiting. He looked over at the safe on the marshal's cart. It was still locked, still inviolate, but within minutes all that would be changed forever.

When he had taken office ten years ago he had sworn to uphold the Constitution and the laws of the United States. A month ago he had flung down Orwell's *1984* on the conference table. Beware! he had cried. And beware of whom? Of Benjamin Edmonds, Ph.D., J.C., Associate Justice of the United States Supreme Court, and psi extraordinary. For he thought it very likely that he was now going to violate his oath, and in so doing, the constitutional rights of another. And thereby he would strike down, besmirch, and discredit for decades the enhallowed institution he had sworn to preserve. For Helen Nord (and how did *she* know?) was right. Tyson had *not* pulled the trigger of that fateful rifle. He *knew*. (And for that matter, how did he know?) And so there remained a thing for him to do, a thing so simple, so devastating, that the Tyson case would be decided instantly and forever. It was not lawful; it had only justice to excuse it.

Edmonds noted that Pendleton seemed to be studying him from the corner of his eye. But then the Chief Justice turned and nodded gravely to Helen Nord, at the far left. She nodded back. She was on her own.

This, thought Edmonds, was the crowning paradox. Helen Nord, who knew that psi existed, had joined with four of her brothers in the majority opinion that would hold, in effect, that psi was unproven. And she would do this because it would free a man whom she thought innocent.

The woman's voice was clear and strong. Briefly she recited the undisputed facts, read the single question certified to the Court, then came directly to the point. "It is the view of a majority of this Court that the search warrant was not issued upon probable cause, as is required by the Fourth Amendment, in that the basis of the information was not explained to the magistrate who issued the warrant. *Aguilar* v. *United States*. This finding requires the further finding that the evidence obtained by the search is inadmissible under the Fifth Amendment. And it must follow that Tyson's conviction must be reversed, and that he is entitled to a new trial, in which this tainted evidence must be excluded."

There was more, but Edmonds now heard only snatches. His eyes were looking into—and through—the eyes of Philip Dopher. In a strange, nearly real sense, both of them were for the next few minutes not even in this great chamber, but in a deserted room in an office building on Manhattan's East Side, where Dopher was kneeling at an open window, caressing a rifle resting on the window sill, and waiting.

Somehow, the voice of Helen Nord floated by, wisplike, fragmented. ". . . the consequences of the reasoning urged by New York . . . the thrust of the constitutional command . . . we do not recede from . . ."

And now he watched the kneeling figure grow tense and still. The bearded cheek lay in lethal affection against the wooden stock, the eye peering through the telescopic cylinder, and the gloved finger beginning to squeeze its unspeakable message to the trigger.

". . . if clairvoyance *does* exist—and this we do not decide—this source of information should have been brought to the magistrate's attention, so that he could fully understand and evaluate what was being sworn to as a fact . . . and assuming *arguendo* that clairvoyance exists, we rule, nevertheless, that it is not such a generally accepted basis for experiential information that the magistrate could take judicial notice of it . . ."

One year and a couple of hundred miles away, a puff of smoke appeared at the muzzle of Dopher's rifle. Ben Edmonds closed his eyes and withdrew from the mind of the murderer.

"In summary, it is the decision of this Court that the warrant did not issue upon probable cause. The judgment of the Court of Appeals of New York is reversed and the cause remanded for further proceedings not inconsistent with this opinion."

She was done.

Everyone in the courtroom knew what had happened. It would be futile for New York to retry Tyson without the evidence of the rifle. He would have to be released, a branded assassin, the mark of Cain on his forehead, with every hand against him. How long had Tyson to live?

Dopher appeared to be reflecting silently. To Edmonds the man seemed only mildly disappointed. Dopher had no way of knowing what had just happened to him: that the image Dopher dreaded most, the horrid secret one, had been carefully lifted from his mind, and had been carried away and laid down in another place, and there made permanent, as a flowing modulated pattern of light-sensitized silver bromide molecules in a gelatin emulsion.

Edmonds knew that his face was covered with tiny drops of perspiration, and that he was cold.

As Helen Nord closed her case folder, the Chief Justice turned and nodded to Oliver Godwin.

The old man's voice rasped out. "I must respectfully dissent from the majority opinion, and my Brothers Moore, Lovsky, and Randolph have authorized me to state that they join in this dissent. We do not contend that the discovery of the rifle justifies the search, but we think this not the point. We think the search was made on a lawfully issued warrant, and that the rifle was properly admitted for that reason. In any event, the matter is procedural. We think, if perchance the constable blundered, this should not set the criminal free. Society has the right to be protected against the return of this man. A great deal has been said about psi and clairvoyance in the proceedings below, and here. Some of the authors of this dissent have asked me to confirm their satisfaction that the record amply supports the existence of psi. Personally, I am far from convinced. But no matter, for our dissent is not founded either on the belief or disbelief in psi. We might observe that the use of psi as a police technique necessarily requires corroboration. But the only useful corroboration necessarily involves the subject matter of the search. It seems to us of the minority, that when the clairvoyant (assuming he was such) has been duly corroborated, the warrant stands self-validated, and further inquiry is superfluous. In our minority view the warrant was issued upon probable cause. We would, therefore, affirm.

"And now, with the consent of our brothers representing the majority opinion, we turn to one final matter. In the record below there is explicit testimony to the effect that the contents of the safe—Exhibit Q—will prove that psi exists. Both majority and minority have of course reached our separate conclusions without benefit of the safe—which, indeed, is not even in evidence and can have no probative value in our decisions. We do now order that the safe be opened. Marshal?"

Walter Sickles leaped to his feet. "Objection, Your Honor! We have had no opportunity to examine the contents!"

"Overruled. Your opportunity will come." The old man added sternly, "And there is no such thing as an objection to this court."

Sickles sat down uncertainly.

"Will the marshal please proceed?" said Godwin testily.

"May I remind Your Honor," said the deputy marshal, "that I do not have the combination."

"Of course. Here it is." Pendleton swiveled his chair around and gave the waiting page an envelope.

In a moment the marshal had the safe open and was staring inside. "It's full— of something, Your Honor."

"Yes. I imagine that's the urethane foam. You'll have to tear it out with your fingers. But be careful when you get to the camera."

The deputy dug in gingerly. Finally he pulled out the camera, still encrusted with adherent bits of plastic foam.

There was a sudden excited buzz in the great chamber.

Pendleton banged twice with his gavel. "Silence! Or I will ask the sergeants to clear the room!" He added quietly to the marshal: "Remove the film. Do you know how?"

"Yes, Your Honor." He pulled the tab, counted off the seconds, then tore off the assembly and stripped the wet print. His eyes widened as he stared.

"If the court please!" Guy Winters was on his feet.

"The court recognizes New York."

"New York requests permission to see the print."

"Granted, Mr. Winters. And I assume Mr. Sickles would like to see it also?"

"Of course, Your Honor."

Together the two lawyers bent over the composite with the marshal, who held the black-and-white print by the tab as the three of them studied it.

Pendleton's voice was under control, but it had now risen by half an octave. He demanded: "What does the print show?"

Winters looked up at the Chief Justice in wonder. "It seems to be—*the* rifle. A puff of smoke . . . just been fired. It's *the* room . . . *the* window. And the man is still aiming . . ."

"Man?" demanded Pendleton.

"Yes, your honor. It looks like . . . Philip Dopher!"

"Dopher? The witness below?"

"Sure looks like him," affirmed Winters in irreverent wonder.

And now a commotion in front of the audience. A stocky bearded man exploded into the center aisle. His right hand held a pistol. The spectators shrank away from him.

He cried out, "Yes! I did it! Long live the revolution!"

The defiant, weaponed fist upraised, in weird confrontation of the ultimate lawless force versus the ultimate force of law.

Everyone in the audience was on his feet. A wide empty circle formed around the intruder.

Dopher boomed out again. "If I killed your President, you think I won't kill you? All of you, possessed by the devil! Only way you could know I did it. I have six bullets. I think maybe I start with your chief, Mr. Pendleton." He waved the pistol. "Nobody move! Maybe I miss, and hit the smart lady judge—you want that, eh?"

Edmonds felt his stomach caving in. The horror was complete. It was futile now, and much too late, to say, never, never again.

But now in the appalling silence, he felt a chill descending into the room. A cold wind struck his face, and he shivered. Behind him, the great maroon drapes were rustling.

He almost forgot Dopher. What? he wondered. Or—who?

"Laura . . . ?" Oliver Godwin, struggling out of his chair, mustaches trembling like questing antennae, had whispered the word. It was at once a statement and a question, fluttering, broken-winged, desolate. It made the hair stand stiff on Edmonds' neck.

Dopher's pistol arm swiveled to the new target. Paralyzed, Edmonds watched the fist squeezing, the dead aim. He heard, unbelieving, the deafening crack, then the reverberations.

Godwin did not fall. Edmonds knew he was untouched, and that a leaden pellet was somewhere sailing, lonely forever in stranger time and space. He turned back to the grotesque figure in the center aisle struggling between the two sergeants-at-arms.

Roland Burke now stumbled to his feet and leveled a shaking finger at Dopher. "*You!* Did *you* kill President Cromway? Answer me!"

"Don't answer that!" Thunder exploded from the throat of Oliver Godwin. He seemed to stand nine feet tall. "In this Court, the rights guaranteed by the Constitution will be respected. I admonish you, sir, to remain silent until you have the benefit of counsel. Be that as it may, Mr. Dopher, if such be your name, I now place you under arrest, on suspicion of murder of President Cromway, and for attempted murder here. We have no place of detention in this building, but in a moment I rather believe the District Police will arrive and transfer you to the District Jail, there to hold you for further proceedings in accordance with law. Mr. Sickles, will you accept Mr. Dopher as your client, until one of you shall request to the contrary?"

"Indeed yes, Your Honor. And I move that the Court impound and preserve this safe, camera, film, and all associated materials."

"Unless my brothers have any objection—" he did not even look at his colleagues. "So ordered."

As Dopher was led out into the main hall, Godwin turned to the Chief Justice. He was at this moment the reincarnation, the fusion, and the voice of all the great justices who in decades past had guided the flow of American legal thought. He was the great Marshall; he was Taney; he was Hughes. He was the immortal Holmes. "I apologize to my Brother Burke for interrupting him, and to the other members of this Court, and most especially to my Brother Pendleton for any undue presumption of authority." But now he stood silent a moment, looking about the great room, wistful, searching. His body bent over a little, and he put a hand on the bench to steady himself. When he spoke again, the few reporters left in the front row had to strain to hear him. "God's blessing on this place . . . on these, my brothers . . ." He looked up at Pendleton. "With the leave of the court, I beg leave to retire."

Pendleton nodded to the clerk. "Adjourn the court."

The reporters, attuned to a generation of Washington arrivals and departures, caught it instantly. "It's *real*. He doesn't just mean retire, he means—*retire*. Godwin's finally retiring!" They were on their way to phones even as the crier was intoning, "All rise . . ."

> *I think it not improbable that man, like the grub that prepares a chamber for the winged thing it never has seen but is to be—that man may have cosmic destinies that he does not understand.*
>
> —Justice Oliver Wendell Holmes

"Thank all of you for coming," said Chief Justice Pendleton to the assembled justices. "After the events of this past noon, I thought it best for one last, highly informal conference, to tie up loose ends on *Tyson*. You've seen the afternoon papers?" He passed the copies around. "There seem to be all kinds of speculation. The *Evening Star* thinks Dopher's companions took the picture and got it into the safe somehow, and so betrayed him. The *Daily News* sees it as a plot to assassinate the Supreme Court. They demand a Congressional investigation with full TV and press coverage. Only the *Post* seems to have noticed that we released Tyson and simultaneously preserved Dopher's constitutional rights. They don't applaud either. But at least we need not be concerned further with Dopher. He's been extradited and is on his way to New York."

"And he'll bring the identical question right back here, evidence obtained by clairvoyance," said Moore.

"Not necessarily," said Pendleton cheerfully. "I think each and every member of this court is automatically disqualified to participate in any future cause of *Dopher* v. *New York*. We were all witnesses. If we ever get a petition for certiorari, we would have to deny."

"So New York will have to handle it all by itself," said Helen Nord thoughtfully. "This time, with a confession in open court, in front of several hundred witnesses, how can Winters lose?"

"Especially if he won't have to worry about an appeal to this court," murmured Blandford.

"Why *are* we here, Mr. Pendleton?" asked Roland Burke.

"Well, I thought we'd have sort of a post-mortem discussion. And when we finish that, I'd like your signatures on a memento for Oliver Godwin. His resignation was effective at the close of court this afternoon."

"High time," breathed Burke.

Pendleton looked at him sharply, then cleared his throat. "A great deal has happened in this case that some of us do not understand. A picture has appeared as if by magic. Two pictures, as a matter of fact."

Burke sat up suddenly. "*Two* pictures?"

Pendleton peered at him noncommittally. "Yes, two. I'll come to that later on. I don't know what it all means, not really. Either we are faced with the most colossal fraud of our careers, a fraud that involves a number of people of good repute, or else . . . we have just experienced a three-ring circus of psi. A pistol was fired point blank at Godwin. But the bullet, if there was a bullet, vanished in midair. Yes, there seems to be a great deal going on around me that I don't know about, and probably wouldn't understand if I did. I want to leave it alone. I will not inquire further. None of this need interfere with, nor is it truly relevant to, the continued performance of this Court. And therefore, in closing, let me assure you that I reprimand no one. Quite the contrary. I think we all owe a great debt to someone, or perhaps to several. Finally, I am very glad we are all alive."

Mr. Justice Burke was perplexed. "You mean that's the end of it? That we went through all that, and we're still not going to decide anything? What kind of logic is *that?* Shouldn't we withdraw our opinion, pull the whole case back for rehearing, and decide something?"

"And just what would we decide?" said Pendleton. "Should we take judicial notice that psi exists?"

"Of course not. You're twisting it all around. All I mean is, we can't dodge it forever. This is only the first case. Next term we'll have half a dozen."

"Exactly what do you think we ought to do, Brother?" asked Blandford.

"I don't know. I do know you're all against me." He stood up. "I would like to be excused from this conference."

"Just one more thing, Mr. Burke." Almost diffidently Pendleton turned around and picked up a portrait folder from the cart behind his chair. He passed it down to the justice. "This is the little farewell memento I mentioned earlier for Oliver Godwin. We wanted to give him a banquet and a suitable gift, but he flatly refuses. It's a photograph, with a signature card on the inside fold. We all plan to sign. Since you are now the Senior Associate Justice, we thought you might like to be the first."

"Of course. Very thoughtful." He opened the boards . . . and stared. "What on earth! Hands? A photograph of somebody holding hands?" He got out his fountain pen and unscrewed the cap, then looked over at Pendleton. "It's an old man's hand—in a black silk sleeve. It's Godwin, in robes, isn't it?"

"Yes."

Burke peered again at the portrait. "The other hand. It's a young woman's. The bracelet looks—familiar. Odd. Who is she?" He looked around the table uneasily. "Where did you get this?"

"It was on the negative from the *Tyson* camera. You may recall, I mentioned two pictures. The FBI developed the whole strip. This was on it, too. Ben Edmonds made the blowup."

"Who *is* she?" whispered Burke. He looked at Helen Nord's wrist. "It wasn't you. *You* don't wear a bracelet like *that* . . . of laurel . . . leaves?" As he considered this, doubt began to undermine doubt, and finally left him at the edge of some awesome mental precipice, unbalanced, and clawing to return to his warm, predictable, three-dimensional continuum. "No!" he gasped. "It can't be. And even if it is, I don't have to believe it!"

Chief Justice Pendleton looked at the gray face. He said soothingly, "Of course you don't, Mr. Burke. In this country, and on this Court, nobody has to believe anything."

And now it seemed to Roland Burke that this cheerful band had been illuminated by a flash of lightning, that he was now seeing their faces for the first time—and they were strangers, knowing, powerful, and he was helpless, and innocent among them. There was something terrifying about it. Nothing could ever be the same again.

Ben Edmonds knew what must be passing through Burke's mind: psi existed. It was a living thing, without boundary of time, space, life, or death. It was not subject to the laws of logic, or to any law made by man. It was without probable cause.

Burke's pen clattered to the floor. From the great black table he picked up the current volume of *United States Reports,* clutched it to his breast as though it were a talisman to ward off a horrifying unknown, and walked slowly from the room.

Edmonds leaned over and took the photograph from Pendleton. "Helen and I will sign first," he said simply. "It would please them."

THE ARAQNID WINDOW

1. Archeology 411

Every morning, for many years, right after he turned off the alarm clock, and whether he was on campus or in the field, Professor Speidel had permitted himself a brief visionary moment.

He saw a list of names:

> *Jean Champollion, Rosetta Stone, 1822.*
> *Sir Henry Layard, Nineveh, 1845.*
> *Heinrich Schliemann, Troy, 1870.*
> *Sir Flinders Petrie, Egypt, 1880.*
> *Sir Arthur Evans, Knossos, 1900.*
> *Sir Leonard Woolley, Ur, 1922.*
> *Hon. Jacques Derain, Ferria, 2095.*
> DR. REITER SPEIDEL, ARAQNIA, 21–.

Yes!

He might have doubts and reservations about some things. He doubted that the terrestrial Stone Age stopped and the Bronze Age began sharply at 2,000 B.C. He doubted that Egypt was older than Sumer. He doubted that the Mayan cities had died because of local soil exhaustion. But there was one thing that he knew for certain, and which he did not doubt. And that was that he, and he alone, was destined to discover the home civilization of the elusive Araqnids. The name of Speidel would be entered in the hall of fame along with other archeological greats. And from this fame would come great influence and power, and money. He would wave his hand, and scores of assistants would put together beautifully illustrated texts on Araqnia. The stereo frontispiece would show him leaning modestly on a shovel, beside a complete piece of the most delicate Araqnid statuary, done doubtless in alabaster. The statue would be sitting on a black velvet cloth spread out at the very spot where it had been teased out of the dig site. He would be smiling. It would be a faint, very wise, very confident smile.

Everything was certain but the date. This morning, as he slowly rose from his cot and fished for his slippers, he had a presentiment that he would make it this summer. He had a good group on this field seminar. One or two exceptions, of course, such as he always had in a group this size. But by and large, most were competent. In a couple of weeks he would be finished here at the base line, and he would send them out in several search parties to other likely sites where Araqnid artifacts had already been found. They knew what to look for. Somewhere on this very Earth-like planet of Ferria were the ruins of a city with a technology so advanced that they had visited all the outlying sun systems of the local star cluster over three thousand years ago. But then, very suddenly, they had disappeared, almost without a trace.

It would have to be this year. He was seventy. The Department was going to retire him. Lack-Coeur, the Departmental Head, had told him so, months before the expedition. "No chance of staying on afterward, Speidel. Nothing in the budget. Sorry."

"But what if I find Araqnia this trip?"

"No. The answer is still the same. Firstly, there's no such thing as Araqnia. Secondly, even if there were, there's still the question of the budget. Thirdly, you are seventy years old."

Well, no matter. He had immediately written all the foundations and museums. Somewhere there must be a place for him. But the replies had come back, one by one, each one a kick in the stomach. Every few days he got another one. "Our staff full for the coming season."

God, it was hell to be old. Thirty years ago, when he had yet to write the first edition of *Comparative Archaeology*, he had got a dozen offers when he closed up his first expedition. There was still hope, of course. He had yet to hear from Interstellar Geographic. They had financed Derain, the discoverer of this planet, fifty years ago. He should have a TX from them any day now. He had given them three proposals of varying scope and expense, all directed to finding the lost city. The third and cheapest proposal was simply to toss up an orbiting satellite to make a combination photo-sonar scan of the entire planet, with computerized enhancements. Geographic was his last hope.

He switched the tent light on, shaved and dressed quickly, and got out his notes for the morning lecture. A few minutes later the twin suns of Algol burst over the horizon like a nuclear explosion. From down the camp street he could hear the chattering begin. Why did young people have to make so much noise?

The youngsters seemed to feel a duty to make a racket day and night. With the lights-out signal, when sane people should be composing themselves for slumber, the camp put on a new burst of energy. Night brought out the guitars, the concertinas, the singers, and the two moons. One big moon and one little moon, skipping and dancing as it orbited the big one. And there was giggling, music, and waltzing on the sward for all hours, probably with liquor. At night he buttoned his tent flap tight and refused to inquire as to what might be going on out there. God knows what all they did. But they looked fresh and bright in the morning. That was what counted. He did not really care what they did so long as they were ready for another good day's work at the dig.

They made him think back to his own student days. He thought of girls, beer, and drinking songs. Why had he never married? He was out in the field too much. It would not have been right to ask a woman to share the hard life at the dig site with him. And yet, these young people today . . . There were plenty of girls in the groups he had brought here, year after year. And several married couples. The Thorins, for example. The girls did not seem to mind the rough life. But of course they would change when the babies started coming. No, archeology was no life for a woman.

He considered the way the young women dressed. Faded blue jeans stretched tightly across their rumps. In his generation it would never have been done. In his student days the girls had worn dresses in the field. Khaki, generally. Occasionally, perhaps a split skirt. Times had changed, but he had not. Did that mean he was truly getting old? He had to turn up something on this trip. Not that it would help him at the University. The course would have a different teacher next summer, no matter what happened. Too bad. He'd taken a group here for twelve years.

Archaeology 411. Excavations on Ferria. Examination of artifacts. Study of parallel evolution of Araqnid-Llanoan culture. 3 credits.

Araqnia, where are you?

He could hear the young voices in the mess tent, half a kilometer away. What were they talking about? Him? Perhaps.

He knew their name for him. Rider the Spider. They thought him a monomaniac. Well, perhaps he was. It was the only way to make a name in this field. Perhaps he was like Captain Ahab in search of the great white whale. He saw good and evil only in terms of what helped or hindered his search for the fabled Araqnia. It permitted a crystal-clear morality. Sometimes he awoke in a sweat at night, dreaming that he had died before he had found the city. Get hold of an obsession and never let go. That was the way the others had done it. And so would he.

He smiled grimly. Let them chirp and chatter, if that is what they had to do. Just so long as they turned up an artifact or two today.

He looked up the camp street. Across the little valley and up in the range of low hills he could make out the scattered buildings of the Wolfram Mining Company. The chief engineer had studied under him, many years ago. Last evening they had sat down to supper together in the crude mining mess hall. The engineer was sympathetic to the professor's problems. "Professor, all you need is to find this city, and then you will have so much fame that every foundation on earth will come looking for you. Maybe you are not digging fast enough. Maybe you should borrow one of my blastavators for a couple of days. Goes through solid rock like butter."

Speidel had laughed. "I appreciate it, Zachary. Truly I do. But I'll have to pass up the offer. If we dig faster than a centimeter an hour, we're sure to miss something."

Zachary Stone shook his head. "Well, if you change your mind, just let me know. I will send a machine anywhere you say, anywhere on the planet."

"I—" Speidel sneezed suddenly, then fished for his handkerchief.

"Gesundheit!" declared the engineer, looking at him narrowly. "Professor, you are catching something."

"Nonsense. It's just the afternoon mistral. Starts up on the Plateau of Sylva. Flows down the valley every afternoon." He blew his nose, then buttoned his jacket carefully around his throat.

"Sylva? The volcano?"

"That area, yes. The cone has been extinct for centuries. The lava flows made the plateau. It's all forested over, now. There's nothing there."

"Maybe we should send a 'vator up. Plow around in the lava a little."

"Not worth it. Araqnia is not on Sylva. All the signs point elsewhere. We've picked up artifacts in a dozen places, but nothing on Sylva."

"Maybe it's there, just buried."

"Then it's no good to me. I've got to locate and catalog things I can find quickly. Unless I get something from Interstellar Geographic, this is my last trip. I've got to show results, and I've got to send the kids out where I know they can find something."

"Sure, Professor. It's your show. Just let me know if I can help."

It was good to have friends. But there was nothing the engineer could do for him. At least not at this dig.

2. Four Hundred Mounds

After breakfast he wound up his morning lecture from the little dais in the mess tent.

"Our topic this morning is the Four Hundred Mounds, located two kilometers north of our camp. As we know, these mounds are lined up neatly in rows, twenty by twenty, and consist mostly of iron oxide, Fe_2O_3. And that was why the great Derain named this planet Ferria. And there the mystery begins. For there were suspicious percentages of other metals along with the iron. Nickel was there, and cobalt, tungsten, molybdenum, chromium. Metals such as are found in our own ferrous metal structures. Our machinery. Our landcraft. Our seacraft. And, most intriguing of all, our spacecraft. Had these rust heaps once been proud ships, challengers of the deeps of space? I am almost certain they were. But the great number troubles me. Had every ship in the Araqnid fleet been caught on the ground by some terrible disaster? Ah, what we would give to know! And somewhere here the answer is waiting for us.

"It has been proposed that this area was indeed the lost city, and that these piles were the houses. Impossible. Iron houses? No. And only four hundred houses? Not acceptable. And not storage sheds or warehouses, either. No, these were space-ships. How do we know this? Next to the area of the four hundred mounds is a concrete apron, several hectares in extent. Like all of this area, it is covered with fifteen centimeters of volcanic ash. Last year we borrowed a remote-control blastavator from the Wolfram Company and scraped off the overburden on a two-meter path, right down to the concrete pads. We took skin samples from the concrete and picked up some nice radioisotopes of alkaline earth silicates. So we are even able to identify their nuclear fuel mix. And not only that, from the isotopic residues we can date their last blast-off. The radiology lab at the University gives it as three thousand plus or minus three hundred years B.P.—before the present. This coincides nicely with data from the other known landing sites on the four other planets, including two on Earth, which is to say, one in the North Sahara and one in California. Students, just imagine those marvelous explorations of thirty centuries ago. They blasted off from this very place, just a few kilometers away, and they landed on our own home planet. You can almost see them. And then . . ." His voice dropped uncertainly. "And then, they disappeared. No more flights to Earth, no more explorations anywhere. Overnight, they vanished. Why? What terrible disaster struck them? Well, perhaps on this trip we shall find out.

"Now then, enough talk. Let's get to work!"

Nevertheless, within the hour the professor found himself making another speech.

"It has been said—" (And here the professor deliberately quoted himself.) "—that archaeology is a process of destruction."

The circle of seminarists dropped spade and sieve and assembled around the savant.

"Destruction, yes," the professor continued grimly. "But we mean *informed* destruction. And don't forget the modifier. Is *this*—" (he pointed to John Thorin's trench) "—*informed* destruction?"

The class looked at the young student in secret sympathy. It was going to be a bad day.

"The Llanoans," continued the professor, "built a wall here. A wall of sun-baked clay bricks. Then the wall crumbled, as such walls do. The desert moved in and covered everything. And now Mr. Thorin comes along with his spade, some four thousand years later, and digs a fine trench. And runs it right through the wall. Mr. Thorin, this is destruction, but it is not informed destruction. May I ask, sir, why your trench did not stop when it came to the wall?"

"I guess, sir, because the wall texture was the same as the soil. I just did not see the line where the soil stopped and the wall began. The bricks were made from the desert soil in the first place, and I guess they sort of weathered back into soil."

"So that you should have been specially careful, eh, Mr. Thorin? Well, then, can you now show the class the wall which you have zoomed right through with such enthusiasm?"

Thorin flushed. Forced to rub his nose in it. Thank God the light was just right. He could barely pick out a band of something about one decimeter thick. But he knew that if the professor had not told him it was there, he would have missed it. He knelt and pointed at the boundary.

"Very good. And now let's trade." He took the spade gently from the student's hands and gave him a digging knife. "You will now proceed to define the wall. Carry on, class."

Thorin sighed. He hoped this wasn't going to set the pattern for the field trip. He was glad his wife had not been present to witness his humiliation. Fortunately, Coret was busy today typing reports in the administration tent.

And that bit with the knife. As though to tell him he couldn't be trusted with anything so gross as a shovel.

He set his jaw philosophically and began to hack away. Just how he was going to run a trench a meter wide down the full length of the wall using only a handknife, he did not know. The shovel was the only way to do it. But he wasn't going to risk the shovel again. The professor might send him home. Even though he was majoring in instrumentation, he needed this 3-hour credit in ark. He had to finish this field trip. No, he could not risk antagonizing the professor.

Digging alternated with lectures.

"On a rock in Tassili, in the northern Sahara, on our home planet, is carved a line drawing of a figure in a space suit. Who were these creatures?" The professor looked across the assembled group, sitting on the ground around the camp fire, and his eye fell on John Thorin.

Thorin knew his lines by heart. "Most likely the Araqnids," he mumbled.

"Most definitely the Araqnids, Mr. Thorin. And there are similar markings in the Tulare region of California. And where did the Araqnids come from, Mr. Thorin?"

Thorin bore it in patience. "Here on Ferria, somewhere."

"Yes. Very definitely. Somewhere here on this very planet. We have already detected several of their rocket sites here. We have found their artifacts here, and fragments of their statues. We have a fair idea of what they looked like. A rather small spider-like people, with tentacles. And just as we ride horses, they rode furry bipeds—the Llanoans. We have established this in drawings on pottery. We postulate a home city for them, which I have named Araqnia. Our prime objective for this seminar is to find Araqnia."

"Good," thought the instrumentalist. "He is off on Araqnia. Nobody will get chewed out for the rest of the lecture."

3. The Wind

Next day, the professor said to Thorin, "I am assigning you to the sifting screen. The excavators will bring you the soil they have dug up, one wheelbarrow after another. They will help you shovel it onto the screen bed. You press the button, here, and the machinery will vibrate the screen. The soil will drop through. Potsherds, small artifacts, anything the shovels missed, will be retained on the screen. When you see anything, pick it up right away and put it on the collection table. This is very simple. A child could do it. Do you think you will have any trouble?"

"Of course not, sir."

"Don't say 'of course not.' I am taking a chance on you. Just do it."

"Yes, sir."

As he expected, there was nothing to it. The hours passed, and the wheelbarrows kept rolling up. He helped them unload. The waste dropped through the sieve into the little mining car, which moved off down the slope to dump its burden, and then rolled back again. Once in a while he caught an over-size pebble on the screen. That was all.

After lunch, it became hotter, but the afternoon breeze from the plateau got stronger and kept the perspiration stripped from his body. The breeze felt fine. He shifted around to windward of the sieve to keep the loess from blowing over him.

At this point an unfortunate thing happened. Coret had wheeled up a load of soil. Together they had shoveled it onto the screen. Then she had turned the wheelbarrow around, and he had switched the shaker on and was watching her push the barrow back down the boarded path. The wind was gusting sharply, and she had to stop for a moment to retie her kerchief about her hair. The bare hint of her jasmine perfume brushed his nostrils. As he faced back to the sifter, there was Professor Speidel, frantically picking things out of the sieve box.

"Turn it off!" cried the professor.

Thorin turned it off. "What's the matter?"

"Do you know what you have just shaken to pieces?" He held up a handful of shards.

"No, sir," gulped Thorin. "What?"

"A pollen box!"

"A pollen box, sir?"

"Yes, 'a pollen box, sir.' Pollen was a delicacy the Araqnids fed their Llanoan mounts, just as we feed pieces of sugar to a horse. They kept it in little pottery boxes. Such as this used to be."

"Well, sir, I will be happy to restore it. I can glue the pieces back together."

"I'd never trust you with it. And even if you knew how, the pollen is gone, totally blown away. The box was full of it. When the box broke, the wind completely scattered it. Not a grain left. Nothing to give our botanists. They could have identified the plants." He studied Thorin glumly, "I am being punished. But why? What have I done to deserve this?" He shook his head and stalked away.

4. The Pack

At the evening lecture the professor expounded on practical matters. "The competent archeologist carries a knapsack into the field. This knapsack should contain the necessary working tools, nothing more. You will need a small folding shovel: the so-called trench shovel. And a mason's pointing trowel. A small hoe. You can make one by sawing off most of the handle of a small garden hoe. Next, a small camp axe. A jackknife. And for cleaning the artifact, a small paint brush. If the artifact is fragile, you may want to strengthen it immediately with celluloid-acetone solution before you even take it from its matrix. We had a case this afternoon . . ." He looked over at John Thorin severely.

The instrumentalist squirmed. The pollen box was all over the camp, now. Was the professor going to bring it up again in front of everybody?

But the professor had other ideas. "Mr. Thorin, do you have a knapsack?"

"Yes, sir. Sort of."

"Sort of?"

"I made my own back-pack, sir."

"It has, of course, the things I just mentioned?"

"Well, perhaps not all of them, sir."

"Could you demonstrate your pack, Mr. Thorin?"

"Well, I guess so. Just a moment, sir, while I get it."

Perhaps this was an opportunity to redeem himself. Actually, he was rather proud of his pack. There were some pieces of special equipment in it that he had made in the tool shop back at the museum. He ran all the way to the tent and back.

"Here, sir." He put it on the lecture table. "It zips open here."

"Yes. And what is this?"

"A coverall, sir. Very light. Folds to a very small size, as you can see. There are gloves, and wrappers for the feet. Covers the body from head to toe."

"Why would one want to cover the body from head to toe, Mr. Thorin?"

"Well, rain, sir?"

"Do you know the last recorded rainfall in this area, Mr. Thorin?"

"No, sir."

"It was before you were born. Well, now. What is this?"

"It is a polarizer, sir. It measures stress in transparent or translucent objects."

"Does it have any significance for an archeologist?"

"Well, suppose he found a piece of glass, or something like that, and he wanted to find out if it was in a stressed condition . . ."

"Next item, Mr. Thorin."

"Well, this is an orientor."

"A compass?"

"No, sir. Actually, it is more than a compass. It is a tiny recording gyroscope. Once you set it you can go on a very winding path, even in three dimensions, and it will record all the twists and turns and guide you back when you are ready to return."

"A compass is much more reliable, Mr. Thorin. But what have we here?"

"A sonar device, sir. It sends sound pulses into rooms and chambers that you can't get into, and it will give the position of things in the chamber." '

"Indispensable, I am sure. And this?"

"I call it a flexiscope. It's a periscopic, extensible probe. An advanced model of the type that Carlo Lerici used to lower into Etruscan graves in the twentieth century."

"Well, possibly. And what's this?"

"Infra-red scope, sir. You can shine it on any surface, and it will reflect back a heat image of anything warm that has recently touched the surface."

"I am sure we have many warm-blooded creatures underground who will appreciate your interest in them. And what have we here?"

"As you can see, sir, it is a pistolet."

"A weapon? My God!" The professor struck his palm to his forehead. "You think the mummies will rise up and attack you? That perhaps the Araqnid skeletons will go after you with their tentacles? How long do you think the government would permit us to continue to excavate if we came out of the digs each morning wearing a gun like your ancient cowboy gangsters? Get that thing out of here! The whole pack!"

After Thorin had slunk away the professor continued his lecture. "It is a great mystery. The Araqnids certainly achieved interplanetary and interstellar travel thousands of years before we did. Their culture and technology was vastly ahead of ours. And when we find their ruins, we may be the first to establish a great archeological paradox: The buried culture is more advanced than that of the diggers. It has never happened before, and even now it is difficult to imagine. For if they were that far advanced, they should have been able to deal with almost any catastrophe. They should have been able to recover from earthquakes, flood, disease, even nuclear warfare." The professor sneezed violently, then blew his nose. "The mistral has given me a cold, students. Take care you keep yourselves warm when you are out in the wind." He returned to his theme.

"We have been able to study at first hand certain of our primitive arrested cultures which exist today as they did five thousand years ago. For example, the Australian aborigines, the Eskimo, the Bedouin, the bird-raisers of the planet Avia, the sea-harvesters of the planet Thallassa. But these cultures have been limited, generally devoid of writing skills, permanent dwellings, or specialized professions. All men were hunters or shepherds, for example. And so it is a bitter irony that these primitive cultures have survived, and the marvellous civilizations of Memphis, Rome, and Araqnia have long vanished. Ah, what were the sounds and smells in the Piraeus on an average day, and what was the chant of the slave gangs that raised the great blocks of Cheops? What were the Araqnids like—the scientists, their women, their families? All is lost, except in our imaginations."

John Thorin had meanwhile crept back, and was listening on the fringes of the circle. The professor was not poetic by nature, and Thorin conjectured that the archeologist must have read this somewhere. No matter. It was all true.

5. The Peculiar Holes

The next morning, while Thorin was scraping (very very carefully) on the soil in his allotted grid, he uncovered a small hole, which seemed to slant tortuously down into the ground. It was about two centimeters in diameter. An animal burrow? He thought not. Rather too small for that, unless of course it was a very small animal indeed. More likely, an insect burrow. Well, he would soon know. He continued to scrape, removing a plane of soil about one centimeter thick at a time, in the approved fashion. And then he uncovered another hole. And then two more. Well, now, he thought, a whole family of whatever it is. We are getting somewhere. I will bet these lead to some sort of central nest. He scraped cautiously. Ah, there it was. The burrows all converged into a larger chamber, somewhat larger than his head. He bent over and peered into this hole. And there seemed to be an even larger cavity below this one. Well, he would soon get to the bottom of the matter. He continued to scrape. In another fifteen minutes he was able to remove completely the dirt defining the upper chamber, and he was well into the lower chamber. At one point he stopped and peered down into the lower hole. To his surprise, it seemed to have four burrows slanting downward from it. More and more interesting. He wondered for a moment whether he should call the professor. But the professor might scold him for the interruption. After all, it was still just a hole. It wasn't as though he had uncovered the top of an artifact.

Just then a shadow fell on him. He looked up. It was the professor. Thorin smiled uncertainly. Then, as he studied the professor's face, his smile vanished.

"Is something wrong, Professor?"

"What is it?" asked the professor hoarsely.

"A hole, sir, that's all. Just a hole."

The professor climbed down into the excavation with him and squinted into the little chamber. After a time he shifted his position and peered down again. "I need more room, please get out for a moment. Do it as carefully as you can."

"Of course."

The professor pulled a handlight from his side pocket, got down on his hands and knees, and made a final examination of the hole. Then he stood up laboriously, pressed a hand to the small of his back, and asked, "There was a chamber just above this one?"

"Yes, sir," said Thorin uneasily.

"And four burrows leading down into that one?"

"Yes, sir. How did you know that?"

The professor groaned. It was a mournful, heartrending sound. Afterwards he was silent for a time.

A cluster of students had now gathered curiously around the pit. Coret put her arm protectively around her husband's waist.

A tear began a zigzag course slowly down the furrows of the professor's cheek. "It is true," said the professor sadly, "archeology is a destruction. But as I have already explained to all of you, it is a controlled, informed, and educated destruction. We destroy the matrix of loess, mud, and gravel in order to recover the primitive skull, the *objet d'art,* the bronze brooch."

"But I didn't destroy anything," protested Thorin. "There was this hole in the subsoil, about one meter down, and I—"

"This *hole,*" said the professor, dignified, but white-faced, "was where an Araqnid statue used to be. Alabaster is slowly soluble. It had been leached away by ground water, probably centuries ago. Only the empty outline was left."

"But surely, the hole wasn't any good," said Thorin.

"Good heavens," whispered the professor.

"You were supposed to fill it up with plaster of paris, dear," said Coret. "That would give you the exact shape of the original statue."

"It would probably have been the first complete reproduction of an Araqnid on his Llanoan mount," said the professor heavily. "Worth the cost of the expedition."

Coret walked her husband back to the tent, so that the professor would not be tempted to do anything foolish.

6. The Fall of Civilizations

Next morning, the professor opened his breakfast lecture with his inevitable theme. "The Araqnid-Llanoan mergence took place about four thousand years B.P. Prior to this time the Araqnids had advanced approximately to the state of our own Egyptiac or Mesopotamian cultures, of say three thousand B.C. They had spears, the crossbow, the battleaxe. They fought battles in chariots. They cultivated plants equivalent to our wheat, corn, and barley, and they had fruit orchards. Curiously enough, the Llanoans were beginning to develop their own very primitive culture. In the preceding hundred thousand years they had evolved from a furry quadruped to a furry biped, although we may speculate that they still had a somewhat shuffling gait and might from time to time touch the ground with their knuckles. Although the Llanoans had no agriculture, they had a varied diet. They ate wild berries and fruits, they trapped and ate small animals. Their only weapons were improvised clubs. The evidence suggests that before the mergence of the races, the Araqnids and the Llanoans were about the same size and build. After the mergence, the Araqnids shrank in size and the Llanoans became taller and heavier. That, of course, was to be expected. The Araqnids became totally parasitical on the Llanoans. We lack concrete evidence as to the mechanism of the Araqnid body structure that permitted this parasitism to function. We speculate, however, that when the Araqnid was mounted on the Llanoan, two or more tubular probes were thrust into the spinal column and the bloodstream of the mount. This system permitted the Araqnid to dispense in large part with a digestive system. In evolving in this direction they might well have lost fifty kilos. In their final form, they must have been mostly head and tentacles.

"It was a strange symbiosis. Exact analogies are lacking in our own terrestrial history. As pairs, we think of *homo sapiens* and *equus,* but the analogy is inexact. The horse never had any culture of its own, and of course there was no blood-to-blood contact between the two animals.

"The Araqnid-Llanoan relationship was unique. Its potentials were immediately recognized by the Araqnids. All manual labor, all menial tasks, were done by their mounts. The master race was freed to think, to create, and to invent. In one thousand years they had steam-powered vehicles. A few hundred years later they were in space. We know they visited several planets in the local sun cluster. And then they vanished. They must have had a great city, with tall buildings and several million inhabitants. But it has vanished without a trace. Civilizations have come to an end before, of course. The Babylonians destroyed Nineveh in 612 B.C., and it never rose again. But at least the ruins are still there. Rome destroyed Carthage, but at least we know the site, and how it happened. Knossos fell beneath a combined earthquake and tidal wave. Angkor Wat has been deserted for a thousand years, but we know where the city is. The Mayan cities of the Yucatan are long deserted, but at least we know they are there, and we can see and touch the buildings and temples. Not only do we not know where Araqnia is, we don't know why it disappeared. Was it flood? War?" He coughed raucously and blew his nose. "Disease? Some nasty virus such as I have? (God protect them!) It might well have been a genocidal epidemic.

"Yes, an epidemic. As we know, the population of Easter Island was wiped out in the early nineteenth century by exposure to Europeans. The Mediterranean area was ravaged by a brand-new disease brought back from the New World by Columbus's sailors. Today we know it as syphilis. Whole tribes of North American Indians have been destroyed by a single exposure to variole, which used to be our mildest form of smallpox." He wiped at his nose. "And even a little thing like the common cold was fatal to thousands of Eskimos when they were first exposed to it by the early explorers looking for the Northwest Passage. As a matter of fact, if I and my cold were transported back into Araqnia of three thousand years ago, I myself might be a contributing cause to their destruction. To them the common cold might be a lot worse than the Black Plague was to Europe in the Middle Ages.

"So much for disease and the fall of civilizations. Next week we shall divide the group into search parties of two or three students, and we will all look for the lost city. And we shall find it. Have no doubts about that. Just think. We shall stand there, looking out into a street that once was filled with these remarkable beings. In our inner ear we shall hear the ordinary street noises of an ordinary Araqnid day. We shall watch their wonderful cars and vehicles move at tremendous speed up and down the airways of the city."

The professor looked dreamily off into the distance. "What we need is a window on the past. A sort of time machine that rolls back a couple of thousand years, and lets us see the natives as they really were, what they wore, how they talked, and the million details of their everyday living."

At this point, unbeknownst to his listeners, he had a momentary flashback into his own past. For he had stood on the steps of the Acropolis and looked down on Athens. He had stood on the steps of the Roman Forum and had looked out on the Via Flaminia. He had looked out on the Egyptian desert from the temple of Karnak. He had stood on the great tragic Mount Masada and looked down on the Dead Sea. He had gazed forth from a ziggurat in Babylon, and from the Temple of the Sun near Mexico City. From all these places he had let the times of the structure take over. The hoverbuses and modern buildings and people in their twenty-second-century clothing had vanished, the millennia had rolled away, and he had seen the ordinary people and carts and wagons and animals of bygone times. And he would do the same here. He would find Araqnia, and a window in Araqnia, and he would look forth upon the remains of the lost city, and for him it would come to life again. And when this happened, it would not matter whether he had found a new post, or whether he would have to take his little University pension and disappear. If he ever found the right window, he just might walk through it and be gone forever.

The professor sighed, then became embarrassed. "Well then, let's be off. All of us have work to do. Dismissed!"

John Thorin looked covertly at his wife. "Nutty as a fruitcake."

"Don't talk like that. He loves his work."

7. Poolside

Next day the sub-groups were named and assigned their search areas.

Thorin and Coret were named as one group. Their assignment was the Plateau of Sylva.

"But Professor, sir!" protested Thorin. "That's the only place on the planet where no Araqnid artifacts have been found!"

"Exactly," said the professor grimly. "It is up to you to remedy the lack."

"But, sir, I need to collect material for my thesis. The plateau is a thousand square miles of virgin forest. Where do I start to dig?"

"Consider it a challenge, young man. Look harder. And since you have so little time, I suggest you start immediately."

"Sir, if it's the Llanoan wall, I can explain—"

"Perhaps you can find another wall, Mr. Thorin."

"And I'm truly sorry about the pollen box, and the holes, or whatever you call it. I'll be very careful, if only you can switch my assignment."

"Check back with me as soon as you turn up something, Mr. Thorin. Someone will be on the TX at all times."

"Yes, sir." Thorin backed out of the tent. This was the end.

Pompeii Jones let the skiff hover over an open place in the forest. "There's a stream, and a pool. You might as well have a decent campsite."

"It's pretty," said Coret gamely. "Take us down, Pom-pom."

"Say a hundred meters or so from the pool," said Thorin. "We don't want to be in the path of animals coming down to drink."

The staff man helped them get their gear out of the luggage rack. "Need any help with your tent?"

"No. It's a pushbutton."

"Don't forget to file your evening report."

"Yeah."

"Well then, see you in a couple of weeks."

"Yeah."

"Sorry, old friend."

"Yeah."

At sunset the instrumentalist filed a nonchalant TX with the professor. "Camping in clearing near pool. Coordinates A26, Q19. Biosensored area for one kilometer diameter. Numerous small avians and herbivores. Nothing dangerous. No trace intelligent life past or present."

That night they cooked over a primitive campfire, and later Thorin got out his concertina and they sang mournful songs by the light of the dying embers.

Finally they yawned, zipped up the electroscreen, and got into their sleeping bags. Thorin had just dozed off when Coret awakened him. "John, there's something out there."

He listened but heard nothing. "Probably an Araqnid. Go to sleep."

"I'm not sleepy."

"Well, I am. Goodnight."

"With the moving and all, I didn't get a shower all day."

"So? I haven't had one this week."

"You don't mind being dirty. I do."

"You can get one in the morning. In the pool. You'll have it all to yourself."

"You're sure there's nothing out there?"

"Just an Araqnid."

"Don't be funny. They're extinct."

"Yeah. Goodnight, Coret."

8. The Creature

It was morning, and he was barely awake when he heard the scream. He squirmed from his sleeping bag and grabbed the pack. Even as he ran out of the tent he began fumbling in the side pocket that held the pistolet. "Coret! I'm coming!"

But there were no more screams. Nothing, until he reached the edge of the pool where Coret had gone for her morning bath.

He saw her at the same instant he got the gun out. She was naked, and running and stumbling up the path away from him. There was something horrid and bristly on her back.

He stood there transfixed for the briefest fraction of a second, as the color left his face. "My God," he whispered. But within the time it took him to set the pistolet to 'stun,' his wife had disappeared around the bend of the path.

He picked up the pack by one strap and dashed off after her.

He cursed himself for letting her go down to the pool without him. But yesterday it had all seemed perfectly safe. He had evidently missed a crucial life form. And the omission might well kill his wife.

Coret had now vanished around a turn in the path. But when Thorin arrived there, seconds later, he saw that it was more than a turn. It was a fork. The path branched off to both the right and the left. And another thing. The main path had been open overhead. But the forks were roofed over with some sort of plastic monofilament.

Coret had taken one of the paths. But which one?

He pulled a handlight from the pack and shone it down each of the paths in turn. He could see nothing, except more of this strange garlanding filament. He would have to chance one or the other. He turned again to the right-hand fork.

And now he noticed something strange. It was an odor. Traces of Coret's perfume were coming from the right-hand path! This was the one, of course. And he was about to dash down this passage, when by chance his eye fell on the soft soil floor of the other path. And there was an incomplete impression of a human foot. Just the ball of the left foot. It had to be Coret, running. And the next footprint would be a couple of meters into the left-hand tunnel. But something . . . someone (the creature?) wanted him to think otherwise, and in fact had immense skills and technology for persuading him. As witness the scent. The realization stunned him. Definitely, the left. But how then could he account for the delicate traces of jasmine wafting eerily from the right-hand fork? A pang of fear shot through his intestines. It was so violent that he bent over for a moment. The . . . thing . . . that possessed Coret was emerging as a fantastically cruel and intelligent adversary. Was it possible that it had already got into Coret's cerebral cortex? And even if the creature knew, in some unexplained way, that Coret used a certain perfume, how had it recreated it? Especially from a different tunnel?

The intimations were . . . appalling. But he refused to think about it. He had to get moving.

He picked the bag up and started into the left branch. And then he stopped suddenly. Something was hanging from the filament-network. The skeleton of a small winged creature. It had apparently got stuck there, and then something had eaten it. Or most of it. One of the wings, fairly intact, had fallen half a meter to the floor, where it was again stuck in the felted mass. And a couple of meters farther on, a pig-size skeleton was netted to the floor. And beyond that, another. The place was full of bones. Animals had wandered in here, and they had been caught in these strands. And then something had eaten them.

He picked up a dead tree branch from the pathside and jabbed it into one of the strands. It stuck instantly. He pulled at it. The strand yielded a few centimeters, then firmed up. He pulled at the branch with all his strength. His efforts served only to force it into contact with other strands. It was held so tightly now that it stuck out into the air.

And yet, Coret had passed untouched through these ghoulish garlands.

He shook his head dizzily. If he were ever going to see his wife alive again, or vice versa, he would have to get a grip on himself before the strands did.

He had no idea how Coret had managed to evade the filaments. Yet, perhaps he had a few tricks, too. He took his cape, gloves, and shoe-wraps from the pack and pulled them on. The garments had been treated with a fluorocarbon polymer so that they could be folded without sticking. The anti-stick property might now come in handy as protection against the webbing. The pack had been likewise treated, so that he did not have to worry about losing it to the filaments.

He took a few steps inside, let the cape contact the wall of strands, and pulled it off again readily. There was no adhesion. He was not going to get stuck.

He opened his pack again, set the orientor, and pulled the bag back again on his shoulders. There might be many twists and turns and forks. He did not trust his memory to guide him back. If he ever came back.

He was a hundred meters into the tunnel, with the entrance-light a tiny disk behind him, when be made his second discovery. The tunnel was made of finished stone, laid with mortar.

This place was not just a natural elongated cave in the side of a hill. Intelligent beings (the Araqnids?!) had made it. It led somewhere. And for the life of him, he did not know whether that was good or bad. It would delight Professor Speidel, of course. But just at this moment he felt no great urge to delight Professor Speidel.

As he trotted, he pulled a lead from the fuel cell in his pack and attached it to his handlight. It would save the batteries in the light, which would otherwise last only a few hours. The fuel cell was good for several days. It might be best not to think what would happen when the main cell failed. Even the orientor would go dead.

How far ahead was Coret? And why was she able to move without getting hung up in this ghastly mess? Undoubtedly, that creature on her back was doing it, doing something to the strands so that she could pass. What manner of creature could alter the laws of adhesive chemistry? And it was really worse than that. What was the nature of this monster who had made this web, and could cause it to synthesize and release complicated molecules identical to Coret's perfume?

He fought a sudden animal urge to turn and run out as fast as he could.

But he hitched the packstraps over his shoulders and pressed on.

9. The Shaft

The next fork astonished him. It was not a right-and-left fork. The bifurcation was vertical. He could climb up or he could climb down. Either way he would have to grasp loose loops of webbing with his gloves.

Which way?

A quick survey with the handlight showed no disturbance in either branch, at least as far as he could see with the light.

Well, there was a thing he could try.

He got the polarizer from his pack. This little instrument gave out a pencil beam of light from an ordinary tungsten filament. The beam passed through a slice of calcite, which polarized it, and thence it could be sent through any semitransparent body, where at least a portion of the beam would be reflected back from the far wall of the body. The reflected beam returned through a receiving lens in the polarimeter, which automatically rotated back and forth seeking a colored path in the object examined. The color would indicate recent stress.

He let the pencil beam dance along the strands of the upper branch. There was no color. Thorin sighed. The upward path might . . . just might . . . have led to some ancient rooftop and to free air. But of course it was too much to hope for. He shone the beam downward. Yes, there were several strands there, definitely stressed. Coret had leaped off the edge of the tunnel lip with great confidence and had caught a strand a good two meters below. And the next stressed strand that he could detect was a good two meters below that one. The thing was barely braking its fall in its flight.

He returned the polarizer to the pack and shone the search beam downward again. All clear. He holstered the pistolet, and holding his light so that it would shine downward, began a slow and careful descent.

His thoughts kept returning to the basic mystery of these strange filaments. He had to assume that the creature was in some way able to protect Coret from getting stuck. But how? What was the creature doing that made the girl immune? He speculated that the immunity might well be local and transitory. Even so, it apparently sufficed. The creature was able to force Coret to move with astonishing speed, headlong, pell-mell, whereas he had to feel his way along, meter by meter. And the very haste of Coret's flight was in itself interesting. Perhaps the creature did not wish to risk an encounter with the pistolet, even turned down simply to stun. And as he considered that one, the implications confirmed his earlier chilling suspicions. Except through Coret the creature had no way to know that he possessed a weapon, and certainly had no knowledge of its capabilities. Not only had it pierced her spinal cord and seized complete control of her motor nervous system: the thing had very definitely plugged in to her mind and memory,

The odds against him were growing. For the first time, he felt intimations of hopelessness. There were probably other creatures. They were waiting to attack him. He would be overwhelmed and enslaved, the same as Coret. Perhaps he should get out now, while he could, and call for help. The other exploration teams could join him within a few days. All together, they could explore all of the dozens, or hundreds, or thousands, of branches and forks of this accursed warren. Eventually they would find the creature. Yes, that was the logical way to do it.

And what would happen to Coret meanwhile? Would the thing permit her to eat and drink? He thought of the skeletons hanging in the tunnel entrance, and he shuddered. And then he trembled once more, because he could not accurately speculate as to whether Coret would be the eater, or the eaten. Or perhaps both. He was sure of only one thing. The creature would not go hungry. And that of itself would impose a double burden on Coret's blood and tissues. While she lived. And these filaments undoubtedly were spun spider-like from the body of the creature, who in turn took whatever it needed from its host.

If he did not find her in a couple of days, she would die.

From somewhere floated peal after peal of wild laughter.

He froze against the wall of the shaft. The hair on his neck stood straight out and goose bumps played in ripples over his paralyzed cheeks.

It was Coret, of course. The creature had found her voice.

And then the screams stopped, as suddenly as they had come. The echoes vanished. The black silence returned.

He clenched his teeth and continued downward. But now he was uncertain once more. For he had the eerie impression that the sound had come from above, not from below. Was it possible? Was he on the wrong path, after all? He decided to trust his instruments. His senses had gone awry in this gloomy place.

He continued down.

And now he came to a fork in the shaft. One fork branched downward to the right, one to the left.

He hung onto a ladder-like loop in the main shaft while he flicked the analyzer over the strands in the right-hand shaft. Several of them showed stress. Good. He was about to replace the instrument when he decided to double check his conclusion by shining the little beam into the left-hand branch also.

The strands there also showed stress, in fact, about twice as much stress as those in the right-hand branch.

He was stunned. Had something heavy gone down both branches? He had speculated that other creatures might roam these dark caverns. Was this concrete evidence of their presence? In fact, did the extra tension in the left-hand strands indicate a second and much heavier creature? He shone the search beam uneasily down the left-hand shaft. Nothing moved.

But then a thought occurred to him. He clambered down the left-hand shaft for a few meters and then explored the strands below with the polarizer. None showed any stress.

So. The creature had climbed down here a short distance, then up again, and finally over into the right-hand branch. Just to throw him off the track. That explained the double stress of the first few strands here. They had been stretched as the creature descended, and then stretched again as the thing went up again.

He climbed up once more and lifted himself over the lip of the other shaft. The thing was making full use of Coret's intelligence. It was going to be tricky. The dimensions of his problem had expanded again. As he descended he tried to sort it out. The creature could move faster than he. The creature could sense his coming through the network of filaments, and could always manage to keep out of pistolet range. Furthermore, the creature would undoubtedly have opportunities to ambush and attack him. He imagined Coret's pearly teeth at his throat, and the thought chilled him. And then, of course, there might be other creatures, with or without host animals, lurking in the strands, waiting to drop on him, even as this one had dropped on Coret. The fluorocarbon cape was no protection against such assault.

The labyrinth itself was a major problem. Undoubtedly it radiated for many kilometers. And substantial portions of it were in three dimensions. He could expect to be in here for many hours. He had emergency food rations in his pack, and of course the little tank of hydrogen, which combined with the oxygen of the air in his fuel cell to give his drinking water as well as his long-term electrical energy.

The creature, he assumed, was even now parasitically feeding on Coret's blood and tissues. The thing was consuming Coret as though she were a seven-course dinner. He did not want to think about it, but he forced himself to consider it. For in that horrid symbiosis lay the only chance he would have of getting Coret out of this dismal place.

The cruel reality was this: he had food and water; Coret had none. And not only that, she had to nourish that horror on her back. He was in hard physical condition; Coret was not. It added up to this: if he could keep moving, not too far behind Coret, never giving them an opportunity to rest, she would eventually drop of exhaustion. Somewhere, eventually, she would collapse on the cavern floor. On her face, perhaps, with the creature still fastened to her body. And so he would find them. His mouth twisted grimly. He would not need to moderate the pistolet beam. And he was an excellent marksman. He would need only one shot.

But all of this was wishful thinking. It might not happen that way at all.

Nevertheless, he knew his plan was basically sound. What was more to the point, it suited his immediate inclination to keep moving. The thought of sitting down somewhere to try to conjure up a better plan was absolutely intolerable.

He came now to the bottom of the shaft and flicked his search beam cautiously around him. It seemed actually to be the crumbling floor of an ancient stone room. He could make out some of the individual blocks. They appeared to be granite. Undoubtedly this planet had had a geological history similar to that of Earth, and the highly cultured beings who had built this vanished city had made full use of their magmatic heritage in laying these cavernous foundations.

This had to be part of the lost city of Araqnia. What irony! He wished he had never heard of the hell-place. And that creature, then, must be a descendant of the once proud Araqnids.

10. The Rustlings

It was then that he heard the rustling. Something was in this room with him. He immediately swept the light toward the sound. There was a dark, shimmering heap in the far corner. Thorin recoiled a step and in a lightning reflex movement, drew his pistolet from its holster. But he did not fire. He leaned forward. The surface of the thing seemed alive, undulant. Otherwise it did not move. Thorin took a couple of steps toward it. Nothing happened. Then another few steps. The rustling was a little louder. Otherwise, there was nothing.

Whatever it was, it was not Coret.

He would hazard a shot, say a stun cone of about ten centimeters diameter. He pressed the trigger. The beam formed and vanished instantly.

Thorin flung his arm over his face and fell back. Things hit his protective cape, and then bounced off again. His heart pounded violently as the light jerked about the room.

Tiny shapes were flying around him, and circling overhead up the shaft.

He knew instantly. Beetles! Hundreds of them. Scavengers. A ghastly thought hit him. No, of course it could not be Coret. Not yet, not yet! He walked over to the thing in the corner. It was a smallish quadruped. Patches of black fur still clung here and there to its eroding skeleton. Doubtless one of the creature's prior mounts. So this was their mounts' ultimate fate. To be devoured by insects. He thought of the dermestes beetle that lived on the desiccated flesh of Egyptian mummies, and he shuddered.

He bent over to inspect the death-remnant. A six-inch circle of dead beetles covered one shoulder, where the stun ray had struck. He picked up one and studied it briefly. How were these things able to live here without getting caught on the strands? He fished in his pack, brought out the little spectroscope, and ignited a sample of the wing. There were strong lines of carbon and fluorine. The things were protected by fluorocarbon polymers, of about the same composition as the coating on his cape. Probably they had evolved in this way in millennia past, simply to serve this ghoulish service. They kept the tunnels clean.

11. A Touch of Warmth

And now, which way? There were three corridors leading out of this room. He inspected each in turn. Each was stone-floored. Here and there, a few filaments slithered across the floor, and numerous strands hung from the ceilings. There was no moss or vegetation on the floors to catch the print of a bare foot. And the polarimeter showed that none of the strands anywhere had been pressed or stretched or, so far as he could tell, even touched. The creature had not permitted Coret to leave any trace of her passing.

And yet, there had to be . . . something. He realized now that this was merely his hope. It was not a certainty. There was no reason at all to assume that there was in fact evidence that she had entered any of the passages, or, if there were evidence, that he would be clever enough to find it. And he knew now from experience, that if he found a trace in one corridor, he might well find the same trace in the other two corridors. The real problem was to find something in one that the other two did not have.

He returned to the tunnel on the right, and knelt down and examined the floor. It was well-laid granite. It had been here for thousands of years, and it was strange that it was not covered with dust. But there was little or no dust. The sticky strands, acting very much like nasal mucosa, had caught every particle. And yet . . .

He pushed the infra-red filter over the lens of his handlight, put the i.r. scope to his eye, and surveyed the floor, foot by foot. Nothing. He retraced his steps and entered the middle corridor. He was a bare meter into the tunnel when he found something. The red blotch in his scope resolved into the ball of a foot, complete with five toes. Coret had been running. This was her route. Still, to be safe, he checked the left-hand tunnel. Nothing. He returned to the middle corridor and began trotting down it.

He was perspiring freely. He wished he could remove his cape, but he knew that was impossible. He would be hung up in the strands in seconds.

He now had an idea how the creature was able to protect Coret from this hideous network. He speculated that the thing was able, by simple touch, to neutralize or "turn off" the adhesive surface of the strands as Coret moved along. Thorin had not got a very good look at the creature in the beginning, but he thought it reasonable that the thing had exterior tentacles, perhaps a meter long, and he could imagine these thin arms reaching out and touching the strands. Perhaps a sort of electrical current passed, which had the effect of altering the surface chemistry of the strands. He carried his speculation further. The strand surface was undoubtedly highly polar. He conjured up several models in his mind. A long-chain linear polymer, certainly. And the simplest kind of high polarity would be oxygen based. Which meant that the polymer probably contained a high percentage of hydroxyl and carbonyl groups. Very sticky indeed. And yet, at the creature's command, these groups were "switched off." How? He visualized a stream of electrons flowing from the creature's arms to a strand. These oxygen groups would thereby be reduced, perhaps for several meters along the strands. The carbonyls would become hydroxyls, and the hydroxyls might lose their oxygen altogether, release it to the air, leaving behind an inert methylene group. It must be something like that. It would seem to follow that the oxygen was very loosely bound to the surface molecules of the strands. A rather mild electrical charge was apparently sufficient to dislodge them and render the strand inert. He turned the thought over in his mind. He would have to figure out a way to verify it. If he ever got a breather, it should be a simple matter to run a C-H-O analysis on a strand fragment before and after passing an electrical current through it. Such a mechanism might explain the jasmine scent at the beginning of the chase. Evidently, the creature could control the entire network of strands from any point within the web, and could generate electrical impulses that released the exact combination of molecules that made up the very complex odor of jasmine.

Well then, suppose he was right, so what? How was it relevant in his battle to recover his wife? That he did not know. Maybe it was not relevant. He was not sure what was relevant and what was not relevant.

The hours wore on. He stopped twice to drink water from his fuel cell, and once he took time to open a tin of emergency rations from his pack. He wasn't hungry, and did it only on principle.

He encountered many more forks. Sometimes the creature tried to deceive him with false trails, sometimes not. He noticed now, when the pursuit led along horizontal runways, that an occasional drop of moisture might be found among Coret's footprints. It showed up as a great bloody blotch in the i.r. scope. This puzzled him. Were these tears? Was Coret weeping? He thought not. The creature probably had sufficient control over her voluntary nervous system to prevent any such emotional display. No, it had to be perspiration. Coret was tiring. In fact, Coret must be very tired indeed. Coret might walk several miles a day in her kitchen, and in cleaning their little apartment, but that was not the kind of exercise that would equip her to run and climb hour after hour. It must eventually happen, as he had foreseen from the beginning: Coret was going to drop. The creature might keep her moving during the initial phases of her exhaustion, by brute application of electrical impulses delivered as overpowering hammer blows to her spinal cord. But finally that would fail. And then he would find her. Dying . . . ? Dead . . . ? He stumbled and nearly fell on his face. Was he going about this in the right way? On the other hand, what other way was there? He set his jaw firmly and plunged on. But now he was thinking even more furiously than before. Alternates! He needed alternates. But there were none.

12. The Balcony Room

He was well into the twentieth hour of pursuit, and he had long ago lost track of the numerous twists and turns, ascents and descents. He relied on the orientor to record his route. Otherwise, even if he found Coret, they might wander here for days, and finally starve or die of thirst.

The way now led ever higher. He suspected that he was in a great building, possibly above ground. It was probably covered with lava and vegetation, and that was why the aerial surveys had missed it.

A muted humming, persistent but not unpleasant, seemed to fill the corridor. He was coming to something. Machinery? No, the sound was more like that from great electrical transformers.

The passageway opened into a great circular chamber. Thorin played his handlight briefly over the expansive walls and high ceiling. Glassed bookshelves lined the walls. Tapestry-covered tables and odd-shaped chairs bordered the sides of the room, and cabinets filled the corners. Some sort of electrical apparatus sat on the far cabinet. Ten casket-like boxes with opened lids clustered in an area to his right. Statues, faintly luminous, graced some of the table centers.

Thousands of years ago intelligent beings had lived here. He couldn't really know exactly what the Araqnids looked like. But evidently they required space, and room to work and live, the same as human beings.

It was then that he noticed the light. Across the great room there was a rectangular opening in the wall, and a gentle luminosity was drifting in through it. A window to the outside world? Was it possible that the creature had fled through here to the outside?

He panned the room quickly with his handlight. He saw no other exits.

He stepped across the room cautiously and stood before the aperture.

He listened. Over the pervasive electronic humming he could hear strange noises. He knew immediately what they were. Street noises. Vehicles moving rapidly up and down streets, clanging at each other. Even occasional squeaky cries.

It was not possible!

The light evidently came from a balcony that overlooked a busy street. He would have to see this!

But if he stepped out there, would the creature be hiding by the side of the balcony doorway, waiting to ambush him?

He hung his light on his belt, grasped his pistolet firmly in his right hand, and stepped carefully to the balcony entrance. The street sounds were much louder. Very slowly, he peered first to the right, then to the left. The little balcony was empty.

And now, even without stepping out onto the balcony, he could see that a marvelous vista lay open before him: greensward and gardens, fountains and colonnades swept down the valley. The great mall was bordered on both sides by majestic white buildings. They were so tall he could not see their top stories. He ducked back on reflex as a great metal shape hurtled past the balcony. His jaw dropped in total awe.

He had found Araqnia.

Beyond this balcony the city had shaken off millennia of desolation and had sprung back to life. It was like some fairy tale left over from his childhood.

He had a sudden impulse to step out to the balcony railing and peer into the streets below. But he did not. There was something wrong here. It was all too, too strange.

The creature had tried to lose him, first in two dimensions, then in three. The next logical step would be a false trail in four dimensions. This balcony led backwards in time. And he suspected it was a one-way passage. If he stepped out there, he would step into this city as it existed thousands of years ago, with no way to get back to the present.

On the other hand, perhaps the creature had forced Coret out there, and was even now laughing at him from the vantage point of distant eons. Was it possible?

From where he stood, he examined the surface of the balcony floor. Like most of the other structures he had encountered, it was stone. It seemed devoid of disturbance, ancient or recent. He played the i.r. scanner over the surface briefly, but without result. No, Coret had not come this way. He could relax on that score.

He stepped back into the room, trying to stay in the same path he had used on entering the room. From the center of the chamber he shone his light slowly, meter by meter, around the walls. The only exit he could see was the doorway whereby he had entered.

He got out the i.r. again and began systematically to cover the floor. He got firm readings only when it touched his own footprints.

And yet Coret's footprints had been in the long corridor. And the corridor led here, and only here.

He returned to the doorway. Here he picked up her last set of footprints with the i.r. In fact there were several prints. She had been standing there, doing something that involved moving her feet a little. And then she had vanished into thin air.

He looked back into the great room. And now in the grayness of the high ceiling, he picked out an irregularity. As he played his light over it, it resolved into a black disk, about a meter in diameter. It was, he suddenly realized, a hole. A hole in the dome of the ceiling. And it had to be Coret's exit from this room.

But how had she reached it? There were no filaments hanging from the ceiling; it was totally bare.

He examined the walls with his light. Here there were no strands, no filaments for her to climb up to reach the ceiling.

And yet, somehow, she had stood here in the doorway and had reached that hole in the ceiling.

And undoubtedly the horror on her neck was at this moment hovering over the edge of the hole, listening, and perhaps even peering cautiously over the ledge when Thorin's back was turned.

He opened his pack once more and pulled out the sonar.

The sonar beam would not make direct contact with Coret's body, of course. But he did not think that was necessary. The beam would go through the hole, hit a surface, perhaps the ceiling of the room above, then be reflected to another surface, then to another, and another, and it would do this perhaps several dozen times. Eventually, however, a reflection would return to the instrument. He would make ten or fifteen readings, and one of them ought to be weaker than the others. And if it were correct, it would be because something—perhaps Coret's body—was shielding out the reflections to a measurable degree.

He found something before he had completed one-third of the circle.

Something.

Coret?

There was no way to know unless he could get up there. And if it were Coret, how had *she* got up there? He thought he knew; but he needed to make an experiment.

He returned to the passageway, and with his pistolet, severed a length of filament. The strand was about 5 mm. in diameter, a dirty translucent gray, except for its core, which was a tiny black thread. It reminded Thorin of something. An insulated electrical conductor? Perhaps. But there might be an even closer analogy. A mammalian neuron: the central axon with its protective myelin sheath. Very likely it was actuated in the same way as a motor nerve. The creature touched it with a tentacle, and a tiny electrical impulse, perhaps measured in milliamperes, passed into the strand. The electrical characteristics of the filament changed. Electrons traveled along its surface, reducing carbonyl groups to hydroxyls, perhaps even releasing loosely-bound oxygen to the atmosphere. And when that happened, the filament, for a couple of meters from the point of contact, was no longer sticky.

This could be easily verified. He plugged conductors into his fuel cell. One conductor end he left bare on the stone floor, to serve as a rather poor ground. The other he touched to one of the strand garlands hanging at the doorway. It adhered tightly. He turned the current delivery knob to one milliamp. The conductor on the strand fell away instantly, bounced off two more strands, and dropped to the floor. That was interesting to know. Neutralizing one strand seemed to neutralize all strands in the some area. Of course, it was not too surprising, since they were all interconnected.

Now he was ready. He repacked the conductors, picked up the piece of strand he had cut, and re-entered the room. He took careful aim and threw the fragment toward the ceiling, near the hole. It stuck there.

And that must have been how the creature had reached the ceiling. It had spun a fresh filament from its own body, and Coret had thrown the strand through the hole, where it had caught, and then Coret had climbed up the filament, hand over hand, through the hole (her palms must be raw flesh), and they had pulled the cord up after them.

The thing was consuming Coret. Her body was being transformed into this horrid network. How much of this could she take? Evidently quite a bit. For she was waiting for him up there, waiting to kill him.

"Earthling!"

"Aie—!" The call was so unexpected that Thorin screamed. He picked the pistolet from its holster and looked up.

A face peered down at him. He did not recognize it at first as belonging to Coret. It was a twisted, animal thing. The hair was bedraggled, held together in front by perspiration. The eyes were not in good focus. One seemed to wander while the other gazed vacantly at his feet.

"Earthling!"

He held the light with his left hand while he raised the pistolet slowly, quietly confirming with a flick of his eye that it was still on "stun."

The face disappeared.

He was not surprised. The creature would not risk paralysis of the host body. The next call was muffled. "Earthling, I mean you no harm. Nor do I understand your persistent attempts to recover your mate. How can you resent my using her? In your own world you ride horses, camels, even elephants. You kill and eat cattle, sheep, pigs, and chickens. And you know you must die. You have very short lives, less than one hundred years. Why be concerned if it is somewhat shorter? In the few days your mate has left, I will give her many lifetimes. I do not have to do this, yet I shall, as a favor to her, and because she has given me a glimpse into another way of life, primitive though it be. For these reasons I have permitted her to see into my mind. And there was much to see, for I have lived three hundred of your Earth years. I am Keeper Number Ten. The ancestor of the Ten Keepers was named Eroch. He was a great scientist. It was he who built this window into time. Before he died he was able to set apart ten egg-sacs, one for each of the ten three-hundred-year periods that would follow on this side of the window. I am the last. Our prime directive is to preserve this room until the Death-One comes. Nothing must change until the Death-One comes. Go, Earthling! If you die here, the Death-One might be warned away."

It was eerie, unnerving, to hear this coming from the lips of Coret. He understood none of it; yet instinctively he felt he had to keep the creature talking as long as possible. He cried, "Am I the Death-One?"

"No."

"How will you know him?"

"Ah! He sprays treacherous death from his mouth! And when he comes, he must die, here in this room. He must not go forth on the balcony."

"Why?"

"There is more, much more. But I cannot remember. Or perhaps I was not told. My ancestors were ready to send forth great ships, to found colonies. And then the Death-One came, and they died."

"Where? Where were they going?"

"Ah, where? What was it? Was I ever programmed to understand? I do not know. But you must not be here when the Death-One comes. Nothing must affright him. When he stands before the balcony, he dies."

Now that was odd. Thorin had walked toward the balcony, and he had not died. There must be a comparator beam that had analyzed him and decided he had not been worth killing. Was there something up there? He played the handlight carefully over the lintel of the balcony entrance. Yes, there was a glassy grid. Some sort of closed-circuit TV. The comparator was evidently waiting for the "Death-One." And if you believed Keeper Number Ten, the comparator had been waiting quite a while . . . three thousand years! It didn't make sense.

The creature was making Coret speak again. "This time he must not get through, to bring death. Ah, foolish young Earthling, you don't answer. You don't understand. So be it. I now leave you. Don't follow. There has been enough death. It would truly sadden me to have to kill you."

Thorin waited a moment. Overhead there was total silence. But the thing might still be there. He made a rapid pan with the sonar. The rim of the hole registered blank. That was not necessarily decisive. The creature might have withdrawn into a nearby doorway.

And then, as he stood there, he realized that the creature had come to this room, this sanctuary, this tiny remnant of a lost civilization, and had found no weapon to counter the pistolet. The evidence was irrefutable: he had been visible to the thing for several minutes and he was still alive. Were weapons unknown to this thing and its culture? Probably not. But probably none were needed at home, and perhaps up to now the creature had seen no reason to keep one in its home. But weapon or no, as long as the thing controlled Coret, he was in great danger. He must follow with great caution.

He fished a tiny barb-ladder out of his pack and fired it into the ceiling hole. He could hear the muffled metallic clank as the sharp teeth struck somewhere out of sight overhead. He dragged the cord until the barbed tines caught, apparently in a crack in the flooring. He fixed the light to his visor, grasped the pistolet in his teeth, and began the ascent. He reached the ceiling and paused a moment before climbing over the edge of the hole.

If he were going to be attacked, it would be here and now. He listened. If Coret were nearby, he should be able to hear her breathing. The creature would not be able to prevent that. But he heard nothing.

He stuck his head up and looked quickly over the edge, front and back. There was no movement in the chamber above him. No sound. Nothing. He clambered out on the floor. The room was empty, save for a few cabinets and shelves at the sides. And there were no filaments. Hence there ought to be dust. And where there was dust he should be able to follow Coret's footprints with his naked eye.

And there they were. The creature had made Coret walk out through the archway at the right.

13. Fatal Contact

He repacked the ladder-barb into his kit, pulled his cape about him, and walked over to the passage. The light reached into another tunnel. Here, there were strands again. It was a puzzle. Why were some areas choked with filaments and some completely devoid of them? Perhaps the stranded areas were the entrance ways, which this Araqnid and his predecessors had lined with webbing both to trap and to bar the wild life of the Ferrian forest. Deep in the interior of the labyrinth it was probably not needed. The Araqnids' historical mounts, the Llanoans, were either all dead or had reverted to the wild, and this last of the race was forced to move on his own spindly legs, except when he found an occasional mount. Well, the thing had one now.

Thorin trembled. Even if he were successful in killing the creature, would Coret recover and live? After seeing her face, he was no longer sure that he would be doing her a favor to rescue her. Perhaps, from her viewpoint—if indeed she still had some sort of mind of her own—she wanted only to die. But it was wasted mental effort even to think about it. He would get her back or be killed. And just now he suspected that the chances of the latter were fairly good.

For his adversary was a three-headed monster. Part of him was Coret and Coret's mind and knowledge of human limitations. Part of him was the creature of the vast culture and technology of Araqnia. And finally, the ultimate and dominant part, the part that controlled everything else, was an insane spider-like beast.

He peered down the empty corridor. His light shone bright and true. There was no movement. The deadly garlands hung limp, silent, waiting for him.

It was a long passageway, and it sloped upward, so that the end, if there was an end, was cut off from view. The creature might have disappeared in that direction. On the other hand, there might be sidepaths. He pulled a set of zoom binoculars from his pack and examined the corridor again. Yes, about halfway down, there appeared to be branch tunnels leading off on each side. And beyond that, another pair.

The thing might have disappeared in any one of five directions.

He clamped his light to his visor once more, got out the i.r. scanner, and, pistolet in hand, proceeded slowly down the way.

The floor was dust-free, and he had to rely almost exclusively on the i.r. Without any attempt at concealment or camouflage, Coret's footprints led into the right branch. And the thought occurred to him that the creature lurked just around the corner, waiting. He stopped in his tracks and listened. Did he hear breathing? He was almost certain he did.

This would be the end. All the creature had to do was tear his cape and hurl him against the wall strands. He would be stuck. And forever. Or worse, he would be the next mount after the creature had finished with Coret.

He knelt down, opened his pack once more, and brought out the flexiscope. This was a flexible tube tipped with a photocrystal, extensible to the length of a couple of meters, and which would turn corners on command. A tiny light beam paralleled the crystal. Thorin snaked out the tube, guided it around the corner, and examined the right-hand corridor. Nothing. Very odd. So, what had he heard? He retrieved the instrument and repacked it.

Then he stepped abruptly into the intersection and shone the handlight down the length of the right-hand branch of the corridor.

A hell-cry burst into his ears from behind him. Something hard and sharp slashed at his right hand. The pistolet sailed down the corridor, where it slammed into a cluster of webbing.

He got up from his knees even as the creature ran past him. He took one step, then in frozen horror saw the creature riding Coret's neck, touching the strands in lightning-like gestures with its thin tentacle-like arms, as Coret ran on her toes. He knew he would lose the race to the weapon. He turned and ran back into the main corridor.

Peals of crazy laughter followed him.

He knew instantly what had happened. There must have been an overhead passage. The creature had gone into the side corridor, taken a flight of stairs overhead, and had come down into the left-hand passage, there to await him from his rear.

Fleet steps would follow him now. The creature knew its own territory, and could make Coret move about it very rapidly indeed. He knew that already. It was pointless to try to outrun this thing.

He slipped into the next side corridor and dropped his pack quickly from his shoulders. He had no real weapon left. Certainly nothing to compete with the pistolet. Still, there was one last thing to try. He opened the face of his fuel pack. If the creature were able to send a modest stream of electrons into the strands and thereby depolarize them to inertness, it just might be possible to neutralize the creature's imposed current with an exactly equal current of opposite polarity. That might make the strands adherent again—even to the Araqnid. He need only reverse the conductors and adjust the amperage. With savage haste he jabbed the clamps at the filaments. There was no current yet; his hand rested on the switch handle. He waited.

Howls reverberated down the corridor. An explosion sounded far beyond him, down the main tunnel. The creature was testing the pistolet. The footsteps were pounding closer.

That was good. He wanted Coret to be running. He wanted the creature to be touching those little strands in rapid succession.

At this moment he ought to be thinking of death and destruction. But all he could think of was Coret. But not this poor ridden wretch waving his pistolet. He remembered Coret on their wedding day: floating in a radiant whiteness, and with tiny red flowers in her hair. Let him die seeing her in perfection.

He pulled the switch.

An inhuman scream.

A grunt.

A body falling.

He stepped out into the main passage.

Coret lay motionless on the floor. Behind her, the creature dangled from the ceiling strands. His four tentacles, torn out at the roots, hung in the filaments a couple of meters behind his body. His thorax was ripped open where it had been fastened to Coret's neck. It gushed a purple liquid in rhythmic spurts onto the floor below. Only the eye-stalks seemed undamaged. It seemed to peer in immense surprise at Thorin, as though to be caught in its own web was totally impossible. A thread of filament oozed slowly from the thing's spinneret and collected in a crazy obscene coil on the cold stone surface.

Thorin knelt over Coret and felt for the artery in her throat. The pulse was strong. He picked up the pistolet, turned the heat gauge up as far as it would go, and incinerated what was left of the Araqnid.

He then tried to lift Coret up. She was stuck to the floor strands, but that was readily fixed. He reversed the conductors again. Now the strands were in their reduced, non-oxygenated phase. Nothing would stick to them.

He folded the cape up, slipped it into his pack, holstered the pistolet, clamped his light in his visor, reversed the orientor, picked his wife up in his arms, and started out. By the time he had lowered her down into the balcony room, she had recovered consciousness and was able to drink some water from the fuel-cell flask.

She coughed, looked up at him, then took the little canteen with both hands. "My . . . God!"

"Yeah. But don't try to talk."

"What *was* it?"

"An Araqnid, I guess. Just rest awhile."

She handed the canteen back. "I saw the city."

He nodded toward the window. "The balcony?"

"No, not the balcony. He was in my brain, and I was in his. They programmed him while he was in his egg-sac. Complete with implanted memories. He was born one hundred percent educated. He knew how it was before the Death-One came. I know just about everything he knew. I can read those books in the balcony room."

"You're talking too much."

"All right. Can we get back?"

"I think so. It may take hours, but the orientor should get us there."

"He doubled back and circled around a lot."

"The orientor can cancel out the doubles and circles."

"I wonder if they've missed us yet."

"I guess so. I'm several hours overdue to make the evening call."

"They'll be there waiting for us."

"Maybe."

"We'd better start."

"You can't even stand."

"Yes I can. Help me up."

"And let me fix your hands. Your fingers are bleeding." He got out the first aid kit. "You'll have to do some climbing in those shafts."

"Do you have an extra cape and gloves?"

"Sure."

"But maybe we don't need them. Couldn't we just leave the power pack up there, plugged in to neutralize the web? Save a little weight that way, too."

"No. Too risky. We'll wear capes and carry the pack. I'll go back and get it. In the first place, the orientor is integral with the pack. Secondly, we may need the fuel-cell water before we get out. Finally, suppose the electrical effect quits?"

"I just asked. Cape and gloves, then. What's the matter?"

"I was just wondering. The web. Maybe it's a good aerial."

"You could get a signal out?"

"Worth a try." He jabbed the aerial probe from his communicator into the nearest strand and adjusted the dials. "Calling Archeology 411. Thorin here."

The receiver crackled almost immediately. "Speidel here. Thorin, are you two all right?"

"Pretty much, Professor. Where are you?"

"I'm at the base. Jones is on his way now to your camp to check up on you. Why didn't you call in?"

"Professor, we've been having a sort of adventure. We couldn't shake free until just now. It's going to take us several hours to get out of here."

"Where are you?"

"Well, I guess you'd call it a network of tunnels and shafts. It used to be connected to Araqnia. Your lost city."

"*Araqnia?* Don't make jokes with me, young man."

"It is . . . it *was* Araqnia, Professor. Right now, I don't really care whether you believe me or not."

"Hmm. Can you make it back to your camp?"

"I think so."

"Meet Jones there. Give him a full report."

"Whatever you say."

14. Spacegrams

TX TO R SPEIDEL
CARE WOLFRAM MINING CORP
FERRIA
TRUSTEES REDUCING EXPEDITION BUDGET THIS SEASON AND NEXT. REGRET NO VACANCIES
INTERSTELLAR GEOGRAPHIC

The professor sat down in the canvas chair. He looked up at Zachary Stone. "You know what it says?"

"Yes. Sorry, Professor."

"Actually, they've got two digs next year. They think I'm too old. Seventy isn't so old."

"Professor, listen to me. A dig is no picnic. You could break a hip real easy."

"A man with fifty years in the field doesn't have silly accidents."

"And right now you have a cold. Your eyes are watering, your nasals are blocked. You're running a degree of fever. You ought to be in bed."

"I can't. I've just contacted the Thorins. They claim they've found something. And perhaps I believe them. Anyway, I have to get up to Sylva." He arose. "But first, a word to Geographic. Could I use your TX again?"

"Of course. Just give the message to the clerk."

The professor wrote it out quickly:

TX TO INTERSTELLAR GEOGRAPHIC
WASHINGTON, D.C.
HAVE A LEAD ON ARAQNIA. DOES THIS CHANGE ANYTHING?
SPEIDEL

As he returned down the path, Stone was waiting for him. "Can I do anything for you, Professor?"

"A couple of things."

"Say on."

"You once offered to lend us a blastovator. Perhaps facetiously?"

"I may have smiled. But it's yours. Just let us know when you want it, and for how long, so we can schedule our stripping operations."

"Can you get it up to Sylva for a couple of hours tomorrow? The Thorins talked about tunnels in the plateau. I'd like to cut through to one of them."

"No problem. We'll run it up on the ore freighter."

"This is a big help to me, Zachary. Perhaps it's just as well you got into mining."

"I was never much good at archeology."

"Not a popular career. Partly my fault. I don't inspire the kids. I see things. I see people moving in the past. But I don't know how to tell them, how to let them see."

"It's not everybody's bag, Professor."

"No. Suppose not. Do you know how many ark majors I have in this group?"

"How many?"

"Not one. I don't count Jones. He's a post-grad assistant. They're all in it for the summer outing and the snap credit."

"You can't blame them, Professor. My summer course with you in '57 was a real treasure. I met my wife there. Do they still have guitars and beer at midnight?"

"Yes, I think they do." The professor tapped his hat on firmly and blew his nose. "Damn cold. Can't throw 'em off the way I used to. The antivirals don't seem to work for me." He let out his breath slowly.

"You ought to try Arizona or New Mexico, Professor. Get out in the desert. Soak up the sun."

"You mean retire."

"Not necessarily. You could try some of the digs there. Cliff dwellers and such."

The professor shrugged. "I won't give up just yet. This lead on Araqnia will reopen the whole thing. Interstellar Geographic is going to change its mind."

"I hope you're right."

"When their offer comes in, could you TX it up to Sylva?"

"Sure, Professor."

"Well, then, I'd better get on up there."

15. The Cut to the Tunnel

With the aid of his orientor Thorin and the survey crew took bearings on the balcony-room corridor inside the hill. The great blastovator then moved up, zeroed in, and began chewing away at the hillside. They got through the overburden in a matter of seconds. The topsoil simply disappeared from in front of the machine and reappeared as a dust storm out of the mouth of the waste conduit two hundred meters down the hillside. The engineer turned on the water spray at the conduit mouth and the dust quickly turned to a dirty gray sludge. And now they hit bedrock. It was lava. The operator turned up the heat, and the water spray below them turned to steam as it hit the white-hot particles of rock spewing out of the waste tube below them.

As the shaft jabbed deeper into the hillside the 'vator moved slowly forward with it. Within a quarter of an hour the operator had shut the cab visor, turned on his air conditioning, and the great machine disappeared into the shaft, dragging the waste tube with it. Fifteen minutes later it backed out again.

The professor ran over. "Did you reach the corridor?"

"Yes. Some kind of tunnel. It dead-ended right inside there. Full of sticky stuff. You through with me now, Professor?"

"If you can wait another ten minutes, I would like Mr. Thorin to check. Make sure this is the right place."

"Lemme hose it down before you go in. It's still hot in there." He closed the visor and the 'vator rumbled forward once more. It disappeared into the shaft amid a cloud of steam, and reappeared a few minutes later.

"Well?" cried the professor.

"You can make it. But you'd better hold your breath while you're in the shaft, and you'd better run until you get into the far corridor."

"Fine. Thank you very much. You and the mining company have done the University a great service. Please express my gratitude to Mr. Stone."

"Sure, Professor." The machine coiled up the waste conduit, turned around, and lumbered off down the valley toward the waiting freighter.

"Well, I think we are ready," said the professor.

"Not quite," said Thorin.

"Why not?"

"Because of the webbing inside the corridor. I'll have to go in first to see if I can neutralize it with my power pack. And even though I may be successful at our entrance here, I'd like to take a cape and check the webbing throughout the entire length of the tunnel."

"Hmm. Yes. A good idea. Please proceed."

The instrumentalist pulled on his cape and entered the shaft. A few minutes later he was back. "All clear." He led the little party through the shaft.

The professor and Pompeii Jones were strangely silent as their handlights flickered over the stone walls of the corridor.

"Here is where I killed the Araqnid," said Thorin laconically. He pointed upward with his light to a great gap in the garlands of webbing. "I had the pistolet on 'high.' It vaporized him and melted the stone ceiling here. He was probably the last of his race."

The professor groaned. "A wanton needless act, Mr. Thorin. He would have been invaluable to us."

Thorin hesitated a moment, then turned around and faced the great man. "Professor Speidel, that is a very stupid remark. That thing nearly killed Coret and me. Now, watch the turn here."

The professor stared at him in amazement. Jones was horrified.

The savant cleared his throat. He said stiffly, "Well, I suppose you and Mrs. Thorin have had a rather trying experience. I can understand that you will need a little time to recover fully. So I am inclined to overlook—"

"The balcony room is straight ahead, and below," said Thorin shortly. "But before you get close to the balcony, there is a thing I have to do. So let me go on ahead."

"No more destruction, I hope," said the professor hurriedly.

"In a moment you can judge for yourself."

They entered the circular chamber.

"Beneath us is the dome room and the balcony," said Thorin. "I will drop this rope ladder down through the hole in the dome. Let me go first, and I will take a look around."

"Go ahead, but don't destroy anything," said the professor. "And, Jones, can you please call outside and tell the base where we are and what's going on."

"You can plug in to the nearest strand," said Thorin. "It's a good conductor and a good aerial."

Jones made immediate contact. He turned to the professor. "Sir, they've been trying to reach us. You have a TX relayed from Wolfram Mining."

"Ah, yes. From Interstellar Geographic?"

"Yes, sir."

"They changed their minds! They finally saw the light!"

Jones looked uncomfortable. "Could you step over here a moment, sir?" He led the professor down the corridor from Coret. "The message said, 'Good luck on Araqnia. Still can't use you.' "

"Ah."

"Sorry, sir."

"It's a disappointment, of course. Too bad, too bad. They were the last, you know, Jones."

"Yes, sir."

"I'm an old man. I'm . . . finished."

The assistant was silent.

Finally the professor asked, "Did you report our present location to the camp?"

"Not yet, sir."

"Tell them we're waiting to go down into some sort of room. With some sort of window."

"Yes, sir."

After a moment Thorin called up. "All clear. Come on down."

The three clambered down the ladder.

The professor looked about in wonder. "Just imagine! A scientific laboratory! Intact. With apparatus and library. And there of course is the balcony. I can hear the street noises. And there's a shadow passing. By the great god Thoth! A window on Araqnia!"

"The window was made by an Araqnid archeologist named Eroch," said Coret. "He built it in order to look out on ancient Araqnia as it existed three thousand years before his time. The Araqnid watchers of our year one thousand B.C., who had attained space travel, looked through that balcony, and saw their ancestors of four thousand B.C. in carts drawn by animals.

"But then, in one thousand B.C., they learned that a nearby volcano was about to erupt. They decided to emigrate. But before they could get away, the Death-One came. And he came to them through this window. He came to Araqnia from our year 2177."

"I must have a look!" cried the professor.

Thorin barred his way. "Just a minute, Professor."

"Stand aside, young man!"

"Not just yet. See that lens over the balcony?" Thorin let the beam of his handlight play on the TV barrel.

"Well, yes. So?"

"The Araqnids put it there deliberately. It is supposed to kill this thing they call the Death-One, so he won't go out on the balcony."

"But you stood here and it didn't kill you."

"True. And it was a stupid thing to do. But as it turned out, the lens rejected me."

"Well, do I look like this . . . whatever it is?"

"Not to me. But you might to them."

"Nonsense. I am going out on the balcony."

"You ought *not* to go out on the balcony. But in any case, before you even get near it, let me shoot out the lens."

"No! Wait—!"

Thorin aimed and fired. There was a tinkle of glass.

"Oh . . . oh . . ." moaned the professor.

"I think you *were* their Death-One, sir," said Coret. "I believe the comparator beam has been waiting for you for three thousand years. It was put there for the sole purpose of detecting you and then killing you, so that you would not go out on the balcony."

"I don't believe it! They never saw me before! And certainly I would not do them the slightest harm. Well, in any case, is it all clear now?"

"I think it is safe for you to stand in *front* of the balcony," said Thorin. He added firmly, "But I don't think you ought to go *out* out on it."

"And why not?"

"Two reasons. Number one, suppose it is a one-way time passage? If that is the case, you're out there in their world of one thousand B.C. and you couldn't get back in here to 2177. Number two, suppose they grab you while you are standing there admiring the view?"

"Young man, why do you force this humiliation on me? Must I plead with you? Don't you realize what has happened? No one will hire me. I've been kicked out of archeology. It doesn't matter what happens out there. It doesn't matter whether I can get back."

"Sorry, professor. I can't let you risk it."

"I'm going out there, Thorin."

"No, you are not, Professor."

16. The Window

Several things happened very suddenly.

The professor dashed for the balcony. Thorin made a flying leap and grabbed him by his left foot. He had him! But now Jones jumped into the melee. Jones grabbed at Thorin's arms. The professor's leg was free. The great man struggled to his feet, flushed, panting, and very angry. "How dare you!" he shouted at the instrumentalist.

"Professor . . ." ventured Thorin. But Jones stepped between them.

Coret spoke up. "Let him go." She held the pistolet loosely, not aiming at anyone in particular. But she was speaking to her husband.

Thorin stared at the weapon incredulously. "Coret . . . but why?"

The professor dusted off his jacket and without a backward glance stepped out on the balcony.

They watched him in awed silence as he leaned over the railing and looked up and down the vista. He interrupted his inspection a couple of times to cough and sneeze. Finally he pulled out his handkerchief and blew his nose with enthusiasm and turned to re-enter the room.

But it was as though be had run into a glass wall. He stepped back, shrugged his shoulders, waved toward them, then turned outward again.

"Coret . . . I tried to tell him," whispered Thorin.

They watched in horror.

"You mean, it really is one-way," said Jones hoarsely.

"Yes, it really is," said Thorin grimly.

In that moment a great shadow filled the balcony. The professor stepped back in hasty reflex. A group of furry things, each carrying a spidery creature on his shoulders, swarmed down an exit ramp out of the hovering airship, and then they hauled the professor back into the ship with them. The professor turned, got one arm free, and waved farewell. They caught wisps of his voice. When last seen, he was evidently trying to explain something to his captors. Then the airship vanished.

"They got him." gurgled Jones. "They took him away."

"Just what he wanted, wasn't it?" said Thorin. He looked over at Coret. He held out his hand and she gave him the pistolet. It was on 'stun.' "I think perhaps you would have shot me if I hadn't let him go on through. Why?"

"It is as I said. He was the Death-One . . . the monster they dreaded. When he walked through, onto the balcony, he carried with him the disease that destroyed them."

"I thought he only had a cold."

"He did. But to them it was the black death. It killed their mounts—the Llanoans. And lacking mounts, they died. They couldn't eat, they couldn't drink."

"But even assuming his cold is what did it, why would you want to let him destroy them?"

"Don't you see, dear? Those four hundred heaps of iron oxide out on the launch pad are what is left of four hundred colonizing ships. The creature told me. If nothing had stopped them, they would have landed in the Nile Valley about one thousand B.C. *Homo sapiens* wouldn't have had a chance. We wouldn't be here today talking about it."

He looked at her wide-eyed. She was right, of course. "But why did they go to all this trouble, leaving behind guardians of the window, and all that? Why not just turn off the time-stream?"

"They didn't know how. Eroch, the builder, was among the first to die. And since the professor came to them from three thousand years in their future, they knew they'd have to stop him—three thousand years in their future. Which for us is right now, this instant. Which meant they'd have to set up the comparator beam *then*, to kill the professor *now*. And they'd need a series of guardians—the Keepers—to see that the system was not disturbed for that three thousand years. It was remarkable that they got all this put together in the little time remaining to them. It was their bitter ironic paradox that their very efforts to destroy their Death-One served to preserve him."

"All right," said Thorin. "The professor is gone. I think we must count him missing in action, possibly dead in the line of duty. And I don't see anything we can do about it." He flicked an inquiring glance over at Jones. "Pom-pom, I don't suppose you would want to go out there and look for him?"

"Not me."

"Then I think all we can do is notify the Interstellar Police and the University and any next of kin, and see if they have any recommendations. Meanwhile, I suggest that we call in the other teams and see how much of this stuff we can haul out of here."

17. A Memorial

Some ten days later, as they were packing the last of the books in the balcony room, Coret called out from the wooden scaffolding they had placed in front of the balcony. "Something is happening out there!"

Thorin came running. "There hasn't been any motion out there for three or four days. What is it?"

"Something is falling in the streets. Not rain. Hail . . . ?"

Jones said uneasily, "That's ashes and lapilli. A volcano is erupting somewhere near here."

"You mean, has already erupted," said Thorin. "Remember, we are looking at something that happened three thousand years ago."

"Wow! Look at that . . ."

"Volcanic bombs," said Jones. "Globs of molten pumice as big as your head."

"And those flashes of light!" cried Coret. "What's happening?"

"It's lightning—from the volcano," said Jones.

"So that's what finished them," said Thorin. "The volcano."

They looked at each other in shocked silence.

"The professor . . . ?" whispered Coret.

"He dies a hero," said Jones.

"Died," said Thorin. "Out there, it's one thousand B.C."

The room began to vibrate.

"I think we have caught a molten flow," said Jones. "It's filling the streets."

"How high can it get?" asked Thorin.

"I don't know. Vesuvius covered Herculaneum to a depth of over ten meters. But lava flows several miles deep are not uncommon."

"I think we had better get out of here," said Coret.

"But all this took place thirty centuries ago," said Thorin. "Here we are in the twenty-second century. It can't touch us."

"Just the same, I think we'd better get out. The window might not hold."

The room began to rumble.

Jones pointed at the balcony. His voice shook. "White-hot! And it's already filled up the street." He dropped his books on the floor and started up the ladder.

The others looked at Thorin. "We can come back tomorrow," said Coret. "If there's anything to come back to."

"Yes. Everybody grab whatever you can carry. Let's go. Women first." He picked up the volumes that Jones had dropped and brought up the rear of the group.

Outside, they dropped their loads on the tarpaulins spread out on the ground and turned back to listen.

Thorin moved over to Coret. "That's why no trace of Araqnia had ever been found here before now. The lava must have covered the city completely."

Coret put a finger to her lips. "Listen!"

They looked up at the entrance to the shaft. The sound began as a barely audible rumble. And then it grew louder, and became a continuing muffled thunder. A cloud of dust swirled out of the tunnel mouth.

Looking back every other step, the group edged uneasily down the slope.

And then the rumble died away.

"I think the window collapsed," said Thorin. He looked at Jones inquiringly.

The other shrugged his shoulders. "Very likely. Perhaps the combination of several thousands of pounds pressure and the white heat were too much for it."

"But why did the lava stop?"

"It probably filled up the room, ran along the corridor for a hundred meters or so, and then it cooled down enough to form a plug."

"The window is gone?"

"Gone," said Jones.

"So this is all we will ever have . . ." Thorin waved his hand at the books and boxes. "Even so, enough for a thesis for all of us."

Jones turned his face away. "Don't expect me to do it."

"But you're the only ark in the group."

"I don't care. And anyway, I'm getting out of ark. A fellow could get hurt in this business. I'm transferring to classical languages."

"All right, Pom-pom. Anybody else? Lots of stuff here. We really ought to do something with it. We owe it to the professor."

They all shook their heads. "I'm in stage design," said one. Another: "I'm phys. ed. I just did this for the easy credit." A third, "This fall, I'm overloaded with Englit."

Thorin lifted his hands in a hapless gesture. "All right, all right. Of the whole bunch here, I'm the one least qualified. But somebody has got to do it. We can't let the professor walk out for nothing. So I'll do it, even if I have to switch my major from instrumentation."

"I can help," said Coret.

"Yeah," said Thorin. "I mean, I really can. I can read Araqnid. I got it from the creature—from Number Ten. You and I can completely reconstruct life in Araqnia. The books tell their technology. Their space drive. It's beyond nuclear: it's an anti-grav system."

"Well, what do you know. Anyone want to join us?" he asked. "Any science majors here? Phys? Chem? Engineering? Instrumentation? Anyone for fame, fortune, and maybe an A+?"

Silence.

"It's all yours," said Jones. "And you've certainly earned it."

"So be it. Well, one last thing. Any art majors here?"

A lone arm thrust up reluctantly.

"We want a memorial for the professor," said Thorin. "See if you can create a design, maybe with a couple of Araqnids in the borders."

"Where's this going to be, and how big?"

"In the rock by the corridor excavation. Let's have a big one, say three meters on a side. We can burn it out with my pistolet."

"What words go on it?"

"Don't really know. But it ought to say something important. Like,

DOCTOR REITER SPEIDEL, ARAQNIA, 2177."

"The Council of Universities would certainly ennoble him," said Coret.

"Yeah. Make that Baron Doctor."

"Anything else?"

Thorin thought of the professor spreading germs in the sacred Araqnid air. "Yeah, add a kind of motto, maybe in small print: 'Archeology is a process of destruction.'"

Summer Solstice

1. The Ship Is Hit

Even as the sleeper lid rose, Khor could see the console lights flashing and could hear the intermittent buzzer.

The break-sleep alarm. Very often the last sound some spacemen ever heard. His blood pressure began to mount. He wasn't even completely awake, and his body was doing this to him. He shuddered. He would not see home again. Never again the stern Zoology Supervisor. ("What, Khor, *still* no featherless biped?") and Queva . . . she had taken the sleep, to wait for him. Beloved Queva. She had given him the key to her casket. "You alone will open. Else I sleep forever." No, Queva, no, no, no . . . I may never return. But she had done it. The female mind . . . beyond all comprehension. Well, my friend, what now?)

He deciphered the alarm code mentally as he clambered up from the cushions: the hydraulic system had been hit, aft. Bad, bad. He had a dreadful premonition of what he would find. Get to it. Know the worst.

He ran a finger around his helmet seal, brushing his scapular feathers. Still air-tight. Next he sat on the side of the casket and wondered whether he should remove his helmet. He decided to leave it on. At least for the moment he wouldn't have to make any decisions about cabin pressure and oxygen.

The alarms—all of them—had now become impatient with him. They had moved from console and wall and had invaded his guts and brain like barbed parasites. "Xeris and Mord," he groaned.

He reached for his heat-suit and simultaneously glanced at the ceiling meter. How long had he been under? Forty cycles. Long time. He closed the suit up and clumped over to the console. First turn off that *pflicht* alarm. Now back to the tail of the ship.

Air pressure apparently holding. Which meant the hole in the ship wall self-sealed in good order. The missile—a meteorite?—couldn't have been too big. So why hadn't internal automatic repair handled the problem? As he rounded the passage, the answer literally hit him in the face. A jet of oil struck his visor. The pin hackles on his neck and face stood out in panic. By reflex his hands grabbed the valve wheel and extinguished the flow. He wiped his visor with his sleeve. "By the egg that bore me!" He felt sick. How much fluid had he lost? From the looks of the balls of glop floating weightlessly around him, at least half. How was it possible? Not just one leak? He played the inspection light along the piping array. The whole tubular system was dripping. Some of the holes were big enough to see. Others were microscopic, hiding behind tiny globules of fluid. The meteorite had evidently struck a brittle section of the ship wall, which then had imploded into a thousand high-velocity fragments. He had warned Maintenance last time in. The skin was fatiguing. The chief mechanic had laughed at him.

He sighed and looked around. Oil everywhere. Mocking clusters. All sizes.

Where could he find make-up fluid in this Zaforsaken comer of the galaxy? And repair-tape? He'd used the last of his tape on the solar batteries . . . how many cycles ago?

"Khor," he muttered gloomily, "you sorry misbegotten space scavenger, you are in serious trouble." He'd have to land. Very funny. (You had to have a sense of humor for these collection missions.) To land, he'd have to find a planet. And not just any planet. One with a civilization sufficiently advanced to supply his needs.

He shuffled back through the collection area, toward the control room. He passed the cage with the ten-legged carnivorous reptile, now quietly sleeping its drugged sleep in the corner. Past the telepathic tree that had tried to charm him into its gluey branches as its next meal. Past the floating head-size ball of fluff that seemed to have no mouth, no food, and no alimentary system, but which had doubled in size since he had first captured it on Sargus-VI. And finally the empty cage: "Featherless biped." Where in the name of Xippor the Remorseless was he to find such an unlikely specimen? You can at least try, the Supervisor had admonished him. There are a lot of unexplored planets out there.

And so to the pilot-console, where he activated the chart screen. Nearest star . . . there we are. Yellow, medium size. Third generation. Has all ninety-two elements. How about planets? Big one. Too big. And too far out. Also that one with the gorgeous ring. No. The red one? No air. Next. There's one . . . plenty of water, probably good air. Life? Maybe. Civilization? Maybe. Go on. Two more. Both too hot. Back up to III. No choice, really. I'm going in.

2. Ne-tiy Introspects

Ne-tiy knelt and stared into the mirroring surface of the lotus-pool. She liked what she saw: a young woman of excellent figure, with a face possibly bordering on the beautiful. That figure was sheathed in the classic linen tube, failing almost to her sandals, and supported by broad shoulder straps covering her breasts.

She touched her cheeks just below the eyes. There was a certain sadness about her eyes. She would like to use a little kohl at the corners for cheerful emphasis, and perhaps a little red iron oxide to highlight her cheeks, but her owner, the great priest, had strictly forbidden it. "You live for one thing, and that is not to adorn yourself." And what was that one thing? If and when the priest gave the signal, she was to offer the poisoned wine to a certain person.

She tried hard not to think about it. But it was no use. She could think of nothing else.

The priest, who served only the sun-god Horus, had bought her in the slave market at On, ten years ago. Her parents had been imprisoned for debt, and she had been turned over to the temple of the cat goddess, Bast. And then things had become blurred. She remembered she had cried a lot. Things had been done to her. In the end she knew only fear, hate, and that she was going to endure.

And then the great inquisitor priest, Hor-ent-yotf, had bought her, and had taught her certain skills." You will enter the house of the Librarian," he had said. "You will listen to all that he does and says."

"Why, my lord?"

"Why is not your concern."

But she knew why. Hor-ent-yotf (the name meant avenger of the father of Horus) was licensed by the Greek pharaoh to sniff out heresy and impiety in the low and the high. Especially in the high, for they were the most influential. Anything demeaning the sun-god Horus was suspect. The penalty was death. She shivered.

If she were called upon to kill Eratosthenes, what would she do?

For six months she had lived as a trusted servant in his house. He knew horses, and had taught her. She had driven his chariot. He liked that. His family raised thoroughbreds, back in Cyrene, where the pasturage was rich and blue-green. When she drove with him, her body rubbed against his within the light wicker framework of the vehicle. Something had awakened within her. And now it had come to this: to be near him was torture, and not to be near him was worse.

She stared down into the pool and passed her fingertips slowly over her abdomen. "How can I ever bear his child? He doesn't know I exist. I need to be rich. I need exalted office. High priestess of some god or other. But it is hopeless, for I am nothing, and I will remain nothing."

A shadow fell on the water. She arose and turned slowly, impassively, head bowed. She did not need to look up. She saw without seeing: the shaven bald pate, eyes lengthened by dark cosmetics, the thin pleated linen skirt with cape, the leopard skin, complete with claws, tail, and fanged, glaring head. His hands hung at his sides. Her eyes rested on his long fingernails.

On his right hand he wore three deaths, shaped as rings, each with its tiny jeweled capsule. First was the copper ring, which had a capsule shaped as Set, the god of darkness. On the middle finger was the silver ring, bearing the face of the evil goddess Sekhmet, who slew Osiris. Finally was the gold ring, on his fourth finger. Its capsule was a sardonic bow to the Greek conquerors, for it bore the face of their god Charon, who ferried their dead across the River Styx to Hades.

The faint north wind moved a sharp blanket of incense around her face. She realized that it had been the smell that had announced him.

"Where is he?" said Hor-ent-yotf.

"He has gone forth into the streets, my lord."

"When does he return?"

"In the afternoon."

"I have reason to think he has found the directions for the tomb of the heretic pharaoh Tut-ankh-amun. Has he mentioned this?"

"No, my lord."

"Be watchful."

"Yes, my lord."

"There is another matter. In a secluded courtyard at the Library he is making a measurement of the disc of Horus. Listen carefully. Let me know if he says anything about it."

"As my lord wishes." She listened to the sandals crunching away down the pea-gravel path. Then she turned back to the pool, as though trying to hide in the beauty of the flowered rim. The Greeks had brought strange and beautiful flowers to Alexandria: asphodels, marigolds, a tiny claret-colored vetch, irises purple and deep blue. Purple and white anemones, scarlet poppies.

She wished she were a simple, mindless blossom, required only to be beautiful.

Ah, Hor-ent-yotf, great Avenger, thou demi-god, I know you well. Your mother was impregnated by the ka of Horus the hawk-god, divine bearer of the sun disc. Flights of golden hawk whirred over your house at your birth, calling and whistling to you. So it was said. As a boy apprentice in the temple at Thebes, you saw the glowing god descend from the sun, and he spoke to you. Avenge me, the god said. Find the tomb of Tut-ankh-amun, who married the third daughter of the heretic pharaoh Ikhnaton, who denied me. Destroy that tomb, and all that is within.

So it was said.

She shivered again.

3. Rabbi Ben Shem

Eratosthenes had been wandering the streets for an hour, vaguely aware of the sights, sounds, and smells of Alexandria at high noon.

The Brucheum, the royal quarter of the great city, was totally Greek, as Greek as Athens, or Corinth, or even far Cyrene, where he was born. As thoroughly Greek as the great Alexander had intended, when he strode about this shore opposite the Isle of Pharos, a bare eighty years ago, and said: build the walls here, the temples there, yonder the theatre, gymnasium, baths. . . . The mole, the Heptastadia, was built from the city out to the island, dividing the sea into two great harbors. Ptolemy Philadelphus kept his warships in the eastern harbor. Commercial shipping used the western harbor.

Alexandria, the greatest city in the world, the Gem of the Nile, the Pearl of the Mediterranean, was indeed Greek. But more than Greek. All races lived here. Egyptians, of course. And Jews, Nubians, Syrians, Persians, Romans, Carthaginians. (Those last two were quite civil to each other here in the city, though several thousand stadia to the west their countrymen were happily slaughtering each other on Sicily and adjacent seas.)

He was passing now through the northeast sector, along the Street of the Hebrews. The Jews had a specially elegant quarter, a politeumata set aside for them by Alexander himself, in gratitude for their help in his Persian campaigns.

"Greetings."

He looked up. Was someone calling to him? Yes, there was the rabbi, Elisha ben Shem, coming down the steps of the synagogue. "Greetings, noble Eratosthenes!"

The geometer-librarian bowed graciously. "Peace to the House of Shem! How goes the translation?"

"Oh, very well indeed." The priest stroked his flowing silver beard and chuckled. "Why I laugh, I do not know. It really isn't funny."

Eratosthenes looked doubtful. "Well, then . . . ?"

Ben Shem grinned. "You have to be Jewish to see it, my friend. You and I converse in Greek, the tongue of the Hellenes. I am also fluent in classical Hebrew, in which our Holy Scriptures were written. I can also speak Aramaic and the other local dialects of Judea. But did you know there are forty thousand Jews here in Alexandria who speak, read, and write Greek and only Greek? They can't read a word of the Books of Moses, and the Psalms of David are mysteries to them."

"I knew that," said the man of measures. "That's why Ptolemy brought seventy scholars from Jerusalem here to translate the Hebrew texts into Greek. Seventy. The Septuagint. Actually, seventy-two, wasn't it?"

Ben Shem sighed. "Ah, Eratosthenes, my dear boy. So learned. So earnest. But think of it! Jews translating Hebrew into Greek for Jews. Where is the subtle sense of irony, the love of paradox, that set your ancestors apart from peasant minds? If you had your way, Achilles would overtake Zeno's hare with a single pulse beat."

"Rabbi . . ."

"Oh, never mind." He turned his head a little. "You are still attempting to determine the size and shape of the Earth?"

"Yes, still at it."

"Are you close to a solution?"

"Now, Rabbi. You know I must report all findings first to His Majesty."

"Yes, of course." He cleared his throat. "You will be at the palace tonight? To celebrate the coming of the Nile flood?" They stopped before the residence of the priest.

"I'll be there," said Eratosthenes.

4. The Stone Cutter

He crossed the great intersection at the magnificent mausolea. Here Alexander was laid to rest, in a marvelous glass-and-gold coffin. And in the tomb adjacent, the first Ptolemy. Beyond, to the west, lay the Rhacotis, originally the haunt of fishermen and pirates. Now, however, eighty years after the Conqueror had paced out the unborn city, it was full of the run-down shops and abodes of artisans, poets (mostly starving), and astrologers, raffish theatres, baths (some clean), slums, and certain facilities for sailors.

And so into the Street of Stone Cutters, and the first shop on the corner. He could hear the strike of chisels well before he entered the work yard. In the center, four slaves stripped to loin cloths chipped away at a copy of the Cnidus Aphrodite. The assistant project master hovered about the crew anxiously, calling, coaxing, occasionally screaming. They all ignored the newcomer. Eratosthenes shrugged and passed on into the shop. Little bells rang somewhere and the man behind the counter looked up, squinting and coughing. Stone dust had long ago impaired his eyes and lungs. "Ah, Eratosthenes," he muttered, rising. "Greetings, and welcome to my humble shop." He groaned softly as he tried to bow.

"And greetings to you, good Praphicles. I trust the gods are kind?"

"Alas, great geometer, business is terrible. When our present commissions are completed I expect that we shall starve."

The visitor smiled. Business was always terrible and starvation always lay in wait for the old fraud. Even in his semi-blindness Praphicles was still the most highly skilled of stone workers in the quarter. He turned away clients, and he owned half the real estate on the waterfront.

"Well, then," said Eratothenes drily, "before the gods utterly abandon you, perhaps we had better conclude our business."

"Ah, yes." The ancient master reached down into a cupboard under the counter, pulled out the work, and laid it carefully on the cedar surface.

It was a statuette of the Titan Atlas, bent, with arms arched backwards and up, as though already holding his great burden, Earth. It was cut from the famous red granite of Syene. The base held an inscription in Greek, which Eratosthenes verified by reading slowly to himself.

The old sculptor's eyes never left him.

"It is beautiful," said the visitor. "The years have not dimmed your hands, old friend. Your fingers grow even more skillful, if that is possible." He pulled a purse from his cloak and dropped it to the counter. "The balance."

Praphicles made no move toward the little leather bag. He said, "The commission was interesting, especially in what was *not* commissioned."

"You don't make sense."

"The Earth that Atlas will hold . . . where is it? Who will supply it?"

"I'll attend to that."

"And what shape will it be? He is positioned to hold a disc, or a cylinder, or a square. Or perhaps even a sphere."

Eratosthenes smiled. "How are the wagers running, good Praphicles?"

"Two to one that you will report to His Majesty the Earth is shaped like a disc. Even odds for a cylinder. Three to one against a square. Ten to one against a sphere." He pushed the bag of staters back to Eratosthenes. "Just give me a hint," he whispered. "And keep your purse."

The geometer chuckled, pushed the money back, and picked up the little statue. "I will pray to the gods to save your business, old friend."

Out again. Still walking west, and getting closer to the Eunostos harbor.

5. The Horoscope

He thought of one of the great Periclean speeches, as recalled (and probably polished up a bit) by Thucydides.

"Each single one of our citizens, in all the manifold aspects of life, is able to show himself the rightful lord and owner of his own person, and do this, moreover, with exceptional grace and exceptional versatility."

Well, Pericles, perhaps that was the way it was with you and your Athenians, but that's not the way with me. When my career—nay, my very skin!—is at risk, I feel neither grace nor versatility. I feel afraid. For I have a fair idea already how my calculations are going to come out. When I make my report, a great many people will be very, very upset. Hor-ent-yotf had warned me not to make any measurements whatever involving the sun. "It is heresy," the priest had said. "Not even a Greek under royal protection may break our religious laws with impunity."

So why am I here, in this street, at this hour? I know very well why.

But I mustn't show my anxiety. What would Marcar think? He and I studied together under the Stoic Ariston, in Athens. After that, we went our separate ways. But now here we are again in Alexandria.

Ah, Marcar, thou man of Mesopotamia, part mystic, part mountebank. Which part dominates? No matter. We have always been able to talk together.

And now it was time to be careful. Not against robbers or pickpockets. That wasn't the problem at all. The problem was simply this: he was now in the Street of the Mathematici Chaldaei, and he would just as soon not be recognized. What would the good rabbi say if he saw the highly rational geometer walking into the shop of an astrologer? The holy man would indeed have his cherished laugh!

Eratosthenes pulled his cloak up around his face and began walking in an anonymous shuffle. He was barely halfway down the street when small dirty urchins began tugging at his tunic. "My lord! Beautiful pictures! Naked ladies! All different positions! Mine are best! Painted directly from Ptolemy's harem. No! Straight from Eratosthenes' secret scrolls at the Library! No pictures! Real live women! No waiting! Cheap! My virgin mother! Only twenty drachmas!"

By Zeus and Hera! He struck out at them, but they scattered nimbly, like a flock of water birds.

A strong hand grabbed his sleeve. "In here, you old lecher!"

"Marcar!" He stepped into the antecourt and his host slammed the great door behind them. "Thanks, old fellow. I was coming to see you, anyhow."

"I know." He motioned to the table and chairs.

"You always say that. Actually, you hadn't the faintest idea I would visit you today."

"Maybe not today, exactly. But soon. You say you don't believe in the stars, august Eratosthenes; yet you come here because you are not completely sure. You are curious." He poured two goblets of Persian wine. "So what do you want of me?"

"Nothing. Everything."

The astrologer smiled faintly. "Translating: Does your horoscope predict anything horrible in your immediate future?"

The geometer gave him a hard look. "Well?"

"But the answer would be meaningless to you, friend, because you do not believe in astrology, or horoscopes, or star-fates."

Eratosthenes sighed. "You're right, you know. I can't have it both ways. I can't denounce horoscopes in one breath and ask for mine in the next. But it's always good to see you, Marcar." He started to rise.

The Chaldean waved him back down. "Not so fast. Tarry a bit. Who requires total belief, old friend? Not I. And what is belief, anyway? A curious mix of tradition, garbled facts, superstition, prejudice—and once in a great while, perhaps a little truth thrown in to thoroughly confuse the picture." He sipped at his cup. "Let us clear the air. I suspected you might come. So this morning I constructed your horoscope."

The Greek looked across the table in surprise, but was silent.

"You might at least ask," said Marcar. "You owe me that much."

The librarian smiled. "I ask."

"Well, then. At the outset, please understand that a horoscope makes no absolute predictions, at least of the type you are thinking about. No chart will ever say to you, Eratosthenes, you will die at sunup tomorrow. At most your chart will say, Eratosthenes, you will be presented with the *possibility* of dying on such and such a day, and perhaps at such and such an hour."

"Go on," said his visitor quietly.

The Mesopotamian shrugged. "You have given the gods much trouble in recent days, and I think that even now the matter is not fully decided. I see Gaea, the Earth goddess. You would strip her naked. You would say, her size and shape are thus and so. I see Cronos, the god of time. You would have lovely naked Gaea turning, turning, turning under the lascivious scrutiny of Cronos. Apollo stands still in the skies, and leers."

Eratosthenes laughed. "What a marvelous way of saying the Earth rotates and moves around the sun."

"Ah yes. The heliocentric hypothesis. But that's only part of the difficulty. The scientific pros and cons are quite beyond me, my esteemed colleague. All I can say is, that's the problem that brings the risk. May I be blunt?"

"It would be most refreshing."

"The wrong answer to your present geodetic research may well get you assassinated."

"By Ptolemy?"

"I don't read pharaoh . . . I see a woman . . . young, beautiful, dedicated."

"So you know about Ne-tiy. Placed in my house by the Horus-priest, Hor-ent-yotf."

"Everyone knows. The female cobra within the flower basket. Why don't you get rid of her?"

"Nonsense. He'd find someone else. Meanwhile, she's where I can keep an eye on her."

Marcar shrugged. "That's up to you, of course. But the risk to your life is not the only matter of significance. There's another thing."

"Oh?"

"You will have a visitor. A most remarkable visitor, from a place far away. I am tempted to say he is a god, but I know how you feel about the gods. Like you, Eratosthenes, he faces a great trouble. But you can help him, and he can help you."

The mathematician chuckled. "Now *that,* friend from the marshes, *is* a prediction. Years away, of course. It's always safe to predict things that happen ten years from now."

Marcar smiled. "According to the signs, he arrives on the first day of the New Year."

"There you go again. *Which* New Year? The New Year when Sirius is first seen in the dawn skies, announcing that the Nile will begin its rise? In fact, tomorrow, in the hour before sunrise? Or do you mean the New Year of the current Egyptian calendar, the first day of Thoth, which is actually two hundred days away? I remind you that the Egyptian calendar is based on 365 days, not 365 and a quarter, as shown by the stars, and that it loses one full year every 1,460 years. The last time the calendar was right was 1,171 years ago. It won't be right again until 289 years from now. So—*which* New Year, most noble charlatan?"

Marcar's eyes gleamed. "Your sign is Cancer. And however you calculate it, O great geometer, Cancer begins at midnight tonight, and announces the first day of the summer solstice. In the dark morning skies Sirius will indeed be seen, heralding the New Year, and the awakening of Hapi, which you Greeks call the Nile, with great festivities beginning in all towns and villages the entire length of the river, and continuing for twenty-one days, with carousing, merriment, and consumption of seas of barley beer."

Eratosthenes laughed heartily. "I take it, most astute astrologer, that buried in that Rhea-flood of rhetoric is an assertion that my relevant New Year is within the small hours of tomorrow morning, beginning with Sirius ascendant?"

"Thou seest all, wise Eratosthenes."

"I see that you are a fraud, more colossal than any pyramid at Gizeh."

"My lord overwhelms me with his flattery." He leaned forward. "Now that your stomach is weak with laughter and your defenses breached, may we talk of your sun-project?"

"It's a bit premature."

"In any case, presumably you have by now determined the shape of the Earth? Perhaps you could tell an old friend?"

"My report goes first to Ptolemy. You know that."

"Of course, of course. Nevertheless, what harm is a hint . . . in strictest confidence?"

The mapmaker grinned. "I hear the odds are disc, two to one; cylinder, even; three to one against a square; and ten to one against a sphere." He rose to leave. "Later, Marcar. Later. I promise."

"If you live," whispered the astrologer.

The visitor stopped. He turned around slowly. "Have you drawn the horoscope of Hor-ent-yotf?" It was a stab in the dark, a flash—of what? Psychic insight? Stupidity?

Marcar peered at him most strangely. Finally he said, "Why do you ask?" "Never mind. Really none of my affair." But he knew. The astrologer had lifted the veil on the sinister Egyptian, and he had not understood what he had seen. It was pointless to press the seer further. One thing was certain: the fates of Eratosthenes and Hor-ent-yotf were inextricably interwoven, like designs into a funerary shroud.

He bowed and left.

6. The Shadow

And so home again, away from smells and noises and dirty streets. Eratosthenes nodded to the gatekeeper and walked up the palm-lined entrance toward the central gardens. He paused under the colonnade and looked out toward the focus of the courtyard. There, as he had ordered, the scribe Bes-lek sat cross-legged in front of the shadow cast by the man-high gnomon, and he was chanting. Bes-lek had selected his own chant, a hymn, really, something addressed to Horus the sun god, a recital not too long, not too short. As the Greek watched, the clerk finished his mumbled litany, dipped his reed pen into the little pot of charcoal ink, and made a tiny dot at the tip of the gnomon shadow on the circular stone flagging. Then he commenced again. "Horus, giver of light, son of Osiris and Isis, shine down upon us in thy journey across the sky . . ." It was in Egyptian, and between the foreignness of the language and the garbled maundering, the sense was largely lost on the librarian.

Eratosthenes walked up the gravel path toward the chanter. Bes looked up and saw him coming, but his droning mumble did not waver. The geometer looked down at the white flagging with critical eye. Bes sat just outside a concave curve of dots. He had begun about an hour before noon, and now it was about an hour after noon. The dots showed longer shadows at the beginning, growing shorter as noon approached, then growing longer again as midday was passed. The dot closest to the gnomon base would be the one for noon. That was the one to measure. "Bes," he said, "my faithful friend, I can see from the marks that you have made a fine record of the god's overhead course. The matter is complete, except for measuring the noon angle. Get up now, stretch your legs, and then help me with the angle rod."

"Aye, thank you, master." The little man groaned with great eloquence as he struggled to his feet. "Such strain, such care. My poor joints. I shall ache for days. For the pain, perhaps my lord could allot two extra puncheons of fine barley beer."

"Two?"

"One for my wife. The dear creature assumes all my pains. And considering that the festivities begin tonight."

"Two, then. Tell the steward. But first, hold the angle rod. Put the point on that inner dot, the one closest to the gnomon. Yes, that's it. Steady, while I rest the upper edge on the top of the gnomon. Fine, fine. A good angle. Now, let me take the precise measurement on the protractor arc. Yes. Seven degrees, twelve minutes. I'll take the rod."

"Is it done, master?"

"One more measurement. I need to know the distance of the dot to the base of the gnomon." He placed the rod at the base of the gnomon and alongside the noon dot. "Hm. Check me here, Bes. What number do *you* read?"

The scrivener squinted. "It is one and a quarter units, and yet it is a generous quarter."

"We'll call it one and a quarter." He doesn't ask why, thought Eratosthenes. He doesn't wonder. He doesn't care. Not one hoot of the owl of Athena in Hades. He gets his daily bread, with an occasional extra ration of beer. He has his gods and his feast-days, and he's happy. A true son of the Nile. Well, why not? It seems to work for him. He said, "Tell the guard of the kitchen I said to give you *three* puncheons of good brown khes, suitable for Ptolemy's own table. One for you, one for your wife, and one to lay on the altar of Horus, the hawk-god of the sun, who has favored us today."

Bes bowed low. "The master overwhelms me."

He's not even being sarcastic, thought Eratosthenes. "Go," he said.

And now back to the calculations. The gnomon was ten units high. The leg measurement was one and a quarter. The tangent of the sun angle was therefore one hundred and twenty-five thousandths. What was the angle? It ought to check out pretty close to seven degrees, twelve minutes. He had trigonometric tables in the library that would give the value. Check. Confirm. Re-check. Pile up the data. It's the only safe way.

Why was he doing this? Who cared whether the Earth was a globe? Who cared what size that globe might be? Not Ptolemy Philadelphus, his lord and master, the pharaoh-god, who had brought him here to run the great library. In fact, Ptolemy had made veiled references to temple pressures. Hor-ent-yotf, the high priest of Horus, was complaining that these studies were demeaning to the hawk-deity and might even foreshadow a revival of monotheism, as attempted by Ikhnaton a thousand years ago. *That* misguided pharaoh had proclaimed, "There is but one god, and he is Aton, the sun. Pull down all other temples." The crazed pharaoh had been slain and his name obliterated from all monuments. Over the years the tombs of all his descendants, direct and collateral, had been searched out and desecrated.

All except one, mused the geometer. The boy pharaoh, who married the third daughter of the heretic. The youth had been assassinated, of course, and then properly and secretly buried, along with suitable treasures, in a hillside in the necropolis at Thebes. However, before the Aton-haters could find the grave, the tomb of the fourth Rameses was dug in the cliffside just above, and the boy-king's grave was buried under the quarry chips. Eratosthenes had seen the maps and read the reports, and then he had hidden them away.

And why was he thinking of the tomb of Tut-ankh-amun? Because it was knowledge that might save his life.

He passed on into the building and walked through silent halls into the mathematics room. Here he found the scroll of trig tables and ran his finger down the tangent columns. The angle whose tan is one hundred twenty-five thousandths, here we are. Seven degrees, seven and one-half minutes. I was looking for seven degrees, twelve minutes. Well, not bad. Within experimental error? And how good are these tables? Some day soon, redo the whole thing. Suppose I take the average. Call it seven degrees, ten minutes, or almost exactly 1/50 of a circle. Baseline, Syene to Alexandria, 5,000 stadia. So if the Earth is a sphere, 5,000 stadia is 1/50 of its circumference, which is, therefore, 250,000 stadia.

Two hundred and fifty thousand stadia.

That's what the numbers said. But was it really so? Such immensity was inconceivable.

He rubbed his chin in perplexity as he walked over to the big table where his map was spread out. His greatest work. Ptolemy himself had praised it, and had accorded the ultimate flattery of reproducing the map in mosaic in the floor of his study. Copyists were turning out duplicates at the rate of one every two weeks, and probably making all sorts of errors in their haste. For which he, the author, would be blamed, of course.

He bent over the sheet.

It had been a magnificent effort, drawn mostly from documents in the library: travelers' reports (especially Herodotus'); terse military accounts; letters; local descriptions; sea captains' logs; census and tax reports. To the west, it showed the Pillars of Hercules; and even beyond that, Cassiterides, the tin-islands discovered by Himilco the Phoenician. To the east, Persia, conquered by Alexander, and on to India and the Ganges River. And beyond *that* a mythic land, Seres, where a fine fabric called silk was woven. Then the legend isles of Cipangu (which he didn't even show). But the whole known world, from west to east, was at most 75,000 stadia—less than one-third of the sphere he had just calculated.

And yet he knew his numbers were right.

There was more to the world than he or anyone else had dreamed.

Was the rest simply water? Vast, barren seas? Or, on that other invisible hemisphere, were there balancing land masses, with peoples and cities and strange gods? His heart began to pound. He knew it was futile to speculate like this, but he couldn't help it. Some day . . .

7. The Light

Khor sniffed the cabin air. Was it going stale? Yes, the CO_2 was definitely building. Which meant the absorbers were very nearly saturated. Why hadn't the alarm sounded? And then he noticed. The purifier bell *was* ringing. And the proper red light was flashing. Swamped by his other troubles, he just hadn't noticed. Alkali. Did he have any more? No. He remembered shaking out the last flecks of sodium carbonate from the container. He had tossed the empty box into the disposal.

Was there any chance of finding alkali down there on that watery little planet? Conserve. Conserve. Breathe slowly, slowly. Khor, you luckless zoologist. Whatever possessed Queva to give you her sleep key? Not very smart of her.

Well, now, Planet III, just what sort of world are you? Is there intelligent life down there, waiting to hand me emergency tape, a barrel of oil (meeting hydraulic spec K-109, of course), and a basket of alkali? And (who knows) maybe they'll hand me a featherless biped as I leave.

How silly can I get?

He watched the 3-D shaper carve out a fist-sized copy of the planet sphere: blue for oceans, brown for continents, white for polar ice. He pulled the ball out of the lathe and studied it. Very, very interesting. How big? No way to tell. All he got was shape and surface. No matter. Maybe he was going to live after all. There had to be *something* down there. He put the ball in a fold of his spacejacket.

Back now to the screen.

Looking visually. Night-side. But no city lights? No civilization? Take her around again. Another orbit. Try north-south. Nothing? Not yet. Night side again. Maybe I'm too high. Lower . . . lower still. Watch out! Water! Slow down. I'm over some kind of sea. Hey—a *light!* A big one! It's a lighthouse! Better switch on my running lights . . . what's the convention? Alternating red . . . green . . . white . . . blue. Plus a forward search beam. By Zaff, I see buildings. Spread out . . . a *city*. Saved!

Where to put down?

8. Arrival

Eratosthenes wrapped his woolen cloak tighter about him as he stared out to sea. It was the last hour of evening and the first of night. Dark sea was indistinguishable from dark sky. The constant north wind pushed back the dubious perfumes of the delta and the royal harbor, to his rear. He inhaled deeply the crisp salt air blowing in from the reefs.

He stood on the balcony of the great light-house, on the Isle of Pharos, that long spit of limestone protecting Alexandria from the encroaching Great Green. He was so high, and the air so pure, that he didn't even have to use mosquito ointment.

Ah, Pharos—isle of strange and diverse fortunes! Menelaus, bound homeward from the Trojan War, blown ashore and becalmed by angry Zeus, nearly starved here, with disdainful Helen. So Homer sang. How long ago? Eight centuries, perhaps nine. But then eighty-two years ago the great Alexander came. "A fine island," he said. "It will shelter a new city, over there on the delta." He paced it out, where to put everything. Everything but the final essential building: his tomb. The first Ptolemy had built that and then had brought the body back.

"Eratosthenes," he said to himself, "you're dodging the issue. You're thinking about everything except the problem." Ah, yes. So he had confirmed (in his own mind at least) that the Earth was a sphere, with a circumference of 250,000 stadia. But it was too much. A globe that size! Incredible. Or was it? There was, of course, a rough check, available to anyone. You didn't have to go to Syene. You didn't have to look down a well at high noon, on the day of the solstice. There was another way. Just an approximation, of course.

He walked a slow circuit of the balcony, pondering vaguely the beauty of the night sea and the twinkling lamps of the city. It was lonely here, and he could think. No one to bother him. The lighthouse keepers knew him as the curator of the great Library, and let him come and go as he pleased. Far below in the courtyard Ne-tiy waited patiently with the chariot.

To the north nothing was visible except the stars and the light shaft thrusting out horizontally from the great concave mirror at the top of the tower. He had come here to think about that light beam. It was supposed to be visible out to sea for 160 stadia. To him, that was one more proof that the Earth was spherical. The light was visible out to sea to the point where the Earth's curvature shut it off. He reviewed the problem in his mind. He saw the diagram again. Circles. Tangents. The height of the Pharos tower, taken with the seaward visibility. That would give an angle—call it alpha—with the horizon. That angle alpha would be identical to the angle—call it beta—at the center of the Earth subtending the 160-stadia chord of the light shaft. The lighthouse was two-thirds of a stadion high. The sine of the angle alpha was therefore two-thirds divided by 160, or 417 hundred thousandths. Next, the angle whose sine was 417 hundred thousandths was about 141/3 minutes, or about 1/1500 part of a circle, and finally, 1500 times 160 gave you 240,000 stadia. Close enough to the Syene measurement of 250,000. So he couldn't be too far wrong. He had done the numerical work already. He knew the result before he came out here tonight. But he still found it hard to believe. The Earth couldn't possibly be that big. Or could it? Had he made an error somewhere? Maybe several errors? Actually, the measurements using the lighthouse were not easy to make. Sighting the Pharos light had to be done at sea from a pitching, bobbing boat. Subtractions had to be made for the height of the perch at the mast top.

He clenched his jaw. He had to believe his numbers. He had to believe his rough check. And he had to believe the only conceivable conclusion that his calculations offered. The Earth was indeed a huge sphere, in circumference 240,000 to 250,000 stadia, more or less.

The question now was, should he so report to Ptolemy, and possibly get himself discharged from his post at the Library. Or worse?

He was due at the palace by midnight. He would have to decide within hours.

He had just turned back, to descend the outer stairway, when something in the dark northern skies caught his eye. Lights, moving, flashing. And different colors. Red . . . green . . . white . . . blue . . . flashing, on and off. And then that terrific shaft of white light . . . brighter even than Pharos . . . *coming straight at him!*

He threw his arm up over his eyes. There was a roar overhead. The tower shook. And then the thing was gone . . . no, not entirely. There it was, over the Library quarter . . . hovering now, stabbing its blinding light beam down. He raced around to the side of the light tower.

What in the name of Zeus!

Was it now over *his* house, the great manse entrusted to him by Ptolemy Philadelphus? He stared in horrified amazement.

By the wine bags of Dionysus, the thing was . . . descending into his fenced park.

For a moment he was paralyzed. And then he recovered and started down the stairs. Outside, he awoke the dozing charioteer. "Ne-tiy! Home! Home!"

9. Encounter

Khor read the preliminary data in the analyzer. Oxygen, nitrogen, air density, viscosity, temperature . . . Nothing obviously toxic. Gravity a little low. No matter. Everything within acceptable limits. He turned off the lights and got out. Fortunately for the ship (not to mention his unwitting host), he had come down in a clearing. There were trees and hedges on all sides. Tiny little things, but they would provide shelter. He had landed within some sort of private estate, and very likely he could complete his repairs without the bother of curious and/or hostile crowds. And what did they look like? If they built cities, they must have hands, and legs to get about, and certainly they were able to communicate with each other. Probably very handy little fellows.

He walked on the cropped turf back to the rear of the ship. Yes, there was the hole. He played the light on it and around it. The outer plate had laminated over nicely. Only the interior would need attention. Well, get with it. Start knocking on doors. "Could I borrow a few hundred xil of adhesive tape? And a load of high-spec hydraulic fluid (you supply the container). Plus a var of sodium carbonate. Just enough to get me to a star some nine light cycles away."

And that raised another problem. What language did these creatures speak? Better get the telepathic head-band. He crawled back up the hatchway and returned with it. Suppose they're unfriendly? Should I bring a weapon? No, I've got to look absolutely peaceful.

His ear tympani vibrated faintly. Noises. Wheels churning in loose gravel. Cries, addressed, he thought, to a draft animal of some sort. Two different voices? They had seen his ship come down, and they had driven here to confront the trespasser.

Fair enough. He unfolded the long veil, starting at his head, over the teleband, and quickly draped his entire body from head down to talons. (No use alarming them right at the outset!) Then he propped up his portable beam between rocks in the clearing so that it would shine on him.

He listened to the cautious steps on the fine pebbles, closer, closer.

And there they were, two of them, standing just outside the light circle.

By the pinions of Pinar! Featherless bipeds!

One seemed calm, the other fearful and fidgety. The calm one stepped out into the light.

Excellent! thought the visitor. It has stereoscopic eyes, nostrils, mouth, ears. Not the most attractive alien he had ever encountered; yet not the ugliest, either. Somewhere in between.

Khor held up both hands to show they were empty, then bowed slowly.

The calm one repeated the gesture with great dignity.

Khor spoke through the tele-band into the mind of his host. "My name is Khor."

The Greek showed his surprise. "You understand Greek? And you are able to speak into my mind? How is this? Whence came you?"

Khor pointed to the band around his head, visible in outline under his body veil.

"Ah," said Eratosthenes. "A mental language device. Fantastic. But where—" He jerked. Strange thoughts . . . strange sounds . . . sights . . . smells . . . were forming in his head. He gasped. "You are from a distant world? A *star?*"

Khor nodded.

The geometer gulped. "Are you a god? The messenger Hermes perhaps?" (How could he be asking this? He didn't believe in gods!)

"No. I am a mortal, like yourself. My people are a little more scientifically advanced than yours, that's all."

"Why are you here?"

"I was on a collection expedition. I work for a museum, the same as you. I was searching for certain plants . . . animals . . . I was loaded up, and on my way home, when a meteorite hit my ship. I had to land for repairs."

"I see. I *think* I see. Can I help you?"

"I don't know. I will need certain things. Certain . . . tapes. Certain oils. Some . . . alkali. And then perhaps some geodetic information."

"Such as?"

"The circumference of your world, Terra, considered as a sphere."

The Greek eyed his visitor sharply.

Khor hesitated. "Have I asked a forbidden question? Is something, how do you say it, taboo? Or perhaps you were not aware that Terra is a sphere?"

"*That* I had indeed surmised. No, I was simply struck by the coincidence. I have been working on the problem for the past several weeks, and very recently, actually within the last few hours, I have obtained some sort of answer. But why do you need to know?"

"I can use Terra's rotational velocity to help fling the ship into escape orbit, when the time comes to leave. To determine that velocity, I need to know Terra's circumference."

"I think I can provide a fair estimate."

"Excellent."

Eratosthenes had to stop and think a moment. Khor needed the velocity of the *rotating* Earth? Well, of course. The Earth rotated. That's why the sun *appeared* to move around the Earth. But that wasn't all. The Earth must revolve around the sun, from a very great distance, once a year. And that's why the sun appeared to move through the zodiac once a year. Actually, it was the Earth that was moving. The sun stood still. The heliocentric hypothesis wasn't a hypothesis. It was a fact. And if the Earth moved around the sun, so did all the five other planets: Mercury, Venus. Mars, Jupiter, Saturn. And so the sun was a star, much like millions of other stars. Did all those other stars out there have planets, with strange life forms, thinking, working, loving? His heart beat faster as he thought about it. Whom could he tell? Nobody. "A visitor from another star told me." Next stop, the madhouse. It made him smile just to think about it.

But back to reality, and the present. "So then, Khor, can I offer you the hospitality of my house? Not a Ptolemaic palace—but yet not a hovel, either. Food of all sorts, wines brought in from all parts of the world. Baths, hot and cold. Servants to assist you. You could relax while we dine, and you could describe your needs to me."

"Your offer is most attractive. Truly, I have a great need. But I do not wish to cause problems for you. I read in your mind certain names: Ptolemy . . . Hor-ent-yotf . . . even the female at your side, Ne-tiy. Who are these people? How can they harm you?"

"Harm me? Perhaps the words are too strong. Ptolemy rules—*owns*—this land, called Egypt. He is a Greek, a foreigner, and he tries to rule softly, and to give no great offense to the people, aside from taking their money. But Hor-ent-yotf, a high priest of the hawk-god Horus, likewise rules, in that he reigns over the minds and souls of the people. Ne-tiy is a slave, put in my house by Hor-ent-yotf. She is his property, even as his clothing and his cosmetic box are his property. Do you read my thoughts in this matter, honored stranger?"

"I do, and I reply with thoughts. You propose to do a thing offensive to Ptolemy, and horrifying to Hor-ent-yotf, and because of this thing the priest may kill you. Or perhaps make the female kill you. Is this the situation?"

"It is so."

"I find this quite alarming. Obviously, I do not understand your ways. Please explain."

"It is a very complex matter, O visitor from great distances. Perhaps we can continue over cakes and wine?"

"Fourteen percent CH_3CH_2OH?"

"I beg your pardon?"

"Just thinking out loud. A pleasure, Eratosthenes. Just let me close up the bucket."

10. Repairs

"To each his own custom," thought Eratosthenes. "We Greeks eat while reclining on an eating couch. The Egyptians sit in chairs. But you stand."

"At all times," replied the thoughts of his visitor. "We stand to eat, drink, study, work, even to sleep. Our skeletal structure requires it." His gloved hand clasped the wine cup and brought it to his lips through a slit in his body veil.

The Greek heard a "clack" as the metal goblet struck something hard." Well then, let us look to your needs. First, strips of adhesive cloth. Tapes, you call them. That we have in abundance. It is the custom of the country to use them as bandages to wrap the bodies of the dead, in preparation for burial." He held up a piece of white cloth. "This is a rather fine linen, woven from the flax plant. Every Egyptian family saves scraps of cloth against the inevitable burials. The pieces are ripped into strips: narrow bandages for the fingers, wider ones for the limbs and torso." He tore off a strip and handed it to Khor, who examined it closely.

"What makes it stick?" asked his visitor.

"They dip it in liquid balsam. It sets up hard in a couple of hours."

"It ought to work," said Khor. "Now, about the oil."

"We have several kinds: olive oil, from the fruits of the olive tree. It's used in cooking and in our lamps. Castor oil . . . several grades. This is from the castor bean. It has medicinal uses, and is also a fine lubricant. The army uses it in the oil packing for its chariot wheels. And linseed oil . . . which we boil and then use in paints and varnishes."

"Back up. This castor oil . . . is there a refined grade?"

"Indeed yes. Settled over charcoal and filtered through fine linen."

"I'd like to try that. And now one more thing. A bit of alkali."

"Alkali . . . ?" The geometer frowned.

"Sodium carbonate would do nicely. Hm. That's making it worse, isn't it? How to describe it . . . let me think. It would be bitter to the taste, very soluble in water, turns red wine blue. Fizzes in vinegar. Can be boiled with fats and oils to make soap . . ."

"Oh! Of course! *Natron!* We use it in embalming. It helps desiccate the corpse. But how would you use natron in your ship?"

"Simple. During wake-periods on my ship, my lungs give off a waste gas, which we call carbon dioxide. It can become toxic if allowed to reach high concentrations. The alkali absorbs it."

"Well then, I think the next step is to gather up these things and take them out to your ship. I'll call the servants. No—I can't. They're all down in the city, celebrating the New Year. You and I and Ne-tiy will have to do it."

"It's just as well. Less risk to the ship."

To the extent that any of the geometer's aplomb had left him, very nearly all of it had by now returned. He said, "As you may have read in my mind, it is the practice for one of our library clerks to go through every incoming ship to look for new books to copy. I wonder . . ."

"Ah, my friend. I have dozens of books, none in any Earth-language. *The Maintenance of Ion Drives . . . Collecting on Airless Worlds . . . Operation of the Sleep Casket.* Some with holos, for which you'd need a laser reader. But I tell you what. You like maps. Before I finally leave, I'll give you a sort of map."

"Fair enough."

An hour later Khor, Eratosthenes, and Ne-tiy had wound the last of the linen strips around the hydraulic tubes, refilled the depleted oil surge tank, and secured the amphora of natron in the storage locker.

"The balsam resin will require a couple of hours to cure and harden," said Eratosthenes. "And I am due at Ptolemy's palace very soon. May I suggest that you join me?"

"Won't I excite comment?"

"Hm. You're a bit taller than average. However, just keep covered with your body cape. I'll tell Ptolemy you're a foreign visitor and your religion requires the covering."

"Is it an offense to you, my host, that I conceal my body from you in this way?"

The Cyrenian smiled. "Since you are my guest, it pleases me that you do as you see fit." He bowed. "This way to the chariot."

11. Ptolemy on His Balcony

On this night of the summer solstice, the beginning of the three weeks of madness celebrating the rising of the river, Ptolemy the Second, called Philadelphus, stood on his balcony and looked out over the royal harbor. Shading his eyes, he could barely make out the tiny light swinging in slow arcs in the blackness. At his request, the captain had fixed the lantern at the top of the mast of the royal barge. Why? No reason given. He had simply said, do it, and it was done. Actually, it was a token of a promise to himself: tomorrow he would be on that ship, headed south on the Nile, with all concerns of state receding sternward.

For five thousand years the rulers of Egypt had made this trip. Tradition held that when the sun ceased his northward journey, Pharaoh would set forth, sailing all the way to Thebes, to ensure a proper flood. If Pharaoh did not thus set forth on the bosom of Hapi, the river would not rise. If the river did not rise, there would be no sowing, and no harvest. Famine would grip the land. The tax gatherers would gather little or nothing. The army could not be paid. The dynasty could fall.

Superstitious nonsense?

Who was he to say?

It was best to go along with it. Anyhow, he always looked forward to the long trip on the river. He just wished Arsinoë were still alive.

Noises in the streets below brought his eyes down to the parade of dancing torches. The annual infection had spread even here, to the guarded serenity of the royal quarter. In a way it was unsettling; yet on the whole it was reassuring that the people were content to stay within their multi-millennial rut. No riots, no revolutions, no marches against the granaries. Not this week, anyhow. Let the beer flow!

He looked around as a woman in an elegant linen dress and cape parted the hangings and stepped out to join him. A thick black wig, artfully dusted with gold powder, fell to her shoulders. She was his concubine of the month. Her name was Pauni, daughter of a noble house. He named them for the current Egyptian month. It was the only way he could attach names to their beautiful faces. And so it had been, since the death of Arsinoë, his true sister-wife. twenty years ago. By Greek ideas, that marriage had been incest; but it was quite in the pharaonic tradition. A bit of irony: in the river tongue, the word for concubine was "sne-t," which meant "sister."

(Ah, Arsinoë, Arsinoë. I loved you greatly. You should not have died. It was the only unkind thing you ever did.)

"Respect their traditions. Respect their religion. Worship their gods," his great father Ptolemy, Alexander's general, had told him. "Be pious. You lose nothing, and you will preserve the dynasty." He took the woman by the arm and they listened in silence to the revelry. "The old man was right," he muttered.

"Who, my lord?" said Pauni politely.

"My father. When the Persians conquered Egypt, they flouted the local religions. Ochus, the satrap, killed the sacred bull. The priests invoked a terrible curse on him, and on his masters in Persepolis. And so Alexander came, and destroyed Persia. He came to Egypt, and gave all honor to the priests. He sacrificed to Apis and other native gods. He made the great journey across the desert, without road or path, to the sanctuary of Ammon at Siwah. There the priests declared his divine descent, and that he was indeed the son of Ammon." He reflected. "Did I ever tell you about Alexander's trip across the desert to Siwah?"

(Several times, my lord.) "No, sire, I don't recall that you did."

"Ah. Well, then. The storms had destroyed the roads. Even the guides were lost. The sun was pitiless, and the men were dropping from heat stroke. But the gods sent a great flock of ravens, who flew in circles overhead, and shaded Alexander. And if the guides made a wrong turn, the birds screamed until they went straight again."

"Amazing," said Pauni.

The royal Greek sighed again. If only he didn't owe so much money to so many people. The Jews had helped him—and his father—finance the great lighttower on Pharos. It had been finished these nine years, and the treasury was still paying. And the Egyptian priests. The public debt was soaring because of their demands for new temples. And then there was the standing army, all mercenaries, and they liked to be paid regularly, in hard clanking brass. And the navy. A thousand years ago Rameses had not been troubled with ships that sailed the Great Green. And *two* thousand years ago the pharaohs didn't even use money. There wasn't any. It hadn't been invented yet. Go, said Khufu to his peasants. Build me a tomb-pyramid. One million men, working twenty years. And they had done it, and not an obol paid out to anyone. Alas, how things had changed. "Who rules Egypt?" he mused softly. "Do I? No. Do the one million Greeks who have settled here? No. Well, then, do the priests and their seven million fellahin? Or is the land a hopeless anarchy?"

By now she was used to this. "Speaking of priests," Pauni reminded him gently, "the high priest of Horus is here. Also Rabbi Ben Shem. And then the other notables: Eratosthenes and his lady. The geometer brings a very strange guest, who covers his body with a long black veil. And then there are the consuls and ambassadors—Claudius Pulcher the Roman, Hamilcar Barca the Carthaginian . . ."

Ptolemy suppressed a groan. Eratosthenes. He had tried to forget him, but of course it was impossible. The man of measures was going to make his report tonight. And what will you say, noble philosopher? How big is the world? As to that, say anything you like. But the *shape!* Declare Earth a flat square, or a disc, or a cylinder. Any of these. But you know you must not say "sphere" or "ball" or "globe." That's heresy, mathematician. Don't betray me, my brother Greek. There is a long line waiting to take your place as curator of the great Library. And it isn't just me you should worry about. If you say "sphere," the local holies will have you floating in the canal before the night is out.

He paused. The girl looked up at him in grave concern. He thought: she knows I am fifty-nine, and that I am dying. Ah, to be young again. No, don't turn back. Let it be finally done. Nothing really matters very much anymore. From here on in, let us have peace. He smiled. "Perhaps we should rejoin our guests."

12. Heresy

A little cluster had already formed around the two ambassadors. The Carthaginian was explaining something. "One of my purposes here is to obtain copies of the world map of Eratosthenes."

"And what good is that?" growled Claudius Pulcher, the Roman.

"Carthage will probably win our present war with Rome, noble ambassador. If so, we will expand into Spain and Gaul. For that we will need good maps. If we lose—may Baal save us!—we will certainly need to recoup our fortunes, and we would look to western Europe for that. Again we would need good maps. Including—" (here he gave the stolid Pulcher a crafty leer) "—a good showing of the passes through the Alps."

"Passes . . . ?"

"For our war elephants."

The Roman general stared at him blankly. Then recognition dawned. "Oh—you mean from Gaul, over the mountains into Italy." He began to laugh. He laughed so hard he spilled his wine. "Excuse me." He walked back to the credentia for a refill.

Ptolemy watched him for a moment, then turned back to the Carthaginian. "The great Alexander was always fearful of war elephants. He never really discovered how to cope with them. Quite an idea, Hamilcar Barca."

"But there's still a problem," said Eratosthenes. "We have several reports by travelers in the Library. They all say the passes are very narrow, barely wide enough for a horse. How will you get your elephants through?"

"You should read more of your own books, learned scroll-master," said Barca. "The mountains are made of calx. Vinegar dissolves calx. We shall bring hundreds of casks of vinegar. The mountains shall melt away, and the great war beasts shall pass."

"Why does Carthage disclose its strategy to Rome in advance?" asked Ptolemy.
The young Carthaginian grinned. "No harm in it at all. First, they think we lie, that we try to deceive them. Therefore, they won't bother to defend the passes. Second, they're so confident that if and when they do fortify the passes they would so tell us. Third, they are incapable of thinking in terms of empire for themselves, so they can't conceive that their enemies would have such impossible ideas. They lack imagination. They don't know what dreams are."

"They seem to have done very well despite these deficiencies," demurred Eratosthenes. "Three hundred years ago they were just a fishing village on the Tiber. Now they rule the entire Italic peninsula. Who needs dreams?"

"You have a point, mapmaker. Well then, reverse the case. We Phoenicians needed dreams, and we produced them. We have established trading outposts at the limits of the known world. We have sailed through the Pillars of Hercules to the Tin Islands. We have circumnavigated Africa. We have traded in the Black Sea. Our ships rule the Western Mediterranean, and business on great waters has made us rich. And all because we had a vision. We still have it, and with it, we shall beat the Romans."

"Peace, gentlemen," said Ptolemy. Wars and rumors of war made him uneasy. "Let us talk of other things. Eratosthenes, how go the angles?"

"Today, my lord Ptolemy, the day of the summer solstice, I measured the angle of the sun at high noon. I found it to be seven degrees and ten minutes."

The Second Ptolemy smiled graciously, yet warily, and with a warning in his eyes. "And pray what is the significance of seven degrees and—what was it—?"

"Ten minutes, my lord. Significance?" The geometer eyed the Greek pharaoh carefully. "To determine the significance, we may need the assistance of the priests"—he bowed gravely to Hor-ent-yotf and Rabbi Ben Shem—"and the historians"—a bow to Cleon, the Homeric exegesist—"and perhaps to other philosophers, living and dead."

Claudius Pulcher had meanwhile returned from the credentia with a wine refill. "Aside from all this assistance, real or threatened," he grumped, "can anyone tell me the significance of seven degrees and ten minutes?"

"By itself, nothing," volunteered Hamilcar Barca. "However, taken with certain other measurements, it could give you the size and shape of the Earth." He said to the librarian: "Am I right?"

Eratosthenes sighed, and glanced at Ptolemy from the corner of his eye,

"Oh, go ahead," said the pharaoh wearily. (And oh, to be on that barge!)

The Greek shrugged. "At Syene, where the finest red granite is quarried, a tall pole casts no shadow at noon on the day of the summer solstice, and the sun shines directly into the wells. This is so because Syene lies almost directly on the Tropic of Cancer. Also, Alexandria lies almost due north of Syene, at a distance of 5,000 stadia. Now seven degrees and ten minutes is about 1/50 of a full circle, so 5,000 is 1/50 of a full circle on the Earth. Thus we multipy 5,000 by 50, and we get 250,000 stadia as the circumference of the Earth."

"One moment," interposed Ptolemy. "You say 5,000 stadia. How did you measure that?"

"From cadasters—registers of land surveys for tax purposes, made by the Second Rameses, over a thousand years ago. The exact dimensions of the nomes are given. It's a matter of simple addition, from Syene to the sea, with certain adjustments."

The Roman frowned. "I still don't see. What's a 'stadia,' anyhow?"

Hamilcar Barca smiled. "The singular is stadion. A bit over eight stadia to your Roman mile. Using your units, General, the world is a sphere about 30,000 miles in circumference."

"Ridiculous," breathed Pulcher. "It can't possibly be that big."

"This is entirely unofficial," interposed Ptolemy hastily. "The Great House takes no position . . ."

Rabbi Ben Shem smiled uneasily. "Dear Eratosthenes . . . the Earth cannot be a sphere. Our Holy Scriptures state, 'the four corners of the Earth.' "

"I think we may be overlooking the obvious," said Hor-ent-yotf. "Our esteemed geometer assumes the sun is so far away that its rays, as received here, are parallel. The assumption is totally unwarranted, as I shall show. There are other, much more reasonable conditions that will give the same data." He pulled a piece of papyrus from his linens and inspected it. "If the sun is 40,000 stadia distant, it will give your same shadow angle of about seven degrees here at Alexandria, will it not, Eratosthenes?"

The mathematician smiled. "Quite so—assuming the Earth is flat."

"As is indeed the case," said the Roman ambassador.

Hamilcar Barca shook his head. "Like the Greeks, we Carthaginians are a seafaring people. On shore, when we watch a ship come in, we see first the tip of the mast, then the sails, then the bow. That means to us that the Earth is a great ball, and that the ship comes up into view over the curvature. It is the same at sea. For example, my trireme arrived here at night. We came in, guided by the great Pharos light tower. At first, our man at mast-top could not see the light at all. And then, suddenly, 'Light ho!' and there it was, just over the belly of the sea."

There was a moment's silence, broken by Ptolemy. His voice was strained. "This is a very interesting discussion; yet I do not feel that we can ignore a thousand years of research and thought that have gone into the problem. Certainly the ancient authorities leave no doubt on the question. Homer said the Earth was a flat disc, bounded by the River Oceanus. A decade before the battle of Marathon, Hecataeus announced the same fact."

"One moment, Your Majesty," said Hamilcar Barca. "Your own Aristotle believed the Earth to be a sphere because of the round shadow on the moon, during lunar eclipse."

Ptolemy shrugged. "Homer's disc, head-on, would cast a round shadow."

"My lords," said Rabbi Ben Shem harshly, "*I* make no attempt to define or deal with impiety. Certainly Greek history provides ample precedent. I have read widely in your Library, Eratosthenes, and I can cite your own laws and applicable cases. Your Anaxagoras propounded a heliocentric system, and wrote that the sun was a big blazing ball, bigger even than the Peloponnesus. He was condemned to prison for his impiety. Pericles was barely able to save his life. Aristarchus also proposed a heliocentric cosmos, and was accused of impiety. Alcibiades was recalled from the Syracuse campaign to face charges of impiety to Hermes: whereupon Athens lost the war. Socrates was executed for impiety. Protagoras confessed agnosticism and fled Athens with a price on his head."

Ptolemy rubbed his chin. "I, for one, believe Homer, who declared the Earth to be flat, with its omphalos—navel—at Delphi. A sphere seems quite impossible. People at the antipodes would walk with their heads hanging down. Trees would grow downward. Rain would fall up. These things cannot be." He fixed a grim eye on Eratosthenes. "The gods gave us a flat world, my young friend. Adjust your numbers to fit the facts, not the other way around." And so having delivered his views, and having thus dried his throat, he and Pauni left the group in search of the wine table.

"Well, then, man of the Library," said Ben Shem, with just a hint of triumph, "you will of course recant?"

Eratosthenes found his body turning, not to face the rabbi, but instead to Hor-ent-yotf. It was to the priest of the hawk-god that he gave his answer: "No. I do not recant. I do not retract. It is as I said." The hawk-priest stared at him without the slightest expression.

"Oh!" said Ben Shem. "You claim the Earth is a sphere?"

"Yes."

"And it circles the sun?"

"Did I say that? If I didn't, I meant to."

"Aiee!" shrieked the rabbi. "Heresy, heresy compounded!" He pulled at his beard, and a few hairs tore loose.

"Sorry," said the Greek apologetically. "I didn't know you'd take it this way." The priest stumbled away, muttering.

Khor shot a thought into the geometer's mind: "Science is a very upsetting subject around here."

"Yes."

Hamilcar Barca broke in. "May I ask a question about your 5,000-stadia measure to Syene?"

"Of course."

"Does that include a rake-off by your local priests? Say, one-sixth?"

"How do you mean?"

"Well, suppose the true measurement is actually 4,285 stadia. Do the priests add one-sixth, or 715, for their share of the grain crops?"

"Yes." It was Hor-ent-yotf who answered. They all looked around at him. "From the time of Menes," said the priest, "the first pharaoh, who united upper and lower Egypt, the temples have taken one-sixth of the crops. We do this painlessly, by telling the farmer his plot is one-sixth larger than it really is."

Eratosthenes was embarrassed. "I am caught in a gross error. The circumference is then 4,285 times 50, not 5,000 times 50. More accurately, the circumference is"—he thought a moment—"214,250 stadia, or about 26,000 Roman miles."

"The one-sixth difference is not significant," said Hor-ent-yotf. "The crux of the matter is, you have attempted heresy of the gravest order." He signaled to

Ne-tiy. She glanced once at Eratosthenes, then followed the hawk-priest away from the group.

"Watch him," warned Khor. "I see into his mind. He has condemned you, and he means to kill you."

The geodesist shrugged. "It had to come."

"Shouldn't you leave now?"

"Why delay the confrontation? It might as well be here. Regardless of what happens to me, Ne-tiy can drive you back to your ship."

"I wasn't thinking of that. When the time comes, I can manage by myself."

"Can you see them?" asked Eratosthenes. "You are taller."

13. Something in the Wine

"I see them both very well. He and the female approach the wine table. He whispers to her. She is to put something in your wine."

"Poison."

"Yes. You are to die by poison. The mind of the female is in a great turmoil. She wants to refuse. But the priest threatens her. Ah, she looks back this way, but she cannot see you. What a strange expression on her face, Eratosthenes. How is one to interpret it?"

"Horror, possibly. She does not really want to kill me. She resists strongly, but I think probably she will make the attempt. From childhood, this is what the temple trained her to do."

"They argue some more. He insists. He says to her, if she fails, servants will bind her mouth and limbs, and carry her in a cart to the temple pool, and the crocodiles will feed. And you will die in any case."

"Pleasant fellow."

"Perhaps you should leave with me, Eratosthenes. As you know, I still seek a bipedal specimen. On my world you need have no fear of assassination."

The librarian laughed forlornly. "Don't tempt me, admirable visitor. What are they doing now?"

"Nothing as yet. I am in the mind of the priest. He is thinking about rings on his fingers, and three white powders. Arsenic . . . strychnine . . . aconite. Arsenic is tasteless, but takes a while, probably too long for what he wants. Also you might get sick and vomit. Strychnine? A good one. Not much is needed. Acts in a few minutes. Whole body goes into mortal spasm. He's seen a man die, lying flat, resting only on his heels and the back of his skull. But strychnine is bitter. You might taste it and not drink the wine. No, no strychnine for you. It's aconite. The deadliest known poison. It is extracted from a delicate plant that looks like a tiny helmet or hood, and which grows in mountains called the Alps, far to the north of the Roman domains. A crystal the size of a grain of sand can be fatal. You are quickly paralyzed. Your heart stops. Death is quick. Ah, he's moving. He cups his hand over a wine goblet. The cap on his golden ring opens. A powder falls into the wine. He gives the goblet to the girl. He snarls at her, and she moves away. Look sharp, Eratosthenes! Here she comes!"

And there was Ne-tiy, standing before him quietly. "I have brought wine, my lord."

He looked at her in glum silence.

She raised the cup to her own lips.

"No!" he cried. He struck the cup away. It clattered to the floor, splashing red liquid over carpet and guests, who stared around in dismay. "Sorry!" cried the geometer. "So clumsy of me!" He called a serving man to bring mop and bucket.

Ne-tiy had not moved. "True, my lord, I could not harm you. Yet, what you have done to me just now is a cruel thing. For now I face a very painful death. The wine would have been . . . like going to sleep."

"Khor, take care of her for a moment." His voice grated harshly in his own ears. "Take her out on the balcony' I'll join you there in a little while." *Now, Hor-ent-yotf, you son of river scum, where are you?*

14. The Bargain

He found him quickly. If Hor-ent-yotf was surprised, he didn't show it.

Eratosthenes controlled his voice carefully, as though he were discussing the weather, the cost of grain, or whether the eastern harbor might need dredging this year. "I understand that Ne-tiy has refused to kill me. This despite your direct order. So that now her own life is forfeit. Is this not so?"

"Why should I stand here, talking to a Greek spawn of Set? Yet it is so. She failed. She dies."

"Let us bargain, high avenger of Horus." Should he include his own life in the negotiations? No. Too demeaning. Just Ne-tiy. He said, "I will buy her."

"Ah?" The small eyes peered suspiciously at the heretic. "With what?"

"Information. I know the burial site of the boy-pharaoh, Tut-ankh-amun."

The eyes of the priest popped. "You lie! You lie most vilely!"

Eratosthenes smiled. "No. It is so. Tut, son-in-law of that great heretic, Ikhnaton, who decreed the worship of Aton, the sun, and desecrated all other temples. Ikhnaton, who built Akhetaton, an entire city devoted to the worship of Aton . . ."

"The City of the Criminal!" breathed the priest. "He died. And we destroyed his city. We destroyed everything of his. All—"

"Except the tomb of Tut . . . who married Ikhnaton's third daughter."

"Prove it!" hissed Hor-ent-yotf. "Prove you *really* know!"

"I have seen the records. The report, for example."

"Report? What report?"

"The one written by the captain of pharaoh's guards. He caught the grave robbers in the act of breaking in. He slew them on the spot, reinforced the entrance, and posted a guard."

"Go on."

"I can give you the record of the final funerary banquet, held within the tomb itself. Eight necropolis officials ate five ducks, two plovers, a haunch of mutton. They drank beer and wine, and they swept up all residue with two small brooms, put the debris in a special jar, and buried the jar in a pit outside the tomb. I have seen the jar."

The Avenger of Horus studied the librarian, and his eyes narrowed in a crafty squint. "How much can you tell me about the location?"

"It's in the Necropolis of Thebes, in the Valley of Kings."

"Hm. That's a big place. Specifically—?"

"No specifics as to place until we have an agreement."

"I see. His queen, the vile spawn of the criminal pharaoh Ikhnaton?"

"Her name was Ankhesenamun. But she was not buried with the boy king."

"Interesting." The priest hesitated. "But certainly the tomb was re-entered subsequently?"

"No. The entrance was later further sealed, one might say almost by accident. I have verified that the seal is undisturbed."

"The last of the Atonist hell-people," muttered the priest. "Pull him out of his death-lair. Burn the infidel mummy. The gold and silver go to the servants of Horus."

"Is it a bargain?"

The holy man hesitated. They both waited for a time in silence.

Eratosthenes sighed. "The excavation will be expensive. A hundred slaves must be rented and housed and fed for several weeks. You will need ready money. I will sign over my Cyrenian estates to you, together with my gold on deposit in local banks."

Hor-ent-yotf still seemed lost in thought.

"If we cannot agree," said the librarian gravely, "I will be forced to take a certain action."

"Oh, really?" The priest's mouth curled. "Exactly what?"

"I will turn over Tut's location to the Council of Antiquities. They will excavate at government expense. There will be great excitement, presaging a revival of Aton-ism."

The priest clenched his fists. "You wouldn't!"

"I would."

"Yes, Greek, I think you would . . . for you are the ultimate obscene evil . . ."

"Well?"

"But hear me well, son of darkness. We speak only of the faithless slave girl. What Horus intends to be *your* fate, only the god can say."

"Such is my understanding."

"Then consider it done." The priest struck his chest with his fist. "I will have the temple clerks draw up the agreement, in hieroglyphics and in Greek, and I will come with it to the Serapeum tomorrow afternoon. We will sign before witnesses."

"Yes." Eratosthenes turned back toward the balcony. The priest hesitated for a moment, then followed at a dozen paces. He swirled his cloak about him as though to minimize contamination from the air the Greek passed through.

15. Sirius Rising

As he stood on the balcony with the girl, Khor found himself thinking of Queva, and Ne-tiy, and how they seemed to blend into one person, one passionate loving mind. "I will wait for you," Queva had said.

He had followed closely the negotiations between Eratosthenes and Hor-ent-yotf. Ne-tiy had saved the Greek's life at apparent cost of her own, and now the man had given up all that he had to save her. Khor would not have believed these creatures capable of such nobility. But there it was. Strong stuff. How was he going to enter this in the ship's log? The Supervisor would neither believe nor understand. So skip it all. Maybe tell Queva someday.

I'm very nearly done here, thought the star-traveler. Just one more little job. Ah, come on out on the balcony, Eratosthenes. And here comes Hor-ent-yotf, right behind you. That's good, very good. He shot a thought to the Greek: "Dawn is coming, friend. Look, there's my home star—rising just over the sea!"

"Sirius?" said Eratosthenes, pointing.

"Sothis!" said Hor-ent-yotf, giving the Egyptian name for the great blue star.

Khor spoke again to the mind of Eratosthenes: "Your Sirius—my home star. And a fine conclusion to a profitable visit. You see the first heliacal rising of Sirius, or Sothis, and you tell me that means the Nile has now started to rise. It means the summer solstice, and great festivities throughout the land, going on for days. Thank you for all your help in repairing my ship, and for your contributions, including this last."

"Our pleasure, esteemed visitor!" Then he stopped. "This . . . last?"

"Especially this last," replied Khor cryptically. "It is time for me to go. If I launch within the next few minutes, my trajectory vectors out directly toward Sirius."

"I'll call Ne-tiy, and she'll run you over to your ship." He was still puzzled.

"No need. I know where it is."

"But how—?"

"Ah, my friend, I see you really didn't know. Well then, in view of what is about to happen, perhaps you should have some important witnesses. Get Ptolemy and one or two others. Quickly now."

Eratosthenes felt a lump of cold lead forming in his stomach.

"Hurry!" said Khor. Through the black body veil the command burst like the hiss of the great gyrfalcon.

"Gods!" thought the Greek. That was an actual shouted command! He's vocalizing! The librarian sliced through the balcony drapes and stumbled into Claudius Pulcher, arm in arm with Ptolemy. "My lords," he gasped, "could you please join me on the balcony?"

"What's up, Eratosthenes?" demanded the Greek pharaoh. "Oh, I know— Sirius is now visible? Is that it?"

"Majesty, if you please . . ." Eratosthenes pulled the drapes aside.

A little crowd was already gathering: Pauni . . . Hamilcar Barca . . . a dozen gilded dignitaries.

The tall shrouded figure faced them all, then bowed especially to Ptolemy. "Thank you for a pleasant evening, ruler of Egypt," he said in harsh sibilant tones. He took his shroud with both hands and in a smooth majestic motion pulled it away from his head and body, then let it fall to the floor.

They stared.

The great head was entirely feathered. The mouth was an amber beak. Feathers scintillated on arms and chest. Some sort of breech-clout covered the groin. The legs terminated in scales and in what were almost human feet, except that the toes were taloned. As in the raptor birds of the Nile, a horizontal fold over each eye gave the face a stern, even fierce expression.

Eratosthenes now realized that the outlander was a consummate actor, that every word, every gesture, was planned for its dramatic effect, and that this terrified audience lay in the hands of Khor.

The mystery-creature now made his feathers vibrate, so that they excited nearby nitrogen atoms, and surrounded his plumaged body in a golden triboluminescent glow.

Ptolemy dropped his wine cup. Even Eratosthenes, who had suspected something like this would happen, was stunned.

"Horus!" gasped Hor-ent-yotf. *"Thou art the god!"*

"Thou sayest, worthy Hor-ent-yotf," hissed the visitor.

"To your knees, everyone," roared the priest.

And so they did. With one exception. Rabbi Ben Shem tore his cloak and ran screaming from the room.

Khor looked full at Hor-ent-yotf. "Come."

Hor-ent-yotf rose and walked forward, as though tranced. Khor took the man in his arms. "Arise, all, and witness," he commanded.

Gigantic wings unfolded from Khor's shoulders. The spread of those great pinions exceeded even the breadth of the balcony.

And now even Eratosthenes was done in. He pronounced slowly, quietly, and with great conviction, his favorite schoolboy oath. "Holy . . . excrement . . . of Zeus!"

Khor ignored him. "Since I take with me this holy man, I must appoint and sanctify a person to take his place, and to rule my holy temples in his stead. I name Ne-tiy. Come forward, child!"

They made way for the slave-girl. She bowed before the winged thing.

"I name thee High Priestess for Horus, for Egypt, and for all the world, exalted above all men, above even my noble son, the pharaoh Ptolemy. Take thee to mate whom thou wilt. Be fruitful, and be merry. I go."

He held the priest with one hand and tossed something to Eratosthenes with the other.

Next, there was a tremendous rush of air from the fantastic wings, and the giant birdman leaped over the balustrade and was gone.

Eratosthenes watched for a moment. At least the coursing creature was headed in the right direction.

Should he feel sorry for Hor-ent-yotf? He decided that maybe he should. However, he didn't. A character flaw, possibly. But who was perfect?

The rest of them joined him at the parapet. All eyes were looking out over the city, searching the skies. And now a collective gasp. "There!" cried someone. "The chariot!" shouted another. "See the lights!" "Straight into the rising sun!"

He turned away and hefted the strange ball Khor had thrown to him. No time now to study it in detail, but he knew intuitively what it was: a model of the Earth.

He raised his eyes. Ne-tiy was standing at the entrance-way, looking at him. The geometer walked toward her. "How it is on *his* world, I do not know. But in Greek lands, the man takes the woman, though she be exalted, and of the highest rank. And so I take thee, Ne-tiy."

She gave him a sweeping bow and a most marvelous smile.

16. The River

"I hope the Horus affair has taught you a lesson," said Ptolemy. "I think you must now be quite convinced."

The two couples rested under the rear canopy of the royal yacht, which was moving upriver with its great red sail stretched tightly by the north wind. Pauni and Ne-tiy were immersed in private murmurs while the men talked intermittently.

"I have learned much," admitted Eratosthenes.

"For myself," continued the Greek pharaoh, "I never had any doubt that the gods were real. It is a bit puzzling, though, that the god would take that priest. I never thought much of Hor-ent-yotf. Always considered him a dangerous fanatic. Shows how wrong even I can be."

"A memorable man," murmured Eratosthenes.

In silence they watched a riverside village pass. The river had now risen to the stage where the house-clusters were accessible only by causeways and moles. The brown people had drawn back into their reed and wattle cone-roofed huts to let father Hapi drop his bounty. In a couple of months the waters would recede. The farmers would sow their wheat and barley, and finally they would reap. Four months of flood and receding water, four months of sowing and growing, four months of harvest and drying up. Then repeat. And repeat. They had been doing this for more than fifty centuries. From time to time conquerors had flowed in, then out again, like waves on the seashore. Nubians . . . Hyksos . . . Assyrians . . . Persians. And now the Greeks. A million Greeks, up and down the river. How long would *we* last? Who throws *us* out? Rome? Carthage? "Majesty," said Eratosthenes, "what happened to those two ambassadors?"

"Interesting, that. They both got word that Panormus, on Sicily, fell to the Roman besiegers. Barca was recalled to Sicily to organize the Carthaginian guerrillas. Pulcher will return to Rome to organize an army to fight Barca. It's all insane, isn't it? What will they do with Sicily? Who cares? But Sicily isn't really the point, is it?"

Eratosthenes shrugged. "No. Actually, there are two points: one is greed, the other conquest. If Carthage wins, her greedy ships will sail west to Cipangu . . . the Indies . . . perhaps in our generation. They sail for trade and profit. If Rome wins, we will not see the antipodes for a thousand years. They go nowhere they cannot conquer. And they move only on roads."

"I fear I must agree," said Ptolemy. "We Greeks used to go out to colonize. But that spirit is dead. It died five hundred years ago." The pharaoh's nose twitched. He looked back toward the incense tripods on the stem of the yacht. "We cover the smell of death with other smells." The braziers burned balsam, carnation, anise, and the blossoms of assorted flowers.

Eratosthenes smiled. He didn't really care for the artificial smells either. Actually, he preferred the river odors: willows, reeds, orchards, palms, fish (living and dead), the dung of humans and beasts, all veneered by this massive rising water and its suggestion of distant melting snows. He studied the beads of condensate on the chill sides of his silver goblet.

Ptolemy was watching him. "It's cooled with crushed ice. Improves the tang and fights the heat. The locals prefer their beer warm. Do you realize they have never seen ice? They don't even have a world for it in their language."

"Curious," said Eratosthenes absently. Ice . . . snow . . . he mused. I made a special map of the Nile, beyond the cataracts, south to the confluence of the Blue and White Nile. Melting snow . . . that's what starts the yearly flood. Snow on far, equatorial mountains. Vast mountain ranges, far to the south. And feeder lakes. Big ones, inland seas. Some day we'll find them.

Ptolemy squinted around toward the ladies. "The priests are putting on quite a show at Thebes, in the great temple of Karnak. We would all be honored if the Betrothed-of-Horus could open the ceremonies."

"So it is written," said Eratosthenes gravely.

"Good. Settled. Religion, true religion, keeps a country alive, don't you agree, dear Eratosthenes?"

"Oh, quite."

"You've read Herodotus, of course. You recall that the Greeks at Marathon called on the great god Pan to terrify the Persians, and he did, and we won."

(Not to mention, we had a very smart general, thought Eratosthenes.)

"And you know," continued Ptolemy, "that Athena herself saved our fleet at Salamis. She was actually seen to alight on the prow of Themistocles' flagship."

"So I recall."

"So then, quite aside from the appearance of Horus last night, it is plain that the gods exist, and have been with us from the beginning. Clearly, they control human affairs. We must yield to the gods in all things, Eratosthenes. When science and religion conflict, science must yield."

Ptolemy took the geometer's silence for assent. "Did I ever tell you of the great Alexander's journey to the shrine of Ammon, at Siwah?"

(Many times, thought Eratosthenes.) "I don't seem to recall . . ."

"Well then. My father, the first Ptolemy, told it to me. Storms had completely obliterated the desert roads. Nothing to be seen but a sandy waste. The priests wanted to turn back. 'No,' said Alexander. 'If I am truly a natural son of Ammon, the god will send a guide.' And no sooner than spoken, here were these two serpents, rising out of the hot sands. 'Follow us,' they said, and off they went . . . "

(Wasn't it two ravens last time? thought Eratosthenes.) "Amazing," he said.

"He said to her, 'Be fruitful; be merry.' "

The map-maker had to think a moment. "Yes, the god Horus, to Ne-tiy."

"Not to you, though, Eratosthenes. Nothing merry about geometry."

"No."

"My father knew Euclid, who wrote his *Elements* back there in Alexandria. Father tried to plow through the *Elements*. Tough going. Complained to the master, there should be an easier way. Euclid replied, 'My lord, there is no royal road to geometry.' Father was so impressed that he founded the chair of mathematics at the Library. We've had a world-renowned geometer there ever since. Including you, young fellow."

"I am honored. And grateful."

"Actually, things turned out rather well for you."

"Yes."

To their rear the young women were talking in low tones. He heard a strange tinkling sound, as of little silver bells. He started to turn, then stopped. He knew what it was. Ne-tiy had laughed. He had never heard her laugh before. He relaxed and looked out over the river, to the west. The sun was a glowing semicircle, growing smaller and smaller as it dropped below the darkening hills.

"Gizeh," said Ptolemy, shading his eyes as he pointed into the sunset. "Have you ever seen the pyramids?"

"Yes, sire. But perhaps the ladies . . ."

The two women were already at the rail, looking out over the distant sands. The men joined them. They were all thralled to silence by the three immense structures.

Egypt, O Egypt, thought Eratosthenes. Land of cyclopean architecture and bestial gods. Where does awe leave off and disgust begin?

Twilight was brief. The sailors were already lighting lamps along the ship's walkways. Upriver, along the shore, more lights were visible. Torches, thought the mathematician. A lot of them. And the sound of sistra and tambourines, with shouting and singing and much merriment. The whole city was turning out to greet the pharaoh.

"We're coming into Memphis," said Ptolemy. "I'll have to join in the temple ceremonies, and Pauni and I will sleep in the palace tonight. You can join us, or you can remain on board."

"If it please you, we'll stay."

"I thought you might. You and the priestess may have my quarters. Everything is prepared. Until tomorrow, then."

17. Khor's Globe

Ne-tiy watched with uneasy curiosity as Eratosthenes opened the chest and carefully removed the little statue of Atlas, his back and arms still bent to receive his as yet invisible burden.

"I see writing on the base. An inscription in Greek," she said. "What does it say?"

"It says, 'Tell my friends I have done nothing unworthy of philosophy.' — Hermius."

"What does it mean? And who was he, this Hermius?"

"Hermius was a Greek who studied with Aristotle, under Plato. He was captured by the Persians and tortured. He said these words, and then he died."

"I see. You admire him."

"Very much." From another compartment he pulled out the ball that Khor had tossed to him on the balcony. Bigger than his fist, smaller than his head. It fit exactly on the titan's back.

"What is *that?*" whispered Ne-tiy.

"The world globe. Khor made it, and gave it to me as he left."

They both studied it in silence. It was clear she did not understand. Perhaps it was just as well. He was not sure *he* understood. It might have been better if Khor had never come. No, that wasn't so. He was very lucky that Khor had come.

But this globe . . . the artifact was far ahead of its time.

(She stole an uneasy look at his face.)

My great world map, he thought, over which I have labored so many years . . . compared to this it is almost nothing. A bare 80 degrees out of 360. We have not even scratched the surface. Most of the world is still out there, unknown, undiscovered. Who will be the first to find it? I wish I were a great sea captain. I'd take a dozen ships. Sail out through the Pillars of Hercules. Due west. Into the western hemisphere. And there meet those two great continents. How to get around them? Perhaps a northwest passage through the north polar sea? Or around the southern tip of the southern land giant? And then on, for a complete circumnavigation of the globe.

He sighed. Not in his lifetime. Perhaps not in a hundred years. Maybe not even in a thousand. But eventually ships would go forth to that new land. And find what? Cities? Savages? Strange animals and plants? No way to tell.

Back to Earth, map-maker! He pressed the globe's north polar cap with his index finger. There was a click, and a tiny spot of light began to pulse, on and off, on the facing side of the sphere.

Ne-tiy gasped. "What is that?"

"The light simply marks the spot where we are. See?" He pointed. "We are *here,* at Memphis. See the river? Yesterday the light point was on Alexandria, on the Great Green. In five days it will be at Thebes. Calm down, it won't hurt you. Down here is the rest of Africa. Above, Italy, Gaul, Iberia, the Tin Islands, Thule. East, India, Seres, Cipangu."

"Are there really such places?"

"Yes. Do you want to see the other side?"

". . . I don't know."

"Well, then, we won't look."

"Can you turn off the little light? It's like the eye of Horus. watching us."

He laughed, but turned it off. "You know what Homer said."

"What did Homer say?"

" 'Though all gods and goddesses look on, yet I gladly sleep with golden Aphro dite.' "

"I have a better one," said Ne-tiy. (For she knew she held the ultimate refutation of all science: geodetics . . . math . . . cartography . . . the rising of stars . . . the solstice of suns.) "*Aie se philo*—I love thee forever." She held out her arms.

This is my historical period. My bemused ancestors fought on both sides during the Civil War. West Virginia (where we came from) seceded from Virginia and joined the Union, but one of my distant Harness uncles organized and outfitted a company with his own money and joined up with General Lee. The Harness house on Route 220 near Moorefield, West Virginia, still stands, with rifle ports in the basement. And George Washington actually did spend the night there on his way to fiasco at what is now Pittsburgh.

QUARKS AT APPOMATTOX

"General Lee." A statement. A greeting. A question. "General" with a hard "g," and each syllable precisely enunciated. And something odd about the accent. More like "Gaynayral Lay."

The two officers in gray jackets stared down from their horses at the stranger who stood by his own mount, a beautiful bay. The soft radiance of the paschal moon revealed a man in uniform, but the jacket and trousers were neither blue nor gray. The newcomer was dressed in black. From his bearing, clearly a soldier. Rank uncertain.

The stranger saluted the tall officer with the white beard. "General Lee. I am Oberst Karl von Mainz, of the Army of West Germany."

If General Lee was puzzled, he concealed it well. He returned the salute and nodded toward his companion. "Colonel von Mainz, my aide, Major Potter." He studied the visitor a moment. "I presume you are a military attaché from His Majesty, King William of Prussia. Welcome, sir. We haven't had an attaché since the British Colonel Freemantle rode with us to Gettysburg. You must have overcome incredible hardships to join me here at Appomattox Court House, and quite possibly to no purpose." He peered through the semi-light. "I don't remember you in Richmond. How did you get through? The roads are jammed with Union troops."

"I used . . . a different approach, Herr General."

"Ah? Well, no matter. Major, would you please extend our hospitality to the colonel?"

His aide sighed. "It's parched corn and creek water, sir. No coffee. No tea. No brandy."

Robert Lee thought back. A Richmond lady had entertained him in her parlor a few months ago. She had given him a cup of real tea, made from what were probably the last genuine tea leaves in the doomed city. She had drunk her own cup of "tea," which he knew to be dark water from the James River. He had never let on. She had sipped, and she had smiled. A true Southern lady. All this was passing away. He said. "By your leave, Colonel, I will now retire. There will be action tomorrow morning that decides whether the war is over or whether it continues."

"Herr General, I know all about that. The Army of Northern Virginia now consists of two small infantry corps—Gordon and Longstreet—and a little cavalry. And you are in a tight box. On your east is General Meade, with the Second and Sixth Corps. To the west is Custer and most of the Union cavalry. To the south is Sheridan's cavalry. That's the bottom of the box, and that's where the Union lines are weakest. You propose to break out through Sheridan, move rapidly south on the Lynchburg Road, join up with General Johnston in North Carolina, and drag the war out until the North is willing to negotiate an honorable peace. But it won't work, Herr General."

General Lee looked at the German for a long time. "Sir, you seem to know a great deal about the tactical situation. So tell me, why can't I break out through the south?"

"Because, Herr General, history has already written the dénouement of this, your last campaign." He did not look at Major Potter. "May we discuss this in private, Herr General?"

Lee shrugged. "Very well." He dismounted and gave the reins to his aide. "Oh, it's perfectly all right, Potter. We'll be in the tent."

A stump of candle was already burning on the cracker box when they went inside. The Confederate officer motioned to the camp chair, then eased himself down on the cot. "I think we can push through Sheridan," he said.

The other nodded. "True, in the dawn fighting you will push back Sheridan's dismounted cavalry. Your boys will cheer. But that's the end of it. General Ord's Fifth Corps arrives just in time to reinforce Sheridan. The great game is over. You send out a rider with a white flag. At eleven tomorrow morning, Palm Sunday, you will send General Grant notice that you would like to meet him to discuss surrender terms. You will accept his demand for unconditional surrender. Tomorrow afternoon, except for a little scattered action in other theatres, the war will be over."

Lee was silent.

Von Mainz shrugged. "You think I am insane? I am not insane, General Lee. I know many events that lie in your future."

"How is this possible?"

"You think of me as a loyal subject of King William of Prussia and an officer of the Prussian army, in this year eighteen hundred five and sixty. Not exactly, General. I am not what you suppose. There are two very basic facts that you must accept. If you can accept these two facts and all that they imply, then you can understand everything you need to know about me. Fact number one, I am from your future. I was born in the year two thousand and thirty. I am thirty-five years old. I left the American Sector of Berlin this morning, April 8, in the year two thousand five and sixty, almost exactly two hundred years in your future. I am indeed a colonel, but not in the Prussian army. I am a colonel in the Neues Schutz-Staffeln—the 'NSS'—an underground paramilitary organization devoted to reuniting West and East Germany." He waited. "You don't believe me? Not just yet? No matter. I assure you, I can provide proof."

"West Germany . . . East Germany?" said Lee. "I don't understand."

"Never mind. It's a long story. With the general's permission, I'd like to state the second fact."

"Proceed. What is your second fact?"

"The second fact is that you can win the war. Not merely the impending battle. You can win the whole war."

Lee looked at him sharply. "How?"

"With a new weapon."

The older man smiled faintly. "Which you brought with you, of course, from your twenty-first century?"

"Of course. And please do not smile, General. It does not become you; nor is it fitting to the occasion."

Lee stood up. "Now, you really must excuse me, Colonel. Tomorrow will be a difficult day." He walked to the tent door. "There's Potter over there, by the napoleon. He'll find a place for you to sleep."

Colonel von Mainz joined him at the tent door and peered out into the moonlight. "A napoleon. Hah! The deadliest cannon of the war. Favored by both sides. Range, one mile. With canister at two hundred yards, wipes out an entire platoon. Like a giant sawed-off shotgun. The difficulty is, Grant has three times as many as you have, as well as plenty of powder and skilled gun crews. But you can even the odds, my General." The stranger flashed black eyes at his reluctant host. "May I demonstrate?"

"Go ahead."

Von Mainz smiled, then held a finger up. "On the other hand, General, it would be more convincing if you performed the experiment yourself."

"Really, Colonel—"

"Would the general please pull out the weapon from my rifle boot."

Lee walked over to von Mainz's horse, pushed the saddle bags aside, and tugged at what appeared to be a plain rifle stock. The thing came out with a long squeak. Lee carried it into a patch of moonlight for a better look. He frowned. "It's not a rifle . . . ?"

"Not exactly. Now then, shall I retire with your Major Potter, or do you want me to tell you about this . . . instrument?"

"Hm. It's a weapon, you said?"

"It is, indeed." The visitor smiled and crossed his arms over his chest.

"What does it fire?" asked Lee.

"Something in the nature of an electric charge."

"Electricity? For heaven's sake! But to what effect?"

"See for yourself. First, ask the good Major Potter to move a few meters away from the napoleon."

"Very well." Lee called out, "Major—move away to your left a bit. There. That's fine."

"Now," said the visitor, "take it to your shoulder and hook your finger around the trigger, just as you would a rifle. Aim it at the cannon barrel."

"What's this on the barrel?" muttered Lee. "A telescopic sight? No—what in the name of heaven! I can see everything, plain as day!"

"A snooperscope," explained von Mainz. "It senses infrared radiation."

"Whatever *that* is," said Lee. He began to perspire.

"A gentle squeeze on the trigger," prompted the German.

Lee felt a faint click as he closed the trigger.

The cannon seemed to vanish. The great Confederate first squinted; then his eyes opened very wide. Something was still there. Dust. Metallic dust glinting in the soft moonlight. Now beginning to settle. And a clatter as the wooden wheel spokes and undercarriage collapsed.

Lee hurried out to the shambles, followed by von Mainz. The general poked into the dust clumps with a boot toe. He bent over, picked up a handful, and smelled it cautiously. A faint odor—something like the residue of a lightning strike. He tossed the dust aside.

Major Potter ran over to Lee. "General! Are you all right? What happened?"

Lee stared first at his aide, then at the German colonel. "Potter, everything's fine. Excuse us, please. The colonel and I still have somewhat to discuss." He handed the strange weapon gingerly to von Mainz and motioned him back into the tent. The candle sputtered at the sudden draft.

"There are five more such weapons in my saddle bags," said von Mainz. "They merely require assembly. So. What do you think? Do you believe me now?"

"I believe," said Lee, "that I have seen a remarkable thing." He sat on the cot and motioned to the chair again. "How does it work?"

"I'm not a technical man—but I think I can give you the basic theory. You've heard of atoms, of course?"

"Yes."

"Atoms are made up mostly of even smaller particles called protons and neutrons. These in turn consist of sub-particles called quarks. These quarks are held together by a thing called the strong force, or color force. It is also called 'gluon,' because it functions like glue in holding the quarks together." He peered over at the tired gray face. "Do you follow me, General?"

"No, I'm afraid not."

"Well, I'm sorry. Shall I go on?"

"Please do."

"Very well, then. It appears that quarks have at least five flavors: up, down, strange, charm, and bottom. But we'll skip all that. The point is, General, that in my birth year, two thousand and thirty, a means was discovered to de-sensitize the gluon associated with the so-called *down* quark, which exists in neutrons of the structural metals. Since neutrons are made of one up-quark and two down-quarks, the consequence was that such metals could readily be caused to disintegrate. Your napoleon is—was—brass, an alloy of copper and zinc. Brass is quite susceptible. But so are musket barrels, swords, all the iron and steel instruments of war. Even the harmless things yield to it: belt buckles, buttons, stirrups, mess kits, telegraph keys, telescope barrels, spectacle rims . . ."

The general patted his jacket pocket uncertainly.

Von Mainz laughed. "Your glasses are safe, General. The weapon never back-fires."

Lee studied his visitor in silence. Finally he said, "The demonstration was indeed a success. Quite remarkable. I accept it as proof that you are from another time and place. But *that* simply raises additional questions. How did you get here from the future? What is it to you whether the South wins or loses? Why did you select me for your presentation?"

"Not so fast, dear General. Good questions, all valid, and there are answers. Why *you*? You are the commander-in-chief of all the armies of the Confederacy, and your army has a very pressing need for the weapon. You were therefore the logical choice.

"Now then, how did I get here? Not quite so easy to answer, but I can try. There is a device—really an entire cellar room—in Berlin. It is associated with an immense power source, all very accurately calibrated. In the center of the room is a sort of plate, a machine, actually, very cleverly constructed. A person stands on that plate, together with certain things he may wish to bring along, even including a horse. Then the dials are set to a specific time and place in the past, a compatriot pulls a switch, and the plate is empty. If the warp is accurate, the person in the chair moves from Berlin twenty sixty-five to . . . wherever, whenever . . ."

"I . . . see," murmured the general. "I think I see." He put his fingers to his forehead. "So here you are. But why? What difference does the outcome of this war make to you . . . to the NSS. . . to the Germany of the twenty-first century?"

"*Why*? Because I—my group—we want to change the past, and hence the future fate of the German people. You and I together can do this."

"Go on."

"I'm sure you realize, General, that in the history about to be written the South loses the war. The Union is reestablished. The United States spreads across the continent 'from sea to shining sea,' as your hymn says. Very quickly America becomes rich and populous. But she is not done with war. There will be a great war in nineteen fourteen to nineteen eighteen: at the start, Germany against England, France, and Russia. We would have won this war, except that America came in against us. Germany rose from the ashes and in nineteen thirty-nine tried again, against almost the same enemies. Again, we almost made it. Our armies lay on the outskirts of Leningrad—oh, St. Petersburg to you. We could see the church spires of Moscow. But once more America came in against us. America sent Russia immense quantities of war materials: shipload after shipload through the Persian Gulf, and in the north by Murmansk. These weapons you would find quite incredible. Self-propelled cannons with iron plating, called 'tanks.' Machines that flew through the air, capable of dropping terrible bombs. And big horseless carriages for moving troops rapidly. Our German armies had these things too, of course, but in nowhere near the numbers the Americans were able to furnish our Russian enemies." He sighed and took a deep breath. "In nineteen hundred three and forty the Russians began a general counterattack across the entire eastern front—some twelve hundred miles long. For us it was the beginning of the end. We gave up two years later."

"But you speak of history. All that will happen whether the South wins or loses."

"No, we think not. Our forecasters have made a number of studies on great machines called computers. The results agree as to several essential points. If America exists in two countries, North and South, neither would possess the industrial and manpower resources to make a difference in the war of nineteen fourteen to nineteen eighteen. Germany would have won. The German emperor—the kaiser—would have stayed in power, and there would have been no need for the war of nineteen thirty-nine to forty-five. Stalingrad . . . Lend Lease . . . our Führer committing suicide in a bunker in Berlin . . . all moot . . . will never happen."

"You are telling me, sir," mused the general, "if the South wins now, in eighteen sixty-five, Germany wins in nineteen eighteen."

"Exactly." The visitor smiled crookedly. "And more than that. The world wins. For twenty million people are scheduled to die in the war of nineteen thirty-nine to forty-five. They would live. And that's not all. America develops a bomb capable of destroying all humanity all over the globe. If the South wins in eighteen sixty-five, that bomb would not be available in nineteen forty-five."

"Interesting. And very curious. I can see that science is due to make immense strides in the decades ahead. But tell me—this present weapon—this strange rifle—what do you call it?"

"Dis. Short for disintegrator."

"Was it—perhaps I should say *will* it—be used in one of your future wars?"

"No, General. Happily—or unhappily—the radiation is readily nullified by insulating the metal with a certain coating."

"Suppose the North discovers this defensive coating?"

"They won't. It requires an alloy that won't be available for a hundred and fifty years." He looked at the general expectantly. "Well, sir?"

Lee seemed lost in thought. Finally he said, "No, I cannot accept the weapon."

Von Mainz was astonished. "But *why?*"

"Colonel, I can say a thing to you, a total stranger, that I cannot say to Mr. Davis, or to any of my own officers, or even to my wife."

"Sir?"

Lee's voice dropped. He said quietly, "I believe that the Almighty wills that the South shall lose."

The man from the future stared at him.

Lee said, almost sadly, "I am convinced at last that God has been trying to give me a message these past four years. I could have won at Sharpsburg in '62, except that one of my officers used my battle plan as a cigar wrapper, and it fell into McClellan's hands. And I would have won at Gettysburg if Stonewall Jackson had been there. But he had been shot at Chancellorsville by his own picket—another freak accident. And last year, in the battle of The Wilderness, victory was within our grasp. Longstreet was reaching out to take it—when he was shot by his own men. Another ghastly and impossible mistake. And that's not the end of it. Last year in his march to Richmond, Grant split his army to cross the North Anna River—Warren on the right, Hancock on the left. I moved in between them, and I could have smashed first one and then the other, except that I fell ill. If we had won on any of these occasions—Sharpsburg or Gettysburg or The Wilderness or on the North Anna—Britain and France would have recognized the South as a new nation. The North would have had to lift the blockade. Money, arms, food, everything would have poured in. We could have negotiated an easy peace with Washington, and we would have remained in permanent fact the Confederate States of America. But Providence intervened. Always at the critical place, the critical hour. I believe it to be the will of the Almighty."

"The will of the Almighty?" Von Mainz's jaw dropped. "Is childish superstition to decide this great struggle? *Gott in Himmel!* Is the strain finally too much?" He peered in hard suspicion at the man on the cot. "Let us face the realities, Herr General. Look at the facts! Lincoln has already carved your beloved state in two. The western section he calls West Virginia. The federals hold your plantation at Arlington. Your wife is an invalid in Richmond, and the city is burning. Are these calamities the will of God? Your son Fitzhugh rots in a federal prison. The war has already killed his wife and two children. And your own daughter Annie. Do you see in this a divine plan, General? Your army is starving. No rations in two days. You are finished. When this is over, General, the best that life can offer you is presidency of a tiny southern college with an enrollment of forty-five students."

"All that you say is true, and it is tragic," said Lee. "But some day the country will be great once again. Lincoln will see to that. He will not permit the South to be ground down like a conquered province."

Von Mainz laughed softly. "Lincoln dies one week from today. He will be assassinated while attending a play at Ford's Theatre in Washington."

The candle flame shuddered as Lee's head jerked up. "No!"

"Yes. History, dear General. And to your beloved South, terrible things are done by Lincoln's successors."

Lee groaned. "But the common people . . . we are of one blood . . . we are brothers."

Von Mainz shrugged.

Lee leaned over, stuffed a loose trouser leg back into a Wellington boot top, then tried to get up. His mouth twisted with pain.

His visitor leaned forward, concerned, but the older man waved him back. "Rheumatism, Colonel. I'm an old man. My joints . . ." He was up. "I cannot take your weapons, Colonel. I will take my chances on breaking out tomorrow. I think it pointless for you to remain any longer. How will you return to your time?"

"No problem, General. I step out into the darkness. There's a sort of gate, near where my horse is tethered. I go through with my weapons, and you never see me again. I'll leave the bay behind. He's yours, if you want him. Remind General Grant that in your army, the horses belong to the men personally, not to the Confederate government."

"If it should come to that."

"It will." The colonel looked overhead at the full moon. "Perhaps it's all for the best. You've heard of Jules Verne?"

"The French science writer? I've heard of him. Never read any of his books, though I understand *Five Weeks in a Balloon* was quite popular with our young people."

"Yes. And this year, *From Earth to the Moon*."

"Wild fantasy, Colonel."

"Is it? Your great *United* States of America will launch a manned ship from Cape Canaveral and it will land on the Moon, following which it will safely return to Earth. It will do that in just about one hundred years from now. And I have seen the return of the first *interstellar* ship. The ion engine was designed in Washington and Lee University."

" 'Ion' engine? All after my time. And I don't believe I know the institution. Any connection with the Lees of Virginia?"

"Very close, General." His guest smiled wryly. "The starship, incidently, was named the *Robert E. Lee. Auf Wiedersehen*, Herr General." He saluted, and disappeared through the tent flap.

The old soldier stared after him. Over a quarter million Southern lads dead in this war. It had lain within his power to make good their sacrifice, and he had thrust it aside. What would Stonewall Jackson think? And Jeb Stuart, and A.P. Hill? Were they all whirling in their graves?

Was he a secret Unionist at heart? Did he see this bountiful land stretching in a single golden band from Atlantic to Pacific, and from New Orleans to the Canadian border? Did he secretly think all men should be free? He had never owned a slave, except briefly, when he inherited a few from his mother-in-law. He had promptly emancipated them.

How much humiliation lay ahead for him, and for the army?

It was morning, and he was looking toward the south with fieldglasses.

"We got through Sheridan," he muttered. "But that's the end of it." He handed the glasses to his aide. "That's Ord coming up, isn't it?"

"Ord? Can't make out the regimentals, sir. Yes, I'm afraid so. A corps, at least."

"Row on row of blue," murmured Lee.

"Sir?"

"Never mind. The war's over, Potter. Signal General Gordon. He knows what to do."

"But—"

"Get on with it, Potter."

Wilmer McLean had a horrid sinking feeling in his gut. He knew now that the Almighty had had his eye on him in this war, from start to finish. On July 21, 1861, General Beauregard had requisitioned McLean's fine farmhouse near Manassas, and had just sat down to dinner, when a cannonball crashed into the dining room fireplace, thereby announcing that the federals were on their way to Richmond. So Wilmer McLean had sold out and moved south and west, to the village of Appomattox Court House, and here had built an even finer house, where by all logic he should have been to farm in peace and quiet, out of the path of armies.

But Fate had decreed otherwise. For just now his carriage circle and his front yard and his porch and his parlor swarmed with more generals and lesser officers—of both sides—than there were bees in his blossoming apple trees.

They all stopped talking a moment and made a path for an unkempt, slouched-over officer in a mud-spattered blue uniform. "Is General Lee up?" he asked. Somebody said yes, and he walked up on the porch and into Wilmer McLean's house.

"The rest is easy, General Lee," said General Gordon. "Our troops just march off down that road there, stack arms in the field at the right, and then they go home."

"There's a line of Yankees along the roadside," said Major Potter uneasily.

"Don't worry, Potter," said Lee. "That's Chamberlain's brigade. Just to keep order. Decent chap, Chamberlain. Used to be a college professor."

"There go my boys," said Gordon. "I'd better get out there with them."

"Yes, of course," said Lee. "Go on."

The officer cantered away.

From somewhere ahead a bugle shrilled. It echoed and re-echoed down the road. Then General Lee and his aide heard a hoarse shout, repeated up and down the blue line along the road, then the slapping of thousands of rifles on hardened palms.

Major Potter stood up in his stirrups. "My God, sir! What—!"

"It's all right, Major," said Lee quietly. "General Chamberlain has just given his Yanks the order for 'carry arms.' It's the 'marching salute'—the highest honor fighting men can give other fighting men." His eyes began to glow. "And look at Gordon. He's standing his horse up. His sword is out, and he's ordering . . . our boys to return . . . the salute." He coughed softly. "Dusty hereabouts, Potter."

"Yes, sir."

The *United* States, thought Lee. Both sides are going to try. We've got the future. It's all ahead of us. There for the taking. Science, that's what we need. Math. Chemistry. Physics. That's the road for our young people. And we need a vision. This fellow Verne has a vision. Get his books.

Potter was trying to ask him something. "What now, sir?"

Back to earth. "Where do you live, Major?"

"Florida, sir. My folks have a little farm on the Atlantic side."

"I was there in '61, trying to strengthen the forts. Where is your farm, Potter?"

"You probably never heard of it, sir, a place called Cape Canaveral."

"Oh, but I have, Potter."

"Really, sir?" The ex-officer looked at the man in gray with pleasure and astonishment, but no explanation was given him.

"Let's go home, Potter." Lee wheeled his horse and cantered off toward Richmond.

GEORGE WASHINGTON SLEPT HERE

1. Oliver Potts

Miss Catlin waited until her employer had laid his briefcase on the credenza and sat himself behind his desk. "Did you win your case, Mr. Potts?"

He beamed up at her. "Of course not, Miss Catlin. Any calls?"

"The local D.A.R. wants you to give a talk . . . preferably something early American. Refreshments."

"What was my last D.A.R. lecture?"

"Termite resistance of white oak log cabins, I believe."

"And that about exhausts my colonial expertise. On the other hand . . . re–freshments, you said?"

"A colonial menu."

"Tell them I'll accept."

"They'll want to know the title of your talk."

"I'll think of something. And don't sound so cynical, Miss Catlin." He squinted at an engraved card on his desk. "What's this?"

His secretary sniffed. "Junk mail, Mr. Potts. I really shouldn't have brought it in. It just means somebody has accessed into the Bar Association roster."

"Gracious, Miss Catlin, it's an invitation. For membership in the Trust for Preservation of Mount Vernon."

"Translation: they want money."

"For a good cause, I'm sure. Wasn't there an enclosure?"

"Oh, Mr. Potts! You're so gullible." She handed him a folder.

"See, they're trying to duplicate some things that turned up missing when Washington died in 1799. Saddle bag, given to him by Congress in 1783. Long underwear, imported from London. A 1795 ten dollar gold piece. And so on. Where's your patriotism, Miss Catlin? They're trying to restore Mount Vernon the way it was when *he* died."

"Patriotism, Mr. Potts—and I remind you I got this from you—is the last refuge of a scoundrel."

"Send them one hundred."

"Mr. Potts. Your office needs painting. The reception room needs new furniture. That sofa is a disgrace. If you want to restore something, start here. Ten dollars. Not a penny more."

"Catlin—oh, the hell with it. Get the phone."

She picked it up. "Oliver Potts law office." After a moment she said to him, "It's Mr. York's secretary, calling from Sena City. She wants to talk to you."

"I'll take it here. Yes, Miss Joyner? Accident? What? *Dead?* Good God." (Potts *never* used profanity) Miss Catlin watched his face in growing alarm as he listened further to the stricken voice in his earpiece. "Due in court this afternoon? But surely . . . the local guys . . . Nobody will take it? The judge . . . Oh. Oh. What a . . ." He mumbled the word as he looked at his watch. "The commuter flights leave on the half hour. I can just make it." He bounded from his chair, grabbed his attaché case, and dashed for the door. He called over his shoulder to Miss Catlin (who was standing there shaking her head): "Phone the printouts in to the plane . . . *Sena* v. *Bridge Authority* . . . Judge Roule . . . g'bye!"

Oliver Potts graduated tenth from the bottom in a law class of one hundred and forty-seven. He accepted his low estate philosophically. When he started his practice he assumed that rich clients with sure winners were not going to flock to his door. In this he was quite right. How then, he asked himself, shall I pay the rent, a secretary's salary, and sometimes eat? It was then that he made a remarkable discovery: for every winning litigant there is a loser. Fifty percent of all those anxious faces are losers. *They* are your clients! The field is white unto the harvest! Go get them, Oliver!

And so he did. Losers, sensing a kindred spirit, brought their cases to him in droves. Incredibly, some of them had money, and paid his fees. And so he acquired a certain reputation, absolutely unique in his county: during his entire professional career, spanning nearly two decades, he had never won a case.

Since he entered each individual contest expecting to lose, the foreseen result rarely surprised or disappointed him. But there was more to it. Opposition counsel dreaded taking the winning side versus Potts. Examples abounded. A prestigious law firm with a sure-win medical malpractice suit, after spending ninety thousand dollars in desk time, won a judgment of three dollars, of which they kept one-third. In another instance Potts lost a famous product liability case because of a local statute-of-limitations, but the notoriety stimulated a dozen additional cases where the statute had not run out.

In a case of alleged failure to pay for a newspaper, he successfully counterclaimed for false arrest, libel, kidnaping, and assault. But his client was still required to pay five cents for the paper.

Perhaps the closest Potts ever came to not losing was his famous hound-dog case. His client, serving a ten-year sentence, had been put in charge of the bloodhound kennels at the prison farm. Soon thereafter he walked out. Since he took all the dogs with him, there was no easy way to track him. Ten years later he was recaptured. Potts, his court-appointed lawyer, argued that the warden was criminally negligent and guilty of entrapment for putting his client in charge of the dogs. Potts argued further that the ten-year sentence must now be considered served, in that his client had cared for the dogs for a full ten years and indeed had set up a nationally known breeding farm based on the original prison nucleus. The care and feeding came to twenty thousand dollars, plus interest. His client went free, the state paid a large sum in settlement; yet Potts felt that he had lost, since his client had to return an equivalent number of dogs to the prison kennels. The warden and D.A. both took early retirement. They went partners on a chicken farm in eastern Maryland and were never heard from again.

The current curse at bar smokers: "May you win against Oliver Potts." Potts accepted their opprobrium with rancorless resignation.

An hour after Potts left his office he was looking down out of the plane window. Below him, meandering off to the right, was the big river. From up here, though, it didn't look too impressive. And there were the twin cantilever towers, one on each side of the river, nicknamed George and Martha by the irreverent. Toys at this height, but soon they'd hold a span between them, and the whole thing would be transformed into the great George Washington Bridge. Not intended to rival the famous George Washington suspension bridge in New York City, of course, but named rather in memory of Washington's early surveying trips into the wilderness. He had crossed the river on a raft when he was eighteen, and on the western side had carved his initials on Sena Rock: "G. W. 1750." The scratches were now covered by steel and concrete of the growing cantilever, but Potts had read that plaster casts of the legend had first been made, and that miniatures (made in Taiwan) could be bought at local souvenir stands.

That tower on the right —"George"—*that* was what all the fuss was about. He tried to remember some of the things he had read in the papers. His friend Fenleigh York had been insane to take the case. Or else the fee had been irresistible.

"Mr. Potts?" called the stewardess. "Mr. Oliver Potts?"

He held up his hand.

"You have a call."

"Thanks." Catlin had got the data already. Nice work. He walked back to the communicator cubicle, pulled the curtain behind him, and pushed the "Come In" button on the keyboard.

He watched intently as the screen came alive. First, the abstract.

Sena v. *Bridge Authority*
Plaintiff petitions order (a) restraining Defendant from taking a certain river-side parcel by eminent domain & (b) requiring Defendant to dismantle cantilever bridge tower from said parcel.

Good Lord! thought Potts. Fen took money for *this?* Well, let's go on. Now we get the people.

There's Judge Maximilian Roule, walking up the courthouse steps. (Nice holo definition.) Nervous springy man. Grim face. Combination of Louis the Fourteenth and Machiavelli. Maybe just the camera angle? Stiffest sentences in the state. Maximum Max. Lines of print now zipping in on the CRT. Net worth: indeterminate. Some sources say near bankruptcy. Others say he has recently recouped lost fortune. Hobby, bridges. Off you go, judge.

Next, Sena. Miss? Mrs.? York's client. And now mine. Is that her first or her last name? Named for Sena City? She's walking across a lawn. That's probably her house? Yes. The Bridge Authority let her move it away from the condemnation site. Fine figure. She turns, waves. Smiles. Beautiful face. Pale coppery complexion. Age, uncertain. Looks to be about twenty-five. Income, independent but modest.

And now, counsel for the opposition, Barton Badging. Bachelor. President County Bar Association. Presiding chairman local chapters FFV, SAR. President, Sena City Numismatic Association. Monographs: *Seventeenth Century Immigrants to Tidewater Virginia; George Washington's Personal Silver Converted to Dismes and Other Coins.* The holo showed Badging making a speech at a banquet table.

"Vocal," prodded Potts.

"Poor audio," apologized the cassette.

"Go ahead."

Scratchy words came from the little figure. "Fellow numismatists, twenty years ago I said to myself, there is a perfect 1795 gold eagle out there, waiting for me. Where? I don't know. All I know is, it's there. Do any of you know its whereabouts? If so, please tell me. Before I die, I want to see that beautiful coin, in proof condition. Not merely extremely fine. Not merely uncirculated. Not even MS—mint state. This coin at the end of the rainbow, this elusive piece of gold, will be in absolutely *proof* condition."

"And *you*," muttered Potts, "are an absolute crock." But then he stopped to think. "On the other hand, maybe this kind of thing is standard at Sena City. Watch out, Ollie."

Next, Marcus Reed, Bridge Authority Chairman. Coming out of the Sena Athletic Club. Looks both ways before he crosses the sidewalk to his limo. Entrepreneur. Politician. Billionaire. Reed is major stockholder in Reed Construction, Inc., building the Bridge.

Potts punched "hold." The little holo figure of Marcus Reed froze, glaring up at him as though affronted by the restraint.

Potts asked the computer, "Who are the other stockholders in Reed Construction?"

"Mrs. Reed . . ."

"And . . . ?"

"There's a twenty-five percent slice, owner unidentified."

"Find out."

"Data insufficient."

He punched "run." The rear door of Reed's car opened, and the great man got in.

Who opened the door for him? thought Potts. Of course, the chauffeur might have done it by remote.

He punched "reverse," then "run."

There. A hand; a blurred face. Potts zoomed in. Poor definition. Yet . . . Was it possible? His heart began to pound. Judge Roule. Maximum Max.

It doesn't necessarily mean a thing, he told himself. Maybe they're old buddies from college. Maybe they're working together on a local charity. And maybe I'm the queen mother.

His voice was a dry crackle. "Breakdown, Roule's assets."

"Unavailable."

"Does Roule have an equity position in Reed Construction?"

"Unavailable."

"Terminate Reed. Give me the police report on the death of Fenleigh York, last night."

He watched the lines scroll up.

"York car accompanied by truck crashed through cable railings on Palisade Drive. York vehicle found on its back at bottom of hill. Truck burned midway to river. Unidentified witness states truck forced the car off the cliff, but locked bumpers with it at the last moment and went over with it. Truck reported stolen Wednesday last."

Then the ambulance report. Hospital report. Both York and truck driver DOA.

"Any holos?" asked Potts.

"No."

"Where was he going?"

"Data insufficient."

"Does Palisade Drive lead to the airport?"

"Yes."

"Did Mr. York hold a reservation?"

"No."

That didn't mean much, one way or the other. On a commuter flight you didn't generally need a reservation.

"Did he make a phone call to Capital City yesterday?"

"Checking. Yes."

"To whom?"

"It's listed simply as the Judicial Grievance Committee."

Oh God. Fenleigh was going to blow the whistle on something or somebody. The judge? Marcus Reed? But they had found out. And they took his whistle away. Permanently. His friend had been murdered.

And where, he mused, does that leave *me?*

"Fasten your seat belts," ordered the bland dead voice of the stewardess. "Extinguish all smoking materials. We are landing at Sena City Airport."

2. Sena

He parked his rental car in a nearby lot, dashed up the courthouse steps, and found the right courtroom by instinct. And so up the aisle and through the swinging gate at the bar.

They were all waiting for him.

The woman was a striking beauty. Light amber complexion, lustrous black hair and eyes. "Oliver Potts," he puffed. "Your new lawyer, if you want me."

She shrugged, as if to say, Do I have a choice? Then her mouth twisted into a half-smile. "Yes, Mr. Potts. Of course I want you."

He nodded, then walked up to the bench. "Oliver Potts, Your Honor, replacing Mr. York."

Judge Roule scowled. "All right. Tell the reporter, Mr. Potts."

On his way back to his seat he gave his card to the court reporter and stopped by to introduce himself to opposing counsel. He noted that Barton Badging was a prim-looking gentleman who wore gold-coin cufflinks, a tie pin fashioned from a coin, and had a gold-coin watch fob dangling from a heavy gold chain stretched across his vest. Opposing counsel stared up at him in grave distaste. "Barton Badging," he said. He made no effort to accept Potts's outstretched hand.

The judge hammered with the gavel. "If the social hour is over, we have a trial in progress." He glared suspiciously at the newcomer. "We know you by reputation, Mr. Potts. But let me tell you right now, I like things clear-cut in my court. A winner wins clean. A loser loses clean, and no funny business. That's it. Black and white. Do you understand, Mr. Potts?"

"I couldn't agree more, Your Honor."

"Good. So sit down, Mr. Potts."

Potts sat down beside his client.

"Motions?" asked Judge Roule.

Potts was immediately up again. His eyes locked with the judge's for one long moment. Patches of goosebumps raced up and down his cheeks, his arms, his back. His biceps contracted. His veins were awash in adrenalin.

It was happening to the judge, too. The lawyer read the body language clearly. The man behind the bench fidgeted, he wet his lips with a thick wet tongue. He fiddled with his gavel. He returned the lawyer's stare uneasily.

In these milliseconds (while no one else in the room noticed) they measured each other like skilled swordsmen. They circled like wolf and prey, like cobra and mongoose. Starfish and oyster. The question was, who was who? Who was hunter, who was hunted? No way yet to tell. But Potts believed he would know very soon.

He spoke, and as he spoke, he opened the lid of his attaché case in a careless absent motion and switched on the tekt-x cube. He said, "Your Honor, as you may be aware, I am absolutely new to the case. So that I can familiarize myself with the issues, I request a continuance for one week."

Judge Roule stared down at the lawyer through wide-spaced eyes set deep under bushy brows. Slowly, his smooth cheek pads pulled back, lifting his mouth into a fanged grin. "No, Mr. Potts, no continuance."

So, thought Potts. Now we know. The roles are defined. You're the heavy. Just as I thought. Did you send out that truck that killed Fenleigh? Okay, Roule. I expect to lose, but in the process, you're going down. He said: "If I cannot have a week, Your Honor, could I have at least one hour with my client?"

"Oh, come now, counselor! Don't you read the papers? Surely you know this is the famous George Washington Bridge case. It's been going on in this very courtroom for days. Look at the reporters behind you, there in the first row." The jurist frowned, then sighed, as though unable to cope with the incompetence of imported counsel. He leaned forward. "Listen carefully, Mr. Potts. You won't need a continuance or a long rambling futile discussion with your client, because I'm going to brief you myself. The Bridge Authority is building a bridge, known as the George Washington Bridge. As a preliminary necessary step, the state has taken by eminent domain certain access properties on both sides of the river. Did the state have the power to condemn and take? That's the main issue, Mr. Potts. Plaintiff claims the taking was improper, in that the parcel on one side of the river included the Sena Rock, given by the United States to a foreign power as site for an embassy or consulate or trading post, or something of the sort. Plaintiff also contends that the Sena Rock lacks the compressive strength to carry the weight of the structures that will eventually rest on it. She tells us that as soon as another five thousand pounds is added to the west cantilever tower—the so-called "George" tower—Sena Rock will collapse and the tower will drop into the river. To prevent this, she asks that I order construction be suspended, and that the bridge site be moved one quarter-mile upriver." He favored the woman sitting next to Potts with a mocking smile. "Have I stated the case, Madame Plaintiff?"

"Yes, Your Honor," she said quietly.

"Then," continued the judge, "believing that the interests of Plaintiff's alleged embassy and of the Bridge Authority will be adequately protected by prompt proceedings, and bearing in mind that this court serves the public interest in searching for an immediate resolution of all issues, I deny Plaintiff's request for a continuance. We will go forward. For your information, Mr. Potts, Plaintiff completed her main case yesterday. Today we hear from the Defendant, the Bridge Authority. Mr. Badging?"

As Potts sat down he flashed a reassuring smile at his client. She did not smile back.

At the other counsel table, Barton Badging got to his feet. "Your Honor, we renew our motion for dismissal. Surely, this farce has gone far enough."

"I appreciate your viewpoint," said Roule. "On the other hand, this is a court of record. You must state your reasons."

"Yes Your Honor. First, the alleged treaty, Plaintiff's Exhibit One. Plaintiff concedes it is written in a foreign language, unreadable by anyone except herself. Indeed, she concedes that the granting party, an alleged tribe of alleged Indians, vanished from this area some three thousand years ago. This alleged treaty is sheer madness, Your Honor." He paused and turned to peer over half-moon spectacles at Oliver Potts. He smiled. "But it doesn't stop there, Your Honor. No indeed. There's the matter of the identity of the foundation rock, the so-called Sena Rock, which Plaintiff urges is the site of her mysterious embassy. This rock, she would have us understand, is not part of the foundation bedrock of the area. It is not, she claims, native basalt, poured up from the bowels of our mother Earth two hundred million years ago, part of several thousand square miles of companion flow. Oh, no indeed. Nothing so geologically banal. *Her* rock is special. It was formed out of nothing; out of blank space, if you will, by esoteric processes known only to Plaintiff's countrymen. And why special?

She does not say. She says only that it will not support the weight of the west tower." Mr. Badging chuckled mournfully. "Really, Your Honor, if you will but look out the window"—he pointed, and they all looked—"you can see that the tower is substantially complete, and that the alien rock—if we may call it that—is holding up nicely." He took the lapels of his jacket in pink hands. "If ever a case should never have come to court, it is this one." He bowed eloquently to the judge, perfunctorily to opposing counsel, and sat down.

Potts, who had been simultaneously reading, listening, and taking notes, now arose. "We oppose the motion to dismiss. The Bridge Authority is attempting to moot this case by completing the west tower during this trial. I remind the Authority that if the treaty is finally upheld, the bridge would be subject to dismantling and removal. At Defendant's expense, I might add. But that problem is minor compared to the risk of life involved with continuing construction. The records show that there are never less than ten workmen on the tower, and that forty or more are not unusual, including riveters, welders, crane operators, painters, and others. If Sena Rock collapses, the cantilever tower comes down, and most of these men will be killed." He took his seat.

The judge seemed to study the oak surface of his bench. Then he looked up and searched out the face of the woman seated by Potts. He said carefully: "The record is not sufficiently complete for me to rule just now on Defendant's renewed motion for dismissal. In any event, I have a couple of questions for Plaintiff. Madame . . . *Sena,* is it?"

She rose gracefully. "Simply Sena, your honor. It is an abbreviation of Asenaa peeneniwa, which, in the tongue of the Algonquian Indians, means 'Spirit-of-the-Rock.' "

"Hm. You are an Indian?"

"No."

"Indeed? Of what race are you? Who are your ancestors?"

"I have no race and no ancestors."

"No games, young woman. Remember, I can hold you in contempt. Everyone has ancestors."

"Not I, Your Honor."

The judge's eyes flashed. "Not even a mother?"

"No."

"Then, how came you into existence?"

"I was made by . . . certain people."

"When?"

She hesitated. "I'm over twenty-one, Your Honor."

The judge sighed. "I see. Let's go on to the Rock. I gather that the people who, ah, 'made' you, also 'made' the Rock."

"Yes."

"When did they make the Rock?"

She shrugged. "Before they made me."

Roule's face reddened. "You are being evasive, young lady. I can accept a certain amount of evasiveness when a lady's age is involved. But the age of Sena

Rock is another matter entirely. If you know when your people made the Rock, I require that you say."

"The Rock is at least ten thousand years old; possibly twelve."

"But not more than twelve?"

"Not more than twelve."

The judge frowned. Then he glared at the tittering courtroom audience, then at Oliver Potts, then back at the woman. "You are aware of the state geologist's report, already stipulated in the pleadings?"

"Yes, sir."

"You know that report states that the bedrock in the abutment area is metamorphosed basalt, which is to say, tough, resistant greenstone, exposed locally some two hundred and thirty *million* years ago?"

"Yes."

"*Not* a mere ten or twelve thousand years ago?"

"True, Your Honor."

"How do you explain the inconsistency?" He leaned back in his plush highback chair, safe in the certainty there could be no rational explanation.

"It's simple, Your Honor. The geologist took rock samples at one-mile intervals. He missed the embassy site altogether."

"The embassy site, which is to say, Sena Rock, is not greenstone?"

"It is not. It just looks like greenstone."

Roule was thoughtful. "Let us back up a bit. Into this 'non-greenstone' the builders have cut great gaping holes. They have sunk giant rebars, they have poured vast volumes of corrosion-resistant concrete. On this basement rock abutment they have built a cantilever, with arms reaching backward from the shore and forward over the river. Sena Rock *looks* like bedrock. It is *acting* like bedrock. The cantilever tower is anchored to it firmly. It is supporting the tower nicely, just as greenstone is supposed to. But you say it isn't greenstone."

"It isn't."

"What is it, then?"

"Synthetic matter, Your Honor."

"Synthetic? You mean like synthetic fabric? Plastics? Something like that?"

"Not at all. The matter was synthesized from nothing . . . from space—using an energy catalyst. The atomic spacings . . . silicon, oxygen, the alkali metals, are quite satisfactory for imitation rock, but they're all wrong for true greenstone."

During this interplay Potts had been dividing his attention between his client, the judge, opposing counsel, and the tekt-x cube in his attaché case. This device was actually a remote laser-reading polygraph. It cast out a 360-degree laser net and brought back modified pulses in the reflected beams that showed the standard vitals in selected nearby personnel: pulse beat, blood pressure, respiration, galvanic skin response, and voice stress. In sum, the reader was a lie detector that operated without attachment to the subject. In prior litigation Potts had used it successfully to conduct simultaneous and continuing screens of the witness in the box, the judge, opposing counsel, and his own client. He had never served in an ongoing trial where everyone told the truth all the time. The fact no longer amazed him. Indeed, he accepted it (with morose reluctance) as a statement about the human condition, probably including himself.

He watched the recessed code lights on the tiny reader panel. He was getting some interesting readings from Barton Badging. His opponent was hiding something. I fear you have not led a lily-white professional life, Mr. Badging. But you're a featherweight compared to what we're getting from Maximum Max. The man was totally corrupt. Have to get back to him. But the judge wasn't the immediate problem. He could cope with corruption. The real trouble was with his client.

Sena wasn't registering at all.

It wasn't a question of under- or overreacting. It was much worse. The tekt-x simply wasn't picking up any readings from her body. Nothing whatsoever. A marble statue would show more activity.

Perhaps the laser net was defective in her direction? He gave the box a quarter turn. Still nothing. He rotated the instrument back. As he did this, he saw she was watching him from the corner of her eye.

Ah, he thought. She's taking it all in. She knows what the tekt-x does. She knows she doesn't register. Now what?

"Sorry," she whispered. "I'll turn on."

The little lights assigned to her suddenly lit up. The base lines for all her vitals showed absolutely normal: pulse, 70; b.p., 125 over 65; respiration, 16; perspiration normal; no voice stress. As if to compensate for her zero emotional level, his own light panel began to flash. *His* pulse, blood pressure, and galvanic skin index readings were jumping off the register. He had stopped breathing, but now his chest was beginning to work again.

"Could I give you a tranquilizer?" she whispered.

"I'm . . . okay."

No. He wouldn't believe it. Somehow, the little machine had malfunctioned. They do that. These modern electronic marvels . . . when they work, they work beautifully. But when they don't, everything comes apart. Maybe a short somewhere. Have the technicians check it out. Seems to be working fine now. I overreacted. What's the matter with me? This woman is insane. How did I get roped into this? Fen was never stupid. Why did *he* take it? Money, probably. And now I've got it, and I've got some kind of duty to this madwoman. The county asylum is supposed to be around here somewhere. Maybe we'll all be in it before this is over.

For the next hour he listened to the drone of the enemy expert, as prodded and led by Badging.

"Now, Dr. Davis, you have heard Plaintiff's testimony that pressure alters the morphology of rocks and minerals?" said Badging.

"Yes, sir."

"Is that a danger here?"

"Not at all."

"Why not?"

"It is only *extreme* pressures that alter the characteristics of materials. At ten thousand atmospheres mercury solidifies at room temperature. At slightly greater pressures, boiling water solidifies, and graphite changes to diamond. At one hundred thousand atmospheres iron becomes non-magnetic. At slightly under one million atmospheres spinel is squeezed into perovskite. All these transformations are readily achieved in a diamond anvil pressure cell, and they all involve reductions in volume. However, such transformations cannot possibly take place under the pressures resulting from the west cantilever, the so-called 'George' tower."

"What *is* the average pressure on the George tower area?" asked Badging.

"Less than sixty pounds per square inch—about four atmospheres."

Sena bent over to Potts. "It's not the average pressure that's critical—it's the total *weight*. And they will indeed exceed *that*."

"Noted," whispered her lawyer. "We'll put you back on for that point during rebuttal." (If we get that far, he said to himself.)

"Your witness," said Badging.

Potts faced the expert. "Just now, Dr. Davis, you have offered considerable engineering data as to the effect of pressure on minerals."

"Yes, sir."

"You did the experiments yourself?"

"Experiments? I don't understand."

"Well, for example, did you go into the laboratory, take a piece of coal, and apply pressure to it, say in a diamond anvil, whereby you noted that at a certain pressure the coal changed to graphite? Is that the kind of thing you did?"

"Oh, no. I just copied some data out of an engineering handbook."

Potts addressed the judge. "All of Dr. Davis's testimony is obviously hearsay, Your Honor. I move it be stricken."

Roule pointed to the computer screen on the comer of his bench. "You see the green light, Mr. Potts. Motion denied."

Potts showed amazement. "But, Your Honor, there's a long line of cases—"

"The computer has spoken, Mr. Potts. In this court admissibility is determined by computer. Our computer accesses *all* relevant cases, and it is infallible. Error is inconceivable; hence no appeal lies to the state supreme court. And certainly in this case it is in the public interest that our decision be final as well as prompt. Do you understand, Mr. Potts?"

"Yes, Your Honor."

"Any further cross?"

"I'd like to pose a hypothetical to Dr. Davis."

"Involving what?"

"Plate tectonics."

Badging cried out, "Objection! Irrelevant."

Roule hesitated. He said, "Let's hear it, then I'll decide."

"Doctor," said Potts, "isn't it true that the Atlantic plate is subject to internal strains?"

"That's the current theory," admitted Dr. Davis.

"Such intra-plate strains, in fact, caused the great Charleston earthquake of 1886?"

"Yes, we think so."

"Now, if 'George' falls, mightn't the collapse trigger plate vibrations that will bring 'Martha' down, too?"

"I repeat my objection!" Badging was on his feet and waving his arms. "This hypothetical is highly improper. Your Honor, there has been no credible testimony that the George tower is any danger whatsoever."

"Ms. Sena has so testified!" insisted Potts.

"No *credible,* I said," reiterated Badging.

"Gentlemen, gentlemen, calm yourselves," rumbled Roule. "I agree with you, Mr. Badging. We'll strike the hypothetical question and answer." The dark eyes gleamed down at the visiting lawyer. "Mr. Potts, the court will take judicial notice that strong ties of love and affection existed between George and Martha Washington, and indeed that, when he died, she soon followed. However, these bonds and identities do not carry over into modern cantilever design, however named."

Potts sighed. "Nothing further, Your Honor."

As he sat down, the woman passed him a scribbled note: "The computer panel is rigged. The judge controls it by buttons under the bench."

Probably true, thought Potts, but how did she know? Did she have strange electronic sensors in her brain and/or body? He nodded to her, then wadded up the note. And there was another puzzle. Since they were going to lose on the merits, why did the judge have to resort to dirty tricks?

After a lunch break Badging put on several more witnesses: a real estate appraiser who testified to the value of the condemned parcel; a bridge engineer who swore the structure design met all codes and was absolutely safe; a gentleman from the U.S. State Department who explained the protocol for selection of sites for embassies and consulates and who denied that the Department had any record of a foreign embassy on Sena Rock; a psychiatrist who refused to look at Sena while he testified that she was ruled by delusions and hallucinations.

Potts objected to one and all, for various reasons, without avail. The green light for admissibility lit up on each and every occasion.

Late in the afternoon Badging said, "That's my case, Your Honor."

"Yes. Hm. A very thorough presentation, Mr. Badging." The judge peered at the clock at the back of the courtroom. "It's six o'clock. Will you have any rebuttal, Mr. Potts?"

"I'd like to consult my client about that, Your Honor. I've had no opportunity—"

"You had a whole hour at lunch to talk to your client, Mr. Potts."

The lawyer stifled a groan.

"But," said the judge, "this is a generous court. We are, above all, fair." The sardonic eyes glinted down at the lawyer. "I'll give you the, weekend. Court adjourned until ten o'clock Monday morning." With a swish of his robe he swept from the dais.

"All rise . . ."

Potts felt a great relief. It could have been worse. At least now he had a couple of days. Weekends are gifts of the gods to lawyers in mid-trial. A time for research, talking to the client, hunting witnesses, finding that crucial bit of data or that milestone citation to spring on Monday. Forty-eight hours to recover from Friday's trauma.

He closed his attaché case carefully. "We have to talk," he told his client.

"Where are you staying?"

"At the Colonial, if they're still holding the room."

"Drive over behind me. I know where it is. There's a good restaurant across the street."

3. Dhorans

She insisted on going up to the room with him. As they stepped inside, she held her finger up to her lips. He looked at her in wonder. She walked over to him and whispered into his ear: "Bugged."

He nodded. Somehow it didn't surprise him. He fished around in his case, brought out a micro-cassette player, and placed it on the night table.

They left quietly, down the back stairs to the street.

"What's on the tape?" she asked as they walked into the rear of the restaurant.

"Some high entertainment. It'll keep the goons glued to their earphones for a couple of hours."

"Standard equipment?"

"I never leave home without it. What's good to eat here, Sena?"

"I like the trout. They don't take them from the river anymore, of course. Probably flown in from Spain or Alaska."

He ordered quickly. "We must talk. Forgive me if I'm blunt and tactless."

"Go ahead."

"How old are you?"

"You heard me tell the judge."

"I'd like to hear it from you."

She would not look at him. "Everyone thinks I'm crazy. Do you?"

"No." (Chalk up one lie, Potts. But what could he say?) "Are you?"

"Sometimes I think I am."

"What are your earliest memories?"

"Is that important?"

"I can appreciate your reluctance." He shrugged. "A young friend once asked me, 'Should I put on my resumé that I have seen a flying saucer?' I told him, 'Don't admit it—to anyone—*ever!*' But since then, I've had second thoughts. Honesty has its points, too. Please answer, if you can."

"I've never told anyone before. Not even *him*." She sighed.

Him? Better not ask just yet. He waited.

"I came out of the Rock at sunrise," said Sena. "That's the first thing I remember. The great ship was there. Three or four of the People were standing around, watching me. I knew they had made me. They had copied an Indian girl of the neighborhood. I also knew they had given me much knowledge, and

I knew what I was supposed to do to preserve the Rock. After a time they got back into the ship, and it made a soft hissing sound, and then it vanished."

"These People . . . what did they look like?"

"They floated . . . they pulsed . . . they vibrated . . . mostly they were balls of light . . . sometimes things stuck out of them, like coiling light rays . . ."

"Go on. What happened next?"

"That morning a herd of great horned creatures came down to the river to drink."

"Deer?"

"Much bigger. The giant bison, I think. Their horns were easily six feet across, point to point."

"Are you sure, Sena? The giant bison became extinct in North America about ten thousand years ago."

"That's what they were, though."

"How about horses? Camels?"

"Those too. And giant sloths. And big cats, what you call saber-tooth tigers. They're all gone, now."

Sandia fauna, thought Potts. All extinct by seven thousand B.C. "You were 'copied' from an Indian girl? Did you have much contact with the early Indians?"

"Not much. But they were there. They hunted the bison and the other hooved creatures."

"With bows and arrows?"

"This was before bows and arrows. But they had spears and were skilled with the atlatl—the spear thrower. And there were cliffs nearby—the Palisades, where Mr. York died. The early people stampeded the herds over the cliffs and took meat and hides down below. The cliffs were much steeper then."

"Why did your People select this particular site for the Rock?"

"It's one of the few places they could bring into focus with a matching plate on Dhora. The plates line up every two hundred years, and make sort of a bridge. Then they can cross over."

"Dhora?"

"Their world."

"I see." (He didn't.) "Why did they make you a female?"

"I believe they thought the Indians would consider me less a threat. In this they were only partly right."

"Oh?"

"At first the Indians wanted to kill me, but then I showed them how I could sink down into the Rock, and after that they were greatly afraid of me. They called me Asenaapeeneniwa, Spirit-of-the-Rock. Later . . . much later, they shortened it to just plain Sena. They brought me meat, still hot on cooking sticks, and later little corn cakes."

"Ah, so you do have an alimentary system?"

"Of sorts. Not like yours, though. I can take it or leave it."

"Let's see if I understand. You're not a true human being. You're really a sort of alien artifact. And so is the Rock."

"That's true."

"And you're about ten thousand years old."

"Yes."

"The river, the town, the county . . . all named after you? Not the other way around?"

"Most improbable, isn't it, Mr. Potts?" She seemed grimly amused.

He sat there, staring at her, rudely, tactlessly. She looked back at him. Finally he took a deep breath. "Your story is indeed improbable. But I would like very much to believe you."

"Then we are making progress."

"You and I, perhaps. But the case, no. There's no way we can stop the construction. If you're right, the Rock is going to collapse, and it'll take the tower with it. If you're wrong, the Bridge goes safely ahead. Either way, you lose. I can do nothing for you. I might as well go back home."

"Perhaps you should. It would be safer for you."

"York was murdered, wasn't he?"

"Yes."

"Why?"

"He found out that the judge owned a big share of the Bridge bonds. He had hard evidence. So go home, Oliver Potts. You can still catch the late flight."

"No. Not yet. In any case, I'm staying for Fenleigh's funeral, tomorrow morning. I can't stop the Bridge, Sena, but perhaps you can think of some small, possible thing I can do for you."

"Not for me, Oliver. But how about the men on the tower? There are two elevators on the tower; traveler creepers, they call them. The first thing Monday morning, ten men will go up to the top of the tower on one creeper. Then the second creeper will be loaded with girders—about two and a half tons, and then it will start up. As soon as it does, the Rock will disappear, the tower will begin to collapse, and those ten men must die. If you're really determined to do something for me, perhaps you can figure out a way to prevent those men from being on the tower when it collapses. Maybe if you explained all this to the judge, he'd order the men not to go up, at least temporarily."

"He'd never do it. He'd consider it an admission your case has possible merit."

"Perhaps you could talk to Mr. Badging?"

"He'd feel even stronger about it." Noting her concern, he added quickly, "But let me think about it."

"Yes."

"Now, we have to make plans. After Fenleigh's funeral tomorrow, I'd like to talk to you again."

"He was your friend?"

"We went through the university together."

"I'm so sorry."

As they left the restaurant, he asked, "What's that big brick building over there, across from the motel?"

"The County Sanitarium," she said dryly. "Maybe we belong there?"

"Not yet, not yet," he said absently. And now he remembered something he had been meaning to ask. "Earlier, you mentioned you hadn't even told *him*. Who was *him?*"

"George. George Washington, that is. We were sort of . . . friends."

"Oh." He looked across the street. The face of the main building was well-lit. Beyond the chain-link fencing and the big iron gate he tried to read the gold letters on the façade, but they were too far away. "Goodnight, Sena."

4. The Black Bag

As the burial crew lowered the casket into the dark empty rectangle, Potts talked quietly to Miss Joyner. "Did he take a retainer?"

"It's in the trunk of my car."

After the service was over they walked to her car together. She opened the trunk and helped him lift out a heavy black leather bag. He laid it on the gravel of the parking lot.

"What in the world . . ." he muttered.

"A lot of old coins," said Miss Joyner. "He was going to have them appraised, but he never got around to it."

Potts studied the bag glumly. The leather was ancient, smelly, and cracking in several places. He sighed. Fen had taken Sena's money, probably old pennies. From the weight, maybe even lead counterfeits. And now Potts was stuck with it.

He said softly: "What did he think of her? Of Ms. Sena?"

York's ex-secretary shrugged. "I don't know. I think sometimes he thought she was crazy. She told him the coins were counterfeit, but contained gold."

"Gold?" He lifted the bag again and fought off an urge to open it on the spot. "You don't think so?"

"I don't know. I'm just a secretary, Mr. Potts."

"And one of the best, Miss Joyner."

"Can I help you carry the bag to your car?"

"Thanks, no." He opened the car door for her and watched her drive away. Next week he'd have to help her wind up Fenleigh's affairs. Just now, he had other problems.

Inside his motel room Potts drew the drapes, chain-locked the door, and very carefully opened the bag. On the very top was a fold of ivory-hued fabric, which he took to be a coarsely-woven mix of linen and wool. He eased it back carefully.

Despite the dim lighting, golden sparkles rose up and dazzled him. He stared, unbelieving. He reached in and picked out a coin at random. He adjusted his spectacles, read the date, then closed his eyes for a moment, then opened them again and read the date once more. This time out loud, as though to convince his ears: "Seventeen ninety-five."

A 1795 gold coin. My goodness!

Rings a bell. In fact, two bells. The Mount Vernon Trust sent me that notice . . . a missing 1795 gold eagle. And Barton Badging. Barton, are you still looking for a 1795 gold eagle? Proof condition?

He replaced the coin and picked up another. Seventeen ninety-five. The next, seventeen ninety-five. And another. The whole bag? Shades of Blackstone! The bag must weigh at least forty pounds. Forty pounds of 1795's? Counterfeits, Miss Joyner had said? Sena, where did you get these?

He picked up the phone and got Catlin at her apartment back home. "I need information about old coins. Look in your access index. I'll wait."

She was back in a few minutes. "There are several sources."

"Top three?"

"American Numismatic Association; Professional Numismatic Guild, Inc.; and National Coin Collectors. And guess who was past president of NCC?"

"Not Barton Badging,"

"Yes, Barton Badging. Mr. Potts, shouldn't this be on scramble?"

He smiled, but his mouth was in a hard line. "Don't bother just yet. Anything more on Badging?"

"He wrote a book, *Grading Guide for Eighteenth Century Eagles. And* he's an Associate Authenticator. He can look at your coin and give you a certificate. He's really into this stuff, Mr. Potts. Go on scramble, now?"

"No, not just yet. Access his book, get what he says about the seventeen ninety-five ten dollar gold eagle."

"Right here. Liberty head. Designed by Robert Scot. Minted at Philadelphia. Seventeen point five grams, thirty-three millimeters diameter, reeded edge. Ninety-one point six seven percent gold, balance copper." She paused.

"How many minted?"

"Five thousand, five hundred and eighty-three."

"What's one worth?"

"The best listed is MS-sixty-five, uncirculated, last auction at one hundred thousand dollars. Mint proof is better than that. Only one known to be struck, and given to George Washington for approval. Whereabouts unknown."

"Very good, Miss Catlin. *Now* we scramble." He placed the electronic device over the phone mouthpiece and waited for the whirring to stop. "You there?"

"Yes, sir."

"The room here is bugged, of course." No problem with that. I've got a cassette override on it. But the interesting thing is, I think we picked up a tag on the computer output as soon as we plugged in to the seventeen ninety-five reference. Can you check it out?"

"I'll try. Hold on. Yes, it's coming in. There *was* a tag. It was routed to Sena City. Somebody there is alerted every time the seventeen nine-five reference is pulled out. But Sena City is as close as I can get. No name. No phone number. Is that any help?"

"Oh, yes indeed. Thank you, Miss Catlin. And goodnight."

Next call to Sena. "Please come over here as fast as you can."

Okay, Badging, he thought. You laid the tag on the circuit. You've got all the questions. Let's see if Sena has any answers.

As soon as she came in the door he showed her a written slip: "Room still bugged. I've put on Entertainment Cassette Number Two. We can talk softly."

He walked back to the leather bag on the floor and lifted the covers. "An extraordinary collection, Sena."

"I trust they are adequate for the retainer?"

He smiled without humor. "I have been given to understand that one coin—just one—would bring in excess of one hundred thousand dollars. And how many are here?"

"Originally there were eight hundred, but over the years I had to spend twenty, maybe twenty-five."

"All identical?"

"Yes."

He grappled with the mental arithmetic. Nearly eighty million dollars. Of course, not that much. After the first few got on the market, the price would begin to drop.

"Oliver," she said gently, "don't even think about it. I told Fenleigh and now I tell you: they're counterfeit."

"Counterfeit. Oh. I see."

"No, you don't see. It's still forty pounds of coin-grade gold bullion, worth about three hundred thousand dollars on the New York market. Of course, there may be a slight problem with the copper content."

He had a feeling he shouldn't ask. "Tell me about the copper."

"They had to program for copper, to conform to the Philadelphia mint formula. Copper is added to coin gold for hardness, you know."

"Go on. There was a problem?"

"We didn't pay much attention to isotopes in those days. Native copper is a mix of Cu-sixty-three with about twenty-nine percent Cu-sixty-five isotope. Our Cu is all Cu-sixty-three."

"Is the lack of Cu-sixty-five detectable?"

"There are ways. First of all, though, you have to know to look for it."

"Would a professional coin authenticator be likely to look for Cu-sixty-five?"

"No. It would be outside his level of expertise. Anyway, he wouldn't have the equipment."

"Interesting." Something else was bothering him now. "Mr. York's secretary said he took your case on contingency. If he lost, you didn't pay. Is that so?"

"Yes, that was our arrangement."

"But you *did* pay. These coins certainly have bullion value, at six hundred dollars an ounce. If we lose, am I supposed to return the coins?"

"No, that wouldn't be necessary. Let me explain. It's true, the coins have bullion value just now. On the other hand, they're part of the Rock. If the Rock collapses, so do they."

Oliver Potts suppressed a moan. "So we're back to *that*. If the Rock goes, they go? Poof?" He pantomimed blowing a feather from his palm. "Like that?" He looked at her with raised eyebrows.

"Poof, like that."

"Hard to get more contingent than that."

"That's true."

"But *how* did you make them, Sena?"

"Actually, Oliver, *I* didn't make them. *They* made them for me. They made them on a matter copier."

"*They* . . . ?"

"The People who made the Rock, and who made me. The Dhorans."

(Was he beginning to *believe*? Potts, *stop*! Remember that big red brick building across the street, with the chain-link fence.) He mused aloud: "And they made the Rock to be the Earth terminus of a bridge—*their* bridge. That's kind of funny, isn't it?"

"You're not laughing, Oliver."

He smiled wanly. "Your original coin was fresh out of the Philadelphia mint when your People copied it. That was two hundred years ago. Have they been here since?"

"No. They're not really due for another couple of months."

"Where do they come from? Where *is* Dhora?"

"Dhora is the second planet of Alpha Centauri."

He had to think about that. "They've done this on other planets?"

"I think so, though I've never seen the other places."

"*Why* do they do it, Sena? What do they want?"

"The Rock is several things. Besides being a bridge terminus, it's also a weather station. It records interspatial dust, cosmic temperatures, interstellar radiation, that sort of thing. They need to know all that, because they have great interstellar commerce. Also, the last several times they were here, the Rock was a big trading post with the Indians. The Dhorans bought beaver furs with knife blades and beads and blankets."

"The beavers are long gone."

"I know; so are the Indians."

"Nowadays, I doubt we'd have anything they'd want."

"I don't know. They're great traders. They'll find something. You have orchids, butterflies, rosewood, seashells. They can give you a list."

"What would they offer in return?"

"Technologies."

Of course. But none of it was going to happen. Not now. "And you, Sena, why are you here?"

"I try to keep the Rock clear, at least for the two-hundred-year entries. Up to now, it's been just a question of clearing away leaves and storm debris. This is the first time the Rock itself has been threatened. As a preserver I'm not doing so well, am I?"

"You're doing fine, Sena." He didn't want to believe. Why was he doing this to himself? He shook his head vigorously, as though to shatter the fantasy. But it didn't shatter. It stayed right there. "The master coin, Sena, where did *it* come from?"

"*He* gave it to me. George."

"George *Washington?*"

"Your first president."

"He was just passing by? In seventeen ninety-five?"

"There was more to it than that. Don't you read your history? They were giving him hell about the treaty John Jay had negotiated with the British finally to end the War and define all the boundaries and commercial rights. The proposed treaty was tearing the country apart. Some told him, the British are stealing us blind, don't sign. The Senate said, sign immediately, before they change their minds. He had to think, weigh all the pros and cons. He got away to Mount Vernon, but they followed him there. And then one weekend he really disappeared."

"He came here?"

"It wasn't the first time. We were . . . old friends."

Potts found himself blushing. "I understand."

She reflected. "That summer, when he was still in Philadelphia, the Director of the Mint, David Rittenhouse, gave him that first gold eagle, struck specially for George's approval. George gave it to me. The Dhorans used it a few weeks later to make the eight hundred copies."

Oliver Potts found himself dreaming. George Washington, General of the Armies, First President, Father of his Country, Model of Morality and Rectitude, easing his fading days with this beautiful woman. Ah, me. "Go on," he said.

"Well, he went back to Philadelphia and signed the Treaty, and so your United States got off to a good start. A few years later he was dead. Do you believe me, Oliver?"

He didn't answer immediately. He was staring at the leather bag. On the near side, something in mottled gold letters. "G.W.," he whispered. "His saddle bag?"

"He forgot it. Today, I guess you'd call it a Freudian wish to return. It made a good coin case."

Potts stared at the bag a long time. Finally he said, "I can't stop the bridge." He pushed at the bag with his toe. "Even with all this."

"No, I guess you can't."

He was frowning, and concentrating. An idea was trying to form. If he could just get it to crystallize . . . "Those men up there on the tower. When the next load of girders is brought up, the cantilever collapses, and they will all be killed." (After he said it, he realized he was not asking a question, but making a statement.)

She watched his face with great interest.

He continued: "And 'George' collapses whether or not the workmen are out on the cantilever arm."

"Yes."

"So it would be a humane act to keep the workmen off the tower until the elevators go up?"

"That's what I've been telling you. But you said you couldn't get an order from the judge—"

"Not the judge. Badging. Maybe." His idea was now almost complete. There was just one more thing. "Is it possible to show that these coins were in fact made in 1795?"

"Yes. By measurement of the copper oxide coating. X-ray apparatus is required, but it's readily available, and the test is simple and non-destructive. It's quite similar to Bragg x-ray crystal analysis."

"Would Badging be likely to have the equipment?"

"I'm sure he would." She studied him with growing surmise. "You have hidden depths, Oliver."

"Why, thank you." He beamed in gratitude. "I could be a real S.O.B. if I put my mind to it. I'll call him now."

A few minutes later he said, "He's home, and he's expecting me."

"Just you?"

"I want to talk to him alone. A thing is going to happen that you shouldn't watch."

"You're the doctor."

"Lawyer."

5. The Coin Room

Barton Badging's eyes flicked from Potts's face to the bag he cradled in his arms. He stared at the bag, speechless.

(He's our chief bugger, thought Potts. Of course, the judge is in on it, too.) "May I come in, Mr. Badging?"

"Oh, of course, of course. I was a bit startled, that was all."

(So you were; but you haven't seen anything yet.)

"Let's go down to the coin room," said Badging. "Bit more private. Do you collect, Mr. Potts?"

"Not really. Don't know a thing about it. We are aware, of course, of your stature in the field. As a matter of fact, that's why I'm here."

"Not about the litigation?"

"No." (Although we may get around to it.)

"Down these stairs, Mr. Potts. Hold the rail. Can I help you with that?"

"Oh, I think I have it."

"You can put it on the table."

"Yes, thanks." Potts looked about the room in genuine appreciation. Glass cases full of coin trays lined the room. Coins were framed in collections that hung from the walls like carefully lighted paintings. His host was indeed a serious collector.

Badging's eyes never left the black bag. He wet his lips. He fingered a necklace strung with odd-looking beads.

(Let's drag it out a bit, thought Potts.) "Interesting necklace," he said.

Badging's head jerked. "Oh. You mean this. It's Iroquois wampum. Very old. Made about sixteen thirty-seven, of shell bits, very carefully cut and polished. Once used as money, legal tender, six white or three purple were worth one English penny." Badging kept his eyes on the black bag, but now he let out a long breath and relaxed a bit. "People don't really appreciate money, Mr. Potts."

"No.

"There's something special about the sight and sound of bright jangling coins. To have, to look at, even to smell."

"Yes, of course." Potts looked across the room at a wall covered by bookshelves. "And to study?"

"And to study. I love books about money, ancient money, modern money. I've written a couple myself. And I have scrapbooks of tours through American and foreign mints."

"That all sounds pretty general. Do you have a specialty?"

"Of course. All serious collectors have a specialty. Mine is Americana, seventeen hundred to eighteen hundred."

"Fascinating, Mr. Badging. However did you get into *that?*"

Badging put his hand out and caressed the bag gently. He said, "It started years ago, when I had just hung up my shingle. I settled an estate, which, alas, turned out to be bankrupt. The widow paid me with the deceased's strong box, 'inherited as is from great-great-Uncle Philip.' I broke it open. One or two gold coins. Hardly worth melting down. And there were several other items. A great disappointment. Still, being a prudent man, I had the batch appraised. The report was a real surprise. There were Spanish reales, Massachusetts Willow Tree shillings, Maryland pennies, Virginia halfpennies, New Yorke tokens, Pitt farthings . . . The appraiser made me a six-figure offer on the spot. I never regretted turning it down. Oh, I may have had one small bad moment as I drove home from the goldsmith's: was I ethically bound to tell the widow about the true value? No, I decided."

(And, thought Potts, your conscience has never troubled you since.) He said, "I see the picture, now. It's inspiring, when we realize that from that nucleus, your present collection has grown. And of course, along the way, you probably became an international expert in early Americana?"

Badging nodded. His hand was on the leather cover. He was about to open the bag.

(It's time, thought Potts. He's going crazy.) "Plastic gloves?" he said quietly.

Silently, Badging opened the desk and brought out two pair. They put them on.

"Go ahead," said Potts. "Open it."

Badging did. With trembling hand he picked out one coin, looked at it, and almost dropped it. He laid it beside the bag and did several things: his eyes glazed, he put his hands under the table, and he stopped breathing.

Potts had watched bird dogs behave quite similarly before they settled into a rigid point. Just don't let him faint, he thought.

Slowly, Badging returned to life. His eyes opened. He whispered: "How many do you have here?"

"About seven hundred and seventy-five, so I'm told."

Badging thought a moment. "About forty pounds?"

"Yes."

"All identical?"

"Yes, I think so."

The coin expert closed his eyes again. They opened. This time his hands were on top of the table, but they were still trembling. "Mr. Potts, would you permit me to take one of the coins into the back room for a closer inspection? I assure you—"

"Oh, you don't need to do that, Mr. Badging. I'm convinced they're counterfeits. I'm sure your tests will show that. That's partly why I'm here."

"Counterfeits?" Badging's cheeks sagged as the blood began to drain away.

"It stands to reason, doesn't it, Mr. Badging? Nearly eight hundred 1795 gold eagles still in mint proof condition after two hundred years? I'm no fool, sir. And neither are you. The problem is how to handle the stuff as bullion."

Potts watched the collector's eyes. I would make a good mind reader, he thought. Greed makes a man deaf, dumb, and blind. He thinks he knows a genuine seventeen ninety-five as Da Vinci knows Mona Lisa, or as Parsifal knows the Holy Grail. I can read him. Just now he's thinking that copper promotes slow oxidation on uncirculated gold coins. The coating is only a few microns thick and it's invisible to the naked eye. However, it is detectable and measurable by techniques well within the scope of his skill and equipment. "Go ahead," said Potts gently. "Prove it to yourself that they're counterfeit."

"Yes. Thank you. Please excuse me." Badging picked up the coin with plastic-sheathed fingers and disappeared into the alcove behind him.

Ten minutes later he was back. He wouldn't look Potts in the eye.

"I'm sorry," said Potts sincerely. "I told you they were counterfeit. Remarkable imitations, though. Now then, could we talk about the bullion value?"

"Bullion . . . ?" It seemed difficult for Badging to concentrate.

"There is a small problem," explained Potts delicately. "Possession."

"Possession . . . ? Oh, you mean possession of counterfeit coins?"

"Yes. Eighteen, U.S.C. 485. The Secret Service may not take kindly to possession of nearly eight hundred counterfeit gold coins. They'll have to be melted down."

Badging turned pale. "Melt . . . ah . . . no . . . well . . ."

Potts watched this with interest. He smiled. "That raises another difficulty. Because of the legal problems, it would have to be done under conditions of great discretion. My client doesn't know any goldsmiths; nor do I. But we thought you might."

The older man's face suddenly shone with a great light. "I know . . . one or two." He coughed delicately. "There would, of course, be a fee."

"My dear Mr. Badging, you don't understand. She wants to be completely rid of the coins. She wants no bullion back. She's simply trying to steer clear of the law."

"*She?* Ah! Madame Sena?"

"Yes."

"The crazy woman."

"So they say."

"What do *you* think, Mr. Potts?"

"She's certainly different."

They looked at each other. Badging sighed. It was coming together. Things said, plus things not said. "What does she want?" He put it almost petulantly.

"Thirty thousand dollars, plus a little favor."

"The money's reasonable. But I can't throw the case, Potts."

"No, of course not."

"So what's this 'little favor'?"

"Monday morning, when the first two loads of girders go up into the west cantilever tower—'George,' they call it—ten men will be at the top waiting with rivet guns. My client believes the tower will crash as soon as those elevators start up, and that those ten men will be killed in the crash. She requests that the men stay off both towers—east and west—until the elevators move on George. After that, you can do anything you like."

"Huh? You mean, the men on both George and Martha wait until the girders go up on George?"

"That's it."

"That's all she wants?"

"Plus the thirty thou, of course. At this point, she's simply trying to save lives. Both towers may be involved because of internal strains in the underlying continental plate."

"*If* George falls, you mean," said Badging.

"*When* George falls," said Potts firmly.

"Oh, God. You too?"

"Me too."

Badging shrank back in his chair. Then he looked at the mythic leather case, and back to Potts. He exhaled slowly. Potts relaxed.

Badging rubbed his chin. "Insanity aside, Potts, I'd have to persuade the on-site engineers. They'll howl, you know. They'll lose fifteen or twenty minutes, getting the men up there after the beams. No rational explanation. There'll have to be pay-offs. Not sure I can swing it."

Potts smiled. "We have faith in you, Badging." He pushed the case toward the other.

His host laid possessory hands on it. "I'll make out a check."

"Do we want to burden the record with a piece of paper?"

"Oh. Ah, no, of course not. Cash. You want it now?"

"That would be fine."

Badging went over to his wall safe and came back with three bundles of one-hundred-dollar bills. "You want to count it?"

"Certainly not, Mr. Badging. You want a receipt?"

"No need for that. I am holding the bag."

Potts smiled. "Why, so you are. Got time for an anecdote?"

"Well, all right."

"It's about that very bag. Outrageous rumor has it that the Continental Congress gave the bag to Washington when he bade farewell to the army at Annapolis, in seventeen eighty-three. I imagine a thorough examination by a competent antiquarian would show the leather is no more than twenty or thirty years old. Those gold initials are probably actually for some chap named Gerald Whipple, or something like that. Are you all right, Mr. Badging?"

"Yes," said his host faintly. "It was listed as missing after his death at Mount Vernon in seventeen ninety-nine."

"What? What was missing?"

"Nothing. Nothing."

Potts arose and pushed his chair under the table. "Oh, there's one thing . . ."

Badging looked up. His mouth twisted into harsh lines. "The catch," he said bitterly. "*Now* we get it."

"The catch," agreed Potts amiably. "I'm informed the coins carry a curse. I promised Sena I would mention it. If the Rock collapses, the coins vanish." He smiled broadly.

They looked at each other. After a moment Badging smiled too. Then he began to chuckle. Then he leaned back and guffawed. Tears ran down his cheeks. Finally the laughter died away. Ignoring his guest, Badging leaned forward and clasped the leather case to his chest and began to shower kisses on it.

"I'll let myself out," whispered Oliver Potts.

6. Sunday at Sena's

Potts accepted Sena's invitation for Sunday dinner.

As she ushered him in, she said, "Actually, Oliver, I should be giving a great festive party in your honor, just as in the old colonial days, when someone important came to visit." She smiled at him as they walked into the dining room.

"That's hardly indicated, Sena."

"You're right, of course. But at least we can have the fixin's, just as they had in the old time: soup, river oysters, fish, roast turkey, chicken, duck, goose, beef, mutton, molded jellies, plum pudding, pies, cakes, tarts, spiced punch . . ."

He stared at her, appalled.

She laughed merrily. "Small wonder the men had gout and the women the dropsy. No, Oliver dear, actually, we'll, have just a little dab of different things, all over on the side table. It's buffet style tonight. Take what you want. Just soup and crackers, if that's your preference."

They got trays and loaded up.

She poured him a tumbler of foamy pinkish liquid. "Sillabub," she explained. "Wine and cream. Old plantation recipe. The lipids in the cream facilitate absorption of the alcohol through the stomach lining. Knocks you on your ear."

"Like a double martini?"

"More like a triple."

Great, thought Potts. Oh well, maybe we can finally get to the bottom of things. As they sat at table, he noted the strange music from the far side of the room. She explained. "That's a 'player' spinet, otherwise genuine for the period. The strings are plucked by little quills."

"What's the tune?"

"That one is *High Betty Martin*. Next you'll hear *Old Father George*."

"G.W. again?"

"No, no connection. Although they *were* very popular in his day, and he *did* love to accompany me on the fife when I played the spinet."

"I didn't know he played anything."

"He wasn't very good at it, but he could pat his foot and keep the rhythm."

"Sounds like a good life."

"It was different. I once had a museum room, where I kept things characteristic of the period. But it all went into storage when I had to move my house."

"What's your house made of?"

"Not wood, or stone, or plastic. It's the same stuff as the Rock. When the Rock goes, so will the house, and everything in it."

He looked around. "Lots of tapestries."

"Actually, those are rugs. In colonial days they were too valuable to walk on. We hung them on walls and put them on tables."

She was in a reminiscent mood. It worried him. He had once observed the same mood in a man awaiting execution. "How did you get along with the early colonials?"

"Pretty well, until they caught religion. Then they decided I was a witch and should be burnt. That was about sixteen ninety. The town fathers chased me out here with torches and blunderbusses. But as they watched, I sank into the Rock. The preacher cursed the place in an elaborate ceremony, and then the warders stripped my house bare and tried to burn it. But it wouldn't burn. I stayed in the Rock for years. When I came out again it was seventeen twenty-five, and all was forgotten. Tea had come to the colony. Cups from France, no handles. When you went to a tea party you brought your own cup and saucer, and you sipped daintily from the saucer, not the cup. It's all different now. "

"Did going into the Rock have any ill effect?"

"It was boring. And I picked up a little radioactivity. But it had a fast half-life and soon faded. I haven't been in the Rock since I emerged in 1725. There's no need, anymore. I'm quite harmless, now, Oliver. You have a higher radiation level than I do."

"Weren't they suspicious when you never aged?"

"Oh, I learned how to handle that. I aged with make-up and gray wigs. When I got *very* old I went away, 'died,' and returned as my 'niece,' to inherit the house and the Rock." She pointed to a framed portrait on the wall. "See over there? I was a 'grande dame' when Stuart painted me in seventeen eighty-two. That big white wig was quite the rage. Cost me four guineas. I slept on a headboard for several nights to preserve my coiffure."

Potts peered at the painting. "Really well done."

"You like it? George thought so, too. He developed into a fair connoisseur."

"He had excellent taste," agreed Potts.

"Some of today's things he would have liked; some not. He was a great dancer. He'd ride miles to a ball. Would you like to dance, Oliver?"

"I'm not so good at the modern steps . . ."

"I'm not either. A colonial favorite, perhaps?"

"Fine."

"*The Rolling Hornpipes.* I take the spinet, he accompanies on the fife. What he lacked in talent, he made up in spirit."

"Huh?"

"George and I played together, back in seventeen ninety-five. I made a life-size holo at the time. I never played it back for him. I didn't think he'd understand." She walked across the room and pressed a switch.

And there they were. The general, standing tall, lips puckered, blowing into the little silver cylinder. Sena's fingers were dancing nimbly over the spinet keyboard. She was looking up gleefully at her musical guest.

Potts jumped up as though stuck with a red-hot needle. "Jesus X. God," he whispered. The tall white-haired man was, save for a towel draped around his middle, totally naked.

The lawyer emerged slowly from his paralysis. He found himself thinking of Hawthorne's famous comment: "Did anybody ever see Washington nude? It is inconceivable. He had no nakedness, but I imagine he was born with his clothes on, and his hair powdered, and made a stately bow on his first appearance in the world."

That's very strong sillabub, thought Potts.

"Come," said Sena. "Let's dance." She took his hand.

"But—"

"I'll explain later."

And, so she led him into the sprightly gyrations of a vanished time to music provided by the Father of His Country.

It came to an end. The holo shut off automatically. The vision of lost centuries vanished.

Potts wiped a sleeve over a damp forehead. "Well?"

"He was out this way for the first time in seventeen fifty, surveying for Lord Fairfax. He was only eighteen, though he looked older. Oh, how handsome he was, with his thick red hair, his fine shoulders, his slim waist. We were lovers, Oliver. There are still some letters spread around in the archives where he mentions me. I was his 'Low Land Beauty.' He capitalized everything. I was not the only woman in his life, but I think I was the first. Sally, Martha, Eliza, all were later."

"He returned?"

"Yes, just that one time, in July seventeen ninety-five. The country was in a horrible mess, the worst since the Revolution. The Jay Treaty was supposed to bring peace with Britain. If we didn't sign, Britain would declare war. If we did sign, we'd face civil war at home. John Jay was hanged in effigy. Alexander

Hamilton tried to defend the Treaty and was stoned. The house of the British minister was insulted by a mob. The British flag was dragged through the streets of Charleston and burnt before the doors of their consul. There was nowhere George could turn for objective advice. Knox and Hamilton had resigned from the cabinet. Only Randolph remained, and he was suspected of treason. And besides the Treaty, George had to go back to Philadelphia that fall and give his Annual Report to Congress. 'Sena,' he said to me, 'what the hell am I to do?' 'George darling,' I said, 'just now the main thing is to keep the *status quo*. Hold off war at almost any cost, at least for fifteen or twenty years. Let this lusty young country grow rich—able to defend itself—against the British, French, Spanish, the Barbary pirates, everybody.' 'But the *South*,' he said. 'They want to ship cotton to Europe, but under Article Twelve of the Treaty they can't, because it would compete with cotton from the British West Indies. The South will scream if I sign.' 'Look, honey,' I said, 'rewrite the West Indies Article, *then* sign the damned Treaty, and get it over to London before Congress reconvenes. The British will sign. Believe me.'

"I remember how he looked at me. He refused to wear his spectacles, so he couldn't really tell whether I looked old or young. Actually, at the time, I was made up to look about forty, but with a nice figure and a good complexion. I applied more pressure. 'George, dear, the British don't want any trouble from us. They've got enough right there in Europe. The French have a bloody revolution in progress. A young artillery captain named Bonaparte has just run the British out of Toulon.' 'You are well informed, my girl.' 'I read the papers, General.' He said, 'And I suppose you have some thoughts about my Seventh Report to Congress?' 'I have indeed. Tell them—and the country—they never had it so good. Wayne's victory over the Indians at Fallen Timbers has brought peace in the southwest. In the northwest the Jay Treaty will bring peace with the British. Also, the Treaty will frighten the pants off the Spanish, and they'll concede commercial rights the full length of the Mississippi. Our population continues to grow, and the country to prosper. New canals and new roads are opening everywhere.' George stared at me. His mouth was wide open, and I could see the silver mechanism on his false teeth. 'Well, by God,' he said. 'You're right! Anything else?' 'My friend,' I said, 'you rode in here shivering even in your long underwear. I remind you it's the middle of July. Even with all the doors and windows open, it's still quite warm. And now you've stopped shivering and you've begun to perspire. I'd be pleased if you would let me launder your linen.' " She stopped and looked at Potts. "I gave him a towel."

"Yes. That's where we came in."

"He just needed a rest. Just a couple of days . . . and nights."

"Yes."

"Actually, I think he forgot some of his linens."

Potts thought about the coin packing. He nodded.

Sena said, "He went back to Philadelphia, signed the Treaty in August, and gave his State-of-the-Nation in December. Of course he had to put it in the stilted formal language of the day: 'I invite you to join me in profound gratitude to the

Author of all good for the numerous and extraordinary blessings we enjoy.' But there it all was."

Potts was thoughtful. "And it all came about just as you predicted."

"Almost exactly. But nowadays, who cares?"

"*I* care."

"You're a good soul, Oliver." She took his hand and led him to the bay window, where the full moon was shining in, sinking slowly but measurably just over the horizon, and just behind the tower, giving the illusion that a colossal skeleton was rising up over the edge of the land. They could almost hear a victory shriek.

Potts felt Sena trembling. "Your people will come for you," he said.

"No, I don't think they care. I'm not really real, you know. I'm just a figment of my own imagination."

"They care, and they'll come."

"Even if they want to, I'm not sure they can. The gate doesn't open for another sixty days."

"This is an emergency. They'll do something special. They'll be here." He held her against him.

"Keep talking," she said. "Tell me how they will come."

"A great big white ship, rockets blazing, will sit down on the courthouse lawn—"

"No, no ship."

"Well, okay, no ship. We're in court, the judge is in the very act of handing down his decision, when suddenly the room is filled with this blazing radiance. It means their bridge has joined up. They call to you. You're not sure you want to go. You explain to them, you want to stay with me, to talk, and dance, and make love. They say, Sena, you *can't* stay. You *must* come with us, for we love you, and we have come a long way for you. You give me an agonized backward glance, and I think for a minute I might go with you. But we both know it wouldn't work. And the next moment you are gone, and the light is gone."

"And the bridge, and the Rock, and my house and everything in it. And the coins."

"Everything. Judge Roule is going to be a mite upset, not to mention Barton Badging."

"When I die I would like to dream. I will dream of you."

"Sena, stop talking like that. You're not going to die."

She ignored him. "But I don't know how to dream. I sleep when I want to, but I don't dream. I don't know how. It's a thing that only you humans do. If I could dream, I couldn't really die, could I?"

He thought, *Somnio, ergo sum.* I dream, therefore I am.

"Perhaps," she said moodily, "it would have been better if I had never met you. It would have been much easier to die. I would have had no regrets. It was cruel of you to come."

"Now you are reasoning like a woman."

"Am I, really? A genuine flesh-and-blood woman? Perhaps I'm changing into a human being. You know, just as Pinocchio changed into a real live boy. Then I'd be safe, wouldn't I?"

He thought of lines from Andrew Marvell. 'The wanton troopers riding by / Have shot my fawn, and it will die.' He said, "You're already safe."

"You can spend the night, can't you?"

He squeezed her hand.

Several hours later, as he was drifting away in sleep, he managed to rouse himself. He tapped her on the shoulder. "Are you awake?" he whispered.

"What is it?"

He hesitated. Still, something had been nibbling at the analytic lawyer-lobe in his cerebral cortex. Out with it, Potts. "Sena, do you remember your radiation level in 1750—when you first met *him*."

In the darkness he sensed her wakening astonishment. "It was still pretty high. George may have picked up several hundred rem. Oh, my . . ."

He tried to recall the relevant numbers. Yes, recommended maximum dose for the general public, one-half rem per year.

"I sterilized him, didn't I?" she murmured in a very small voice.

"Go to sleep, Sena." (It's all ancient history, now.)

He lay there thinking. She *had* sterilized the youthful George. And since he could not have sons of his own, the young officers of the Continental Army became his sons: Hamilton, Lafayette, Greene, Wayne, Fitzgerald, Benjamin Lincoln . . . All of them. Small wonder he could dissolve mutinies with a gesture. Small wonder the men in epaulettes wept when he bade farewell at Fraunces Tavern. And as President he adopted the entire population as his family. Of *course* he was the Father of His Country—which he would never have been if he had had children of his own body. So curious the chain of causation! This woman, lying here beside me, made a great man greater, thereby winning a long and desperate war for independence, and ensuring the successful birth and infant years of the new nation. Without you, "Low Land Beauty," we might still be vassals of Great Britain. Or worse.

And so thinking, he smiled and went to sleep.

7. Case Dismissed

The courtroom, three minutes before ten.

He felt her knee touch his under the table. He realized at once the contact was not meant to be seductive. Sena was seeking reassurance. He reached over and patted her hand.

Then he looked up. Badging was standing by the table, looking about the area nervously. "Potts, just a quick question about the coins." He added diffidently: "If you have a moment."

"Sure, Badging. You want to back out of the deal? No problem. Here's—"

"No. No, nothing like that. But the coin wrappings. They look like long underwear, homespun linen, as a matter of fact, for a rather tall man. Do you know anything about them?"

"All I can do is repeat the tradition. George rode off without his drawers. Old wives' tale, Badging. Absolutely nothing to it."

"Yes, of course. Thank you, Potts, oh thank you, thank you." His face was glowing. He returned slowly to his table.

Glad I can bring a bit of cheer to you, thought Potts, even if it's only temporary.

"All rise!" intoned the bailiff. "This honorable court is now in session. Honorable Maximilian Roule presiding. *Sena* versus *Bridge Authority.*"

Roule swept in, glared around the courtroom, then sat down and glared once more, this time at Plaintiff and her counsel. "Any rebuttal, Mr. Potts?"

"Yes, Your Honor. I'd like to show some holos."

"Of what?"

"Various bridge collapses. How they came about. What caused them."

"How is that relevant here, Mr. Potts? The conditions are not the same at all."

"The Quebec bridge *is* quite similar, Your Honor. Bedrock under the south cantilever was unstable. The rock dropped one-quarter inch. The cantilever weighed twenty thousand tons, the same as the cantilever in issue here. The center span in the Quebec bridge was nevertheless installed—some five thousand tons. Whereupon the whole bridge collapsed, killing a number of men."

Badging was on his feet. "Your Honor!"

"Mr. Badging?"

"Plaintiff insists that another five thousand pounds of girders on our western cantilever is enough to overload the underlying greenstone, causing the Rock to collapse and the tower to fall. Now, Defendant does not agree with Plaintiff's assertion of human risk. Not one whit. Nevertheless, out of the boundless goodness of his heart, Defendant has agreed to clear men from both towers while the next load of girders is going up on the west tower."

Roule scowled at Potts. "That will have to satisfy you, Mr. Potts. It's a very generous concession; Defendant has no obligation to make it. I hold your proposed holos inadmissible. Anything further, Mr. Potts?"

The visiting lawyer sagged a little. "No, Your Honor."

Roule smiled at him coldly. "Well, don't look so hang-dog. You did fine, considering there was nothing you could do. Don't sit down just yet. Mr. Badging?"

"Yes, Your Honor?"

"Since Mr. Potts had no rebuttal, you have no surrebuttal. Now, Mr. Potts, back to you. Do you have a closing statement?"

"Yes, Your Honor." He began slowly. "First, this court is without jurisdiction in the subject matter of this case. Sena Rock is the territory of a foreign country, namely the Dhorans, an extra-stellar people. It was acquired by them by treaty with the Indians, thousands of years ago. That treaty was automatically assumed by the United States when it assumed sovereignty over the Rock. Foreign territory cannot be taken by eminent domain, but only by war or treaty, or abrogation of a treaty. None of these things have occurred."

"Just a minute," demurred Roule. "You're familiar with 33 U.S.C. 532?"

"Yes. It gives the states and state-authorized bodies power to acquire property for bridges. And I presume Your Honor is familiar with 33 U.S.C. 531, which says 532 doesn't authorize the construction of any bridge that would connect the United States to any foreign country."

Roule rolled his eyes upward. "There you go again, Mr. Potts. You persist in thinking the Rock was the terminus for a bridge connecting the United States with outer space?"

"Yes, Your Honor."

"Mr. Potts, do you realize that the County Sanitarium is just up the road?"

"I am aware of it, Your Honor."

"Anything further, counselor?"

"One more point, Your Honor. The case presents a corollary question. In taking the Dhorans' Rock, this court has taken property without due process of law, in violation of the Fifth Amendment to the Constitution. There is thus a second federal question. With all due respect, Your Honor, this case should never have come to a state court. Only the federal courts have jurisdiction. Thank you." He sat down.

"And thank *you*, Mr. Potts, for a most original presentation. Mr. Badging?"

"Your Honor, at the beginning of this trial, I moved to dismiss. Following the completion of Plaintiff's main case, I renewed this motion. I now renew once again."

"Before I decide your motion, Mr. Badging, I have some comments about bridges, and especially their construction and design. Actually, design has improved to the point where collapse is pretty much a thing of the past. Engineering skills have improved. Materials have improved. The designers autopsied their catastrophes, and they learned." The judge seemed to be in great good humor. "The big changes came in the late nineteenth century, when the bridge builders were trying to figure out how to handle the weight of bigger and bigger trains. Granted, they had a lot to learn. For in the decade eighteen seventy to eighty, four hundred bridges collapsed. But that sort of thing is all in the past. Bridges are no longer dangerous. Today we understand the basic principles of design.

"But of course, these are generalities and do not address the particulars of Mr. Badging's motion. To do that, we must refer to the evidence of record. And here we encounter a very basic threshold question, which sounds in the law of evidence, to wit, what weight are we to give to the sworn testimony of a witness who claims she is ten thousand years old, that she was made by creatures from outer space, and that Sena Rock is about to collapse. I say she is either lying or insane, or both, and that all of her testimony is therefore to be ignored."

He leaned back. "And having decided *that*, we come now to the final question, namely, whether the Rock is owned by aliens aforesaid, and if so, whether they have certain rights by treaty. I think to state the question is to answer it. And the answer must be, and is, no.

"I will now rule on Mr. Badging's motion to dismiss:

"Motion granted. Case dismissed. No appeal." He glowered at Potts and Sena once more, as though they were guilty of unspeakable offenses against law and humanity. "I want to see both counsel in chambers. You too, Ms. Sena. Just give me five minutes. I have to make a phone call. Court adjourned." He banged the gavel and arose from the bench.

Sena looked up at Potts anxiously. "It's all over. So what's he up to, now?" Nothing good, thought the lawyer. "We'll just have to go in and see."

8. Bridges That Made History

"Now that it's all over," said Roule, "I thought we might watch the load limit here in chambers, on closed-circuit TV." He looked at his watch. "The creeper travelers are loaded with five thousand pounds of steel. No men are on either tower—courtesy of Mr. Badging, I understand. And in exactly twenty minutes the lift motors will turn on and the elevators are going to start up on 'George.' So, we have to kill a little time. I've noticed that you, Mr. Potts, and you, Ms. Sena, have been looking, a bit covertly, I might add, at my pictures hanging on the walls. All bridges, aren't they? And very particular bridges, with one very interesting feature in common. All of them collapsed. Yes, Mr. Potts, that's what bridges do. Bridges collapse. Lawyers orate, grass grows green, women have babies, the sun shines, and bridges collapse. It's simply the thing that they do. But come along. While we wait for the George Washington Bridge to collapse, I'll give you the guided tour.

"We'll start way back. Here's Xerxes' bridge over the Hellespont, which he built for his invasion of Greece. Blown away by a storm in 481 B.C. Next, a fictional item: Wilder's bridge of San Luis Rey, just before it breaks. Those six people will be killed in the chasm below. Wilder believed God was doing them all a favor. And here we have a genuine historical structure, a truss bridge designed by Ithiel Town for rail traffic over Catskill Creek in New York state. It collapsed in 1840 and killed a workman; first railroad bridge fatality in the U. S.

"And here's my pride and joy. The photo is 'before,' of course. On December 29, 1876, this bridge fell into this gorge, near Ashtabula, Ohio. With it dropped two locomotives and eleven cars. Eighty died, not counting the bridge inspector, who committed suicide. Amasa Stone, the builder, was disgraced. We still don't know the cause.

"And here's another 'before.' In England, in 1879, this beautiful iron bridge over the Firth of Tay collapsed with a train, killing seventy-five people.

"We pass on. *This* is the Quebec Bridge, over the St. Lawrence. You mentioned this one, Mr. Potts. Actually, the facts were considerably more horrendous than you indicated. The first collapse was in 1907. The south cantilever fell during construction. Seventy-five men died. And, as you noted, the builders actually had prior warning: under the weight of the south arm, the abutment foundation did in fact drop one-quarter inch. After the collapse of the cantilever, they rebuilt, but then in 1916, as they were hoisting the central span, *it* dropped, killing eleven men.

"Next we see 'Galloping Gertie,' the suspension bridge over the Puget Sound Narrows at Tacoma, Washington. After gyrations worthy of a hula dancer, it fell into the abyss."

Potts had witnessed mockery before, including some directed toward him. There were different kinds: some (at one extreme) playful and teasing (as between lovers and good friends); some (at the other extreme) cruel and moronic, as Christ's crown of thorns. But never before had he encountered anything so devastatingly cynical, savage, and sadistic as Roule's present exposition. It was a mockery multiplied by malignance. He found it horrifying.

Roule looked back at the trio. "There are several more, but time is running out, and I'm going to pass on to the final item." They followed him to the far wall. "It's the architect's rendition of our own George Washington Bridge." He added roguishly, "After completion, but before collapse." He leered at Potts from eyes half-hidden under the deep brow ridge. "Impressed, counselor?"

"I am, judge."

"And time is growing short. Let's return to our chairs and watch the screen. The big show is about to begin."

As they took their seats, Potts studied the TV screen. The view was excellent: the giant west tower of the criss-crossing steel girders. Strong and light. But not nearly strong enough, and not nearly light enough to survive the collapse of the Rock. From this graceful structure the engineers intended that great wings would form, aft for the Bridge access to the land, forward to connect with the east cantilever already reaching out from the opposite shore.

It saddened him. The engineers intended . . . the state and county planners intended . . . merchants and bankers and builders of villages and shopping centers intended . . . And all these fine intentions would go down the drain.

Sena reached over and took his hand. "Where are they?" she whispered.

"They'll come," he said. But he didn't really believe it. He already counted her as dead.

"I see that the creepers are loaded and ready," observed Roule. "And I'm sure all of you are wondering what's going to happen when they start on their way up the tower. Well, madame, gentlemen, I'll tell you. Nothing is going to happen. And that will prove that you, Ms. Sena, and you, Mr. Potts, are both insane." He smiled wolfishly at the two of them. "Young woman, you're not worth bothering with. But your lawyer is quite another matter. Potts, I've already called the sanitarium. I'm having you committed. The straitjacket boys will be here in ten minutes. Of course, if you want to leave now, your car's out front, and you can make the noon flight."

So *that* was your call, thought Potts. I might have known. He murmured, "It's an interesting coincidence, isn't it. Fenleigh York was on his way to the airport when his car was run off the cliff."

Roule sighed. "Yes, I suppose you have a point. It was most unfortunate. Would you believe, Potts, your friend thought he had uncovered some tasty evidence of corruption in the Bridge Authority. Something about sale of a big block of bonds to me for one dollar. Blatantly libelous. We tried to reason with him. But no. He was determined to take it to the Judicial Grievance Committee, and to the papers. So naive. What a pity. Sad, sad. Don't you agree, Mr. Potts?"

Most interesting, thought Potts. Barton Badging is sitting here, a witness to all this. Either the judge doesn't mind living dangerously, or else the coin expert is inextricably involved in the whole rotten scheme. He tried to catch Badging's eyes, but the other lawyer would not look at him.

The judge was talking to him. "I said, Mr. Potts, don't you agree?"

Potts shrugged. "Whatever," he said absently. His attention was momentarily focused on the TV screen. A man standing by the creeper traveler was waving to another out of camera view. The traveler was evidently about to begin its upward journey.

Roule looked at Potts sharply. "Have a care, sir. I can include your client in the certif—" His admonition was chopped off in midsyllable.

Simultaneously Badging jerked, and his elbow knocked an ashtray off the arm of his chair. But the ashtray didn't fall. It just seemed to hang there, spilling ashes that didn't fall, either. Very curious, thought Potts. He looked over at the judge, who was now simply a very odd-looking statue. The man's face and eyes showed no particular emotion: no fear, no alarm. Then Potts realized that all sound had ceased. The judge . . . Badging . . . the whole room . . . everything was like a still photograph, framed in dead time. He whirled and looked at Sena. She stared back, wide-eyed, then shrugged, as though to say, Don't ask *me!*

Well, at least the two of them seemed to be free. How about outside? How about the Bridge? He looked across the room. No sound was coming from the TV; the scene on the screen was motionless. The foreman's arm was still lifted in immutable signal to someone unseen, presumably the elevator operator. A group of men in hard hats, who had been walking toward the tower base, had come to a complete stop, as though caught in a snapshot.

It was like a scene in *The Sleeping Beauty,* where the fairies cast a spell, and all motion ceases. The king and queen go to sleep. The knights and ladies stop in mid-motion. The butcher's cleaver halts in mid-descent. An enchantment of great power falls on everything.

Potts's jaw dropped. Then he slowly closed it. For now he understood. The Dhorans are coming. Maybe they are already here. They have come for Sena. In the nick of time. His thoughts were confused and blurry. How will they do this? What do they look like? He stole a look at the woman. She was peering . . . outward . . . at what? And now it was *he* who was afraid. He held her hand tighter.

The judge's library wall began to glow. The entire section of *Atlantic Reports, 2nd,* shone, then glittered, then vanished. Potts could see through the wall. See what? Certainly not the parking lot, nor the street, nor the Domestic Relations Annex. He saw things for which he had no name. Brilliant fleeting lights . . . strange-colored, glowing frondy things. And sounds . . . weird, tinkly, harmonious. He knew there was nothing like this on Earth.

Sena let go his hand, stood up, then bent over to kiss him. "I'm leaving now, Oliver."

"They cannot save the Rock?"

"No, it is too late. If I stay, I die when the Rock vanishes. From the Rock, I was made." She hesitated. "Oliver, in all these ten thousand years you are the only person I have ever been able to talk to. There are many wonderful things on Dhora. We could be happy together there. Please come with me."

"No, you know I can't. It wouldn't work. You are immortal, Sena. You would stay young forever, but I would grow old and die. Go, Asenaapeeneniwa, Spirit-of-the-Rock, and let us remember each other."

She gave a wild desolate cry and ran into the radiance.

Atlantic Reports, 2nd, instantly rematerialized.

Life resumed.

The TV screen showed that the creeper traveler, carrying five thousand pounds of steel girders, had begun its ascent.

At this instant the Rock vanished.

For a moment the cantilever tower carelessly and impiously named George seemed motionless, suspended over thirty feet of absolute nothing, as though it had forgotten all about the teachings of Sir Isaac Newton. Or perhaps it thought itself hung from some colossal sky hook. But then reality overtook it, and it dropped, silently and leisurely at first, and straight down. There was a brief time lag between sight and sound, as though the makers of this scenario had ineptly failed to synchronize these vital elements of the performance. But finally everything came together, and the impact was seen, heard, and felt in some sort of ragged order in Roule's chambers. The vibrations nearly knocked the TV set off its stand.

In horror and fascination, the three men watched. Sena's absence went unnoted.

True bedrock at the site, thirty feet below the now-vanished Rock, sloped down toward the river, so that the river-side floor of the tower had farther to drop. This caused the tower to fall toward the water. It did not fall in one piece. The skyward sections had farther to go, and they could not be hurried. George in his final Virginia Reel, thought Potts. Truly a titan. The tower broke ultimately into three major pieces, all of which collapsed with grand gestures, as though waving at Martha across the river. Great Soul crying out to Great Soul, mused Potts. The upper sections fell finally into the river with tremendous prolonged splashes that drenched TV crewmen on the Bridge approaches half a mile back from the water.

The earth tremors continued, and the catastrophe now became quixotic. The TV cameras zoomed in on Martha across the river. The companion tower had begun to sway in a slow grand manner, as if opening a stately minuet. It was a strange and complicated movement, combining a sort of back-and-forth rocking with a side-to-side quiver. Things began to fall from the tower, girders, apparently. At first, slowly, and one by one. Then the tempo of destruction picked up, as though a gust of wind were blowing dead leaves out of a tree in late autumn.

With a great sigh Martha shook herself. She collapsed not as an integral piece of lacey steel, but as a jumble of awkward giant jackstraws.

Barton Badging turned slowly to face Potts. The mouth of the President of the Sena City Numismatic Association was a big slack O, and at first the words wouldn't come out properly. "My— My— The— What—?"

Potts waited sympathetically, but there was really nothing he could do.

Finally Badging screamed, then dashed out of the room. "My coins! My ninety-fives! The curse!"

The judge watched this with a chalk-white face. He staggered back to his chair, but he collapsed on the floor before he could reach it. He lay there in a heap by his desk.

Potts shook his head. A stroke? Better call an ambulance. And what a bad time for it! Bet they're all headed out to the Bridge. He started toward the judge's phone, but stopped when he heard steps behind him.

Two burly young men in white jackets stood there, looking at him, then at the figure of the floor.

"Sanitarium?" asked Potts. "Judge Roule's commitment order?"

"Yeah."

"There's your man, on the floor. You'll need a stretcher. And he ought to have immediate medical attention."

"Okay, chief. You got the papers."

"We'll send them over later."

"Fair enough. We'll have him out in a jiffy. You see the Bridge fall?"

"I did. But it was no big deal. That's what bridges do. Women have babies, grass grows green, lawyers orate, bridges fall."

The two attendants looked at each other as though asking, Do we have the right guy?

Potts appreciated their problem. He smiled, then shrugged, as though to say, It's a good question. "Oh, just one more thing." He strode quickly to the wall and took down the architect's picture of George Washington Bridge. "When he comes to, he'll want this. Just prop it up on his night-stand. Should have a great calming effect on him."

9. 'S' for Sillabub

"Well, Mr. Potts, how was the case in Sena City?" Miss Catlin sensed that Mr. Potts's mind was far away, and had been ever since his return that morning, and she put the question carefully.

"Sena. Fine."

"They treated you all right?"

"Oh, yes indeed. Memorable reception. The judge was remarkably hospitable— wanted to give me free room and board. Opposing counsel unusually helpful. Client's story ultimately understood by everyone. All very much like right here at home."

There was something not quite right in his answer, but she couldn't put her finger on it. She said, "Did you see the bridge fall? They interrupted TV programs all over the country to show it."

"Yes, I saw it."

"Are you all right, Mr. Potts?"

"Certainly. And it's time to get back to Earth. Where were we, before I rushed out last Friday?"

She examined a page in her notebook. "You had just asked me to send a ten-dollar check to the Mount Vernon Trust, and then you got that terrible phone call about Mr. York."

"I remember. Ten dollars?"

"Yes, sir."

"That makes me a member?"

"I suppose. Whatever *that* is."

"I want a second membership, actually a co-membership, for a couple of clients."

"Oh?"

"On the check, just say, 'For Sena and George.' Send the Trust ten thousand dollars."

"Mr. Potts! Are you crazy! You don't have ten thousand dollars!"

With careless nonchalance he handed her the big envelope. "Here's thirty thou, Miss Catlin. It might be best to deposit it before writing any checks. Also, would you please send ten thousand to Fenleigh York's executor."

She eyed him suspiciously. "Can we keep the other ten thousand, Mr. Potts?"

"By all means, Miss Catlin."

"Am I to understand you *won?*"

"No. I lost. The case was dismissed. My record remains unblemished."

She never knew when he was being sarcastic. "I understand there was some more excitement, following the bridge collapse." She watched him closely.

He looked back in total innocence. "Really?"

"I saw in the newscasts something about important people leaving the country. Marcus Reed, Chairman of the Bridge Authority."

"Yeah. To Brazil."

"And Mr. Badging went with him?"

"That's the rumor," said Potts.

"And we don't have an extradition treaty with Brazil? Mr. Potts?"

"Oh. No, I guess not."

"And that poor man, Judge Roule, still completely paralyzed from his stroke."

"So they say."

She bit her lip. He just wasn't going to talk. All right, then. Back to business here. "There was also the matter of the D.A.R. They wanted you to give a talk. You accepted. They want to know the talk title so they can put it on their programs. Preferably something early American."

"Ah, yes." He interlaced his fingers behind his head and leaned back and studied the ceiling. (Catlin was right, it needed painting.) He closed his eyes, and he saw that tall figure once again. George with a towel about his middle, playing the fife while his underwear dried. Sena at the spinet. That priceless holo—gone now, with Sena's house. So be it. He could still hear the tune. He began to pat his foot. Ah Sena, did you (like Sally Fairfax, like Eliza Powel) ever enliven the Old Boy's dreams in that upper bedroom at Mount Vernon? I hope so!

And so crashing back. Alas. "Tell them the title will be, *1795—Year of Crisis.*"

She beamed at him. She hadn't expected it would be so easy. Maybe he was going to behave, after all. "And now just a little housekeeping matter. Where shall I file this new case folder? Under 'S' for Sena? 'B' for Bridge Authority? 'Y' for York? Or—?"

" 'S,' " he said dreamily, "for Sena. For spinet. For saddlebag. For seventeen ninety-five. For sterility. But most of all for sillabub."

She might have known. Back to normal.

This is about my high school English teacher. I adored her. She once went out on a limb for me—to my eternal shame: she gave me a final grade that included a nonexistent term paper on Browning. I had promised I would write it and turn it in, but I delayed and dawdled and never did.

(So, my lyric love, here it finally is. With compound interest. You are long dead, but deathless.)

This one led me into research about Florence, the Renaissance, and ultimately to "The Tetrahedron."

O LYRIC LOVE

I had long ago realized that Professor Mae Leslie identified strongly with the Victorian poet Elizabeth Barrett. She looked like Barrett and dressed like Barrett. Like Barrett's, her hair dangled in long ringlets about a pale but lively face. Like the poet, she wore no make-up. She out-Barretted Barrett in one respect: an adolescent maltreated bout with polio confined her to a wheelchair, which she maneuvered with great skill and energy. As we know, the British poet had a spinal problem and was in bed a lot, but she was certainly ambulatory on her wedding day. Which brings me to the next similarity: both women (in their own way, and in their own time) loved Robert Browning.

And I loved Mae Leslie. How do I love thee? Let me count the ways! First as a beautiful woman. Consider the stark black hair, artfully contrived into those curls. The flashing green eyes. The naturally red lips between the translucent cheeks. That body. I imagined marvelous breasts, smooth, semi-firm, capped by roseate buds. Then the erotic sweep of belly. Her hands were sonnets. And yet she was virginal. I doubted that any male hand had ever been laid on her in lust. What a waste!

For years I had gone to sleep thinking of her. She was older than I—by six or seven years. It didn't matter to me. Her erudition was formidable, but that didn't matter either. Recognized authority on minor Victorian poets. She had written books. She lectured by video terminal all over the world: Oxford, the Sorbonne, Moscow U., and (would you believe it!) M.I.T.

She knew something about everything. The universal doctor. She could even hold her own when we discussed my undergraduate specialty, which was quantum physics, and how certain theoretical sub-particles could move forward and backward along a time axis (the "Feynman minuet"). She appreciated me. She encouraged me. As my senior year in college closed, she helped me get the graduate scholarship.

Aye, there's the rub.

So here we were in her little office in the Fine Arts Building, once again after all these years, and I knew exactly what she was thinking.

The Browning paper.

I had relived that last conference five years ago a dozen times. She had been quite disturbed, and she kept fiddling with the controls on her wheelchair. "You need an A in this course if you are going to get that scholarship in quantum physics. Are you making any progress with your paper on Browning?"

How much was any? "Some," I said. Where had the time gone? Time time time. I had six end-of-term assignments and projects. Too much time on the time project. And now Browning was left. An Appreciation of Robert Browning. Term paper for Eng Lit 205. How could it have happened? I loved this lovely stricken woman. I knew it hurt her to deny me that A and the scholarship. Well, it hurt me too. I was hurting all over. For me, for her, for my future.

"What are you doing this summer?" she had asked.

I had shrugged. "Nothing."

She brightened. "I'll give you an A. Now. You'll get the scholarship. Finish the paper this summer. Let me have it by the end of August. Promise?"

"Of course!" I had been surprised and grateful. I had stretched out my hand, as though to shake on the deal, and probably by simple reflex she had given me hers. But then I had taken that hand in both of mine, and I had laid the fingers out flat, and I had kissed the palm, and given it back to her, and left, picking my way through the stacks of books and papers.

Five years ago.

The Browning paper.

I had tried. For the next two weeks of that summer I had kept the library terminals hot, collecting data, getting microprintouts. I had even drafted a couple of preliminary pages. Who the hell was this guy Robert Browning? The husband of Elizabeth Barrett: that was his only claim to fame. In fact, a lot of the computer entries called him Robert Barrett.

"He wrote beautiful things, significant things," Mae had insisted (arguing so futilely at the cold bar of history). "That's how they met, in the first place. She was already a great poet, and she understood *his* poetry: 'My Last Duchess.' ('She liked whate'er she looked on, and her looks went everywhere.') 'How They Brought the Good News from Ghent to Aix.' ('I galloped, Dirck galloped, we galloped all three.') 'Home Thoughts from Abroad.' ('Oh to be in England, now that April's there.') 'Pippa Passes.' ('God's in his heaven— All's right with the world.') And of course that remarkable little thing, 'The Pied Piper of Hamelin.' All before he met Elizabeth Barrett."

I looked it all up. Robert declared his love. At first Elizabeth rejected him. My father will never consent, she said. Besides, I am a semi-invalid. I would be a burden to you. Consent be damned! declared Robert. Arise! She did. And so they were married, and moved to Italy, and she continued her career with the greatest love poems of the nineteenth century: *Sonnets from the Portuguese*. And all the other marvels: *Aurora Leigh, A Musical Instrument, De Profundis, Bianca Among the Nightingales*. But Robert just faded away. He wrote and was ignored. *She* wrote and flourished.

At one of our early conferences Mae had posed an interesting speculation. "If Robert had written one really significant long poem, it might have been enough to ignite well-deserved interest in his earlier works. He might have got an entry in *Poets' Dictionary*, and perhaps a half column in the *Encyclopedia of English Poets*. But no. 'The Pied Piper' has survived, and that's all."

So now it was five years later, and I had brought Dr. Mae Leslie, plus wheelchair, in my van to my laboratory. She hadn't wanted to leave her campus cubbyhole at first. She was still mad at me. She still felt betrayed. Because to this very day I hadn't finished my Appreciation of Robert Browning. As it turned out, I had had to drop my Browning research in the middle of that first summer and get a job, or starve. That fateful August had passed, and no paper. But I had got the A, and then the scholarship. We hadn't spoken since, except for my call to her yesterday.

I got her out of the van and onto the sidewalk. She checked the controls on her wheelchair. "Lead on. I'm right behind you."

And so on into the entrance way, past the offices ("Hold my calls." "Yes, Mr. Roland"), and into the back of the main building.

She was impressed. "Is all this your lab?"

"This is it. We make things here, such as electronic gadgets for NASA, and we have several classified government research projects. All this exists because you gave me an A in Eng Lit 205."

"Which you did not earn. You still owe me a Robert Browning."

"I'm coming to that." We stood before a locked door, which I opened with a signal from a pen-light. We stepped inside. "The transmission room."

"What in the world?"

I could understand her wonder. It didn't look like much. Just a big room, nearly empty. It held a couple of tables, a computer console, and a chair or two. A few books and some apparatus lay on one of the tables, which also carried a switch panel. Soft shadowless radiants provided anonymous illumination.

I looked at my watch. I had it timed well. If it worked. And I knew it would. "Look at the table," I told her. "A book will appear on the dais in the center." As we watched, a paperback volume did in fact materialize on the raised area.

I heard her sharp intake of breath. "How did you do that?"

"It wasn't easy." I walked over and picked the book up. "It's the undergraduate catalog." I peeked into the Eng Lit section. I hesitated very briefly as a truly astonishing entry struck my eye. Then I closed it up quickly and handed it to her. "Care to check?" She flipped the pages at random, then looked up. "So what's the point?"

"Just a little preliminary test demonstration." I picked up another volume from the table. "*This* is the identical catalog. At three P.M., one hour from now, as we leave, I shall put it here on the dais—we call it the Feynman plate—and it will be sent into the past, which is of course here and now, at two P.M. It materializes—*has* materialized—on the table. In a word, it time-travels."

She just looked at me. I couldn't tell whether she believed me or not. She said noncommittally: "Go on."

"The plate is capable of transmitting up to one kilo of matter, backward in time, up to two hundred years, and to anywhere in the world."

She had to think about that. She temporized. "I suppose it's silly of me to ask if this has something to do with Robert Browning." It wasn't really a question. It was almost as though she was thinking out loud.

"We're going to send him something." I watched her face. She was not completely successful in masking her thoughts, which said, *you are crazy*. She asked politely, as though we were assembling a seminar agenda, "Just exactly what are you going to send him? The college catalog?"

"No." I took the catalog from her and handed her a second book. "This."

She put it in her lap and opened the stiff vellum-veneered cover. Her eyes widened. "Well now, what have we here? Title page—handwritten. And in Italian! Concerning the trial of Count Guido Franceschini and four confederates for murder, and their conviction and execution." Very carefully she turned a few more pages. "Now we get into printed Latin. Paper old, very old, edges crumbling. Depositions . . . dated . . . good heavens! . . . 1698!" She peered up at me a moment, intrigued, puzzled, then continued leafing through the book. "And finally, more handwritten pages." She closed the volume cautiously. "Bernard, what is it? What is this all about?"

"*That*," I said, "is the keystone in our campaign to rehabilitate your friend Robert Browning. The people really lived. The godawful things reported there really happened. May I tell you the story?"

"Please do."

"Well, there was this Guido Franceschini, a bachelor, and a sort of second-class Italian nobleman, and he was broke, and looking for a bride with money. A middle-aged bourgeois couple by the name of Camparini had a young and beautiful daughter, Pompilia, and the parents had a big block of treasury bonds. The bond income was to continue for the life of their children—which meant during Pompilia's life. The Camparinis wanted the prestige of being in-laws to nobility. Besides which, Guido claimed to be rich in his own right. And so the marriage was duly arranged and the income assigned over to Guido. Then came trouble. Mama and Papa Camparini visited the newlyweds at the gloomy Franceschini castle in Arezzo, near Rome, and there their eyes were opened. The Franceschinis were at the bottom of the list of petty nobility; except for the bond income they were paupers; and they insulted the Camparinis at every turn. Mama and Papa returned to Rome, furious, and vowing vengeance. They filed a suit in the Roman court, asking that the bond income be revoked, on the ground that Pompilia was not their daughter. Actually, they had bought her as a newborn infant from a woman of the streets and passed her off as their own child to extend the period of bond income. And now it was Guido Franceschini's turn to be furious. He threatened to kill Pompilia. Terrified, she escaped from Arezzo with the help of a priest, Giuseppi Caponsacchi. Guido rode off in pursuit, and overtook them at an inn. Adultery! he howled. A big row. Police called in. A clerical court considered the case. Pompilia was finally released to the custody of her parents, in Rome. Caponsacchi was exiled to Civita for three years. Count Guido was told to go home. And so he did. But he couldn't leave it alone. He gathered up four local cutthroats, rode to Rome, burst in on the Camparinis—father, mother, daughter—and killed the three of them. The five were caught, tried, and executed. Guido was beheaded, to give credit to his claim to nobility. The other four were hanged. All as reported in this old yellow book. You note here the depositions of the witnesses, the statement of the prosecutor, the pleas of defense counsel, judgment of the court, Guido's appeal to the Pope, and the three-line affirmation of His Holiness."

"Impressive." She was still noncommittal.

"There's just one little difficulty."

"Oh?"

"It's all forgery. Every page. Every word."

She opened the book at random and studied the pages again. Then she shook her head. "Forgery? I've seen old documents before. It certainly *looks* genuine."

I smiled. It was good to hear her say that. "The paper was made last month from a mix of rags, old paper, fish nets, and flax, pulped by hand in mortar and pestle, tub-sized with alum, then hand-laid. An old Italian recipe. The type was very recently reconstructed from a Manutius font characteristic of the period. The Latin and Italian texts were prepared by scholars at Columbia and Fordham. After binding in vellum, the whole was aged by exposure to u.v. light and steam. The finished product was delivered to me yesterday. Whereupon I promptly called you."

"And you're going to send it back in time to Robert Browning?"

"Yes."

"How can you be so sure he'll get it? And what is he supposed to do with it?"

"There's a lot more. Let me give you the whole picture."

"I'd like that."

"To start, take note that my Barrett-Browning data bank includes everything known today about either or both of the poets. I've pieced together comprehensive personality profiles from old letters—theirs and others; their literary output; reviews; biographical sketches of Elizabeth (Robert had none); maps of places and cities where they lived or visited; her surviving medical files; histories of the times; and so on. Where data are missing, I have asked the computer to give its best estimate. We can fairly predict what each of them would do or say under certain given circumstances. In this way, we can determine that on the morning of June 15, 1860, a Friday, Robert will be out for a walk in downtown Florence, Italy. The weather is clear and hot. He is timing his outing so as to be home and have a late lunch with Elizabeth. She has not been feeling well, and he wants to spend the afternoon with her. His return route lies through the square of San Lorenzo. There's a cart in the middle of the square loaded helter-skelter with pots and pans, old clothes, books, all kinds of junk. On this hot midday, this old yellow book will land on top of the heap. Browning will see it and buy it. The computer now predicts his actions, right down to the trifling sum, one lira, that he will offer for the book. (He is a man of careful economies!) My forgery will fascinate him. He'll read it as he walks home. He'll pass the Strozzi palace, cross the Arno on the San Trinita bridge; he walks down the Via Maggio; and by the time he reaches home at Casa Guidi, he'll have finished it. In his head is crystallizing the dramatic background for a magnificent work, the thing that will eventually transform the husband of Elizabeth Barrett to Robert Browning, major Victorian poet, and rival of Tennyson, Wordsworth, Byron, Shelley . . ." I paused.

She was still not convinced. "If you can really do this kind of thing . . . send matter back through time, why haven't you sent a bomb back to Hitler's bedroom, say about 1935?"

I shrugged. "I thought of that. But I'm afraid to change history so drastically. With no Hitler, would we have the modern state of Israel? And suppose I altered the past in such a way that my parents never met? No. We've got to limit the transmission to non-historic matters."

"Suppose Browning checks up on your alleged facts?"

"I'm sure he will. And he'll find the story is completely true. My material is based on data in a volume in the Royal Casanatense Library in Rome, identified as Miscellaneous Ms. 2037, '*Varii successi curiosi e degni di esser considerati.*' And there are unrelated supporting reports, such as the baptismal records of the child-wife Pompilia, of the hero priest Caponsacchi, of the villainous husband Franceschini, and so on. I have photocopies. Do you want to see them?"

"Never mind." She kept looking at me, puzzled, thoughtful. "Assume it works. Assume Browning is stimulated to write his magnum opus, his masterpiece, and it makes him famous. I keep coming back to my basic question. Why are you doing this, Bernard?"

"I owe you. With interest."

"Not this much."

"Yes, this much. This is my term paper, An Appreciation of Robert Browning. I have the facilities, the money, the technology. I can do it, finally. Permit me to pay my debt."

Debt? Ha! There was more to it than that. I had a secondary object, like a wheel within a wheel, or, as the computermen say, a nested loop. And it was this: I wanted Robert Browning to compose some lines for me that would show my love for Mae Leslie. I would call on him to declare, in exquisite rhyme or blank verse or whatever, feelings I did not know how to express. I would go to him as an illiterate peasant in the streets of Calcutta or Quito or Morocco goes to a commercial letter writer, to compose a dulcet message to a beloved. I was like the dull and inarticulate de Neuvillette, persuading Cyrano de Bergerac to compose love letters to Roxane. Robert, old friend, say this to her, that she is like a song, a lyric. She is part angel, part bird. And tell her, O age-lost ghost writer, that I have a wild and wonderful hunger for her.

Was this possible? I doubted it. But it was worth a try.

Mae broke in on my reverie. "Well then, let's see where it stands. Browning buys the book, reads it, is impressed. He visualizes a great poetic drama. What then? Does he start drafting right away?"

"I think not. It has to simmer a bit. He has to sort out the players, define their roles. He will be Caponsacchi. Edward Barrett, Elizabeth's father, will be the tyrannical Guido Franceschini. The pure and innocent Pompilia will be Elizabeth. We bear in mind that Elizabeth has barely a year to live. She dies in June, 1861. Browning will see this much clearer following her death."

Mae sat there in her chair, silent, probably inwardly grieving at my insanity. "There's a terminal with a CRT just behind you," I said. "Before we send the old yellow book down the time tube, you might want to see what one of the standard references has to say, as of this day and this hour, about friend Robert."

"I know already. Well, okay, for the record . . ." She revolved toward the terminal and tapped away at the keyboard. "I'm accessing *Encyclopedia of English Poets*. Ah, here we are. It says 'Browning, Robert. See Barrett, Elizabeth.' Satisfied? Or shall I go for *her?*"

"No. Just print the entry. When we finish, we can call him up again and compare. Before and after, as it were. I think we're about ready. Shall I pull the switch?"

But she temporized. I could sense a growing unease, as though finally she was thinking, maybe he's right . . . maybe it really will work. But . . . but . . . "Bernard, have you ever done this . . . transmitted matter . . . before?"

"You saw the college catalog, and there were several times before that." (Paper clips, a pencil, a coin, traveling at farthest from one end of the table to the other, over a time span of a few hours.)

"So it's perfectly safe?"

"Well . . ." (Now it was my turn to hesitate. I knew a tremendous surge of energy would be required to send a full kilo back nearly two hundred years, and across nearly five thousand miles. I had never transmitted on this scale before.) I said, "There may be certain holographic hallucinations, but there is nothing physically harmful." (I hope.)

She sighed. (Had she noted the edge of uncertainty in my assurance?) "Go ahead." She rolled away from the console.

I laid the forgery on the Feynman plate. "Mae," I said, "nothing is going to happen to us, but just in case . . . I want you to know that I love you." I pulled the switch.

"Bernard!"

The room began to vibrate. She shrieked. There was a tremendous crash and a blinding light. We threw our arms up over our eyes. It wasn't supposed to do this. Had a time-tesseract collapsed somewhere? My head was going around crazily. Mae . . . I had to reach Mae . . .

Things steadied. I stood up and looked about in the semi-dark.

Mae? No Mae. No tables. No computers . . . no lab . . .

I am standing on a sort of terrace-balcony. Somewhere, somewhen. I lean on the railing while I wait for my head to stop spinning. A gibbous moon lights up an eerie scene outside. Across the street, a church dome. San Felice. I hear the muted chant of nuns drifting out of the square windows. People with lanterns and torches moving in the street. A fiesta. I tug at my beard. Some time ago, as a whim, when it was black, I shaved it off. When it grew out again it was gray. "Distinguished!" Elizabeth said.

I love this view. We're fortunate to live here at Casa Guidi, the townhouse of faded Florentine nobility. Thirteen years. Living, writing, loving. The reviewers were ecstatic over *Aurora Leigh*. And she's hard at work on "Bianca."

Night and people. Everything brings me back to the medicinal leaves of that strange yellow book. I see the people so clearly. Pompilia fleeing for her life. I mark

her route from Arezzo. Perugia . . . Camoscia . . . Chiusi . . . Foligno . . . Castelnuovo
. . . ah, now she is exhausted, and Caponsacchi insists they stop and rest. A grave
mistake. Only four hours from Rome. Couldn't they have made it? I think the inn
still stands at Castelnuovo. And there Guido overtakes them. And then one thing
led to another . . . and finally to that final frightful night. She had twenty-two stab
wounds. Or was it the father? Check that.

I walked slowly back into the bedroom. Mae lay on the divan, sleeping quietly with the thin blue coverlet rumpled around her legs. Dim-lit by moonlight.
No, not Mae. Elizabeth. Though the ringlets make the faces almost identical.
How had Hawthorne described her? 'A pale small person, scarcely embodied at
all . . . elfin, rather than earthly . . . sweetly disposed towards the human race,
though only remotely akin to it.' What an astonishing person you are, Elizabeth. My angel. My bird uncaged, singing your sweet lyrics. My love.

I listened to the silences within the house. Son Pen, asleep in his little room.
Wilson's night off. She's out somewhere with her young man.

My head begins to whirl again. I am moving forward in time. Months are
flitting by like uncertain moths. We are still in Casa Guidi, and it is still night,
and the noises within the cavernous rooms are still faint, a dark gentle background to the tragedy unfolding in the bedroom.

I hear Mae's guttural whisper. "Robert . . ." I hurry back in. Last night she
told Pen she felt better. But I don't know. I sit in bed with her and she snuggles
up across my chest. My hand rests over her heart. The beat is faint and irregular.

Is she conscious? Does she know where she is? I say softly, "Do you know
me?" "Oh Robert, I love you, I love you." She kisses me. She says, "I must tell
you something." "Yes?" She whispers, "Our lives are held by God." She puts her
arms around me happily. She says, "God bless you." It is incredible. I say, "Are
you comfortable?" "Beautiful."

She smiles. Her head falls forward. At first I think she may have fallen asleep.
At worst, fainted. Anything else, unacceptable. But I know. She is dead. It is
four in the morning, June 29, 1861. Tears define nothing. A time for auguries
and comets.

The mists slowly cleared.

Mae was no longer in my arms. (Was she ever?) She was in her wheelchair, and
we were back in my lab, and staring at each other.

She spoke first."I thought I was . . . you were . . ."

"Illusions," I said. "I mentioned the possibility."

"Illusions . . . God! At the last, there, I thought I had died." Her voice faded
away and she passed translucent fingers over her brow. Her face was wet, and her
long curls clung plastered to her cheeks. I passed a roll of paper towels to her,
and she daubed at her face and hair. "Now what?" she asked. "Besides wrecking
my hair-do and scaring me out of my wits, what have you accomplished? Everything around here seems the same."

First things first. "How do you feel?"

"All right. Just a little shaky. I need to think."

I could appreciate that. So did I.

Her thinking was not hard to follow. I had had the same thoughts many times. Consider the various possibilities. First—the project hadn't worked. Because if it had, Robert Browning would today be a famous poet, and we would know it. But we don't know it, so he isn't, so it didn't work. Second—but if perchance somehow it *had* worked, there must now be two parallel worlds, one with and one without the great forgery; one world in which Browning is a great poet, and one world in which he's a virtual nonentity, known only as Elizabeth's husband. Two such worlds would reconcile all the facts. (But if there are two, may there not be three . . . or four . . . or a million? Where does it stop?)

Too much of this could drive her crazy. And me too. I had to break it up. I said, "Have you recovered enough to work with the terminal again?"

She blinked. "Oh . . . the terminal. I think so." She rubbed her fingers together, then rolled back to the console. "For a strict comparison let's check the *Encyclopedia of English Poets* once more."

"Good idea."

She tapped the keys. The CRT sprang to life. "Good God!" she muttered. "Look at that!" The screen filled up. Then line after line, it overflowed. This went on for several minutes. "All about Robert Browning."

"Get a print-out," I said.

The laser printer began to hum. I walked over to the collection basket and, as the sheets folded and dropped, I dug under the pile for the very bottommost, the original encyclopedia entry. Was it still there? Was there any place in this new parallel world for a reference identifying Robert as simply the husband of Elizabeth Barrett? Aha! There it was! "Browning, Robert. See Barrett, Elizabeth." I put it back out of sight and faced her. "What did he call it?"

"Call what? Oh, the new magnum opus." Her eyes became suddenly sly. She was getting into the spirit. "Not so fast. What did your computer *predict* he would call it?"

"*The Ring and the Book.*"

"Quite plausible. The ring would be from the inscription the Florentines made for Elizabeth on the wall of Casa Guidi: '. . . she made of her verses a golden ring between Italy and England.' The book would be your famous forgery. And of course the initials of the title would probably be R for Robert and B for Browning. Well, let's check. What *did* he call it? And there it is: *The Ring and the Book.* Bullseye! Twenty-one thousand lines. First published by Smith and Elder in four volumes, at monthly intervals, starting 21 November 1868."

I said, "Look for some contemporary reviews."

"Coming up." (She was with it now, a believer. How could she ever have doubted?) "*Fortnightly Review, London Quarterly, Revue des Deux Mondes*—all unstinting praise. Ah, listen to what the *Edinburgh Review* says about Pompilia, Caponsacchi, and the Pope: 'In English literature the creative faculty of the poet has not produced three characters more beautiful or better to contemplate than these three.' And the *Athenaeum*, the lordly arbiter of English criticism, says, '. . . *The Ring and the Book* is beyond all parallel the supremest poetical achievement of our time . . . it is the most precious and profound spiritual treasure that England has produced since the days of Shakespeare.' " She looked up at me in wonder and silence. Finally, she turned back to the computer. "And now, how do we stand with Elizabeth Barrett?"

"Don't, Mae."

"I've got to know." She typed briefly at the keyboard. "Look at *that*. It says, see Elizabeth Barrett Browning."

I didn't know what to say. Keeping quiet just now was one of the few smart things I've done in my life.

"It was a risk we ran," she said thoughtfully. "They were one entity, really. The more of her, the less of him. And vice versa. Each wanted the other to be appreciated and understood and famous. This was her wish for him, and his for her. She would have wanted it this way. Hm. *The Ring and the Book*. I want to read this great thing."

I said, "The computer predicted he would dedicate it to her. For now, why don't we just look for the dedication? Plug in the poem. The dedication ought to be somewhere near the beginning."

"All right. Here we go.

PART 1

> *Do you see this ring?*
[I'm skimming," said Mae.]

.   .   .

> *Do you see this square old yellow book?*
[And on, and on. Robert takes his time. Makes it all clear. Ah, here we are, these lines to Elizabeth, closing Part 1:]
> *O lyric love, half angel and half bird,*
> *And all a wonder and a wild desire—*

Her voice broke. "I can't. It's too personal. She had been dead several years when he wrote that. All for her. He remembered . . . everything. He opened his heart. Oh, Bernard, what have we done?"

Well, Robert, I thought, you got my message, loud and clear. And you magically transformed it. But it was *my* message, to *Mae,* and now was the time to tell her. I wanted to say, Mae darling, that dedication was my declaration to *you.* But I couldn't speak. Mae saw it as a love letter to Elizabeth. And of course the lines were no longer just for Elizabeth: they had now entered the public domain and were the sacred property of every woman who was ever loved, or ever would be. So be it.

I tried to reassure her. "We did exactly what they both wanted. And the world is better for it."

"Do you think so? Well . . ." She shrugged. (Was she still bothered about Elizabeth, fading into the background?) She studied the CRT. "He didn't stop with the *Ring*. A lot of later things. Everything works now, everything sells. Browning clubs at Oxford and Cambridge. They explain *Sordello* to the mystified. Swinburne is elated with 'Fifine at the Fair': '. . . far better than anything Browning has yet written.' The Browning Society of London is chartered in 1881. Oxford and Cambridge give him honorary degrees."

I broke in. "Anything about what finally happened to the old yellow book?"

"Hold on. Here we are. After his death his son donated it to the library of Balliol College, at Oxford."

"What do you have on his death?"

"He died while visiting Venice, 12 December 1889. He had wanted to be buried next to Elizabeth, in the Protestant Cemetery at Florence, but because of Italian regulations and red tape, this was not possible. So he was buried in the Poets' Corner in Westminster Abbey, next to Tennyson, and facing Chaucer." She paused. There was not much more to say. "I guess that's the end of it. Somehow, I'll have to catch up with Robert. Read the *Ring*, of course, and all his later poems. Study his bio. And the critics, contemporary and modern. He seems to have aged well."

"I know a good start," I said. "It's right here in the catalog."

"Really?"

The game was not over. An hour ago I had noted a fascinating entry in the time-traveled college catalog. Eros had one more shaft in his quiver. I said, "Remember, in our new parallel world, our little catalog reflects all changes resulting from Robert's rehabilitation. Ah, here. Eng 301, Travel Seminar, Summer Session. An appreciation of Elizabeth Browning, minor Victorian poetess, wife of Robert Browning. Visit scenes of her childhood, youth, and marriage: Hope End, Wimpole Street. The marriage flight. Then that week in Paris. Next, Pisa, and finally Casa Guidi in Florence."

"Curious. Who's the tour instructor?"

"You are."

"No!" She grabbed the catalog, read slowly aloud, while she turned white. "I *can't*. I'm a semi-invalid."

"So was Elizabeth. I'll go with you. I'll help you up and down all those stairs. I'll take the questions about Robert. Where did they stay in Paris? The Hôtel de Ville, in the Rue d'Evêque, both now long gone." I may have regarded her with a look more leer than lyric (this being the nature of a man of purpose). "Do you know what they did on their last night there?"

She studied me with an innocence suggestive of Pompilia Franceschini, but with just a touch of Mata Hari and Lucrezia Borgia (such being the nature of a woman of purpose). "I know that it's exactly one minute before three o'clock, and that if you don't put that catalog on your funny time-plate, we may both wind up in a world where none of this ever happened."

THE TETRAHEDRON

1. Elizabeth

Elizabeth sat tightly in her chair—a chair ordinarily occupied only by very important people.

The man on the other side of the desk, the senior-most partner of the most prestigious law firm in Washington, D.C., had called her in from her little cubbyhole. Why? What horror had she, a mere junior associate, committed that required the personal attention of Barrington Wright? She was going to be fired. She just knew it.

Cocooned in tight invisible armor, Wright peered over at her somberly. "Ms. Gerard, do you know what TM is?

TM? She thought. What the hell was *that?* Was she *supposed* to know? She suspected no. So just tell him the truth. "No, sir. I don't think I've ever heard of it."

She watched his face covertly. Yes, the muscles around his mouth seemed to relax. She had passed some sort of test. She hadn't known what TM was, and for some reason that was good.

He said in a soft monotone, "There are only ten persons in the world with TM clearance. That number includes myself—and now, you."

She blinked. They were not about to fire her. Quite the contrary.

" 'TM,' " said Wright, watching her, "means time machine."

She knew she heard him clearly, but it made no sense. She waited.

"A client," he said, "has invented a time machine. Theoretically, it works. Our Mr. Pellar prepared and filed a patent application on it." He paused and looked at his watch. "I had expected him to sit in with us, but he has been delayed coming in from the airport. So we'll go ahead with the preliminaries. To continue, the patent office has placed our patent application in interference with another application, earlier filed, and directed to the same invention." He paused and looked over at her.

She nodded. C. Cuthbert Pellar was evidently one of the charter members of this TM club. Pellar the Couth. Wright's clone, they called him—but not to his face.

Wright was saying something to her. "Do you follow?"

"Yes, sir. We're junior party. To win the interference, we have to prove that our client is the first inventor."

"And what would that involve?"

"We'd need at least a prior conception, properly confirmed, with a good showing of diligence leading to actual reduction to practice."

"And what if the client can't do any of that?"

"Then somebody should tell him he can't win. At least save him the cost of useless litigation."

"That's good advice, ordinarily. But here it's a bit more complicated. Our client is the Department of Defense."

"And Defense won't let you give up?"

"Exactly. So what do we do now, Ms. Gerard?"

"Find some really close prior art, then move to dissolve the interference, as unpatentable to either party. That way, nobody gets a patent, but DOD will be free to use the invention."

She knew very well they didn't have any "really close prior art," and that somehow she would be involved in remedying the omission. It was beginning to come together.

The intercom buzzed. "Yes?" said Wright, without turning.

"Mr. Pellar, sir," said a disembodied female voice.

"Send him in."

C. Cuthbert Pellar smiled ingratiatingly at the man who could make him partner, frowned remotely at Elizabeth, and took the indicated chair.

"Nothing?" said Wright

"Nothing, sir. We've searched the entire field of U.S. and foreign patents, and all the scientific literature. We've spent three months and three million dollars looking for a reference to prove the TM is old in the art. We found nothing." He looked over at Elizabeth. His expression said plainly, "And she can't help."

"As I explained earlier," said the older man, "the DOD has examined the *curricula vitae* of every employee of the firm, including the associates, not only for security reasons, but also looking for special skills." He held up a printout, adjusted his spectacles, and studied the sheet. "Colonel Inman has called my attention to certain interesting facets in Ms. Gerard's background. She got her master's degree in assembling and translating ancient manuscripts. She has stack privileges in major international libraries. She is reasonably fluent in several foreign languages."

"Sir," said Pellar, "I don't understand."

Yeah, thought Elizabeth. Me either.

"Simple," said Wright. "We've exhausted the printed art; now we go farther back—into the manuscripts."

"But—" began Pellar.

"The client has requested it, Mr. Pellar," said Wright firmly. "Please describe the machine to Ms. Gerard, so that she can go to work."

"Oh, yes, sir. Of course, sir. We can start with the interference count. I quote." He half-closed his eyes and began to rattle away in a rhythmic sing-song. "Apparatus for shifting the space-time axis consisting of (a) silver tubes containing heavy water and positioned to form a tetrahedral framework; (b) a source of EMF adapted to cause an electrical current to flow through said framework; (c) a cubical crystal of uraninite; and (d) a mammal in cerebral electrical contact with said EMF source and said uraninite.'"

Son-of-a-gun, thought Elizabeth. He's memorized it. And meanwhile, she was thinking . . . a *tetrahedron?* Had she seen something . . . somewhere?

Pellar leered at her. "Well? Did you get it?"

He's mad at me already, she thought. The first team spent three million and crapped out. So now the problem is handed over to one lone female junior associate. And the worst is yet to come, Cuthbert, because I do indeed remember something. "Just a minute, please." She let an image form in her mind. Four equilateral triangles made of silver tubes . . . Where had she seen this? Something in manuscript. She remembered the strange writing. She ran down a mental list of the major medieval mathematicians. Geber . . . Kashi . . . Copernicus. No, none of them. How about the minors? Biagio da Ravenna . . . Paolo dal Pozzo Toscanelli . . . two of the finest mathematicians of Renaissance Italy, and both had taught the boy Leonardo da Vinci.

Of course.

That's where she had seen the sketch. In a copy of a page from one of Leonardo's many notebooks. Which one? There were dozens, and they were scattered in libraries all over the world Yes, she had it now. The *quaderno* so recently bought by the Library of Congress. "Gentlemen," she said, "your time machine may indeed have been described in the unprinted literature."

The two men stared at her in puzzled silence.

Pellar was the first to move. He looked over at Wright. It was an expressive look, and it said, "You see, Mr. Wright, this is what you get when you bring in a woman."

Elizabeth blushed, and fought the urge to clench her fists. *This is the twenty-first century. Why do we still have to put up with this?*

"Ms. Gerard," said Wright gently, "would you excuse us for a moment?"

"Of course." She rose from her chair. They had decided she was useless, and they were going to take her off the case before she was ever really on it.

Like hell they were.

2. The Fax

She turned when she reached the door. "Before I go, I'd like to mention that Leonardo da Vinci described an apparatus very similar to that of the interference count in Notebook 23, Codex IV, pages forty and forty-one. It's in the data banks at the Library of Congress, and you can call up a fax in seconds, if you're interested." She started out into the reception room.

"Ms. Gerard," Wright called quickly. "Just a minute, please."

"Oh?"

Wright nodded toward his credenza. "Use my fax."

She walked back in, punched in the call, and the printer lasered the reply in less than three minutes. The two men hovered over the machine. No room for Elizabeth. No matter. She had caught a glimpse: a sketch of a tetrahedron, plus lines of tiny elegant letters.

"Interesting," admitted Wright. "Very. What does the writing say?" He handed it over to Pellar.

The associate shook his head. "It's all gobbledegook. Illegible. Worthless!"

"He wrote right to left," explained Elizabeth. "You read it with a mirror. I assume there's one in Mr. Wright's washroom?"

"Sir?"

"Go ahead."

"It's—" began Elizabeth.

Pellar pushed her aside, but after a moment he wailed from the little room: "I *still* can't read it."

"It's in Italian," said Elizabeth. She walked up behind him. "It says, 'A tetrahedron is required, of a size such that a man can stand within. The four triangles are formed of silver tubes filled with water distilled from forty tuns by the alchemist. The traveler stands in the center of the base triangle. He attaches the headband. He holds the black cube, and he attunes his mind to the . . . (hmm—strange word here . . . ah . . .) *back-time*. He sees a—hmm . . . *scacchiera* . . . yes, chessboard. By means of this assembly I was able to finish the *Cenacolo* for the friars in Milan!' "

"Chay-nak-olo?" said Pellar. "What's *that?*"

"*The Last Supper,*" explained Elizabeth. "He painted it on a monastery wall in Milan in the late 1400s."

"He used the apparatus to complete a painting?" asked Wright. "How? Why?"

"I don't know," said Elizabeth. "He doesn't say."

"But, sir," Pellar said, "five hundred years ago how could anybody know anything about space-time and quantum physics? And especially this fellow Leonardo? He was just a painter."

"Leonardo had an ultra-genius I.Q.," Elizabeth answered stoutly. "Some psychologists place it at 250, some even at 300, beyond Einstein. He had brainpower adequate to create your TM. From the description that he left, it appears that he did just that."

"*Appears?*" sneered Pellar.

"I think we can nail it down, one way or the other," declared Elizabeth.

Wright swiveled his chair to face her. "How?"

"Go back. Ask him."

"Him?" said Pellar blankly. "Who?"

"Leonardo," explained Wright dryly. "Take his deposition."

Pellar was now totally bewildered. "I thought he was dead!"

"She means," Wright explained patiently, "use the TM. Go back to Leonardo's time. Find him. Take his deposition. Ask him to explain his sketch. Is that it, Ms. Gerard?"

"Yes, sir."

"Fascinating," mused Wright. "It might give us the exact art we need to dissolve the interference. When did Leonardo make this sketch, Ms. Gerard? Any way to tell?"

"The date can be fixed only roughly. It was almost certainly after he finished *The Last Supper,* in Milan, in 1498, but probably before he started the *Mona Lisa* in Florence, which we think was 1503."

"So, where would we find Leonardo in 1503?"

"From March to June, 1503, he was in Florence. He had a studio in the house of an affluent friend."

Wright regarded her with interest. "What would the locals think about the machine? And its crew, for that matter. Could you get in and out again safely?"

"There's some risk, but it could be minimized. Our Italian associates could provide a list of alberghi—inns—complete with piazzas, that have been in existence in Florence since 1500. We would come in on the piazza, just before dawn. It would be dark for a few more minutes. We dismantle the TM, pack it away, and present ourselves, properly dressed, to the innkeeper."

"So we check in," demanded Pellar. "Then what?"

"We locate Leonardo, find a local lawyer to swear him in, and proceed with the deposition."

Wright studied the ceiling. "It just might work." His eyes dropped back to her. "Ms. Gerard, just how did you become interested in medieval manuscripts?"

"Well, sir, to sort of sum it up and cut some corners, at American U. two of my Professors were international authorities in the Renaissance and its incunabula. It seemed the natural thing to do."

Wright nodded. "Yes. Undoubtedly a wise decision. Still, quite a coincidence that it should offer such possibilities in a patent interference." He leaned forward, and now his tone and manner were all business. "I'd like you to prepare a memorandum stating the essentials we'll need to consider for this deposition. I'll go over it with Mr. Pellar and Colonel Inman, our contact at Defense. Further, would you please prepare the necessary deposition notices."

"Yes, sir." As she closed the door behind her, she heard:

"Mr. Pellar, if you could stay a moment . . ." The syllables were harsh, clipped.

As she walked away she visualized the probable tableau now going on behind her. Wright wouldn't even raise his voice, but Pellar would perspire and wonder if he could still make partner. Finally, Wright would suggest to Pellar that he prepare a suitable memo to Colonel Inman of the DOD, explaining why he, Pellar, had wasted three million dollars before getting around to the Leonardo proposal. It made absolutely no difference that Pellar was essentially blameless; it was simply the way things worked.

Anyhow, she was too exhilarated by her new assignment to feel very sorry for Pellar. All that effort in the Renaissance was finally paying off. She knew medieval Florence backwards and forwards. She knew how to dress, what to wear. She could walk across the Piazza del Signoria in 1500 and be taken for an average housewife on her way to the *panetteria*. And the way things were going, it seemed quite likely that something like that was going to happen.

She floated all the way back to her minuscule office. "Office" by courtesy, that is. It lay between the copier room and the men's washroom. Actually it had originally been the anteroom to the men's washroom, but it had been remodeled for her, because there was nowhere else to put her. The male associates had to walk behind her desk to get to the washroom door.

There were two pictures on her desk. One was a good miniature of the *Mona Lisa*, the other a photo of the house where she had been born and raised, back in Naples, Texas. She required the first because in her estimation the Lady Lisa was the most beautiful woman in history. She kept the second as a substitute for the real thing. She dreamed of going home again, but she knew she probably never would. She couldn't face her mother's highly vocal accusation: "Twenty-eight and still not married!"

Meanwhile, stop dreaming and get out the form book! Fix up a notice for Mr. Wright to sign and send to . . . who was opposing lead counsel? Larvey? Yes, Ralph Larvey, of Getterfield, White. Right down the street. Welcome to 1503, counselor!

3. Like a Smothered Mate

At the appointed time Elizabeth and Pellar drove out to the army complex near Manassas, Virginia, to meet Colonel Inman and receive instruction in operating the TM.

The colonel was a tall, thin, gray-haired man. Elizabeth knew very little about him, just that he was married, with children grown and gone away. He had several graduate degrees, including physics and law, and now he ran Special Assets.

She also knew that the colonel's consuming interest just at present was to resist buying the opposing Rosso patent application, which had been offered to the Army for one hundred million dollars.

The officer led them down a gravel path to a Quonset hut. He unlocked the door, flipped a light switch, and they walked in. A seven-foot plywood tetrahedron stood in the center of the chamber.

"I thought the TM was just a framework of tubing," Elizabeth said.

"The real thing is," explained Inman. "What you see here is just a trainer, to familiarize you with the controls. We want to minimize use of the real thing. You've heard of the 'space-break' theory?"

Elizabeth nodded. One of the top DOD physicists had a theory the TM could break the time-space barrier only a limited number of times. After that, the TM wouldn't work.

"Where *is* the real thing?" asked Pellar.

Elizabeth had already figured that out. Over against the far wall stood a nondescript leather valise. By her calculations, if the tubes of the framework were unscrewed into quarters and stored with battery pack and computer console, it all ought to fit into that valise.

"It's in a safe place," answered Inman noncommittally. He held open the door of the simulator and turned on a small fluorescent. They joined him inside.

"There's room for three travelers and these two cases," he said. "One case can hold the dismantled tetrahedron, including the console and battery pack. The other is intended for materials you'll need for your deposition. Take a look." He asked Elizabeth, "Is one case big enough for your needs?"

"Hm. The IBM translator and printer will fit nicely, but there may be a space problem with our power pack. Do you think we could use the TM pack?"

"What power will you need?" asked Inman.

"One hundred watts, for probably two to three hours."

"The TM pack can easily provide that. Now then, let's go on. I'm sure you both know the theory of the invention. It's based on the University of Arizona process of cold fusion. In that process, heavy water fuses to helium-four and makes heat. Simple, eh? Actually, not so simple. More heavy water was disappearing than could be accounted for in recovered helium-four. Asa Green, our inventor, discovered the loss was going into positive He-4—antimatter—which was not detectable because it was being consumed by driving the synthesis apparatus into the past. In the interests of efficiency and control, Green developed the tetrahedral frame of silver pipes. The heavy water circulates in each fractional pipe section. For control of gross movement he uses a crystal of black uranium oxide, linked to the console and framework by an electrical conductor. For fine tuning he uses a headband"—he indicated a circlet of thin gold braid— "also linked to the console. This way the 'driver' maintains continuing contact with the synthesis process within the silver tubes."

"Just exactly what does this 'continuing contact' feel like?" asked Elizabeth.

"It's a visual thing," said Inman, "experienced by images created in the occipital lobe. Sort of like getting conked on the head and seeing stars, except there's no pain, and instead of stars you see shifting geometric patterns. Do you play chess?"

She had taken first prize in the D.C. Open last year. She said cautiously, "I know the moves."

"So do I!" Pellar chimed in.

"Very good. Look at it this way: time moves in quanta—seen mentally as frames of a chessboard. Each moment differs from the next by changes in position of the 'chess pieces' on the frames. As you stand in the TM and approach your destination, it may seem that the pieces are clumping around a central point, rather like pawns and pieces sheltering a king at chess. It's up to you to select the final point in time. Quite like cross hairs in the center of a bull's-eye, or a knight making a smothered mate. If you're a fair chess player you'll have no trouble running the TM. So let's start."

"Me first," said Pellar.

Inman smiled faintly as he handed the lawyer the small black cube of uraninite, and then a gold circlet. Both were attached to the console by insulated wires. "Ready?"

"Ready."

There was a sharp metallic click as Inman closed the triangular door.

Pellar jerked. "Hey!" He dropped the black crystal. "You didn't say it was going to be like *this!*"

Inman grinned. "Try again, Mr. Pellar. This time, close your eyes and imagine you're a class master, playing blindfold."

Pellar tried a few more times, achieved a debatable competence, then passed the headband and crystal over to Elizabeth.

She caught the hang of it in seconds. She asked Inman, "When we return, do we use the same technique?"

"No. Coming back is much simpler. You don't need the headband or the crystal. You just slam the tetrahedral 'door,' and you zoom right back. You'll come to a jarring halt at your exact starting time and place." He looked at them both and smiled. "I think we're ready for Florence."

4. Florence

Elizabeth, Pellar, and the colonel were drinking cappucinis under the awning of an outdoor cafe on the Piazza del Signoria.

Pellar kept glancing at his wristwatch. "Larvey's late."

Inman shrugged. "Do you know him?"

"Only by reputation."

"Same here. Apparently he's a deposition wizard. I've studied all his past depositions that I can find. He's clever, sneaky, dangerous, slippery, treacherous."

"Yeah," said Pellar sincerely. "A credit to the bar."

Inman looked across the table at Elizabeth. His mouth twitched.

She smiled faintly back at him. She knew that Inman had insisted she take the TM training along with Pellar and that she be a member of the time travel group. Pellar had resisted bitterly, and finally they had compromised. Pellar could drive the machine. She would be the language link with Leonardo and the other Florentines.

"This may be our boy now, coming across the square," said Pellar. "Yes, it's Larvey." He stood up and waved.

Elizabeth observed the approaching lawyer carefully. He was about forty, hair thinning but no gray. A wide smile. Too wide, she decided.

Pellar made the introductions. He explained and excused Elizabeth's presence: "She speaks medieval Italian. Sort of a tour guide."

Let it stand, she thought.

They got down to business. Next stop, the costumer's.

"Attire must be simple, yet elegant," Elizabeth explained. "For you chaps, tunics and tights, with citizen's caps and soft leather boots. Tunics may be silk brocade, stitched with gold thread, with fur trim on cuffs and collars. Matching cloaks recommended. I shall wear gray silk, covering a plurality of petticoats, with a single strand of pearls. All these things are available locally."

"For the costume ball at the embassy?" the shop manager asked politely.

"Something like that," said Elizabeth. She watched the two men preen in the fitting room. Pellar had a good figure. His legs modeled beautifully in the close-fitting tights—tights rather like a woman's panty hose, except of heavier material. The tunic design was truly exquisite: red roses woven into a light blue background, and embroidered with gold and silver threads and paste diamonds and pearls. The outfit was completed with Gucci shoes of soft black leather, and for the tunic, a big gold buckle. As they watched, the tailor draped a knee-length cloak over the lawyer and turned him into the mirror.

Impressive, thought Elizabeth.

Larvey was similarly dressed. He caught the spirit, and pirouetted like a ballet dancer.

The once-piazza of the *Cigno Nero,* now a fifty-car parking lot, was duly cleared and closed for the night, and in the cover of darkness the TM crew set up the big canvas tent and brought in the two cases. Under Elizabeth's critical eye Pellar opened the case containing the knocked-down TM and began reassembly. Colonel Inman looked on silently. Twenty minutes and a few bungles and curses later, it was ready. And now a last-minute flashlight inspection of her two companions. Clothing, hats, cloaks, all OK. Next, the travel case. She unbuckled the leather straps, raised the lid, and pushed aside shaving kits and extra underwear. The IBM translator/camcorder was in place. Everything ready? she asked herself. Not necessarily. She stood up and faced the men. "I think we should make sure the IBM is still in working order."

"I already tested it," Pellar said stiffly.

"Here?"

"No, back in D.C."

"It's had several plane rides and taxi rides since then."

"If it bothers you," mumbled Pellar, "go ahead. Test it again."

Silently, she removed the unit from the case, then opened the TM storage locker, got out the power pack, plugged it into the side of the IBM, and flipped the switch. A green LED flashed in front of the translator box. "IBM," she said, "are you operational? *Per italiano?*"

A well-modulated baritone rose from the box. "Yes. I'm ready. *Posso chiederle chi è?*"

"I don't believe we've met. *Io sono la signorina* Elizabeth Gerard."

"Ah, Signorina Gerard, sono molto licto di fare la sua conoscenza."

"Grazie. Do you feel competent to take a patent deposition in Italian?"

"Si."

"Knock it off, Elizabeth," growled Pellar. "The machine is working. Let's go!"

"Yes," she said. "See you later, Mr. IBM."

"Arrivederci, signorina."

She pulled the plug and repacked everything. "Gentlemen," she told the two lawyers, "you may get inside." She moved in with them, handed the flashlight out to Inman, picked up the unlit lantern from the TM console, and looked around for the tinder box with its flint and steel. She found it, flicked away for a moment, and got plenty of sparks, none of which ignited the exposed wick. She paused, frustrated.

"Hey, no problem," said Larvey. He pulled out a cigarette lighter, flicked it once, and touched the flame to the wick. She took the lighter from him and stuck it into her waist-purse. "By golly, Ralph," she said thoughtfully, "if you do that in 1500 Florence, they will probably lay a commemorative plaque for you."

"A plaque?" He smiled uncertainly.

"A plaque. It would read, 'Here we burned the English sorcerer, Raphael of Larvey.' "

"Oh. Sorry."

She closed the triangular door with a satisfying click. "OK, Cuthbert, take it away."

The lawyer pulled the circlet over his forehead, then plugged it into the console. He began adjusting dials.

In the semi-dark she stole covert glances at Pellar and Larvey. Were they as scared as she? Quite likely, she thought. She took a long deep breath. Out beyond the silver tubes she thought she could make out the vague form of the colonel. He kept fading in and out.

At that instant Inman, the tent, everything outside the tetrahedron—shimmered and vanished.

5. Where Is 1503?

She watched Pellar as he studied the dials with apparent competence. The days were whizzing by like strobe lights. The retinal lag soon merged everything into a gray twilight.

She. leaned forward and watched the three chronometer dials: year . . . day . . . hour. 1575 . . . 1570 . . . 1565 . . . 1560. So far so good, she thought. But— is he *slowing?* No, Cuthbert, don't slow *here.* He's almost stopping! Water's seeping in! She spoke loudly in his ear. "Cuthbert, keep moving! *Move!*"

There was a jar. "Cuthbert," she wailed, "you've hit the Great Flood of 1558. *Keep moving!* If you stop here, we'll drown!" She scurried to the rear of the tetrahedron and plucked the battery pack out of the water.

It took a moment for the message to sink in; then the senior associate accelerated so fast that it made Elizabeth's head snap.

"Too fast, Cuthbert," she cried. "You'll overshoot!"

"Shut up!" he shouted. "*I'm* driving!" But finally he eased to a stop.

They looked out through the silver rods. It was early morning. The piazza was empty. Save for one . . . man? . . . lying face down a few yards away.

"Ssh . . ." She held her finger to her lips in a call for silence. She listened. No sounds anywhere. She sniffed the air. It was sour, sickening.

She looked out toward the body again and her throat tightened. She forced a squeaky question. "Cuthbert, are you sure we're in the right time frame?"

He muttered, "Yeah, I *guess* so."

"What year? Check your chronometer."

"Check it yourself if you're so interested."

Idiot, she thought. She replaced the power pack in its frame and was about to start forward to the chronometer panel when she noted motion out in the piazza. It was a rat, and it was headed for them.

Meanwhile Pellar, perhaps influenced by a tremolo in her voice, had returned to the instruments. "Thirteen forty-eight," he called back. "Are you happy now?"

Her calm astonished her. "Cuthbert, get us out of here."

The lawyer responded blithely. "Maybe we should get out and look around."

"Dammit, Cuthbert, will you listen? Thirteen forty-eight is the year of the Black Death. Half the city died. That's one of the dead ones over there. The plague is spread by fleas on rats. Like the one coming now. *There!*" She pointed.

"Cuthbert," urged Larvey, "let's get the hell out!"

Pellar stared open-mouthed at the oncoming rodent.

"Cuthbert?" said Larvey weakly.

Elizabeth glided quietly over to Pellar, eased the control band from his skull, and pulled it down over her head. He didn't protest. She doubted that he realized she had taken over. She adjusted the indicators quickly. The chessboard patterns began to come in. Slowly at first. A day. Another day. Then faster and faster. Flash flash flicker flicker. A week, a month. Faster. A year.

She visualized the cross-hairs lining up in her occipital lobe. The right year. 1503. She checked the chronometer panel. The right month. April. And then the right day and the right hour—minutes before daybreak.

They were there. She unplugged the cable but left the gold circlet on her head.

Pellar flashed a look of utter hatred at her.

6. *Il Cigno Nero*

She held the lantern high and looked through the silver framework out into the darkened piazza.

No movement anywhere. No sounds. That would change very soon. Dawn would be here in a very few minutes. The watch would open the city gates. The streets would begin to fill with people and carts. She looked at the men. "All clear, boys. Let's move!" She held the light while the two men unscrewed the tubing and loaded it into the TM case. "OK, now let's rouse *il locandiere.*" She rattled the handle of the great iron-studded portal.

"Hey, it's locked!" complained Pellar. "Now what?"

"We knock." She picked up the bronze hammer, dangling from its chain, found the approximate center of the knocker plate, and gave it a hefty bang. The door rattled and sang with the stroke, and the piazza reverberated. She banged again. And again.

In the middle of the last assault the peep door beside the plate opened, and two bleary eyes peered out. A hidden mouth rasped: *"Non c'è stanza . . . non c'è stanza . . . va . . . va . . . va!"* No room . . . go away!

She reached into her pocket bourse and picked out a freshly minted gold florin. With her other hand she held up the lantern. The coin flashed.

"We shall require the entire first floor," she declared in firm Italian. In the local custom, she knew, that meant the second floor.

"All taken . . ." gurgled the innkeeper. But his eyes never left the coin.

"*Quanti clienti?*" she asked. How many guests?

"*Otto.*" Eight.

"How much for each, the night?"

"Forty soldi."

"You mistake yourself, innkeeper. I know it to be ten soldi, rules of the Innkeepers Guild. No matter. Return their money. Double it. Nay, triple it. Roust them out. For your trouble take the florin."

She heard the creak of sliding bars and chains being unlatched. The door opened a crack. "*Signorina*, come around here, *per favore.*"

She took a step to the right and held the coin up by thumb and forefinger. A fat bare arm flashed out. The coin vanished. The door clanged shut. After a moment the door grated fully open. The innkeeper, still in the process of trying to fasten his tunic belt, looked out into the courtyard. "*Dov'è la vostra carrozza?*" Where is your carriage?

"On its way back to Pisa. Now, will we come in, or not?"

"Oh, *sì sì*. Come in, *signorina, signori*. Wife, get their bags."

Elizabeth asked, "How do you call yourself?"

"Antonio—Tony—*signorina*, at your service. And this is my wife, Anna." They both bowed laboriously.

"And who, *signorina*," asked the innkeeper, "honors my humble *albergo?*"

"A commission from His Majesty, Henry, King of England," she said calmly. "I shall explain certain things to you at the proper time."

"Of course, *signorina*, of course." Host and hostess ran greedy eyes over the newcomers, noting the rich clothing and especially the string of pearls around the woman's throat.

Wife pulled husband aside and held a hurried discussion with him. He turned back to Elizabeth with a face radiant with woe. "I had forgotten various extra expenses."

"How much?" she said dryly.

"Two additional florins. Three altogether."

She handed over the coins. "Now, Tony, let this be the end of it. It would grieve me to have to report you to the *Signoria*."

He listened uneasily. "No, *signorina*, no need for that. Here—" He handed back one coin. "You see, because of my love for your King Henry, I am willing to lose money."

Like hell, she thought.

She looked around. They had entered the main room, a combined kitchen with fireplace, dining room, and recreation room. There were several tables with benches. Cuts of meat and fowl, together with garlands of garlics, leeks, and onions, hung from hooks on the walls. Overhead, chickens roosted in the eaves.

She took a deep breath. These were the sights and smells of barnyard and kitchen on Grandfather Gherardini's farm back in Texas. She was home.

She noted that her two companions were absorbing all this in growing horror. She suppressed a grin.

On the far side of the room a black-bearded man sat at a table, staring at them. Correction. Staring at *her.* Oh well, have to expect it. Strangers in town. Very strange strangers. But he was a bit odd, himself. For there was no plate or knife in front of him. Instead, a chess board.

She turned back to Tony. "We would like the rooms as soon as possible."

"Of course! Of course!" He wiped his hands on his apron and smiled effusively. "My wife will prepare your chambers. There may be a slight delay. She will have to, ah, *negotiate* with each of our patrons. While we wait, would the *signorina* and her noble companions care for wine?"

"We decline for the moment. We will talk later of wine and other matters."

"The gentlemen do not speak our language?" asked the innkeeper.

"No, they speak only English. I interpret and translate. I am called Elisabetta, and I am daughter of the English ambassador in Napoli. This gentleman is Lord Cut'berto, of Georgetown; the other gentleman is Lord Raphael, of Arlington."

"Ah . . . I see." He looked them over shrewdly, then back to her. "You are here to see—*him.*"

"*Him?*" She knew exactly what he meant.

"Leonardo, *signorina*. Great men, rich men, they come to him. *Maestro,* they beg, paint me, paint my wife, my daughter, my favorite greyhound. But no. He paints only as he pleases. Meaning no disrespect, milady, but I think if you even try to find him, he will vanish."

"But *you* could find him?"

He shrugged. "Perhaps."

They were interrupted by an outburst of howls, shrieks, and imprecations from the rooms overhead.

7. A View of the River

The innkeeper smiled apologetically but did not look up. "My good wife is negotiating the refunds. Your rooms will be ready very soon."

"What's all that racket?" demanded Pellar. "What's going on?"

Elizabeth pointed. A loud, disconsolate procession was stumbling down the broad oaken stairs: six men, two women, their nakedness covered in varied degrees. Their complaints died away when they beheld the three regal visitors.

"Former occupants," explained Elizabeth quietly. "Checking out."

Eyes downcast, the ex-guests filed respectfully past the newcomers. Two or three turned off toward the kitchen; the rest shuffled out the front door and disappeared.

Elizabeth faced Tony. "You have done well. Here's your florin back. For this I want you to send up various things to eat and drink. We would like warm red wine, and various meats and fruits, together with butter, cheese, and fresh-baked bread. You can manage that?"

"Of course, noble lady."

Half an hour later, when they were property installed upstairs, they reassembled in Elizabeth's room. She handed the waiting innkeeper a little package. "Five ducats for you, Tony, if you place this in the hands of Leonardo within the hour."

"Count it done, noble *signorina*." He turned to go.

"Wait—there is a second matter."

"Oh?"

"Involving litigation. We require a notary, a member in good standing of the Guild of Judges and Notaries."

"A notary . . . Hm. There are several good ones, milady. What will be expected of him?"

"It is a matter of legal deposition. I will be putting questions to a witness, and Lord Raphael will cross-examine. Everything must be done in accordance with certain rules."

"I see," said Antonio. "Let me think a moment. Yes, the best for this sort of thing is probably *Signor* Rucellai."

"Rucellai? How long has he been a notary?"

"Over twenty years, milady."

"He comes in here to dine occasionally?"

"Often, milady."

"He appreciates a good table?"

"He does, he does."

Very good. A profile was beginning to emerge. She sensed a complaisant functionary who would render the necessary services without asking unnecessary questions and who could be relied upon to spend most of his time at the side table. "His Christian name?"

"Biagio, if you please."

"He's our man, Tony. Please send for his excellency, *Messer* Biagio Rucellai. You may tell him that our great King Henry appreciates prompt service."

After he left, she noted that the two men were nibbling at things on the side table.

The morning was warming up. She walked over to the little window and looked out. *Il Cigno Nero* was on a slight rise, and she had a nearly panoramic view of the city. There was the great cathedral, with Brunelleschi's famous dome. Beyond that, Giotto's campanile tower. And then the Arno and its beautiful bridges. Downriver somewhere was the estate of Francesco Giocondo, whose wife Lisa would soon enter immortality at the hands of the great Leonardo. Leonardo had sworn to paint no more women, but he had seen La Gioconda, and he had changed his mind.

Pellar walked up behind her. "You really ought to keep us better informed, Elizabeth. What was in the package? Where's it going?"

"Oh, sorry, Cuthbert. Our landlord claims Leonardo sees no one. I figured we needed something special to attract his attention. So I took Ralph's lighter and wrapped it in a photocopy of page forty-one of the TM fascicle, and held it all together with a rubber band. A gift to Leonardo."

"I don't get it," said Larvey.

"It's easy, Ralph. Your lighter tells him we're from his future, and page forty-one tells him how we got here. Even the rubber band says something. He'll add it up, and he'll come. Also, Ralph, I should mention I've sent for a local officer of the court. Meanwhile, we'd better get the IBM set up. Cuthbert, would you please put it under this little table. You can drape a cloth over the table to hide it, but make sure the lens has a good view. Ralph, would you close the door."

Larvey had hardly shut the door when there was a knock on the other side. He opened it a crack. It was the innkeeper.

Elizabeth came over to the door and held a brief discussion with Antonio.

8. A Member of the Guild

"What'd he say?" demanded Larvey.

"The notary's downstairs. Are we ready?" She examined the center table critically. The cloth seemed to hide the IBM translator adequately. She turned back to Antonio. "Will you please bring him up?"

A moment later the innkeeper returned with a short, fat, well-dressed gentleman. *"Signorina, signore,"* said Tony with great composure, "my privilege to introduce a leading notary of our fair city, the most learned, brilliant, and wise *Messer* Biagio Rucellai."

"We thank you for your kind assistance, Antonio," said Elizabeth. She added with calm hauteur: "You may leave us now."

The innkeeper bowed once more and closed the door behind him.

Elizabeth turned to the newcomer and inspected the distinguished *Messer* Rucellai in silence. It had evidently been a considerable labor for him to mount the stairs, and he was still puffing. He wore the characteristic four-cornered hat of a working Renaissance lawyer, a deliberately ambiguous forked beard, and finally, and most importantly, the notary's robe, grave and somber with its broad black stripes on dark red background. A leather pouch hung from a strap over one shoulder.

She smiled graciously. "We are honored, *Messer* Rucellai. I am Lady Elisabetta of Napoli, daughter of the English ambassador there. I am interpreter for these two gentlemen, who speak only English. This gentleman is Lord Cut'berto of Georgetown, and the other gentleman is Lord Raphael of Arlington."

The notary bowed deeply. "Milady . . . milords."

Elizabeth continued. "We are here on a commission to see a certain citizen of Florence."

"Oh, Of course. You wish to commission a painting? A statue?"

Elizabeth interrupted. "No, nothing like that."

"No? Ah, I see. You wish to *sue* a Florentine. Yes?"

"Dammit, Elizabeth," complained Larvey. "What's going on? I'm entitled to know."

She turned back to him. "Of course you are, Ralph. Just turn on the IBM. The remote is there on the table. You can sit over there by the window and get a good readout on the CRT. You too, Cuthbert."

And back to the notary. "Excuse the interruption, *Messer* Rucellai. The gentlemen are fatigued and wish to rest."

"Of course," he said dubiously.

"But you and I will continue. Sue, you ask? No, not that, either. We merely require a deposition—a sworn statement from one of your citizens. The statement must be made in the presence of a member of the Guild of Judges and Notaries, which is to say, yourself. The final document will require your seal."

"I am never without my seal." He patted the leather pouch.

"Excellent, *messer*. These are bothersome little details, but I'm sure that an official of your standing is familiar with all of them."

He bowed. "Naturally." He looked about the room. "But where is your deponent?"

"A messenger has been sent for him. We expect him at any moment." She paused. "And now, *Messer* Rucellai, we come to the matter of your fee."

"Fee? Fee? Oh, milady, you cut me to the quick. Members of the Guild serve all, rich or poor, without charge or fee." He drew closer and whirled his cloak so that the side pocket gaped at her. "Yet, noble *signorina*, we acknowledge that sometimes, completely unsolicited and totally unbeknownst to us, a grateful client may press a modest retainer upon us . . . such as may be within his means . . . or hers. A ducat for the day, as it were." He watched her, at first with mild anticipation, and then with growing fascination as with slow hypnotic gestures she loosed the drawstring of her waist-bourse. He sensed the thud of a heavy coin in his cloak pocket. He stifled a gasp. That was no mere ducat! That was—*gold!* A florin! Was it possible?

He gathered all his courage and continued hoarsely: "Two, if the matter be complex."

Clink!

Madre di Dio!

He closed his eyes. "And for the guarantee of satisfaction in all details, major and minor, for assurance of complete harmony in all matters, expected or unexpected—"

Clink!

Messer Rucellai began to perspire; he decided to quit while he was ahead. He sighed and closed up his fee pocket. "If milady will excuse the question, we come now to the crux of the matter. Who is your deponent?"

"Leonardo da Vinci."

He thought about that. "I must warn you, milady, Leonardo is a very independent man. If he refuses to come, I will refund—"

"No need for that, *Messer* Rucellai," said Elizabeth. "In any case, I am certain that he will come."

There was a heavy knock at the door.

"*Entri!*" called Elizabeth.

The door opened. A tall bearded man in a rose-colored cloak stood in the doorway. Gray hair fell loosely to his shoulders. He took off his cap and looked about the room with cool blue eyes. His shoulders were broad; his hands surprisingly large. Elizabeth was ready to believe the stories that he could straighten horseshoes with his bare hands. Yet his features were fine, patrician, almost feminine.

His eyes came back to her.

9. Leonardo

For a full moment, with shameless candor, the trained anatomist examined her. He seemed to take mental measurements of throat, breasts, waist. Then back to the face, estimating proportions of cheek, brow, nose, lips.

He spoke in a low resonant voice. "You are very beautiful. I will paint you." He held up Larvey's lighter. "In time, how far away?"

Messer Rucellai watched all this with open mouth.

Elizabeth found a small squeaky voice. "*Messer* Leonardo, I am not beautiful, and I cannot imagine why you would want to paint me. Aside from that, and before I answer your second question, please indulge me a moment. I am called Elisabetta. And here is Raphael, and there Cut'berto." They all traded bows. "And you may know our honorable notary, *Messer* Biagio Rucellai?"

Artist and lawyer exchanged nods.

She continued. "*Messer* Rucellai has not yet had breakfast. Our host has provided certain nutriments, all on the side table, with fine Tuscan breakfast wine. We will excuse you, *Messer* Rucellai, while you attend to your breakfast."

The notary got the message. Actually, he had had bread and sausage within the hour, but he didn't like to oppose this golden client. He hurried to the table and fell to.

Elizabeth returned her attention to the artist. "*Messer* Leonardo, we are from the year 2003. We live in the New World, discovered by Cristoforo Colon in 1492. In our day the New World has grown very populous, and inventors have made great discoveries in the sciences. In my country we have a system of laws that grants an inventor a seventeen-year monopoly on his invention. Our government issues a document—a patent—to the inventor certifying to his monopoly. Sometimes two inventors seek patents on the same invention. The government must then consider all facts, and issue the patent only to the first inventor."

"But suppose neither is the first inventor?"

"In that case nobody gets a patent." He catches on fast, she thought.

"And that's why you are here?" He held up the photocopy of page forty-one.

"You think *I* invented the machine?"

"Did you?"

"Yes."

She took a deep breath. "Maestro, will you testify to that? We have a device here that will record everything you say, translate it into English, and will finally make a printout."

" 'Printout'?"

"Like the pages in the books of your *Signor* Manutius."

"I see." He was thoughtful. "Your civilization seems quite advanced. All right. I will do it."

"Thank you. First, the notary will have to swear you." She called over to the banquet bench. "*Messer* Rucellai?"

The lawyer turned and acknowledged her signal with a sonorous belch.

Pellar shuddered.

"*Messer* Rucellai," she said, "will you please administer the oath to *Messer* Leonardo?"

The notary wiped his mouth on his sleeve, then, aided with a mouthful of mutton, he mumbled a polysyllabic litany.

"Thank you, *Messer* Rucellai," said Elizabeth. "In a little while we will need you again, to swear our recorder."

Leonardo looked puzzled, "You will swear a *machine* to tell the truth?"

"Something like that. The device is not only a recorder, it also serves as an interpreter. It translates my questions and your answers into English, so that Cut'berto and Raphael may follow the course of the deposition. Under our Code an interpreter has to be sworn just as any other witness."

The artist shook his head in wonder.

She called over to the notary. "*Per favore, Messer* Rucellai."

"*Monna?*"

"Please swear our interpreter."

The notary looked about the room, then back to Elizabeth.

"He's under the table," explained Elizabeth. "You can't see him for the cloth."

"Oh. That's the way it's done in England? How does he call himself?"

"*Signor* Ibi Emme."

The notary called out: "*Signor* Ibi Emme!"

From under the table: "*Presente!*"

"*Signor* Ibi Emme, do you solemnly swear to translate accurately and completely, in full idiom, from one tongue to another, as required, adding nothing and omitting nothing, so help you God?"

"I do."

"*Grazie.*"

"*Prego,*" said *Signor* IBM.

Messer Rucellai exchanged nods with Elizabeth, then returned to his table.

10. The Deposition

"I will speak in English for the benefit of attending counsel," Elizabeth told Leonardo, "and the IBM machine will immediately translate into vocal and printed Italian. *Messer* Larvey will follow the same procedure. Your responses will be in Italian, and they will be similarly translated into English. Is that satisfactory?"

The artist nodded. "Of course."

She began. "Please state your full name and your residence."

"Leonardo da Vinci. I live in the house of Andrea Martelli, in the Street of Brickmakers, Florence."

"What is your occupation?"

"Painter, sculptor, civil and military engineer, architect, inventor."

"*Messer* Leonardo, I hand you a sheet of paper purporting to show a geometric figure. Can you identify this?"

"Yes. It's a copy of a page from one of my notebooks."

"Showing—what?"

"A sketch of a tetrahedral machine for going back in time."

"Did you actually make such a machine?"

"Yes."

"When?"

"At Easter, in the year 1498."

"Please describe that machine."

"As you see from the sketch, it was shaped as a tetrahedron, forming a framework of silver tubes. These tubes were four ells on a side."

"Empty tubes?"

"No. They were filled with special water."

"Water from where?"

"From Dr. Marcos, a local alchemist. He had started with one hundred thousand jars of well water, and over a period of ten years, he boiled it and boiled it, until only five jars were left."

"Objection," intoned Larvey. "Hearsay."

Elizabeth said: "Let the record show that the specification of the party Rosso described such residues as a source of heavy water. Let us continue. *Messer* Leonardo, what, if anything, was associated with the framework?"

"A collection of alternating plates of copper and zinc. The plates were half an ell square and were separated by thick felt paper soaked in vinegar. The collection was about two ells high. I attached a silver wire to the topmost plate, which was copper, and another silver wire to the bottommost plate, which was zinc."

"What, if anything, did you do with this collection of metal plates?"

"I attached one of the silver wires to the upper apex of the tetrahedron and the other to another apex."

"Go on."

"I clasped the black cube in one hand."

"Describe the cube, please."

"Half a finger on a side. Heavy for its size. Strange texture, somewhat reminiscent of pitch. It was mined at Jachymov, in Bohemia, and was presented to Duke Ludovico as a mineral rarity."

"Let the record show that the witness has described uraninite, or pitchblende. Now then, *Messer* Leonardo, how did you come to invent your time machine? What was your purpose?"

The artist thought for a long time. "It goes back to the cenacolo."

"Meaning *The Last Supper?*"

"*The Cenacolo,* yes. The Duke Ludovico asked me to paint a cenacolo for the Dominicans at their monastery in Milan, and I began the preliminaries in 1495."

"When did you finish?"

"In ninety-eight."

"There were delays?"

"Actually, except for two faces, the work was completed within the first year."

"Which two faces?"

"Our Lord . . . and Judas. I could not visualize the divinity of the one, nor the evil of the other. So I delayed."

"But eventually you visualized the two?"

"I *saw* them. All of them: Jesus and the twelve."

She frowned. What was he saying?

He continued. "That's why I made the time-tetrahedron. So I could go back."

"To when? And where?"

"To the Upper Room of the Last Supper. Nearly 1,500 years ago. I saw them all. Then I returned to Milan, and I finished the faces."

"So you found . . ." But the words faded in midsentence. Hold on here! she thought. Other than the final trip to France, where he died, there was no record that he had ever left Italy. And yet . . . and yet . . . she knew he was telling the truth. In that year of the Crucifixion, he had been in Jerusalem. *How?* she thought. How had he done this impossible thing? There was only one way. He had set up his machine in Milan, and from there he moved practically instantaneously in both time *and space!*

The man understood things about the TM beyond their wildest imaginings.

Her companions were watching her in silence. Pellar's expression showed that he was merely curious as to why she had stopped. Larvey's mouth was curled in a sardonic grin. *He* knows, she thought. He saw it almost as soon as I did. You're good, Ralph.

She began quietly. "Is it your testimony, Maestro, that you saw Jesus and the twelve disciples at the, shall we say, *original* Last Supper, in Jerusalem, in the year 33 A.D.?"

"Yes. Except the year was 29 A.D. The early Christian fathers miscalculated the year of His birth."

"You were actually *there?*"

"Yes."

And now Pellar was waking up. He shot a warning glance at her. It said, he's lying! Back off!

Interesting. Larvey's face held the exact opposite message: Right on, Gerard! Go on! You're already in over your head. Screw it up!

Maybe Cuthbert's right, she thought. Maybe I should quit while I'm ahead. But then she caught Larvey's wordless sneer. Wordless? No, it was full of words: You're a weak, timid, incompetent *female*.

OK, Ralphie, that did it!

Back to the artist. "*Messer* Leonardo, how far is Jerusalem from Milan?"

He gave her a congratulatory smile. "As the crow flies, about 650 leagues."

Larvey folded his arms over his chest and watched with narrowing eyes.

She said with calm fatalism, "How did you get your machine to Jerusalem?"

"Willpower, *Monna*."

Willpower? With that answer, had her witness thrown away his hard-earned claim to credibility?

Can't quit now, she thought. "Willpower, *messer?*"

"It is no great thing, milady. With a little practice, any left-handed person of fair intelligence can do it."

"Clarify, please."

"Yes. My studies of the human brain indicate that each of the two hemispheres has its own set of special functions. The right hemisphere controls the left side of the body. It also controls our sense of pattern, geometries, visual arrangements, spatial positions. I'm sure all this is well known to your physicians and savants who work with the mind. Is it not so?"

"Much recent work has been done," agreed Elizabeth. "Go on."

"Well, first, I set up the machine."

"Where?"

"In my studio in the Sforza palace, in Milan."

"What next?"

"I connected the wires, held the black crystal tightly, and then I concentrated on moving in both time and space. I had already decided that the journey toward Jerusalem of 29 A.D. should be made with movement of two years and three months per league. Do you want the itinerary?"

"If you please."

"Well, past Florence, down the ridge of the Appenines, past Ravenna, over the Adriatic, through the Straits of Otranto. Then over Macedonia and the land of the Ottomans. Next, the Sea of Crete. The year is now about 765, and I'm halfway there. Athens—now a part of the Byzantine Empire—is next. Then into the eastern Mediterranean, or Mare Internum, as the Romans called it. By the time I passed Rhodes, I was in the era of the Caesars. Suddenly it's the first century and I'm over Jerusalem. I find the Garden of Gethsemane. I leave the tetrahedron there. It was the time of Passover, and everything is a busy mess. The cooks and servants ignore me. I take an apron. I walk up those stairs." He paused, as though thinking back on what he had seen next, then he took a deep breath. "The whole thing was over within the hour."

Elizabeth said: "So you found what you needed? Jesus? And Judas?"

"Yes, I found them, but I did not understand what I had found. Judas? I looked at that face, and I looked for evil. I do not know. It was the face of horror, of despair."

"And Jesus?" Elizabeth asked carefully.

The artist looked up at the ceiling. "It is not easy to speak of this. After Judas left the table, I saw the face of Jesus that I needed for the cenacolo: a sublime sadness. It was that face that I tried to paint. I failed. That face defied painting."

"*Messer* Leonardo, when you returned from Jerusalem to Milan, what did you do with the machine?"

"I destroyed it. My intrusion was a terrible thing. Never again."

"Thank you, Maestro. That completes my direct. Cross, Mr. Larvey?"

"Yes, thank you, Ms. Gerard." He faced the artist.

11. Larvey on Cross

"Just a couple of short questions, *Messer* Leonardo." He folded his arms as he waited for the translation. "Is it your testimony that you journeyed some 1,500 years through time and some 650 leagues over land and sea, all within a fragile metal framework?"

The artist pondered that. "Rather incredible, isn't it? And yet, surely it is more probable than your claim to have journeyed from a time that does not exist."

"I . . . well then, this Last Supper. Did they see you?"

"They paid no attention to me. I wore an apron. I carried in a plate of bread."

"And a slice of lemon?"

"Lemon?"

"In copies of the painting that I have seen, there's a lemon slice on the table. Do you realize that lemons weren't introduced into the Mediterranean area until the twelfth or thirteenth century?"

"No. I didn't know that."

"And you put everyone on one side of the table. It wasn't really that way, was it? They were spaced all around the table?"

"In the Upper Room, they were spaced around on both sides of the table. But in the painting I put them all on the far side so the monks could see the faces."

"And in that alleged Upper Room, did they actually sit on a long bench?"

"No. They sat on straw mats, on the floor."

"Your painting lied?"

"No. In the painting it was easier to see them, sitting on benches."

"Did Judas actually put his bag of silver on the table?"

"No. That was symbolic."

"So there were many differences in what you saw, or thought you saw, and what you painted?"

"Yes."

Larvey sneered. "You're a real bastard, aren't you, Leonardo?"

"Objection," said Elizabeth indignantly. "Counsel is insulting the witness."

Leonardo shrugged. "Oh, I am not offended, *Monna*. True, I was born out of wedlock, but I honor both my parents. I am especially proud of my mother, Caterina. She was a servant girl in an albergo where my father stopped one night. *That* developed into an ardent love affair, but my grandfather da Vinci forbade marriage. Thus, in 1452, I was born illegitimate."

"*Messer* Leonardo," said Larvey, "you have admitted your illegitimacy, and you have admitted falsehoods in your paintings. I put it to you that you are not merely a bastard—you are a *deceptive* bastard."

"Objection," declared Elizabeth. "Counsel is again insulting the witness. If you keep this up, Mr. Larvey, we shall terminate this deposition on the grounds of grossly improper conduct by the party Rosso."

"I can *prove* deception, Ms. Gerard."

"Then do it."

"I will. *Messer* Leonardo, you have filled a number of notebooks with sketches and written comments?"

"Yes."

"But your writing is not easily read?"

"I can read it."

"But the ordinary layman needs a mirror? Because you write deceptively—from right to left?"

"I go right to left because I am left-handed. That's the easy way for me."

"Let it pass," Larvey said huffily. "You draw from life, *Messer* Leonardo?"

"Preferably."

"But you like to draw demons and dragons?"

"On occasion."

"Have you ever seen a demon or a dragon?"

"No."

"They're simply images in your head—illusions?

"Yes."

"Like your illusions of building a time-space machine and visiting Jerusalem?"

"Objection," called Elizabeth.

"Withdraw the question, and that completes my cross."

"I have no redirect," said Elizabeth. "It appears that we are finished, *Messer* Leonardo."

The Florentine stood up. "So now you will be going back with your friends?"

"Yes, tomorrow."

"I take weeks . . . to paint a woman's face."

"I know."

He sighed. "Well, it must be. You say we are finished here? I can leave?"

"Let me check." She looked over at Larvey. "I think the printout is finished. Do you want him to read and sign?"

"No. I want him out of here."

"*Messer* Leonardo," she said, "you have the right to read and sign the record. Do you want to do that?"

"No, I'd just as soon not, but I'd like to see what it looks like."

"Of course. Please come over here. Just let me get one more entry into the record." She spoke quietly. "The parties and the witness waive reading and signature." She waited a moment, then pulled the fan-fold pack from the printer basket. "This is the record. See, two columns, Italian and English. All our questions, all your answers."

"My congratulations," he said softly.

They watched in silence as he closed the door quietly behind him.

12. A Motion to Suppress

Elizabeth called over to the credenza. "*Messer* Rucellai, can you join us here for a moment?"

He walked over, holding a mutton chop in one hand and a half-capon in the other.

"We now need a certificate from you," she explained, "to the effect that you duly administered the oath to *Messer* Leonardo before the commencement of testimony."

"Easily provided, *Monna.*"

"You mean you actually have with you such a form?"

"Yes, indeed." He placed chop and drumstick on the table top, wiped his fingers on the cloth, and pulled a sheaf of papers from the folds of his cloak. "Let's see. Eviction, divorce, complaint for money owed, deed for the sale of land, ah, here we are, certificate for a deposition."

She read it carefully. "Very good, *messer.* It conforms nicely. Will you please fill in *Messer* Leonardo's name, then sign and date it, and affix your seal? Should I send down for pen and ink?"

"No need, *Monna.*" From another cavity in his clothing he pulled a little ivory box, and from this a small quill and stoppered vial of black liquid. He filled in the blanks with a flourish, waved the paper in the air to dry the ink, then pulled his seal from its leather pouch and pressed it into the corner of the form. "Anything further, *Monna?*"

"No, that's all, I think."

He looked down at the half-eaten fowl and chop.

"Please," she said.

He picked them up, then studied the table and its draping cloth. "Could I say goodbye to *Messer* Ibi Emme?"

"Of course."

The notary called out to the invisible translator. "*Arrivederci, Messer Ibi Emme.*"

The reply floated up from under the table. "*Arrivederci, Messer Commendatore Notario. Sono molto lieto di fare la sua conoscenza. Tante cose alla famiglia!*"

"*Piacere! Ciao!*" The Florentine walked toward the door.

"What the hell was that all about?" asked Pellar.

"They were just saying goodbye," said Elizabeth.

The door closed behind Rucellai, and the three were alone.

"We're still on the record?" asked Larvey.

She looked down at the green light on the IBM. "Yes."

He said calmly. "I move to suppress the entire deposition."

Elizabeth and Pellar exchanged glances. The partner-aspirant shrugged. That nonchalant lift of the shoulders translated into, "Elizabeth, you got us into this. You get us out."

She said, "Mr. Larvey, will you please state the basis of your motion?"

"I certainly shall. You are familiar with 17 CFR 1.674(b)(3)?"

"I'm familiar with the sense of the section. A person who is an employee or agent of a party is disqualified as an officer for conducting the deposition. So?"

"An interpreter is considered an officer of the court. The IBM interpreter is your property and under your control. Hence it is your employee and agent. Hence disqualified." He smiled at her.

"Ownership does not make the machine either our employee or our agent. In any case, the IBM is not a 'person' as called for under the relevant CFR section."

"He has third level A.I.," countered Larvey. "That's enough to give him a personality, and a biased personality, at that."

She considered her opponent thoughtfully. Here, she told herself, is a bitter, vengeful man. He knows his only recourse now is to try to discredit the record. "Mr. Larvey, when did you discover this disqualification in the IBM interpreter?"

"In the beginning."

She said, "Mr. IBM, will you please quote 37 CFR 1.685(c) in pertinent part for Mr. Larvey?"

"Of course. 'An error or irregularity in the manner in which testimony is handled by the officer is waived unless a motion to suppress the deposition is filed as soon as the error or irregularity is discovered.' "

Elizabeth smiled agreeably. "Mr. Larvey, if you ever had any right to suppress, you waived it by not making your motion at the beginning of the deposition." She paused. There was a silence. "Surrebuttal, Mr. Larvey?"

He gave her a long strange look. For once she was glad for Pellar's presence in the room. She sensed that Ralph Larvey very much wanted to beat her brains out. Larvey turned his face to the window and did not reply.

She faced the IBM and spoke in a low monotone. "The Party Rosso offers no surrebuttal. These proceedings are terminated." She added, "And I think we might as well disconnect the machine. We'll need all that's left in the power pack for the return trip." She leaned down and pressed the switch. The little green LED went off.

What now?

She walked over to the credenza. The table was nearly stripped. *Messer* Rucellai had been thorough. Where had he put it all? She wasn't hungry, but in discharge of her maternal duties she would reorder for the two men. Not that they deserved anything.

13. The Bridge

She joined Pellar for supper in the adjacent sitting room. It was a chilly evening, and she added a couple of split oak logs to the fire before she sat down at the table.

Pellar was expansive. "Well, Elizabeth, I did it. I pulled it off. I won. I'll make partner."

She took a deep breath. *Get control, Elizabeth!* "Where's Ralph?"

"Sulking in his room, probably plotting something wicked." He looked around the table. "Where are the forks?"

"Forks won't be invented for another fifty years. Use your fingers."

"Damn primitives," he muttered. He tore a leg off his roast capon and started nibbling at it. "Good stuff, Elizabeth."

"Cuthbert," she said evenly, "if we are able to prevent Rosso from getting his patent, it will be largely because of *my* efforts. *I* found the relevant notebook pages. *I* located Leonardo. *I* persuaded him to testify, and *I* conducted the deposition."

Pellar replaced the half-eaten bird on his plate, wiped his fingers on the table cloth, took a sip of wine, and studied his recalcitrant companion with judicious male eyes. "Of *course*, Elizabeth, of *course*. You were a big help to me. So relax, and eat your supper."

Like a good girl, she thought. "Cuthbert," she said, "because of my work, you'll soon be a partner, with a big corner office where you can see the river, and with a staff of juniors and secretaries. If anybody deserves to make partner, it should be me."

He stared at her, astonished. "But, Elizabeth," he sputtered, "you're a *woman!*"

She got to her feet unsteadily. "I think I'll go for a walk."

Brooding, she wandered the deserted twilight vias, letting her thoughts and feet go where they would. The narrow streets, most of them barely alleys, arched overhead with timbered walkways that made a fretwork pattern against the darkening skies.

She passed the old stone *bottega* where the youthful Leonardo had been apprenticed to the great Verrocchio. Art historians claimed the High Renaissance—the *terza maniera*—had been born in that shed. She sighed and went on.

You might as well accept it, she told herself. You will hang your tail between your legs, and you will trail Pellar back to your office next to the men's washroom, and there you will finally fade away.

She stopped and looked around. It was getting dark. Was she lost? No, wait, there's the approach to a bridge. Must be the Ponte Vecchio, "Old Bridge." Very old, in fact. The foundation arches had been laid by the Romans.

Downstream (she knew), bordering both sides of the Arno, began the considerable estates of Francesco del Giocondo, the husband of Mona Lisa. Oh, *Signora,* how I wanted to meet you!

She squinted down river, but it was too dark to see anything, except maybe a half dozen lanterns just off shore. Fishermen, at night? A bit strange. But she didn't really care anymore.

She returned to the arches, pulled off her slippers, and tossed them over the stone rail. Then she clambered over the railing, screamed once, and dropped.

14. Francesco

She flailed and thrashed, now under, now breaking the tumultuous surface. Her struggles were irrelevant. Even if she now changed her mind, and wanted to live, she knew it was not possible.

She awoke in fits and starts.

Her throat burned. Her gut ached.

She felt a flicker of heat on her cheeks. She tried to sit up. She groaned and sank back into the cushions of the great chair.

She was wrapped in blankets, and she was facing an oversized fireplace, afroth with flame.

Behind her, someone spoke. It was a male voice, authoritative, yet gentle. She caught the words: "See if she is waking."

The face of a child—a girl of some ten or twelve years—peered into hers, and broke into a happy smile. "Yes, Father, she wakes!"

Elizabeth winced as her diaphragm muscles cramped. Under the blankets, she put her hand on her bare belly. *I'm nude.* She tried to turn around to face the man.

"No, *Monna*," he said quickly. "Don't move. We will adjust the chair."

Human forms materialized from nowhere and lifted and angled the chair so that she faced away from the fireplace. A man stepped forward and bowed. "*Monna*, I am called Francesco."

She beheld a tall man in his early forties, with dark hair and bushy black eyebrows. She imagined great strength in the arms and shoulders. Warm intelligent eyes studied her face.

He nodded toward a short skinny man with bushy white hair and a black cloak that seemed to swallow him. "This is Doctor Marcos, who brought you back to life."

The doctor bowed modestly. (Marcos? Leonardo's alchemist? Oh, doc, she thought, how could you?) But she pulled herself together and inclined her head in silence. And now she understood why her abdomen hurt. Marcos had used the current system of artificial respiration: they had draped her over a horse, and they had trotted the poor animal in a circle until all the water in her lungs had been jolted out.

"My daughter Dianara," continued the master.

The child curtsied. Elizabeth nodded gravely.

"And my overseer, Lucas, and his wife Lucrezia. Becco, who helps in the stables, and Maria, the finest cook in Tuscany."

She nodded as appropriate, all the while thinking, Francesco . . . Dianara . . . ? Could it be? She whispered hoarsely, "Francesco del Giocondo?"

"The same, *Monna*."

"Your lady," she blurted, "*Monna* Lisa? She is perhaps away?"

He frowned, puzzled. "*Monna*, I am a widower. There is no *Monna* Lisa in my house."

Elizabeth blushed under her pallor. God, what a *faux pas!* He hasn't met her yet. "Oh, I'm sorry . . ."

Her confusion embarrassed him. "You are not from these parts?"

"No. I am called Elisabetta. I am from Napoli."

"Wha—? Oh, *Napoli!*" said Giocondo. "Of course! You're the interpreter with the Englishmen, at the *Cigno Nero*."

It was an invitation to talk but she didn't feel like talking. "I must be getting back," she said.

"*Monna* Elisabetta," said Giocondo doubtfully, "it is long after curfew. You must stay here tonight."

He was right. "Can a message be sent to the inn?"

"That we can do. A mounted courier with sword and lighted pistolet will escort the good doctor to his home and then go on to the inn. What message shall we take?"

"Just say I'm safe and will return in the morning."

"It will be done. And while I make the arrangements, the doctor would like you to take a little wine. It's the red wine of Cyprus, thick, and mulled with pistachios and cloves. After that we will take you upstairs to your room." He handed her a silver cup, half-full. It was warm to the touch. She took a sip. It was delicious.

She was only vaguely aware when someone took the cup from her hand, lifted her up, tucked the blanket decently about her throat, and started upstairs with her. *Messer* Francesco, she thought dreamily, you have a wonderful male smell.

She was lowered gently into something soft. Somebody—the cook—was pulling a nightdress over her, and tucking coverlets around her chin. She heard a little girl's awed whisper, "Oh, Maria, she is so beautiful. Do you think she will stay?"

The responding voice sounded dubious. "All will be as God wills. Come, child." She slept.

15. *Monna* Lisa

A noise—*noises*, rather—awakened her.

She listened to the sounds. They were coming from downstairs. These were *kitchen* noises. Pots and pans. Cutlery.

She remembered now that she had eaten nothing at all yesterday. With or without an invitation, she was going down into that kitchen.

Where had they put her clothes? She looked over at the draped alcove. She surmised that it was actually a dressing room, hopefully with commode and wash basin. She walked barefoot over to the little cubicle and pulled the drapes aside. In the dim light she could see that her clothes had been washed, dried, touched here and there with a warm iron, and hung with great care on wooden rods.

No shoes, but there was a pair of brand new slippers, evidently measured exactly to size.

She opened the commode lid. The bowl contained a scented liquid. Violets? And there, on the table, was a roll of fluffy linen paper.

She sighed. *Ah, that Francesco!* Is *he* why *Monna* Lisa smiled?

And it's really very curious. Where *is* Lisa? He hasn't met her yet. But all the chronologies put her in this house—*now.*

She pulled her nightgown off and dressed quickly. She brought a measure of order to her hair with the comb and brush she found on the washstand. She examined herself in the dressing-room mirror. Plain but tidy. She stepped out into the room and looked around. Her headband lay on a night stand by the bed. She picked it up and pulled it on over her forehead.

That's when it hit her. She gasped once, then grabbed her abdomen in a struggle to breathe.

She saw it all, complete: an integrated panorama. She will marry this good man. She will bed him. His hands, his mouth, will be all over her, touching, caressing, stroking, kissing. . . . She will glow, radiant as the full Moon. Truly, she will be beautiful. Truly, Leonardo will paint her. Truly there will be a marvelous portrait, and it will eventually hang in the Louvre. For who is *Monna* Lisa? *I am.*

Not so fast, Elizabeth!

There was just one little problem: According to well-authenticated history, *Monna* Lisa would accompany her husband on a trip to southern Italy some forty months from now, and there she would die of a fever.

Well, so be it. At least those forty months would be spent with people who loved her. And that's not all. Tradition even gave her a seasonable pregnancy and a little son.

So, *Monna* Lisa-to-be—or Mona, as the English say—let's get the show on the road. Still breathing hard, she pinched both cheeks delicately, just enough to give a spot of pink. Then she opened the door and walked out into the hall.

She smelled it instantly. Coffee! In Italy so soon? She started slowly down the stairs.

There was a scurry down below. Evidently someone had been set to watch for her.

And there, very suddenly, was Francesco Giocondo at the bottom of the stairs, holding out his arms in wide and cheerful greeting. "*Monna* Elisabetta! *Buon giorno!* How did you sleep?"

She smiled at him. "I slept wonderfully well, *Messer* Francesco."

"Then let us sit down a moment and have something to drink, with bread and honey . . . or whatever would please you."

She took a seat on the bench across the table from him. Maria sidled up behind her with plate, knife, and spoon. "What to drink, madonna?" she asked softly. "Milk? Wine? Water?"

Elizabeth looked over at the dark liquid in Francesco's cup. What did they call it? Not coffee. That came from the french word *cafe*, a century later. "What drinks milord?" she asked.

"It is called mocha. The Venetians bring it in as beans from Mocha, the Arabian port. Maria roasts and grinds the beans, and makes an infusion with boiling water. It is a new thing. It helps one to wake up in the morning."

"Really? May I have a taste?"

"Of course." He passed the cup over. "Careful. It's hot, and you may find it somewhat bitter."

She took a sip. "Ah!" She passed the cup back to Francesco, then looked up at the hovering Maria. "I liked that, Maria. Now, could you pour me some, perhaps in a smaller cup, with this much milk?"

"Right away, madonna!" She was soon back.

Elizabeth found the honey jar and stirred in a spoonful.

Francesco watched all this with great interest. "A taste, milady?"

She handed it over. He sipped noisily. "Oh . . . good, *good!* Milk and honey much improve the taste!"

Elizabeth slapped butter and grape jelly on her bread and began the best breakfast she had had since Texas. And while she had him here, she might as well clear up a few points. "*Messer* Francesco, about last night. Would you mind if I asked some questions?"

"Go ahead!" He leaned forward, almost eagerly.

Well, I'll be darned, she thought. *He's* the one who should be asking the questions, like, *signorina,* how did you come to be in the river? But he's not going to pry. She took a long pull at the mocha, then exhaled slowly. "*Messer* Francesco, you were on the river rather late yesterday."

"Yes, madonna, fishing after sunset *is* unusual. It is hard to see anything, even with good lanterns. But last night was special."

"Special?"

He pulled a piece of folded paper from his pocket and handed it over to her. She read:

Fisherman! Tonight the House of Venus stands in the sign of Pisces.

"Your horoscope?"

He nodded. "Doctor Marcos."

She handed it back. Things were clearing up just a little. "Please continue. Pisces? Something about fish?"

"*Perhaps* fish. And there was still the question of Venus. She rose from the waters, you'll recall. But the only water around here is the Arno. So, Monna Elisabetta, mostly because of my very great curiosity, I was there on the river bank, watching our *pescatori.* Sure enough, they hauled you out."

She smiled. "I'm very glad you went fishing, *Messer* Francesco."

"So am I." He paused. "We must do something about names. I am simply Francesco."

"And my friends call me Lisa." *From now on, that is!*

"Lisa," he murmured. He rolled the word in his mouth, as though he were sampling a new wine. "Yes, Lisa. I like that very much. *Monna* Lisa."

It was official.

He said slowly, "I suppose you must return to your friends this morning. I will order a carriage soon. Meanwhile, do we have time to show you my house?"

"Plenty of time. And certainly, I would like to see Dianara again."

16. The Flowers

"This is the central bedchamber," he explained. He pointed to the gigantic four-poster in the center of the room. "Dianara was born in that bed. It is not used at present. The nursery was through that door."

He opened one of the double doors in the east wall, and they stepped out into an expansive loggia that ran half the length of the house. He pointed to a brilliant patch of sunlight on a nearby hill. She gasped; it was gorgeous.

He looked at her and smiled. "Dawn comes first through that gap in the hills, and covers the slope, there, where you see the flowers. Dianara loves to walk there. She brings home dozens of bouquets, but for every flower she cuts, ten more spring up."

They heard throat-clearing sounds in the chamber behind them. They turned to see Dianara with a basket full of irises. The girl curtsied deeply. "They are for you, milady."

"Ah!" Elizabeth radiated pleasure. As she held out her hands for the basket, she noted that the child's feet were wet. Obviously she had gone into the fields barefoot so as not to risk her shoes and stockings. "They are beautiful!" On sudden impulse she bent over and kissed the girl on the mouth.

Dianara grabbed her around the neck, noisily returned the kiss, then turned and ran out of the room, singing, *"Rimarrà, rimarrà!"* She will stay, she will stay!

Elizabeth looked down at the imprint of small bare feet in the deep pile of the rug, then quizzically up at Francesco. His face seemed a blend of awe and pleasure.

She did not know what to say. He wants me, she thought. His daughter wants me. I want them. Why isn't something happening?

The man led her down the hall. They stopped by a glass-fronted bookcase. She pointed to one of the books. "May I?"

He pulled it out for her. "It's a book about the game of chess, by the Spaniard, Luis de Lucena. Very instructive, if you like chess, that is."

She opened the flyleaf. On the left a copper plate engraving of a somber bearded man stared up at her truculently. That face, she thought . . . looks familiar. Where have I seen him? Ah, yes. The man at the chess table at the *Cigno Nero!* The staring man. The great Lucena, champion of Spain, France, and Italy, playing the locals for a few ducats? Singing for his supper, as it were?

She looked further. On the right, the author and title: Luis Ramirez de Lucena/*Repetición des Amores e Arte de Axedres*/Lambert Palmart, *Impresar*/Valencia/1497. Discourse on Love, and Art of Chess. It was actually two books in one binding. The first, the Discourse, would eventually attain fame as the most virulent anti-feminist document of all Spanish literature. Already she detested Luis Lucena.

She replaced the volume, then stood and faced her host squarely. "Francesco, you have a great need for a woman in your home, a wife for you, a mother for your daughter, someone to manage the house and the servants. But you hold back, because it would be your third marriage, and you think you might be condemning the woman to death. You, a mortal, cannot be blamed for what is ordained. You should make the most of what remains." She almost glared at him. Dammit, she thought, *propose to me!*

He took an immense breath, then grasped her hands firmly. "Listen to me, Monna Lisa. You know I have buried two wives . . . two very good women, whom I loved dearly. And you must know I am bad luck. Yet I ask you, despite all this, will you marry me?"

She knew what her answer was going to be; yet she too had to be honest—up to a point. "Before I answer, let me explain something. On occasion, my ways may seem a bit strange to you. I am from another country, you know."

"Understood."

"Secondly, there can be no dowry."

He shook his head. "It is not required."

Fine, she thought. Forget the dowry. But with her next statement she knew she was dealing from strength. "Leonardo wants to paint me."

He looked at her in amazement. "Lisa *cara*, you are a very beautiful woman. But I am a merchant, and Leonardo paints only noblewomen."

"I am not beautiful, Francesco. I must correct you there. Still, he wants to paint me. He asked yesterday morning, but I had to decline, because our commission was scheduled to return today. But now I shall stay, and Leonardo will paint my portrait."

"God is bountiful," he muttered. "The wife of Giocondo, painted by the great Leonardo! I must begin now, assembling the fee."

"No fee, my friend."

"How can you say that? He does not paint for nothing."

"He will paint me for nothing, but he will keep the portrait."

"Ah. I see. Well, most remarkable." He laughed a short half-believing chuckle. "Leonardo resumes painting, and he paints La Gioconda! So now, Monna Lisa, will you marry me?"

Still holding hands with him, she bowed slightly. "Milord, you do me great honor to ask me to be your wife. I accept with pleasure."

He embraced her warmly, then held her by the shoulders. "We must send word to your legation to delay departure, so that they can attend the wedding."

She thought, Cuthbert Pellar attend the wedding of a third-chair associate? Fat chance! "They cannot stay, dear Francesco. Their high liege lords require their immediate return."

"Oh? Too bad. Well, then, we must at least tell them the good news. I'll send now for the carriage."

17. Lucena

The *carrozza* pulled into the piazza of the *Cigno Nero* and stopped near the big iron doors.

"Please wait here," she told him. "I have to explain things and say goodbye."

"Of course. Take all the time you need."

Pellar was waiting for her inside. "Dammit, Elizabeth, we've been worried sick about you!"

She was immediately suspicious. "Cuthbert, what the hell is going on?"

He managed a feeble grin. "First of all, Elizabeth, I'd like you to meet *Señor* Lucena."

Lucena? She looked around. A gloomy bearded man was shouldering his way through the front circle of idlers. Yes, it was he—the great chess master and anti-feminist. A few meters behind him she noted the two TM cases and the bag of florins.

She further noted that Ralph Larvey was standing off to one side, arms folded across his chest. His face was wreathed in a smile of cold triumph.

A heavy gray lump of concrete began to solidify in her stomach.

The Spaniard bowed deeply and gracefully. *"Señorita, sono lieto di conoscerla."*

She ignored him. She whirled on Pellar. "He suckered you into a game of chess, didn't he?"

The lawyer said weakly. "He was just a local *potser,* Elizabeth, but he got lucky."

"Lucky? Godalmighty, Cuthbert! Do you know who he is?"

"What do you mean?"

"This is Luis de Lucena, currently chess champion of Europe!"

"Jesus, Elizabeth, how was I to know? But actually, there's no need to get in an uproar. We can get everything back. All we have to do is, you spend an hour with him upstairs."

She stared at his averted face for a full minute. "Start at the beginning."

"Well, as I said, he suggested we play."

She said, "First, though, Ralph and Lucena had a little discussion, probably using an interpreter. Right?"

"Well, yeah. How did you know?"

So this is Ralph's revenge, she thought. "Then Ralph came over and said here was a local *potser,* and you could beat him easy. Right?"

Pellar nodded dumbly.

"And you beat him, that first game."

"I did. And it was easy."

"Then he suggested a little wager."

"Yeah. I won again."

"Then you started doubling, and redoubling, and you began losing."

"Yeah."

"And you lost everything."

He shrugged.

What was left to say? When Larvey came over, she murmured, "My compliments, Ralph. That was very neatly done."

He smiled. "It's nice to be appreciated."

Pellar looked at both of them, puzzled. "Honestly, Elizabeth, I tried everything. I think Tony even sent for Leonardo, but—"

"Elisabetta."

She whirled. *"Leonardo!"* So he *had* come; but how could he help?

The artist took her by the elbow and moved her out of earshot of Lucena. He spoke quickly. "First, a question. How were you able to guide your machine to the day and hour?"

"I received special training in pattern shifting; it's much like chess play."

"Are you fairly good at chess?"

"I'm very good, Leonardo."

"Then you must challenge him. His stake will be your cases and money. Can you raise a stake?"

She thought a moment. "Yes. And, Maestro, would you be so kind as to be my second?"

"Yes, milady." He stepped over to the Spaniard, and they entered into a heated discussion, with much waving of arms. Finally Leonardo returned. "He will play one game, for all that he has taken from Lord Cut'berto, provided your stake is acceptable."

"Thank you, *Messer* Leonardo." Now it was time to confront the chess lord of Europe. *"Señor* Lucena."

He bowed. *"Señorita.* What stake, please?"

She placed both hands behind her neck and unclasped the string of pearls. "They are valued at ten thousand florins. Examine, if you like."

Pellar gasped. "No! No! Elizabeth, they're *rented!"*

The Spaniard scowled. "What does he say?"

"He says that he is certain I shall grind the bottom of the Spanish pig into little sausages."

"Ha! Does he now?" There was an ugly scrape of metal as the Spaniard pulled his rapier several inches out of its scabbard. Elizabeth gulped. "Listen, why don't we start?" She handed the strand of pearls to Leonardo. "There. Leonardo will hold the stake."

"Then let us draw for color," growled the chess master.

Color was important. She was thinking hard. She needed a sure-fire opening, something truly murderous. If she had the white pieces, she could lead the game into the deadly Evans Gambit, invented by Captain William Evans of the Royal

Marines in 1824. But—to play the Evans she had to have the white pieces. There was only one sure way to get white: as odds-giver.

She said, "There's the question of odds."

His face hardened. "I do not give odds."

"You? No, of course not *you*. As the stronger player, *I* give odds."

"You!" He laughed in cold disbelief.

"Myself."

"You are *loca*. All right, what odds do you give?"

"I shall play *bendato*."

He looked puzzled. "Blindfold?"

"Yes. Without sight of board or pieces."

It gave her great pleasure to listen to the gasps. Evidently none of them had ever heard of blindfold chess. She pulled a white silk handkerchief from her bodice, tied it about her eyes, and took a chair facing away from the chess table. "Set up the pieces. As odds-giver, I take white."

"But how will you know my moves?"

"You will call them over to me, and I shall do the same for you."

She listened to the rattling of the chessmen as they were set up behind her.

"Ready," called Lucena. "Your move."

"Pedone al quarto scacco del re," she called. Pawn to king four.

He replied instantly. "And pawn to my king's fourth square."

And the game was on.

On her fourth move she called out, *"Pedone al regina cavaliere quattro."* Pawn to queen knight's fourth. *That* was the critical move in the Evans opening: the pawn offer.

There was a dead silence. Ha, she thought, he's never seen the Evans before! The question now is, will he take the bait?

Finally Lucena called out, "Bishop takes pawn."

She had him.

The game proceeded. The Spaniard's replies began to slow. He was in trouble, but he was fighting. He clustered his pieces in a protective shield about his king.

Elizabeth paused a moment and considered. The position cried out for a smothered mate. Yes, there it was. She called out in a firm clear voice, "I announce checkmate in two moves."

Silence. What was going on? Could she have been mistaken? No! She got up and removed her blindfold and walked over to the table. The position was exactly right. The smother was there.

Lucena looked up grimly. "There is no mate in two, *señorita*. There is not mate at all. You forfeit."

"*Señor*, there *is* a mate in two." She captured a defending bishop with her queen. "You must recapture, yes?"

He grunted. "So I recapture, and you are a queen down, and there is still no mate."

"Your bishop no longer protects this square, *señor*. My knight moves in, and mates—so." She moved the piece. *"Scacco matto!"* Checkmate.

The bearded man stared at the board, then at her. His cheeks turned red. He scowled. "All right, it's checkmate. But one game decides nothing. We shall play two out of three."

"No!"

There was a commotion at the doorway.

It was Francesco, with Leonardo right behind him. The artist had evidently gone out for reinforcements. She groaned. She hadn't wanted to involve her fiance.

Giocondo took in the situation at a glance. He faced the chess master. The room grew still as he spoke slowly, quietly, and with great presence. *"Signor,* in matters involving my betrothed, you may address *me."* His right hand rested lightly on the pommel of his sword.

The Spaniard looked dubiously at the newcomer, then at Elizabeth, then back at the glowering merchant. He took one fast longing glance toward the gold-bag, then bowed deeply to them all, and he left.

Elizabeth let out a deep breath.

Francesco bent over her. "Are you all right?"

"I am fine." He had asked no questions, and he asked none now. He had simply waded in and protected her. She said, "Soon, I will explain everything. Just now I must say farewell to my friends upstairs."

"Of course, Lisa. Oh—*Messer* Leonardo asked that I return these to you." He handed her the strand of pearls. "I will wait here."

Pellar had already recovered his aplomb. Larvey favored her with a thinly-veiled scowl. But each of the two picked up a valise and followed her silently up the stairs.

Down below, Francesco was calling for the innkeeper. "Tony! Wine for everyone! Set 'em up!"

Just like the Old West, she thought.

18. Decision

UNITED STATES ARMY

Memorandum
TO: A. G. Perry, General, Pentagon, Division of Special Assets
FROM: K. R. Inman, Colonel
RE: Project TM; Patent Interference, *Green v. Rosso*

The Patent Office has formally dissolved this interference, as unpatentable to either party. The decision is perhaps moot, since we are advised by our technical people that the TM cannot be used again for an indefinite period, owing to strains in the space-time fabric created by our last use. Certain other aspects of the Project are best reviewed off the record.

(K.R. Inman)

19. A Smile

She sat again in the comfortable straight-back chair in Leonardo's *bottega*. It was early afternoon. The light was soft, clear, luminous, relaxing—just right for painting.

On the carpet off to the left, Dianara played with the beautiful long-haired cat. Outside in the garden a small fountain splashed. From behind the screen off to the right two unseen musicians were playing quietly, one on pipes, the other with a lyre of the artist's own invention.

Leonardo stood aside from his *cavaletto*—the three-legged easel—and considered her. "And now," he said, "we need a smile." Already he was sketching in the outlines of her face with light strokes of the charcoal pencil. As he worked, he murmured to her, almost as though talking to himself. "Dwell thou on the happiest moment of thy life. Thy nuptial day, perhaps? Or rescue from the river?"

He watched the subtle change in her face with wonder and delight.

Her happiest moment? Ah, she remembered. Pellar and Larvey had stood inside the TM, ready to leave, in their upper room back at the Black Swan, and waiting impatiently for her to join them. Pellar had motioned to her with an imperious jerk of his chin. She had put her left hand on the handle of the door and she had swung the panel back and looked at both of them.

"That's *it!*" marveled Leonardo. "Hold that expression." Oh, yes! This woman was saying something wonderful about life. And death, love, suffering, endurance, all woven together, and emergent in fantastic unity in that smile. What memory, what thought—*thoughts*—had brought this transfiguration?

She was standing just outside the TM, and Pellar had shouted, "Dammit, Gerard, *get in here!*"

And she had calmly replied, "No, Cuthbert, I will not get in there. If you have further business with me, look for me in the Louvre."

Pellar's mouth had dropped. "The Louvre? Wha—?"

(Her happiest moment? Oh yes, she remembered!)

Next, she had finished what she had come to say, and they had both looked at her, first in blank disbelief, and finally in pink-cheeked horror.

"And now may I suggest," she had said sweetly, "that the two of you, jointly and severally, go fuck yourselves." Then she had slammed the frame door. The TM had shimmered . . . and vanished.

20. *Déjà Vu*

C. Cuthbert Pellar and his new bride spent their honeymoon in Paris, and on this particular day in June, mostly because Mrs. Pellar insisted on it, they found themselves in the Louvre.

They proceeded with the standard treasures, the Venus de Milo, the Nike of Samothrace, the Hera of Samos.

"Yes, dear?" he said.

"Are we supposed to meet someone here? You keep looking around."

(Look for me in the Louvre, she had said.)

"No, we're not meeting anyone. I'm just trying to see what there is to see."

God, what a mess *that* had been, when they got back, and no Elizabeth. It had taken the entire upper echelons of the Pentagon, working with Barrington Wright and the FBI and the CIA, to hush the thing up. Fortunately, Colonel Inman was on their side. It was almost as though he had expected Elizabeth to stay behind. He had provided the basic story, with supporting documents: Elizabeth Gerard was on the passenger list of Italia 816, the ill-fated Concorde blown up over Lisbon by a terrorist bomb. Wright had appointed Pellar to notify Elizabeth's next of kin. After which the associate had made partner.

Mrs. Pellar said, "They've got some famous paintings in here," she said. "What's that thing by Leonardo da Vinci?"

"There were several."

"The most famous one of all. You know . . ."

"The *Mona Lisa?*"

"That's it. Let's find the *Mona Lisa*. We'll have to ask someone."

Together they walked up to the *Renseignements* desk, occupied by a bored youth reading a paperback.

"*S'il vous plaît, monsieur,*" said Pellar politely, "*où se trouve La Mona Lisa?*"

The boy didn't look up. He pointed off to his left with a thumb. "Down that hall, turn right at the second corridor. No flash."

A moment later they stood before the masterpiece. "The greatest painting in the world," he said softly. "I met him, you know, Leonardo."

"I thought he was dead."

Pellar was silent. He didn't want to go into that. Besides, he was studying the portrait. That face . . . had he met her during the time of the deposition? La Gioconda? The wife of a rich Florentine named Giocondo? He was pretty sure he hadn't met any such woman. And yet, it nagged at him. He *had* seen this face—this transcendent beauty—before. Where? When?

Think back. Back. The women there . . .

There had been a servant girl, practically a child. And the wife of Tony the innkeeper. And the cook, an old woman. The only other female on the scene had been . . . *she?* Look hard. *On her forehead.* Is that the TM head-band?

Oh, great God! Don't let it be *she!* Oh no no no *no.* He closed his eyes and moaned.

Mrs. Pellar looked up in alarm. "Cutie—?"

He turned his back to the portrait. "Let's get out of here."

"But . . . oh, all right." She looked back. Wasn't there something about a smile? Was the lady smiling? Hard to say.

LETHARY FAIR

1. The Alien Arrives

At about noon on the second day of July, 2198, (I quote from Constable Ned Packle's report) Mistress Erithra Dollkin (age 83) had just emerged from Garshmeyer's Deli, where she had bought some herbal tea, when she noted this strange shadow moving slowly on the sidewalk in front of the deli.

She looked up.

Some sort of vehicle was dropping down rapidly into the street right into the No Parking zone in front of Garshmeyer's. It landed there with a hard *clump.*

That violation of a highly respected City Ordinance apparently not sufficing, the driver of the strange vehicle (which was topless now, with the roof rolled back), after loosening his seat belt, took a moment to adjust his clothing in such a way that he exposed his bare buttocks. Whereupon Mistress Dollkin shrieked, dropped her bag of tea, and covered her eyes.

Constable Packle was just down the Square in O'Malley's Barber Shop. He heard Mistress Dollkin's cry, and he rushed out, whereupon he observed her shaking finger and averted eyes. He listened two or three times to her stammered accusation, and then stepped forward and arrested the surprised felon, who had two heads.

Now, I think I can state it as a fact, the general citizenry of Lethary had never before seen a two-headed person. Of course, there were those rumors about one of the old baron's freak descendants, but that's all, just rumors. Yes, our two-headed visitor was a great novelty.

But mooning a respected citizen of Lethary while simultaneously parking illegally was just icing on the criminal cake. For alas, in the Alien's precipitous descent (that's what he turned out to be—an Alien) his craft landed on Dr. Dennis Banchou, an aged Buddhist monk. When they got the craft lifted up and hauled away, the old scientist-monk was dead.

Additionally, and perhaps of even greater concern to some, was what happened to Sara, a very beautiful geisha android owned by the Sixtrees Bar-Del-O. Apparently she was routinely headed for Garshmeyer's to pick up Percy Sixtrees's lunch when she looked overhead just in time to get herself knocked down and crushed.

Since the jail was just down the Square it was a simple matter for Constable Packle to march the criminal over and lock him up.

The miscreant (who spoke a broken English—which apparently he had picked up while orbiting the planet) claimed his/their name(s) was/were "John-Claude Berg." At least that's what Ned finally made out, and wrote in the police blotter. John was the head on the Alien's right, Claude was the other.

Me. My name is William Moncrief Whitmore. Call me Bill. Bachelor, age thirty-eight. I'm a lawyer, and that's how I got involved with the Alien.

I knew I was in line for court-appointment. The pay was nominal, the case was a sure loser, I had to get out of town—fast. But Judge Martin Cloke was faster. He strode into my office just as I was making a reservation at the Surf and Sand, a seashore resort in Galveston.

The judge didn't sit down, he didn't even take off his hat. He spoke first, and he was using his mean grim tone of voice. "He needs somebody like you, William."

"Judge—"

"Arraignment tomorrow morning, 9 o'clock. Be there."

"Now wait a—" But I was talking to a closing door.

Now, I don't want to give the impression that Martin Cloke is *actually* mean. He isn't. He's a very decent man with a thankless job and a mortgage just like the rest of us. On the bench he's totally fair.

As a youth he had wanted to be a painter, and indeed while he was still in junior high school he had painted a masterpiece. He had been painting by the numbers, and accidentally moved everything up one number, so that cobalt blue became saffron yellow, and yellow became red, and so on. The astonishing result won first prize in the Provincial School Exhibit. His parents were of course delighted. Forthwith they got him the Van Gogh–Gauguin cerebral implant, plus all the accessories, palette, paints, beautiful white canvas smock, and so on. But somehow the implant wiring went awry: the chroma networks failed to connect properly, and there was loss of color reception in the occipital lobe, with the result that the young aspirant could see, paint, and think only in black and white. So his parents switched him to law, which paid better anyway. But the chroma problem never went away. As a lawyer, and later as a judge, he tended to see things only in black and white, with no intermediate shades of gray.

Not a man to waste a thing as valuable as an artist's smock, the judge had in fact put it to extraordinary use. He had printed all his favorite Latin phrases on it in indelible black ink. He wore the over-printed smock only in his most important cases, and in these only on the last day, when he was about to hand down a portentous decision and was in need of the support of appropriate citations.

For his study of the law Martin's parents bought for him the prestigious Harvard Lexus Implant, with Latin Addenda and a lifetime subscription to Connaught's Legal Updates. Equipped with these and a high native intelligence, he was easily the most erudite jurist in the Province.

I'll get to the Alien and his trial soon, but first some more history, starting with me.

My paternal grandfather, Hondo Whitmore, was a sergeant in the militia during the Border Wars. In *which* militia? Hard to say. Sometimes he fought *for* the baron, sometimes against, depending on where the money was. When he lay dying in the Old Soldiers Home, he called me to his deathbed. "Dear boy, there will be no more money." (He had been drawing pensions and disability from both sides.) "You're on your own. Go into the law. Become a respected scoundrel." And with a gurgly chuckle, he died.

And so for the next six years I clerked in the law offices of Pillfeder and Wantech, and I learned the law.

As old Mr. Amos Pillfeder explained when I reported for work, "There is nothing strange, peculiar, or illogical about the law. You just have to understand that things are rarely what they seem. Generally, they're something else."

He was right. At first the law made no sense, but as the months passed it suddenly all came together. In the sixth year I took and passed the Provincial Bar exam and was duly admitted to the bar. I left Pillfeder and Wanntech, opened my own office, and for the first month I starved.

And now back to the Alien. We had to be in court tomorrow morning, and I had yet to meet him.

Manslaughter—that accidental killing of the old Buddhist savant Dr. Banchou—was of course pretty bad. For this the Alien was looking at a ten-year prison sentence. But destruction of Sara might prove even worse, because she was owned by the Sixtrees.

Sara was an exquisite creation, and I had secretly admired her for more than thirty years. For me her demise was a painful personal loss, like watching the Mona Lisa pass through a shredder, or a Gutenberg Bible go up in flames.

I first saw her when I was ten years old. Word had got around that she worked for the Sixtrees in the upper floors of the Bar-Del-O. Even we kids knew what that meant. Once in a while we saw some of those girls. They might emerge in the early afternoon, looking very pretty, but dressed modestly in flowered prints. They might stroll around the Square, or beyond, generally in pairs. Sara was an exception. When she came out she was always alone. We knew she was a geisha android and was supposed to have special talents, but we never saw her dressed up in her geisha garb. Outside she always wore simple street clothes, much like the other girls.

The other girls came and went, but Sara stayed. What was Sara's specialty? What was it that set her off from other girls and other androids? There were all sorts of rumors, but nothing factual ever seemed to filter down.

Even as a boy I had this thing about her. Years later, when I started my law practice, I still fantasized. I wanted her, but I could not bear the thought of sharing her with other men. Maybe one day, when I was very rich (now *there* was a fantasy!), I would buy her, have her all to myself.

And now she was gone. No more fantasies. Sad, sad.

Back to now. I called over to the court clerk, Enos Phlutter, and got the details about her that I'd need for the trial. Enos read snatches from the Android Registrations. Sara, registered as Sakurako ("Cherry Blossom") had been made by

Tokyo Androids, Ltd. and had been sold to a syndicate of Japanese metal consultants in Houston in 2065.

"For how much?" I asked.

"Three hundred thousand kroner."

I swallowed hard. "Three . . . hundred . . ."

"Thousand," finished Enos. "The entry says she was programmed with some sort of high-tech specialty."

"Worth three hundred thou? Some specialty! Then what?"

"Burl Dogger bought her at auction in 2088 for ten thousand kroner. He died in 2098. His will gave all his property, including Sara, to his first male descendant to reach twenty-one under the conditions of the will."

I thought about *that*. This was the famous Sixtrees will. I knew all about it, or thought I did. Actually, I didn't. Just then, all I could think was, my mysterious client was headed for prison. For such was the law. And the Sixtrees and their hired gun, Provincial Prosecutor Dave Clatchett, dearly loved the law.

2. Arraignment

Early the next morning I walked over to the jail. The Square was already full of people waiting for the courtroom doors to open, about half being our local citizenry and half out-of-towners who had come for the Fair. They all now welcomed the forthcoming trial as a free side-show.

And the minions of the media were also arriving. Word of the two-headed Alien had traveled around the world.

"Midnight" Madison, our local TV reporter, was already arguing loudly with Deputy Lon Satters, insisting on the right to interview the prisoner with his camera crew, but Lon was not impressed.

As I worked my way through the crowd, my attention was drawn to overhead, where a copter was hovering and making a great racket. The markings were clearly visible: "MBC," meaning Mogul Broadcasting Company, or, as some claimed, Mather's Bullshit Capers. Whichever, our Alien was now officially newsworthy. For MBC *was* Randolph Mather.

I watched his show later that day. There, he's interviewing our famous seer, Madame Batsky, in the courthouse corridor. She's barely recognizable. Mather evidently uses the new auto-makeup cameras. The machine erased forty pounds and forty years and changed her into a brisk day suit from the couturiers of Paris. Our famous seer was presented to the world as an attractive, well-dressed young business woman. She predicted "some surprises."

Now back in real time. I see Mather talking to Dave Clatchett in the courthouse foyer. Dave is looking very serious and grim. I'm actually headed for the jail stairs, but I can't help overhearing their last words. Mather says, "Mr. Prosecutor, do you think you'll get a conviction?" "Absolutely," Dave says. And that's all he says. But the way it came out on TV, the camera-modifier had Dave saying, "Absolutely, Ran. I have yet to lose a homicide case. I hope MBC is there when the guilty verdict is handed down."

Oh, well . . .

Lon Satters was the deputy on duty. He was waiting for me, and took me on back to the cells, where the new boarder was finishing up breakfast. Lon introduced me and left. The prisoner and I shook hands. He/(they?) had a firm five-fingered grip, same as any ordinary man.

What did he look like? Well, he was clean-cut, graceful, and immensely self-confident. Except for that second head, and aside from his clothes, he looked like a recent college graduate. Of course, those clothes—pants, shirt, jacket—*were* a mite distinctive. They seemed to change color from time to time, like a chameleon.

The blond blue-eyed head was John, the other, the brunette hazel-eyed head, was Claude. According to John-Claude two heads were the norm on his planet.

How had he come to Earth? His story: He was a geologist looking for certain metals in nearby solar systems when he discovered that his fuel gauge wasn't working. It read half full when actually he was down to his last few drops. He headed immediately for the nearest sun and went into orbit around what appeared to be a likely planet—Earth, hopefully a source of fuel.

He explained what he meant by "fuel." It wasn't gasoline or diesel oil or uranium. The ship's nuclear packet still had several centuries of life. "Fuel" was the stuff in the guidance system, the brains of his ship. It was some sort of oil, volatile, odorous. Quite common on his planet. But here? By way of description he took my pen and drew this on my yellow legal pad:

"We call it 'one-legged man,' " he said.

I got it. The "Y" sitting on a torso represented two heads, normal for his people. A chemical formula, maybe? Something to look into later. Just now we had higher priorities.

And so (he explained) he had stayed in orbit for several days, trying to learn the language from media broadcasts. There were several different languages, but he finally picked ours—English—mainly because we seemed to be the civilization most likely and most able to help him. He put the ship on an auto-landing program, with the top down. The next thing he remembered he was standing in his ship trying to adjust his trousers. Nearby a lady was screaming. Seconds later Constable Ned Packle was handcuffing him.

"We're very sorry about this," John said. "We thought we were clear. Apparently the screens failed." Claude added, "We're especially sorry about Sara."

I looked at him sharply. There was no way he could know my feelings for the elegant android. Doubtless he referred to their own legal exposure.

Anyhow there was Ned, unlocking the cell door with his big iron key. "It's five of nine, Billy. We got to git on up there."

He put cuffs on John-Claude, and we followed him up the stairs to the courtroom. "What's all that banging?" I asked.

"Hammers," said Ned. "Carpenters. They're fixing up the Baron's Box."

Interesting. And just a bit alarming. Of course the Sixtrees had a legitimate interest in the case, since the Alien had demolished an expensive piece of Sixtrees property. Still—(I checked it later) no sitting baron had ever before attended court here.

Let me explain about the Baron's Box.

You'll find one in nearly every public auditorium. There's a Box in the opera house, one in the university assembly hall, the lecture auditoriums, the churches, anywhere the public might gather. This includes courtrooms. The fact that the baron rarely (or never) occupied his boxes seemed irrelevant to their continuing existence.

In Judge Cloke's courtroom the Baronial Box was in the middle of a rear balcony looking down at the bar and bench.

"Ned," I said quietly, "what's going on?"

He hesitated a moment, then replied in a subdued monolog. "They installed a one-way visi screen."

That meant whoever was in the Box could see us, but nobody in the courtroom—not even the judge—could see *them*. Curiouser and curiouser. And totally out of character with Cecil, Lord Sixtrees. The current baron loved being seen. *Why* was a puzzle. He was not a handsome man. He was fat. I mean *fat*. No, the party in the Box wasn't Cecil. Anyhow, he was presently in California making a movie.

So who would it be? Even if we had been out on the street with the mob of spectators, we wouldn't have been able to see anybody enter the Box, because the entrance to the Box is completely sheltered. The baron's car (windows up) drives into the secured underground garage, and from there one goes by private elevator straight up into the Box, and the public sees nothing.

Ned led us into the courtroom through the side door, and John-Claude and I sat ourselves down at the defense table and looked around. The prosecution table was loaded. There was Dave Clatchett, of course. Plus two other chaps, very well-dressed, very dignified. I recognized one of them right away—J. Killian Murfree, a partner in a famous Chicago law firm. This was strange. So strange that it—the situation—talked to me. It said, there's something going on here, something beyond Sara. So what was it?

I looked around and up at the Baron's Box. Was *that* part of the mystery? The carpenters no longer hammered. They were gone. Did that mean the invisible occupant(s) had arrived? And if so, who . . . and why?

And now Lon opened the main courtroom doors and people began streaming in, mediamen first. In another five minutes we all rose for the entry of Judge Cloke. He banged his gavel once or twice and ordered his clerk to call the case.

"People versus John-Claude Berg," droned Enos. "Arraignment."

The judge said, "Will John-Claude Berg please rise."

My client and I got up together.

The judge studied his case file a moment. "John-Claude Berg, you are charged with, first, murder; second, felonious destruction of property exceeding in value one hundred kroner; third, indecent exposure; and fourth, illegal parking. How do you plead, counts one through four, guilty or not guilty?"

The two heads spoke in unison. "Not guilty, Your Honor."

"So noted." The judge closed his case folder. "Jury selection, tomorrow morning, nine o'clock." He started to get up.

I stopped him. "Your Honor, there's the matter of bail."

Dave Clatchett objected immediately. "Capital case, Your Honor. No bail."

"No prior record," I cut in. "And the city has seized his vehicle. He can't go anywhere. Furthermore, the jail is hot and humid. Matt Rootner still hasn't fixed the air conditioning. Constable Packle sits there in his office under a circulating fan, and he sweats. It's cruel and unusual punishment back there in the cells. (Actually I didn't think John-Claude would be too uncomfortable. His remarkable clothes were temperature self-adjusting. He was better off than Ned or his deputies.) "Under the circumstances, we ask for release on his own recognizance."

The judge sat back down. He thought for a while. And we were all thinking, bail could indeed be a problem, for, as we all knew, the Alien had no money at all. (Actually, he had what he *claimed* was money, but it was good only on his home planet, back there on something he called Centaurus. His alleged money was thick gold discs, stamped with the bust of some two-headed chap. No good here, of course. All three hundred of them wouldn't buy you a cup of coffee at Garshmeyer's.)

"How about his vehicle?" asked the judge. "Can't he sell it?"

"We looked into that, Your Honor. Several of the area junk dealers have examined the craft, but not one has shown any interest. The Science Commission of Zurich has called and wants to look it over, with a view to making a bid. They seem to think the shell may be made of something they call 'colonium.' But they haven't arrived yet."

At this point in the proceedings my client seemed to jerk, as though startled by some sudden strange sight or sound. (I heard nothing out of the ordinary, just the continuing white-noise buzz of the courtroom.) Then he rose half-way in his chair and looked back toward the Baronial Box. For a long moment he stared at the visiplate there. Then he straightened out and sat back down again, and when he did, little smiles were dancing on both his faces. Something was going on, of course. I'd probably eventually find out, but just now we had other problems.

The judge looked right down at me and didn't bat an eyelash. "Bail set at one million kroner." He sounded grim and final. High, but then again, the Sixtrees were involved. So much for bail.

I said, "Your Honor?"

He sighed and sat back down again. "What is it, counselor?"

"Regarding jury selection. Under our laws, my client is entitled to a jury of his peers—two-headed people, that is. But there are no two-headed people on our jury rolls. So I move for a change of venue, with the trial to take place on his home planet, which is populated with two-headed people."

"Out of the question. The alleged offenses took place in this Province, and the trial must be held in the situs of the offense. The most I can do for you, both parties agreeing, is to have the matter tried to the court, without a jury."

Clatchett and I looked at each other. Neither wanted to do the other any favors, but we both saw advantages in a juryless trial. We spoke simultaneously. "We agree, Your Honor."

Judge Cloke eyed us suspiciously. Finally he said, "All right, trial set for tomorrow morning, nine o'clock."

And he whirled around and vanished into his chamber, whereupon my chief investigator, young Cassius Reevers, began tugging at my sleeve. I left with him, and Ned Packle returned the prisoner to his cell.

Cass had a tale to tell about the Baron's Box. We went over to Garshmeyer's for coffee while he explained.

3. Spectators in the Box

Cass Reevers explained: His little brother Ben, and Ben's close chum, Dick Kabell, had climbed through the air duct, all the way from the engineering room, across the courtroom ceiling, and down through the intake shaft in the private garage. According to Ben, he and Dick were in fact trying to force the vent grate to get down into the garage when the baronial limo rolled in. They watched from behind the grate, scared but curious.

The garage doors slid shut. The limo door opened, the driver got out, looked all around, then went over to the elevator and punched a button. The elevator door opened. A heavily-veiled woman got out of the car.

"Go on."

"She walked over to the elevator and got in and went on up. The chauffeur got an electro-reader out of his pocket and leaned against the car, and yawned and began to read. Ben and Dick decided to go back the way they had come."

"And—?"

"The woman. She was young. She wore a funny looking veil that came down over both heads." He watched me to observe the effect.

"Two . . . heads?"

"It's true. Dick Kabell tells the same story."

I looked around. Nobody was paying any attention to us. A two-headed Sixtrees woman? Well, there was that rumor . . . But it was supposed to have happened ages ago, when old Burl Dogger was trying to preserve his genes to make a post-humous test-tube baby. The experiment, if you can call it that, may have gone slightly but tragically awry. Something wrong with the baby. Weird rumors, now pretty much buried and forgotten.

"We've got to swear the boys to secrecy," I said.

"I already did. They're now Junior Lizards."

A two-headed lady as a secret spectator in the trial of the century? This in itself invited examination. Who was this strange genetic offshoot of the thorny Sixtrees brambles? Name(s)? Age? Medical reports?

Cass was watching my face as I was thinking about these things. "Boss, I'll look into it. How high can I go?"

I studied him a minute. He studied me right back.

"A hundred kroner. And don't get caught."

Before we left Garshmeyer's I ordered a liter thermos of iced tea. "Take this over to Ned, from us, it might help him through the heat of the day. And tell him, as a personal favor to him, I have invoked a voodoo spell, guaranteed, money-back, and that the AC will surely come back on sometime tonight."

Cass gave me a funny look.

"And one more thing. Right after supper, have your two new Junior Lizards go back down into the courthouse engineering room and put the plug of the air conditioner cord back into its socket."

"Hm. They had to turn it off to get through the fan blades and into the air duct, didn't they?"

"No comment."

"Chief, you did the same thing when you were a kid?"

"Get out of here. We both have work to do."

I remained standing for a moment in front of Garshmeyer's, looking down at the chalk-lined spot where John-Claude's ship had smashed poor Dr. Banchou. It is cruel, and it is sad, but I am bound to report that that outline made a lot of people very happy.

And for Sara? Nothing. She was only an android. The only memorial lines for her were in my head. They would be there a long time.

Cassius Reevers was indeed busy during the night.

On my desk early next morning was a photocopy of a couple of pages of letterheads of the old Cosby Clinic (torn down and replaced by the Lethary Central Hospital before I was born). The pages held writing so nearly illegible it had to be Dr. Cosby's own notes. That would have been Cosby Senior, who brought my father into the world, and who has been long dead.

I made a fairly clean translation with the aid of a Thessaly Interpreter, somewhat as follows.

. . . "She" has one rib cage, three lungs, two hearts, one liver, two gall bladders, two stomachs, one large intestine, one small intestine, three kidneys, one pelvis . . . Above the waistline she is two people; below, one.

"They" have distinct and separate personalities, preferences, tastes. These differences may become more pronounced as she moves into puberty. (Presently ten years old.) Both have IQ's exceeding 200. Total, 400+?

***[Cass's note: "apparently several pages missing"]

. . . there appear to be strong connections between the two brains, but how this is accomplished is not clear. Telepathy, not unusual in twins, has been suggested . . .

There were a few more lines describing the doctor's treatment for what was probably the common cold—acetylsalicylic acid, citrus, bed rest, lots of liquids. It was signed R. Cosby MD with a scraggly date, xx Jan, 2109.

Cass had added a half-page with his own analysis: "Chief, this is absolutely all there is. There is only one two-headed person in Sixtrees history, and that one (and this child) is the lady in the Box."

When I read that I had to smile. Obviously, the report dealt with a two-headed child, born probably in 2098 shortly before Burl Dogger died. If alive today she'd be nearly a hundred. She would not—*could* not—be the mysterious two-headed beauty of the Baronial Box. For once, Cassius, you are wrong.

An invoice was attached to the little packet.

The Lizard
Private Investigator
We Go Places You Wouldn't Dare

To recovery of Cosby documents thought destroyed by the
Clatchetts, at great personal risk and peril................. Kr 100.00

I sighed. Well, maybe Cass The Lizard was worth it. If *I* had tried to get those papers, Ned Packle would have caught me, sure.

But what did all this prove? I couldn't see any immediate connection with the trial. On the other hand Dave Clatchett had evidently ordered all copies of Doc Cosby's report destroyed. Why? He must have had a reason. Keep digging . . .

A word about Dave Clatchett. The Clatchetts have been in the service of the barony for several generations. Some say they have some secret hold on the barony, but nobody can point to anything definite.

Anyhow, some Clatchett or other has always served as overseer for the baronial estates, collecting taxes, auctioning the various Provincial offices, raising dowries for the daughters, keeping the sons out of jail, and so on.

4. Dr. Banchou's Report

Back in January I had learned that Dr. Banchou had written a scientific monograph that referred to a member of the Sixtrees family and that Dave Clatchett had confiscated all copies. And further that Dave's report to Baron Cecil concluded, "We were glad to learn that his kidney condition is terminal."

So who was this Dr. Banchou, who was an offense to the Sixtrees and whose life was accidentally snuffed out yesterday by my client?

We are told that Dr. Dennis Banchou accepted an offer to retire to the Buddhist Monastery in Lethary for several reasons: because the food and lodgings were free; because he loved the loose saffron robes of the monks. Further, since he was already bald, he fitted in effortlessly with the community of shaven heads. And finally and very importantly, he could continue to work on his hominid evolution thesis.

Well now, what was in this monograph that so greatly incensed the Sixtrees and their watchdog? Surely there was *one* copy left, somewhere.

[Note by The Lizard: Three front pages missing.]

One hundred years ago the U.S. nuclear submarine *Minnow* was sailing out to sea past Battery Park, when something went wrong. It detonated and vanished, taking Manhattan, Staten Island, Brooklyn, and much of New Jersey with it. Forty million men, women, and children died instantly. Body parts were found as far east as Boston and in front yards in Milford, Pennsylvania. Traces of the immense dust cloud still circle the globe.

We have heard all this before. See for example, the footnote in Gaskell's *History* (5:3.1) which explains the mechanisms that made the catastrophe inevitable, what with the coffee pot so close to the Destruct Switch. However, save for the consequent radiation, none of that is relevant to this report. As the then American President said, "A tragic accident, but these things happen."

Hominid history shows a sequence of beneficial mutations, each arriving after a period of time shorter than the one before. This acceleration is particularly evident in the last million years. During this period each advance has brought a crucial cultural contribution that enabled each new species to dominate and replace the prior species . . . .

[Some pages missing here.]

And here's the point: *The hominid line is still evolving.*

If evolution of the hominid line were proceeding on normal schedule we should not expect *homo superior* to appear until some fifty to seventy-five thousand years hence. But conditions are not normal. We refer, of course, to the mutagenic radiation from *Minnow,* which early spread to all quarters of the globe.

And so, considering the accelerated pace of the evolutionary process, our successors may be living among us at this very moment. Indeed, he/she may live today in this very Province of Lethary. Evolutionary statistics suggest that the first such child will be a female, as favoring rapid reproduction of the new species. How will we know her? It would appear safe to say that, although *homo superior* (let's call "her" that) will probably possess many physical characteristics in common with us, she will nevertheless *look* different. Within her environment she may even be regarded as somewhat a freak (two heads?), and be kept in seclusion as much as possible. Further, she may be expected to have a prolonged childhood and a delayed maturation, both of which would permit an extended learning process. We might predict puberty at fifty years, adulthood at one hundred, with a fertile maturity perhaps continuing for several centuries. She would probably demonstrate early skills beyond anything possible for *h. sapiens.*

An ever-increasing brain size has always been crucial in successful hominid evolution. But now, for us to evolve even bigger heads with even more gray matter, we encounter a serious problem: the female pelvis is already at its maximum. Bigger infant heads cannot pass through the pelvic cradle. Is hominid big-brain evolution therefore at a dead end? Surely not. We speculate as to physical differences that might achieve increased brain volume. Suppose *h. superior* is conceived with two heads? At birth, first one head passes through the pelvic orifice, then the other, then the rest of the baby. One head with the cranial volume of two heads wouldn't be able to pass through, but *two* heads, *seriatim,* surely could.

What advances will our new *h. superior* bring to the hominid line? We can only speculate. Looking back, "Lucy's" people, *Australopithecus afarensis,* were the bright stars of our hominid ancestry for 900,000 years. But think of the awe with which they might view the crude stone tools of their successors, *homo ergaster!*

The point is, the successor's accomplishments would be beyond the comprehension of their ancestors. And so with us, *homo sapiens,* as we speculate about *homo superior* and her world. When *homo superior* arrives, she will bring with her gifts queerer than we can possibly imagine.

[Note by The Lizard: Here follows a comment evidently in
the handwriting of the Buddhist Abbot, Father Fois-Coeur.]

"Brother Banchou: Naming the two women will certainly bring down on us the wrath of the Sixtrees. I strongly urge that you withdraw the paper."

[The bottom third of the last page of
the document was torn off here.]

Well, it looks like Cass the Lizard is right. There was and is only *one* two-headed Sixtrees, and she was born a hundred years ago, and she is the lady of the Baronial Box.

5. The Cremation of Dr. Banchou

Before we get back to the trial, I'd like to explain how Dr. Banchou was connected to the Fair.

Our Provincial Fair is held in late June and early July in the fields east of Lethary, and climaxes on July 4 in the Square itself. The town overflows, and the excess population finds bed and board in local residences or lives in tents or on the bare ground. The baron takes his share of the Fair proceeds in all sorts of ways, but even after that, there's still generally enough to pay city expenses: the officials, schools, roads, utilities, etc.

Every year on the last day of the Fair, July 4, there is a special event. Last year, we had a man being shot out of a cannon and almost caught in midflight by a myopic trapeze artist. This year the spectacle was to be the cremation of the remains of Dr. Banchou in the Square, with guaranteed visible flight of his soul from the ashes. Front row seats, fifty kroner, bleachers, 5 to 25 kroner, depending on how far up.

Public cremation with visible ascent of soul was certainly a novelty, and the Fair business office sold over twenty thousand tickets even before the Fair opened.

But later on both the City Council and the Fair Trustees agreed that maybe the idea was flawed. Back in January, though, it seemed like a winner. Clearly, the old savant-turned-monk was on his death bed. The mourning friars had given him the last rites and wept copious (lachrymator-induced) tears over the shriveled body. The doctors gave him only hours to live.

But the hours stretched into the next day, and the next day into the next week, and the next week into February. They checked on him daily, but he showed no signs of imminent demise. Quite the contrary. He started putting on weight. From a wizened 80 pounds in January he went to 105 in February. In mid-March he rose from his bed. A week later he made a shaky circuit of the Square. The officials were in despair. To do this to them after all the trouble they had gone to!

For indeed they *had* gone to all kinds of trouble. Just to name one or two problems, they had had to get an Impact Statement from the Provincial Environmental Protection Agency: They would have to do something to mask the odor of burning human flesh. The Buddhists recommended a special oil of mint, and so the Budget Office bought a few kilos of the oil, but then immediately got slapped with an injunction by our prolific resident inventor, Peter Fahrni, who had a patent on this particular mint oil. They settled that for a few hundred kroner, only to encounter another problem, which was the old man's weight. He now weighed 110 pounds. But the Environmental permit covered only 100 pounds, so even if he died right then and there, he could not legally be incinerated. More kroner laid in the proper hands finally fixed *that*.

June came. The retired anthropologist was now jogging around the Square twice a day, yellow robes flapping triumphantly.

One group (headed by Cecil Sixtrees) tried to persuade the scientist to promise to go through with it *live*, in the event he couldn't see his way clear to actually dying in timely fashion. Lord Cecil (who owned the franchise on the front row seats) held up to the little man historic examples of saintly Buddhist monks who dosed themselves with gasoline and lit a match. The candidate listened politely, but said no. The Sixtrees scion referred him to the ancient Hindu ceremony of suttee, wherein surviving widows of the deceased maharajah were burnt alive on the pyre along with their late husband. Girl stuff, said the prospect. No.

Others took over. They tried to awaken in him a dormant loyalty to his Order that had made his comfortable retirement possible. They reminded him that Buddha himself had been cremated. (Perhaps overlooking the fact that the Holy Founder was dead at the time.) They pointed out that thousands of kroner had been spent on advertising the event. They explained how the Fair Band (already in rehearsal) would march around the leaping blazes playing Wagner's Magic Fire music, from *Die Walküre.*

No.

Darker solutions were quietly considered.

A team headed by Lord Cecil drove down to Black River, on the Loosianna border, to consult a famous obeahman. I give here Cecil's report. (Obtained in the usual way.)

> The three of us entered the back room, where we were asked to sit on the floor by a side wall. The room was poorly lit by an oil lantern sconced on the wall opposite us, where an old black man sat on the floor. He lifted his head, and spoke: "Why have you come?"
>
> "We need help," I said. "The Fair climaxes July 4. We had expected the monk Banchou to be dead by then, and we had planned to cremate the body in the Square on July 4. If we cannot do this, the Fair will have to refund a great deal of money. We will be bankrupt."
>
> Dave Clatchett explained further, "So you see, it is important that this very troublesome fellow die in time for his cremation."
>
> The old man said, "So laser him."
>
> We were horrified. I said, "We can't do *that.* It's got to be natural causes."
>
> Our host was silent for a long time. Then he said, "I will need something of his . . . a drop of his blood . . . ?"
>
> "Sir," I said, "that might be hard to get."
>
> "A lock of hair?"
>
> "He's bald."
>
> "Nail clippings?"
>
> "A problem there, too. Isn't there some other way?"
>
> "Alternates, yes. But not always entirely satisfactory. I am a very strong obeahman, but I say to you, beware, you may get your wish, and then some. Shall I go on?"
>
> We had no choice. "Yes, please."
>
> "Very well, you have been warned. Ten thousand kroner."
>
> I handed him my plastic, and he ran it through the counter dangling from his neck as a pendant in a necklace of shark teeth. He returned my card and almost simultaneously he was holding a squawking chicken by the neck. Next, her head seemed to leap from her body in a shower of blood.

He held her with both hands and let the blood spurt down on the sawdust floor. He began to chant something. We finally made it out. "Jooli-duh . . . jooli-duh . . . jooli-duh . . ."

Flickering images formed around the blood drops. Miniature trees? I counted six trees, in two rows of three, the kind a child would have in a play village.

The chanting stopped. Everything was very quiet.

Between the tree rows we could see a tiny bald-headed figure in a yellow robe. He looked up, and just then something resembling a little metal boat seemed to materialize out of nowhere, hovering above the toy figure and the toy trees, and then it dropped with a hard plop and crushed everything beneath it, trees and doll-monk together. And then everything seemed to dissolve into the floor. The witch-man was gone.

We stared. At the time we had no idea what was happening. Later, we understood the little boat-thing was the Alien's ship, and that it had dropped out of the sky and had killed Dr. Banchou. The obeahman had done it all with holograms, of course. But how had he known? We continued to sit there for a while, just peering at each other in the dark. Somebody murmured, "Jooli-duh . . . Juli deux . . . *July two* . . . ? Of course! That's when it will happen!"

"M'lord," Dave Clatchett whispered in a shaky voice, "let's get out of here." We did, fast.

So Cecil brought back a report that reassured most of the Fair trustees. However, just for confirmation, they checked in also with two highly reputable Los Angeles astrologers, both of whom claimed that the holy man would indeed leave this life on July 2, and could thereafter be peaceably and profitably cremated.

Mid-morning of July 2 came, and we must now report a final causative event— the incident that sealed the fate of the scientist-turned-friar.

Peter Fahrni had formulated a pill that allegedly suspended Murphy's Law, which says (you'll recall), if anything can go wrong, it will.

Now, as an inducement to Fairgoers to buy the more expensive front-row box seats to watch the forthcoming cremation, the Committee bought several hundred Anti-Murphy pills and encapsulated a pill with each front-row ticket. You could buy the happy combination in a vending machine in front of Garshmeyer's.

Dr. Banchou, in an ultimate sardonic gesture, bought a ticket to his own cremation (Front Row, Center). He didn't stop there. With a supremely confident sneer (according to witnesses) he tore the Anti-Murphy pill from the ticket and tossed the pill into the gutter.

Ah, woe! It was a challenge even a most indulgent and charitable Fate could not ignore.

In that last moment of his life the old man stepped down from the curb and stood there for a moment thumbing his nose at the pile of wood and the drums of kerosene and the tins of mint oil stacked in the center of the Square. Then he moved aside a little to let Sara pass, and in the next instant he was smashed. Old Doc Turner, our part-time coroner, said it surely happened too fast for him to feel any pain.

6. The Trial Begins

And so, at 9 o'clock on the morning of July 4, the trial of Jean-Claude Berg began. As before, the proceedings played to a packed courtroom. So as not to conflict with the cremation scheduled for noon, the judge had already agreed to recess the trial early.

Prosecutor Clatchett and I bowed with false courtesy to each other, and I noted that the Sixtrees were still surrounding him with big-city talent. At least, I thought, if he fails today he can share the blame.

Shortly after Ned Packle led us in, John-Claude turned around and both of his heads stared up at the Baronial Box, and then both heads nodded and smiled. At what? Was *she* in there, looking down on us? Probably.

Judge Martin Cloke entered. Everybody rose. A couple of warning bangs of the gavel, and everybody sat down again, except me.

I had a preliminary motion. "Your Honor, my client is charged with, and admits, illegal parking. The penalty is three days in jail or a five-kroner fine. Since he has been in jail now for three days, I request the charge be dismissed."

"Agreed," muttered Prosecutor Clatchett.

"That one dismissed," said Cloke. "Next, we have the charge of homicide, in that the vehicle in question fell on the Buddhist friar Dr. Banchou, knocking him down and killing him. Opening statement, Prosecutor?"

I'll skip the opening statements, mine and Clatchett's, both of which were pretty much routine. And now:

Judge Cloke: "Mr. Clatchett, call your first witness."

Prosecutor Clatchett: "I call Mistress Spring Stabler."

According to the police report Spring Stabler, a retired schoolteacher, had been on the sidewalk just a few yards from the event and had seen everything.

The crime of Vehicle Homicide requires that the defendant be positively identified as the man at the controls at the time of the death. As for Mistress Stabler (and in fact for the next several prosecution witnesses), my job was simple: they must not be permitted to identify John-Claude as the driver.

I rose slowly, sadly. I hated to do this, but I had a client accused of murder. "Objection. Mistress Stabler cannot testify."

Clatchett looked genuinely surprised. "And why not?"

"Because," I said, "she is a convicted felon. Under the Rules of Court, a felon may not testify." I walked up to the bench and gave a copy of the record to the judge, then back to the Prosecutor's table with another copy.

"Yes, I remember," said the judge. He looked over at Spring. "A mugger attacked you. You defended yourself with a hatpin, punctured his gut, and he ran away. You were arrested and found guilty of carrying a concealed weapon. I gave you 90 days, suspended. Right?"

"Yes, Your Honor."

"Well, I'm sorry, but you must understand, as a felon, you cannot testify."

She shrugged, turned and left the courtroom. As she passed the defense table she gave me a bitter look. For which I didn't blame her. But nobody said life was fair.

"Next witness?" asked Judge Cloke.

Clatchett gave me an uneasy glance. "I call Evan Byron."

Evan Byron had once been rich, and had given lavishly of his bounty to the community. It was his last gift that had got him into trouble.

"Unacceptable," I said.

"That tax thing?" asked Clatchett.

"Yes." Evan, in a burst of religious generosity, had donated all his assets, down to the last farthing, to the Provincial Tax Board, and had claimed the donation as a charitable gift. But he had gone over the limit deductible for charities, and the excess had been disallowed. The Board demanded that he pay taxes on it. Plus interest and penalties. He couldn't pay. He actually served a year and a day in Hoban Pen for tax fraud.

"Unacceptable," agreed Cloke. "Next?"

"I call Mistress Dollkin."

He led her carefully through the horrifying moments of that morning in front of Garshmeyer's Deli, then turned her over to me for cross.

"Just a couple of short easy questions, Mistress Dollkin." I smiled agreeably, but she wasn't fooled a bit. She looked back at me suspiciously. "You never saw his faces, did you?"

"No, of course not. How could I? He was facing away."

"To be sure. But later, perhaps, you picked him out of a line-up at the Constabulary?"

"A . . . line-up?"

"You know, where they line up six or seven men, have them face away, and take down their pants, and you see if you identify what you saw on July second?"

She blushed deep red. "Oh, you mean, showing their . . . ?"

"Exactly, Mistress Dollkin, showing their respective backsides."

"Oh dear, no!"

"But perhaps Constable Packle showed you his Interpol Mooner File, holos of internationally known mooners?"

"Interpol? No . . ."

"He just said, go on home? He'd let you know when to appear in court?"

"Yes, sir, that's all he said."

I shook my head in wonder. "Nothing further."

"Any more witnesses?" Cloke asked.

Clatchett called Constable Packle. Of course Ned hadn't been an eye-witness, and I wouldn't let him say much on direct. Clatchett gave up and let me have him for cross.

"Constable," I said, "can you drive your car while mooning?"

He thought about that. "No."

"Nothing further," I said.

"Any more witnesses, Mr. Prosecutor?"

"Yes, Your Honor." This time he radiated victory. "I call Mistress Wanda Nagel."

I said, "Your Honor, a preliminary question?"

"Go ahead."

I faced Clatchett. "Mistress Nagel was physically out of the Province at the time of the incident?"

"Quite true. She observed the incident because she had an out-of-body experience that placed her in front of Garshmeyer's Deli at the time. And her OB travel fee is paid up, I might add. Further, though she is registered for OB only in Louisimiss, our respective provinces have a reciprocity agreement that validates her OB travel within our area." He folded his arms and rocked on his heels in cold triumph.

"But," I said, "she didn't arrive OB in time to see the actual incident?"

"No. Her testimony will not be directed to the *happening* of the incident, but to its aftermath. She will testify to what the android, Sara, said in the last seconds of Sara's life."

"Hearsay again? It's inadmissible." I thought that would deflate him. I was wrong.

He smiled in unfriendly fashion. "It's admissible as one of the hearsay exceptions. What the android said was a dying declaration."

Well, I miss one once in a while. Not often. But this one was a big one, and somehow it had slipped through. My esteemed opponent had been saving the best for the last. So I smiled tolerantly as my mind whizzed around and around and tried to dredge up everything I knew about dying declarations.

"Your Honor," I began, "as the learned Prosecutor points out, one of the exceptions to the hearsay rule is the so-called dying declaration. The exception is founded on the premise that a dying person, approaching the gates of Heaven, will not expire with a lie on his lips. Given this, we still have serious threshold problems: Sara was an android, not a human being; she has no expectation of an afterlife and had no deathbed pressures to tell the truth. Her so-called dying declaration fails the basic premise on which the exception is based and is therefore inadmissible." I sat down. Let them chew on *that*.

Judge Cloke thought about it. "Mr. Prosecutor?"

Dave Clatchett rose, gave me his most forgiving smile, and addressed the bench. "Sara was an android, true, but an android with Class-5 AI. She had an IQ of 140. She had an emotional life. She had nobility. In the Richfield mine disaster, she saved lives at risk of her own. She loved life, even as you and I. There is not the slightest reason to doubt that she told the truth. Her statement is clearly admissible." He arched his eyebrows at me and took his seat.

I was immediately on my feet. "Your Honor, even assuming all that, we still have a problem. Admissibility requires that the dying declaration identify the killer. Sara never identified anybody. In fact, so far as can be determined, she never said a word. She died in silence." I sat down.

It took a moment for the judge to digest that. "Now, wait a minute . . . you mean . . . ?"

Clatchett never let him finish. "Your Honor, I must protest counsel's attempt to mislead the court. As counsel well knows, there was indeed a dying declaration. In her last moment, as she lay under the vehicle, her right arm was free, and she held up two fingers, thus." (He demonstrated.) "Obviously, she was telling the world, the killer has two heads." He glowered at me and remained standing.

I laughed. "We certainly applaud Mr. Clatchett's imagination, and I'm sure I can never achieve a fantasy so charming. But alas, we find ourselves tied to the humdrum realities of the real world. There's no evidence that the two-fingered gesture was anything more than the last twitch of an expiring body."

"Two fingers . . . two heads . . . maybe . . ." muttered Cloke, as he studied the Latin phrase on his gavel. When he does this, I know he is flipping through the entries in his Harvard Lexus Implant, with the Updates. In all that, is there a file, 'Androids'? I grit my teeth. We wait.

His Honor sighed, then lifted his eyes and seemed to focus at a point in space over Clatchett's table. This was bad. It meant that he had come to a decision, and it would be for Clatchett. He was going to rule that the android's two-fingered signal was admissible as identifying my client as the driver of the vehicle. (Which of course the prisoner was, but legal proof is quite another thing.)

Cloke said, "There appears to be no reported case involving the dying declaration of an android. Well, then what do we have to guide us? Comparison with human models? Speculative extrapolations? Yes, both. So guided, we conclude that—"

We needed a miracle.

Which my client provided. John-Claude grabbed my sleeve and shouted, "What's that *odor!*"

Everybody gasped and stared at him. Me too. I couldn't think coherently for a few seconds. Then it hit me. The smell was burning mint oil. Which meant—

Judge Cloke banged his gavel a couple of times. "Counselor! Control your client!"

I was on my feet. "Your Honor, it's nearly twelve! They've started the cremation!"

His Honor muttered something. People were already heading for the door. He called out, "Recess until tomorrow morning nine o'clock!"

"All rise," the bailiff intoned to a nearly empty room.

And now my client was behaving very strangely. The eyes in both heads were closed tight. His fists were clenched. Very obviously he was concentrating . . . on *what?* Both pairs of lips were whispering, "Banchou . . . Banchou . . . wake up! *Wake up!*" Sweat formed on both foreheads and their sleeves wiped it away. And then it was over, and they were relaxed, and smiling.

"What was *that* all about?" I asked.

"Better get on out there, Mr. Whitmore," said John. "Don't want to miss the cremation," added Claude.

Clearly, they were teasing me. But they were right, I didn't want to miss the big show. Cass had already left.

And thus the decision on whether Sara's two-finger gesture was admissible as identifying John-Claude as the driver was left hanging. The ruling, when it came, would also bear heavily not only on whether John-Claude was responsible for

Dr. Banchou's death but also for Sara's destruction. Not to mention the question of indecent exposure. My work was laid out for me.

As Ned led John-Claude out of the room, I noticed that my client kept looking up at the Baron's Box, and smiling.

Something was going on, something involving my client and the invisible female occupant of the Box. But no point in thinking about it right now. I had more serious priorities. I had to get back to the office.

7. The Square

At this point let me explain a bit of local geography. The Square, I mean.

Starting with Archives in the northwest corner, we proceed clockwise and in near alphabetical order with the Bar-Del-O, the Buddhist Monastery, the Bus Station, the Catholic Church, the Courthouse, Garshmeyer's, the Jail, Lawyer's Building, License Bureau, Methodist Church, Presbyterian Church, the Unity Church, and on around to the last office, Private Investigations, Tom Dorsey, Prop.

That office has been empty ever since I can remember. Make that *maybe* empty. For the place is supposed to be haunted by the ghost of Tom Dorsey, our first and original and perhaps overly zealous private eye. Tom was found one morning long ago hanging by his neck from a rafter in his office basement. It wasn't suicide. He had been shot three times through the head with heavy-duty lasers, following which, as though to teach him a lesson, he had been strung up.

On a dare I once spent a night in the old building. There were some strange noises, but the ghost never showed. Or if he did, I was asleep. I did a lot of exploring next day with a flashlight. I found old papers, fliers, ads, and so on, that nobody had bothered to clean up.

Here's one:

Tom Dorsey, Private Investigator
On the Square

In litigation? Witnesses provided, prosecution and/or defense, authentic, reliable. Substance-free blood, urine specimens. We can match any DNA.

Substitute papers. More authentic than originals. All documents. Licenses. Passports. Birth, marriage, death certificates. Expert calligraphy.

We can protect you. Guard dogs, clean or rabid. Cobras.

Surplus property discreetly disposed of.

Specialties: Involuntary weddings, Yale locks, undetectable poisons, Harvard diplomas, notarized horoscopes for resumes, collections by kneecap.

Liquidations, clueless but cheap. Let us bid on your contract. Satisfaction guaranteed.

I know now, ninety years later, who killed him, and why. We'll come to that. Let's back up. The Bus Station. Its history for the last hundred years is intertwined with that of the Fahrni family. The story is, the great-grandfather, Eric Fahrni, then a young man, had walked into town looking for work and was tired and was about to sit down on the bench in front of the little building that eventually grew into the Bus Station, when he was distracted by gunfire within the building. Two men staggered out and dropped dead in front of him. At that moment the bus drove up.

A lady stepped over the corpses. "What's the fare to Clarksville?" she asked Eric. "Two-eighty," he said. He knew, because he had read the schedule, and that was where he was eventually headed.

She gave him her kroner card, he slid it through his pocket register and returned it to her.

"Linthicum?" asked the boy behind her.

Linthicum wasn't on the schedule, and Eric had no idea where it was. "One-seventy," he said in his best agent's voice. The boy looked at him funny. "Special rate, today only," Eric explained. The boy paid.

By then Eric knew he was on to a good thing. He called the hearse, had the ex-proprietors hauled away, and put up a sign, Lethary Bus Station, Eric Fahrni, Prop. As we know, he and his descendants prospered. It wasn't long before they bought the bus line, and so on.

Anyway, it's easy to understand why great-grandson Peter could always count on lavish displays of his inventions in the Station. We'd like to report that Peter made a lot of money with them. But we can't. He didn't. Except maybe with his pregnancy testing apparatus, better known as the "P-Machine."

Peter's P-Machine involved nothing really new. As we all know, shortly after a woman's ovum is fertilized, it releases a hormone called "CG"—chorionic gonadotropin, which carries the word that her body is now under new management. CG is what the gynecologists test for, and so does (or did) Peter's P-Machine. The only difference is, his machine reports back within seconds.

Here's how it worked. The woman sticks her index finger into Slot A, where a sterile needle draws a drop of blood, which is mixed automatically with a solution of certain of Peter's unique chemicals. The mixture then gives a reaction, which is either positive or negative, and a little card pops out of Slot B. If the test is positive, the card says "Pregnant," and if negative, "Not Pregnant." Simple, huh?

Well, Peter installed his machine in the Bus Station in time for the Fair of 2185. It had heavy use there and appeared to be at least as accurate as the test offered by the local clinic.

But then came the Fair of last year, 2197. Ms. Hattie MacArthur, a widow of uncertain years, took the test "for fun." She was astonished and alarmed at the result. When she told Constable Packle, her current gentleman friend, Ned fainted and had to take to his bed. Within hours six beaming ladies (including two he didn't know) brought him tuna casseroles, flowers, and offers to sit up with him during the night.

Ms. Hattie was not alone in her agitation. It was high Fair-time, and a lot of girls had sneaked in for the test. Every one received a positive card. Word got around fast. Ned Packle became suspicious when his granddaughter stuck the finger of her doll Bubbles in Slot A and got a positive reading. He took the test himself. He was positive. They then found that all the cards were positive. Pregnant or not, if you took the test, you came out positive.

Who had engineered this ghastly joke? Suspicion fell on various possible culprits: the new Baptist minister (fourteen overnight marriages, where the brides refused to face their regular ministers); Dr. Weinbaum, the gynecologist (the line into his office stretched around the block); the Bus Company (fifteen young men left town the next day and another twelve the day following); and so on.

They were all wrong. The trickster was actually Jed Stark's boy Bitsey, playing around with his new toy printing press. He had replaced all the cards with his own newly printed positives.

Peter closed down the P-Machine, and life in Lethary eventually settled back down into a wary equilibrium.

But I seem to have digressed a bit.

Let's get back to real time and the cremation.

8. Surprises in the Square

I stood for a moment on the Courthouse portico and looked down into the Square. The stands lining the Square hid the crematory pyre in the center of the plaza, where a column of black smoke was rising. I shuddered.

Just then a roar rose up from the crowd. Every man, woman, and child in the stands was on his feet, and screaming. From where I was, their backs were to me and I couldn't see much. I crawled underneath the stands and was soon out into the open. Everybody was yelling and jumping and pointing. What they were pointing at was someone standing bewildered in the center of the pile. The flames hadn't reached him yet.

Then, while everybody was staring goggle-eyed, a familiar figure ran out into the Square and into the flames. He grabbed the creature, tossed him over his shoulder, and dashed out again. In seconds the two were inundated by dozens of eager helpers. The hero was of course Cassius, my ubiquitous assistant, and the man on the death-fire was of course Dr. Banchou.

John-Claude's little space ship had not killed him? Had it merely knocked him unconscious for two days? No. He had been dead, and I mean *dead* dead. And then what? I vividly recalled John-Claude's moment of deep concentration. I remembered their tense repeated command, "Banchou, *wake up!*" Something supernormal was afoot here. And was it just John-Claude, or was that entity in the Baronial Box also part of the act? Too deep for me!

Meanwhile, the crowd, on further reflection, began to mutter. While most individuals congratulated the little monk on his new life, some did not. They had paid good money to see cremation of a holy man, to be climaxed by his soul

rising out of the ashes in the form of a white dove. So where was their cremation? Where was the departing soul?

Lacking a monk (for he had presciently vanished), a group of rowdies looked
about for a substitute. They found Master of Ceremonies Buford Snyder, and
despite his protestations of innocence they began dragging him toward the flames.
But just as they were about to toss him on the fire, the timer on the dove-pen at
the head of the pyre went off, releasing the dove in front of the bullies, and so
startling and confusing them that they dropped Buford, whereupon he escaped
into the crowd and was able to get home, where he stayed locked in his room for
the next several days.

Now, back to Cass. Do you think my factotum extraordinaire got a nice thank-
you note from Dr. Banchou? No. A "local hero" write-up in the *Lethary Lancet*?
No, not that either. What he got was, arrested by Deputy Constable Bubba Cauker
for interfering with a licensed civic event. I followed as Bubba led Cass off to jail in
handcuffs. This was Bubba's first arrest, and the young deputy was very proud of it.
Fortunately Chief Constable Packle was there. Ned didn't want to overrule his deputy,
but we arrived at a solution that saved face all around. Cass promised he would
never again rescue anybody from a burning funeral pyre, and they let him go.

I had to figure out what to do next. Since there had been no homicide, there
was no longer any reason to hold my client. We headed back into the cells.

John-Claude knew I was coming, of course. But when I told him I'd have him
out in an hour, he just laughed. John said, "And then what? Where would we go?
Rooms are sold out all over town. It's comfortable here. Another night won't hurt."
Claude added, "Anyhow, you need to get to work on that big damage claim."

He had a point.

And now they both gave me a hard serious look. "But before you go," John
said, "tell us, what, exactly, is this 'rule against perpetuities'?"

That one floored me.

"You've been thinking about it in connection with the trial," Claude said.

I took a long deep breath. "It involves a delayed transfer of property, like by
gift during life, or a bequest after death. Vesting must take place within a life in
being plus twenty-one years, or the transfer is void."

"As in Burl Dogger's will?" said John. "He willed almost his entire estate to a
male child—who turned out to be Lord Harry." "To vest on his twenty-first
birthday," added Claude.

"True," I said. This was getting interesting. "But before the twenty-one years
could run, there was a 'life in being,' namely the child who was conceived one
hundred years ago *in vitro*—by artificial means, that is."

"Mary-Louise Sixtrees," said John.

Now *that* was a very intriguing statement. Where had they got the information? Especially that name. Almost certainly from the lady in the Baronial Box.
Which merely confirmed that which I strongly suspected by now, that he—or
she—or both—or all four—were telepathic. I shrugged. "So it is rumored."

"Now, for the bequest to be valid, was it essential that she be alive at Burl's
death?" asked Claude.

"Well, yes. Or at least *conceived.*" I was beginning to see where this was going. "If there was a gap between Burl's death and Mary-Louise's conception, Clause One of the will fails."

"But *why?*" asked John. Claude echoed, "*Why* must Mary-Louise have been conceived before Burl died for Lord Harry to inherit?"

I shrugged. "It's supposed to make for clarity and predictability. There has to be a designated life in being at the time the will speaks. It goes way back into the foundations of English common law. If there was a life in being, the bequest was valid."

"Well then," said John, "if valid, Clause One gave Sara to Harry Sixtrees."

"But if *not* valid," said Claude, "he did not receive title, nor do his descendants, and the Sixtrees have no case. Right?"

"A correct statement of the law," I said, "but we have no proof of any such time gap. So forget it." I rose to go.

"Wait," John said. "Mary-Louise tells us there *is* proof . . . a record—she thinks an old video cassette—that the Clatchetts keep hidden away in the Archives."

"It's their hold over the barony," added Claude. "A sort of blackmail."

Just then I had a very strange thought: I recalled Lord Cecil's visit to the voodoo man, and the image of the little ship crushing not only the miniature monk figure, but also the six trees.

"She knows where they keep it," said John, "and she'll help you get it."

That didn't make any sense. "Now wait a minute. She's a Sixtrees. Why should she take our side against a kinsman?"

Cassius had been listening quietly. He now made his contribution. "Boss, if you can ask that, you just haven't been paying close attention."

Oh? I stopped a moment and studied the faces of my client(s). *Oho!* He was right. These . . . *four* . . . were in love. Good God! "Right," I said weakly. "Right, so *how* can she help us?"

"Early tomorrow morning," said Claude, "you'll find her in the baronial garage. Meet her there at eight. You know how to get in."

"Yes. But we're due in court at nine. Can't she start earlier?"

"She'll be busy all night," John said cryptically.

Doing what? I wondered. No answers, of course.

"The Archives are next door to the garage," said Claude. "She knows a way through the vents into the back rooms."

"Got it." And I was also thinking, meanwhile I still had a bit of research to do.

"For which you have the rest of the night," observed John cheerfully. He was the humorist of the pair.

So Cass and I started back to the office together. The Square was still in a turmoil. And we noted a very interesting sight. The Sixtrees chauffeur walked up to the row of mint oil cans, grabbed a three-liter tin by the handle, and nonchalantly walked away with it. Amazing. Why? Certainly not for himself. This was surely on orders of his mistress.

And so, as we weaved through the crowd in the general direction of my office, I was asking myself some new questions.

Had Jean-Claude asked Mary-Louise to get the mint oil? Was it perchance the exact oil he needed for his ship? I could go back and ask him, of course. But just now I didn't want him to suspect that I suspected anything. Maybe I should just ignore the whole thing. But no—that oil. It was important to my client, and I wanted to know how and why. Where to start?

I recalled the description he had provided for his oil, the stick figure he had drawn, "man-on-one-leg." Meaning what? I didn't know. Maybe I'd get some hints if I did some research.

And now about my office. It's on the second floor of the Lawyer's Building, between Elshea's Beauty Parlor and Ben's Shoe Repair. You enter a reception room, where you're greeted by Grazia, our built-into-the-wall frozen-face android. Beyond is a hall, and the first door on the right is our info room, where we have all the standard junk: terminals for hitting the Webnet, VR and holo demos, sample jury box. Next, into the conference room, then the library (mostly disc loads), and on into a machine and tool room. Down the hall again, to Cass's cubicle, more like a closet, with desk and chair. By certain contortions of his long legs he can lean the chair back, prop his feet on the desk, and take a nap and/or read one of his genuine paper comic books.

So now we are in the info room, and I am sitting at a terminal, and thinking. In court this morning John-Claude had been the first to notice the odor of burning mint oil. He almost certainly recognized the odor. So now, just to confirm something, I punched some keys and called up the negotiations of the Fair Trustees with Peter Fahrni in the patent infringement action involving the mint oil. Cass hovered over my right shoulder and watched with great interest.

First there were just a lot of words bouncing back and forth, the formal complaint, the formal answers, the subpoenas, motions, interlocutory decisions . . . and finally, what I was really looking for, the patent.

I scrolled the text carefully, line by line. Aha! And there it is, the structural formula of this special mint-scented oil:

$$
\begin{array}{c}
CH_3 \\
| \\
CH \\
H_2C \diagup \quad \diagdown CH_2 \\
| \qquad\qquad | \\
H_2C \diagdown \quad \diagup CHOH \\
CH \\
| \\
CH \\
H_3C \diagup \quad \diagdown CH_3
\end{array}
$$

I sighed. "That can't be John-Claude's oil."
Cass grinned. "Oh, yes, it is."

I hated it when he did this. I didn't look up. We both waited. I gave in. "Cass—"

"Just turn it upside down."

I pushed the rotate key. And sure enough, there it was, the two-headed man on one leg. "Thank you," I said coldly. Everything fell together now. I continued, "Her chauffeur stole a can of oil, and I'll bet he's headed for the Impound Lot right now."

"Not exactly, chief. Forget the chauffeur. Yeah, he took the oil, but he's out of it now. He gave the oil to *her*. *She* has it, and *she's* headed for the Impound Lot."

"The ship is heavily guarded."

"So what? She's Mary-Louise Sixtrees."

I nodded. "She'll fill the control cup, but she won't take the ship. Not yet, anyhow?"

"Right. She has to clear John-Claude first."

I told him, "You might as well go on home. Before you go, though, would you get me a Fahrni Flashlight Kit."

That puzzled him. My turn to grin. "I'll be here a while. Early tomorrow morning I'll be out there somewhere with Ms. Mary-Louise. See you in court."

9. Some History

After Cass left I sat there thinking. I ought to go on home, too. Get a little sleep, get up early and be back at 8. Except that the adrenalin was still pumping, and I knew I wouldn't be able to sleep. So I would simply sit here in front of the TV, review things in my mind, maybe doze a little. Better set the alarm. Next time I'm up.

I let my mind idle along, thinking about Mary-Louise Sixtrees and her very odd ancestry. Her father, old Burl Dogger, died before she was born. And her mother, Lady Ditmars? We knew little or nothing about her. Not that it matters now. Save for Mary-Louise they're all long dead.

Also I'm thinking about my own family history. My maternal ancestors, the Moncriefs, owned a lot of land on the outskirts of Lethary, but lost it all during the Border Wars. Bluntly put, Burl Dogger, the first Baron Sixtrees, just plain stole it by force of arms, all under a thin veneer of legality. I'll get back to him shortly. But first, some more history.

The Border Wars didn't start as a secession. No, in the beginning, it involved an expulsion. Who was first? Some say it was Mississippi, some say Montana, some swear it was Texas. (I claim it was Montana, and that's how I'm telling this.) The story was that the town militia refused to let FBI agents arrest Mrs. Sadie Barrow for unlicensed possession of a starter's pistol, which she used to scare crows in her corn field. Worse, she had a bad attitude. Well, there had been a lot of such incidents lately, and this time the Federal Government was determined to do something about it.

The United States Senate voted to expel the offending state from the United States of America. (A surprise: Montana's two senators and all Montana congressmen likewise voted for the Expulsion.)

That was sort of like breaking a log jam. After that, there was an Expulsion vote every few days, often brought on motion by the state in question. The end came when neither house of Congress could muster a quorum. And so the Union died.

As might be expected, there was at first a bit of looting and vandalism in the ex-capital. The great bronze statue of J. Edgar Hoover (in his famous drag disguise) was toppled from its pedestal in front of the FBI building. Washington's homeless moved from the streets into the mostly vacant federal buildings. For fuel that winter they chopped down the sacred cherry trees lining the Tidal Basin, and they had a tendency to burn the wood in ancient fireplaces that had long been sealed up. Several buildings were lost this way, including the White House.

Of course today, a hundred years later, everything has long been cleaned up, and Washington is again a beautiful international tourist attraction. The White House is back, completely rebuilt and restored. Operated by a Japanese syndicate, it is now one of the best hotels on the East Coast.

At the beginning, though, there were border skirmishes, all kinds of trouble, fighting, chaos. Blood flowed. When things finally quieted down my ancestors found they weren't living in the State of Oklahoma anymore. No, it was now the Province of Lethary. Oh, it had *some* of Oklahoma, and some of what used to be the State of Arkansas, and it had lost a lot of land to what used to be the State of Texas.

The Moncriefs woke up to find that they no longer owned oil fields, acres of alfalfa, cattle, and such as that. No, somehow, legally or otherwise, it had wound up in the bloody hands of old Burl Dogger. Not satisfied with stealing those things, he then took "Sixtrees" as his new baronial name. Now "Sixtrees" was what the Moncriefs called their big manor house west of Lethary. It was named after the six big oaks at the gate house. This was bald insult laid on mayhem and theft. A Moncrief killed Burl's son in a duel, and that seemed to bring the feud to a festering conclusion. No, one thing more. In Burl Dogger's will, he bequeathed the Dogger dung heap to mother's grandfather, Bascomb Moncrief.

But to conclude my thoughts about history, the atomized country did in fact finally coalesce back together as the very loose Confederation of Provinces, and the penitent prodigals became almost law-abiding.

Back to Burl Dogger. What was he doing before he came to Lethary? The records show he was released from prison under the general amnesties of 2068, when most provinces, bankrupted by the Border Wars, decided it was cheaper to turn the criminals loose than feed them.

Burl found employment as a driver for the Borzoi Transportation Company, in which capacity he was able to notify his old gang as to shipments of payrolls, valuable cargoes, and so on. Yep, just as in the Old West.

On this particular day Burl was driving Coach Number Three, Tulsa to Houston. He had only one passenger, a young woman named Karen Bight, who was thought to be carrying a map showing a valuable mineral deposit. A few hours into the route Burl pulled into a side field just west of Lethary, and there he was met by his associates.

They searched Ms. Bight. No maps were found. The frightened courier explained that it was actually a cranial implant, readable only on a special scanner in Houston. They could remove the implant, but if they tried to read it with a commercial scanner it would self-destruct.

The conspirators conferred. Zilch Clatchett, their intellectual (having almost finished fourth grade), pretty much verified Ms. Bight's evaluation of the situation. They conferred some more. They couldn't go on to Houston. They couldn't turn Karen loose. So they sort of settled down right where they were, hoping that one day they could find a suitable reading machine, and meanwhile turning their activities toward more profitable enterprises, such as robbing my ancestors.

They never did find a proper reading machine, and when Karen died giving birth to Roark they buried her in an unmarked grave.

While I'm thinking these deep historical thoughts I punch the remote to the local news channel. I'm looking for "Midnight" Madison, our very own anchorman.

Here he is, in living holo, nonchalant, vaguely contemptuous. "A group of famous scientists arrived last night. Of course everything in Lethary is full up on account of the Fair, and so they had to take rooms in Mrs. Cotly's Bed and Breakfast, way over in Glendale. They finally rented a car (actually, Vincent Finewater's second hearse) at considerable expense, and eventually showed up at the jail and demanded to see our two-headed prisoner, who calls himself—or *them*selves?—John-Claude Berg. Ned Packle turned them away.

"The leader of the visiting scientists is, or rather *was*, Dr. Berzelius Aston, Director of the International Space Agency. It is our understanding that it was he who first suggested that the ship is made of colonium. We are told that Dr. Aston tried various ways to obtain a tiny sample of metal from the ship, but to no avail. This reporter has further been informed that when Dr. Aston's bribe offer of ten thousand kroner for a piece of the ship was refused in turn by Ned Packle, Judge Cloke, and the City Council, Dr. Aston broke down right there in the Council conference room and had a fatal apoplectic fit. Luckily, their rented hearse was waiting at the curb."

Midnight shakes his head, continues. "Why is colonium so important? Let's find out. I turn you over now by recent file tape to Dr. Henry Strope, our science editor.

Dr. Strope: "Between 2175 and 2195 the International Space Agency launched twenty-three probes built of the strongest known metal alloy and equipped with the new Delmar drive. Seventeen were sent toward next-door Alpha-Centaurus, four toward distant Rigel, and two toward the Andromeda Nebula.

"Hours after launch, each ship shifted into maximum velocity of two-thirds the speed of light. During the first day each reported good hourly progress. During the second day, however, each began to report problems. A meteorite the size of a marble, moving at a relative velocity of 200 km/second, had blasted away the fuel tank of Number One. For Number Two it was the gyroscope. In Number Three the hydraulic system. By the third day radio feedback had vanished for all ships.

"All space scientists agree that for such speeds a much stronger, more resilient shell is essential. Specifications have been drawn up, and it is now apparent that no such metal has ever existed, and perhaps in fact cannot exist. No matter. They call it 'colonium' and keep looking."

I yawn.

". . . all . . . agree that only a ship built of . . . colonium can survive interstellar flights . . . zzz . . . zzz . . . zzz . . ."

"Bill Whitmore! Wake up! Five minutes of eight! Get over here!"

"Wha—? Who?" I was *asleep?*

The screen is projecting a miniature holo of a very pretty two-headed lady. (And I still don't know how she did it.)

I jump up. "On the way!"

10. In the Archives

At that moment my office door opened and Cass walked in. "Chief . . . ?"

"Overslept," I mumbled.

He blew on his electric shaver, then tossed it to me.

I was quickly becoming almost alert. "Cass, nine o'clock you go into court and try to stall the proceedings until I arrive with Mary-Louise and the tape. Maybe. Go!" I ran.

On the way out I picked up the Fahrni Flashlight Kit, which he had indeed found somewhere and left for me. Cass, you did good. What I also needed was a cup of coffee. But at least I can shave, approximately.

Three minutes later I scrambled out of the air duct and onto the floor of the Baronial garage, and there they were.

And that's how I met the mythical Lady Mary-Louise Sixtrees.

She was a very beautiful woman, nearly as tall as I, erect, marvelous figure. One head was blonde, the other brunette, and each was coiffured in its own individual style.

I got to my feet and bowed deeply. "Milady, I'm Bill Whitmore, John-Claude's attorney. Call me Bill. And I have lots of questions."

The blonde said, "I'm Mary. She's Louise. Thank you for coming, Bill." She held out her right hand, and we shook hands. Then she held out her other hand. A tiny white pill nestled in the palm. "Caffeine," said Louise.

Remarkable. I took it and swallowed it with spit.

Mary said, "There'll be time to talk later. Right now we have to go into the air duct system. This way."

I handed her a flashlight from my kit and climbed up right behind her into the duct. She led the way on hands and knees in the wavering darkness.

"Through here," said one of them. We stirred up clouds of dust as we climbed down into a dim-lit room. I looked about quickly. It was filled with rows of metal filing cabinets. I sensed intuitively that the crucial tape would not be trusted to such commonplace surroundings.

Did they know where it was, I wondered. And if they did know, *how?* Maybe they had touched the mind of the Chief Archivist, the ancient but indomitable Nora Clatchett?

Mary-Louise had evidently been following my unspoken question. "Tom Dorsey, the P.I., told us about it," Mary said. Louise added, "We were about ten years old at the time."

Huh? "I thought he was murdered a few months after you were born."

"True," Mary agreed. "But his spirit . . . ghost? . . . was still around," Louise said. "He talked to us a lot. Still does. The Clatchetts killed him, you know, when they caught him sniffing around here. They knew what he was after."

"What *was* he after?"

"Same thing we are," said Louise, "the tape that proves I was conceived *after* old Burl died. Tom told us, if that ever came out, it would invalidate the will."

"Shh!" We were now in the central file room, and we had to be quiet. I guess we were not quiet enough.

A thin scratchy voice called out, "Who's there?" Simultaneously a laser beam swept the cluster of filing cabinets that sheltered us. It was of course the Chief Archivist, Nora Clatchett.

I called out, "Ms. Clatchett? Lawyer Bill Whitmore over here, with Lady Mary-Louise Sixtrees."

A dim light came on in the general area of our interrogator, revealing the bent form of a very old woman. In one hand she held a flashlight, in the other a hand weapon. "How did you get in? Well, no matter, you'll have to go. Nobody permitted back here, not even you, milady. So go on, now, both of you." She took a couple of steps toward us. We were now about three meters apart. Although our row of filing cabinets offered a considerable measure of protection for our chests, I took uneasy notice that her weapon was pointed at my head.

"Ms. Clatchett," I said reasonably, "this is an emergency. We need a cassette, which we believe is in your files."

"What cassette?"

"A video record of my conception," Mary said.

The archivist started, and her eyes seemed to widen briefly. "No . . . no . . . We have no such record. Now go. Get out, or I will shoot you both."

I whispered to my companion, "When I jab your arm, duck down and cover your eyes with your hands. Understand?"

They whispered back, "Of course."

And here I must pause, and take a moment to describe the Fahrni Flashlight Kit that I carried strapped around my waist. Actually it was just a canvas bag with four pockets.

Go back five years, when Peter Fahrni made a survey of one hundred Lethary households, asking: "How many flashlights do you have to have in order to be sure to find *one?*" He got answers ranging from 1 to 5. He added up all the answers, divided by 100, and came up with 3.3. Statistically speaking, if the home owner was to be certain of finding one flashlight, he needed to keep 3.3 flashlights in the house. Whereupon Peter offered for sale his famous Flashlight Kits, which contained 3 whole flashlights plus 3/10 of a third. ("A flashlight always guaranteed at hand!") We accepted his statistics but not his Kits. To his astonishment they were unsaleable. So he finally gave them away, which is how I had this one.

And here it gets interesting. The flashlights were laser-powered, of course, and it was a fact that 3/10 of a unit, if held in a certain interlocking way against the base of a whole flashlight, will drive the wattage way beyond the rated capacity of the unit. And *then*—

I jabbed Mary-Louise in the arm. We ducked down behind the filing cabinet and bent our heads and covered our eyes. I lifted the superpowered flashlight over the cabinet and pointed in the general direction of Nora Clatchett. The beam exploded in a blast of light.

The blinded archivist howled in pain and fired her weapon several times, but didn't really come close to us. Then she sank down near the wall and lay there, sobbing.

Mary-Louise and I got to our feet. "She'll recover in ten or fifteen minutes," I said. "We don't have much time."

The room was still vaguely luminous from residual laser activation. We picked our way over to the fallen crone, and I relieved her of her necklace of keys and her little weapon. She barely noticed.

"This way," Mary said. We proceeded on back.

Louise pointed to a metal door. "Through there. The cassette is in a safe in that room."

I tried a couple of keys before I found the right one. The lock responded with protesting squeaks. I reached for the door handle.

"Wait," Mary said. She cocked her head, as though listening. "Tom says, if we do it wrong, the door explodes."

"Tom?"

Louise explained, "Tom Dorsey." Mary added, "He's been with us all along." If they said so . . . "All right, what does he recommend?"

Louise said, "First you *push* on the handle, *hard*. Push, Bill."

I did. We heard a faint metallic click from somewhere inside the door. "*Now* pull," they said in unison.

I pulled. The door creaked and groaned and swung out. A tiny fluor light came on somewhere. We brushed away some spider webs and cautiously stepped inside.

"Nora's awake," said Mary. "And she's calling the police," Louise said.

They shone their flashlight around the room. It was a small chamber, about four meters square, bare except for the formidable-looking safe that sat in the middle. I took a step toward it.

"*Wait up!*" Their mutual command was explosive.

I froze.

Mary explained, "Tom says this is where he got killed."

Oh, fine. I thought of the three holes in his skull.

"We can deal with it," soothed Louise. "Tom says, there are three motion-sensitive lasers, two in the walls, one in the ceiling. Once fired, they require three minutes to recharge. So here's what you do." "Take off your jacket," continued Mary, "wad it up, throw it at the safe."

Which I did. And it got blasted with three beams before it hit the safe.

"Come on in," they said.

I studied the iron cube. "What's the combination?"

"We don't know," Louise said. "However—" Mary began.

Just then we heard a series of muted bell-like tinglings coming from inside the safe. I said, "I believe Nora has just now booby-trapped it."

"Quite right," agreed Mary. "Just touching the safe," said Louise, "will detonate a bomb. This could be a problem."

I thought about that and the equally drear facts that the three guard lasers were merrily recharging and that anyway nobody knew the combination. "It's all over?"

"Not necessarily," Mary said. Louise added, "We need a moment with Tom Dorsey and John-Claude. Don't worry, we can figure this out."

One hundred and ten seconds for a five-way telepathic conference that included a ghost. I waited.

"All right," Mary said. "We have it. Stand over here, please." Louise pointed to a spot in front of the safe. Mary continued, "John-Claude and we are going to warp time. Recall the sequence a century ago, in the original scenario. The safe door stands open. The Chief Archivist places the cassette inside, then the bomb, then closes the safe door and gives the dial a couple of turns. So we think there will be about ten seconds when the cassette is in the safe with the door open, before the bomb is inserted. During those ten seconds you must reach in and take the cassette."

Louise tried to reassure me. "You'll not be touching the safe in real time. The bomb won't blow."

"Do you understand?" They peered up at me earnestly in the dim shifting light.

"Yes." Meaning, I knew what to do, but *how* they were going to do it, I hadn't the foggiest idea. The only thing I was sure about, if I fouled up in the next 30 seconds, the bomb would detonate. In real time. And if the bomb didn't get me, the lasers probably would.

"Get ready," Mary said. "At the count of three, reach in and *grab*. One . . . two . . . *three.*"

It was insane. It was impossible. In a jerky nervous motion I reached back a hundred years and into the blurry outlines of unsolid iron. I grasped a little oblong box. "Got it!" I jumped back.

At that instant three laser beams intersected where my head had just been. Their meeting point glowed a dazzling blue, then vanished with an audible "pop."

"Let's go!" said Mary.

Oh, I was ready! I held the cassette carefully in one hand as we scrabbled along. "There's something—an envelope?—taped to the box . . . What—"

"We think we know what it is," said Mary. "We think it may be Karen Bight's implant," finished Louise. "The guide to the lost mineral deposit."

"Can you ladies decrypt it?"

"No," said Mary, "but we think we know who can." "May we have it, please?" added Louise.

"Of course." I tore the envelope off the cassette, felt something hard and needle-like, and handed it to them. "If you can decode it, I'd like a copy."

"You'll be the first."

John-Claude had known we were coming, of course, and when Mary-Louise and I pushed into the courtroom through the side entrance it didn't really sur-prise me that he was standing and looking towards the opening door. I stood there a moment with her.

John-Claude stared at her and she stared back, and then a weird blue light *crackled* between the two, and they laughed softly, in a strange shimmering quartet. And then it was over.

Love at first sight, I thought. But which one is in love with which one? None of my business!

John-Claude (both of him, that is) grinned, turned around, and sat down again at the defense table facing Judge Cloke—who was staring at us wide-eyed, like most everybody else in the room.

At first all was silence. Then you detected a few raspy breaths. And then the whispers, and then the muted exclamations.

I left Mary-Louise at the witness bench next to Cassius, who carefully did not stare at her, and then I proceeded on past the bar and took a seat at the defense table next to John-Claude. He reached back over the bar and for a moment they held hands.

11. The Tape

By now Judge Cloke had pretty much recovered. "Counselor, we congratulate ourselves that you are finally able to join us."

I stood up. "My apologies, Your Honor. Extenuating circumstances."

"Well, let's get on with it. You had a motion, I think?"

As planned I began our third day in court with a couple of motions. "Your Honor, the court is asked to take judicial notice that Dr. Banchou is still alive and that there was therefore no homicide. Accordingly I move that the charge of homicide be dismissed and that Mr. Berg be released from prison."

"Agreed," mumbled Clatchett.

"So ordered," said Cloke.

I continued. "Also, Your Honor, since there was no homicide, Sara's two-fin-ger gesture is not a dying declaration identifying a killer, and is therefore *not* an exception to the hearsay rule, and is inadmissible. And since there is no other evidence identifying my client as a mooner, I move that the charge of indecent exposure be dismissed."

Clatchett shot me a venomous look. "The People concur, Your Honor."

"The charge of indecent exposure is dismissed," said Cloke. "And now, let's see, what does that leave us?" He peered at his case folder. "Yes, the civil case, Sixtrees versus Berg, destruction of property, to wit, the android Sara, valued at ten thousand kroner. For plaintiff—?"

Clatchett's companion stood. "I'm J. Killian Murfree, Your Honor, Chicago Bar. I will represent Lord Sixtrees, with Mr. Clatchett as co-counsel."

"Opening statement, Mr. Murfree?"

"Yes, Your Honor. Under the law, identification of the driver is unnecessary. Liability attaches to the vehicle and its owner—both already stipulated by Mr. Whitmore as Mr. Berg. The only questions remaining are proof of value and how Mr. Berg proposes to pay." He gave me an exotically wicked leer.

"Your Honor," I said, "the plaintiff claims a value of ten thousand kroner, and we will so stipulate."

This astonished both judge and opposing counsel. "So how can he pay?" blurted Cloke.

I smiled amiably. "There's nothing to pay, Your Honor. My client owes the plaintiff nothing. In fact, the plaintiff has no standing to sue for the loss of Sara. He does not own Sara. He never did."

"This is absurd," cried Murfree. "We trace ownership back to the will of Lord Burl Dogger Sixtrees."

"Your Honor," I said meekly, "may I please go forward with my client's case?"

"And it had better be good," growled Cloke. "And I mean, really good."

"Of course, Your Honor. So, with the court's permission, let me start with a bit of well-known history."

"Objection," grumbled Murfree. "Irrelevant."

"Relevance will be clear, if I am permitted to continue."

"Go ahead," Cloke said.

"The story that I am going to tell is well-known, a tradition firmly established in the annals of our community. It is not offered in evidence as facts, but simply as a background for matters that will be offered later on in evidence."

"Most irregular," mumbled Murfree.

I ignored him. "In his closing years Burl Dogger gave considerable thought as to who should succeed him in the barony. Roark, his son by Karen Bight, had been killed in a duel with Giles Moncrief, who had then prudently disappeared. Roark left three daughters. There could be no more sons with Karen; she had died in giving birth to Roark.

"Burl remarried. He expected that his second wife, the Lady Ditmars, would give him a son. But five years passed, and no children at all. His thoughts turned back to Roark's three daughters, now grown. So how about grandsons, or even great-grandsons? *But* (the lawyers told him) you can't delay transfer of the property indefinitely. The law gives you a fixed term within which the transfer must vest—within a life or lives in being plus twenty-one years. It's called the Rule against Perpetuities.

"That was fine with Burl. The life in being could be the life of any of his children with Ditmars. Make it (he said) the first male descendant born during the life or lives of my children with Ditmars, and when he reaches 21, he gets it all."

Dave Clatchett yawned loudly; the judge shot him a warning glare.

I continued. "But, they said, the Lady Ditmars has no children. We're still trying, Burl said. Also (he explained) I have a deposit at the Sperm Bank. If she and I don't have a child in the usual way, I'll give her a test tube baby. Preferably male, but it really makes no difference. If the baby is male, he takes the barony. If female, surely Roark's line will eventually give us a boy."

J. Killian Murfree stood up, opened his mouth, got an imperious signal from His Honor, sat down again.

I said, "And with that explanation, it's easy to understand the rather involved language of the will. Clause One says, 'I devise and bequeath the properties listed in Appendix A to the first of my male descendants to reach 21 and born during the life or lives of my children by the Lady Ditmars.' Appendix A listed the entire assets of the barony except for one item, stated in Clause Two. In Clause 2 Burl revenges the death of son Roark. We'll get to that.

"But now, back to the old baron. He lies on his deathbed. The succession is now an urgent matter. They review the will. The lawyers suddenly realize that none of the several living male contenders qualify. Why not? Because none were born during the life of a child of the Lady Ditmars, for indeed Ditmars has had no children. But how about future heirs? It is indeed the eleventh hour, but the hole can still be plugged if they act quickly."

The room had become very quiet. Clatchett and Murfree had turned toward me and were listening intently.

I went on. "And so history tells us that a test-tube baby, whom we know today as Lady Mary-Louise, was duly conceived and born, and that when she was five years old, Lord Harry was born to Roark's second daughter, and that twenty-one years later, with all legal requirements apparently satisfied, he succeeded to the estate and the title. All that was nearly a hundred years ago. Today Lord Cecil alleges ownership by descent."

"Alleges?" whispered Murfree loudly. Cloke quickly shushed him.

I gave the visiting lawyer a nice smile. "Those are the events that explain the language of Clause One of the will. We now turn to Clause Two. As we know, Appendix A to Clause One inventoried all assets except one. That one exception is stated in Clause Two."

I looked up at the judge. "For a clear understanding of this exception I will ask that the court take judicial notice that there was a history of bad blood between the Moncriefs and the Doggers, and that the feud climaxed when Giles Moncrief killed Roark Dogger in a duel."

"Objection," Mr. Murfree called out. "All ancient history. None of this is relevant."

"It's highly relevant," I said. "It explains Clause Two of the will."

"I'll let it in," said Cloke.

"Thank you, Your Honor. Clause Two, the second and final grant in the will, simply says, and I quote, 'I give to my dear friend Bascomb Moncrief all the rest and residue of my estate.' Sounds like a lot, doesn't it? Well, we ask, what did the 'rest and residue' consist of? The answer is simple. It consisted of the only piece of property that old Burl did *not* list in Appendix A, to wit, a heap of barnyard manure, piled up against a fence on Barham Road." I set my jaw grimly. "Revenge was sweet. 'Dear friend' indeed!"

Murfree was on his feet. "Your Honor, there's really no need to take this any further. Counsel himself has traced the chain of title of our unfortunate android. Ownership is not in doubt. I move for summary judgment."

I laughed at him. "Your Honor, as to chain of title, learned counsel is absolutely right. But he errs as to where the chain terminates. I am not done. May I continue?"

"Please do." Cloke looked bemused. "And start making sense."

"Of course. Simply stated, Clause One of the will violates the Rule against Perpetuities and is therefore invalid."

I had thought the statement might bring on another period of dead silence; I was wrong. Clatchett had a sudden loud coughing spasm. Judge Cloke just stared at me, wide-eyed, open-mouthed.

I looked up at him almost apologetically. "Our Provincial Code 2112 adopts the rule and states it succinctly: 'No interest is good unless it must vest, if at all, not later than twenty-one years after some life in being at the creation of the interest.' " I looked over at Lawyer Murfree and smiled. He did not smile back. He just looked puzzled. As did most everybody else. A long steady buzz in the courtroom.

The judge tapped his gavel on the bang-plate. "Counselor, would you kindly explain *why* you think Clause One violates the Rule?"

"It involves the '*life in being*,' Your Honor, also called 'the measuring life.' It's a very crucial requirement in this type of postponed vesting. First and foremost, that life had to be identified. And here it was identified as the child of Burl and Ditmars, the Lady Mary-Louise Sixtrees, whom we had all presumed to have been conceived prior to Lord Burl's death. That's what the old baron and his lawyers were counting on, over one hundred years ago. If that's true, then certainly Clause One of the will would appear valid. But—is it true? We think not."

I paused to catch my breath. Cloke and the other lawyers realized that I had finally come to the point. They were listening and frowning. I let them stew a few more seconds, and then I continued.

"We have mentioned Burl's deposit in the Sperm Bank. It's a matter of undisputed history that it was to be used if Burl was dying and had no children then alive. The sperm was to fertilize *in vitro* an egg taken from his very young wife, Lady Ditmars, and returned to her uterus. This would have given the lawyers a life in being during which the hoped-for male heir would be born. That was the expectation. It failed. We now examine how it failed."

Clatchett and Murfree stood up together. Cloke made a slicing motion across his throat. They sat down.

I said, "I offer in evidence a certified copy of the report of the Sperm Bank laboratory." I gave the original to the judge, and a copy to Murfree. "You will note on page two, Your Honor, that the Lab Director, Dr. Arthur Thompson, received a call at 11:15 p.m., May 10, 2098, from the old baron's physician, Dr. Milton Newbury, stating that Burl was not expected to last the hour, and they should start the *in vitro* fertilization immediately. Which they did.

"The sperm was of course kept frozen in liquid nitrogen, and it took several minutes to thaw it. In the further course of testimony we will show the act of contact of individual sperm and ovum, which is to say, fertilization. I now call the Ladies Mary-Louise Sixtrees."

Clatchett and Murfree were bending towards each other and whispering. Murfree seemed to moan faintly.

Mary-Louise was duly sworn in. "Ladies," I said, "I show you what purports to be a video cassette, sealed with the certificate of the Office of Archives. Can you further identify it?"

Mary took the question. "I saw you withdraw it from Archives about thirty minutes ago."

"Please read the label."

Louise took this one. "It says, 'Conception of Mary-Louise Sixtrees.' "

Whispers began sizzling all over the courtroom. The judge banged away and the noise faded.

"With the court's permission," I continued, "we will play the tape."

Murfree was up and howling. "No authentication! Maybe it's a fake. Where's the original cameraman? And in any case, it's irrelevant!"

"It's an entry made in the regular course of business," I said. "As such, it's entitled to a presumption of veracity."

"But how is it relevant?" asked Cloke.

"What it shows," I said, "bears directly on who owns Sara. This will become apparent if we are permitted to run the cassette."

"All right," said Cloke thoughtfully. "Yes, I think we ought to see it. I'll let it in." He nodded to the bailiff, who brought the monitor over and then darkened the room.

"The course of the run was followed by recording microscope," I said. "Times are marked on the frames. "As you will note, at 11:59 p.m. May 10, Day One, the spermatazoa were brought into the proximity of the ovum. One sperm penetrated the shell of the ovum at 12:01 a.m., May 11, Day Two, with characteristic symptoms of satisfactory fertilization." I motioned to the bailiff, who turned the machine off.

"According to the records of the Sperm Bank, at 12:10 a.m. Day Two the fertilized egg was transferred to Lady Ditmars's waiting uterus, and nine months later her grace, Lady Mary-Louise Sixtrees, our present witness, was born."

Murfree had about reached his limit. "Your Honor, why do we have to listen to this? What's any of this got to do with the Rule against Perpetuities?"

"Mr. Whitmore," asked the judge, more curious than condemning, "what *is* the point?"

"The point, Your Honor, is the 'life in being' has to exist at the moment the alleged interest in Sara is created—that is, at the moment the will becomes effective, which, as we know, is at the instant of the testator's death. The old baron died at midnight, May 10, 2098. Conception came next day, at 12:01 a.m., one minute after midnight. There was no designated life in being at the moment of Burl's death. Therefore Clause One, the bequest of the items in Appendix A of Burl's will, including Sara, violates the Rule against Perpetuities, and is therefore invalid, and Cecil does not own Sara." I was almost out of breath when I got to the end.

Clatchett jumped up, but Cloke waved him back down. "Everybody wait a minute." He frowned, then leveled his eyes down at me. "Counselor, you claim that Mary-Louise missed conception prior to Burl's death by one minute, therefore there was no 'life in being,' therefore the will was invalid, therefore Burl's great-grandson Harry should not have inherited, and therefore the estate, including Sara, should not have passed through succeeding generations down to Cecil. Is that about it?"

"Precisely and beautifully stated, Your Honor."

Probably the sincerest (and maybe first) praise the jurist had received during his entire career at the bench. I caught the barest flicker of a smile.

Adverse counsel missed nothing of this. Murfree took the floor. "Your Honor, this is absurd. We're talking here of just one minute—sixty seconds. Will we let one infinitesimal fragment of time upset a chain of title that has been in place for a hundred years? Ridiculous!"

Cloke sighed. "Just speaking hypothetically for the moment, if the Clause One grant *is* invalid, who owns Sara?"

I looked up modestly. "The answer lies in the will, Your Honor. If Clause One is inoperative, we are left with Clause Two, which provides that all the rest and residue of the estate goes to my ancestor, Bascomb Moncrief, and then, by the laws of descent, on down to me. *I* own all the items listed in Appendix A, including Sara."

Clatchett gave me a bitter look. "You are incredible!"

"Pure fantasy!" cried Murfree. (But I could tell he was worried.)

"Gentlemen," declared the judge sternly, "no more of that. I gather both sides rest? Very well, I will give you my decision this afternoon. The witness may step down. Recess until one-thirty." He rose and strode through the door into his chambers, shaking his head.

As the courtroom cleared, Clatchett and Murfree got up and came over to my table. Clatchett tried to smile, but succeeded only in hurting his face. "Can we deal?"

I looked up. "What's your offer?"

John-Claude and Mary-Louise watched this with interest.

Clatchett groaned. "I'll try to persuade Lord Cecil to give you a full one percent of the Sixtrees estate." He tried to look magnanimous, but he had never done it before, and he simply looked funny.

I laughed. "Don't bother, Dave. This afternoon, Cloke is going to give me the whole thing."

"Bill," said Clatchett quietly, "you know the baron controls the local police and the Provincial Militia."

"True, but right now he and his Zouaves are in California making a movie."

"He's flying back at this very moment, and the militia will follow as soon as he can arrange transportation. I hope we can work something out."

He and the prosecution crew left, probably headed for lunch at the Bar-Del-O. I had a very strong suspicion that no matter what Clatchett and I decided, my client and Mary-Louise would have the final word. I started gathering up my files.

"Lunch, chief?" asked Cass.

"Oh, yeah. Sure. Mary-Louise? John-Claude? Any choice?"

"Your office, Bill," said Louise. Mary added, "Perhaps Mr. Reevers can bring something in from Garshmeyer's?"

"Chinese?" asked John. "With iced tea," said Claude.

Learning fast, I thought. "Cass?" But he was already gone.

12. Decision

So, back to my office, where we sat around our conference table and ate pu pu platter, wonton soup, moo goo gai pan, and things I couldn't name. My client and his girlfriends dove in with a relish.

We got into other matters quickly. "What's the story about the baron's militia?" asked John. Then Claude, "If the judge finds for us, could Cecil use his army to cancel the decision? Anybody?"

"Under extreme circumstances," said Louise, "we believe Nephew Cecil might well attempt to overrule the judge by brute force." "So," said Mary, "we have to consider carefully the baron's personal army, his Zouaves, about a thousand men and women."

"The army is a colorful lot," continued Louise, "with their bright red baggy trousers, brilliant blue jackets, white leggings, and black turbans, just as in the French Algerian armies of old. The baron, after experimenting with various uniforms, picked out the zouave style himself. And with good reason." Mary laughed. "When he wears ordinary trousers he can't bend over without splitting his pants. But the zouave britches have plenty of room, and so that's what he and his army wear."

"But his army is presently out-of-town?" John said.

Louise explained: "He leased his army to Nonco Pictures, in Hollywood, to make the new TV miniseries, 'The Blood-and-Iron Brigade,' with the baron as the Field Marshal."

"So," said Claude, "can Cecil just pack up his army and dash home and by force reverse the judge?"

"Not likely!" declared Louise. Mary said, "We have it on good authority that the army likes it out there and will probably stay for sequels regardless of what Cecil wants."

"Well then," observed John, "it appears that, at least for the foreseeable future, Cecil can't count on his army. But how about the Fair guards?"

"Interesting question," said Louise. "When Cecil took his militia to Hollywood, he was mindful that the Fair itself would require police presence. Accordingly, before he left he had Ned Packle swear in fifty new deputies. This was no casual affair. Each of the new deputies had to have a special training implant inserted while reciting and imprinting the loyalty oath: 'I swear to uphold the laws of the Province . . . and so on.' "

Mary added, "It's a known medical fact that any conscious attempt to violate the imprint will result in copious perspiration followed by violent disabling headaches, leading to convulsions and even death if the mental conflict persists."

"Too bad we can't continue this," I said, "but it's time to start back. Perhaps we can sum up: Judge Cloke can't be overruled by an army half a continent away, and Ned and his fifty deputies can be predicted to support Cloke. Agreed? Let's go!"

The courtroom was again packed, as expected. I ushered my brood in at exactly one-thirty. Clatchett and Murfree were already sitting at plaintiff's table, and Dave and I exchanged insincere nods.

We left Cass and Mary-Louise in the row behind the bar and I led John-Claude over to our table.

"All rise!" And so Enos Phlutter announced the arrival of His Honor, who told us to be seated and himself did likewise.

Cass leaned over the bar and whispered in my general direction: "Smock!"

My assistant is forever fearful that I may overlook the obvious. But I had already noted the smock, and I had already groaned an appropriate groan.

I have mentioned the judge's white smock—a relic of his artistic career, saved, and now totally covered with Latin quotations. Wearing the smock meant the judge was going to hand down a thoroughly reasoned decision, lavishly sprinkled with gems in Latin in support of all points as he went along. It could also mean we were in for a long afternoon.

A hush falls over the courtroom. Judge Cloke is checking out something on the flap of his smock. "In the matter of Sixtrees versus Berg, *Per quod servitium Sara amisit*—whereby he lost the services of his servant Sara, we find we are forced to answer a threshold question: *Does Plaintiff own Sara?*" He leaned back and looked very thoughtful.

I relaxed a little. He was starting out very sensibly, and translating his quotes for us. Hope he keeps it up. About the only Latin I knew was *Illegitimi non carborundum:* Don't let the bastards grind you down.

And now the judge is studying the right sleeve of his smock. "We do not make new law. We but seek to know what the law already is. *Sequamur vestigia patrum nostrorum.* Let us follow in the footsteps of our fathers. *Stare decisis.* We stand by past decisions. *Misera est servitus, ubi jus est incertam.*" He looked over the room and smiled. "It's a wretched business where the law is uncertain."

I think I heard Cass's gentle snort behind me. I ignored him and sank a few inches down into my chair. By now, poor Dave Clatchett was probably trying to explain to unbelieving very expensive big city co-counsel how the afternoon would go.

Just then John-Claude leaned over, and John whispered into my ear. "Cecil . . . driving in from the airport."

"Gotcha."

"To answer our threshold question," continued Cloke, "we must examine certain other matters of both law and fact. It is undisputed that Sara was listed in the Sixtrees assets on the death of the original Baron Sixtrees, Burl Dogger, and was bequeathed to his son Harry in Clause One of the Dogger will. But the validity of Clause One has been queried, on the theory that it must fail under the Rule against Perpetuities, as provided in 33 Provincial Code 2112. More specifically, a time gap is alleged between the effective date of the will and the conception of the designated life in being, to wit, one Mary-Louise Sixtrees. Times are evidently critical, and we must examine them with care.

"Now, as we all know, a will speaks from the time of death. *Testamentum, omne morte consummatur.* According to the records, Burl Dogger died at midnight on May 10, 2098. Surely no problem there. We next examine the life-in-being, *videlicet,* that of Lady Mary-Louise Sixtrees. *Qui in utero est pro jam nato habetur.* She who is in the womb is held as already born. We have clear testimony that she was conceived at exactly 12:01 a.m., May 11, one minute after the old baron's death. Is this fact dispositive?" He looked up and over the courtroom as though someone out there might have the answer.

Murfree jumped up. "Your Honor! It's just one minute—sixty seconds! *De minimis non curat lex!* The law takes no heed of little things!"

Now that was downright stupid. Bad enough to interrupt the judge in the very act of handing down his decision. But *nobody* quotes Latin back to Judge Cloke. Julius Caesar himself would not have dared. It was like telling Praxiteles how to design the Acropolis, or Leonardo da Vinci how to paint the Mona Lisa.

His honor seemed momentarily struck dumb by the effrontery.

John whispered, "Murfree is . . . how you say? trying to delay . . . stall, until Cecil gets here."

That made sense. I whispered back, "How about his army?"

"Still in Los Angeles," said Claude, "but we think he will bring in some Fair police."

I nodded, took a deep breath.

The judge sighed, laid his notes aside and checked something on the hem of his smock. "*Multa in jure . . .* etc. etc." (it was a long one, and I won't finish it. What it meant was, there's a lot of illogical stuff in the common law, so what?) "So sit down, Mr. Murfree."

Clatchett pulled his colleague back into his chair.

Then—*crash!*

Every eye in the courtroom looked around as the door burst open and Lord Cecil Sixtrees stumbled in, followed by three Fair guards.

13. Changes

During my lifetime I had not seen Lord Cecil more than half a dozen times, and never before this close. He was huffing and puffing, and his bloated cheeks were scarlet. Black spots burned in the centers of his eyes, which now darted about the crowded room.

Judge Cloke recovered first. And why not? This was his turf. "Leave the room!" he ordered the newcomers.

"No!" cried the intruder. "You must stop this silly trial!"

Dave Clatchett shriveled into his seat. Murfree seemed paralyzed. And now Cecil spotted Mary-Louise, and he hesitated. His eyes widened still further. "Aunt Mary-Louise? What are *you* doing here?"

She replied in a calm clear voice. "I'm a witness in this trial, nephew. My testimony may help Mr. Berg."

"And destroy the barony," muttered Clatchett.

"You shouldn't be *out*," protested Cecil. "You should be *home*."

But now it was clear that Cecil's whole world was at risk, and he'd have to attend to her later. He pointed to the judge. "Arrest that man!" he ordered his three policemen.

That was not smart. The guards looked at Cecil, at each other, at the judge, back to Cecil, and they began to sweat.

I noted that Ned Packle had his hand on his laser holster, and I wondered, are we about to revert to the Border Wars, where disputes are settled with guns? Oh God no! How to defuse this insanity?

In my loudest whoop-'n-holler voice I called out to the judge: "Your Honor! I request a conference in chambers!"

And so we all followed the judge back into his inner sanctum—with Ned Packle but minus the policemen. We got His Lardship inside and seated on the sofa.

"Dave," I said, "would you bring His Grace up-to-date?"

The prosecutor's face went through several contortions before it finally settled down. "It appears," Clatchett said mournfully, "that the judge *may* be about to rule that you don't own Sara . . ."

"What? I don't own Sara? That's ridiculous!" Cecil's belly heaved in slow rhythmic indignation.

"And *that*," Clatchett continued fatalistically, "is just the tip of the iceberg. For if you don't own Sara—and I repeat, *if*—it's because Clause One of the will is invalid."

"Invalid?" sputtered Cecil. "Impossible!"

"It seems that the Clause might be invalid in view of a statute," Clatchett said, dripping woe, "the so-called Rule against Perpetuities. That would leave only Clause Two in the will, and since that gave all the rest and residue of the estate to Bascomb Moncrief, *he* would have taken all property listed in the Appendix, including Sara."

It sank in. Cecil turned white. He said to the judge, "But you haven't ruled yet? None of this is final?"

"No." Cloke's voice was a deadly calm. "I haven't ruled yet. I was about to rule when you interrupted the proceedings."

"Well, you're not going to make any ruling," declared Cecil. "This case is hereby dismissed. It is no longer before the court. Everybody will leave this room . . . go home . . . wherever . . . *Now!*" With an immense effort he stood up.

But nobody moved.

"Will I have to call my guards?" he demanded.

Back to square one? I wondered.

"That would be quite foolish," Cloke observed mildly. "The Fair guards are conditioned to obey the law as I pronounce it. If you and I disagree, it is I whom they will obey, not you." His voice took on an icy edge. "And to clarify matters and bring this litigation to an end, I will now officially state my decision."

The room was suddenly quiet.

As though showing respect for the silence, Cloke's voice was surprisingly soft. "I hold Clause One of the Sixtrees will to be invalid as violating the Rule Against Perpetuities, 33 Provincial Code 2112, whereby all items listed in the Appendix, including the android Sara, fall within the rest and residue of the Sixtrees estate, and thus became the property of Bascomb Moncrief and his heirs."

He looked up momentarily with narrowed eyes at the fat man. "It follows that Sara—or whatever is left of her—is presently the property of William Moncrief Whitmore by descent from Bascomb Moncrief, and that you, Cecil Sixtrees, have no property interest in Sara or anything else listed in the Appendix. Judgment for defendant." He gave Cecil an almost sympathetic look. "Since you are now a pauper, the court will waive costs."

We all noted he had stopped addressing the chief complainant as 'Your Grace.' In Cloke's eyes, and I guess in most everybody else's, Cecil was no longer baron. Then who was? Maybe nobody. For that matter, we didn't really need a baron. Burl Dogger had taken the title long ago as a matter of vanity, and it had sort of stuck.

I studied the opposition. Hard to say who looked sadder, Clatchett or Cecil or Murfree.

"I can take it all back," Cecil said weakly. "My army . . . in L.A . . . they'll come . . ."

"Nephew," interposed Mary, "your militia will do nothing for you." Louise finished: "They are going to do two more series. We believe they will remain in Hollywood indefinitely."

Clatchett talked briefly with his client. When they finished, Cecil's lower lip was trembling.

Mary-Louise leaned over toward me and we had a short three-way conversation. I said mostly, yeah, yeah . . .

I turned back to the fat man. "Cecil," I said, "by this decision I now own everything that you used to own. You will however continue to own the Bar-Del-O, which should provide income sufficient for your personal needs."

He chewed it over thoughtfully. "Can I keep my uniform?"

"Of course."

The room was quiet. "That about it?" asked Cloke.

Clatchett looked resigned, Murfree looked bemused. Cecil had stopped understanding anything long ago.

"There is one more thing," said Mary, "but we have to wait for John-Claude's ship to arrive."

"Your ship is over at the Impound Lot," said Ned Packle. "I can run you over there, no trouble."

"Thank you, constable," John said, "but that won't be necessary." Claude explained, "A friend is bringing the ship here."

Ned looked blank. "Somebody knows how to drive it?"

Just then the door opened and a resplendent vision walked in. "*I* know how!" she declared proudly.

"*SARA!*" I cried.

14. Cherry Blossom

We all stared. All of us, that is, except Mary-Louise.

I was probably the first to get it. Sara as a mass of hopeless junk had been tossed into the Miscellaneous Bin in the Impound Lot, and Mary-Louise had spent nearly all last night rebuilding and dressing her. And then had spent perhaps a few minutes more recharging the mint oil reservoir and tuning the engines of the space vehicle. That's why she had been unable to meet me in Archives until early morning. But why all the effort with Sara? Was she determined to repair John-Claude's damage before they left? Logical. But I sensed there was also another reason, and that before the day was out we'd know a lot more.

But back up. I remember that when Sara was crushed she had been wearing a white blouse, gray suit-jacket, and a simple matching skirt (split down the left thigh, a modest statement of her profession). Indeed, on the few times I had seen her in the past, she had worn something equally drab and unobtrusive. So now the contrast of past and present was startling.

For with the aid of fabrics and make-up Sara had truly bloomed into her full name, Sakurako, "Cherry Blossom." Mary-Louise had dressed her as a beautiful geisha.

Soft white synthetic skin covered her stainless steel body. As undergarment she wore a red silk kimono, and over that, a gorgeous black and purple silk outer kimono, embroidered with designs of trout and insects emblematic of summer. Then the wide *obi*—a sash wrapped around her waist and tied in a square pack in the small of her back, and all held in place with a slender red cord.

She began walking toward me in mincing steps. Split-toed socks covered feet that fit naturally and elegantly into high wooden clogs and were intermittently visible.

All this liquid rippling and flowing of fabric was stunning, but her face was the real knockout. It was painted an eye-scorching white, the "bee-sting" lips were a bright crimson, and the eyes and eyebrows were lined with red and black.

And then the hair! A magnificent mass of contoured black, evidently spray-lacquered to hold it in an upswept chignon.

At this point I stole a glance at Mary-Louise. The expressions on her faces were protean. First, a sly amusement, then pleasure at our reaction to "her" handiwork. In particular she seemed to be watching *me*. Pretty clear, she knew, and had known, how I felt about Sara. But that was only part of it. I sensed that there was more to come, a lot more.

Sara stood in front of me. She seemed to study my face a moment. Then she knelt gracefully and bowed her head.

"Sara," I said, "that's not necessary. Please get up."

She did. "Master, I now belong to you. It is my pleasure to serve you. What do you ask of me?"

I closed my eyes and prayed for an answer. "Sara, you are now free. You belong only to yourself."

" 'Free?' I do not understand. During all my life, others have told me what to do. All my life, the barons held me in *kakae*—strict captivity. For them I made much money. If it be your will, William Whitmore, I can continue this for you."

"No more, Sara. Your life is your own. You can go, you can stay, all as it may please you. What would you like to do? Perhaps we can help."

She appeared to reflect. The white make-up on her brow creased delicately. "I think, my lord *danna*, I would like to leave forever the *karyakai*—the flower-and-willow world." Her clear gray eyes burned into mine. "It would please me greatly if my master never again sold my body."

"It will be so, even as you wish. Your body is your own."

"My lord is generous. May I continue to say what would please me?"

"Of course."

"I would like to move into my lord's house. I can be of much service there, for I can cook, I can clean the house, do the laundry, go to the stores." (She now spoke in a rush.) "I play the shamisen. I am skilled in bed, and with my tongue I can tie the stem of a cherry into a knot . . ."

I cleared my throat hurriedly. "Sara—!"

She looked up at me, puzzled. "My lord is displeased?"

"Not at all. It's just that—"

"Or perhaps I can help in your office? I can file, I can work the computer, I can answer the phone, write down messages. I can take papers to court. I can clerk for you for six years, then take the bar, and be a junior lawyer with you."

She stared up at me brightly, and I caught a brief vision of Sara in full regalia pleading a case before a bemused Judge Cloke and twelve goggle-eyed jurors.

Mary called over to us. "I hate to break this up, but John-Claude and we will be leaving very soon, and before we go we'd like to clear up the matter of Karen Bight's implant."

I laughed. "The gold mine."

She ignored me and addressed Judge Cloke. "Your Honor, what I have to say now is an interesting footnote to this litigation. It should take but a moment. If Your Honor will indulge us?"

"Without objection, please go ahead."

"Thank you, Your Honor," said Louise. "We start with a bit of history. In the closing years of the twenty-first century a team of Japanese geologists surveyed the entire globe via satellite, looking for deposits of colonium. In New York their director encrypted their findings in a cerebral implant, which they inserted in the brain of a qualified courier, one Karen Bight. She was to take the strip to Houston, where it would be decrypted in special decoding apparatus by the local survey team. The implant never reached its destination. The courier was waylaid by Burl Dogger and his gang. He had no means of translating the implant, so he held Karen in captive concubinage until she died in childbirth, giving Burl's son Roark to the world. On her death Burl cut the implant from her brain and filed it away for safekeeping. *This* is the implant." They held up for our inspection a thin sliver of glinting titanium.

"It is the only record of the Japanese survey," said Mary. All other notes, records, and relevant personnel were lost over a hundred years ago when the *Minnow* blew up and took metropolitan New York with it." She handed the strip to Sara. "Sara was the decrypting apparatus that waited long years for this in Houston. It never came. But here she is now, hopefully once more in good working order, and we will ask her to decrypt it, if she can."

With a graceful, almost languid motion the geisha android worked her hand into the folds of her kimono and thrust the metal strip into an invisible slit somewhere in her chest.

At this moment I realized that Sara's rumored high-tech specialty was simply the ability to decode certain encrypted implants. It had nothing to do with sex. I felt oddly relieved.

Some seconds later she pulled out a tiny roll of white parchment and handed it to me. It had numbers and markings on it, but they meant nothing to me.

Mary said, "May I?"

I gave it to her. She and Louise stretched it out with both hands and examined it carefully. Louise said, "Three deposits. Gives latitude and longitude, precise to the meter. Number one—Pacific Ocean—looks like seven miles down, to the bottom of the Marianas Trench. Hopeless for present technology. Number two—50 kilometers from the North Pole, inaccessible under Arctic ice."

As they studied the rest of the tape Mary seemed to be making various mental calculations. Finally she finished, and both heads turned to me with wide grins. Mary said, "Number three, in a field just west of Lethary, on Barham Road. It's the corner under your dung heap." Louise added, "According to this, the deposit is extensive. Most of it lies near the surface and can be readily strip-mined."

John Berg commented: "The deposit must be considered priceless." Claude added, "Certainly worth several times the entire tax base of Lethary Province."

"Word will get around," said John. "Buyers will come in from star systems not yet entered in your catalogs."

"You'll need a good-sized space-port," said Claude. "Some of the ships from Andromeda are as big as the town Square."

I groaned. I didn't want this. I just wanted to be a country lawyer with a reasonable case load, not too light, not too heavy. Life in the middle lane. But I could see that wasn't going to be possible. Not anymore. And they weren't through yet.

"You'll be building your own ships," observed John casually. "We'll leave you three basic designs," said Claude. "The motors for two will be FTL—faster than light—which of course you'll need for inter-galactics."

"Of course," I said.

"You can do it," said Mary. "Hire some of the old NASA people," suggested Louise. "There's got to be a lot of engineering talent out there, just waiting to go to work."

"Any questions?" asked John.

Nobody dared.

"Some dung heap," muttered Cecil. "Not enough to *give* it away? For good measure we had to lose it to the law." After that the room was very still for what seemed a long time. I noticed then that Cecil had taken something from a jacket pocket: a small canister. I recognized it—Fahrni's Canned Laughter, recommended for use when you sense the situation calls for hilarity, but you can't seem to get started. He sprayed it straight into his face. We all watched, fascinated. First we heard only a low dismal chuckle, but this rapidly grew in volume and soon changed into peal after peal of hysterical guffaws.

Ex-Lord Cecil was now laughing so hard that he had to hold his great belly with both hands, else it would bound away from him. And even when he finally quit, his stomach kept going for several minutes, like diminishing seismic aftershocks.

After that, as though waiting for him to finish, the two-headed lovers walked through the doorway, and a few minutes later we heard the thrumming of the ship as it lifted off. All was silent again. Where were they headed? It was anybody's guess.

Everybody now seemed to be looking at me expectantly. Why? I had no plans, no sense of direction, no instructions for anybody. I was tired, totally beat. I had to get away.

I looked around the room. Was this the end of it? Cecil looked sad, numb. Clatchett, grim, anxious. Murfree looked resigned, and was probably wondering whether Cecil had enough cash flow remaining to pay his considerable fee.

And our notable provincial justice? He looked not only happy, he looked wise. He now uttered what was to be his last Latin pronouncement of the day: *"Molae deorum molent tarde sed molent subitissime."* I worked it out in my head. The mills of the gods grind slowly, but they grind exceeding fine.

Directly in point, Your Honor.

"Sara," I said, "come with me. You and I are going to Galveston."

That evening I began packing again. I was absolutely starting for my little seaside cabin within the hour and Sara was going with me. Cass would have to handle the office all by himself for the next twenty-one days. I figured we would stay in touch and he could do no real harm.

Sara finished her own packing quickly. "I shall take only what I carry onto the plane, including my see-through red silk. A single pull will undo the *obi*. In our cabin, I will show you."

I loved to hear her prattle. Ah, Sara . . . perhaps I'm not as old as I think. I've been a bachelor all my life. I've never lived with a woman. Not sure I know how. Of course, they could argue, you're not a woman. They would be wrong!

A knock on the door. I looked up. I had a terrible suspicion.

I sat down on my suitcase. I refused to answer the door.

"Bill?" It was Martin Cloke. He spoke loudly. "You've got to help. Cecil's charged with fraud and embezzlement. You have to take his case. Come on, Bill, open the door."

"No! He doesn't need me. He's got his own hot-shot lawyers."

"No, he doesn't. Dave Clatchett's facing jail. Murfree has high-tailed it back to Chicago."

"Judge, be reasonable! I've got this reservation for a beach cabin—"

"Bill, let's look at this another way. I haven't yet signed the Agreement we hammered out this afternoon. And even when I do, don't forget you'll need over fifty licenses and permits just for your colonium mine, not to mention what you'll need for your factories and buildings. And guess who's still Chairman of the License Board?"

I didn't answer. I was thinking hard.

He went on. "You want to give *everything* back to Cecil? Manor house, your six big oak trees?"

I thought about the surf at Galveston.

"Bill, you want to cancel the deal, throw it all away for a few days lying around getting sunburned?"

No answer.

"You have an obligation to the bar, William Whitmore. Especially since all this is your fault anyhow."

How did he figure *that* one? But I didn't nibble.

He played his ace. "Suppose I gave it all back to Cecil, what would old Bascomb Moncrief think?"

Oh, unfair!

I knew what my great-grandfather would think. And do. His grave was in the family cemetery in the grove just west of the old manor house. That grave would explode. Dirt and casket shards everywhere.

I took the damn case.

Later, much later . . .

The Parole Board released Cecil for reasons of health after a lugubrious tenancy of six months. In that time he had lost 180 pounds, and they didn't want him dying in prison. No matter. Ultimately with the help of the Bar-Del-O kitchen he got it all back.

Dave Clatchett is still doing time at Hoban. Nora visits him regularly. He wishes she wouldn't.

Cherry Blossom Industries Inc. launched its first ship last week, and our intrepid Captain Reevers expects to rendezvous with John-Claude and Mary-Louise in about two months. The *Lizard* is loaded with a lot of things she left behind, or didn't think about at the time, such as a couple of trunks of her baby clothes.

CELEBRATING
CHARLES L. HARNESS

GEORGE ZEBROWSKI

Charles L. Harness published his first story, "Time Trap," in the August 1948 issue of *Astounding Science Fiction*—and this story immediately set the pattern for the reception of his work: less than overwhelming initial response to any particular work, followed by a continuing series of rediscoveries by readers, editors, and publishers that continues to this day and can almost be plotted on a time chart.

"Time Trap" makes one wonder whether its time travel loop somehow started the way that the reading world continues to return to Harness's work, as if following a program set by this first story.

Other oddities attend this story. It was first reprinted in an unexpected place, against the prejudices and preconceptions of the time, when the "New Wave" of the 1960s was proclaimed as being antithetical to "hard science fiction," especially to anything published in John W. Campbell's *Astounding Science Fiction*, recently transformed into *Analog*. Michael Moorcock reprinted "Time Trap" in his "radical" *New Worlds* (May 1965), and no one cried foul.

Robert Silverberg reprinted the story in his anthology *Alpha One* (1970). There were further reprints of the story in 1966, 1968, and 1981. Please note the long gaps between these rediscoveries of Harness's work; they mark its staying power.

"The New Reality," from *Thrilling Wonder Stories*, December 1950, followed a similar pattern of "rediscovery," with reprints in a best-of-the-year anthology in 1951, then nothing until 1966 and 1967, followed by reprintings in 1974, 1977 (in Silverberg's *Alpha Eight*), 1982, 1984, and 1988.

"The New Reality" is justly one of Harness's legendary stories, one of several that have been described as intellectually challenging and thought-provoking, even though few critics have ventured to say wherein these qualities consist. The striking central conception of "The New Reality" takes its strength from the dynamic fact of human scientific development, by which the growth of our knowledge is linked to new ideas and imaginings.

523

Harness makes this growth an actual physical process in his story. The universe changes as our ideas change. Now this *is* what happens, psychologically, to people who are faced with major conceptual changes in the sciences; and this kind of change has often been a wrenching one indeed. The dethroning of the Earth as the center of the universe was one such disturbance; the germ theory of disease another; evolution by natural selection horrified many people; the demise of Newton's absolute space and time in Einstein's reconfiguration is still poorly understood even among educated people; and, finally, the entrance of quantum mechanics into physics made even Einstein wary. The psychology of this process is reflected in the television series and book by James Burke, appropriately titled *The Day the Universe Changed.*

The collision that occurs when a better scientific model meets a previously established conception is hilariously exampled in Poul Anderson's novel, *The High Crusade* (1960), in which a starship takes a group of medieval people into space—and one character expects to hear the breaking of Aristotle's crystalline spheres as the ship heads outward; but what shatters instead is a mind that is hopelessly unprepared for new ideas. A reader who needs to ask "What are crystalline spheres?" is in deep trouble. Another story, Philip José Farmer's "Sail On! Sail On!" (1952), destroys the characters' expectations in reverse, as the technologically advanced clerics of an alternate reality actually sail off the edge of the world! Both Anderson's novel and Farmer's short story are later brothers to "The New Reality," in varying degrees of perversity. With Harness's story, they belong to a select group of science fictions that mirror the sciences in making us properly uneasy and methodically doubtful of whatever bombshells await us in our only provisionally settled forms of knowledge. It is this intellectual penetration of our philosophies of science, in what is otherwise an extravagant fiction, that makes this story so extraordinary. Readers who are knowledgeable enough to pick up the subtleties are startled, and those who only sense the authenticity of deeper issues are merely dazzled.

Now eighty-three, Charles L. Harness is still in the midst of a period of productivity that resumed in the 1970s, with a new novel and stories appearing every two years. He belongs to a select group of writers, among them William Tenn, James Gunn, Ward Moore, Chad Oliver, and others who began to publish in the 1940s, and whose accomplishments easily rank with the masters of SF, even while the vagaries of publishing have made it difficult for these talents to find their audiences, much less to make these audiences grow.

Two of Harness's later novels, *Krono* (1988) and *Lurid Dreams* (1990), were highly praised by publications as diverse as *Locus* and *The New York Times,* and yet were neglected by his publishers, even as the chorus of praise for his entire body of work (begun in the 1950s and '60s by Damon Knight, Judith Merril, Arthur C. Clarke, James Blish, Michael Moorcock, and Brian W. Aldiss, to name a few of the most prominent) became louder and more articulate.

The Paradox Men, one of the most unusual science fiction novels ever published, first saw print in the May 1949 *Startling Stories* magazine under the title *Flight Into Yesterday.* In 1953, a badly edited, poorly proofread and printed hardcover of the expanded version was published under the same title. Ace Double

Novels published the book in 1955 as *The Paradox Men,* the title under which the book is known today; the flip side of this format presented Jack Williamson's *Dome Around America.* Although the novel's colorful ideas, energy, and unusual conviction were recognized (it draws on the author's deeps of personal remembrance, trauma, and love), the book went out of print in the United States.

Following Michael Moorcock's reprinting of Harness's early stories in *New Worlds* during the mid-sixties, there was a renewed interest in his work. A new edition of *The Paradox Men,* with an appreciative introduction by Brian W. Aldiss, was published by Faber. A British science fiction book club edition followed in 1966, with paperback editions in 1967. In 1976 Brian W. Aldiss and Harry Harrison reintroduced the novel to British readers in the SF Masters Series from New English Library, but there was no new American edition.

Harness's best known work, a short novel entitled *The Rose,* had been ignored by American publishers, and had finally appeared in the British magazine *Authentic Science Fiction Monthly* in March 1953; but it was not until 1966 that there was a book edition. It included two stories, "The New Reality" and "The Chessplayers." It was published, through the efforts of Michael Moorcock, by Compact Books, which was also the publisher of *New Worlds.* Strangely enough, but typically for Harness, this paperback edition was followed by a Sidgwick & Jackson hardcover in 1968. An American paperback finally appeared from Berkley in 1969, possibly because Harness had been published in Damon Knight's *Orbit* series of original anthologies from the same house, where Knight had been an editorial consultant. It followed Compact's inclusion of the two additional stories. Panther did a paperback in Britain in the same year, and reprinted it in 1970 and 1981. According to the author, all these editions reprint the magazine version that he cut from a longer manuscript, which even in later years proved intractable, despite efforts at revision, and which Harness finally set aside. The text in this collection is the first fully corrected, definitive edition of the story.

But throughout this period there was still no new edition of *The Paradox Men.* Brian Aldiss intrigued new readers by reprinting a chapter in his anthology *Space Opera* (Doubleday, 1974). A number of critics, reviewers, and editors whetted readers' appetites by citing this now legendary novel. Robert Silverberg, in his editorial note to "Time Trap" in *Alpha One* (1970), described *The Paradox Men* as a "dizzyingly intricate novel, which repays close study by anyone wishing to master the craft of plotting." A decade later there was still no new edition. Collectors knew that this was a novel not to be missed, if they could only find a copy. Harness continued to grow as a writer, with *two* legendary books to his name, yet still there was no new edition of *The Paradox Men.*

In 1979, as Harness began his current period of sustained creativity, *The Science Fiction Encyclopedia,* edited by Peter Nicholls, described him as "a highly imaginative writer whose relative neglect in his own country is difficult to understand." The newest edition of this reference work repeats the same statement, word for word.

In 1984, I included the novel in my ten-volume set for Crown, *Classics of Modern Science Fiction;* all the volumes sold out, but were not kept in print. I learned from Harness at that time that his original title for this novel was *Toynbee Twenty-Two,* which refers to the British historian's numbering of civilizations that have come and gone. T-21 is the future civilization in the story, which is struggling to avoid the decline predicted by Arnold Toynbee's theory of history. The Toynbean philosophers in Harness's story hope that space travel, by means of a faster-than-light starship, the T-22, will serve as a bridge to a new culture. In our world, Arthur C. Clarke and others have expressed the hope that the opening of space will liberate human creativity and spark a new renaissance, as we move beyond a planet of limited economic horizons and power struggles.

I also learned that *Flight Into Yesterday,* both the magazine and first hardcover title of this same novel, was the title chosen by Sam Merwin, then editor of *Startling Stories.* Donald A. Wollheim, the editor of Ace Books at the time, changed the title to *The Paradox Men,* which is perhaps the most intriguing of the novel's three titles, because it accurately describes the ambiguous predicament of the story's major characters. For this reason, and to avoid confusion among readers and bibliographers, the author finally chose to keep the title of the novel's largest edition; but he retained his original title as the title of Chapter 22.

In preparing the Crown edition, the author and I gave the novel a careful line by line reading, correcting dropped punctuation, typos, and wrong words. Harness took the opportunity to expand overly compressed scenes, and made important details more lucid through a judicious updating of terms, as well as improving the general movement of the story. The purely mechanical defects of previous editions had been a needless obstacle for readers. In effect, the Crown edition was given the normal book editing that was not always available in the science fiction field of the 1940s and '50s. Crown's edition, with some 3500 words of restored and revised material, was the first definitive version of a genuine SF classic, replacing the previous editions. The Easton Press Masterpieces of Science Fiction leatherbound edition of 1992 corrected the typos of the Crown edition, and included a newly revised afterword by the author, as well as a revised introduction by me.

Reactions to the novel's first book publication were mixed. Groff Conklin seemed baffled in his January 1954 *Galaxy* review, but found the novel "pretty astonishing, if only because of the cauldronful of ideas and fantasies that are mixed up in it." P. Schuyler Miller's review in the April 1954 *Astounding* described the novel as an "action entertainment," but he failed to notice the story's compulsive, dreamlike power and treatment of serious issues. Anthony Boucher's review in *The Magazine of Fantasy & Science Fiction* for September 1953 found the book to be a "fine swashbuckling adventure of space-and-time travel, the politics of tyranny, and the identity problems of an amnesiac superman . . ." and compared the work to A.E. van Vogt's two "Weapon Shops" novels; however, Boucher also found the story to be too intricate and its science confusing and perhaps mistaken. In this last criticism he was wrong, since there are solutions to equations involving travel near and beyond light speed that permit the result that Harness elects to have in his novel; whether this is physically true or not is irrelevant to the use of this result for dramatic "what if" purposes. Harness's use of both science and technology follows Arthur C. Clarke's Third Law—"that any sufficiently advanced technology is indistinguishable from magic." Harness is aware of what it might take to have the effects he wants, but he does not always elaborate on the details or dwell on them. A good example of this kind of fictional use of stylized science and technology is Clarke's *Against the Fall of Night* (1953).

When Harness's novel came out in paperback three years later as *The Paradox Men,* Damon Knight, the most influential science fiction reviewer of the time, hailed it (in *Infinity Science Fiction,* February 1956) as "the brilliant peak of Charles L. Harness's published work," and described it as being "symmetrically arranged, the loose ends tucked in, and every last outrageous twist of the plot justified in science and logic," and "you can trust Harness to wind up this whole ultracomplicated structure, somehow, symmetrically and without fakery. Finally, when it's all done, the story means something." He used similar words in his review of Alfred Bester's *The Stars My Destination,* 1956. Knight goes on to conclude that "Harness's theme is the triumph of the spirit over flesh . . . This is the rock under all Harness's hypnotic cat's cradle of invention—faith in the spirit, the denial of pain, and the affirmation of eternal life."

Manipulated by a player whose identity is hidden from both the protagonist and the reader, Alar the Thief survives a series of life-threatening encounters, each of which develops his concealed nature further and moves him closer toward death and transfiguration, all in the cause of breaking humanity out of its *cul-de-sac* of cyclical history.

One of Harness's major concerns in his fiction is with the unsatisfactory state of human nature, which many of his protagonists seek to transcend. It is this theme that gives his stories their mythic character, while the scientific and technological details weave a poetic fabric of glittering plausibility. That we could be different, that our societies could be different, that our histories might have been otherwise, that creative change is possible—these are the siren songs of science fiction, whether heard in an extravagant mood or with the hope that genuine possibilities wait only for our will and hand. In *The Paradox Men* a casual reader will find epic poetry, an ecstasy of ideas, and a critical view of his own humanity. The deep currents of personal history out of which Harness writes, together with his background in patent law and chemistry, make for a powerful melodrama that is compelling and enigmatic even after several readings.

Michael Moorcock, in his 1968 introduction to *The Rose,* emphasizes that "Harness chose to write SF in the magazine style popular at the time (although he is, as 'The Chessplayers' shows, quite happy to write in a more 'sophisticated' style if it suits him) and at first glance most of his work appears to be nothing more than good, baroque SF adventure fiction. A closer look shows nuances and throw away ideas revealing a serious mind operating at a much deeper and broader level than its contemporaries in the SF field. Behind all the extravagance, and making full use of it, is Harness's mind, reasoning (where normally the SF writer rationalizes or reacts) and concerned (where much SF rejects) with the fundamental issues of human existence. That sounds pompous—but *The Rose* is never pompous, never pretentious, and this, too, gives it an edge over a lot of better-known SF novels."

An admirer of A. E. van Vogt, Harness built on that author's dream-like scenarios and wheels-within-wheels plotting, and achieved what James Blish called "the extensively recomplicated plot." *The Paradox Men* is comparable to Alfred Bester's *The Demolished Man* (1953) and *The Stars My Destination* (1956, as *Tiger! Tiger!* in Britain) in its sweep and color, especially in the ethereal beauty of Harness's closing pages. *The Rose* and *The Paradox Men* stand in relation to Harness's short fiction as do Bester's two novels to his short fiction. All four draw resourcefully on genre materials and visual possibilities; and while Bester may have the purely stylish edge, Harness has both style and substance.

The Stars My Destination does seem to owe to Harness's novel; and there is more than a bit of Harness and van Vogt in Kurt Vonnegut's *The Sirens of Titan* (1959). Gully Foyle and Winston Niles Rumfoord are kindred to Alar the Thief, who is kin to Gilbert Gosseyn in van Vogt's *The World of Null-A* (1948). Like his brother heroes, Alar is scattered in agony across a swath of space-time, but is striving to learn more about himself and to reform a recalcitrant human nature, although Alar seems more ethical than the nihilists Foyle and Rumfoord and the confused Gosseyn, and is finally more effective than all of them.

In his introduction to the first British hardcover edition, Brian W. Aldiss wrote: "Of all the types of science fiction story, my favorite is the wine-dark patch in which we find Charles Harness's novel, *The Paradox Men*. Here we find tales that challenge us with their wildness, only to sweep us away into belief on a tide of excitement and convincing detail. Though their themes may be unified, they are built from a number of strange and unexpected things. They combine madness and logic, beauty and fear. They are not fantasy, nor are they scientific fiction. These pure science fiction novels may be categorized as Widescreen Baroque. They like a wide screen, with space and possibly time travel as props, and at least the whole solar system as their setting." Aldiss adds that "for all its slam-bang action, *The Paradox Men* holds a particular enchantment. I have likened it to novels I admire, *The Stars My Destination* and *The Sirens of Titan;* but they lack the tenderness for humanity that gives the present book its freshness and its last scenes their conviction. Unlike the science fiction being written in England, America, and Russia, the values here are not purely materialistic."

To this I can only add that no SF hero ever remade human history as flamboyantly, as thoroughly, or as movingly as Alar the Thief: he steals the way to human progress. The full meaning of this is for the reader to discover, but I promise that you'll want to make the trip more than once. I have long suspected that readers who admire Philip K. Dick's works might also enjoy those of Harness, and this collection makes for a wonderful starting place. What both authors have in common is a "tenderness for humanity" and a dazzling "wildness" of ideas and action.

Praise for Harness's work became even more vocal in the 1980s and '90s, with critics and fans calling for more intelligent publishing support of his work, and lamenting that there has never been a volume of his collected stories. In the last twenty years *The Rose* and *The Paradox Men* have appeared on lists of all-time best SF novels, and together with his short fiction have been highly praised in every reference work. The consensus today is that the already high opinion of Harness's work can only increase.

And now, wonder of wonders, Charles Harness has his first volume of collected short fiction, with *The Rose* as a bonus bouquet, in a volume as permanent, well made, and pleasing as anyone might wish. We might have had such a collection twenty years ago, except for the excuses of publishing economies, which look at past sales records with no regard for what goes on between an author and his readers or with any faith in the author's future. As with illicit love affairs, the publisher is always the last to know! The myth of sales records deserves to be exploded, since it is clear that in a statistical sense publishers would do just as well to be guided by merit alone as by commerce; they might even do better to let the "free market" of taste do its work instead of trying to fix the horse race. An obvious contradiction thus exists at the heart of the business machine, which prattles about "free enterprise" but in truth skews the outcomes.

NESFA Press has to date done very well in keeping distinction and merit in print, and I believe this volume will stay in print forever once the word gets out, confirming the persistence of Harness's past and present admirers among readers, editors, and critics, and winning him new ones. Here is a volume that displays five decades of creativity paralleling the author's career as a novelist.

As I write these words, I have just talked with the author and learned that new stories are to be published in the near future, new novels await a publisher, and from the vigor in his voice I know that Charlie Harness is a mere youth *following* the unstoppable ninety-year-old Jack Williamson, who is still writing. When I asked Harness whether he had any favorites in this collection, he said, "George, I liked them all equally well when I was writing them!" And when I asked him what about his overly modest statement which he likes to make, that he did it for the money, he hems and haws—and I know the truth: he just couldn't help being Charles L. Harness, with his intelligence and talent, and he was unable to keep from growing and developing his skills and doing as well as he did, and he can't hide the love that sings from his stories.

A new story, "Lethary Fair," closes this volume. I rest my case.

George Zebrowski
Delmar, New York, Spring 1998

BIBLIOGRAPHY

PRISCILLA OLSON

"1894"
> Analog, August 1994

"The Alchemist"
> Analog, May 1966

"The Araqnid Window"
> Amazing, December 1974

"Biofeedbach"
> Fantasy Book, December 1985

"Bookmobile"
> Worlds of IF, November 1968
>> *School & Society through Science Fiction,* ed. by John D. Olander and Martin H. Greenberg, Random House, 1974

"The Bug, the Mouse and Chapter 24" (nonfiction)
> Analog, Mid-December 1994

"Bugs"
> F&SF, August 1967

"The Cajamarca Project"
> Analog, February 1985

"The Call of the Black Lagoon" (with Blandford B. Harness)
> Avon Science Fiction and Fantasy Reader, January 1953

The Catalyst
> Pocket Books, 1980

"The Chessplayers"
> F&SF, October 1953
>> *The Rose* (collection), 1966
>> *SF Oddities,* ed. by Groff Conklin, Berkley, 1966
>> *Out of This World 10,* ed. by A. Williams-Ellis and Michael Pearson, Blackie, 1973
>> *The Best Animal Stories of Science Fiction and Fantasy,* ed. by Donald J. Sobol, Warner, 1979

"Child by Chronos"
>> F&SF, June 1953
>> *The Best from F&SF—Third Series,* ed. by Anthony Boucher and
>>>> J. Francis McComas, Doubleday 1954
>> *Love 3000,* ed. by Martin H. Greenberg and Charles G. Waugh,
>>>> Elsevier, 1980

Cybele, with Bluebonnets
>> Old Earth Books, 1999

"Even Steven"
>> Other Worlds, November 1950

"The Fall of Robin Arms" (with Blandford B. Harness)
>> F&SF, March 1984

Firebird
>> Pocket Books, 1981
>> SFBC, 1981

"The Flag on Gorbachev Crater"
>> Asimov's Science Fiction, June 1997

Flight into Yesterday (AKA *The Paradox Men*)
>> Startling Stories, May 1949
>> Bouregy & Curl, 1953

"Fruits of the Agathon"
>> Thrilling Wonder Stories, December 1948
>> Science Fiction Yearbook #1, 1967

"George Washington Slept Here"
>> Analog, July 1985

"The Guac Bug"
>> Analog, June 1998

"H-TEC"
>> Analog, May 1981

"Heritage"
>> F&SF, Fall 1950
>> *Tomorrow's Universe,* ed. by H. J. Campbell, Hamilton, 1954

"I Did It for Money" (autobiographical comment)
>> *Twentieth-Century S-F Writers:* Second Edition, Macmillan, 1986

"The Improbable Profession" (as by Leonard Lockhard)
>> Astounding SF, September 1952

Krono
>> Franklin Watts, 1988
>> Avon, 1989

"The Lab Assistant" (with Shiloh Erin Cullen)
>> Analog, January 1994

"Lethary Fair"
>> *An Ornament to His Profession,* ed. by Priscilla Olson, NESFA, 1998

Lunar Justice
>> Avon, 1991

Lurid Dreams
  Avon, 1990
"The Million Year Patent"
  Amazing, December 1967
"The New Reality"
  Thrilling Wonder Stories, December 1950
  Best SF Stories and Novels, ed. by E. F. Bleiler and T. E. Dikty, Frederick
    Fell, Inc., 1951
  Isaac Asimov Presents the Great SF Stories: 12 (1950), ed. by
    Isaac Asimov and Martin H. Greenberg, DAW, 1984
  The Rose (collection), 1966
  The Shape of Things, ed. by Damon Knight, Popular Library, 1967
  Alpha 8, ed. by Robert Silverberg, Berkley, 1977
  Isaac Asimov Presents the Golden Years of Science Fiction: 6th
    Series, ed. by Isaac Asimov and Martin H. Greenberg,
    Crown/Bonanza, 1988
  The Last Man on Earth, ed. by Isaac Asimov, Martin H.
    Greenberg, and Charles D. Waugh, Fawcett, 1982
  As Tomorrow Becomes Today, ed. by Charles W. Sullivan,
    Prentice-Hall, 1974
"O Lyric Love"
  Amazing, May 1985
"An Ornament to His Profession"
  Analog, February 1966
  SF 12, ed. by Judith Merril, Delacorte, 1968; Mayflower, 1970
    (as *The Year's Best SF 12*)
  A Science Fiction Argosy, ed. by Damon Knight, Simon &
    Schuster, 1972
  Demons!, ed. by Jack Dann and Gardner Dozois, Ace, 1987
An Ornament to His Profession (collection with critical material, 17 works, and 7
  introductory pieces by Harness), ed. by Priscilla Olson, NESFA, 1998
The Paradox Men (AKA *Flight into Yesterday*)
  Bouregy & Curl, 1953
  Ace, 1955 (#118, bound with *Dome Around America* by Jack Williamson)
  Faber & Faber, 1964
  UKSFBC, 1966
  Four Square, 1967
  New English Library, 1976
  Space Opera, ed. by Brian W. Aldiss, Orbit, 1974
  Crown, 1984 [extensively revised, includes some critical material]
  Easton Press, 1992
"The Picture by Dora Gray"
  Analog, December 1986
"The Poisoner"
  F&SF, December 1952

"Probable Cause"
    Orbit 4, ed. by Damon Knight, Putnam, 1968
"Quarks at Appomattox"
    Analog, October 1983
    The Fantastic Civil War, ed. by Frank D. McSherry, Jr., Charles G.
        Waugh, and Martin H. Greenberg, Baen, 1991
Redworld
    DAW, 1986
The Ring of Ritornel
    Gollancz, 1968
    Berkley, 1968
    Panther, 1974
"The Rose"
    Authentic Science Fiction, March 1953
    The Rose (Harness collection), 1966
    Science Fiction Special 4, Sidgwick & Jackson, 1971
The Rose (collection) (with "The Rose," "The Chessplayers," "The New Reality")
    Compact, 1966
    Sidgwick & Jackson, 1968
    Berkley, 1969
    Panther, 1969
    Granada, 1982
"Signals"
    Synergy: New Science Fiction, Vol. 1, ed. by George Zebrowski,
        HBJ Harvest, 1987
"Stalemate in Space" (AKA "Stalemate in Time")
    Planet Stories, Summer 1949
    Commando Brigade 3000, ed. by Martin H. Greenberg and
        Charles G. Waugh, Ace, 1994
"Stalemate in Time" (AKA "Stalemate in Space")
    New Worlds, August 1966
"Summer Solstice"
    Analog, June 1984
    Terry Carr's Best Science Fiction of the Year #14, ed. by Terry Carr,
        Tor, 1985
"That Professional Look" (with Theodore L. Thomas) (as by Leonard Lockhard)
    Astounding SF, January 1954
"A Thesis for Branderbook" (with Blandford B. Harness)
    Thrilling Wonder Stories, June 1951
"The Tetrahedron"
    Analog, January 1994
"Time Trap"
    Astounding SF, August 1948 (December 1948 in UK)
    New Worlds #150, May 1965
    Alpha One, ed. by Robert Silverberg, Ballantine, 1970

First Voyages, ed. by Damon Knight, Martin H. Greenberg, and
Joseph D. Olander, Avon, 1981
SF Reprise 5, ed. by Michael Moorcock, Compact, 1966
The Traps of Time, ed. by Michael Moorcock, Rapp & Whiting, 1968
The Venetian Court (expanded version of novella)
Del Rey, 1982
"The Venetian Court" (expanded into novel)
Analog, late March 1981
"Waiting for Things to Work" (nonfiction)
SFWA Bulletin, Spring 1984
Wolfhead
Berkley, 1978
"Wolfhead" (serial)
F&SF, November and December 1977

Non-genre (for the Bureau of Mines)

"Marketing Magnesite and Allied Products" (with Nan C. Jensen), 1943
"Mining and Marketing of Barite," 1946

Other material of interest

Afterword in The *Paradox Men* (Crown edition)
Author's note in *Redworld*
Introduction to "Time Trap" (in *First Voyages*)

Reference materials

"Charles L. Harness: Attorney in Space: A Working Bibliography," Galactic
Central Publications #44, Phil Stephensen-Payne, 1992

"Chronography: A Chronological Bibliography of Books by Charles L.
Harness," by T. Koppel, Chris Drumm Books, 1993

"Charles Harness," (interview from radio show) in *The Sound of Wonder* (vol. 1)
by Daryl Lane, William Vernon, and David Carson, Oryx Press, 1985

"Charles L. Harness," in *The Science Fiction Source Book,* ed. by David
Wingrove, Van Nostrand Reinhold Co., 1984

Foreward by Brian W. Aldiss in *The Paradox Men* (Faber and UKSFBC, and as
afterword in Crown, 1966)

Introduction by Michael Moorcock in *The Rose* (1966)

The Flight into Tomorrow," by Brian Aldiss in *The Paradox Men* (as introduction, 1976), and in *This World and Nearer Ones,* Weidenfeld & Nicolson, 1979

Foreword by George Zebrowski in *The Paradox Men* (Crown), 1984

Numerous reviews

"Charles L. Harness: The Flowering of Melodrama," by N. L. Hills, Extrapolation, May 1978

Bibliography, and "Charles L. Harness, the Paradox Man," by William D. Vernon, Science Fiction Collector #14, May, 1981

Biolog by Jay Kay Klein, Analog, March 1981

"Harness, Charles L(eonard)," by W. D. Stevens, in *The New Encyclopedia of Science Fiction,* ed. by James Gunn, Viking Penguin, Inc., 1988

"Harness, Charles (Leonard)," in *The Encyclopedia of Science Fiction,* by John Clute and Peter Nicholls, St. Martin's Press, 1993

"Harness, Charles L(eonard)," in *St. James Guide to Science Fiction Writers,* Fourth Edition, ed. by Jay P. Pederson and Robert Reginald, St. James Press, 1996

"*The Paradox Men* by Charles L. Harness," in *Science Fiction: The 100 Best Novels,* by David Pringle, Xanadu Publications, 1985

Entry by Brian Ash, in *Who's Who in Science Fiction,* Taplinger, 1976

Entry by Brian Stableford, in *The Encyclopedia of Science Fiction,* Nicholls, Granada, 1979

Entry by Charles Cushing, in *Twentieth-Century Science Fiction Writers,* Second Edition, Macmillan, 1986

Entries on *The Catalyst, Firebird, Flight Into Yesterday, The Paradox Men, Redworld, The Ring of Ritornel,* and *The Rose* in *Anatomy of Wonder: A Critical Guide to Science Fiction,* Third Edition, ed. by Neil Barron, R. R. Bowker Co., 1987

Entries on *The Catalyst, Flight Into Yesterday, Krono, The Paradox Men, Redworld, The Ring of Ritornel, The Rose, The Venetian Court,* and *Wolfhead* in *The Ultimate Guide to Science Fiction,* Second Edition, by David Pringle, Scolar Press, 1995

Entries by Brian Stableford on *The Paradox Men* and *The Rose* in *Magill's Guide to Science Fiction and Fantasy Literature,* ed. by T. A. Shippey and A. J. Sobczak, Salem Press, Inc., 1996 (first publication, vol. 4, 1979)

Notes

"The Call of the Black Lagoon," "The Fall of Robin Arms," and "A Thesis for Branderbook" were based on short stores Blandford B. Harness wrote for a creative writing class at TCU in 1924 when he was 18. He died of inoperable brain tumors in 1932.

"The Curious Profesion" is commonly credited to "Charles L. Harness with Theodore L. Thomas" (as Leonard Lockhard; a pseudonym composed of their middle names). It is the third of a series: the first ("The Improbable Profession") was written by Charles Harness, the second ("That Professional Look") was co-authored, and "The Curious Profession" was written by Thomas alone (who continued the series in later Analogs).

The New England
Science Fiction Association (NESFA)
and NESFA Press

Recent books from NESFA Press:

- *First Contacts: The Essential Murray Leinster* $25.00
- *Frankensteins and Foreign Devils* by Walter Jon Williams $23.00
- *His Share of Glory: The Complete Short SF of C.M. Kornbluth* .. $27.00
- *Entertainment* by Algis Budrys (trade paperback) $14.00
- *The Armor of Light* by Melissa Scott and Lisa A. Barnett $23.00
- *The Silence of the Langford* by Dave Langford
  (trade paperback) $15.00
- *The White Papers* by James White $25.00
- *Ingathering: The Complete People Stories of Zenna
  Henderson* $25.00
- *Norstrilia* by Cordwainer Smith $20.95
- *The Rediscovery of Man: The Complete Short Science
  Fiction of Cordwainer Smith* $25.00
- *From the End of the 20th Century* by John M. Ford................. $21.00
- *Making Book* by Teresa Nielsen Hayden (trade paperback) $11.00
- *The Best of James H. Schmitz*... $18.95

Books may be ordered by writing to:
> NESFA Press
> PO Box 809
> Framingham, MA 01701

We accept checks, Visa, or MasterCard. Please add $2 postage per order in the U.S., and $4 for foreign orders.

The New England Science Fiction Association:

NESFA is an all-volunteer, non-profit organization of science fiction and fantasy fans. Besides publishing, our activities include running Boskone (New England's oldest SF convention) in February each year, producing a semi-monthly newsletter, holding discussion groups relating to the field, and hosting a variety of social events. If you are interested in learning more about us, we'd like to hear from you. Write to our address above, or visit us on the Web at www.nesfa.org.

Acknowledgments

David Hartwell—who encouraged me to get started, put me in touch with the right person, and wrote a wonderful introduction.

Linn Prentis—the "right person". Agent extraordinaire, who helped make it all happen.

George Zebrowski—source of fascinating bits of hidden information. For support, enthusiasm, and well-reasoned critique (and a finely done afterword, as well.)

James Daugherty and Jane Dennis—for creativity and grace.

The NESFA side:

Mark Olson—for being there (not to mention computer support whenever I panicked).

George Flynn—for exceptional poorfraeding, and making me do (most) things correctly.

Tony Lewis—NESFA Press Czar, who demanded timely reports.

Proofing by: Lisa (and Liana) Hertel (very special thanks, and congratulations!) and many others: Mark Olson, Bonnie Atwood, Elisabeth Carey, Pam Fremon, Deb Geisler, Rick Katze, Sharon Sbarsky, and Tim Szczesuil.

This book was typeset using Adobe Pagemaker and the Adobe Garamond typeface. The chemical structures in "Lethary Fair" were created using CambridgeSoft's ChemDraw Pro.

— Priscilla Olson
June, 1998